The
Wascana Anthology
of Short Fiction

ഉൗൽ

The
Wascana Anthology
of Short Fiction

ഇൽ

edited by

Ken Mitchell, Thomas Chase, and Michael Trussler
Department of English, University of Regina

CANADIAN PLAINS RESEARCH CENTER 1999

Canadian Plains Research Center
University of Regina
Regina, Saskatchewan S4S 0A2
Canada
Tel: (306) 585-4758
Fax: (306) 585-4699
e-mail: canadian.plains@uregina.ca
http://www.cprc.uregina.ca

Canadian Cataloguing in Publication Data

The Wascana anthology of short fiction

(University of Regina publications, ISSN 1480-0004 ; 3)

ISBN 0-88977-113-8

1. Short stories. I. Mitchell, Ken, 1940-
II. Chase, Thomas, 1957-   III. Trussler, Michael
Lloyd, 1960-   IV. University of Regina. Canadian
Plains Research Center.   V. Series

PN6120.2.W38 1999   808.83'1   C99-920071-2

Cover Design: Donna Achtzehner
Cover Photograph: "Trinity" by Bob Howard, courtesy of Bob Howard.

Printed and bound in Canada by
Hignell Printing Limited, Winnipeg, Manitoba

Printed on acid-free paper

TABLE OF CONTENTS

PREFACE

With the successful introduction of *The Wascana Poetry Anthology* in 1996, the University of Regina English Department launched plans for this companion edition, *The Wascana Anthology of Short Fiction*. Like the poetry text, this book is designed for first-year university students.

The selection process was pragmatic, rather than predetermined. I began by canvassing the teaching faculty for the stories they used most often or "found most useful" in class. That is, I sought out stories that have proven themselves effective models of analysis and teaching in the university classroom. The survey extended not only through the English Department, but also to colleagues teaching at Luther, Campion, and the Saskatchewan Indian Federated College. From this survey a master list of preferred stories was drawn up. I was astonished by the degree of consensus on this list, which included a very wide range of international literature — Gogol, Hemingway, Mansfield, Poe, Chekhov, Joyce and others. But it also showed a bias toward story-tellers of Western Canada and the States — that is, the Plains region. I take this, for two reasons, as a healthy sign of the genre's continuing vitality. First, experience shows that first-year students respond enthusiastically to the contemporary literature of their communities. Second, this most modern (and ancient) of literary forms continues to grow and change in response to the needs of different cultures and times.

Many years separate Geoffrey Chaucer and Guy Vanderhaeghe, but many strands connect them, for human nature changes slowly, if at all. I hope these forty stories will demonstrate the important linkage between the study of canonical ("classical") art and the evaluation of contemporary narratives. There is no single thematic preoccupation that I can see, or any ideological preference. What these tales have in common is the way they grip us from beginning to end, and — in many cases — long afterward.

It should be clear that our anthology is less intent on charting the historical evolution of the short story than demonstrating the variety of its styles and subjects. The commentaries following each story have been contributed by my colleagues in English at the University of Regina, and in themselves reveal the variety of approaches to studying the story form. They are not intended to fix critical or theoretical attitudes toward individual stories, nor do they claim to provide a "correct" or preferred response. Rather, they anticipate questions that students invariably ask, and indeed pose new queries.

Because the book is directed primarily to students, a principal goal of its publication was to provide an affordable first-year anthology. I believe this is an important accomplishment, though the economic limitation did affect the editorial selection to some extent, as a couple of choices simply could not be obtained for publication. I might as well identify them, for they explain something about the challenges of editing such an anthology. Franz Kafka's "The Metamorphosis" could not be included because of the cost of reprint rights to the English translation. (It is a superb irony that the translator's version of Kafka's story costs more than almost all of the other stories combined; and this version has a virtual monopoly of the North American market. Kafka died in poverty, little rewarded for his art.) A similar difficulty with publishers prevented us from including "Babylon Revisited" by F. Scott Fitzgerald.

In the end, this anthology's worth will be determined by its practicality as an instrument of instruction, so if your best teaching story is not included here, please nominate it for inclusion in the next edition. In the meantime, try reading one less familiar to you, and be prepared for a pleasant surprise.

Of course there can never be final agreement on which (or who) should be in, and who (or which) left out, but the buck stopped with me. I evade some responsibility by emphasizing that this project was accomplished though the applied wisdom of the entire English Department, and truly has been a collective creation in which I served as mediator of the last resort, while everyone else did all the work. I want especially to thank department members who wrote the endnotes to the stories. They include Gail Bowen, Nils Clausson, Troni Grande, Rick Harvey, Gerry Hill, Susan Johnston, Cameron Louis, Alex MacDonald, Cindy MacKenzie, Greg Maillet, Nick Ruddick, Bernie Selinger, Jeanne Shami, Garry Sherbert, Florence Stratton, Andy Stubbs, Jo-Ann Thom, Kathleen Wall, and Peggy Wigmore. The glossary was done by graduate student Conny Ratt, working on a student assistantship from the Faculty of Graduate Studies.

It has been a pleasure working with the publisher, the Canadian Plains Research Center. The support of Brian Mlazgar and Donna Achtzehner has maintained the project from its beginnings. Donna Achtzehner's resourcefulness and accuracy have been crucial to the timely publication of this text, and her production office quickly became a guiding light. Above all, I am grateful for the unflagging energy and encyclopedic knowledge of my co-editors, Thomas Chase and Michael Trussler, whose practicality and good sense actually made the anthology happen.

I can't think of a better vehicle for introducing the stories than Frank O'Connor's superb essay "The Lonely Voice." Many, many theories attempt to define the essential nature of the short story, and its universal appeal. Other critics lament its death, and still others its continuing popularity. But for a commentary on the social purpose of the short story form, it seemed appropriate to turn to a master. I believe that O'Connor's vision of "the little guy" speaking for a submerged population resonates even more powerfully than it did in 1962. In retrospect, it certainly informs this collection, though the "little guy's" gender and identity undergo continuing transformation.

Ken Mitchell

Frank O'Connor

The Lonely Voice

"By the hokies, there was a man in this place one time by the name of Ned Sullivan, and a queer thing happened him late one night and he coming up the Valley Road from Durlas."

That is how, even in my own lifetime, stories began. In its earlier phases storytelling, like poetry and drama, was a public art, though unimportant beside them because of its lack of a rigorous technique. But the short story, like the novel, is a modern art form; that is to say, it represents, better than poetry or drama, our own attitude to life.

No more than the novel does it begin with "By the hokies." The technique which both have acquired was the product of a critical, scientific age, and we recognize the merits of a short story much as we recognize the merits of a novel — in terms of plausibility. By this I do not mean mere verisimilitude — that we can get from a newspaper report — but an ideal action worked out in terms of verisimilitude. As we shall see, there are dozens of ways of expressing verisimilitude — as many perhaps as there are great writers — but no way of explaining its absence, no way of saying, "At this point the character's behaviour becomes completely inexplicable." Almost from its beginnings the short story, like the novel, abandoned the devices of a public art in which the storyteller assumed the mass assent of an audience to his wildest improvisations — "and a queer thing happened him late one night." It began, and continues to function, as a private art intended to satisfy the standards of the individual, solitary, critical reader.

⋘

Yet, even from its beginnings, the short story has functioned in a quite different way from the novel, and, however difficult it may be to describe the difference, describing it is the critic's principal business.

"We all came out from under Gogol's 'Overcoat' " is a familiar saying of Turgenev, and though it applies to Russian rather than European fiction, it has also a general truth.

Read now, and by itself, "The Overcoat" does not appear so very impressive. All the things Gogol has done in it have been done frequently since his day, and sometimes done better. But if we read it again in its historical context, closing our minds so far as we can to all the short stories it gave rise to, we can see that Turgenev was not exaggerating. We have all come out from under Gogol's "Overcoat."

It is the story of a poor copying clerk, a nonentity mocked by his colleagues. His old overcoat has become so threadbare that even his drunken tailor refuses to patch it further since there is no longer any place in it where a patch would hold.

Akakey Akakeivitch,[1] the copying clerk, is terrified at the prospect of such unprecedented expenditure. As a result of a few minor fortunate circumstances, he finds himself able to buy a new coat, and for a day or two this makes a new man of him, for after all, in real life he is not much more than an overcoat.

Then he is robbed of it. He goes to the Chief of Police, a bribe-taker who gives him no satisfaction, and to an Important Personage who merely abuses and threatens him. Insult piled on injury is too much for him and he goes home and dies. The story ends with a whimsical description of his ghost's search for justice, which, once more, to a poor copying clerk has never meant much more than a warm overcoat.

There the story ends, and when one forgets all that came after it, like Chekhov's "Death of a Civil Servant," one realizes that it is like nothing in the world of literature before it. It uses the old rhetorical device of the mock-heroic, but uses it to create a new form that is neither satiric nor heroic, but something in between — something that perhaps finally transcends both. So far as I know, it is the first appearance in fiction of the Little Man, which may define what I mean by the short story better than any terms I may later use about it. Everything about Akakey Akakeivitch, from his absurd name to his absurd job, is on the same level of mediocrity, and yet his absurdity is somehow transfigured by Gogol.

> Only when the jokes were too unbearable, when they jolted his arm and prevented him from going on with his work, he would bring out: "Leave me alone! Why do you insult me?" and there was something strange in the words and in the voice in which they were uttered. There was a note in it of something that roused compassion, so that one young man, new to the office, who, following the example of the rest, had allowed himself to mock at him, suddenly stopped as though cut to the heart, and from that day forth, everything was as it were changed and appeared in a different light to him. Some unnatural force seemed to thrust him away from the companions with whom he had become acquainted, accepting them as well-bred, polished people. And long afterwards, at moments of the greatest gaiety, the figure of the humble little clerk with a bald patch on his head rose before him with his heart-rending words "Leave me alone! Why do you insult me?" and in those heartrending words he heard others: "I am your brother." And the poor young man hid his face in his hands, and many times afterwards in his life he shuddered, seeing how much inhumanity there is in man, how much savage brutality lies hidden under refined,

---

[1] "The Overcoat" comes to us in translation, of course, and in this essay, O'Connor's references to "The Overcoat" are from a translation other than the one by David Magarshack reprinted in our volume. Thus, "Akakey Akakeivitch" here is "Akaky Akakyevich" in the translation beginning on page 172; likewise, the "Chief of Police" is the "police commissioner" and the "Important Personage" is the "Very Important Person." Compare the lengthy quotation above with the corresponding section of the story on page 174.

cultured politeness, and my God! even in a man whom the world accepts as a gentleman and a man of honour.

One has only to read that passage carefully to see that without it scores of stories by Turgenev, by Maupassant, by Chekhov, by Sherwood Anderson and James Joyce could never have been written. If one wanted an alternative description of what the short story means, one could hardly find better than that single half-sentence, "and from that day forth, everything was as it were changed and appeared in a different light to him." If one wanted an alternative title for this work, one might choose "I Am Your Brother." What Gogol has done so boldly and brilliantly is to take the mock-heroic character, the absurd little copying clerk, and impose his image over that of the crucified Jesus, so that even while we laugh we are filled with horror at the resemblance.

Now, this is something that the novel cannot do. For some reason that I can only guess at, the novel is bound to be a process of identification between the reader and the character. One could not make a novel out of a copying clerk with a name like Akakey Akakeivitch who merely needed a new overcoat any more than one could make one out of a child called Tommy Tompkins whose penny had gone down a drain. One character at least in any novel must represent the reader in some aspect of his own conception of himself — as the Wild Boy, the Rebel, the Dreamer, the Misunderstood Idealist — and this process of identification invariably leads to some concept of normality and to some relationship — hostile or friendly — with society as a whole. People are abnormal insofar as they frustrate the efforts of such a character to exist in what he regards as a normal universe, normal insofar as they support him. There is not only the Hero, there is also the Semi-Hero and the Demi-Semi-Hero. I should almost go so far as to say that without the concept of a normal society the novel is impossible. I know there are examples of the novel that seem to contradict this, but in general I should say that it is perfectly true. The President of the Immortals is called in only when society has made a thorough mess of the job.

But in "The Overcoat" this is not true, nor is it true of most of the stories I shall have to consider. There is no character here with whom the reader can identify himself, unless it is that nameless horrified figure who represents the author. There is no form of society to which any character in it could possibly attach himself and regard as normal. In discussions of the modern novel we have come to talk of it as the novel without a hero. In fact, the short story has never had a hero.

What it has instead is a submerged population group — a bad phrase which I have had to use for want of a better. That submerged population changes its character from writer to writer, from generation to generation. It may be Gogol's officials, Turgenev's serfs, Maupassant's prostitutes, Chekhov's doctors and teachers, Sherwood Anderson's provincials, always dreaming of escape.

"Even though I die, I will in some way keep defeat from you," she cried, and so deep was her determination that her whole body shook. Her eyes glowed and she clenched her fists. "If I am dead and see him becoming a meaningless drab figure like myself, I will come back," she declared. "I ask God now to give me that privilege. I will take any blow that may fall if but this my boy be allowed to express something for us both." Pausing uncertainly, the woman stared about the boy's room. "And do not let him become smart and successful either," she added vaguely.

This is Sherwood Anderson, and Anderson writing badly for him, but it could be almost any short-story writer. What has the heroine tried to escape from? What does she want her son to escape from? "Defeat" — what does that mean? Here it does not mean mere material squalor, though this is often characteristic of the submerged population groups. Ultimately it seems to mean defeat inflicted by a society that has no signposts, a society that offers no goals and no answers. The submerged population is not submerged entirely by material considerations; it can also be submerged by the absence of spiritual ones, as in the priests and spoiled priests of J.F. Powers' American stories.

Always in the short story there is this sense of outlawed figures wandering about the fringes of society, superimposed sometimes on symbolic figures whom they caricature and echo — Christ, Socrates, Moses. It is not for nothing that there are famous short stories called "Lady Macbeth of the Mtsensk District" and "A Lear of the Steppes" and — in reverse — one called "An Akoulina of the Irish Midlands." As a result there is in the short story at its most characteristic something we do not often find in the novel — an intense awareness of human loneliness. Indeed, it might be truer to say that while we often read a familiar novel again for companionship, we approach the short story in a very different mood. It is more akin to the mood of Pascal's saying: *Le silence éternel de ces espaces infinis m'effraie.*

I have admitted that I do not profess to understand the idea fully: it is too vast for a writer with no critical or historical training to explore by his own inner light, but there are too many indications of its general truth for me to ignore it altogether. When I first dealt with it I had merely noticed the peculiar geographical distribution of the novel and the short story. For some reason Czarist Russia and modern America seemed to be able to produce both great novels and great short stories, while England, which might be called without exaggeration the homeland of the novel, showed up badly when it came to the short story. On the other hand my own country, which had failed to produce a single novelist, had produced four or five storytellers who seemed to me to be first-rate.

I traced these differences very tentatively, but — on the whole, as I now think, correctly — to a difference in the national attitude toward society. In America as in Czarist Russia one might describe the intellectual's attitude to society as "It may work," in England as "It must work," and in Ireland as "It can't work." A young American of our own time or a young Russian of Turgenev's might look forward with a certain amount of cynicism to a measure of success and influence; nothing but bad luck could prevent a young Englishman's achieving it, even today; while a young Irishman can still expect nothing but incomprehension, ridicule, and injustice. Which is exactly what the author of *Dubliners* got.

The reader will have noticed that I left out France, of which I know little, and Germany, which does not seem to have distinguished itself in fiction. But since those days I have seen fresh evidence accumulating that there was some truth in the distinctions I made. I have seen the Irish crowded out by Indian storytellers, and there are plenty of indications that they in their turn, having become respectable, are being out-written by West Indians like Samuel Selvon.

Clearly, the novel and the short story, though they derive from the same sources, derive in a quite different way, and are distinct literary forms; and the difference is not so much formal (though, as we shall see, there are plenty of formal differences) as ideological. I am not, of course, suggesting that for the future the short story can be written only by Eskimos and American Indians: without going so far afield, we have plenty of submerged population groups. I am suggesting strongly that we can see in it an attitude of mind that is attracted by submerged population groups, whatever these may be at any given time — tramps, artists, lonely idealists, dreamers, and spoiled priests. The novel can still adhere to the classical concept of civilized society, of man as an animal who lives in a community, as in Jane Austen and Trollope it obviously does; but the short story remains by its very nature remote from the community — romantic, individualistic, and intransigent.

ʘ

But formally as well the short story differs from the novel. At its crudest you can express the difference merely by saying that the short story is short. It is not necessarily true, but as a generalization it will do well enough. If the novelist takes a character of any interest and sets him up in opposition to society, and then, as a result of the conflict between them, allows his character either to master society or to be mastered by it, he has done all that can reasonably be expected of him. In this the element of Time is his greatest asset; the chronological development of character or incident is essential form as we see it in life, and the novelist flouts it at his own peril.

For the short-story writer there is no such thing as essential form. Because his frame of reference can never be the totality of a human life, he must be forever selecting the point at which he can approach it, and each selection he makes contains the possibility of a new form as well as the possibility of a complete fiasco. I have illustrated this element of choice by reference to a poem of Browning's. Almost any one of his great dramatic lyrics is a novel in itself but caught in a single moment of peculiar significance — Lippo Lippi arrested as he slinks back to his monastery in the early morning, Andrea Del Sarto as he resigns himself to the part of a complaisant lover, the Bishop dying in St. Praxed's. But since a whole lifetime must be crowded into a few minutes, those minutes must be carefully chosen indeed and lit by an unearthly glow, one that enables us to distinguish present, past, and future as though they were all contemporaneous. Instead of a novel of five hundred pages about the Duke of Ferrara, his first and second wives and the peculiar death of the first, we get fifty-odd lines in which the Duke, negotiating a second marriage, describes his first, and the very opening lines make our blood run cold:

> That's my last Duchess painted on the wall,
> Looking as if she were alive.

This is not the essential form that life gives us; it is organic form, something that springs from a single detail and embraces past, present, and future. In some book on Parnell there is a horrible story about the death of Parnell's child by Kitty O'Shea, his mistress, when he wandered frantically about the house like a ghost, while Willie O'Shea, the complaisant husband, gracefully received the condolences of visitors. When you read that, it should be unnecessary to read the whole sordid story of Parnell's romance and its tragic ending. The tragedy is there, if only one had a Browning or a Turgenev to write it. In the standard composition that the individual life presents, the storyteller must always be looking for new compositions that enable him to suggest the totality of the old one.

Accordingly, the storyteller differs from the novelist in this: he must be much more of a writer, much more of an artist — perhaps I should add, considering the examples I have chosen, more of a dramatist. For that, too, I suspect, has something to do with it. One savage story of J.D. Salinger's, "Pretty Mouth and Green My Eyes," echoes that scene in Parnell's life in a startling way. A deceived husband, whose wife is out late, rings up his best friend, without suspecting that the wife is in the best friend's bed. The best friend consoles him in a rough-and-ready way, and finally the deceived husband, a decent man who is ashamed of his own outburst, rings again to say that the wife has come home, though she is still in bed with her lover.

Now, a man can be a very great novelist as I believe Trollope was, and yet be a very inferior writer. I am not sure but that I prefer the novelist to be an inferior dramatist; I am not sure that a novel could stand the impact of a scene such as that I have quoted from Parnell's life, or J.D. Salinger's story. But I cannot think of a great storyteller who was also an inferior writer, unless perhaps Sherwood Anderson, nor of any at all who did not have the sense of theatre.

This is anything but the recommendation that it may seem, because it is only too easy for a short-story writer to become a little too much of an artist. Hemingway, for instance, has so studied the artful approach to the significant moment that we sometimes end up with too much significance and too little information. I have tried to illustrate this from "Hills Like White Elephants." If one thinks of this as a novel one sees it as the love story of a man and a woman which begins to break down when the man, afraid of responsibility, persuades the woman to agree to an abortion which she believes to be wrong. The development is easy enough to work out in terms of the novel. He is an American, she perhaps an Englishwoman. Possibly he has responsibilities already — a wife and children elsewhere, for instance. She may have had some sort of moral upbringing, and perhaps in contemplating the birth of the child she is influenced by the expectation that her family and friends will stand by her in her ordeal.

Hemingway, like Browning in "My Last Duchess," chooses one brief episode from this long and involved story, and shows us the lovers at a wayside station on the Continent, between one train and the next, as it were, symbolically divorced from their normal surroundings and friends. In this setting they make a decision which has already begun to affect their past life and will certainly affect their future. We know that the man is American, but that is all we are told about him.

We can guess the woman is not American, and that is all we are told about her. The light is focused fiercely on that one single decision about the abortion. It is the abortion, the whole abortion, and nothing but the abortion. We, too, are compelled to make ourselves judges of the decision, but on an abstract level. Clearly, if we knew that the man had responsibilities elsewhere, we should be a little more sympathetic to him. If, on the one hand, we knew that he had no other responsibilities, we should be even less sympathetic to him than we are. On the other hand, we should understand the woman better if we knew whether she didn't want the abortion because she thought it wrong or because she thought it might loosen her control of the man. The light is admirably focused but it is too blinding; we cannot see into the shadows as we do in "My Last Duchess."

> She had
> A heart — how shall I say? — too soon made glad,
> Too easily impressed; she liked whate'er
> She looked on, and her looks went everywhere.

And so I should say Hemingway's story is brilliant but thin. Our moral judgment has been stimulated, but our moral imagination has not been stirred, as it is stirred in "The Lady With the Toy Dog" in which we are given all the information at the disposal of the author which would enable us to make up our minds about the behaviour of his pair of lovers. The comparative artlessness of the novel does permit the author to give unrestricted range to his feelings occasionally — to *sing*; and even minor novelists often sing loud and clear for several chapters at a time, but in the short story, for all its lyrical resources, the singing note is frequently absent.

୧

That is the significance of the difference between the *conte* and the *nouvelle* which one sees even in Turgenev, the first of the great storytellers I have studied. Essentially the difference depends upon precisely how much information the writer feels he must give the reader to enable the moral imagination to function. Hemingway does not give the reader enough. When that wise mother Mme. Maupassant complained that her son, Guy, started his stories too soon and without sufficient preparation, she was making the same sort of complaint.

But the *conte* as Maupassant and even the early Chekhov sometimes wrote it is too rudimentary a form for a writer to go very far wrong in; it is rarely more than an anecdote, a *nouvelle* stripped of most of its detail. On the other hand the form of the *conte* illustrated in "My Last Duchess" and "Hills Like White Elephants" is exceedingly complicated, and dozens of storytellers have gone astray in its mazes. There are three necessary elements in a story — exposition, development, and drama. Exposition we may illustrate as "John Fortescue was a solicitor in the little town of X"; development as "One day Mrs. Fortescue told him she was about to leave him for another man"; and drama as " 'You will do nothing of the kind,' he said."

In the dramatized *conte* the storyteller has to combine exposition and development, and sometimes the drama shows a pronounced tendency to collapse

xv

under the mere weight of the intruded exposition — " 'As a solicitor I can tell you you will do nothing of the kind,' John Fortescue said." The extraordinary brilliance of "Hills Like White Elephants" comes from the skill with which Hemingway has excluded unnecessary exposition; its weakness, as I have suggested, from the fact that much of the exposition is not unnecessary at all. Turgenev probably invented the dramatized *conte*, but if he did, he soon realized its dangers because in his later stories, even brief ones like "Old Portraits," he fell back on the *nouvelle*.

The ideal, of course, is to give the reader precisely enough information and in this again the short story differs from the novel, because no convention of length ever seems to affect the novelist's power to tell us all we need to know. No such convention of length seems to apply to the short story at all. Maupassant often began too soon because he had to finish within two thousand words, and O'Flaherty sometimes leaves us with the impression that his stories have either gone on too long or not long enough. Neither Babel's stories nor Chekhov's leave us with that impression. Babel can sometimes finish a story in less than a thousand words, Chekhov can draw one out to eighty times the length.

One can put this crudely by saying that the form of the novel is given by the length; in the short story the length is given by the form. There is simply no criterion of the length of a short story other than that provided by the material itself, and either padding to bring it up to a conventional length or cutting to bring it down to a conventional length is liable to injure it. I am afraid that the modern short story is being seriously affected by editorial ideas of what its length should be. (Like most storytellers, I have been told that "nobody reads anything longer than three thousand words.") All I can say from reading Turgenev, Chekhov, Katherine Anne Porter, and others is that the very term "short story" is a misnomer. A great story is not necessarily short at all, and the conception of the short story as a miniature art is inherently false. Basically, the difference between the short story and the novel is not one of length. It is a difference between pure and applied storytelling, and in case someone has still failed to get the point, I am not trying to decry applied storytelling. Pure storytelling is more artistic, that is all, and in storytelling I am not sure how much art is preferable to nature.

Nor am I certain how one can apply this distinction if one can apply it at all. In trying to distinguish between Turgenev's novel and *nouvelles*, Dmitry Mirsky has suggested that the *nouvelles* omit conversations about general ideas which were popular in the nineteenth-century Russian novel. I have tried to assimilate this to my own vague feelings on the subject by suggesting that this is merely another way of saying that the characters in the *nouvelles* were not intended to have general significance. In a marvelous story like "Punin and Baburin," the two principal characters seem to have no general significance at all as they would have been bound to have had they been characters in a novel. In fact when they do appear in a novel like "On the Eve" they have considerable general significance, and the reader is bound to take sides between them. The illegitimate defender of human liberty and the gas-bag poet are not people we take sides with. We sympathize and understand, all right, but they both remain members of a submerged population, unable to speak for themselves.

Even in Chekhov's "Duel," that fantastic short story which is longer than several of Turgenev's novels, the characters are too specific, too eccentric for any real generalization, though generalized conversations are strewn all over the place. We look at Laevsky and Nadyezhda Fyodorovna as we look at Punin and Baburin, from outside, with sympathy and understanding but still feeling, however wrongly, that their problems are their own, not ours. What Turgenev and Chekhov give us is not so much the brevity of the short story compared with the expansiveness of the novel as the purity of an art form that is motivated by its own necessities rather than by our convenience.

As I have said, this is not all gain. Like the Elizabethan drama the novel is a great popular art, and full of the impurities of a popular art, but, like the Elizabethan drama, it has a physical body which a purer art like the short story is constantly in danger of losing. I once tried to describe my own struggle with the form by saying that "Generations of skilful stylists from Chekhov to Katherine Mansfield and James Joyce had so fashioned the short story that it no longer rang with the tone of a man's voice speaking." Even in the nineteenth century there were writers who seem to have had the same uncomfortable feeling. One is Leskov, the only great Russian writer whose work has not been adequately translated.

Even from the miserable number of his stories that have been translated it is clear that he wanted literature to have a physical body. He has tried to revive the art of the folk storyteller so that we can hear the tone of a man's voice speaking. The folk storyteller, because his audience (like a child listening to a bedtime story) can only apprehend a few sentences at a time, unlike a reader who can hold a score of details before his mind simultaneously, has only one method of holding its attention, and that is by piling incident on incident, surprise on surprise. One old folk storyteller, who got someone to read him a couple of my stories, said sadly, "There aren't enough marvels in them." In Leskov's "Enchanted Wanderer" he would have found enough marvels to satisfy even him.

Leskov had also the popular taste for excess. He liked people to be full-blooded. When they were drunk he liked them very drunk, and when they fell in love he did not care for them to be too prudent. "Lady Macbeth of the Mtsensk District" is no understatement as a title. The heroine, consumed by passion, first murders her father-in-law, then her husband, then her co-heir, and finally in destroying herself murders her lover's mistress as well. I think my old friend the folk storyteller would have smacked his lips over that, but I cannot bear to imagine his disappointment over "The Lady With the Toy Dog." "And no one got killed at all?" I can almost hear him cry. He could not have told it to an audience in his little cottage without adding two farcical incidents, two murders, and at least one ghost.

But if this were all, Leskov would be merely a Russian Kipling, and so far as my understanding of his work goes, beyond the superficial resemblances — the episodic treatment and the taste for excess — he had very little in common with Kipling. Kipling, I should say, took the superficial things that belong to oral storytelling without that peculiar sense of the past that illuminates its wildest extravagances. In one very amusing story Kipling describes the native descendants of an Irish rebel in the British forces in India singing "The Wearing of the Green" before a Crucifix and a cap badge at the time of the Angelus, but in his usual way he vulgarizes it, throwing the Crucifix, the Angelus, the cap badge, and the Irish rebel song in with the mutilation of cattle as the essential Irish things — a mistake that Leskov would not have made. Superficially, there is little to distinguish Leskov's "Lady Macbeth" from "Love-O'-Women," but you could put the former into an Icelandic family saga without anyone's noticing anything peculiar about it. Try to think of someone putting the latter in without someone's noticing that "I'm dyin', Aigypt, dyin' " is not the language of saga! It is irremediably the language of the gin palace.

No, Leskov is important because he is really defining a difference of outlook not between an English Conservative and an English Labour man but between two types of human being. Kipling loves the physical only if the physical happens to be his side and to be well equipped with repeating rifles. Leskov loves it for his own sweet sake. Both to Turgenev and to Chekhov flogging was a horror — to Turgenev because he felt that history had cast him for the part of the flogger, to Chekhov, the slave's grandson, because he felt that every blow of the whip was directed at his own back. Leskov, without prejudice — we might as well face it — found the whole vile business vastly entertaining. To him flogging was an endurance test like any other, and the essence of masculinity was the capacity to endure. He would probably have defended torture on the same grounds.

> They gave me a terrible flogging, so that I could not even stand
> on my feet afterwards, and they carried me to my father on a piece of
> straw matting, but I didn't mind that very much; what I did mind was
> the last part of my sentence, which condemned me to go down on my
> knees and knock stones into a garden path. . . . I felt so bad about it
> that after vainly casting about in my mind how to find a way out of
> my trouble I decided to do away with myself.

That is an extraordinary attitude which you can find in at least one other story of Leskov's, and quite characteristic of him. For instance when the hero of "The Enchanted Wanderer" has gambled away his boss's money he realizes that the only punishment that fits his case is a flogging, so he goes to his boss with bowed head.

> "What are you up to now?" he asked.
> "Give me a good beating at any rate, sir," I said.

Now, this is not mock-heroics; it is not the maunderings of a sexual pervert; it is identical with the extraordinary scene in Gauguin's *Journal* when his mistress, who has been unfaithful to him, asks to be beaten, not so much because she feels any particular guilt about her own behaviour as that she knows instinctively that Gauguin will feel better afterward. It is part of the primitive childish psychology of Lawrence's "Tickets, Please!" and between grown-up, civilized people there is literally nothing to be said about it. It is a fact of childish and primitive psychology, but it means that Leskov is often right about that when liberals and humanitarians like Turgenev and Chekhov are wrong.

It must be twenty years since I read a story of Leskov's called "The Stinger" that reminded me at once of Chekhov's "At the Villa." Chekhov's is a tragic story of a civilized engineer who, with his wife and family, is trying to do everything for the unenlightened peasants about him but incurs their scorn, and is driven out of his home by their malice. Leskov's, as best I can remember it, is about a civilized English factory manager in Russia who replaces the barbaric floggings with mild and meaningless punishments. The peasants, who had hoped that the Englishman would treat them like a father and beat them when they did wrong, are absolutely horrified when they are bidden to stand in a corner, and finally, in despair, burn the Englishman's home about him. The same story, but this time told from inside.

Once again, we could argue till the cows came home and get no nearer a solution. The principal difference is that Leskov, by his very extravagance, convinces us that he knows the peasants, while Chekhov, the saintly doctor, trying to help them from without, simply has no clue to the workings of their minds. Russian and all as he is, he is simply an alien in the world of Leskov and Gauguin.

I do not like that world, but about certain things Leskov is the truer artist.

∞

The battle has gone against the traditionalists, and for the reason which I stated in the opening paragraphs of this chapter. The form itself is modern. It is possible to give a primitive art like the theatre a new slant in the direction of a more public statement, but experiment in storytelling is nearly always in the other direction. Leskov, as great a writer as Chekhov if one accepts the views of Russian critics, is practically unknown outside Russia. Kipling, a remarkable storyteller with some of Leskov's virtues, has had little influence outside the English-speaking countries, and even in them it would be hard to deduce from the work of any serious storyteller that such a writer as Kipling had ever existed. Even in his own country he has had no influence on Lawrence, Coppard, or Pritchett.

In Ireland, one could certainly deduce his influence on Edith Somerville and Martin Ross, the authors of *The Irish R.M.,* but the history of their work in their own country is almost an object lesson in the way storytelling develops.

The Irish R.M. — to adopt a general title for the books of stories that began with "Some Experiences of an Irish R.M." — is one of the most lovable books I know. Edith Somerville was an art student in Paris and came under the influence of the French Naturalists, as we can see from a novel like *The Real Charlotte.* George Moore, another member of the Irish landowning class, was also an art student, and also came under the influence of Naturalism, and his novel *Muslin* stands comparison with *The Real Charlotte.* But there the similarity ends. When Somerville and Ross wrote stories, they forgot all they had ever learned from the French Naturalists and apparently wrote just to enjoy themselves. George Moore did not forget, and the influence of Flaubert, Zola, and the Goncourts — even of Turgenev — can be seen even in the slightest of the stories in *The Untilled Field.*

The contrast between these two books is extraordinary. I have reread *The Irish R.M.* off and on for forty years for the mere pleasure of it. The stories in it are yarns, pure and simple. They have a few of the virtues of Leskov's stories; they are of the open air, of horses and animals, and people who have much in common with both. The humour is of the slapstick variety I remember from boys' books of my childhood. The supreme moment of fun comes when the hero breaks his eyeglasses or puts his foot through the barometer. The number of mishaps that occur at the local agricultural show pass all reckoning. The water jump dries up and the distracted stewards fill it with lime.

If, as I suppose, the object was to delude the horses into the belief that it was a water jump, it was a total failure; they immediately decided it was a practical joke, dangerous and in indifferent taste. If, on the other side, a variety entertainment for the public was aimed at, nothing could have been more successful. Every known class of refusal was successfully exhibited. One horse endeavoured to climb the rails into the Grand Stand; another, having stopped dead at the critical point, swung round and returned in consternation to the starting point, with his rider hanging like a locket round his neck. Another, dowered with a sense of humour unusual among horses, stepped delicately over the furze-bushes, and amidst rounds of applause, walked through the lime with stoic calm. . . .

It is only when one asks oneself what the stories are about that one begins to have doubts of one's own judgment. There, indeed, is a man's voice speaking — or a woman's — and it calls for an audience, but take the audience away and what are we left with? Nothing, certainly, that responds to analysis. Years ago, I was disturbed by the reading of one story called "Harrington's" and sat down to analyze it. It turned out to be a funny story crossed with a ghost story, and the result resembled a bad accident at a level crossing. The Chimney Sweep comes to the home of the Resident Magistrate, and, knowing the nature of sweeps, the R.M. and his family leave home for the day, having first refused the loan of their long ladder to a humorous neighbour. They call on two spinsters who run a chicken farm and eventually find them at an auction in Harrington's, the house of a mine manager who has committed suicide. One of the spinsters is playing the piano while beside her stands a man in a yachting cap. While the R.M. is purchasing another long ladder (to lend to the neighbour as requested) his little boy disappears, and the spinster confesses to having seen him cross the fields with a man in a yachting cap.

At this point it is obvious to the meanest intelligence that the man in the yachting cap is the deceased mine manager and that he intends some harm to the R.M.'s little boy. The child is rescued with nothing worse than a broken collarbone, and at this point the R.M. discovers that the ladder he has just bought for thirty shillings is his own.

In a story like this, of course, there is scarcely a hint of a work of art. It has no intellectual framework and is nothing when studied alone by the cold light of day. It needs candles and firelight and above all a receptive audience.

But if one turns from it to a story like George Moore's "Home Sickness" in *The Untilled Field* one realizes that Moore's story does not need fire nor candlelight nor any audience other than oneself. It is the simple story of a New York barman who is sent back to Ireland to regain his health and falls in love with an Irish girl. He is hindered from settling down with her by a suspicion of his neighbours' timidity and the loutishness of the local priest. One day, haunted by the memory of frank and friendly discussions in America, he slips back to New York, and at the end of the story, whenever he thinks of Ireland he thinks of the girl he abandoned there to the loneliness and cowardice of her world, and his memories have a new poignancy. Contrast the cool and sympathetic intelligence of Moore's final paragraph with the schoolgirl high jinks of the passage from Somerville and Ross:

> There is an unchanging, silent life within every man that none knows but himself, and his unchanging, silent life was his memory of Margaret Dirken. The bar-room was forgotten and all that concerned it and the things he saw most clearly were the green hill-side, and the bog lake and the rushes about it, and the greater lake in the distance, and behind it the blue line of wandering hills.

Here there is no contrivance, not so much as a single coincidence. The narrative line is merely a pattern: the pattern of human life as we have all experienced it — nostalgia and disillusionment and a fresh nostalgia sharpened by experience. It has the absolute purity of the short story as opposed to the tale, and it bears the same relationship to "Harrington's" that a song of Hugo Wolf's bears to "Du Lieber Augustin." You may like or dislike it — and my own attitude to the short story is somewhat ambivalent — but as a piece of artistic organization it is perfect. It represents an art form as elaborate as the sonnet, and — what is much more important to a student of the form — it points out the direction that the Irish short story would take. Though I suspect that for one copy of *The Untilled Field* you can find, you will find a hundred of *The Irish R.M.,* Irish literature has gone Moore's way, not Somerville and Ross's.

It is right that Moore should get the credit which at present goes to his unruly disciple Joyce, for though, as the work of the two men developed, it showed great differences — Moore giving way to his passion for polemic, Joyce to his for formal experiment — the early stories in *Dubliners* derive much from Moore.

So, I believe, do the stories of Liam O'Flaherty, though O'Flaherty might easily never have read Moore. His novels, at least, suggest as much, but whereas in O'Flaherty's novels he makes mistakes that Moore could never have made, in his stories he avoids all the mistakes that Moore would certainly have made. If one wished to write a thesis to show that the novel was not an Irish form but that the short story was, one could do worse than take O'Flaherty for text. His subject is instinct, not judgment. "When O'Flaherty thinks, he's a goose, when he feels, he's a genius," is how George Russell, the poet, summed him up. His best stories deal with animals, and the nearer his characters approach to animals the happier he is in dealing with them. With his passion for polemic, Moore in "Home Sickness" could not ignore the fact that emigration is largely caused by the sheer boredom of an authoritarian religion. With his own natural innocence O'Flaherty in a story like "Going Into Exile" could ignore everything except the nature of exile itself —a state of things like love and death that we must all endure.

And one can easily imagine the sort of mess that George Moore would have made of O'Flaherty's "Fairy Goose," one of the great Irish short stories. It is the story of a feeble little goose whom the superstition of her owner turns into the divinity of an Irish village. She makes the fortune and turns the head of her owner until the parish priest decides to break up the cult, and the village louts stone the poor little goose to death. In essence, it is the whole history of religion, and it screams for a George Moore, an Anatole France, or a Norman Douglas, but because he is feeling rather than thinking, O'Flaherty never permits the shadow of a sneer to disturb the gravity of the theme. We laugh, all right, much louder than Moore or France or Douglas ever made us laugh — but at the same time we are moved, and eventually the impression left on our minds is something like that left by Turgenev's "Byezhin Prairie" — "the eternal silence of those infinite spaces terrifies me."

ᴄᴚ

If I knew as much about American literature as I do about Irish literature, I feel I should probably be able to put my finger on Sherwood Anderson's *Winesburg, Ohio,* and say, "This is to America what *The Untilled Field* is to Ireland." The date itself — 1919 — is as significant as the date 1903 on the title page of Moore's book. Participation in the First World War had made Americans conscious for the first time since the Civil War that they were isolated, unique, and complacent; and the dissatisfaction it roused in them turned them into a generation of displaced persons, at home neither in America nor on the Continent. The year 1919 and Sherwood Anderson signaled the beginnings of a new self-consciousness; by 1920 Scott Fitzgerald was describing the return of the troops and the fresh complications this was creating, and within a couple of years Hemingway and Faulkner were sketching out the new literature.

When I said that I could think of no great storyteller who was not a great writer, I excluded Anderson, who did not really begin to write till he was in his forties. But few writers have had so clear a vision of what the short story could do. With absolute certainty he marked out his own submerged population — the lonely dreamers of the Middle West. Their loneliness is deeper and more tragic than that of George Moore's priests or Joyce's clerks, perhaps because, like Anderson himself, they come of pioneering stock, confident, competent men and women who do not understand what it means to be beaten almost from birth. There is an interesting comparison to be drawn between Joyce's "Eveline" and Anderson's "Adventure." Both deal with sensitive women who for one reason or another have been left on the shelf. Eveline is waiting to go with the man she loves to Buenos Aires, but when the boat is on the point of departure she leaves him and runs home, beaten before she starts at all. Alice Hindman, who has waited hopelessly for the return of a man she loves, strips herself and runs out into the street one rainy night to offer herself to the first man she meets, but he turns out to be old and deaf and says nothing but "What? What say?" So Alice returns to the house, goes to bed, and "turning her face to the wall, began trying to face bravely the fact that many people must live and die alone, even in Winesburg." It is a terrible moment for the American when his clear-sighted optimism gives place to an equally clear-sighted despondency. Anderson's characters understand their own hopeless position so well that I sometimes find myself wondering whether they are not really examples of that passive suffering which Yeats maintained was no material for art.

Those two terrible words, "alone" and "lonely," ring out in almost every story in *Winesburg, Ohio,* and with them the word "hands" — hands reaching out for a human contact that is not there. Yet contact itself is the principal danger, for to marry is to submit to the standards of the submerged population, and for the married there is no hope but to pass on the dream of escape to their children. The danger is the theme of the beautiful story "The Untold Lie," and of a later, inferior story, "The Contract." The hope transmitted to the children is the theme of Anderson's finest story, "Death." In this, George Willard's grandfather, distrusting his son-in-law, leaves his daughter eight hundred dollars to be "a great open door" to her when the time comes for her to escape. Elizabeth, defeated in her turn, has saved it to be "a great open door" to her son, George, and hidden it a week after her marriage in a wall at the foot of her bed, where at the end of the story it still lies, plastered up and forgotten.

It is from this remarkable little book that the modern American short story develops, and the Americans have handled the short story so wonderfully that one can say that it is a national art form. I have given one reason for the superiority of the American short story over all others that I know, but of course, there are several reasons, and one is that America is largely populated by submerged population groups. That peculiar American sweetness toward the stranger — which exists side by side with American brutality toward everyone — is the sweetness of people whose own ancestors have been astray in an unfamiliar society and understand that a familiar society is the exception rather than the rule; that strangeness of behaviour which is the very lifeblood of the short story is often an atavistic breaking out from some peculiar way of life, faraway and long ago.

One of the many stories of my American students which I remember better than I do my own is one written by a Jewish boy about a woman who kept an old junk shop in New York and whose son stole quarters and fifty-cent pieces from the till for his own amusements. One evening he comes home and finds the till broken into and his mother unconscious. She had been mugged by another Jew whom she recognized. But when her son tries to call the police she goes mad. "Isn't it bad enough for poor Mrs. Birnbaum she should have a son a dirty thief without my sending the police to her?" "After that," the story ends, "I gave up stealing from the till."

Oh, Jews, you say! But that story isn't merely Jewish any more than Saroyan's loveliest stories are merely Armenian, or, indeed, Katherine Anne Porter's stories merely Negro or Irish. It is a voice from other worlds, like that of the little copying clerk in Gogol's "Overcoat" crying, "I am your brother."

That, I fancy, is the importance of J.F. Powers' stories to me. It is not a racial one, though, judging by his name, Mr. Powers must be even more Irish than I am. The best of his stories deal with priests or would-be priests, intruders on a money society, though the money society has left the mark of its dirty paws on the Church to which they belong. Powers has discovered a genuine submerged population as disturbing as Saroyan's Armenians, Willa Cather's spoiled artists, and Anderson's spoiled romantics, and again, across the abyss that separates me from them I seem to hear the voice of Gogol's copying clerk, crying, "I am your brother."

But, at the time of writing, the most typical of modern American storytellers is J.D. Salinger. It is not only that he has developed the form itself as no one since Chekhov had done or that in his work it stands out as precisely what it is — the anti-novel. What makes him typical is that though his theme is still human loneliness the loneliness is specific instead of generalized.

True, he makes a bold bid for our sympathy by producing characters who are the product of a Jewish-Irish marriage — the loneliest combination of submerged populations one can imagine. But in spite of this he has no submerged population, no objectivization for the loneliness in himself that he externalizes: all his characters are Hamlets. This may account for his popularity among young people who always tend to regard themselves as Hamlets. Zachary Glass is a grown man and apparently a very successful figure in a highly competitive commercial occupation — television — yet he is as isolated in his private world as any adolescent. Apparently, he doesn't get drunk and say silly things as some of us do, nor does he go home with the secretary to her apartment. One would like to know how he does it.

We can see the development in Salinger's work. In the most beautiful of the early stories — "For Esme, With Love and Squalor," a masterpiece if ever there was one — a conversation with a pert little English child saves the reason of an American soldier stationed abroad. In "A Splendid Day for Banana Fish" such a conversation does not save Seymour Glass from suicide. In "Franny" a girl on the verge of a nervous breakdown comes to a college match to meet the young man she is in love with and then cracks up in the women's lavatory and just recites, "Jesus, have mercy on me."

And already, in three stories we have run into serious critical difficulty. When "Franny" appeared college students and teachers split on the question of whether Franny was pregnant or not. This was not clumsiness on the part of the author, nor overcleverness on the part of readers. It was a real critical awareness on the part of the readers that somehow the story was insufficiently motivated — a point that is fully demonstrated by its sequel, "Zooey," in which Zachary Glass tries to deal with his sister's breakdown. For Zooey, like Franny, seems to have no animal existence. This was what the original readers were attempting to supply when they plumped for Franny's pregnancy. Pregnancy is a fact of animal life, and subconsciously they were aware that this was missing.

It is implied if not stated in "Franny" that she and her young man are lovers. At least they have been keeping company for a year and it had apparently not dawned on the young man that she was frigid. She is fastidious about animal food but there is no hint that she is repelled by animal contact. Franny, so far as I can see, is enduring a moral crisis without a morality. Her "Jesus" is completely disembodied, unrelated to any spiritual inadequacy in herself and to any possible roots this might have in her animal nature.

This becomes clearer in the long and beautifully composed sequel. Zooey is twenty-eight; he is a successful actor in a television performance that he despises.

At his age he is presumably not sexually innocent. Like Franny and their dead brother, Seymour, he is a God-seeker, yet never once are we told that his quest for ultimate reality affects his sexual life or his attitude to his work. Spiritual dissatisfaction does not drive him to leave his job and take up something that might satisfy him spiritually.

My only doubt about the Glass family is that they seem to me already perfect, and what is perfect can only fade.

◌

We have been told that the novel is dead, and I am sure that someone has said as much for the short story. I suspect that the announcement may prove a little premature, and I should be much readier to listen to an argument that poetry and the theatre were dead. I should not be too enthusiastic about that either, but I should be prepared to admit that since they are both primitive arts there would be some sort of case to answer. But the novel and the short story are drastic adaptations of a primitive art form to modern conditions — to printing, science, and individual religion — and I see no possibility of or reason for their supersession except in a general supersession of all culture by mass civilization. I suppose if this takes place, we shall all have to go into monasteries, or — if mass civilization forbids — into catacombs and caves, but even there, I suspect, more than one worshipper will be found clutching a tattered copy of *Pride and Prejudice* or *The Short Stories of Anton Chekhov*.

July 21, 1962

◌

The Approximate Size of My Favourite Tumour

A fter the argument that I had lost but pretended to win, I stormed out of the HUD house, jumped into the car, and prepared to drive off in victory, which was also known as defeat. But I realized that I hadn't grabbed my keys. At that kind of moment, a person begins to realize how he can be fooled by his own games. And at that kind of moment, a person begins to formulate a new game to compensate for the failure of the first.

"Honey, I'm home," I yelled as I walked back into the house.

My wife ignored me, gave me a momentary stoic look that impressed me with its resemblance to generations of television Indians.

"Oh, what is that?" I asked. "Your Tonto face?"

She flipped me off, shook her head, and disappeared into the bedroom.

"Honey," I called after her. "Didn't you miss me? I've been gone so long and it's good to be back home. Where I belong."

I could hear dresser drawers open and close.

"And look at the kids," I said as I patted the heads of imagined children. "They've grown so much. And they have your eyes."

She walked out of the bedroom in her favourite ribbon shirt, hair wrapped in her best ties, and wearing a pair of come-here boots. You know the kind with the curled toe that looks like a finger gesturing *Come here, cowboy, come on over here*. But those boots weren't meant for me: I'm an Indian.

"Honey," I asked, "I just get back from the war and you're leaving already? No kiss for the returning hero?"

She pretended to ignore me, which I enjoyed. But then she pulled out her car keys, checked herself in the mirror, and headed for the door. I jumped in front of her, knowing she meant to begin her own war. That scared the shit out of me.

"Hey," I said, "I was just kidding, honey. I'm sorry. I didn't mean anything. I'll do whatever you want me to."

She pushed me aside, adjusted her dreams, pulled on her braids for a jumpstart, and walked out the door. I followed her and stood on the porch as she jumped into the car and started it up.

"I'm going dancing," she said, and drove off into the sunset, or at least she drove down the tribal highway toward the Powwow Tavern.

"But what am I going to feed the kids?" I asked, and walked back into the house to feed myself and my illusions.

After a dinner of macaroni and commodity cheese, I put on my best shirt, a new pair of blue jeans, and set out to hitchhike down the tribal highway. The sun had gone down already so I decided that I was riding off toward the great unknown, which was actually the same Powwow Tavern where my love had escaped to an hour earlier.

As I stood on the highway, with my big, brown, and beautiful thumb showing me the way, Simon pulled up in his pickup, stopped, opened the passenger door, and whooped.

"Shit," he yelled. "If it ain't little Jimmy One-Horse! Where you going, cousin, and how fast do you need to get there?"

I hesitated at the offer of a ride. Simon was world famous, at least famous on the Spokane Indian Reservation, for driving backward. He always obeyed posted speed limits, traffic signals and signs, even minute suggestions. But he drove in reverse, using the rearview mirror as his guide. But what could I do? I trusted the man and when you trust a man you also have to trust his horse.

"I'm headed for the Powwow Tavern," I said, and climbed into Simon's rig. "And I need to be there before my wife finds herself a dance partner."

"Shit," Simon said. "Why didn't you say something sooner? We'll be there before she hears the first note of the first goddamned song."

Simon jammed the car into his only gear, reverse, and roared down the highway. I wanted to hang my head out the window like a dog, let my braids flap like a tongue in the wind, but good manners prevented me from taking the liberty. Still, it was so tempting. Always was.

"So, little Jimmy Sixteen and One-Half Horses," Simon asked me after a bit, "What did you do to make your wife take off this time?"

"Well," I said. "I told her the truth, Simon. I told her I got cancer everywhere inside me."

Simon slammed on the brakes and brought the pickup sliding to a quick but decidedly cinematic stop.

"That ain't nothing to joke about," he yelled.

"Ain't joking about the cancer," I said. "But I started joking about dying and that pissed her off."

"What'd you say?"

"Well, I told her the doctor showed me my X-rays and my favourite tumour was just about the size of a baseball, shaped like one, too. Even had stitch marks."

"You're full of shit."

"No, really. I told her to call me Babe Ruth. Or Roger Maris. Maybe even Hank Aaron 'cause there must have been about 755 damn tumours inside me. Then, I told her I was going to Cooperstown and sit right down at the lobby of the Hall of Fame. Make myself a new exhibit, you know? Pin my X-rays to my chest and point out the tumours. What a dedicated baseball fan! What a sacrifice for the national pastime!"

"You're an asshole, little Jimmy Zero-Horses."

"I know, I know," I said as Simon got the pickup rolling again, down the highway toward an uncertain future, which was, as usual, simply called the Powwow Tavern.

We rode the rest of the way in silence. That is to say that neither of us had anything at all to say. But I could hear Simon breathing and I'm sure he could hear me too. And once, he coughed.

"There you go, cousin," he said finally as he stopped his pickup in front of the Powwow Tavern. "I hope it all works out, you know?"

I shook his hand, offered him a few exaggerated gifts, made a couple of promises that he knew were just promises, and waved wildly as he drove off, backward, and away from the rest of my life. Then I walked into the tavern, shook my body like a dog shaking off water. I've always wanted to walk into a bar that way.

"Where the hell is Suzy Boyd?" I asked.

"Right here, asshole," Suzy answered quickly and succinctly.

"Okay, Suzy," I asked. "Where the hell is my wife?"

"Right here, asshole," my wife answered quickly and succinctly. Then she paused a second before she added, "And quit calling me *your wife*. It makes me sound like I'm a fucking bowling ball or something."

"Okay, okay, Norma," I said, and sat down beside her. I ordered a Diet Pepsi for me and a pitcher of beer for the next table. There was no one sitting at the next table. It was just something I always did. Someone would come along and drink it.

"Norma," I said. "I'm sorry. I'm sorry I have cancer and I'm sorry I'm dying."

She took a long drink of her Diet Pepsi, stared at me for a long time. Stared hard.

"Are you going to make any more jokes about it?" she asked.

"Just one or two more, maybe," I said, and smiled. It was exactly the wrong thing to say. Norma slapped me in anger, had a look of concern for a moment as she wondered what a slap could do to a person with terminal cancer, and then looked angry again.

"If you say anything funny ever again, I'm going to leave you," Norma said. "And I'm fucking serious about that."

I lost my smile briefly, reached across the table to hold her hand, and said something incredibly funny. It was maybe the best one-liner I had ever uttered. Maybe the moment that would have made me a star anywhere else. But in the Powwow Tavern, which was just a front for reality, Norma heard what I had to say, stood up, and left me.

☙

Because Norma left me, it's even more important to know how she arrived in my life.

I was sitting in the Powwow Tavern on a Saturday night with my Diet Pepsi and my second-favourite cousin, Raymond.

"Lookit, lookit," he said as Norma walked into the tavern. Norma was over six feet tall. Well, maybe not six feet tall but she was taller than me, taller than everyone in the bar except the basketball players.

"What tribe you think she is?" Raymond asked me.

"Amazon," I said.

"Their reservation down by Santa Fe, enit?" Raymond asked, and I laughed so hard that Norma came over to find out about the commotion.

"Hello, little brothers," she said. "Somebody want to buy me a drink?"

"What you having?" I asked.

"Diet Pepsi," she said, and I knew we would fall in love.

"Listen," I told her. "If I stole 1,000 horses, I'd give you 501 of them."

"And what other women would get the other 499?" she asked.

And we laughed. Then we laughed harder when Raymond leaned in closer to the table and said, "I don't get it."

Later, after the tavern closed, Norma and I sat outside on my car and shared a cigarette. I should say that we pretended to share a cigarette since neither of us smoked. But we both thought the other did and wanted to have all that much more in common.

After an hour or two of coughing, talking stories, and laughter, we ended up at my HUD house, watching late-night television. Raymond was passed out in the backseat of my car.

"Hey," she said. "That cousin of yours ain't too smart."

"Yeah," I said. "But he's cool, you know?"

"Must be. Because you're so good to him."

"He's my cousin, you know? That's how it is."

She kissed me then. Soft at first. Then harder. Our teeth clicked together like it was a junior high kiss. Still, we sat on the couch and kissed until the television signed off and broke into white noise. It was the end of another broadcast day.

"Listen," I said then. "I should take you home."

"Home?" she asked. "I thought I was at home."

"Well, my tipi is your tipi," I said, and she lived there until the day I told her I had terminal cancer.

☙

I have to mention the wedding, though. It was at the Spokane Tribal Longhouse and all my cousins and her cousins were there. Nearly two hundred people. Everything went smoothly until my second-favourite cousin, Raymond, drunk as a skunk, stood up in the middle of the ceremony, obviously confused.

"I remember Jimmy real good," Raymond said, and started into his eulogy for me as I stood not two feet from him. "Jimmy was always quick with a joke. Make you laugh all the damn time. I remember once at my grandmother's wake, he was standing by the coffin. Now, you got to remember he was only seven or eight years old. Anyway, he starts jumping up and down, yelling *She moved, she moved*."

Everyone at the wedding laughed because it was pretty much the same crowd that was at the funeral. Raymond smiled at his newly discovered public speaking ability and continued.

"Jimmy was always the one to make people feel better too," he said. "I remember once when he and I were drinking at the Powwow Tavern, when all of a sudden, Lester FallsApart comes running in and says that ten Indians just got killed in a car wreck on Ford Canyon Road. *Ten Skins?* I asked Lester, and he said, *Yeah, ten*. And then, Jimmy starts up singing, *One little, two little, three little Indians, four little, five little, six little Indians, seven little, eight little, nine little*

Indians, ten little Indian boys."

Everyone in the wedding laughed some more, but also looked a little tense after that story, so I grabbed Raymond and led him back to his seat. He stared incredulously at me, tried to reconcile his recent elegy with my sudden appearance. He just sat there until the preacher asked that most rhetorical of questions:

"And if there is anyone here who has objections to this union, speak now or forever hold your peace."

Raymond staggered and stumbled to his feet, then staggered and stumbled up to the preacher.

"Reverend," Raymond said. "I hate to interrupt, but my cousin is dead, you know? I think that might be a problem."

Raymond passed out at that moment and Norma and I were married with his body draped unceremoniously over our feet.

ᕲ

Three months after Norma left me, I lay in my hospital bed in Spokane, just back from another stupid and useless radiation treatment.

"Jesus," I said to my attending physician. "A few more zaps and I'll be Superman."

"Really?" the doctor said. "I never realized that Clark Kent was a Spokane Indian."

And we laughed, you know, because sometimes that's all two people have in common.

"So," I asked her. "What's my latest prognosis?"

"Well," she said. "It comes down to this. You're dying."

"Not again," I said.

"Yup, Jimmy, you're still dying."

And we laughed, you know, because sometimes you'd rather cry.

"Well," the doctor said. "I've got other patients to see."

As she walked out, I wanted to call her back and make an urgent confession, to ask forgiveness, to offer truth in return for salvation. But she was only a doctor. A good doctor, but still just a doctor.

"Hey, Dr. Adams," I said.

"What?"

"Nothing," I said. "Just wanted to hear your name. It sounds like drums to these heavily medicated Indian ears of mine."

And she laughed and I laughed too. That's what happened.

ᕲ

Norma was the world champion fry bread maker. Her fry bread was perfect, like one of those dreams you wake up from and say, *I didn't want to wake up.*

"I think this is your best fry bread ever," I told Norma one day. In fact, it was January 22.

"Thank you," she said. "Now you get to wash the dishes."

So I was washing the dishes when the phone rang. Norma answered it and I could hear her half of the conversation.

"Hello."

"Yes, this is Norma Many Horses."

"No."

"No!"

"*No!*" Norma yelled as she threw the phone down and ran outside. I picked the receiver up carefully, afraid of what it might say to me.

"Hello," I said.

"Who am I speaking to?" the voice on the other end asked.

"Jimmy Many Horses. I'm Norma's husband."

"Oh, Mr. Many Horses. I hate to be the bearer of bad news, but, uh, as I just told your wife, your mother-in-law, uh, passed away this morning."

"Thank you," I said, hung up the phone, and saw that Norma had returned.

"Oh, Jimmy," she said, talking through tears.

"I can't believe I just said *thank you* to that guy," I said. "What does that mean? Thank you that my mother-in-law is dead? Thank you that you told me that my mother-in-law is dead? Thank you that you told me that my mother-in-law is dead and made my wife cry?"

"Jimmy," Norma said. "Stop. It's not funny."

But I didn't stop. Then or now.

‹∅›

Still, you have to realize that laughter saved Norma and me from pain, too. Humour was an antiseptic that cleaned the deepest of personal wounds.

Once a Washington State patrolman stopped Norma and me as we drove to Spokane to see a movie, get some dinner, a Big Gulp at 7-11.

"Excuse me, officer," I asked. "What did I do wrong?"

"You failed to make proper signal for a turn a few blocks back," he said.

That was interesting because I had been driving down a straight highway for over five miles. The only turns possible were down dirt roads toward houses where no one I ever knew had lived. But I knew to play along with his game. All you can hope for in these little wars is to minimize the amount of damage.

"I'm sorry about that, officer," I said. "But you know how it is. I was listening to the radio, tapping my foot. It's those drums, you know."

"Whatever," the trooper said. "Now, I need your driver's license, registration, and proof of insurance."

I handed him the stuff and he barely looked at it. He leaned down into the window of the car.

"Hey, chief," he asked. "Have you been drinking?"

"I don't drink," I said.

"How about your woman there?"

"Ask her yourself," I said.

The trooper looked at me, blinked a few seconds, paused for dramatic effect, and said, "Don't you even think about telling me what I should do."

"I don't drink either," Norma said quickly, hoping to avoid any further confrontation. "And I wasn't driving anyway."

"That don't make any difference," the trooper said. "Washington State has a new law against riding as a passenger in an Indian car."

"Officer," I said. "That ain't new. We've known about that one for a couple hundred years."

The trooper smiled a little, but it was a hard smile. You know the kind.

"However," he said. "I think we can make some kind of arrangement so none of this has to go on your record."

"How much is it going to cost me?" I asked.

"How much do you have?"

"About a hundred bucks."

"Well," the trooper said. "I don't want to leave you with nothing. Let's say the fine is ninety-nine dollars."

I gave him all the money, though, four twenties, a ten, eight dollar bills, and two hundred pennies in a sandwich bag.

"Hey," I said. "Take it all. That extra dollar is a tip, you know? Your service has been excellent."

Norma wanted to laugh then. She covered her mouth and pretended to cough. His face turned red. I mean redder than it already was.

"In fact," I said as I looked at the trooper's badge, "I might just send a letter to your commanding officer. I'll just write that Washington State Patrolman D. Nolan, badge number 13746, was polite, courteous, and, above all, legal as an eagle."

Norma laughed out loud now.

"Listen," the trooper said. "I can just take you both in right now. For reckless driving, resisting arrest, threatening an officer with physical violence."

"If you do," Norma said, and jumped into the fun, "I'll just tell everyone how respectful you were of our Native traditions, how much you understood about the social conditions that lead to the criminal acts of so many Indians. I'll say you were sympathetic, concerned, and intelligent."

"Fucking Indians," the trooper said as he threw the sandwich bag of pennies back into our car, sending them flying all over the interior. "And keep your damn change."

We watched him walk back to his cruiser, climb in, and drive off, breaking four or five laws as he flipped a U-turn, left rubber, crossed the center line, broke the speed limit, and ran through a stop sign without lights and siren.

We laughed as we picked up the scattered pennies from the floor of the car. It was a good thing that the trooper threw the change back at us because we found just enough gas money to get us home.

෪

After Norma left me, I'd occasionally get postcards from powwows all over the country. She missed me in Washington, Oregon, Idaho, Montana, Nevada, Utah, New Mexico, and California. I just stayed on the Spokane Indian Reservation and missed her from the doorway of my HUD house, from the living room window, waiting for the day that she would come back.

But that's how Norma operated. She told me once that she would leave me whenever the love started to go bad.

"I ain't going to watch the whole thing collapse," she said. "I'll get out when the getting is good."

"You wouldn't even try to save us?" I asked.

"It wouldn't be worth saving at that point."

"That's pretty cold."

"That's not cold," she said. "It's practical."

But don't get me wrong, either. Norma was a warrior in every sense of the word. She would drive a hundred miles round-trip to visit tribal elders in the nursing homes in Spokane. When one of those elders died, Norma would weep violently, throw books and furniture.

"Every one of our elders that dies takes a piece of our past away," she said. "And that hurts more because I don't know how much of a future we have."

And once, when we drove up on a really horrible car wreck, she held a dying man's head in her lap and sang to him until he passed away. He was a white guy, too. Remember that. She kept that memory so close to her that she had nightmares for a year.

"I always dream that it's you who's dying," she told me, and didn't let me drive the car for almost a year.

Norma, she was always afraid; she wasn't afraid.

ca

One thing that I noticed in the hospital as I coughed myself up and down the bed: A clock, at least one of those old-style clocks with hands and a face, looks just like somebody laughing if you stare at it long enough.

ca

The hospital released me because they decided that I would be much more comfortable at home. And there I was, at home, writing letters to my loved ones on special reservation stationery that read: FROM THE DEATHBED OF JAMES MANY HORSES, III.

But in reality, I sat at my kitchen table to write, and DEATH TABLE just doesn't have the necessary music. I'm also the only James Many Horses but there is a certain dignity to any kind of artificial tradition.

Anyway, I sat there at the death table, writing letters from my deathbed, when there was a knock on the door.

"Come in," I yelled, knowing the door was locked, and smiled when it rattled against the frame.

"It's locked," a female voice said and it was a female voice I recognized.

"Norma?" I asked as I unlocked and opened the door.

She was beautiful. She had either gained or lost twenty pounds, one braid hung down a little longer than the other, and she had ironed her shirt until the creases were sharp.

"Honey," she said. "I'm home."

I was silent. That was a rare event.

"Honey," she said. "I've been gone so long and I missed you so much. But now I'm back. Where I belong."

I had to smile.

"Where are the kids?" she asked.

"They're asleep," I said, recovered just in time to continue the joke. "Poor little guys tried to stay awake, you know? They wanted to be up when you got home. But, one by one, they dropped off, fell asleep, and I had to carry them off into their little beds."

"Well," Norma said. "I'll just go in and kiss them quietly. Tell them how much I love them. Fix the sheets and blankets so they'll be warm all night."

She smiled.

"Jimmy," she said. "You look like shit."

"Yeah, I know."

"I'm sorry I left."

"Where've you been?" I asked, though I didn't really want to know.

"In Arlee. Lived with a Flathead cousin of mine."

"Cousin as in cousin? Or cousin as in I-was-fucking-him-but-don't-want-to-tell-you-because-you're-dying?"

She smiled even though she didn't want to.

"Well," she said. "I guess you'd call him more of that second kind of cousin."

Believe me: nothing ever hurt more. Not even my tumours, which are the approximate size of baseballs.

"Why'd you come back?" I asked her.

She looked at me, tried to suppress a giggle, then broke out into full-fledged laughter. I joined her.

"Well," I asked her again after a while. "Why'd you come back?"

She turned stoic, gave me that beautiful Tonto face, and said, "Because he was so fucking serious about everything."

We laughed a little more and then I asked her one more time, "Really, why'd you come back?"

"Because someone needs to help you die the right way," she said. "And we both know that dying ain't something you ever done before."

I had to agree with that.

"And maybe," she said, "because making fry bread and helping people die are the last two things Indians are good at."

"Well," I said. "At least you're good at one of them."

And we laughed.

&)(&

Hoping that assimilated Indians would stay in the cities and abandon the resource-rich reservation lands, the U.S. Bureau of Indian Affairs persuaded many Indian people to move away from their homes to pursue a university education. Not surprisingly, then, the

*best known Native American authors — Momaday, Silko, Erdrich, Welsh, and Vizenor —
are well-educated academics. That makes Sherman Alexie, who is not a scholar, something
of an anomaly in the world of contemporary Native American literature. Like Jimmy Many
Horses, the protagonist of this story, Alexie is just a really funny guy from "the rez." Yet
even though both Alexie and Jimmy are funny, "The Approximate Size of my Favourite
Tumour" is not, at first glance, a very funny story. Jimmy Many Horses' life is bleak, but he
uses humour, albeit to excess, to cope with cancer, poverty, and racism. Showing readers
the humour that has helped Native Americans survive 500 years of oppression, Alexie
continues his battle to explode the Hollywood stereotype of the stoic Indian by introducing
readers to endearing and enduring Native Americans who, like Jimmy, have not vanished
from this continent.*

                                                                              J.T.

JAMES BALDWIN *(1924-1987)*

Sonny's Blues

I read about it in the paper, in the subway, on my way to work. I read it, and I couldn't believe it, and I read it again. Then perhaps I just stared at it, at the newsprint spelling out his name, spelling out the story. I stared at it in the swinging lights of the subway car, and in the faces and bodies of the people, and in my own face, trapped in the darkness which roared outside.

It was not to be believed and I kept telling myself that, as I walked from the subway station to the high school. And at the same time I couldn't doubt it. I was scared, scared for Sonny. He became real to me again. A great block of ice got settled in my belly and kept melting there slowly all day long, while I taught my classes algebra. It was a special kind of ice. It kept melting, sending trickles of ice water all up and down my veins, but it never got less. Sometimes it hardened and seemed to expand until I felt my guts were going to come spilling out or that I was going to choke or scream. This would always be at a moment when I was remembering some specific thing Sonny had once said or done.

When he was about as old as the boys in my classes his face had been bright and open, there was a lot of copper in it; and he'd had wonderfully direct brown eyes, and great gentleness and privacy. I wondered what he looked like now. He had been picked up the evening before, in a raid on an apartment downtown, for peddling and using heroin.

I couldn't believe it: but what I mean by that is that I couldn't find any room for it anywhere inside me. I had kept it outside me for a long time. I hadn't wanted to know. I had had suspicions, but I didn't name them, I kept putting them away. I told myself that Sonny was wild, but he wasn't crazy. And he'd always been a good boy, he hadn't ever turned hard or evil or disrespectful, the way kids can, so quick, so quick, especially in Harlem. I didn't want to believe that I'd ever see my brother going down, coming to nothing, all that light in his face gone out, in the condition I'd already seen so many others. Yet it had happened and here I was, talking about algebra to a lot of boys who might, every one of them for all I knew, be popping off needles every time they went to the head. Maybe it did more for them than algebra could.

I was sure that the first time Sonny had ever had horse, he couldn't have been much older than these boys were now. These boys, now, were living as we'd been living then, they were growing up with a rush and their heads bumped abruptly against the low ceiling of their actual possibilities. They were filled with rage. All they really knew were two darknesses, the darkness of their lives, which was now closing in on them, and the darkness of the movies, which had blinded them to that other darkness, and in which they now, vindictively, dreamed, at once more together than they were at any other time, and more alone.

When the last bell rang, the last class ended, I let out my breath. It seemed I'd been holding it for all that time. My clothes were wet — I may have looked as though I'd been sitting in a steam bath, all dressed up, all afternoon. I sat alone in the classroom a long time. I listened to the boys outside, downstairs, shouting and cursing and laughing. Their laughter struck me for perhaps the first time. It was not the joyous laughter which — God knows why — one associates with children. It was mocking and insular, its intent was to denigrate. It was disenchanted, and in this, also, lay the authority of their curse. Perhaps I was listening to them because I was thinking about my brother and in them I heard my brother. And myself.

One boy was whistling a tune, at once very complicated and very simple, it seemed to be pouring out of him as though he were a bird, and it sounded very cool and moving through all that harsh, bright air, only just holding its own through all those other sounds.

I stood up and walked over to the window and looked down into the courtyard. It was the beginning of the spring and the sap was rising in the boys. A teacher passed through them every now and again, quickly, as though he or she couldn't wait to get out of that courtyard, to get those boys out of their sight and off their minds. I started collecting my stuff. I thought I'd better get home and talk to Isabel.

The courtyard was almost deserted by the time I got downstairs. I saw this boy standing in the shadow of a doorway, looking just like Sonny. I almost called his name. Then I saw that it wasn't Sonny, but somebody we used to know, a boy from around our block. He'd been Sonny's friend. He'd never been mine, having been too young for me, and, anyway, I'd never liked him. And now, even though he was a grown-up man, he still hung around that block, still spent hours on the street corners, was always high and raggy. I used to run into him from time to time and he'd often work around to asking me for a quarter or fifty cents. He always had some real good excuse, too, and I always gave it to him, I don't know why.

But now, abruptly, I hated him. I couldn't stand the way he looked at me, partly like a dog, partly like a cunning child. I wanted to ask him what the hell he was doing in the school courtyard.

He sort of shuffled over to me, and he said, "I see you got the papers. So you already know about it."

"You mean about Sonny? Yes, I already know about it. How come they didn't get you?"

He grinned. It made him repulsive and it also brought to mind what he'd looked like as a kid. "I wasn't there. I stay away from them people."

"Good for you." I offered him a cigarette and I watched him through the smoke. "You come all the way down here just to tell me about Sonny?"

"That's right." He was sort of shaking his head and his eyes looked strange, as though they were about to cross. The bright sun deadened his damp dark brown skin and it made his eyes look yellow and showed up the dirt in his kinked hair. He smelled funky. I moved a little way away from him and I said, "Well, thanks. But I already know about it and I got to get home."

"I'll walk you a little ways," he said. We started walking. There were a couple of kids still loitering in the courtyard and one of them said goodnight to me and looked strangely at the boy beside me.

"What're you going to do?" he asked me. "I mean, about Sonny?"

"Look. I haven't seen Sonny for over a year, I'm not sure I'm going to do anything. Anyway, what the hell *can* I do?"

"That's right," he said quickly, "ain't nothing you can do. Can't much help old Sonny no more, I guess."

It was what I was thinking and so it seemed to me he had no right to say it.

"I'm surprised at Sonny, though," he went on — he had a funny way of talking, he looked straight ahead as though he were talking to himself — "I thought Sonny was a smart boy, I thought he was too smart to get hung."

"I guess he thought so too," I said sharply, "and that's how he got hung. And how about you? You're pretty goddamn smart, I bet."

Then he looked directly at me, just for a minute. "I ain't smart," he said. "If I was smart, I'd have reached for a pistol a long time ago."

"Look. Don't tell *me* your sad story, if it was up to me, I'd give you one." Then I felt guilty — guilty, probably, for never having supposed that the poor bastard *had* a story of his own, much less a sad one, and I asked, quickly, "What's going to happen to him now?"

He didn't answer this. He was off by himself some place. "Funny thing," he said, and from his tone we might have been discussing the quickest way to get to Brooklyn, "when I saw the papers this morning, the first thing I asked myself was if I had anything to do with it. I felt sort of responsible."

I began to listen more carefully. The subway station was on the corner, just before us, and I stopped. He stopped, too. We were in front of a bar and he ducked slightly, peering in, but whoever he was looking for didn't seem to be there. The juke box was blasting away with something black and bouncy and I half watched the barmaid as she danced her way from the juke box to her place behind the bar. And I watched her face as she laughingly responded to something someone said to her, still keeping time to the music. When she smiled one saw the little girl, one sensed the doomed, still-struggling woman beneath the battered face of the semi-whore.

"I never *give* Sonny nothing," the boy said finally, "but a long time ago I come to school high and Sonny asked me how it felt." He paused, I couldn't bear to watch him, I watched the barmaid, and I listened to the music which seemed to be causing the pavement to shake. "I told him it felt great." The music stopped, the barmaid paused and watched the juke box until the music began again. "It did."

All this was carrying me some place I didn't want to go. I certainly didn't want to know how it felt. It filled everything, the people, the houses, the music, the dark, quicksilver barmaid, with menace; and this menace was their reality.

"What's going to happen to him now?" I asked again.

"They'll send him away some place and they'll try to cure him." He shook his head. "Maybe he'll even think he's kicked the habit. Then they'll let him loose" — he gestured, throwing his cigarette into the gutter. "That's all."

"What do you mean, that's *all*?"

But I knew what he meant.

"I *mean*, that's *all*." He turned his head and looked at me, pulling down the corners of his mouth. "Don't you know what I mean?" he asked, softly.

"How the hell *would* I know what you mean?" I almost whispered it, I don't know why.

"That's right," he said to the air, "how would *he* know what I mean?" He turned toward me again, patient and calm, and yet I somehow felt him shaking, shaking as though he were going to fall apart. I felt that ice in my guts again, the dread I'd felt all afternoon; and again I watched the barmaid, moving about the bar, washing glasses, and singing. "Listen. They'll let him out and then it'll just start all over again. That's what I mean."

"You mean — they'll let him out. And then he'll just start working his way back in again. You mean he'll never kick the habit. Is that what you mean?"

"That's right," he said cheerfully. "*You* see what I mean."

"Tell me," I said at last, "why does he want to die? He must want to die, he's killing himself, why does he want to die?"

He looked at me in surprise. He licked his lips. "He don't want to die. He wants to live. Don't nobody want to die, ever."

Then I wanted to ask him — too many things. He could not have answered, for if he had, I could not have borne the answers. I started walking. "Well, I guess it's none of my business."

"It's going to be rough on old Sonny," he said. We reached the subway station. "This is your station?" he asked. I nodded. I took one step down. "Damn!" he said suddenly. I looked up at him. He grinned again. "Damn it if I didn't leave all my money home. You ain't got a dollar on you, have you? Just for a couple of days, is all."

All at once something inside gave and threatened to come pouring out of me. I didn't hate him any more. I felt that in another moment I'd start crying like a child.

"Sure," I said. "Don't sweat." I looked in my wallet and didn't have a dollar, I only had five. "Here," I said. "That hold you?"

He didn't look at it — he didn't want to look at it. A terrible, closed look came over his face, as though he were keeping the number on the bill a secret from him and me. "Thanks," he said, and now he was dying to see me go. "Don't worry about Sonny. Maybe I'll write him or something."

"Sure," I said. "You do that. So long."

"Be seeing you," he said. I went on down the steps.

™

And I didn't write Sonny or send him anything for a long time. When I finally did, it was just after my little girl died, he wrote me back a letter which made me feel like a bastard.

Here's what he said:

> Dear brother,
> You don't know how much I needed to hear from you. I wanted to write you many a time but I dug how much I must have hurt you and so I didn't write. But now I feel like a man who's been trying to

climb up out of some deep, real deep and funky hole and just saw the sun up there, outside. I got to get outside.

I can't tell you much about how I got here. I mean I don't know how to tell you. I guess I was afraid of something or I was trying to escape from something and you know I have never been very strong in the head (smile). I'm glad Mama and Daddy are dead and can't see what's happened to their son and I swear if I'd known what I was doing I would never have hurt you so, you and a lot of other fine people who were nice to me and who believed in me.

I don't want you to think it had anything to do with me being a musician. It's more than that. Or maybe less than that. I can't get anything straight in my head down here and I try not to think about what's going to happen to me when I get outside again. Sometime I think I'm going to flip and *never* get outside and sometime I think I'll come straight back. I tell you one thing, though, I'd rather blow my brains out than go through this again. But that's what they all say, so they tell me. If I tell you when I'm coming to New York and if you could meet me, I sure would appreciate it. Give my love to Isabel and the kids and I was sure sorry to hear about little Gracie. I wish I could be like Mama and say the Lord's will be done, but I don't know it seems to me that trouble is the one thing that never does get stopped and I don't know what good it does to blame it on the Lord. But maybe it does some good if you believe it.

Your brother,
Sonny

Then I kept in constant touch with him and I sent him whatever I could and I went to meet him when he came back to New York. When I saw him many things I thought I had forgotten came flooding back to me. This was because I had begun, finally, to wonder about Sonny, about the life that Sonny lived inside. This life, whatever it was, had made him older and thinner and it had deepened the distant stillness in which he had always moved. He looked very unlike my baby brother. Yet, when he smiled, when we shook hands, the baby brother I'd never known looked out from the depths of his private life, like an animal waiting to be coaxed into the light.

"How you been keeping?" he asked me.

"All right. And you?"

"Just fine." He was smiling all over his face. "It's good to see you again."

"It's good to see you."

The seven years' difference in our ages lay between us like a chasm: I wondered if these years would ever operate between us as a bridge. I was remembering, and it made it hard to catch my breath, that I had been there when he was born; and I had heard the first words he had ever spoken. When he started to walk, he walked from our mother straight to me. I caught him just before he fell when he took the first steps he ever took in this world.

"How's Isabel?"

"Just fine. She's dying to see you."

"And the boys?"

"They're fine, too. They're anxious to see their uncle."

"Oh, come on. You know they don't remember me."

"Are you kidding? Of course they remember you."

He grinned again. We got into a taxi. We had a lot to say to each other, far too much to know how to begin.

As the taxi began to move, I asked, "You still want to go to India?"

He laughed. "You still remember that. Hell, no. This place is Indian enough for me."

"It used to belong to them," I said.

And he laughed again. "They damn sure knew what they were doing when they got rid of it."

Years ago, when he was around fourteen, he'd been all hipped on the idea of going to India. He read books about people sitting on rocks, naked, in all kinds of weather, but mostly bad, naturally, and walking barefoot through hot coals and arriving at wisdom. I used to say that it sounded to me as though they were getting away from wisdom as fast as they could. I think he sort of looked down on me for that.

"Do you mind," he asked, "if we have the driver drive alongside the park? On the west side — I haven't seen the city in so long."

"Of course not," I said. I was afraid that I might sound as though I were humouring him, but I hoped he wouldn't take it that way.

So we drove along, between the green of the park and the stony, lifeless elegance of hotels and apartment buildings, toward the vivid, killing streets of our childhood. These streets hadn't changed, though housing projects jutted up out of them now like rocks in the middle of a boiling sea. Most of the houses in which we had grown up had vanished, as had the stores from which we had stolen, the basements in which we had first tried sex, the rooftops from which we had hurled tin cans and bricks. But houses exactly like the houses of our past yet dominated the landscape, boys exactly like the boys we once had been found themselves smothering in these houses, came down into the streets for light and air and found themselves encircled by disaster. Some escaped the trap, most didn't. Those who got out always left something of themselves behind, as some animals amputate a leg and leave it in the trap. It might be said, perhaps, that I had escaped, after all, I was a school teacher; or that Sonny had, he hadn't lived in Harlem for years. Yet, as the cab moved uptown through streets which seemed, with a rush, to darken with dark people, and as I covertly studied Sonny's face, it came to me that what we both were seeking through our separate cab windows was that part of ourselves which had been left behind. It's always at the hour of trouble and confrontation that the missing member aches.

We hit 110th Street and started rolling up Lenox Avenue. And I'd known this avenue all my life, but it seemed to me again, as it had seemed on the day I'd first heard about Sonny's trouble, filled with a hidden menace which was its very breath of life.

"We almost there," said Sonny.

"Almost." We were both too nervous to say anything more.

We live in a housing project. It hasn't been up long. A few days after it was up it seemed uninhabitably new; now, of course, it's already rundown. It looks like a parody of the good, clean, faceless life — God knows the people who live in it do their best to make it a parody. The beat-looking grass lying around isn't enough to make their lives green, the hedges will never hold out the streets, and they know it. The big windows fool no one, they aren't big enough to make space out of no space. They don't bother with the windows, they watch the TV screen instead. The playground is most popular with the children who don't play at jacks, or skip rope, or roller skate, or swing, and they can be found in it after dark. We moved in partly because it's not too far from where I teach, and partly for the kids; but it's really just like the houses in which Sonny and I grew up. The same things happen, they'll have the same things to remember. The moment Sonny and I started into the house I had the feeling that I was simply bringing him back into the danger he had almost died trying to escape.

Sonny has never been talkative. So I don't know why I was sure he'd be dying to talk to me when supper was over the first night. Everything went fine, the oldest boy remembered him, and the youngest boy liked him, and Sonny had remembered to bring something for each of them; and Isabel, who is really much nicer than I am, more open and giving, had gone to a lot of trouble about dinner and was genuinely glad to see him. And she's always been able to tease Sonny in a way that I haven't. It was nice to see her face so vivid again and to hear her laugh and watch her make Sonny laugh. She wasn't, or, anyway, she didn't seem to be, at all uneasy or embarrassed. She chatted as though there were no subject which had to be avoided and she got Sonny past his first, faint stiffness. And thank God she was there, for I was filled with that icy dread again. Everything I did seemed awkward to me, and everything I said sounded freighted with hidden meaning. I was trying to remember everything I'd heard about dope addiction and I couldn't help watching Sonny for signs. I wasn't doing it out of malice. I was trying to find out something about my brother. I was dying to hear him tell me he was safe.

"Safe!" my father grunted, whenever Mama suggested trying to move to a neighbourhood which might be safer for children. "Safe, hell! Ain't no place safe for kids, nor nobody."

He always went on like this, but he wasn't, ever, really as bad as he sounded, not even on weekends, when he got drunk. As a matter of fact, he was always on the lookout for "something a little better," but he died before he found it. He died suddenly, during a drunken weekend in the middle of the war, when Sonny was fifteen. He and Sonny hadn't ever got on too well. And this was partly because Sonny was the apple of his father's eye. It was because he loved Sonny so much and was frightened for him, that he was always fighting with him. It doesn't do any good to fight with Sonny. Sonny just moves back, inside himself, where he can't be reached. But the principal reason that they never hit it off is that they were so much alike. Daddy was big and rough and loud-talking, just the opposite of Sonny, but they both had — that same privacy.

Mama tried to tell me something about this, just after Daddy died. I was home on leave from the army.

This was the last time I ever saw my mother alive. Just the same, this picture gets all mixed up in my mind with pictures I had of her when she was younger. The way I always see her is the way she used to be on a Sunday afternoon, say, when the old folks were talking after the big Sunday dinner. I always see her wearing pale blue. She'd be sitting on the sofa. And my father would be sitting in the easy chair, not far from her. And the living room would be full of church folks and relatives. There they sit, in chairs all around the living room, and the night is creeping up outside, but nobody knows it yet. You can see the darkness growing against the windowpanes and you hear the street noises every now and again, or maybe the jangling beat of a tambourine from one of the churches close by, but it's real quiet in the room. For a moment nobody's talking, but every face looks darkening, like the sky outside. And my mother rocks a little from the waist, and my father's eyes are closed. Everyone is looking at something a child can't see. For a minute they've forgotten the children. Maybe a kid is lying on the rug, half asleep. Maybe somebody's got a kid in his lap and is absent-mindedly stroking the kid's head. Maybe there's a kid, quiet and big-eyed, curled up in a big chair in the corner. The silence, the darkness coming, and the darkness in the faces frightens the child obscurely. He hopes that the hand which strokes his forehead will never stop — will never die. He hopes that there will never come a time when the old folks won't be sitting around the living room, talking about where they've come from, and what they've seen, and what's happened to them and their kinfolk.

But something deep and watchful in the child knows that this is bound to end, is already ending. In a moment someone will get up and turn on the light. Then the old folks will remember the children and they won't talk any more that day. And when light fills the room, the child is filled with darkness. He knows that every time this happens he's moved just a little closer to that darkness outside. The darkness outside is what the old folks have been talking about. It's what they've come from. It's what they endure. The child knows that they won't talk any more because if he knows too much about what's happening to *them*, he'll know too much too soon, about what's going to happen to *him*.

The last time I talked to my mother, I remember I was restless. I wanted to get out and see Isabel. We weren't married then and we had a lot to straighten out between us.

There Mama sat, in black, by the window. She was humming an old church song, *Lord, you brought me from a long ways off*. Sonny was out somewhere. Mama kept watching the streets.

"I don't know," she said, "if I'll ever see you again, after you go off from here. But I hope you'll remember the things I tried to teach you."

"Don't talk like that," I said, and smiled. "You'll be here a long time yet."

She smiled, too, but she said nothing. She was quiet for a long time. And I said, "Mama, don't you worry about nothing. I'll be writing all the time, and you be getting the checks. . . ."

"I want to talk to you about your brother," she said, suddenly. "If anything happens to me he ain't going to have nobody to look out for him."

"Mama," I said, "ain't nothing going to happen to you *or* Sonny. Sonny's all right. He's a good boy and he's got good sense."

"It ain't a question of his being a good boy," Mama said, "nor of his having good sense. It ain't only the bad ones, nor yet the dumb ones that gets sucked under." She stopped, looking at me. "Your Daddy once had a brother," she said, and she smiled in a way that made me feel she was in pain. "You didn't never know that, did you?"

"No," I said, "I never knew that," and I watched her face.

"Oh, yes," she said, "your Daddy had a brother." She looked out of the window again. "I know you never saw your Daddy cry. But *I* did — many a time, through all these years."

I asked her, "What happened to his brother? How come nobody's ever talked about him?"

This was the first time I ever saw my mother look old.

"His brother got killed," she said, "when he was just a little younger than you are now. I knew him. He was a fine boy. He was maybe a little full of the devil, but he didn't mean nobody no harm."

Then she stopped and the room was silent, exactly as it had sometimes been on those Sunday afternoons. Mama kept looking out into the streets.

"He used to have a job in the mill," she said, "and, like all young folks, he just liked to perform on Saturday nights. Saturday nights, him and your father would drift around to different places, go to dances and things like that, or just sit around with people they knew, and your father's brother would sing, he had a fine voice, and play along with himself on his guitar. Well, this particular Saturday night, him and your father was coming home from some place, and they were both a little drunk and there was a moon that night, it was bright like day. Your father's brother was feeling kind of good, and he was whistling to himself, and he had his guitar slung over his shoulder. They was coming down a hill and beneath them was a road that turned off from the highway. Well, your father's brother, being always kind of frisky, decided to run down this hill, and he did, with that guitar banging and clanging behind him, and he ran across the road, and he was making water behind a tree. And your father was sort of amused at him and he was still coming down the hill, kind of slow. Then he heard a car motor and that same minute his brother stepped from behind the tree, into the road, in the moonlight. And he started to cross the road. And your father started to run down the hill, he says he don't know why. This car was full of white men. They was all drunk, and when they seen your father's brother they let out a great whoop and holler and they aimed the car straight at him. They was having fun, they just wanted to scare him, the way they do sometimes, you know. But they was drunk. And I guess the boy, being drunk, too, and scared, kind of lost his head. By the time he jumped it was too late. Your father says he heard his brother scream when the car rolled over him, and he heard the wood of that guitar when it give, and he heard them strings go flying, and he heard them white men shouting, and the car kept on a-going and it ain't stopped till this day. And, time your father got down the hill, his brother weren't nothing but blood and pulp."

Tears were gleaming on my mother's face. There wasn't anything I could say.

"He never mentioned it," she said, "because I never let him mention it before you children. Your Daddy was like a crazy man that night and for many a night thereafter. He says he never in his life seen anything as dark as that road after the lights of that car had gone away. Weren't nothing, weren't nobody on that road, just your Daddy and his brother and that busted guitar. Oh, yes. Your Daddy never did really get right again. Till the day he died he weren't sure but that every white man he saw was the man that killed his brother."

She stopped and took out her handkerchief and dried her eyes and looked at me.

"I ain't telling you all this," she said, "to make you scared or bitter or to make you hate nobody. I'm telling you this because you got a brother. And the world ain't changed."

I guess I didn't want to believe this. I guess she saw this in my face. She turned away from me, toward the window again, searching those streets.

"But I praise my Redeemer," she said at last, "that He called your Daddy home before me. I ain't saying it to throw no flowers at myself, but, I declare, it keeps me from feeling too cast down to know I helped your father get safely through this world. Your father always acted like he was the roughest, strongest man on earth. And everybody took him to be like that. But if he hadn't had *me* there — to see his tears!"

She was crying again. Still I couldn't move. I said, "Lord, Lord, Mama, I didn't know it was like that."

"Oh, honey," she said, "there's a lot that you don't know. But you are going to find it out." She stood up from the window and came over to me. "You got to hold on to your brother," she said, "and don't let him fall, no matter what it looks like is happening to him and no matter how evil you gets with him. You going to be evil with him many a time. But don't you forget what I told you, you hear?"

"I won't forget," I said. "Don't you worry, I won't forget. I won't let nothing happen to Sonny."

My mother smiled as though she were amused at something she saw in my face. Then, "You may not be able to stop nothing from happening. But you got to let him know you's *there*."

◌ℜ

Two days later I was married, and then I was gone. And I had a lot of things on my mind and I pretty well forgot my promise to Mama until I got shipped home on a special furlough for her funeral.

And, after the funeral, with just Sonny and me alone in the empty kitchen, I tried to find out something about him.

"What do you want to do?" I asked him.

"I'm going to be a musician," he said.

For he had graduated, in the time I had been away, from dancing to the juke box to finding out who was playing what, and what they were doing with it, and he had bought himself a set of drums.

"You mean, you want to be a drummer?" I somehow had the feeling that being a drummer might be all right for other people but not for my brother Sonny.

"I don't think," he said, looking at me very gravely, "that I'll ever be a good drummer. But I think I can play a piano."

I frowned. I'd never played the role of the older brother quite so seriously before, had scarcely ever, in fact, *asked* Sonny a damn thing. I sensed myself in the presence of something I didn't really know how to handle, didn't understand. So I made my frown a little deeper as I asked: "What kind of musician do you want to be?"

He grinned. "How many kinds do you think there are?"

"Be *serious*," I said.

He laughed, throwing his head back, and then looked at me. "I *am* serious."

"Well, then, for Christ's sake, stop kidding around and answer a serious question. I mean, do you want to be a concert pianist, you want to play classical music and all that, or — or what?" Long before I finished he was laughing again. "For Christ's *sake*, Sonny!"

He sobered, but with difficulty. "I'm sorry. But you sound so — *scared!*" and he was off again.

"Well, you may think it's funny now, baby, but it's not going to be so funny when you have to make your living at it, let me tell you *that.*" I was furious because I knew he was laughing at me and I didn't know why.

"No," he said, very sober now, and afraid, perhaps, that he'd hurt me, "I don't want to be a classical pianist. That isn't what interests me. I mean" — he paused, looking hard at me, as though his eyes would help me to understand, and then gestured helplessly, as though perhaps his hand would help— "I mean, I'll have a lot of studying to do, and I'll have to study *everything*, but, I mean, I want to play *with* — jazz musicians." He stopped. "I want to play jazz," he said.

Well, the word had never before sounded as heavy, as real, as it sounded that afternoon in Sonny's mouth. I just looked at him and I was probably frowning a real frown by this time. I simply couldn't see why on earth he'd want to spend his time hanging around nightclubs, clowning around on bandstands, while people pushed each other around a dance floor. It seemed — beneath him, somehow. I had never thought about it before, had never been forced to, but I suppose I had always put jazz musicians in a class with what Daddy called "good-time people."

"Are you *serious*?"

"Hell, *yes*, I'm serious."

He looked more helpless than ever, and annoyed, and deeply hurt.

I suggested helpfully: "You mean — like Louis Armstrong?"

His face closed as though I'd struck him. "No. I'm not talking about none of that old-time, down home crap."

"Well, look Sonny, I'm sorry, don't get mad. I just don't altogether get it, that's all. Name somebody — you know, a jazz musician you admire."

"Bird."

"Who?"

"Bird! Charlie Parker! Don't they teach you nothing in the goddamn army?"

I lit a cigarette. I was surprised and then a little amused to discover that I was trembling. "I've been out of touch," I said. "You'll have to be patient with me. Now. Who's this Parker character?"

"He's just one of the greatest jazz musicians alive," said Sonny, sullenly, his hands in his pockets, his back to me. "Maybe *the* greatest," he added, bitterly, "that's probably why *you* never heard of him."

"All right," I said, "I'm ignorant. I'm sorry. I'll go out and buy all the cat's records right away, all right?"

"It don't," said Sonny, with dignity, "make any difference to me. I don't care what you listen to. Don't do me no favours."

I was beginning to realize that I'd never seen him so upset before. With another part of my mind I was thinking that this would probably turn out to be one of those things kids go through and that I shouldn't make it seem important by pushing it too hard. Still, I didn't think it would do any harm to ask: "Doesn't all this take a lot of time? Can you make a living at it?"

He turned back to me and half leaned, half sat, on the kitchen table. "Everything takes time," he said, "and — well, yes, sure, I can make a living at it. But what I don't seem to be able to make you understand is that it's the only thing I want to do."

"Well, Sonny," I said gently, "you know people can't always do exactly what they *want* to do —"

"*No*, I don't know that," said Sonny, surprising me. "I think people *ought* to do what they want to do, what else are they alive for?"

"You are getting to be a big boy," I said desperately, "it's time you started thinking about your future."

"I'm thinking about my future," said Sonny, grimly. "I think about it all the time."

I gave up. I decided, if he didn't change his mind, that we could always talk about it later. "In the meantime," I said, "you got to finish school." We had already decided that he'd have to move in with Isabel and her folks. I knew this wasn't the ideal arrangement because Isabel's folks are inclined to be dicty and they hadn't especially wanted Isabel to marry me. But I didn't know what else to do. "And we have to get you fixed up at Isabel's."

There was a long silence. He moved from the kitchen table to the window. "That's a terrible idea. You know it yourself."

"Do you have a *better* idea?"

He just walked up and down the kitchen for a minute. He was as tall as I was. He had started to shave. I suddenly had the feeling that I didn't know him at all.

He stopped at the kitchen table and picked up my cigarettes. Looking at me with a kind of mocking, amused defiance, he put one between his lips. "You mind?"

"You smoking already?"

He lit the cigarette and nodded, watching me through the smoke. "I just wanted to see if I'd have the courage to smoke in front of you." He grinned and blew a great cloud of smoke to the ceiling. "It was easy." He looked at my face. "Come on, now. I bet you was smoking at my age, tell the truth."

I didn't say anything but the truth was on my face, and he laughed. But now there was something very strained in his laugh. "Sure. And I bet that ain't all you was doing."

He was frightening me a little. "Cut the crap," I said. "We already decided that you was going to go and live at Isabel's. Now what's got into you all of a sudden?"

"*You* decided it," he pointed out. "*I* didn't decide nothing." He stopped in front of me, leaning against the stove, arms loosely folded. "Look, brother. I don't want to stay in Harlem no more, I really don't." He was very earnest. He looked at me, then over toward the kitchen window. There was something in his eyes I'd never seen before, some thoughtfulness, some worry all his own. He rubbed the muscle of one arm. "It's time I was getting out of here."

"Where do you want to *go*, Sonny?"

"I want to join the army. Or the navy, I don't care. If I say I'm old enough, they'll believe me."

Then I got mad. It was because I was so scared. "You must be crazy. You goddamn fool, what the hell do you want to go and join the *army* for?"

"I just told you. To get out of Harlem."

"Sonny, you haven't even finished *school*. And if you really want to be a musician, how do you expect to study if you're in the *army*?"

He looked at me, trapped, and in anguish. "There's ways. I might be able to work out some kind of deal. Anyway, I'll have the G.I. Bill when I come out."

"*If* you come out." We stared at each other. "Sonny, please. Be reasonable. I know the setup is far from perfect. But we got to do the best we can."

"I ain't learning nothing in school," he said. "Even when I go." He turned away from me and opened the window and threw his cigarette out into the narrow alley. I watched his back. "At least, I ain't learning nothing you'd want me to learn." He slammed the window so hard I thought the glass would fly out, and turned back to me. "And I'm sick of the stink of these garbage cans!"

"Sonny," I said, "I know how you feel, but if you don't finish school now, you're going to be sorry later that you didn't." I grabbed him by the shoulders. "And you only got another year. It ain't so bad. And I'll come back and I swear I'll help you do *whatever* you want to do. Just try to put up with it till I come back. Will you please do that? For me?"

He didn't answer and he wouldn't look at me.

"Sonny. You hear me?"

He pulled away. "I hear you. But you never hear anything *I* say."

I didn't know what to say to that. He looked out of the window and then back at me. "OK," he said, and sighed. "I'll try."

Then I said, trying to cheer him up a little, "They got a piano at Isabel's. You can practise on it."

And as a matter of fact, it did cheer him up for a minute. "That's right," he said to himself. "I forgot that." His face relaxed a little. But the worry, the thoughtfulness, played on it still, the way shadows play on a face which is staring into the fire.

CR

But I thought I'd never hear the end of that piano. At first, Isabel would write me, saying how nice it was that Sonny was so serious about his music, and how, as soon as he came in from school, or wherever he had been when he was supposed to be at school, he went straight to that piano and stayed there until suppertime. And, after supper, he went back to that piano and stayed there until everybody went to bed. He was at the piano all day Saturday and all day Sunday. Then he bought a record player and started playing records. He'd play one record over and over again, all day long sometimes, until he'd improvise along with it on the piano. Or he'd play one section of the record, one chord, one change, one progression, then he'd do it on the piano. Then back to the record. Then back to the piano.

Well, I really don't know how they stood it. Isabel finally confessed that it wasn't like living with a person at all, it was like living with sound. And the sound didn't make any sense to her, didn't make any sense to any of them — naturally. They began, in a way, to be afflicted by this presence that was living in their home. It was as though Sonny were some sort of god, or monster. He moved in an atmosphere which wasn't like theirs at all. They fed him and he ate, he washed himself, he walked in and out of their door; he certainly wasn't nasty or unpleasant or rude, Sonny isn't any of those things; but it was as though he were all wrapped up in some cloud, some fire, some vision all his own; and there wasn't any way to reach him.

At the same time, he wasn't really a man yet, he was still a child, and they had to watch out for him in all kinds of ways. They certainly couldn't throw him out. Neither did they dare to make a great scene about that piano because even they dimly sensed, as I sensed, from so many thousands of miles away, that Sonny was at that piano playing for his life.

But he hadn't been going to school. One day a letter came from the school board and Isabel's mother got it — there had, apparently, been other letters but Sonny had torn them up. This day, when Sonny came in, Isabel's mother showed him the letter and asked where he'd been spending his time. And she finally got it out of him that he'd been down in Greenwich Village, with musicians and other characters, in a white girl's apartment. And this scared her and she started to scream at him and what came up, once she began — though she denies it to this day — was what sacrifices they were making to give Sonny a decent home and how little he appreciated it.

Sonny didn't play the piano that day. By evening, Isabel's mother had calmed down but then there was the old man to deal with, and Isabel herself. Isabel says she did her best to be calm but she broke down and started crying. She says she just watched Sonny's face. She could tell, by watching him, what was happening with him. And what was happening was that they penetrated his cloud, they had reached him. Even if their fingers had been a thousand times more gentle than human fingers ever are, he could hardly help feeling that they had stripped him naked and were spitting on that nakedness. For he also had to see that his presence, that music, which was life or death to him, had been torture for them and that they had endured it, not at all for his sake, but only for mine. And Sonny couldn't take that. He can take it a little better today than he could then but he's still not very good at it and, frankly, I don't know anybody who is.

The silence of the next few days must have been louder than the sound of all the music ever played since time began. One morning, before she went to work, Isabel was in his room for something and she suddenly realized that all of his records were gone. And she knew for certain that he was gone. And he was. He went as far as the navy would carry him. He finally sent me a postcard from some place in Greece and that was the first I knew that Sonny was still alive. I didn't see him any more until we were both back in New York and the war had long been over.

He was a man by then, of course, but I wasn't willing to see it. He came by the house from time to time, but we fought almost every time we met. I didn't like the way he carried himself, loose and dreamlike all the time, and I didn't like his friends, and his music seemed to be merely an excuse for the life he led. It sounded just that weird and disordered.

Then we had a fight, a pretty awful fight, and I didn't see him for months. By and by I looked him up, where he was living, in a furnished room in the Village, and I tried to make it up. But there were lots of other people in the room and Sonny just lay on his bed, and he wouldn't come downstairs with me, and he treated these other people as though they were his family and I weren't. So I got mad and then he got mad, and then I told him that he might just as well be dead as live the way he was living. Then he stood up and he told me not to worry about him any more in life, that he *was* dead as far as I was concerned. Then he pushed me to the door and the other people looked on as though nothing were happening, and he slammed the door behind me. I stood in the hallway, staring at the door. I heard somebody laugh in the room and then the tears came to my eyes. I started down the steps, whistling to keep from crying. I kept whistling to myself, *You going to need me, baby, one of these cold, rainy days.*

CR

I read about Sonny's trouble in the spring. Little Grace died in the fall. She was a beautiful little girl. But she only lived a little over two years. She died of polio and she suffered. She had a slight fever for a couple of days, but it didn't seem like anything and we just kept her in bed. And we would certainly have called the doctor, but the fever dropped, she seemed to be all right. So we thought it had just been a cold. Then, one day, she was up, playing, Isabel was in the kitchen fixing lunch for the two boys when they'd come in from school, and she heard Grace fall down in the living room. When you have a lot of children you don't always start running when one of them falls, unless they start screaming or something. And, this time, Grace was quiet. Yet, Isabel says that when she heard that *thump* and then that silence, something happened in her to make her afraid. And she ran to the living room and there was little Grace on the floor, all twisted up, and the reason she hadn't screamed was that she couldn't get her breath. And when she did scream, it was the worst sound, Isabel says, that she'd ever heard in all her life, and she still hears it sometimes in her dreams. Isabel will sometimes wake me up with a low, moaning, strangled sound and I have to be quick to awaken her and hold her to me and where Isabel is weeping against me seems a mortal wound.

I think I may have written Sonny the very day that little Grace was buried. I was sitting in the living room in the dark, by myself, and I suddenly thought of Sonny. My trouble made his real.

ᑕᖇ

One Saturday afternoon, when Sonny had been living with us, or, anyway, been in our house, for nearly two weeks, I found myself wandering aimlessly about the living room, drinking from a can of beer, and trying to work up the courage to search Sonny's room. He was out, he was usually out whenever I was home, and Isabel had taken the children to see their grandparents. Suddenly I was standing still in front of the living room window, watching Seventh Avenue. The idea of searching Sonny's room made me still. I scarcely dared to admit to myself what I'd be searching for. I didn't know what I'd do if I found it. Or if I didn't.

On the sidewalk across from me, near the entrance to a barbecue joint, some people were holding an old-fashioned revival meeting. The barbecue cook, wearing a dirty white apron, his conked hair reddish and metallic in the pale sun, and a cigarette between his lips, stood in the doorway, watching them. Kids and older people paused in their errands and stood there, along with some older men and a couple of very tough-looking women who watched everything that happened on the avenue, as though they owned it, or were maybe owned by it. Well, they were watching this, too. The revival was being carried on by three sisters in black, and a brother. All they had were their voices and their Bibles and a tambourine. The brother was testifying and while he testified two of the sisters stood together, seeming to say, amen, and the third sister walked around with the tambourine outstretched and a couple of people dropped coins into it. Then the brother's testimony ended and the sister who had been taking up the collection dumped the coins into her palm and transferred them to the pocket of her long black robe. Then she raised both hands, striking the tambourine against the air, and then against one hand, and she started to sing. And the two other sisters and the brother joined in.

It was strange, suddenly, to watch, though I had been seeing these street meetings all my life. So, of course, had everybody else down there. Yet, they paused and watched and listened and I stood still at the window. *"Tis the old ship of Zion,"* they sang, and the sister with the tambourine kept a steady, jangling beat, *"it has rescued many a thousand!"* Not a soul under the sound of their voices was hearing this song for the first time, not one of them had been rescued. Nor had they seen much in the way of rescue work being done around them. Neither did they especially believe in the holiness of the three sisters and the brother, they knew too much about them, knew where they lived, and how. The woman with the tambourine, whose voice dominated the air, whose face was bright with joy, was divided by very little from the woman who stood watching her, a cigarette between her heavy, chapped lips, her hair a cuckoo's nest, her face scarred and swollen from many beatings, and her black eyes glittering like coal. Perhaps they both knew this, which was why, when, as rarely, they addressed each other, they addressed each other as Sister. As the singing filled the air the watching, listening faces underwent a change, the eyes focusing on something within; the music seemed to soothe a poison of them; and time seemed, nearly, to fall away from the sullen, belligerent, battered faces, as though they were fleeing back to their first condition, while dreaming of their last. The barbecue cook half shook his head and smiled, and dropped his cigarette and disappeared into his joint. A man fumbled in his pockets for change and stood holding it in his hand impatiently, as though he had just remembered a pressing appointment further up the avenue. He looked furious. Then I saw Sonny, standing on the edge of the crowd. He was carrying a wide, flat notebook with a green cover, and it made him look, from where I was standing, almost like a schoolboy. The coppery sun brought out the copper in his skin, he was very faintly smiling, standing very still. Then the singing stopped, the tambourine turned into a collection plate again. The furious man dropped in his coins and vanished, so did a couple of the women, and Sonny dropped some change in the plate, looking directly at the woman with a little smile. He started across the avenue, toward the house. He has a slow, loping walk, something like the way Harlem hipsters walk, only he's imposed on this his own half-beat. I had never really noticed it before.

I stayed at the window, both relieved and apprehensive. As Sonny disappeared from my sight, they began singing again. And they were still singing when his key turned in the lock.

"Hey," he said.

"Hey, yourself. You want some beer?"

"No. Well, maybe." But he came up to the window and stood beside me, looking out. "What a warm voice," he said.

They were singing *If I could only hear my mother pray again!*

"Yes," I said, "and she can sure beat that tambourine."

"But what a terrible song," he said, and laughed. He dropped his notebook on the sofa and disappeared into the kitchen. "Where's Isabel and the kids?"

"I think they went to see their grandparents. You hungry?"

"No." He came back into the living room with his can of beer. "You want to come some place with me tonight?"

I sensed, I don't know how, that I couldn't possibly say no. "Sure. Where?"

He sat down on the sofa and picked up his notebook and started leafing through it. "I'm going to sit in with some fellows in a joint in the Village."

"You mean, you're going to play, tonight?"

"That's right." He took a swallow of his beer and moved back to the window. He gave me a sidelong look. "If you can stand it."

"I'll try," I said.

He smiled to himself and we both watched as the meeting across the way broke up. The three sisters and the brother, heads bowed, were singing *God be with you till we meet again*. The faces around them were very quiet. Then the song ended. The small crowd dispersed. We watched the three women and the lone man walk slowly up the avenue.

"When she was singing before," said Sonny, abruptly, "her voice reminded me for a minute of what heroin feels like sometimes — when it's in your veins. It makes you feel sort of warm and cool at the same time. And distant. And — and sure." He sipped his beer, very deliberately not looking at me. I watched his face. "It makes you feel — in control. Sometimes you've got to have that feeling."

"Do you?" I sat down slowly in the easy chair.

"Sometimes." He went to the sofa and picked up his notebook again. "Some people do."

"In order," I asked, "to play?" And my voice was very ugly, full of contempt and anger.

"Well" — he looked at me with great, troubled eyes, as though, in fact, he hoped his eyes would tell me things he could never otherwise say — "they *think* so. And *if* they think so —!"

"And what do *you* think?" I asked.

He sat on the sofa and put his can of beer on the floor. "I don't know," he said, and I couldn't be sure if he were answering my question or pursuing his thoughts. His face didn't tell me. "It's not so much to *play*. It's to *stand* it, to be able to make it at all. On any level." He frowned and smiled: "In order to keep from shaking to pieces."

"But these friends of yours," I said, "they seem to shake themselves to pieces pretty goddamn fast."

"Maybe." He played with the notebook. And something told me that I should curb my tongue, that Sonny was doing his best to talk, that I should listen. "But of course you only know the ones that've gone to pieces. Some don't — or at least they haven't *yet* and that's just about all *any* of us can say." He paused. "And then there are some who just live, really, in hell, and they know it and they see what's happening, and they go right on. I don't know." He sighed, dropped the notebook, folded his arms. "Some guys, you can tell from the way they play, they on something *all* the time. And you can see that, well, it makes something real for them. But of course," he picked up his beer from the floor and sipped it and put the can down again, "they *want* to, too, you've got to see that. Even some of them that say they don't — *some*, not all."

"And what about you?" I asked — I couldn't help it. "What about you? Do *you* want to?"

He stood up and walked to the window and remained silent for a long time. Then he sighed. "Me," he said. Then: "While I was downstairs before, on my way here, listening to that woman sing, it struck me all of a sudden how much suffering she must have had to go through — to sing like that. It's *repulsive* to think you have to suffer that much."

I said: "But there's no way not to suffer — is there, Sonny?"

"I believe not," he said and smiled, "but that's never stopped anyone from trying." He looked at me. "Has it?" I realized, with this mocking look, that there stood between us, forever, beyond the power of time or forgiveness, the fact that I had held silence — so long! — when he had needed human speech to help him. He turned back to the window. "No, there's no way not to suffer. But you try all kinds of ways to keep from drowning in it, to keep on top of it, and to make it seem — well, like *you*. Like you did something, all right, and now you're suffering for it. You know?" I said nothing. "Well you know," he said, impatiently, "why *do* people suffer? Maybe it's better to do something to give it a reason, *any* reason."

"But we just agreed," I said, "that there's no way not to suffer. Isn't it better, then, just to — take it?"

"But nobody just takes it," Sonny cried, "that's what I'm telling you! *Everybody* tries not to. You're just hung up on the *way* some people try — it's not *your* way!"

The hair on my face began to itch, my face felt wet. "That's not true," I said, "that's not true. I don't give a damn what other people do, I don't even care how they suffer. I just care how *you* suffer." And he looked at me. "Please believe me," I said. "I don't want to see you — die — trying not to suffer."

"I won't," he said, flatly, "die trying not to suffer. At least, not any faster than anybody else."

"But there's no need," I said, trying to laugh, "is there? In killing yourself."

I wanted to say more, but I couldn't. I wanted to talk about willpower and how life could be — well, beautiful. I wanted to say that it was all within; but was it? Or, rather, wasn't that exactly the trouble? And I wanted to promise that I would never fail him again. But it would all have sounded — empty words and lies.

So I made the promise to myself and prayed that I would keep it.

"It's terrible sometimes, inside," he said, "that's what's the trouble. You walk these streets, black and funky and cold, and there's not really a living ass to talk to, and there's nothing shaking, and there's no way of getting it out — that storm inside. You can't talk it and you can't make love with it, and when you finally try to get with it and play it, you realize *nobody's* listening. So *you've* got to listen. You got to find a way to listen."

And then he walked away from the window and sat on the sofa again, as though all the wind had suddenly been knocked out of him. "Sometimes you'll do *anything* to play, even cut your mother's throat." He laughed and looked at me. "Or your brother's." Then he sobered. "Or your own." Then: "Don't worry. I'm all right now and I think I'll *be* all right. But I can't forget — where I've been. I don't mean just the physical place I've been, I mean where I've *been*. And *what* I've been."

"What have you been, Sonny?" I asked.

He smiled — but sat sideways on the sofa, his elbow resting on the back, his fingers playing with his mouth and chin, not looking at me. "I've been something I didn't recognize, didn't know I could be. Didn't know anybody could be." He stopped, looking inward, looking helplessly young, looking old. "I'm not talking about it now because I feel *guilty* or anything like that — maybe it would be better if I did, I don't know. Anyway, I can't really talk about it. Not to you, not to anybody," and now he turned and faced me. "Sometimes, you know, and it was actually when I was most *out* of the world, I felt that I was in it, that I was *with* it, really, and I could play or I didn't really have to *play*, it just came out of me, it was there. And I don't know how I played, thinking about it now, but I know I did awful things, those times, sometimes, to people. Or it wasn't that I *did* anything to them — it was that they weren't real." He picked up the beer can; it was empty; he rolled it between his palms: "And other times — well, I needed a fix, I needed to find a place to lean, I needed to clear a space to *listen* — and I couldn't find it, and I — went crazy, I did terrible things to *me*, I was terrible *for* me." He began pressing the beer can between his hands, I watched the metal begin to give. It glittered, as he played with it, like a knife, and I was afraid he would cut himself, but I said nothing. "Oh well. I can never tell you. I was all by myself at the bottom of something, stinking and sweating and crying and shaking, and I smelled it, you know? *my* stink, and I thought I'd die if I couldn't get away from it and yet, all the same, I knew that everything I was doing was just locking me in with it. And I didn't know," he paused, still flattening the beer can, "I didn't know, I still *don't* know, something kept telling me that maybe it was good to smell your own stink, but I didn't think that *that* was what I'd been trying to do — and — who can stand it?" and he abruptly dropped the ruined beer can, looking at me with a small, still smile, and then rose, walking to the window as though it were the lodestone rock. I watched his face, he watched the avenue. "I couldn't tell you when Mama died — but the reason I wanted to leave Harlem so bad was to get away from drugs. And then, when I ran away, that's what I was running from — really. When I came back, nothing had changed, *I* hadn't changed, I was just — older." And he stopped, drumming with his fingers on the windowpane. The sun had vanished, soon darkness would fall. I watched his face. "It can come again," he said, almost as though speaking to himself. Then he turned to me. "It can come again," he repeated. "I just want you to know that."

"All right," I said, at last. "So it can come again, All right."

He smiled, but the smile was sorrowful. "I had to try to tell you," he said.

"Yes," I said. "I understand that."

"You're my brother," he said, looking straight at me, and not smiling at all.

"Yes," I repeated. "yes. I understand that."

He turned back to the window, looking out. "All that hatred down there," he said, "all that hatred and misery and love. It's a wonder it doesn't blow the avenue apart."

℘

We went to the only nightclub on a short, dark street, downtown. We squeezed through the narrow, chattering, jam-packed bar to the entrance of the big room, where the bandstand was. And we stood there for a moment, for the lights were very dim in this room and we couldn't see. Then, "Hello, boy," said a voice and an enormous black man, much older than Sonny or myself, erupted out of all that atmospheric lighting and put an arm around Sonny's shoulder. "I been sitting right here," he said, "waiting for you."

He had a big voice, too, and heads in the darkness turned toward us.

Sonny grinned and pulled a little away, and said, "Creole, this is my brother. I told you about him."

Creole shook my hand. "I'm glad to meet you, son," he said, and it was clear that he was glad to meet me *there*, for Sonny's sake. And he smiled, "You got a real musician in *your* family," and he took his arm from Sonny's shoulder and slapped him, lightly, affectionately, with the back of his hand.

"Well. Now I've heard it all," said a voice behind us. This was another musician, and a friend of Sonny's, a coal-black, cheerful-looking man, built close to the ground. He immediately began confiding to me, at the top of his lungs, the most terrible things about Sonny, his teeth gleaming like a lighthouse and his laugh coming up out of him like the beginning of an earthquake. And it turned out that everyone at the bar knew Sonny, or almost everyone; some were musicians, working there, or nearby, or not working, some were simply hangers-on, and some were there to hear Sonny play. I was introduced to all of them and they were all very polite to me. Yet, it was clear that, for them, I was only Sonny's brother. Here, I was in Sonny's world. Or, rather: his kingdom. Here, it was not even a question that his veins bore royal blood.

They were going to play soon and Creole installed me, by myself, at a table in a dark corner. Then I watched them, Creole, and the little black man, and Sonny, and the others, while they horsed around, standing just below the bandstand. The light from the bandstand spilled just a little short of them and, watching them laughing and gesturing and moving about, I had the feeling that they, nevertheless, were being most careful not to step into that circle of light too suddenly: that if they moved into the light too suddenly, without thinking, they would perish in flame. Then, while I watched, one of them, the small, black man, moved into the light and crossed the bandstand and started fooling around with his drums. Then — being funny and being, also, extremely ceremonious — Creole took Sonny by the arm and led him to the piano. A woman's voice called Sonny's name and a few hands started clapping. And Sonny, also being funny and being ceremonious, and so touched, I think, that he could have cried, but neither hiding it nor showing it, riding it like a man, grinned, and put both hands to his heart and bowed from the waist.

Creole then went to the bass fiddle and a lean, very bright-skinned brown man jumped up on the bandstand and picked up his horn. So there they were, and the atmosphere on the bandstand and in the room began to change and tighten. Someone stepped up to the microphone and announced them. Then there were all kinds of murmurs. Some people at the bar shushed others. The waitress ran around, frantically getting in the last orders, guys and chicks got closer to each other, and the lights on the bandstand, on the quartet, turned to a kind of indigo. Then they all looked different there. Creole looked about him for the last time, as though he were making certain that all his chickens were in the coop, and then he — jumped and struck the fiddle. And there they were.

All I know about music is that not many people ever really hear it. And even then, on the rare occasions when something opens within, and the music enters, what we mainly hear, or hear corroborated, are personal, private, vanishing evocations. But the man who creates the music is hearing something else, is dealing with the roar rising from the void and imposing order on it as it hits the air. What is evoked in him, then, is of another order, more terrible because it has no words, and triumphant, too, for that same reason. And his triumph, when he triumphs, is ours. I just watched Sonny's face. His face was troubled, he was working hard, but he wasn't with it. And I had the feeling that, in a way, everyone on the bandstand was waiting for him, both waiting for him and pushing him along. But as I began to watch Creole, I realized that it was Creole who held them all back. He had them on a short rein. Up there, keeping the beat with his whole body, wailing on the fiddle, with his eyes half closed, he was listening to everything, but he was listening to Sonny. He was having a dialogue with Sonny. He wanted Sonny to leave the shoreline and strike out for the deep water. He was Sonny's witness that deep water and drowning were not the same thing — he had been there, and he knew. And he wanted Sonny to know. He was waiting for Sonny to do the things on the keys which would let Creole know that Sonny was in the water.

And, while Creole listened, Sonny moved, deep within, exactly like someone in torment. I had never before thought of how awful the relationship must be between the musician and his instrument. He has to fill it, this instrument, with the breath of life, his own. He has to make it do what he wants it to do. And a piano is just a piano. It's made out of so much wood and wires and little hammers and big ones, and ivory. While there's only so much you can do with it, the only way to find this out is to try; to try and make it do everything.

And Sonny hadn't been near a piano for over a year. And he wasn't on much better terms with his life, not the life that stretched before him now. He and the piano stammered, started one way, got scared, stopped; started another way, panicked, marked time, started again; then seemed to have found a direction, panicked again, got stuck. And the face I saw on Sonny I'd seen before. Everything had been burned out of it, and, at the same time, things usually hidden were being burned in, by the fire and fury of the battle which was occurring in him up there.

Yet, watching Creole's face as they neared the end of the first set, I had the feeling that something had happened, something I hadn't heard. Then they finished, there was scattered applause, and then, without an instant's warning, Creole started into something else, it was almost sardonic, it was *Am I Blue*. And, as though he commanded, Sonny began to play. Something began to happen. And Creole let out the reins. The dry, low, black man said something awful on the drums, Creole answered, and the drums talked back. Then the horn insisted, sweet and high, slightly detached perhaps, and Creole listened, commenting now and then, dry, and driving, beautiful and calm and old. Then they all came together again, and Sonny was part of the family again. I could tell this from his face. He seemed to have found, right there beneath his fingers, a damn brand-new piano. It seemed that he couldn't get over it. Then, for awhile, just being happy with Sonny, they seemed to be agreeing with him that brand-new pianos certainly were a gas.

Then Creole stepped forward to remind them that what they were playing was the blues. He hit something in all of them, he hit something in me, myself, and the music tightened and deepened, apprehension began to beat the air. Creole began to tell us what the blues were all about. They were not about anything very new. He and his boys up there were keeping it new, at the risk of ruin, destruction, madness, and death, in order to find new ways to make us listen. For, while the tale of how we suffer, and how we are delighted, and how we may triumph is never new, it always must be heard. There isn't any other tale to tell, it's the only light we've got in all this darkness.

And this tale, according to that face, that body, those strong hands on those strings, has another aspect in every country and a new depth in every generation. Listen, Creole seemed to be saying, listen. Now these are Sonny's blues. He made the little black man on the drums know it, and the bright, brown man on the horn. Creole wasn't trying any longer to get Sonny in the water. He was wishing him Godspeed. Then he stepped back, very slowly, filling the air with the immense suggestion that Sonny speak for himself.

Then they all gathered around Sonny and Sonny played. Every now and again one of them seemed to say, amen. Sonny's fingers filled the air with life, his life. But that life contained so many others. And Sonny went all the way back, he really began with the spare, flat statement of the opening phrase of the song. Then he began to make it his. It was very beautiful because it wasn't hurried and it was no longer a lament. I seemed to hear with what burning he had made it his, with what burning we had yet to make it ours, how we could cease lamenting. Freedom lurked around us and I understood, at last, that he could help us to be free if we would listen, that he would never be free until we did. Yet, there was no battle in his face now. I heard what he had gone through, and would continue to go through until he came to rest in earth. He had made it his: that long line, of which we knew only Mama and Daddy. And he was giving it back, as everything must be given back, so that, passing through death, it can live forever. I saw my mother's face again, and felt, for the first time, how the stones of the road she had walked on must have bruised her feet. I saw the moonlit road where my father's brother died. And it brought something else back to me, and carried me past it, I saw my little girl again and felt Isabel's tears again, and I felt my own tears begin to rise. And I was yet aware that this was only a moment, that the world waited outside, as hungry as a tiger, and that trouble stretched above us, longer than the sky.

Then it was over. Creole and Sonny let out their breath, both soaking wet, and grinning. There was a lot of applause and some of it was real. In the dark, the girl came by and I asked her to take drinks to the bandstand. There was a long pause, while they talked up there in the indigo light and after awhile I saw the girl put a Scotch and milk on top of the piano for Sonny. He didn't seem to notice it, but just before they started playing again, he sipped from it and looked toward me, and nodded. Then he put it back on top of the piano. For me, then, as they began to play again, it glowed and shook above my brother's head like the very cup of trembling.

ᔑᓄᘿᘏ

Born in Harlem, African-American writer James Baldwin is remembered less for his novels than for his essays and for this story, which appeared in the collection Going To Meet the Man *(1965). "Sonny's Blues" remains Baldwin's most intensely realized fiction less for its unsentimental "ghetto realism" than for the interweaving of light and dark through which Harlem is rendered. Baldwin does not simply oppose the two, as the narrator's image of "an animal waiting to be coaxed into the light" might suggest; rather, he deploys light itself as death-dealing, from "the vivid, killing streets" into which boys "came down . . . for light and air and found themselves encircled by disaster" to that light which, in "fill[ing] the room . . . [fills the child] with darkness." Illumination, in other words, is dearly bought; the narrator must enter the darkness of the jazz club to see this, to know that "if they moved into the light too suddenly, they would perish in flame." And indeed Sonny perishes, like the other jazzmen "keeping it new, at the risk of ruin, destruction, madness, and death" so that the narrator may see and know. Sonny brings grace, where Grace has died; Sonny is the sacrifice, the darkness that grounds the light. Baldwin's complication of this simple opposition may represent his resistance to easy divisions between the aesthetic concern with image and the social concern with race, a resistance that allows "Sonny's Blues" to transcend both.*

S.J.

Sandra Birdsell *(b. 1942)*

Disappearances

With the way things were going with his head, Donald thinks this could well end up being their last motoring trip. And so, when they stopped at Virden for gas earlier, he decided to take a southerly route along the U.S. border. Best, he told Frances, to avoid the heavier traffic on the Canada number 1. Donald's intention is to enjoy a more leisurely pace and to delay their arrival in Saskatoon.

There are few settlements straddling this highway, and fewer gas stations, and the road looks used up and abandoned. Lambs-quarters clump along the fencelines which form a straggled delineation of the groomed fields beyond and the wilderness that bursts up from the ditches, encroaching on the road with weedy patches of purslane and wild aster. Here, the highway seems a grey corridor, cracked, but inexorably straight and bound for the horizon and the clouds hanging above it. While the landscape makes Frances feel untethered and weightless, Donald feels gathered in, enclosed in a circumference of light. His head will not act up on him here, Donald thinks.

"You'd think there was a bug going around," Frances says. She puts aside a newspaper she's been reading since their stop at Virden for gasoline and to let Buster, their schnauzer, out for a widdle.

"How's that?" Donald inclines a grey shoulder speckled with dandruff, and invites Frances to elaborate. Donald is a grey man in a grey suit. People tell him he resembles Alfred Hitchcock.

"There's another person gone missing," Frances says. "A woman, this time round. Went for a walk three miles down a road to visit her mother and never got there. Had a tiff with the hubby, apparently. She was forty-two. Same age as Marjorie," she adds.

At the mention of their daughter's name Donald blinks rapidly, as though to clear a speck of dust. Rolling hills appear suddenly, greening dromedaries loping towards the horizon. Flat one moment, hilly the next, Donald thinks. The sight of them catches in his throat, and he feels the knot of words stuck there, stories, poems perhaps.

"You recall in winter," Frances says, "there was that man and his son?" So they will not be overtaken by thoughts of Marjorie and the girl, Frances wants to build on the virus theory, a virus that makes people disappear. "The house burned down and no remains were ever found. And then there was that case last autumn. The man who went off to a meeting of some sort. I don't think they've found him, yet."

"A church meeting," Donald says, "if I remember correctly. I think he was a deacon." As Buster, their dog, rearranges himself on the back seat, Donald hears the clink of his chain collar and feels a pang of guilt. He should, for the sake of the dog, turn on the air conditioner. He can take off his suit jacket if it gets too close in the car, but the wee fella, he thinks, can't do anything but bear it.

They approach what was once a homestead, a square of overgrown vegetation with a house in its centre, its windows framing an interior that looks gutted, blackened by age and the elements. Its door, askew on its hinges, gives the appearance of a toothless mouth, wry with objection as they pass by.

"Looks to me like caragana gone wild," Frances says. "It's all they seem to know on the prairie. That, or honeysuckle."

"Likely," Donald says.

From the strict look of the house, its front door gaping in midair, Frances supposes its inhabitants were from among the Galician or Ukrainian. More than likely. More than likely people who hadn't thought twice about eating gophers during the Depression. Loud-spoken and hot-blooded people who might well have a tiff with the hubby, go for a walk and not return.

Last spring, Frances remembers, according to a newspaper account, a woman in Alberta had gone rolling in mud. She'd returned home after being missing for several days covered in clay and bits of twigs and dried weeds stuck to her hair and clothing. She needed a breather, a family spokesperson had said, and didn't invite further questions. Frances would have loved to be a fly on that wall. Then, there was that winter thing near Saskatoon. The parks person grooming ski trails and hearing a snorting in the underbrush. Thinking it was a deer or something, until he saw the woman's naked body thrashing about in the snow. When Frances read about it, her heart had been in her mouth, fearing, what with all of Marjorie's problems with the girl, it might be Marjorie who had gone rolling in snow.

"Frostbite to her extremities," Frances says, and giggles. The hospital spokesperson had not elaborated. She is caught by her reflection in the side mirror, a younger face flitting away as soon as her eyes meet it. She approves of the soft arrangement of silver curls across her forehead and the cluster of coral at her ears. The peach top, which she plans on wearing to the preliminary hearing. She simply cannot imagine being inside a courtroom.

"What was that?"

"Don't forget about those two women, disappeared," Frances says.

"Which ones would that be?"

"The landscape artists," Frances says, as she has come to refer to the women. Making mud and snow angels in the wilderness for others to come upon and wonder what kind of animal had been there.

"I don't believe," Donald says and stops. They have had this conversation before, he thinks, or is it *déjà vu*? Or is it one of those things with his head, beginning to happen?

"Mind you, I could be wrong," Donald says carefully, listening for what he's supposed to say next. "But the landscape women didn't disappear. They came back, didn't they? You oughtn't trust my memory, though," he says with a rueful smile, before she can say it.

"Of course they came back," Frances says. "How else would the newspaper know they'd been out making their mark? But it's as though they disappeared because they couldn't remember a thing about it. Not how they'd got there, or where they'd been. Or why they'd been rolling." Frances has made this point before. She suspects Donald's forgetfulness. She suspects that Donald's fulfilment of the pattern of what happens when a man retires is her punishment for wanting to sell the house and move into the Oaks and Pond enriched housing.

"Yes, I suppose you're right," Donald says. "If they couldn't remember where they'd been, it would seem as though they had disappeared, at least to them, it would."

But Donald can always remember where he's been. He remembers being in the Centennial library paging through back copies of the *National Geographic* and attending a wine and cheese party at the same time. He'd seen himself put in the request for the magazines, heard himself speak to the library clerk while engaging in conversation with someone at a wine and cheese reception. A short woman, a round face turned up to his, framed by a slash of blonde bangs. During the bus ride home from the library, he emerged from both worlds uncertain whether he would find scraps of notes or a cocktail napkin in his pockets. It's as though he sometimes finds himself on both sides of a window, looking out, looking in. What happens is not memory lapse or Alzheimer's, the doctor said, so you can put that worry out of your head. We could do tests, the doctor said, but I'm almost certain we wouldn't find anything. The doctor told Donald about other cases that had come to him recently. A young woman, a professor, he said, whose children noticed she wasn't there and brought her in to see him. She was away for over two hours, the doctor said. It was something he was seeing more and more frequently. Donald wonders if the times are grinding down and glitches are occurring in the system; the creator blinks and laws are suspended and, for moments, some of us are left dangling, he thinks.

"They'll likely be coming down for tea now," Frances says.

"It's that time, isn't it?" Sunlight glides across the dashboard; he feels its heat on his hands. They are managing nicely, so far, Donald thinks. There's a bit of a headwind, but still getting around 150 clicks per quarter-tank with the air conditioner shut down. Donald grows anxious whenever the needle on the gauge drops to the halfway point. It comes from being raised on the prairies, Frances used to say, gaily. Years later, Donald hears the apology in her voice when she says it, the regret, an indication that allowances must be made. Perhaps it explains his lumpiness and lack of colour.

"Time for your snooze, you mean," Frances says.

"I just can't get used to tea and visiting in the middle of the afternoon," Donald says, as though it puzzles him why he can't.

Gone only half a day and already Frances misses the apricot brocade armchairs, the mint-green walls, and the satiny sheen of light on water in the pond beyond the lounge windows. A bit of a problem, our Marjorie needs us, Frances had told the doctor. He was a retired general practitioner, another happy inmate of the Oaks and Pond was how he'd introduced himself, as though the doctor knew Marjorie and had been there as she stumbled her way through childhood. Beyond the car window, the humpbacked hills vanish suddenly to a flatness, and oil pumps, prehistoric cranes, poke their beaks into the earth. Frances fears the distance between where they have come from and where they are going to; the trip, the car's wheels thumping against the cracked pavement, white sound covering the rift widening at their backs. If she turns and looks, she'll see Tyndall stone cliffs, the Oaks and Pond tumbling into the abyss. The images blur as Frances's eyes fill.

"Donald, for pity's sake, will you just look at yourself, you're dripping," Frances says. "Turn on the danged air conditioner."

"I hadn't thought of that," Donald says. A metaphysical or mystical disappearance, if not an actual one, he thinks.

"May I ask, just what was the point in buying a car with air conditioning if we never use it?"

As Donald plucks a tissue from a packet clipped to the visor, Frances smells him; body talc, aftershave lotion, a yeasty odour that drycleaning fails to remove from his favourite suit. What was the point in buying the new jackets and slacks at Tip Top? Jackets and ties, suitable attire for the dining room, the director informed them when they'd come for their orientation tour of the Oaks and Pond towers. Dressy pantsuits for the ladies were, of course, acceptable. You folks going on a cruise? the salesman wanted to know, and Donald had said, it's kind of like a cruise, isn't it? Except that you can never get off the ship. Donald's new wardrobe remained in garment bags in his closet.

"I, for one, intend to enjoy what I paid for," Frances says. "Right, Buster?" The dog raises his head, his eyes swivelling across her face.

"Why not crank down the window a bit?" Donald says.

"It'll hit me square in the neck. I'll wind up stiffer than a board."

The air conditioner drones to life and an air freshener clamped to a vent exudes the spicy scent of lavender.

A ridge of budding trees appears and, above it, mallard ducks. Six drakes, Donald counts, pursuing a female. Must be water beyond the trees.

"How long do you think it'll go on?" Frances asks, as the ducks pass overhead and disappear from view.

"How's that?" Assiniboia, Donald thinks, if he remembers correctly, is the next major town along the way; he'll be able to gas up there, if it gets too low.

"The court hearing."

Donald bunches his hands around the wheel, his grip tightening as the car meets a pothole. He braces himself against the possibility of a deer bounding up from a ditch and into their path, their forward movement stopped abruptly by the solidness of an animal's body.

"I don't rightly know," Donald says.

"I'd like to put that girl over my knee," Frances says. She sees the fiery cloud of the girl's hair, the chin clamped to her chest, an emaciated shoulder jerking away from a touch. Frances recalls the feeling of impotence, of being unable to satisfy, no matter what. It was as though the girl was born not knowing the word *contentment* and was always looking off to the side of every moment, pining for what she imagined she was missing elsewhere.

CR

"Just look at all the American clunkers," Frances says as they walk along Main Street in the town, past cars parked diagonally into the curb. As Buster stops to urinate against a building, Donald shoves his hands deep into his jacket pockets and glances up and down the street. A car passes by, and heads turn in their direction.

"Why not let him off the leash?" Donald says. "I don't think anyone would pay any mind." Dogs in prairie towns often run loose behind packs of children, Donald remembers, or imperiously stare down pedestrians from the backs of pickup trucks.

"I haven't got a plastic bag," Frances says, slapping her coat pockets.

"Yes, you're right. Better not. We can stop on the way out of town," Donald says.

"I can't for the life of me imagine anyone wanting to call a place like this home," Frances says, as they continue their stroll. When Donald had left engineering at Dorval airport to teach electronics in various community colleges, he'd had the luxury of uniformity, a community of fellow workers, a common language, while Frances had had to battle it out with Marjorie and Aaron in strange prairie cities. It took some getting used to, after being raised in a city like Montreal. But it's given her a broader view, she thinks, a tolerance for the inconsistencies in people, an ability to live and let live. When she takes inventory, the nights when she lies awake in her new, wide room at the Oaks and Pond, listening to the thrum of traffic on the city bypass, she counts her blessings. She names them out loud. Donald, first of all. She knows she has wound up among the fortunate in life.

As they pass by a store, the door opens and two people emerge. A man, tanned face shiny with perspiration, scowls as he steps into the sunlight. He adjusts his distended paunch as he walks towards them, legs bowed as though by the weight of his blue chequered stomach. A spindly woman skips up from behind him and latches onto his arm. Green plastic earrings the size of bread-and-butter plates, Frances notes, as well as the slash of grey at the woman's part, carrot-coloured hair sticking out from the sides of her head in springy curls. As they meet on the sidewalk in front of a café window, the man lurches to a stop and Frances is forced to avoid coming up against his belly. She is aware of people in the café, sitting at the window, watching.

"I've got one of those," the man says. He squints at their dog through a spiral of cigarette smoke. "Identical. Same markings and everything."

"Oh, do you?" Frances exclaims and Donald notes the forced brightness. Since their move she dresses beautifully, he knows, as well if not better than most. But she looks and sounds tense, he thinks, like someone uncertain whether or not they have overdressed for a party.

"It's not the same," the woman says. Her caved-in mouth is an orange smear drawing down at the corners. She tugs at the man's arm to draw him away.

"Identical." But the man's dark eyes waver and slide away from the dog as though he's beginning to have doubts.

"His name is Buster," Frances says. "Schnauzers are such wonderful dogs, aren't they?"

The man clicks his tongue and pats his knee for Buster to come over. His brown and slender fingers rove through the animal's coat and stop to scratch its ears. When he straightens, his breathing is a whistling sound, as though he has a hole in his throat and the air is escaping.

"Yours is not one of them schnauzers. It's a good old Heinz 57," the woman says. The comment is a rebuff intended for Frances. The woman holds a smugness, and her unwillingness to look Frances in the eye is a kind of belligerence. Frances knows she has, for some reason, offended her.

"Did you get yours from a breeder?" Frances asks.

The man struggles to reply and gives up with a look of impatience. He slaps the air and turns away. "You should bathe it," he mumbles. "I'm going home to do mine, now."

"Yes, it's that time of year, isn't it? Time for the spring grooming," Frances says.

"Lyme disease," the man calls as he crosses the street. "Wood ticks are the dickens. You bathe that mutt if you don't want it getting the Lyme disease."

"Emphysema," Donald says. "He meant well."

Donald notices the women sitting at the table in front of the café window, one of them licking an ice cream. He rubs his palms. "This looks like the place to be on a Saturday afternoon," he says. "What do you say we go in and have a bite to eat?"

"It'll be dark before we hit Saskatoon," Frances says. "You know how you are for night driving." A television screen inside the café blinks with the light of a baseball game, and when Frances sees it, it occurs to her how a picture would connect them with the girl. A television news report. A picture of Marjorie. Donald and herself, at Marjorie's side, leaving or entering a courtroom.

"All right," Frances says. They could stop at a motel somewhere along the road and stay overnight. A breathing spell, Frances thinks, a bit more time to consider how to prepare Donald.

"Now that's what I call a good dog," one of the women sitting at the table in front of the café window calls as they enter. She nods her approval at Buster, who is beside a bicycle rack, his leash lying loose on the pavement beside him.

"Oh, he's good when he wants to be," Frances says. "But if he takes a notion not to, let me tell you," she says, and rolls her eyes, grateful for the woman's generosity.

The three women nod and smile knowingly, and for a moment, Frances fears they may invite them to share their table. She notices their similar hairstyles, permed and clipped to sharp points at the ear, teased high on the forehead, their oversize T-shirts drawing attention to their trouble spots. A man and a boy sit at one of several tables along a wall. Across from it is a counter, a high glass case, which, except for a plate of bran muffins, appears empty.

Frances chooses a table beside the door so she can watch Buster. Wall panelling near the ceiling has swelled and sprung loose at the seams, and the floor tiles, maroon and grey, are rippled and chipped. The café feels temporary, Frances thinks, a summer place given over to the frost in winter. Vegetarian burrito, the lunch special of the day, is posted on a chalkboard and, as Frances sees it, she suddenly feels hungry.

"You folks are from Manitoba," the ice-cream-eating woman says. She nods in the direction of their Accord parked across the street.

"From Winnipeg," Frances says.

"Winnipeg," another of the trio says, "I've never been there. Not yet, anyways."

"We're heading up to Saskatoon," Donald says, and Frances sends him a darting, cautionary look.

"Saskatoon," the women repeat, as though they find it surprising anyone would want to go there.

"It's a beautiful city," Donald says. He likes walking early in the morning with Marjorie along the river. He likes the way the river bisects the city, its connecting bridges. He thinks of silt drifting, a mirror reflecting the glass towers and church spires.

"I've got a sister lives in Winnipeg," the woman who eats the ice-cream says. "In West Kildonan."

"West Kildonan can be very nice," Frances says. "Lots of trees there."

"Water beds in every room," the woman continues, as though Frances hasn't spoken. "I couldn't get a proper night's sleep because of it. That and the noise of traffic."

The man sitting at the table with the boy snorts at this. "I wouldn't give you a dime for one of those things. Harder on the back than anything. You can't beat a futon for the back."

The three women nod. "Or a piece of plywood under the mattress."

"Pretty far south for Saskatoon, aren't you?" the man asks Donald. A hard-looking small man with a day's growth of beard so dark it looks blue. The boy with him turns sideways in his seat and stares at Frances.

The boy has the same skin as the girl had when she was his age, Frances notices, the colour of skim milk; she can see the veins in his neck shining through it. It was as though the girl was determined to be undernourished, different, just for the sake of it. The air moved when she entered rooms, a blur of motion. Flying up the stairs to change her clothes, pester Marjorie for money, and be off again. Hi, Gran Whitmore. A cool, meagre little mouth set against Frances's chin, a smile that opened up only wide enough to display her front teeth. A mouth shaped like her own.

"You doing home schooling again this year, Fred?" a clear, young voice calls out from behind the counter, startling Frances.

"You can bet on it," the man called Fred answers. "Plan on keeping Joey with me for as long as I can. Right, buddy?"

The child, still turned in his chair, nods, dark eyes steady on Frances's face. There is something not quite right, Frances thinks. His eyes. The way his heavy eyebrows flare up like wings.

"I sure admire you for that," the voice behind the counter calls out.

"Oh, this place must be self-serve," Frances says, apologetic, as though they've been in error for assuming to be waited on.

"Shelley, you've got customers," one of the women says, and a young face peers across the glass counter, bushy hair caught up in a ponytail at the back of her head.

"Tell me what you'd like, old girl, and I'll go on over and order," Donald says, rising, clamping a hand around Frances's shoulder, giving it a light squeeze.

Frances senses the women's attentiveness, a stillness. She leans on her arms, fingers clasped and at rest against the table. The fullness of her brushed silk skirt drapes from her hips in gentle folds. Frances knows she was never beautiful, her face is far too long and bony, her eyes set too deeply for that. Handsome at times, graceful, she hopes, brave enough to have attempted elegance, even when in her early twenties and lugging groceries, a squirming Marjorie under the arm, Aaron hanging on to her coattail, three floors to their walk-up in Montreal.

Donald returns to the table, dabbing at his forehead with a handkerchief. Too pale, Frances thinks. It's as though his features are layered with white dust and blunted. Donald is shedding, dissolving at the edges, becoming translucent.

"They're out of the special," Donald says.

"It's all right, dear," Frances says, because he looks worried. "Why don't we share a burger?" It's her fault, she thinks, for being too optimistic, hoping she'd get anything else in a place like this.

"With or without onions," Donald wants to know.

"Without." As he returns to the counter, Frances notes how his suit jacket has creased from the trip and rides up his back.

She packed his blazer with the Legion crest on its breast pocket. She had decided to wear a mother-of-pearl pendant with the peach top. She thought it couldn't do any harm; that it might make an impression, for Marjorie's sake. The closer they get to Saskatoon, the more she recognizes the weakness of her thinking, the frivolity of it, as if their presence in the courtroom counted a hoot in the scheme of things. Except for Marjorie, of course. Since this latest episode, Frances can't bring herself to say the girl's name. Can't imagine them ever having been related.

"Would you be wanting mustard and relish?" Donald asks, startling Frances.

"Oh, Don, for goodness' sake," Frances says. "You should know by now." She attempts a bit of laughter for the sake of the women who, she knows, are listening. Men do that, she wants to confide in them, as he returns to the counter. They conveniently escape into clogged arteries and foggy memories, leaving us to take care of the details.

Donald returns once again. "The grill's turned off," he says.

Frances raises her chin, and her eyes become the colour of pewter. "That's strange," she says. "I seem to remember this place had a sign on it outside that said SNACK BAR."

"Shelley's Lunch Bar," the young woman behind the counter says, and Frances recognizes the eyes have gone wide with a feigned innocence, a mocking smile lingering beneath the surface.

"May I enquire if you have tomatoes?"

"I think so." The girl nods and flounces her ponytail for emphasis.

"And do you have bread?"

"Yah. Likely."

"We could go somewhere else," Donald says.

"Well, if it's not too inconvenient, we'll have a tomato sandwich," Frances says.

"The Duchess of Windsor with a shovel up her bum," the ice-cream-eating woman says *sotto voce* as she lights a cigarette. The women's breasts jiggle as they chuckle silently and become preoccupied with the appearance of someone passing in the street.

Though her neck stings with heat, Frances tells herself she does not need their approval. It has become unnecessary at this point. There is no virtue in playing down to win the approval of anyone, she thinks. This is what the Oaks and Pond has given her. A community of the fortunate who are not inclined to apologize for it. And why should they? she thinks.

"Would that be with, or without, mayo," the young woman says.

"And I'll have an ice cream cone," the boy chirps at Donald.

"Hey, button 'er up there," the man called Fred says to the boy. His gruffness is filled with pride.

"I'd like to do that," Donald says. "Let me treat the lad."

The child slides from his chair and goes over to the glass case next to Donald. He peers down into the glass counter at the tubs of ice cream. Donald feels the heat of the child radiate against his leg.

"What'll it be, big fella?" Donald says. A ceiling fan turns, and he hears the soft whirring sound of it, the sound of the television, the roar of the crowd. *I'll have vanilla*, Donald hears himself say, years ago. He's in another room, similar, but the light has changed as though a blind has been drawn on the window. He sees a grainy silhouette of a man wearing a billed cap, standing in front of it.

"I want lime and I want chocolate chip," the boy says.

"Here now, one scoop, you little beggar," the father calls from the table.

Donald hears denim whisper, sees a hand spotted with cinnamon-coloured freckles emerge from a pocket, a coin rests in callused folds; he inhales and smells the familiar dusty odour of alfalfa, the sweat of horse in the denim coveralls of the man standing beside him. Donald wants strawberry, he wants lemon, so why does the word "vanilla" always come out?

"Why not have both?" Donald says to the boy.

A hand comes towards Donald, bearing ice cream, and Donald reaches up, as tall as he can make himself, to receive it.

"Do you folks have relatives in Saskatoon?" the young woman asks, as she hands a double-decker cone to the boy.

The grainy silhouette of the man in front of the window fades.

"Yes," Donald says. He blinks at the sight of a shelf lined with food containers, a clock above it emerging where the other world vanished. It leaves me bewildered, he told the doctor. But it's not the right word to describe what he feels when this happens. Discombobulated, he'd said, to make light of it. It's as though he has been held between sleep and waking, or being and not being.

"So, do you go up to visit them often?"

Donald sees the girl's red mouth moving.

"Who?"

"Your relatives in Saskatoon."

"Yes," Donald says. "My daughter and granddaughter." He is relieved, as the room jumps forward with clarity, brightness of light and sharp edges. Sunlight glances off arborite, cigarette smoke trails across the windowpane.

"My daughter, Marjorie, and Samantha. Prokipchuk," Donald says, forgetting what he is not to say.

"Samantha Prokipchuk?" the child's father asks. The question holds the room still. Donald feels their faces turn away, hears the clink of the chain on the ceiling fan against the metal blades.

"Yes," Donald says.

"That's not the same girl who beat that old couple to death up in Saskatoon?" the man says.

She was not alone, Donald wants to say. There were two others, boys. She happened to be at the wrong place at the wrong time with the wrong kind of people. He sees Frances rise and flee, the dog scrambling after her, its leash trailing. Donald sees the flap of Frances's blue skirt, her flat heels kicking pale blue waves as she runs across the street.

୯ଌ

"I wish I could die," Frances cries. Her voice is ripe with phlegm. She wishes for the oblivion of unconsciousness, and yet she clings to her skirt, its blue silk bunched in her fists and twisted into knots. Frances hangs on for dear life, or risks flying from the face of the earth.

Donald watches a row of sparrows lift from a telephone wire; the birds' wings, jittery dark commas, hook for a piece of the sky. Bewildered, Donald thinks, lost; he has seen the worry in the girl's eyes on family get-togethers, as though she knew she should be able to make sense out of a room full of people, but failed to. He sees the scuffed underside of her shoes as she climbs the steps of a slide in a playground. He remembers her fierce concentration on the ride down it, her noisy objection to being caught in his arms. There are many things Donald does not understand because he has not been made privy to them. He has been spared, he knows, the details of Marjorie's unlucky choice in husbands. Samantha's growing truancy and shoplifting. The drugs. Day-care, Donald thinks, a poor substitute. Television. Food allergies; he has often wondered. He keeps remembering her as a lurching, determined child and can't believe she is guilty.

"Turn this car around," Frances says. "We're not going to Saskatoon."

"It doesn't matter what those people think, Fran. They're strangers. We'll never see them again."

"As if it was only that," Frances says. "Oh, god. Think of it, Donald. Manslaughter," she says, her voice breaking. *Man slaughter*, Frances thinks, and feels her body go rigid. The word, split open like that, brings the taste of blood to her mouth. A man bludgeoned with a tire iron, a baseball bat, his attackers' boots. The woman's windpipe broken by a telephone receiver.

Frances and Donald had watched the newscast, had seen the police rolling out the stretchers, the mounds in body bags, a man with a large stomach, the woman stricken with arthritis. Chosen because they were defenceless, Frances had said, and thank god for the security system, the video cameras and guards at the Oaks and Pond. Frances and Donald had clamped their jaws shut at the sight, not knowing there would be any connection to them.

"If you don't turn around, I'll jump out of this car," Frances says. She draws away as Donald tries to touch her.

"Marjorie needs us."

"You know what Marjorie needs," Frances says, bitterly. "What Marjorie needs is our chequebook." Once a parent, always a parent, the retired general practitioner had said; even on the deathbed, the kids are either demanding you live or die, for their sake. But there are limits, Frances believes. It begins with a man and a woman and it should end that way.

"We will do what we have to do," Donald says.

"We are not going to throw good money after bad."

"She's one of ours, Fran."

"Jesus bloody Murphy," Frances says, her voice rising. "She helped kill two people, Donald."

"We don't know that," Donald says, so softly Frances can barely take it in. "That's what this hearing is about."

"We know," Frances says. "I know. Marjorie knows."

Donald is drawn by the clouds hanging above the watery horizon; the slice of moon, its faint horns defining the space between them. Don't, Donald thinks. Please don't.

He will soon find out anyway, she thinks. There is no way around it. "They found hair. Blood and tissue. On the girl's boots."

The drone of the engine fills Donald's head, circles around and around his brain, echoes in his ears; telephone poles spring up from the earth and fling themselves at him. Trees topple backwards into the horizon.

"Of course. She was there, but that doesn't mean. . . ," he says. "Does it?" It sounds like a plea and not a question.

"And fingerprints. Hers. On the receiver of the telephone. Look, whether or not we believe it won't change a thing," Frances says. "Facts are facts and we have to face up to them."

Donald pinches his eyelids, rubs them to ease the strain. Jack Sprat could eat no fat, Donald thinks, his wife could eat no lean. The words of the rhyme come to him, unbidden.

"Why do you think Marjorie needs the best money can buy? They'll plead not guilty, but she *is* guilty."

Something moves beyond, on the shoulder of the highway, as Frances speaks. A brown spot, Donald thinks, and watches to see if the light will dim or rise, for the colours of whatever place will emerge from the highway in front of the car. The spot jiggles, grows elongated, becomes a strange-looking creature.

"Look," Frances says, as she sees the creature, too. What appear to be coattails flap as it lopes down the shoulder towards them. Then the animal begins to run, an awkward but resolute sideways gallop, as though having confirmed its recognition of them it hurries now to greet them. What looked like coattails become gangly limbs and a tasselled tail, flying in all directions.

"It's a calf," Donald says, and his shoulders drop with relief. He steers the car onto the shoulder and stops.

Frances sees its pricked ears come forward, a startled look, and then the animal lowers its head, as though disappointed. The calf backs into a ditch and stands halfway down among the reeds, studying them. Buster leaps up and sniffs at the window.

"It must have got out through a hole in a fence," Donald says, as he notices a herd of cattle in a pasture beyond. He gets out of the car.

Was that it? Frances wonders. A matter of a hole in a fence, inattentiveness?

The calf stands shoulder-deep among the reeds, and as Donald comes round to the front of the car, the animal sees him and begins to swing its head, backing away, deeper into the rushes.

"It'll wind up hit by a car," Donald says to Frances, who has rolled down the window. He looks for a stone, finds one, and pockets it.

"There's not been a whole lot of traffic, so far," Frances says.

"A man loses a calf, it could mean his profit for the entire year," Donald says. He begins wading, thigh-deep, through the weeds along the edge of the ditch. He means to give the animal lots of room, skirt around it and get it in the rump. The animal stands motionless, peering out at Donald, as though calculating what he will do next.

"For pity's sake, Donald, there's likely water down there," Frances calls. "You'll ruin your shoes."

The whine in Frances's voice sets Donald's teeth on edge. He would like to smash something. Slam his fist down hard, punch a hole in a window.

"They're my shoes, Frances, and if you don't mind, I'll take the risk of ruining them."

His anger sets Frances's heart racing. It's unfair, she thinks, to take it out on her. Put it where it belongs, squarely on the girl's shoulders.

As Donald steps lower down into the rushes he doesn't feel the chilly water filling his shoes and rising to his shins. He sees patches of the animal, a flank, its taffy ribs heaving. A cow moos, a baleful groan from among the herd on the other side of the highway. Over there, you little bugger, Donald thinks. He heaves the stone and it flies too far, splashing down beyond the animal. The calf swings away from the sound and crashes through the reeds towards him. Grab an ear, Donald thinks. Both ears, turn it by the head, and send it up past the car and onto the other side. He smells the animal's heat, sees in its limpid eyes a blindness brought on by fear.

"Here, boss!" Donald calls and waves his arms. "Go! Over there! Here, boss! Go, boss!" The calf stumbles and lunges towards him, the reeds flattening as the animal's legs fold up beneath it and it goes down. "Go!" Donald shouts, as the rank water swirls around its silky brown neck. The animal snorts, and frothy bubbles clump its nostrils and mouth. "Get! You get!" Donald says, not realizing he is weeping as he grabs hold and feels its ears, warm flaps of skin and gristle in his hand. The animal scrambles up, its flanks dripping algae and mud. It shakes his hands off and backs away and, for a moment, Donald fears it means to charge him, but it veers around him, up and out of the ditch. Donald stands for moments, watching, aware now of the chill and wetness creeping in, and he shivers. The calf lopes across an open field, growing smaller. Then a silence moves in, a stillness he has heard only on the prairies. A quiet so intense and full that he used to think he could scoop it out of the air and cup it in his hands. A red-winged blackbird flits down onto a fencepost. The calf stops, turns to look at Donald, raises its head in a plaintive bellow. Go on, you little bugger, Donald thinks. Make a noise, it's not going to get you where you want to go.

His chest tightens from exertion as he climbs out of the ditch. He notices a house down the highway, a bungalow half-concealed by trees. The least he can do is let someone know they have a calf on the loose. His shoes squelch with water and sour-smelling muck smears the car seat as he slides across it.

"The silly thing would sooner go up a chimney," he says. "I tried, but it wasn't having anything to do with it."

Frances sees the soft pleat of skin beside his mouth, the nest of grey hair inside his ear, his chest rising and falling as he waits to catch his breath. She sees him as he must have been as a boy in a country school, dozy from being up early with morning chores, chewing on a ragged sweater cuff. Solid, profoundly loyal.

"We've got to get you out of those wet trousers," she says.

"Yes," Donald says. "Yes."

The farmyard they drive onto is weedy, spotted with patches of mallow, the grey earth trampled by feet and worn to a shine. The bungalow sits on a slight rise, straw bales banked up its sides. It exudes stillness; the windows reflect the clouded sky. Children's toys, bright pieces of plastic, lie scattered beyond the back step as though the children were called suddenly from their play. Frances notices a brackish dug-out pond off to the side of the car, set down against a backdrop of white birch. Its surface, black and oily-looking, suggests a great depth. And no fence, Frances thinks, noting the children's toys lying about the yard. Is it any wonder, she thinks, the frequency of the accounts of farm accidents? Words, warnings, were not enough to keep a curious or determined child away. Or a fence, either, for that matter; an attraction to some.

She watches Donald standing on the back steps, hands on his hips, gazing across the yard as though he expects an answer to his knock may emerge from the shed in a field beyond the garden. Alfred Hitchcock, Frances thinks. A rumpled man in a grey suit. Ashes holding the shape of what was once a solid chunk of wood. Daydreaming, or forgetting more than likely, why he'd gone to the door in the first place.

And I am not the Duchess of Windsor, Frances thinks. But no matter how she tries, the rigid stance is there, she knows. She knows too well how she appears to others. She has never been able to do much about their misconceptions but accept them.

"Don!" Frances calls. It's somewhat like learning of an unexpected pregnancy, she thinks. The dread, fear, anger perhaps, but then you get on with it.

What choice do you have? And it's inevitable, they *will* get on with the trip to Saskatoon. It pains her to think what it may cost in the end. But they will do it. He's right, she thinks, Samantha is ours, like it or not. She can only hope for explanations for the evidence, reasons she can grow into and come to believe. She must remember the child, how she enjoyed holding her. As much as one of her own. She recalls the girl's energy, her spirit beating against its cage of bones. She could feel it in her own hands. Frances used to think she understood the perplexed look in Samantha's green eyes, a pleading for acceptance and understanding.

As he comes down the stairs and begins to walk across the yard, Donald waves, wearing a smile that is wide and sunny and crinkles his eyes. Frances thinks he may have read her mind, and is pleased that she has decided they will do what Marjorie expects of them. His step becomes energetic, jaunty even, as his arms swing and the sodden, stained trousers flap about his muddied shoes. He waves again, and calls hello. Frances returns his wave, but he seems to be looking beyond her and so she turns, expecting to see someone, the owner perhaps, coming through the white birch beyond the pond.

આ

Donald feels a chilly, autumn wind off the lake. Grey pebbles roll underfoot as he carries a jacket for Aaron, a sweater for Marjorie, both of whom are hunched like spotted toads at the end of the pier, absorbed in counting their toes, Donald supposes, or perhaps a fish has just glided into the shadows near the dock.

Frances rolls down the window and searches the stand of birch where its leaves, dots of light, begin to flutter as a breeze moves in from the fields. Leaves flipping white and then silver and white again, stippling the surface of the black water with light as Donald marches towards the dug-out pond, his grey shoulders squared. She thinks she hears Donald whistling, but it's not that, it can't be. Donald has never whistled.

"Don!" Frances calls, unable to take in what she sees, Donald's forward motion, his lack of hesitancy as his feet rise and fall. She sees how they lift, how they come down. She sees the outline of his thin legs in the wet trousers, his hips, his waist, shoulders. She sees Donald, disappearing.

ฬગ

"Disappearances" is the most recently published story in this anthology. Sandra Birdsell was introduced to the subject of disappearing when she was appointed writer-in-residence by the Saskatoon Public Library in 1995. Shortly after, she began noticing various local accounts of people who disappeared. She says:

> *There were many victims, including two people who vanished after a house fire. It was a social phenomenon. Another woman returned home naked, covered in twigs and leaves, with no memory of where she had been. It set me thinking about disappearances, about being and not-being, about women who "disappear" and are never seen again. About the same time, I was driving through southern Saskatchewan — a phenomenal landscape — very flat,*

huge sky, low rolling hills. Lo and behold, a calf suddenly appeared beside the road, out of nowhere. At the time I was finishing my book of stories, The Two-Headed Calf. *There was a black pond on a nearby farm. It was like a gift, the elements of the story combining right in front of me. The calf was the final piece of a narrative puzzle which tied the book together.*

    This story is about a journey not completed. I've never been interested in arriving. I'm more intrigued by what's not there than what's there. In this story, the absent people are the most powerful.

Born in Hamiota, Manitoba, Sandra Birdsell presently lives and writes in Regina. Her first book, Night Travellers *(1982), announced the arrival of a major new writer of stories.* The Two-Headed Calf *was published in 1998.*

K.M.

BETH BRANT (b. 1941)

Swimming Upstream

Anna May spent the first night in a motel off Highway 8. She arrived about ten, exhausted from her long drive — the drive through farmland, bright autumn leaves, the glimpse of blue lake. She saw none of this, only the grey highway stretching out before her. When she saw the signs of a motel she stopped, feeling the need for rest. It didn't matter where.

She took a shower, lay in bed, and fell asleep, the dream beginning again. Her son — drowning in the water, his skinny arms flailing the waves, his mouth opening to scream but no sound coming forth. She, Anna May, moving in slow motion running into the waves, her hands grabbing for the boy and feeling only water run through her fingers. She grabbed and grabbed but nothing held to her hands. She dove and opened her eyes underwater and saw nothing. He was gone. She dove and grabbed, her hands connecting with sand, with seaweed, but not her son. He was gone. Simon was gone.

Anna May woke. The dream was not a nightmare anymore. It had become a companion to her. A friend, almost a lover, reaching for her as she slept; making pictures of her son, keeping him alive while recording his death. In the first days after Simon left her, the dream made her wake screaming, sobbing, arms hitting at the air, legs kicking the sheets, becoming tangled in the material. Her bed was a straitjacket, pinning her down, holding her until the dream ended. She would fight the dream then. Now she welcomed it.

During the day she had other memories of Simon. His birth, his first pair of shoes, his first steps, his first word *Mama*, his first book, his first day of school. Now that he was dead, she invented a future for him during the day. His first skating lessons, his first hockey game, his first reading aloud from a book, his first . . . But she couldn't invent beyond that. His six-year-old face and body wouldn't change in her mind. She couldn't invent what she couldn't imagine. The dream became the final video of her imagining.

She hadn't been there when Simon drowned. Simon had been given to her ex-husband by the courts. She was unfit — because she lived with a woman, because a woman, Catherine, slept beside her, because she had a history of alcoholism. The history was old. Anna May had stopped drinking when she became pregnant with Simon, and she had stayed dry all those years. She couldn't imagine what alcohol tasted like after Simon came. He was so lovely, so new — the desire for drink evaporated every time Simon took hold of her finger, or nursed from her breast, or opened his mouth in a toothless smile. She had marveled at his being, this gift that had come from her own body. This beautiful being who had formed inside her, had come with speed through the birth canal to welcome life outside her; his face red with anticipation, his black hair sticking straight up as if electric with hope, his little fists grabbing, his pink mouth finding her nipple and holding on for dear life. She had no need for alcohol — there was Simon.

Simon was taken away from them. But they saw him on weekends, Tony delivering him on a Friday night, Catherine discreetly finding someplace else to be when his car drove up. They still saw Simon, grateful for the two days out of the week they could play with him, they could delight in him, they could pretend with him. They still saw Simon, but the call came that changed all that. The call from Tony saying that Simon had drowned when he fell out of the boat as they were fishing. Tony sobbing, "I'm sorry. I didn't mean for this to happen. I tried to save him. I'm sorry. Please Anna, please forgive me. Oh God, Anna, I'm sorry, I'm sorry."

So Anna May dreamed of those final moments of a six-year-old life. And it stunned her that she wasn't there to see him die when she had been there to see him come into life.

Anna May stayed dry but she found herself looking into cupboards at odd times. Looking for something. Looking for something to drink. She thought of ways to buy wine and hide it, taking a drink when she needed it. But there was Catherine. Catherine would know and Catherine's face, already so lined and tired and old, would become more so. Anna May looked at her own face in the mirror. She was thirty-six and looked twenty years older. Her black hair had grey streaks she hadn't noticed before. Her forehead had deep lines carved into the flesh, and her eyes — her eyes that had cried so many tears — were a faded and washed-out blue. Her mouth was wrinkled, the lips parched and chapped. She and Catherine were aged and ghostlike figures walking through a dead house.

Anna May thought about the bottle of wine. It look on large proportions in her mind. A bottle of wine, just one, that she could drink from and never empty. A bottle of wine — that sweet, red kind that would take away the dryness, the wrinkled insides of her. She went to meetings but never spoke, only saying her name and "I'll pass tonight." Catherine wanted to talk, but Anna May had nothing to say to this woman she loved, who slept beside her, who shared the same dream. Anna May thought about the bottle of wine. The bottle, the red liquid inside, the sweet taste gathering in her mouth, moving down her throat, hitting her bloodstream, warming her inside, killing the deadness.

She arranged time off work and told Catherine she was going away for a few days — she needed to think, to be alone. Catherine watched her face, the framing of the words out of her mouth, her washed-out eyes. Catherine said, "I understand."

"Will you be all right?" Anna May asked of her.

"I'll be fine," Catherine said. "I'll see friends. We haven't seen our friends in so long, they are concerned about us. I'll be waiting when you get back. I love you so much."

Anna May got in the car and drove up 401, up 19, over to 8 and the motel, the shower, the dream.

Anna May smoked her cigarettes and drank coffee until daylight. She made her plans to buy the bottle of wine. After that, she had no plans, other than the first drink and how it would taste and feel.

She found a meeting in Goderich and sat there, ashamed and angered with herself to sit in a meeting and listen to the stories and plan her backslide. She thought of speaking, of talking about Simon, about the bottle of wine, but she was afraid they would stop her or say something that would make her stop. Anna May didn't want to be stopped. She wanted to drink and drink and drink until it was all over. "My name is Anna May and I'll just pass." Later, she hung around for coffee, feeling like an infiltrator, a spy, and a woman took hold of her arm and said, "Let's go out and talk. I know what you're planning. Don't do it. Let's talk." Anna May shrugged off the woman's hand and left. She drove to a liquor outlet, *vins et spiritueux*. "Don't do it." She found the wine, one bottle, that was all she'd buy. "Don't do it." One bottle, that was all. She paid and left the store, the familiar curve of the bottle wrapped in brown paper. "Don't do it." Only one bottle. It wouldn't hurt and she laughed at the excuses bubbling up in her mouth like wine. Just one. She smoked a cigarette sitting in the parking lot, wondering where to go, where to stop and turn the cap that would release the red, sweet smell of the wine before the taste would overpower her and she wouldn't have to wonder anymore.

She drove north on 21 heading for the Bruce Peninsula, Lake Huron on her left, passing the little resort towns, the cottages by the lake. She stopped for a hamburger and without thinking, got her thermos filled with coffee. This made her laugh, the bottle sitting next to her, almost a living thing. She drank the coffee, driving north along 21, thinking not of Simon, not of Catherine, but thinking of her father. Charles, her mother had called him. Everyone else had called him Charley. Good old Charley. Good-time Charley. Injun Charley. Charles was a hard worker, working at almost anything, construction being his best and favourite. He worked hard, he drank hard. He attempted to be a father, a husband, but the work and the drink took his attempts away. Anna May's mother never complained, never left him. She cooked and kept house and raised the children and always called him Charles. When Anna May grew up, she taunted her mother with the fact that *her Charles* was a drunk and why didn't she care more about her kids than her drunken husband? Didn't her mother know how ashamed they were to have such a father, to hear people talk about him, to laugh at him, to laugh at them — the half-breeds of good-old-good-time-Injun-Charley?

Anna May laughed again, the sound ugly inside the car. Her father was long dead and, she supposed, forgiven in some way by her. He was a handsome man back then, and her mother a skinny, pale girl, an orphan girl, something unheard of by her father. How that must have appealed to the romantic that was her father. Anna May didn't know how her mother felt about the life she'd had with Charles. Her mother never talked about those things. Her mother, who sobbed and moaned at Simon's death as she never had at her husband's. Anna May couldn't remember her father ever being mean. He just went away when he drank. Not like his daughter, who'd fight anything in her way when she was drunk. The bottle bounced beside her as she drove.

Anna May drove north and her eyes began to see the colours of the trees. They looked like they were on fire, the reds and oranges competing with the yellows and golds. She smoked her cigarettes and drank from the thermos and remembered this was her favourite season. She and Catherine would be cleaning the garden, harvesting the beets, turnips, and cabbage. They would be digging up the gladioli and letting them dry before packing the bulbs away. They would be planting more tulips because Catherine could never get enough of tulips. It was because they had met in the spring, Catherine always said. "We met in the spring and the tulips were blooming in that little park. You looked so beautiful against the tulips, Simon on your lap. I knew I loved you."

Last autumn Simon had been five and had raked leaves and dug holes for the tulip bulbs. Catherine had made cocoa and cinnamon toast and Simon had declared that he liked cinnamon toast better than pie.

Anna May tasted the salt tears on her lips. She licked the wet salt, imagining it was sweet wine on her tongue. "It's my fault," she said out loud. She thought of all the things she should have done to prevent Simon's leaving. She should have placated Tony, she should have lived alone, she should have pretended to be straight, she should have never become an alcoholic, she should have never loved, she should have never been born. Let go! she cried somewhere inside her. Let go! Isn't that what she learned? But how could she let go of Simon and the hate she had for Tony and for herself? How could she let go of that? If she let go, she'd have to forgive — the forgiveness Tony begged of her now that Simon was gone. Even Catherine, even the woman she loved, asked her to forgive Tony. "It could have happened when he was with us," Catherine cried at her. "Forgive him, then you can forgive yourself." But Catherine didn't know what it was to feel the baby inside her, to feel him pushing his way out of her, to feel his mouth on her breast, to feel the sharp pain in her womb every time his name was mentioned. Forgiveness was for people who could afford it. Anna May was poverty-struck.

The highway turned into a road, the trees crowding in on both sides of her, the flames of the trees almost blinding her. She was entering the Bruce Peninsula, a sign informed her. She pulled off the road, consulting her map. Yes, she would drive to the very tip of the peninsula and it would be there she'd open the bottle and drink her way to whatever she imagined was there. The bottle rested beside her. She touched the brown paper, feeling soothed, feeling a hunger in her stomach.

She saw another sign — SAUBLE FALLS. Anna May thought this would be a good place to stop, to drink the last of the coffee, to smoke another cigarette. She pulled over onto the gravel lot. There was a small path leading down onto the rocks. Another sign: ABSOLUTELY NO FISHING. WATCH YOUR STEP — ROCKS ARE SLIPPERY. She could hear the water before she saw it.

She stepped out of the covering of trees and onto the rock shelf. The falls were narrow, spilling out on various layers of rock. She could see the beginnings of Lake Huron below her. She could see movement in the water going away from the lake and moving toward the rocks and the falls. Fish tails flashed, catching lights from the sun. Hundreds of fish tails moving upstream. She walked across a flat slab of rock and there, beneath her in the shallow water, salmon slowly moving their bodies, their gills expanding and closing as they rested. She looked up to another rock slab and saw a dozen fish congregating at the bottom of a water spill — waiting. Her mind barely grasped the fact that the fish were migrating, swimming upstream, when a salmon leapt and hurled itself over the rushing water above it. Anna May stepped up to another ledge and watched the salmon's companions waiting their turn to jump the flowing water and reach the next plateau. She looked down toward the mouth of the lake. There were other people, like her, standing and silently watching the struggle of the fish. No one spoke, as if to speak would be blasphemous in the presence of this. She looked again into the water, the fish crowding each resting place before resuming the leaps and the jumps. Here and there on the rocks, dead fish, a testimony to the long and desperate struggle that had taken place. They lay, eyes glazed, sides open and bleeding, food for the gulls that hovered over Anna May's head. Another salmon jumped, its flesh torn and gaping, its body spinning and turning until it made it over the fall. Another one, its dorsal fin torn, leapt and was washed back by the power of the water. Anna May watched the fish rest, its open mouth like another wound. The fish was large, the dark body undulating in the water. She watched it begin a movement of tail. Churning the water, it shot into the air, twisting its body, shaking and spinning. She saw the underbelly, pale yellow and bleeding from the battering against the rocks, the water. He made it. Anna May wanted to clap, to shout with elation at the sheer power of such a thing happening before her. She looked around again. The other people had left. She was alone with the fish, the only sound besides the water was her breath against the air. She walked farther upstream, her sneakers getting wet from the splashing of the fish. She didn't feel the wet, she only waited and watched for the salmon to move. She had no idea of time, of how long she stood waiting for the movement, waiting for the jumps, the leaps, the flight. Anna May watched for Torn Fin, wanting to see him move against the current in his phenomenal swim of faith.

Anna May reached a small dam, the last hurdle before the calm waters and the blessed rest. She sat on a rock, her heart beating fast, the adrenaline pouring through her at each leap and twist of the fish. There he was, Torn Fin, his last jump ahead of him. She watched, then closed her eyes, almost ashamed to be a spectator at this act of faith, this primal movement to get to the place of all beginning — only knowing he had to get there. He had to push his bleeding body forward, believing in his magic to get him there. Believing, believing he would get there. No thoughts of death, no thoughts of food, no thoughts of rest, no thoughts but the great urging and wanting to get there, get *there*. Anna May opened her eyes and saw him, another jump before being pushed back. She held her hands together, her body willing Torn Fin to move, to push, to jump, to fly! Her body rocked forward and back, her heart beating madly inside her breast. She rocked, she shouted, "Make it, damn it, make it!" The fish gathered at the dam. She rocked and held her hands tight, her fingers twisting together, nails scratching her palms. She whispered, "Simon. Simon." She rocked. She rocked and watched Torn Fin's fight to reach his home. She rocked and whispered the name of her son into the water, "Simon. Simon." Like a chant, "Simon. Simon. Simon," into the water, as if the very name of her son was magic and could move the salmon to their final place. She rocked. She chanted. "Simon. Simon." Anna May rocked and put her hands in the water, wanting to lift the fish over the dam and to life. Just as the thought flickered through her brain, Torn Fin slapped his tail against the water and jumped. He battled the current. He twisted and arced into the air, his great mouth gaping and gasping, his wounds standing out in relief against his body, the fin discoloured and shredded. With a push, he turned a complete circle and made it over the dam.

"Simon!" Torn Fin gave one more slap of his tail and was gone, the dark body swimming home. She thought . . . she thought she saw her son's face, his black hair streaming behind him, a look of joy transfixed on his little face before the image disappeared.

Anna May stood on the rock, hands limp at her sides, watching the water, watching the salmon, watching. She watched as the sun fell behind the lake and night came closer to her. She walked to the path and back to her car. She looked at the bottle sitting next to her, the brown paper rustling as she put the car in gear. She drove south, stopping at the telephone booth.

She could still hear the water in her ears.

ℰↃᏅ

What is life if not a "swim of faith" against a current that at times malevolently seeks to destroy us? Middle-aged Anna May has fought every inch of the way, from a childhood overshadowed by her hard-drinking and often absent father, through her own adult struggles with alcohol, prejudice, and love, to the unimaginable grief of losing her only child to a sudden accident. Such blows would destroy many of us, but Anna May has not given up. Beth Brant builds her story of faith around elemental images of water and rock, light and dark. At once life-giving and life-taking, water recurs throughout the narrative. The promise of a blue lake's surface sparkling in the sun coexists with the nightmare of drowning in deep, dark water, the victim unable to find a rock to stand on. Memories and nightmares inscribe Anna May's struggle to understand and — perhaps — forgive. As the story nears its end, however, these things give way to an intensely depicted vision conveyed in prose of incantatory power. Anna May experiences a vivid epiphany uniting water and rock, light and dark, an epiphany that holds the promise of new life.

Of Mohawk ancestry, Beth Brant ("Degonwadonti") was born in Detroit. She now divides her time between Canada and the United States. Brant began writing at the age of forty and has published poetry and essays as well as short fiction. "Swimming Upstream" appeared in the 1991 anthology Talking Leaves.

T.C.

BONNIE BURNARD

(b. 1945)

Joyride

She drives the highway to the lake half dreaming, watching the sun, hoping to catch the exact moment of connection between the warm round base and the flat wheat fields hundreds of miles away on the horizon. It's a game she plays whenever she can. She has always believed there are other people who do it with her, though their horizons would be their own. The grey truck appears from nowhere.

He accelerates and pulls around in front of her and she gives him her full attention, expecting him to pull away and perhaps lift some stones, throw them against her windshield. When he settles in just yards ahead and stays there, she wonders why he has passed at all. Then she sees him grin into his rearview mirror and wave and she knows the signal is not meant for her. The other truck is there, nestled snugly behind her.

The grey truck is old, with rounded edges and high wooden sides, perhaps for livestock, though it seems clean. She thinks the driver might be in his late thirties. His hair is closely cropped, has been recently shaved around his ears and up his neck to expose the two thick muscles running toward his skull. His shoulders are very steady.

The other truck is blue, of all colours, and newer and sharp-edged. The chrome on the grill reflects the sunlight. The driver is fair, his face wide and heavily boned; his passenger has a softer, smaller face.

The boys are out for a ride, she thinks.

She could have waited for morning, as her husband suggested, but she wanted to get to the lake ahead of all the other weekend people. She's not all that comfortable in heavy traffic. She wonders about double clutching and the other tricks; she is sure there are other tricks that good drivers know.

She tries to pass. She pulls out carefully, afraid she might clip the back of the grey truck but she gets clear, out into the passing lane. He simply accelerates and pulls out ahead of her; child's play, she thinks. She doesn't rule out the possibility of trying again.

There is colour in the sky, mauve and pink and orange, swirling together with the clouds, but the source is gone. She ignores the word *trapped* because she knows where she is and has lots of gas and fairly good tires and the car has never really failed her. She has never had to pull over to the side of any road and wave down assistance. Just to be safe though, she locks all the doors she can; the rear passenger door on the far side is beyond her reach, even after she throws off her seat belt. When she finishes reaching and twisting to get at the locks, she notices laughter and the slapping of shoulders in the blue truck. The muscled driver of the grey truck doesn't move at all and she begins to think of him as a granite mannequin.

A car passes them from the other direction. She digs into her purse for her cigarettes, puts one in her mouth and punches the lighter on the dash. The wide-jawed driver behind her sits up at his wheel and takes a new grip. She feels a bump, and then another bump. They want me to know how much they can see, she thinks, how much they can do. She throws the cigarette to the floor.

She is beginning to imagine things, specific things; she's lost that battle. Rape jumps easily to mind. She imagines a darning needle and strong thread; how she would, if it were possible, sew herself shut.

Dusk has muted the colour in the sky. She puts her headlights on.

Death moves into her imagination much more reluctantly. She has never had so much as a broken arm, has not bled any more than an ordinary person should, small careless gashes that quickly healed over with the simple assistance of cleanliness. She tries to visualize the exact thickness of the skull. A quarter of an inch perhaps? Thicker in places? Thinner? Hard enough to withstand the force of a kick from a man weighing maybe two hundred pounds? Possibly. But not hard enough to withstand dozens of kicks, from several boots, with God knows what kind of force behind them.

She is almost sure they don't have guns; she's seen no racks and handguns are not at all common in this country. There may be knives, though, hunting knives or jack-knives with pictures of fish and grizzly bears on the handles. This is insane, she says, aloud. She is pleased with the reasoned tone in her voice.

The blue truck is pulling up beside her now and the passenger leans out his window. For all the softness of his face, his arm is heavily muscled and dark with hair and sun. He does have a knife, though he is not threatening her with it, is very casual in fact, waves it around conversationally. She can't understand what he is shouting at her. When he sees she can't, he thrusts the knife up into the air several times. She notices that the blade isn't clean. She shows all the fear she feels and more, trying to appease. I'm scared. You can stop now. You can leave me now. This horrid concentration, this effort to give them what she thinks they need is taking more skill and energy than she imagined she had.

She hates these bastards. She imagines them beaten by fathers in sweaty undershirts; she imagines teachers with rulers and clenched fists. She doesn't care. It's not her fault. She is innocent. A full-colour fantasy comes to ease her: there is a crash; they remain in a bloody heap of steel and intestines while she slips free.

The truck moves back into position behind her and she thinks maybe there is another car approaching but it is only a sharp curve in the road and they take it together. They are still miles from the lake, miles from the prairie town settled in the valley cut by the chain of lakes. They have already passed several narrow dirt roads meeting the highway, each one marked by the illumination of a single Department of Highways light before receding back through the dark empty fields, and there will be more. She fights down the image of the nest of people awaiting her at the cottage, husband and children and perhaps a friend, stopped in to welcome her and share a beer. She fights down the image of the girls in their new flannel nighties, playing Scrabble at the kitchen table, of her son being coaxed from his sandbox and hosed down on the deck.

She knows a lot will depend on what kind of men they are. And on the thrill threshold they've established. She knows there is no real way to measure pain, not from the outside. She will whimper and cry, more than she needs to, from the beginning. If they have among them some acceptable level of achievement, she will guess at it and give it to them, whether or not they have earned it.

She has urinated but they can't know that. The smell fills the car and she imagines that it gives an extra edge to her reflexes.

The grey truck is braking now, chugging, forcing her to do the same. The blue truck puffs alongside, ready to show her something else. This time he bends to the floor of the truck and sits up again with his large hand wrapped around the body of a doll. He extends his arm to her. Where the doll's head should be is the head of a cat. She can see dried blood on the chest and shoulders. He is laughing, banging his head against the rear window. She discovers something new in the pit of her stomach and she begins to gag.

The sudden screech of brakes stops the gagging and the blue truck swerves, nearly broadsiding her, and tucks back in behind again. There must be a car this time. She prepares herself. There is a car and it's beside her and gone and she floors the gas pedal and pulls out and around and she is free. She is in the lead, the grey truck not as alert as the blue truck might have been.

She watches in her mirror as the blue truck passes its companion. With any luck she'll be able to stay beyond his reach. There is a shudder moving through the car but she doesn't lift her foot. She can see only what her headlights show her, the dotted yellow line moving ahead and the gravel shoulder on her right. They guide her. She thinks about the RCMP detachment on the main street of the town. She thinks about everyone she's ever cared about, recites their names.

She is across the tracks, past the gas station and she slows finally because she will have to make a turn soon. Down to sixty, fifty, forty. The blue truck is there, right behind her. She makes the turn and the rear end goes out from under her but she has watched *Knight Rider* so often with her son that she knows what to do and she does it well, steering into the skid, straightening. She is on a residential street and is grateful for the street lights and the lawn sprinklers. She takes the last corner. There are no cruisers parked in front of the detachment, no lights in the windows. She goes down a darker block, around and over to the main street, turning in to angle park in front of the pizza place. She thinks she will leap from the car but she stumbles out and walks to the wooden restaurant door. The blue truck has parked across the street and the men are climbing out of it.

In the washroom, she strips off her skirt and panties and rinses the urine away. She punches the hand dryer over and over, holding her clothes up to the warm air. When they are nearly dry she remembers herself, realizes how lucky she's been that no-one has come in to see her standing there half-naked. She puts her clothes on. She looks at her face in the mirror and wonders where her make-up has gone. There is nothing left. Three heavily made-up, giddy teenagers come swinging into the washroom, giving her an immediate deference, and she tries to smile at them as she pulls open the door.

In the dining room there are several university students carrying trays of pizza high over their heads. There are children. She can see glasses of chocolate milk, with straws in them.

All three men sit at a table close to the washroom. The one from the grey truck sees her first and he is out of his chair and beside her, pinching her arm. He whispers, "No harm done, eh?"

The other two are watching her, moving spoons slowly through white mugs of coffee, leaning across the table toward each other.

She knows it won't be long until she is with her own people, bathed and cried out and resting. She knows she should act, now, while they are close. She imagines them driving down the highway in some direction. Though she can't name the law they've broken, she is almost sure there is one, and she can hear the statement she'll make composing itself in her head. The dry details will matter to someone and that someone will get in a car and look for the trucks and find them, likely not far away. She will be able to identify them.

She walks into the kitchen. The red-haired waiter, the one the kids like so much, calls her, miraculously, by name. "Do you want Frank?" he asks. Frank is the owner, she thinks. Frank is likely sane. "Yes," she answers.

When he comes through the doors, his dark chin leading his face officiously, she begins to cry, just a little. She can smell her stench rising with the steam in the kitchen and she knows she has not been successful in rinsing the urine out of her clothes.

"You tell me," Frank says. "You tell me what happened." He yells at a waiter. "Get me a glass of cold water here."

She sits where Frank has put her, beside an open back door, sipping at the water the young man has offered. Frank is talking to her, making a point of looking very forcefully at her face, as if this will help. She leans over and turns her head to look out through the door. It's only an empty alley; she can see the decrepit backs of buildings and above them the black prairie sky. Moths thud repeatedly against the bare lightbulb above the door and a cold breeze wraps itself around her shoulders.

℘ℭ℞

A terse compression marks this story, whose present-tense narration encourages readers to experience its events vicariously, as if they are unfolding before our eyes on a television or cinema screen. In this stark account of sudden terror Bonnie Burnard allows us no respite: only three narrative sentences are allowed to set the scene — a woman making a quiet evening car trip to join her family at the lake — before the calm is shattered. Out of nowhere appear two trucks: "the boys are out for a ride."

Who these men are neither we nor the terrified woman learn. In the end, the tormentors' identities are not relevant, just as the identity of their victim bears no significance for them. Burnard's story hinges on the random threat that can without warning invade anyone's life. In this case, the threat comes from the pleasure three cowards take in terrifying a solitary victim during a chance encounter. There is no justice here, no explanation: what happens, happens. As one of the tormentors whispers threateningly, "No harm done, eh?" The imagery of the story's conclusion — the "black prairie sky" and the "cold breeze" that chills the woman — further holds little promise of comfort, restoration of order, or retribution.

Bonnie Burnard has published two collections of short stories. Women of Influence *(1988), in which "Joyride" appears, won the Commonwealth Best First Book Award. Her subsequent collection,* Casino and Other Stories *(1994), was shortlisted for the Giller Prize.*

T.C.

Cathedral

This blind man, an old friend of my wife's, he was on his way to spend the night. His wife had died. So he was visiting the dead wife's relatives in Connecticut. He called my wife from his in-laws'. Arrangements were made. He would come by train, a five-hour trip, and my wife would meet him at the station. She hadn't seen him since she worked for him one summer in Seattle ten years ago. But she and the blind man had kept in touch. They made tapes and mailed them back and forth. I wasn't enthusiastic about his visit. He was no one I knew. And his being blind bothered me. My idea of blindness came from the movies. In the movies, the blind moved slowly and never laughed. Sometimes they were led by seeing-eye dogs. A blind man in my house was not something I looked forward to.

That summer in Seattle she had needed a job. She didn't have any money. The man she was going to marry at the end of the summer was in officers' training school. He didn't have any money, either. But she was in love with the guy, and he was in love with her, etc. She'd seen something in the paper: HELP WANTED — *Reading to Blind Man*, and a telephone number. She phoned and went over, was hired on the spot. She'd worked with this blind man all summer. She read stuff to him, case studies, reports, that sort of thing. She helped him organize his little office in the county social-service department. They'd become good friends, my wife and the blind man. How do I know these things? She told me. And she told me something else. On her last day in the office, the blind man asked if he could touch her face. She agreed to this. She told me he touched his fingers to every part of her face, her nose — even her neck! She never forgot it. She even tried to write a poem about it. She was always trying to write a poem. She wrote a poem or two every year, usually after something really important had happened to her.

When we first started going out together, she showed me the poem. In the poem, she recalled his fingers and the way they had moved around over her face. In the poem, she talked about what she had felt at the time, about what went through her mind when the blind man touched her nose and lips. I can remember I didn't think much of the poem. Of course, I didn't tell her that. Maybe I just don't understand poetry. I admit it's not the first thing I reach for when I pick up something to read.

Anyway, this man who'd first enjoyed her favours, the officer-to-be, he'd been her childhood sweetheart. So okay. I'm saying that at the end of the summer she let the blind man run his hands over her face, said goodbye to him, married her childhood etc., who was now a commissioned officer, and she moved away from Seattle. But they'd kept in touch, she and the blind man. She made the first contact after a year or so. She called him up one night from an Air Force base in Alabama. She wanted to talk. They talked. He asked her to send him a tape and tell him about her life. She did this. She sent the tape. On the tape, she told the blind man about her husband and about their life together in the military. She told the blind man she loved her husband but she didn't like it where they lived and she didn't like it that he was a part of the military-industrial thing. She told the blind man she'd written a poem and he was in it. She told him that she was writing a poem about what it was like to be an Air Force officer's wife. The poem wasn't finished yet. She was still writing it. The blind man made a tape. He sent her the tape. She made a tape. This went on for years. My wife's officer was posted to one base and then another. She sent tapes from Moody AFB, McGuire, McConnell, and finally Travis, near Sacramento, where one night she got to feeling lonely and cut off from people she kept losing in that moving-around life. She got to feeling she couldn't go it another step. She went in and swallowed all the pills and capsules in the medicine chest and washed them down with a bottle of gin. Then she got into a hot bath and passed out.

But instead of dying, she got sick. She threw up. Her officer — why should he have a name? he was the childhood sweetheart, and what more does he want? — came home from somewhere, found her, and called the ambulance. In time, she put it all on a tape and sent the tape to the blind man. Over the years, she put all kinds of stuff on tapes and sent the tapes off lickety-split. Next to writing a poem every year, I think it was her chief means of recreation. On one tape, she told the blind man she'd decided to live away from her officer for a time. On another tape, she told him about her divorce. She and I began going out, and of course she told her blind man about it. She told him everything, or so it seemed to me. Once she asked me if I'd like to hear the latest tape from the blind man. This was a year ago. I was on the tape, she said. So I said okay, I'd listen to it. I got us drinks and we settled down in the living room. We made ready to listen. First she inserted the tape into the player and adjusted a couple of dials. Then she pushed a lever. The tape squeaked and someone began to talk in this loud voice. She lowered the volume. After a few minutes of harmless chitchat, I heard my own name in the mouth of this stranger, this blind man I didn't even know! And then this: "From all you've said about him, I can only conclude —" But we were interrupted, a knock at the door, something, and we didn't ever get back to the tape. Maybe it was just as well. I'd heard all I wanted to.

Now this same blind man was coming to sleep in my house.

"Maybe I could take him bowling," I said to my wife. She was at the draining board doing scalloped potatoes. She put down the knife she was using and turned around.

"If you love me," she said, "you can do this for me. If you don't love me, okay. But if you had a friend, any friend, and the friend came to visit, I'd make him feel comfortable." She wiped her hands with the dish towel.

"I don't have any blind friends," I said.

"You don't have *any* friends," she said. "Period. Besides," she said, "goddamn it, his wife's just died! Don't you understand that? The man's lost his wife!"

I didn't answer. She'd told me a little about the blind man's wife. Her name was Beulah. Beulah! That's a name for a coloured woman.

"Was his wife a Negro?" I asked.

"Are you crazy?" my wife said. "Have you just flipped or something?" She picked up a potato. I saw it hit the floor, then roll under the stove. "What's wrong with you?" she said. "Are you drunk?"

"I'm just asking," I said.

Right then my wife filled me in with more detail than I cared to know. I made a drink and sat at the kitchen table to listen. Pieces of the story began to fall into place.

Beulah had gone to work for the blind man the summer after my wife had stopped working for him. Pretty soon Beulah and the blind man had themselves a church wedding. It was a little wedding — who'd want to go to such a wedding in the first place? — just the two of them, plus the minister and the minister's wife. But it was a church wedding just the same. It was what Beulah had wanted, he'd said. But even then Beulah must have been carrying the cancer in her glands. After they had been inseparable for eight years — my wife's word, *inseparable* — Beulah's health went into a rapid decline. She died in a Seattle hospital room, the blind man sitting beside the bed and holding on to her hand. They'd married, lived and worked together, slept together — had sex, sure — and then the blind man had to bury her. All this without his having ever seen what the goddamned woman looked like. It was beyond my understanding. Hearing this, I felt sorry for the blind man for a little bit. And then I found myself thinking what a pitiful life this woman must have led. Imagine a woman who could never see herself as she was seen in the eyes of her loved one. A woman who could go on day after day and never receive the smallest compliment from her beloved. A woman whose husband could never read the expression on her face, be it misery or something better. Someone who could wear makeup or not — what difference to him? She could, if she wanted, wear green eye-shadow around one eye, a straight pin in her nostril, yellow slacks and purple shoes, no matter. And then to slip off into death, the blind man's hand on her hand, his blind eyes streaming tears — I'm imagining now — her last thought maybe this: that he never even knew what she looked like, and she on an express to the grave. Robert was left with a small insurance policy and half of a twenty-peso Mexican coin. The other half of the coin went into the box with her. Pathetic.

So when the time rolled around, my wife went to the depot to pick him up. With nothing to do but wait — sure, I blamed him for that — I was having a drink and watching the TV when I heard the car pull into the drive. I got up from the sofa with my drink and went to the window to have a look.

I saw my wife laughing as she parked the car. I saw her get out of the car and shut the door. She was still wearing a smile. Just amazing. She went around to the other side of the car to where the blind man was already starting to get out. This blind man, feature this, he was wearing a full beard! A beard on a blind man! Too much, I say. The blind man reached into the back seat and dragged out a suitcase. My wife took his arm, shut the car door, and, talking all the way, moved him down the drive and then up the steps to the front porch. I turned off the TV. I finished my drink, rinsed the glass, dried my hands. Then I went to the door.

My wife said, "I want you to meet Robert. Robert, this is my husband. I've told you all about him." She was beaming. She had this blind man by his coat sleeve.

The blind man let go of his suitcase and up came his hand.

I took it. He squeezed hard, held my hand, and then he let it go.

"I feel like we've already met," he boomed.

"Likewise," I said. I didn't know what else to say. Then I said, "Welcome. I've heard a lot about you." We began to move then, a little group, from the porch into the living room, my wife guiding him by the arm. The blind man was carrying his suitcase in his other hand. My wife said things like, "To your left here, Robert. That's right. Now watch it, there's a chair. That's it. Sit down right here. This is the sofa. We just bought this sofa two weeks ago."

I started to say something about the old sofa. I'd liked that old sofa. But I didn't say anything. Then I wanted to say something else, small-talk, about the scenic ride along the Hudson. How going *to* New York, you should sit on the right-hand side of the train, and coming *from* New York, the left-hand side.

"Did you have a good train ride?" I said. "Which side of the train did you sit on, by the way?"

"What a question, which side!" my wife said. "What's it matter which side?" she said.

"I just asked," I said.

"Right side," the blind man said. "I hadn't been on a train in nearly forty years. Not since I was a kid. With my folks. That's been a long time. I'd nearly forgotten the sensation. I have winter in my beard now," he said. "So I've been told, anyway. Do I look distinguished, my dear?" the blind man said to my wife.

"You look distinguished, Robert," she said. "Robert," she said. "Robert, it's just so good to see you."

My wife finally took her eyes off the blind man and looked at me. I had the feeling she didn't like what she saw. I shrugged.

I've never met, or personally known, anyone who was blind. This blind man was late forties, a heavy-set, balding man with stooped shoulders, as if he carried a great weight there. He wore brown slacks, brown shoes, a light-brown shirt, a tie, a sports coat. Spiffy. He also had this full beard. But he didn't use a cane and he didn't wear dark glasses. I'd always thought dark glasses were a must for the blind. Fact was, I wished he had a pair. At first glance, his eyes looked like anyone else's eyes. But if you looked close, there was something different about them. Too much white in the iris, for one thing, and the pupils seemed to move around in the sockets without his knowing it or being able to stop it. Creepy. As I stared at his face, I saw the left pupil turn in toward his nose while the other made an effort to keep in one place. But it was only an effort, for that eye was on the roam without his knowing it or wanting it to be.

I said, "Let me get you a drink. What's your pleasure? We have a little of everything. It's one of our pastimes."

"Bub, I'm a Scotch man myself," he said fast enough in this big voice.

"Right," I said. Bub! "Sure you are. I knew it."

He let his fingers touch his suitcase, which was sitting alongside the sofa. He was taking his bearings. I didn't blame him for that.

"I'll move that up to your room," my wife said.

"No, that's fine," the blind man said loudly. "It can go up when I go up."

"A little water with the Scotch?" I said.

"Very little," he said.

"I knew it," I said.

He said, "Just a tad. The Irish actor, Barry Fitzgerald? I'm like that fellow. When I drink water, Fitzgerald said, I drink water. When I drink whiskey, I drink whiskey." My wife laughed. The blind man brought his hand up under his beard. He lifted his beard slowly and let it drop.

I did the drinks, three big glasses of Scotch with a splash of water in each. Then we made ourselves comfortable and talked about Robert's travels. First the long flight from the West Coast to Connecticut, we covered that. Then from Connecticut up here by train. We had another drink concerning that leg of the trip.

I remembered having read somewhere that the blind didn't smoke because, as speculation had it, they couldn't see the smoke they exhaled. I thought I knew that much and that much only about blind people. But this blind man smoked his cigarette down to the nubbin and then lit another one. This blind man filled his ashtray and my wife emptied it.

When we sat down at the table for dinner, we had another drink. My wife heaped Robert's plate with cube steak, scalloped potatoes, green beans. I buttered him up two slices of bread. I said, "Here's bread and butter for you." I swallowed some of my drink. "Now let us pray," I said, and the blind man lowered his head. My wife looked at me, her mouth agape. "Pray the phone won't ring and the food doesn't get cold," I said.

We dug in. We ate everything there was to eat on the table. We ate like there was no tomorrow. We didn't talk. We ate. We scarfed. We grazed that table. We were into serious eating. The blind man had right away located his foods, he knew just where everything was on his plate. I watched with admiration as he used his knife and fork on the meat. He'd cut two pieces of meat, fork the meat into his mouth, and then go all out for the scalloped potatoes, the beans next, and then he'd tear off a hunk of buttered bread and eat that. He'd follow this up with a big drink of milk. It didn't seem to bother him to use his fingers once in a while, either.

We finished everything, including half a strawberry pie. For a few moments, we sat as if stunned. Sweat beaded on our faces. Finally, we got up from the table and left the dirty plates. We didn't look back. We took ourselves into the living room and sank into our places again. Robert and my wife sat on the sofa. I took the big chair. We had us two or three more drinks while they talked about the major things that had come to pass for them in the past ten years. For the most part, I just listened. Now and then I joined in. I didn't want him to think I'd left the room, and I didn't want her to think I was feeling left out. They talked of things that had happened to them — to them! — these past ten years. I waited in vain to hear my name on my wife's sweet lips: "And then my dear husband came into my life" — something like that. But I heard nothing of the sort. More talk of Robert. Robert had done a little of everything, it seemed, a regular blind jack-of-all-trades. But most recently he and his wife had had an Amway distributorship, from which, I gathered, they'd earned their living, such as it was. The blind man was also a ham radio operator. He talked in his loud voice about conversations he'd had with fellow operators in Guam, in the Philippines, in Alaska, and even in Tahiti. He said he'd have a lot of friends there if he ever wanted to go visit those places. From time to time, he'd turn his blind face toward me, put his hand under his beard, ask me something. How long had I been in my present position? (Three years.) Did I like my work? (I didn't.) Was I going to stay with it? (What were the options?) Finally, when I thought he was beginning to run down, I got up and turned on the TV.

My wife looked at me with irritation. She was heading toward a boil. Then she looked at the blind man and said, "Robert, do you have a TV?"

The blind man said, "My dear, I have two TVs. I have a colour set and a black-and-white thing, an old relic. It's funny, but if I turn the TV on, and I'm always turning it on, I turn on the colour set. It's funny, don't you think?"

I didn't know what to say to that. I had absolutely nothing to say to that. No opinion. So I watched the news program and tried to listen to what the announcer was saying.

"This is a colour TV," the blind man said. "Don't ask me how, but I can tell."

"We traded up a while ago," I said.

The blind man had another taste of his drink. He lifted his beard, sniffed it, and let it fall. He leaned forward on the sofa. He positioned his ashtray on the coffee table, then put the lighter to his cigarette. He leaned back on the sofa and crossed his legs at the ankles.

My wife covered her mouth, and then she yawned. She stretched. She said, "I think I'll go upstairs and put on my robe. I think I'll change into something else. Robert, you make yourself comfortable," she said.

"I'm comfortable," the blind man said.

"I want you to feel comfortable in this house," she said.

"I am comfortable," the blind man said.

◌◌

After she'd left the room, he and I listened to the weather report and then to the sports roundup. By that time, she'd been gone so long I didn't know if she was going to come back. I thought she might have gone to bed. I wished she'd come back downstairs. I didn't want to be left alone with a blind man. I asked him if he wanted another drink, and he said sure. Then I asked if he wanted to smoke some dope with me. I said I'd just rolled a number. I hadn't, but I planned to do so in about two shakes.

"I'll try some with you," he said.

"Damn right," I said. "That's the stuff."

I got our drinks and sat down on the sofa with him. Then I rolled us two fat numbers. I lit one and passed it. I brought it to his fingers. He took it and inhaled.

"Hold it as long as you can," I said. I could tell he didn't know the first thing.

My wife came back downstairs wearing her pink robe and her pink slippers.

"What do I smell?" she said.

"We thought we'd have us some cannabis," I said.

My wife gave me a savage look. Then she looked at the blind man and said, "Robert, I didn't know you smoked."

He said, "I do now, my dear. There's a first time for everything. But I don't feel anything yet."

"This stuff is pretty mellow," I said. "This stuff is mild. It's dope you can reason with," I said. "It doesn't mess you up."

"Not much it doesn't, bub," he said, and laughed.

My wife sat on the sofa between the blind man and me. I passed her the number. She took it and toked and then passed it back to me. "Which way is this going?" she said. Then she said, "I shouldn't be smoking this. I can hardly keep my eyes open as it is. That dinner did me in. I shouldn't have eaten so much."

"It was the strawberry pie," the blind man said. "That's what did it," he said, and he laughed his big laugh. Then he shook his head.

"There's more strawberry pie," I said.

"Do you want some more, Robert?" my wife said.

"Maybe in a little while," he said.

We gave our attention to the TV. My wife yawned again. She said, "Your bed is made up when you feel like going to bed, Robert. I know you must have had a long day. When you're ready to go to bed, say so." She pulled his arm. "Robert?"

He came to and said, "I've had a real nice time. This beats tapes, doesn't it?"

I said, "Coming at you," and I put the number between his fingers. He inhaled, held the smoke, and then let it go. It was like he'd been doing it since he was nine years old.

"Thanks, bub," he said. "But I think this is all for me. I think I'm beginning to feel it," he said. He held the burning roach out for my wife.

"Same here," she said. "Ditto. Me, too." She took the roach and passed it to me. "I may just sit here for a while between you two guys with my eyes closed. But don't let me bother you, okay? Either one of you. If it bothers you, say so. Otherwise, I may just sit here with my eyes closed until you're ready to go to bed," she said. "Your bed's made up, Robert, when you're ready. It's right next to our room at the top of the stairs. We'll show you up when you're ready. You wake me up now, you guys, if I fall asleep." She said that and then she closed her eyes and went to sleep.

The news program ended. I got up and changed the channel. I sat back down on the sofa. I wished my wife hadn't pooped out. Her head lay across the back of the sofa, her mouth open. She'd turned so that her robe had slipped away from her legs, exposing a juicy thigh. I reached to draw her robe back over her, and it was then that I glanced at the blind man. What the hell! I flipped the robe open again.

"You say when you want some strawberry pie," I said.

"I will," he said.

I said, "Are you tired? Do you want me to take you up to your bed? Are you ready to hit the hay?"

"Not yet," he said. "No, I'll stay up with you, bub. If that's all right. I'll stay up until you're ready to turn in. We haven't had a chance to talk. Know what I mean? I feel like me and her monopolized the evening." He lifted his beard and he let it fall. He picked up his cigarettes and his lighter.

"That's all right," I said. Then I said, "I'm glad for the company."

And I guess I was. Every night I smoked dope and stayed up as long as I could before I fell asleep. My wife and I hardly ever went to bed at the same time. When I did go to sleep, I had these dreams. Sometimes I'd wake up from one of them, my heart going crazy.

Something about the church and the Middle Ages was on the TV. Not your run-of-the-mill TV fare. I wanted to watch something else. I turned to the other channels. But there was nothing on them, either. So I turned back to the first channel and apologized.

"Bub, it's all right," the blind man said. "It's fine with me. Whatever you want to watch is okay. I'm always learning something. Learning never ends. It won't hurt me to learn something tonight. I got ears," he said.

જી

We didn't say anything for a time. He was leaning forward with his head turned at me, his right ear aimed in the direction of the set. Very disconcerting. Now and then his eyelids drooped and then they snapped open again. Now and then he put his fingers into his beard and tugged, like he was thinking about something he was hearing on the television.

On the screen, a group of men wearing cowls was being set upon and tormented by men dressed in skeleton costumes and men dressed as devils. The men dressed as devils wore devil masks, horns, and long tails. This pageant was part of a procession. The Englishman who was narrating the thing said it took place in Spain once a year. I tried to explain to the blind man what was happening.

"Skeletons," he said. "I know about skeletons," he said, and he nodded.

The TV showed this one cathedral. Then there was a long, slow look at another one. Finally, the picture switched to the famous one in Paris, with its flying buttresses and its spires reaching up to the clouds. The camera pulled away to show the whole of the cathedral rising above the skyline.

There were times when the Englishman who was telling the thing would shut up, would simply let the camera move around over the cathedrals. Or else the camera would tour the countryside, men in fields walking behind oxen. I waited as long as I could. Then I felt I had to say something. I said, "They're showing the outside of this cathedral now. Gargoyles. Little statues carved to look like monsters. Now I guess they're in Italy. Yeah, they're in Italy. There's paintings on the walls of this one church."

"Are those fresco paintings, bub?" he asked, and he sipped from his drink.

I reached for my glass. But it was empty. I tried to remember what I could remember. "You're asking me are those frescoes?" I said. "That's a good question. I don't know."

The camera moved to a cathedral outside Lisbon. The differences in the Portuguese cathedral compared with the French and Italian were not that great. But they were there. Mostly the interior stuff. Then something occurred to me, and I said, "Something has occurred to me. Do you have any idea what a cathedral is?

What they look like, that is? Do you follow me? If somebody says cathedral to you, do you have any notion what they're talking about? Do you know the difference between that and a Baptist church, say?"

He let the smoke dribble from his mouth. "I know they took hundreds of workers fifty or a hundred years to build," he said. "I just heard the man say that, of course. I know generations of the same families worked on a cathedral. I heard him say that, too. The men who began their life's work on them, they never lived to see the completion of their work. In that wise, bub, they're no different from the rest of us, right?" He laughed. Then his eyelids drooped again. His head nodded. He seemed to be snoozing. Maybe he was imagining himself in Portugal. The TV was showing another cathedral now. This one was in Germany. The Englishman's voice droned on. "Cathedrals," the blind man said. He sat up and rolled his head back and forth. "If you want the truth, bub, that's about all I know. What I just said. What I heard him say. But maybe you could describe one to me? I wish you'd do it. I'd like that. If you want to know, I really don't have a good idea."

I stared hard at the shot of the cathedral on the TV. How could I even begin to describe it? But say my life depended on it. Say my life was being threatened by an insane guy who said I had to do it or else.

I stared some more at the cathedral before the picture flipped off into the countryside. There was no use. I turned to the blind man and said, "To begin with, they're very tall." I was looking around the room for clues. "They reach way up. Up and up. Toward the sky. They're so big, some of them, they have to have these supports. To help hold them up, so to speak. These supports are called buttresses. They remind me of viaducts, for some reason. But maybe you don't know viaducts, either? Sometimes the cathedrals have devils and such carved into the front. Sometimes lords and ladies. Don't ask me why this is," I said.

He was nodding. The whole upper part of his body seemed to be moving back and forth.

"I'm not doing so good, am I?" I said.

He stopped nodding and leaned forward on the edge of the sofa. As he listened to me, he was running his fingers through his beard. I wasn't getting through to him, I could see that. But he waited for me to go on just the same. He nodded, like he was trying to encourage me. I tried to think what else to say. "They're really big," I said. "They're massive. They're built of stone. Marble, too, sometimes. In those olden days, when they built cathedrals, men wanted to be close to God. In those olden days, God was an important part of everyone's life. You could tell this from their cathedral-building. I'm sorry," I said, "but it looks like that's the best I can do for you. I'm just no good at it."

"That's all right, bub," the blind man said. "Hey, listen. I hope you don't mind my asking you. Can I ask you something? Let me ask you a simple question, yes or no. I'm just curious and there's no offense. You're my host. But let me ask if you are in any way religious? You don't mind my asking?"

I shook my head. He couldn't see that, though. A wink is the same as a nod to a blind man. "I guess I don't believe in it. In anything. Sometimes it's hard. You know what I'm saying?"

"Sure, I do," he said.

"Right," I said.

The Englishman was still holding forth. My wife sighed in her sleep. She drew a long breath and went on with her sleeping.

"You'll have to forgive me," I said. "But I can't tell you what a cathedral looks like. It just isn't in me to do it. I can't do any more than I've done."

The blind man sat very still, his head down, as he listened to me.

I said, "The truth is, cathedrals don't mean anything special to me. Nothing. Cathedrals. They're something to look at on late-night TV. That's all they are."

It was then that the blind man cleared his throat. He brought something up. He took a handkerchief from his back pocket. Then he said, "I get it, bub. It's okay. It happens. Don't worry about it," he said. "Hey, listen to me. Will you do me a favour? I got an idea. Why don't you find us some heavy paper? And a pen. We'll do something. We'll draw one together. Get us a pen and some heavy paper. Go on, bub, get the stuff," he said.

So I went upstairs. My legs felt like they didn't have any strength in them. They felt like they did after I'd done some running. In my wife's room, I looked around. I found some ballpoints in a little basket on her table. And then I tried to think where to look for the kind of paper he was talking about.

Downstairs, in the kitchen, I found a shopping bag with onion skins in the bottom of the bag. I emptied the bag and shook it. I brought it into the living room and sat down with it near his legs. I moved some things, smoothed the wrinkles from the bag, spread it out on the coffee table.

The blind man got down from the sofa and sat next to me on the carpet.

He ran his fingers over the paper. He went up and down the sides of the paper. The edges, even the edges. He fingered the corners.

"All right," he said. "All right, let's do her."

He found my hand, the hand with the pen. He closed his hand over my hand. "Go ahead, bub, draw," he said. "Draw. You'll see. I'll follow along with you. It'll be okay. Just begin now like I'm telling you. You'll see. Draw," the blind man said.

So I began. First I drew a box that looked like a house. It could have been the house I lived in. Then I put a roof on it. At either end of the roof, I drew spires. Crazy.

"Swell," he said. "Terrific. You're doing fine," he said. "Never thought anything like this could happen in your lifetime, did you, bub? Well, it's a strange life, we all know that. Go on now. Keep it up."

I put in windows with arches. I drew flying buttresses. I hung great doors. I couldn't stop. The TV station went off the air. I put down the pen and closed and opened my fingers. The blind man felt around over the paper. He moved the tips of his fingers over the paper, all over what I had drawn, and he nodded.

"Doing fine," the blind man said.

I took up the pen again, and he found my hand. I kept at it. I'm no artist. But I kept drawing just the same.

My wife opened up her eyes and gazed at us. She sat up on the sofa, her robe hanging open. She said, "What are you doing? Tell me, I want to know."

I didn't answer her.

The blind man said, "We're drawing a cathedral. Me and him are working on it. Press hard," he said to me. "That's right. That's good," he said. "Sure. You got it, bub. I can tell. You didn't think you could. But you can, can't you? You're cooking with gas now. You know what I'm saying? We're going to really have us something here in a minute. How's the old arm?" he said. "Put some people in there now. What's a cathedral without people?"

My wife said, "What's going on? Robert, what are you doing? What's going on?"

"It's all right," he said to her. "Close your eyes now," the blind man said to me.

I did it. I closed them just like he said.

"Are they closed?" he said. "Don't fudge."

"They're closed," I said.

"Keep them that way," he said. He said, "Don't stop now. Draw."

So we kept on with it. His fingers rode my fingers as my hand went over the paper. It was like nothing else in my life up to now.

Then he said, "I think that's it. I think you got it," he said. "Take a look. What do you think?"

But I had my eyes closed. I thought I'd keep them that way for a little longer. I thought it was something I ought to do.

"Well?" he said. "Are you looking?"

My eyes were still closed. I was in my house. I knew that. But I didn't feel like I was inside anything.

"It's really something," I said.

ℰ)ℭ

Reacting against what he saw as postmodernism's self-absorption, Raymond Carver created a finely honed realism that speaks to the concerns of everyday life in its own language. Attuned to the spiritual needs of people impoverished by the "Greed Decade" of the 1980s, his stories explore how narrative can help us to make sense of ourselves and others, but can also deceive us, compounding our isolation. "Cathedral" occupies familiar Carver territory: a domestic rift, much alcohol, a plot grounded in conversation. Subterranean narratives are picked up, then dropped. Men bond in this story, women are absent through sleep or death. Loyal to Hemingway's theory of "omission," Carver creates a narrator whose painful honesty about the present completely hides his past. His revelation at the story's end is a Joycean epiphany in its purest form. "Cathedral" reaches back to the genre's origins, in that it is also a parable. Carver uses ekphrasis — *literature describing a visual image, in this instance, television — to investigate the notion of Otherness. Is it possible for a man to understand a dying woman? Can a secular and technologically inundated society perceive what it meant to live in an age of faith? Ultimately, the sheer impossibility of portraying a cathedral to a blind man suggests a parallel with the writer's difficulty in communicating to an audience. But the story is deeply affirmative, as the meaning of a cathedral is passed on. Communication does occur; alienation is overcome for both the characters and the reader.*

M.T.

The Miller's Tale

Heere bigynneth the Millere his tale.

	Whilom ther was dwellynge at Oxenford	
	A riche gnof,° that gestes heeld to bord,	*churl*
3189	And of his craft he was a carpenter.	
	With hym ther was dwellynge a poure scoler,	
	Hadde lerned art, but al his fantasye	
	Was turned for to lerne astrologye,	
	And koude° a certeyn of conclusiouns,°	*knew/operations*
	To demen° by interrogaciouns,	*determine*
3195	If that men asked hym, in certein houres	
	Whan that men sholde have droghte or elles shoures,	
	Or if men asked hym what sholde bifalle	
	Of every thyng; I may nat rekene hem alle.	
	This clerk was cleped° hende° Nicholas.	*called/courteous*
3200	Of deerne° love he koude and of solas;°	*secret/pleasure*
	And therto he was sleigh and ful privee,°	*discreet*
	And lyk a mayden meke for to see.	
	A chambre hadde he in that hostelrye	
	Allone, withouten any compaignye,	
3205	Ful fetisly° ydight° with herbes swoote;	*elegantly/decorated*
	And he hymself as sweete as is the roote	
	Of lycorys or any cetewale.°	*ginger-like spice*
	His Almageste, and bookes grete and smale,	
	His astrelabie, longynge for his art,	
3210	His augrym° stones layen faire apart,	*counting*
	On shelves couched at his beddes heed;	
	His presse° ycovered with a faldyng° reed;	*cupboard/coarse cloth*
	And al above ther lay a gay sautrie,°	*psaltery*
	On which he made a-nyghtes melodie	
3215	So swetely that all the chambre rong;	
	And *Angelus ad virginem*° he song;	*a hymn*
	And after that he song the Kynges Noote.°	*a song*
	Ful often blessed was his myrie throte.	
	And thus this sweete clerk his tyme spente	
3220	After his freendes fyndyng° and his rente.	*support*
	This carpenter hadde wedded newe a wyf,	

72

Which that he lovede moore than his lyf;
Of eighteteene yeer she was of age.
Jalous he was, and heeld hire narwe in cage,
For she was wylde and yong, and he was old

3226 And demed hymself been lik a cokewold.° — *cuckold*
He knew nat Catoun,° for his wit was rude, — *Cato*
That bad man sholde wedde his simylitude.
Men sholde wedden after hire estaat,

3230 For youthe and elde is often at debaat.
But sith that he was fallen in the snare,
He moste endure, as oother folk, his care.
    Fair was this yonge wyf, and therwithal
As any wezele hir body gent and smal.

3235 A ceynt° she werede, barred al of silk, — *belt*
A barmclooth° as whit as morne milk — *apron*
Upon hir lendes,° ful of many a goore.° — *loins/flounce*
Whit was hir smok, and broyden al bifoore
And eek bihynde, on hir coler aboute,
Of col-blak silk, withinne and eek withoute.

3241 The tapes° of hir white voluper° — *ribbons/cap*
Were of the same suyte of hir coler;
Hir filet° brood of silk, and set ful hye. — *headband*
And sikerly° she hadde a likerous° ye; — *certainly/flirtatious*

3245 Ful smale ypulled were hire browes two,
And tho were bent and blake as any sloo.° — *sloe*
She was ful moore blisful on to see
Than is the newe pere-jonette° tree, — *pear*
And softer than the wolle is of a wether.

3250 And by hir girdel heeng a purs of lether,
Tasseled with silk and perled° with latoun.° — *adorned/brass-like alloy*
In al this world, to seken up and doun,
There nys no man so wys that koude thenche° — *imagine*

3254 So gay a popelote° or swich a wenche. — *doll*
Ful brighter was the shynyng of hir hewe
Than in the Tour the noble yforged newe.
But of hir song, it was as loude and yerne° — *eager*
As any swalwe sittynge on a berne.
Therto she koude skippe and make game,

3260 As any kyde or calf folwynge his dame.
Hir mouth was sweete as bragot° or the meeth,° — *a drink/mead*
Or hoord of apples leyd in hey or heeth.
Wynsynge° she was, as is a joly colt, — *skittish*
Long as a mast, and upright as a bolt.

3265 A brooch she baar upon hir lowe coler,

As brood as is the boos° of a bokeler.°   *centre/shield*
Hir shoes were laced on hir legges hye.
She was a prymerole, a piggesnye,
For any lord to leggen in his bedde,
3270 Or yet for any good yeman to wedde.
        Now, sire, and eft, sire, so bifel the cas
That on a day this hende Nicholas
Fil with this yonge wyf to rage and pleye,
3274 Whil that hir housbonde was at Oseneye,
As clerkes ben ful subtile and ful queynte;°   *clever*
And prively he caughte hire by the queynte,
And seyde, "Ywis, but if ich have my wille,
For deerne love of thee, lemman, I spille."
And heeld hire harde by the haunchebones,
3280 And seyde, "Lemman,° love me al atones,   *lover*
Or I wol dyen, also God me save!"
And she sproong as a colt dooth in the trave,°   *frame for shoeing horses*
And with hir heed she wryed° faste awey,   *twisted*
And seyde, "I wol nat kisse thee, by my fey!
Why, lat be!" quod she. "Lat be, Nicholas,"
3286 Or I wol crie 'out, harrow' and 'allas'!
Do wey youre handes, for youre curteisye!"
        This Nicholas gan mercy for to crye,
And spak so faire, and profred him so faste,
That she hir love hym graunted atte laste,
And swoor hir ooth, by Seint Thomas of Kent,
3292 That she wol been at his comandement,
Whan that she may hir leyser° wel espie.   *opportunity*
"Myn housbonde is so ful of jalousie
3295 That but ye wayte wel and been privee,
I woot right wel I nam but deed," quod she.
"Ye moste been ful deerne,° as in this cas."   *secretive*
        "Nay, therof care thee noght," quod Nicholas.
"A clerk hadde litherly biset his whyle,°   *badly used his time*
3300 But if he koude a carpenter bigyle."
And thus they been accorded and ysworn
To wayte a tyme, as I have told biforn.
Whan Nicholas had doon thus everideel
And thakked° hire aboute the lendes° weel,   *patted/loins*
He kiste hire sweete and taketh his sawtrie,°   *psaltery*
3306 And pleyeth faste, and maketh melodie.
        Thanne fil it thus, that to the paryssh chirche,
Cristes owene werkes for to wirche,
This goode wyf went on an haliday.

3310 Hir forheed shoon as bright as any day,
So was it wasshen whan she leet° hir werk.   *left*
Now was ther of that chirche a parissh clerk,
The which that was ycleped Absolon.
Crul° was his heer, and as the gold it shoon,   *curly*
And strouted° as a fanne large and brode;   *stretched out*
3316 Ful streight and evene lay his joly shode.°   *hair part*
His rode° was reed, his eyen greye as goos.   *complexion*
With Poules wyndow corven on his shoos,
In hoses rede he wente fetisly.°   *elegantly*
3320 Yclad he was ful smal and proprely
Al in a kirtel° of a lyght waget;°   *tunic/blue*
Ful faire and thikke been the poyntes° set.   *laces*
And therupon he hadde a gay surplys
As whit as is the blosme upon the rys.°   *twig*
3325 A myrie child he was, so God me save.
Wel koude he laten blood, and clippe and shave,
And maken a chartre of lond or acquitaunce.
In twenty manere koude he trippe and daunce
After the scole of Oxenforde tho,
3330 And with his legges casten to and fro,
And pleyen songes on a smal rubible;°   *fiddle*
Therto he song som tyme a loud quynyble;°   *falsetto*
And as wel koude he pleye on a giterne.
In al the toun nas brewhous ne taverne
3335 That he ne visited with his solas,°   *pleasure*
Ther any gaylard tappestere° was.   *merry barmaid*
But sooth to seyn, he was somdeel squaymous°   *a little squeamish*
Of fartyng, and of speche daungerous.°   *fastidious*
    This Absolon, that jolif was and gay,
3340 Gooth with a sencer° on the haliday,   *vessel of incense*
Sensynge the wyves of the parisshe faste;
And many a lovely look on hem he caste,
And namely on this carpenteris wyf.
To looke on hire hym thoughte a myrie lyf,
She was so propre and sweete and likerous.
3346 I dar wel seyn, if she hadde been a mous,
And he a cat, he wolde hire hente° anon.   *seized*
This parissh clerk, this joly Absolon,
Hath in his herte swich a love-longynge
3350 That of no wyf took he noon offrynge;
For curteisie, he seyde, he wolde noon.
    The moone, whan it was nyght, ful brighte shoon,
And Absolon his gyterne hath ytake;

	For paramours° he thoghte for to wake.°	*the sake of love/stay up*
3355	And forth he gooth, jolif and amorous,	
	Til he cam to the carpenteres hous	
	A litel after cokkes hadde ycrowe,	
	And dressed hym up by a shot-wyndowe°	*hinged window*
	That was upon the carpenteris wal.	
3360	He syngeth in his voys gentil and smal,	

For paramours° he thoghte for to wake.° — *the sake of love/stay up*

3355 And forth he gooth, jolif and amorous,
Til he cam to the carpenteres hous
A litel after cokkes hadde ycrowe,
And dressed hym up by a shot-wyndowe° — *hinged window*
That was upon the carpenteris wal.
3360 He syngeth in his voys gentil and smal,
"Now, deere lady, if thy wille be,
I praye yow that ye wole rewe on me,"
Ful wel acordaunt to his gyternynge.
This carpenter awook, and herde him synge,
3365 And spak unto his wyf, and seyde anon,
"What! Alison! Herestow nat Absolon,
That chaunteth thus under oure boures wal?"
And she answerde hir housbonde therwithal,
"Yis, God woot, John, I heere it every deel."
This passeth forth; what wol ye bet than weel?
3371 Fro day to day this joly Absolon
So woweth hire that hym is wo bigon.
He waketh al the nyght and al the day;
He kembeth his lokkes brode, and made hym gay;
3375 He woweth hire by meenes and brocage,° — *agent*
And swoor he wolde been hir owene page;
He syngeth, brokkynge° as a nyghtyngale; — *singing*
He sente hire pyment,° meeth,° and spiced ale, — *sweet wine/mead*
And wafres, pipyng hoot out of the gleede;° — *fire*
And, for she was of town, he profred meede;° — *money*
3381 For som folk wol ben wonnen for richesse,
And somme for strokes,° and somme for gentillesse. — *force*
Somtyme, to shewe his lightnesse and maistrye,
He pleyeth Herodes upon a scaffold hye.
3385 But what availleth hym as in this cas?
She loveth so this hende Nicholas
That Absolon may blowe the bukkes horn;° — *go whistle*
He ne hadde for his labour but a scorn.
And thus she maketh Absolon hire ape,
3390 And al his ernest turneth til a jape.
Ful sooth is this proverbe, it is no lye,
Men seyn right thus: "Alwey the nye slye
Maketh the ferre leeve° to be looth." — *loved one*
For though that Absolon be wood° or wrooth, — *mad*
3395 By cause that he fer was from hire sight,
This nye Nicholas stood in his light.
Now ber thee wel, thou hende Nicholas,

For Absolon may waille and synge "allas."
And so bifel it on a Saterday,

3400   This carpenter was goon til Osenay;
And hende Nicholas and Alisoun
Acorded been to this conclusioun,
That Nicholas shal shapen hym a wyle°   *trick*
This sely° jalous housbonde to bigyle;   *innocent*

3405   And if so be the game wente aright,
She sholde slepen in his arm at nyght,
For this was his desir and hire also.
And right anon, withouten wordes mo,

3409   This Nicholas no lenger wolde tarie,
But dooth ful softe unto his chambre carie
Bothe mete and drynke for a day or tweye,
And to hire housbonde bad hire for to seye,
If that he axed after Nicholas,
She sholde seye she nyste° where he was;   *knew not*
Of al that day she saugh hym nat with ye;

3416   She trowed° that he was in maladye,   *thought*
For, for no cry hir mayde koude hym calle,
He nolde answere for thyng that myghte falle.
      This passeth forth al thilke Saterday,

3420   That Nicholas stille in his chambre lay,
And eet and sleep, or dide what hym leste,
Til Sonday, that the sonne gooth to reste,
This sely carpenter hath greet merveyle
Of Nicholas, or what thyng myghte hym eyle,°   *ail*
And seyde, "I am adrad, by Seint Thomas,

3426   It stondeth nat aright with Nicholas.
God shilde that he deyde sodeynly!
This world is now ful tikel,° sikerly.   *ticklish, uncertain*

3429   I saugh today a cors° yborn to chirche   *corpse*
That now, on Monday last, I saugh hym wirche.
      "Go up," quod he unto his knave anoon,
"Clepe at his dore, or knokke with a stoon.
Looke how it is, and tel me boldely."

3434   This knave gooth hym up ful sturdily,
And at the chambre dore whil that he stood,
He cride and knokked as that he were wood,
"What, how! What do ye, maister Nicholay?
How may ye slepen al the longe day?"
      But al for noght; he herde nat a word.

3440   An hole he foond, ful lowe upon a bord,
Ther as the cat was wont in for to crepe,

And at that hole he looked in ful depe,
And at the laste he hadde of hym a sight.
This Nicholas sat evere capyng° upright,   *gaping*
As he had kiked° on the newe moone.   *gazed*
Adoun he gooth, and tolde his maister soone
In what array he saugh this ilke man.
  This carpenter to blessen hym bigan,
And seyde, "Help us, Seinte Frydeswyde!
A man woot litel what hym shal bityde.°   *what shall happen to him*
This man is falle, with his astromye,
In some woodnesse° or in som agonye.   *madness*
I thoghte ay wel how that it sholde be!
Men sholde nat knowe of Goddes pryvetee.
Ye, blessed be alwey a lewed° man   *uneducated*
That noght but oonly his bileve° kan!°   *creed/knows*
So ferde another clerk with astromye;
He walked in the feeldes for to prye
Upon the sterres, what ther sholde bifalle,
Til he was in a marle-pit° yfalle;   *clay-pit*
He saugh nat that. But yet, by Seint Thomas,
Me reweth soore of hende Nicholas.
He shal be rated° of his studyyng,   *scolded*
If that I may, by Jhesus, hevene kyng!
Get me a staf, that I may underspore,°   *pry up*
Whil that thou, Robyn, hevest up the dore.
He shal out of his studyyng, as I gesse."
And to the chambre dore he gan hym dresse.
His knave was a strong carl° for the nones,   *fellow*
And by the haspe he haaf it of atones;°   *heaved it off at once*
Into the floor the dore fil anon.
This Nicholas sat ay as stille as stoon,
And evere caped upward into the eir.
This carpenter wende he were in despeir,
And hente hym by the sholdres myghtily,
And shook hym harde, and cride spitously,°   *loudly*
"What! Nicholay! What, how! What, looke adoun!
Awak, and thenk on Cristes passioun!
I crouche° thee from elves and fro wightes."   *bless*
Therwith the nyght-spel° seyde he anon-rightes°   *prayer/right away*
On foure halves of the hous aboute,
And on the thresshfold of the dore withoute:
"Jhesu Crist and Seinte Benedight,
Blesse this hous from every wikked wight,
For nyghtes verye, the white *pater-noster!*°   *Our Father*

3445
3450
3455
3460
3465
3470
3475
3480
3481
3485

Where wentestow,° Seinte Petres soster?"   *did you go*
    And atte laste this hende Nicholas
Gan for to sik° soore, and seyde, "Allas!   *sigh*
3489 Shal al the world be lost eftsoones now?"
    This carpenter answerde, "What seystow?
What! Thynk on God, as we doon, men that swynke."°   *work*
    This Nicholas answerde, "Fecche me drynke,
And after wol I speke in pryvetee
Of certeyn thyng that toucheth me and thee.
3495 I wol telle it noon oother man, certeyn."
    This carpenter goth doun, and comth ageyn,
And broghte of myghty ale a large quart;
And whan that ech of hem had dronke his part,
This Nicholas his dore faste shette,
3500 And doun the carpenter by hym he sette.
    He seyde "John, myn hooste, lief and deere,
Thou shalt upon thy trouthe swere me heere
That to no wight thou shalt this conseil wreye,°   *reveal*
For it is Cristes conseil that I seye,
3505 And if thou telle it man, thou art forlore;
For this vengeaunce thou shalt han therfore,
That if thou wreye° me, thou shalt be wood."   *betray*
"Nay, Crist forbede it, for his hooly blood!"
3509 Quod tho this sely man, "I nam no labbe,°   *blabbermouth*
Ne, though I seye, I nam nat lief to gabbe.
Sey what thou wolt, I shal it nevere telle
To child ne wyf, by hym that harwed° helle!"   *harrowed*
    "Now John," quod Nicholas, "I wol nat lye;
I have yfounde in myn astrologye,
3515 As I have looked in the moone bright,
That now a Monday next, at quarter nyght,
Shal falle a reyn, and that so wilde and wood
That half so greet was nevere Noes flood.
This world," he seyde, "in lasse than an hour
3520 Shal al be dreynt, so hidous is the shour.
Thus shal mankynde drenche,° and lese hir lyf."   *drown*
    This carpenter answerde, "Allas, my wyf!
And shal she drenche? Allas, myn Alisoun!"
3524 For sorwe of this he fil almoost adoun,
And seyde, "Is ther no remedie in this cas?"
    "Why, yis, for Gode," quod hende Nicholas,
"If thou wolt werken after loore° and reed.°   *learning/advice*
Thou mayst nat werken after thyn owene heed;
For thus seith Salomon, that was ful trewe:

'Werk al by conseil, and thou shalt nat rewe.'
3531 And if thou werken wolt by good conseil,
I undertake, withouten mast and seyl,
Yet shal I saven hire and thee and me.
3534 Hastow nat herd hou saved was Noe,
When that oure Lord hadde warned hym biforn
That al the world with water sholde be lorn°?"   *lost*
"Yis," quod this Carpenter, "ful yoore° ago."   *long*
"Hastou nat herd," quod Nicholas, "also
The sorwe of Noe with his felaweshipe,
3540 Er that he myghte gete his wyf to shipe?
Hym hadde be levere, I dar wel undertake,
At thilke tyme, than alle his wetheres blake
That she hadde had a ship hirself allone.
And therfore, woostou what° is best to doone?   *what do you think*
3545 This asketh haste, and of an hastif thyng
Men may nat preche or maken tariyng.
"Anon go gete us faste into this in°   *house*
A knedyng trogh, or ellis a kymelyn,°   *beer tub*
For ech of us, but looke that they be large,
In which we mowe swymme as in a barge,
3551 And han therinne vitaille suffisant
But for a day — fy on the remenant!
The water shal aslake and goon away
3554 Aboute pryme° upon the nexte day.   *9:00 a.m.*
But Robyn may nat wite of this, thy knave,
Ne eek thy mayde Gille I may nat save;
Axe nat why, for though thou aske me,
I wol nat tellen Goddes pryvetee.
Suffiseth thee, but if thy wittes madde,°   *go mad*
3560 To han as greet a grace as Noe hadde.
Thy wyf shal I wel saven, out of doute.
Go now thy wey, and speed thee heer-aboute.
"But whan thou hast, for hire and thee and me,
3564 Ygeten us thise knedyng tubbes thre,
Thanne shaltow hange hem in the roof ful hye,
That no man of oure purveiaunce espye.
And whan thou thus hast doon as I have seyd,
And hast oure vitaille faire in hem yleyd,
3569 And eek an ax to smyte the corde atwo,
Whan that the water comth, that we may go
And breke an hole an heigh, upon the gable,
Unto the gardyn-ward, over the stable,
That we may frely passen forth oure way,

Whan that the grete shour is goon away.
Thanne shaltou swymme as myrie, I undertake,
3576 As dooth the white doke after hire drake.
Thanne wol I clepe, 'How, Alison! How, John!
Be myrie, for the flood wol passe anon.'
And thou wolt seyn, 'Hayl, maister Nicholay!
3580 Good morwe, I se thee wel, for it is day.'
And thanne shul we be lordes al oure lyf
Of al the world, as Noe and his wyf.
    "But of o thyng I warne thee ful right:
Be wel avysed on that ilke nyght
3585 That we ben entred into shippes bord,
That noon of us ne speke nat a word,
Ne clepe, ne crie, but be in his preyere;
For it is Goddes owene heeste° deere.   *command*
    "Thy wyf and thou moote hange fer atwynne;°   *apart*
3590 For that bitwixe yow shal be no synne,
Namoore in lookyng than ther shal in deede.
This ordinance is seyd. Go, God thee speede!
Tomorwe at nyght, whan men ben alle aslepe,
Into oure knedyng-tubbes wol we crepe,
3595 And sitten there, abidyng Goddes grace.
Go now thy wey; I have no lenger space
To make of this no lenger sermonyng.
Men seyn thus, 'sende the wise, and sey no thyng.'
Thou art so wys, it needeth thee nat teche.
3600 Go, save oure lyf, and that I the biseche."
    This sely carpenter goth forth his wey.
Ful ofte he seide "Allas and weylawey,"
3603 And to his wyf he tolde his pryvetee,
And she was war, and knew it bet than he,
What al this queynte cast° was for to seye.   *plot*
But nathelees she ferde as° she wolde deye,   *behaved as if*
And seyde, "Allas! go forth thy wey anon,
Help us to scape, or we been dede echon!
3609 I am thy trewe, verray wedded wyf;
Go, deere spouse, and help to save oure lyf."
    Lo, which a greet thyng is affeccioun!°   *emotion*
Men may dyen of ymaginacioun,
So depe may impressioun be take.
This sely carpenter bigynneth quake;
3615 Hym thynketh verraily that he may see
Noees flood come walwynge° as the see   *surging*
To drenchen Alisoun, his hony deere.

He wepeth, weyleth, maketh sory cheere;
3619 He siketh with ful many a sory swogh;°   *groan*
He gooth and geteth hym a knedyng trogh,
And after that a tubbe and a kymelyn,
And pryvely he sente hem to his in,
And heng hem in the roof in pryvetee.
3624 His owene hand he made laddres thre,
To clymben by the ronges and the stalkes°   *uprights*
Unto the tubbes hangynge in the balkes,°   *beams*
And hem vitailled, bothe trogh and tubbe,
With breed, and chese, and good ale in a jubbe,°   *jug*
Suffisynge right ynogh as for a day.
3630 But er that he hadde maad al this array,
He sente his knave, and eek his wenche also,
Upon his nede° to London for to go.   *business*
And on the Monday, whan it drow to nyght,
He shette his dore withoute candel-lyght,
3635 And dressed alle thyng as it sholde be.
And shortly, up they clomben° alle thre;   *climbed*
They seten stille wel a furlong way.°   *couple of minutes*
        "Now, *Pater-noster*, clom°!" seyde Nicholay,   *hush*
And "Clom!" quod John, and "Clom!" seyde Alisoun.
3640 This carpenter seyde his devocioun,
And stille he sit, and biddeth his preyere,
Awaitynge on the reyn, if he it heere.
        The dede sleep, for wery bisynesse,
Fil on this carpenter right, as I gesse,
3645 Aboute corfew-tyme,° or litel moore;   *dusk*
For travaille of his goost° he groneth soore,   *spirit*
And eft he routeth,° for his heed myslay.°   *snores/lay awkwardly*
Doun of the laddre stalketh Nicholay,
And Alisoun ful softe adoun she spedde;
Withouten wordes mo they goon to bedde,
3651 Ther as the carpenter is wont to lye.
Ther was the revel and the melodye;
And thus lith Alison and Nicholas,
In bisynesse of myrthe and of solas,
3655 Til that the belle of laudes° gan to rynge,   *church service at about 4:30 a.m.*
And freres in the chauncel gonne synge.
        This parissh clerk, this amorous Absolon,
That is for love alwey so wo bigon,
3659 Upon the Monday was at Oseneye
With compaignye, hym to disporte and pleye,
And axed upon cas° a cloisterer   *by chance*

Ful prively after John the carpenter;
And he drough hym apart out of the chirche,
And seyde, "I noot; I saugh hym heere nat wirche
3665 Syn Saterday; I trowe that he be went
For tymber, ther oure abbot hath hym sent;
For he is wont for tymber for to go
And dwellen at the grange a day or two;
Or elles he is at his hous, certeyn.
3670 Where that he be, I kan nat soothly seyn."
      This Absolon ful joly was and light,
And thoghte, "Now is tyme to wake al nyght,
For sikirly I saugh hym nat stirynge
Aboute his dore, syn day bigan to sprynge.
      "So moot I thryve, I shal, at cokkes crowe,
3676 Ful pryvely knokken at his wyndowe
That stant ful lowe upon his boures wal.
To Alison now wol I tellen al
My love-longynge, for yet I shal nat mysse
3680 That at the leeste wey I shal hire kisse.
Som maner confort shal I have, parfay.
My mouth hath icched al this longe day;
That is a signe of kissyng atte leeste.
3684 Al nyght me mette° eek I was at a feeste.   *dreamed*
Therfore I wol go slepe an houre or tweye,
And al the nyght thanne wol I wake and pleye."
      Whan that the firste cok hath crowe, anon
Up rist this joly lovere Absolon,
And hym arraieth gay, at poynt-devys.°   *in every detail*
3690 But first he cheweth greyn and lycorys,
To smellen sweete, er he hadde kembd his heer.
Under his tonge a trewe-love° he beer,   *sprig of herb-paris*
For therby wende he to ben gracious.
3694 He rometh to the carpenteres hous,
And stille he stant under the shot-wyndowe —
Unto his brest it raughte,° it was so lowe —   *reached*
And softe he cougheth with a semy° soun: *gentle*
"What do ye, hony-comb, sweete Alisoun,
3699 My faire bryd, my sweete cynamome?
Awaketh, lemman myn, and speketh to me!
Wel litel thynken ye upon my wo,
That for youre love I swete ther I go.
No wonder is thogh that I swelte and swete;
3704 I moorne as dooth a lamb after the tete.
Ywis, lemman, I have swich love-longynge

That lik a turtel trewe is my moornynge.
I may nat ete na moore than a mayde."
    "Go fro the wyndow, Jakke fool,"° she sayde;   *you idiot*
"As help me God, it wol nat be 'com pa me.'°   *'come kiss me'*
I love another — and elles I were to blame —
3711 Wel bet than thee, by Jhesu, Absolon.
Go forth thy wey, or I wol caste a ston,
And lat me slepe, a twenty devel wey!"
    "Allas," quod Absolon, "and weylawey,
3715 That trewe love was evere so yvel biset!
Thanne kysse me, syn it may be no bet,
For Jhesus love, and for the love of me."
    "Wiltow thanne go thy wey therwith?" quod she.
    "Ye, certes, lemman," quod this Absolon.
    "Thanne make thee redy," quod she, "I come anon."
3721 And unto Nicholas she seyde stille,
"Now hust, and thou shalt laughen al thy fille."
    This Absolon doun sette hym on his knees
And seyde, "I am a lord at alle degrees;
3725 For after this I hope ther cometh moore.
Lemman, thy grace, and sweete bryd, thyn oore!"°   *mercy*
    The wyndow she undoth, and that in haste.
"Have do," quod she, "com of, and speed the faste,°   *hurry up*
3729 Lest that oure neighebores thee espie."
    This Absolon gan wype his mouth ful drie.
Derk was the nyght as pich, or as the cole,
And at the wyndow out she putte hir hole,
And Absolon, hym fil no bet ne wers,
But with his mouth he kiste hir naked ers
3735 Ful savourly, er he were war of this.
Abak he stirte, and thoughte it was amys,
For wel he wiste a womman hath no berd.
He felte a thyng al rough and long yherd,
And seyde, "Fy! allas! what have I do?"
    "Tehee!" quod she, and clapte the wyndow to,
3741 And Absolon gooth forth a sory pas.
    "A berd! A berd!"° quod hende Nicholas,   *a beard! a trick!*
"By Goddes corpus, this goth faire and weel."
    This sely Absolon herde every deel,
3745 And on his lippe he gan for anger byte,
And to hymself he seyde, "I shal thee quyte."°   *pay back*
    Who rubbeth now, who froteth° now his lippes   *rubs*
With dust, with sond, with straw, with clooth, with chippes,
But Absolon, that seith ful ofte, "Allas!"

3750 "My soule bitake I unto Sathanas,
But me were levere than al this toun," quod he,
"Of this despit awroken° for to be.   *avenged*
Allas," quod he, "allas, I ne hadde ybleynt!"°   *turned away*
His hoote love was coold and al yqueynt;°   *quenched*
For fro that tyme that he hadde kist hir ers,
3756 Of paramours he sette nat a kers,
For he was heeled of his maladie.
Ful ofte paramours he gan deffie,
And weep as dooth a child that is ybete.
3760 A softe paas he wente over the strete
Until a smyth men cleped daun Gerveys,
That in his forge smythed plough harneys;
He sharpeth shaar° and kultour° bisily.   *ploughshare/plough blade*
3764 This Absolon knokketh al esily,°   *gently*
And seyde, "Undo,° Gerveys, and that anon."   *open up*
    "What, who artow?" "It am I, Absolon."
"What, Absolon! for Cristes sweete tree,
Why rise ye so rathe°? Ey, benedicitee!   *early*
What eyleth yow? Som gay gerl, God it woot,
3770 Hath broght yow thus upon the viritoot.
By Seinte Note, ye woot wel what I mene."
    This Absolon ne roghte° nat a bene   *cared*
Of al his pley; no word agayn he yaf;
3774 He hadde moore tow° on his distaf   *flax*
Than Gerveys knew, and seyde, "Freend so deere,
That hoote kultour in the chymenee heere,
As lene it me; I have therwith to doone,
And I wol brynge it thee agayn ful soone."
    Gerveys answerde, "Certes, were it gold,
3780 Or in a poke° nobles alle untold,   *bag*
Thou sholdest have, as I am trewe smyth.
Ey, Cristes foo! What wol ye do therwith?"
    "Therof," quod Absolon, "be as be may.
I shal wel telle it thee to-morwe day" —
And caughte the kultour by the colde stele.
3786 Ful softe out at the dore he gan to stele,
And wente unto the carpenteris wal.
He cogheth first, and knokketh therwithal
Upon the wyndowe, right as he dide er.
    This Alison answerde, "Who is ther
That knokketh so? I warante it a theef."
    "Why, nay," quod he, "God woot, my sweete leef,
I am thyn Absolon, my deerelyng.

Of gold," quod he, "I have thee broght a ryng.
3795 My mooder yaf it me, so God me save;
Ful fyn it is, and therto wel ygrave.
This wol I yeve thee, if thou me kisse."
    This Nicholas was risen for to pisse,
And thoughte he wolde amenden al the jape;
3800 He sholde kisse his ers er that he scape.
And up the wyndowe dide he hastily,
And out his ers he putteth pryvely
Over the buttok, to the haunche-bon;
And therwith spak this clerk, this Absolon,
"Spek, sweete bryd, I noot nat where thou art."
3806   This Nicholas anon leet fle a fart
As greet as it had been a thonder-dent,°   *thunder-stroke*
That with the strook he was almoost yblent;°   *blinded*
And he was redy with his iren hoot,
3810 And Nicholas amydde the ers he smoot.
    Of gooth the skyn an hande-brede aboute,
The hoote kultour brende so his toute,°   *bum*
And for the smert he wende for to dye.
3814 As he were wood, for wo he gan to crye,
"Help! Water! Water! Help, for Goddes herte!"
    This carpenter out of his slomber sterte,
And herde oon crien° "water!" as he were wood,   *someone shouting*
And thoughte, "Allas, now comth Nowelis flood!"
3819 He sit hym up withouten wordes mo,
And with his ax he smoot the corde atwo,
And doun gooth al; he foond neither to selle,
Ne breed ne ale, til he cam to the celle
Upon the floor, and ther aswowne he lay.
3824   Up stirte hire Alison and Nicholay,
And criden "Out" and "Harrow" in the strete.
The neighebores, bothe smale and grete,
In ronnen for to gauren° on this man,   *gaze*
That yet aswowne lay, bothe pale and wan,
For with the fal he brosten° hadde his arm.   *broken*
But stonde he moste unto his owene harm;
3831 For whan he spak, he was anon bore doun
With hende Nicholas and Alisoun.
They tolden every man that he was wood;
He was agast so of Nowelis flood
3835 Thurgh fantasie that of his vanytee
He hadde yboght hym knedyng tubbes thre,
And hadde hem hanged in the roof above;

And that he preyed hem, for Goddes love,
To sitten in the roof, *par compaignye.*°   *to keep him company*
3840   The folk gan laughen at his fantasye;
Into the roof they kiken° and they cape,   *stare*
And turned al his harm unto a jape.
For what so that this carpenter answerde,
It was for noght; no man his reson herde.
3845   With othes grete he was so sworn adoun
That he was holde wood in al the toun;
For every clerk anonright° heeld with oother.   *immediately*
They seyde, "The man is wood, my leeve brother";
And every wight gan laughen at this stryf.
3850   Thus swyved° was this carpenteris wyf,   *screwed*
For al his kepyng and his jalousye,
And Absolon hath kist hir nether ye,°   *lower eye*
And Nicholas is scalded in the towte.
This tale is doon, and God save al the rowte!

Heere endeth the Millere his tale.

სⴰ

    Long before the advent of the modern short story, there were many forms of narrative in verse. One of these was the medieval fabliau, a versified comic story with peasant or middle-class characters, which turns on a far-fetched plot. The best of the fabliau is Chaucer's Miller's Tale, *which combines two folk motifs — the duping of the jealous husband with a false prediction of a flood, and the coercive planting of the ignominious kiss. The tale skillfully interweaves these two plots and brings them together in an uproarious climax, in which all the characters save one receive their just comeuppance. Also exceptionally crafted are the detailed, individualized characterizations and the realistic village setting. Geoffrey Chaucer is often credited with making literature written in the English language a respectable field of endeavour, as most of the literary work of his time was composed in Latin or French. A busy civil servant and retainer to the king, he wrote as a hobby in order to entertain the members of the court. His most famous work, of which this tale is a part, is the* Canterbury Tales. *Pilgrims on their way to the shrine of St. Thomas at Canterbury tell tales to amuse each other. The Miller, a boisterous and irreverent drunk, is the second to tell a story, which he uses as a subtle put-down of the stately romance just told by the Knight, and as a not very subtle dig at the Reeve, who is by profession a carpenter.*

                                       C.L.

Anton Chekhov

(1860-1904)

Gooseberries

The sky had been overcast since early morning; it was a still day, not hot, but tedious, as it usually is when the weather is grey and dull, when clouds have been hanging over the fields for a long time, and you wait for the rain that does not come. Ivan Ivanych, a veterinary, and Burkin, a high school teacher, were already tired with walking, and the plain seemed endless to them. Far ahead were the scarcely visible windmills of the village of Mironositzkoe; to the right lay a range of hills that disappeared in the distance beyond the village, and both of them knew that over there were the river, and fields, green willows, homesteads, and if you stood on one of the hills, you could see from there another vast plain, telegraph poles, and a train that from afar looked like a caterpillar crawling, and in clear weather you could even see the town. Now, when it was still and when nature seemed mild and pensive, Ivan Ivanych and Burkin were filled with love for this plain, and both of them thought what a beautiful land it was.

"Last time when we were in Elder Prokofy's barn," said Burkin, "you were going to tell me a story."

"Yes; I wanted to tell you about my brother."

Ivan Ivanych heaved a slow sigh and lit his pipe before beginning his story, but just then it began to rain. And five minutes later there was a downpour, and it was hard to tell when it would be over. The two men halted, at a loss; the dogs, already wet, stood with their tails between their legs and looked at them feelingly.

"We must find shelter somewhere," said Burkin. "Let's go to Alyohin's; it's quite near."

"Let's."

They turned aside and walked across a mown meadow, now going straight ahead, now bearing to the right, until they reached the road. Soon poplars came into view, a garden, then the red roofs of barns; the river gleamed, and the view opened on a broad expanse of water with a mill and a white bathing-cabin. That was Sofyino, Alyohin's place.

The mill was going, drowning out the sound of the rain; the dam was shaking. Wet horses stood near the carts, their heads drooping, and men were walking about, their heads covered with sacks. It was damp, muddy, dreary; and the water looked cold and unkind. Ivan Ivanych and Burkin felt cold and messy and uncomfortable through and through; their feet were heavy with mud and when, having crossed the dam, they climbed up to the barns, they were silent as though they were cross with each other.

The noise of a winnowing-machine came from one of the barns, the door was open, and clouds of dust were pouring from within. On the threshold stood Alyohin himself, a man of forty, tall and rotund, with long hair, looking more like a professor or an artist than a gentleman farmer. He was wearing a white blouse, badly in need of washing, that was belted with a rope, and drawers, and his high boots were plastered with mud and straw. His eyes and nose were black with dust. He recognized Ivan Ivanych and Burkin and was apparently very glad to see them.

"Please go up to the house, gentlemen," he said, smiling; "I'll be there directly, in a moment."

It was a large structure of two storeys. Alyohin lived downstairs in what was formerly the stewards' quarters: two rooms that had arched ceilings and small windows; the furniture was plain, and the place smelled of rye bread, cheap vodka, and harness. He went into the showy rooms upstairs only rarely, when he had guests. Once in the house, the two visitors were met by a chambermaid, a young woman so beautiful that both of them stood still at the same moment and glanced at each other.

"You can't imagine how glad I am to see you, gentlemen," said Alyohin, joining them in the hall. "What a surprise! Pelageya," he said, turning to the chambermaid, "give the guests a change of clothes. And, come to think of it, I will change, too. But I must go and bathe first, I don't think I've had a wash since spring. Don't you want to go into the bathing-cabin? In the meanwhile things will be got ready here."

The beautiful Pelageya, with her soft, delicate air, brought them bath towels and soap, and Alyohin went to the bathing-cabin with his guests.

"Yes, it's a long time since I've bathed," he said, as he undressed. "I've an excellent bathing-cabin, as you see — it was put up by my father — but somehow I never find time to use it." He sat down on the steps and lathered his long hair and neck, and the water around him turned brown.

"I say —" observed Ivan Ivanych significantly, looking at his head.

"I haven't had a good wash for a long time," repeated Alyohin, embarrassed, and soaped himself once more; the water about him turned dark blue, the colour of ink.

Ivan Ivanych came out of the cabin, plunged into the water with a splash and swam in the rain, thrusting his arms out wide; he raised waves on which white lilies swayed. He swam out to the middle of the river and dived and a minute later came up in another spot and swam on and kept diving, trying to touch bottom. "By God!" he kept repeating delightedly, "by God!" He swam to the mill, spoke to the peasants there, and turned back and in the middle of the river lay floating, exposing his face to the rain. Burkin and Alyohin were already dressed and ready to leave, but he kept on swimming and diving. "By God!" he kept exclaiming. "Lord, have mercy on me."

"You've had enough!" Burkin shouted to him.

They returned to the house. And only when the lamp was lit in the big drawing room upstairs, and the two guests, in silk dressing-gowns and warm slippers, were lounging in armchairs, and Alyohin himself, washed and combed, wearing a new jacket, was walking about the room, evidently savouring the warmth, the cleanliness, the dry clothes and light footwear, and when pretty Pelageya, stepping noiselessly across the carpet and smiling softly, brought in a tray with tea and jam, only then did Ivan Ivanych begin his story, and it was as though not only Burkin and Alyohin were listening, but also the ladies, old and young, and the military men who looked down upon them, calmly and severely, from their gold frames.

"We are two brothers," he began, "I, Ivan Ivanych, and my brother, Nikolay Ivanych, who is two years my junior. I went in for a learned profession and became a veterinary; Nikolay at nineteen began to clerk in a provincial branch of the Treasury. Our father was a *kantonist*, but he rose to be an officer and so a nobleman, a rank that he bequeathed to us together with a small estate. After his death there was a lawsuit and we lost the estate to creditors, but be that as it may, we spent our childhood in the country. Just like peasant children we passed days and nights in the fields and the woods, herded horses, stripped bast from the trees, fished, and so on. And, you know, whoever even once in his life has caught a perch or seen thrushes migrate in the autumn, when on clear, cool days they sweep in flocks over the village, will never really be a townsman and to the day of his death will have a longing for the open. My brother was unhappy in the government office. Years passed, but he went on warming the same seat, scratching away at the same papers, and thinking of one and the same thing: how to get away to the country. And little by little this vague longing turned into a definite desire, into a dream of buying a little property somewhere on the banks of a river or a lake.

"He was a kind and gentle soul and I loved him, but I never sympathized with his desire to shut himself up for the rest of his life on a little property of his own. It is a common saying that a man needs only six feet of earth. But six feet is what a corpse needs, not a man. It is also asserted that if our educated class is drawn to the land and seeks to settle on farms, that's a good thing. But these farms amount to the same six feet of earth. To retire from the city, from the struggle, from the hubbub, to go off and hide on one's own farm — that's not life, it is selfishness, sloth, it is a kind of monasticism, but monasticism without works. Man needs not six feet of earth, not a farm, but the whole globe, all of Nature, where unhindered he can display all the capacities and peculiarities of his free spirit.

"My brother Nikolay, sitting in his office, dreamed of eating his own *shchi*, which would fill the whole farmyard with a delicious aroma, of picnicking on the green grass, of sleeping in the sun, of sitting for hours on the seat by the gate gazing at field and forest. Books on agriculture and the farming items in almanacs were his joy, the delight of his soul. He liked newspapers too, but the only things he read in them were advertisements of land for sale, so many acres of tillable land and pasture, with house, garden, river, mill, and millpond. And he pictured to himself garden paths, flowers, fruit, birdhouses with starlings in them, crucians in the pond, and all that sort of thing, you know. These imaginary pictures varied with the advertisements he came upon, but somehow gooseberry bushes figured in every one of them. He could not picture to himself a single country-house, a single rustic nook, without gooseberries.

" 'Country life has its advantages,' he used to say. 'You sit on the veranda having tea, and your ducks swim in the pond, and everything smells delicious and — the gooseberries are ripening.'

"He would draw a plan of his estate and invariably it would contain the following features: a) the master's house; b) servants' quarters; c) kitchen-garden; d) a gooseberry patch. He lived meagerly: he deprived himself of food and drink; he dressed God knows how, like a beggar, but he kept on saving and salting money away in the bank. He was terribly stingy. It was painful for me to see it, and I used to give him small sums and send him something on holidays, but he would put that away too. Once a man is possessed by an idea, there is no doing anything with him.

"Years passed. He was transferred to another province, he was already past forty, yet he was still reading newspaper advertisements and saving up money. Then I heard that he was married. Still for the sake of buying a property with a gooseberry patch he married an elderly, homely widow, without a trace of affection for her, but simply because she had money. After marrying her, he went on living parsimoniously, keeping her half-starved, and he put her money in the bank in his own name. She had previously been the wife of a postmaster, who had got her used to pies and cordials. This second husband did not even give her enough black bread. She began to sicken, and some three years later gave up the ghost. And, of course, it never for a moment occurred to my brother that he was to blame for her death. Money, like vodka, can do queer things to a man. Once in our town a merchant lay on his deathbed; before he died, he ordered a plateful of honey and he ate up all his money and lottery tickets with the honey, so that no one should get it. One day when I was inspecting a drove of cattle at a railway station, a cattle dealer fell under a locomotive and it sliced off his leg. We carried him in to the infirmary, the blood was gushing from the wound — a terrible business, but he kept begging us to find his leg and was very anxious about it: he had twenty rubles in the boot that was on that leg, and he was afraid they would be lost."

"That's a tune from another opera," said Burkin.

Ivan Ivanych paused a moment and then continued:

"After his wife's death, my brother began to look around for a property. Of course, you may scout about for five years and in the end make a mistake, and buy something quite different from what you have been dreaming of. Through an agent my brother bought a mortgaged estate of three hundred acres with a house, servants' quarters, a park, but with no orchard, no gooseberry patch, no duck-pond. There was a stream, but the water in it was the colour of coffee, for on one of its banks there was a brickyard and on the other a glue factory. But my brother was not at all disconcerted: he ordered a score of gooseberry bushes, planted them, and settled down to the life of a country gentleman.

"Last year I paid him a visit. I thought I would go and see how things were with him. In his letter to me my brother called his estate 'Chumbaroklov Waste, or Himalaiskoe' (our surname was Chimsha-Himalaisky). I reached the place in the afternoon. It was hot. Everywhere there were ditches, fences, hedges, rows of fir trees, and I was at a loss as to how to get to the yard and where to leave my horse. I made my way to the house and was met by a fat dog with reddish hair that looked like a pig. It wanted to bark, but was too lazy. The cook, a fat, barelegged woman, who also looked like a pig, came out of the kitchen and said that the master was resting after dinner. I went in to see my brother, and found him sitting up in bed, with a quilt over his knees. He had grown older, stouter, flabby; his cheeks, his nose, his lips jutted out: it looked as though he might grunt into the quilt at any moment.

"We embraced and dropped tears of joy and also of sadness at the thought that the two of us had once been young, but were now grey and nearing death. He got dressed and took me out to show me his estate.

" 'Well, how are you getting on here?' I asked.

" 'Oh, all right, thank God. I am doing very well.'

"He was no longer the poor, timid clerk he used to be but a real landowner, a gentleman. He had already grown used to his new manner of living and developed a taste for it. He ate a great deal, steamed himself in the bathhouse, was growing stout, was already having a lawsuit with the village commune and the two factories and was very much offended when the peasants failed to address him as 'Your Honour.' And he concerned himself with his soul's welfare too in a substantial, upper-class manner, and performed good deeds not simply, but pompously. And what good works! He dosed the peasants with bicarbonate and castor oil for all their ailments and on his name day he had a thanksgiving service celebrated in the center of the village, and then treated the villagers to a gallon of vodka, which he thought was the thing to do. Oh, those horrible gallons of vodka! One day a fat landowner hauls the peasants up before the rural police officer for trespassing, and the next, to mark a feast day, treats them to a gallon of vodka, and they drink and shout 'Hurrah' and when they are drunk bow down at his feet. A higher standard of living, overeating and idleness develop the most insolent self-conceit in a Russian. Nikolay Ivanych, who when he was a petty official was afraid to have opinions of his own even if he kept them to himself, now uttered nothing but incontrovertible truths and did so in the tone of a minister of state: 'Education is necessary, but the masses are not ready for it; corporal punishment is generally harmful, but in some cases it is useful and nothing else will serve.'

" 'I know the common people, and I know how to deal with them,' he would say. 'They love me. I only have to raise my little finger, and they will do anything I want.'

"And all this, mark you, would be said with a smile that bespoke kindness and intelligence. Twenty times over he repeated: 'We, of the gentry,' 'I, as a member of the gentry.' Apparently he no longer remembered that our grandfather had been a peasant and our father just a private. Even our surname, 'Chimsha-Himalaisky,' which in reality is grotesque, seemed to him sonorous, distinguished, and delightful.

"But I am concerned now not with him, but with me. I want to tell you about the change that took place in me during the few hours that I spent on his estate. In the evening when we were having tea, the cook served a plateful of gooseberries. They were not bought, they were his own gooseberries, the first ones picked since the bushes were planted. My brother gave a laugh and for a minute looked at the gooseberries in silence, with tears in his eyes — he could not speak for excitement. Then he put one berry in his mouth, glanced at me with the triumph of a child who has at last been given a toy he was longing for and said: 'How tasty!' And he ate

the gooseberries greedily, and kept repeating: 'Ah, how delicious! Do taste them!'
"They were hard and sour, but as Pushkin has it,

The falsehood that exalts we cherish more
Than meaner truths that are a thousand strong.

I saw a happy man, one whose cherished dream had so obviously come true, who had attained his goal in life, who had got what he wanted, who was satisfied with his lot and with himself. For some reason an element of sadness had always mingled with my thoughts of human happiness, and now at the sight of a happy man I was assailed by an oppressive feeling bordering on despair. It weighed on me particularly at night. A bed was made up for me in a room next to my brother's bedroom, and I could hear that he was wakeful, and that he would get up again and again, go to the plate of gooseberries and eat one after another. I said to myself: how many contented, happy people there really are! What an overwhelming force they are! Look at life: the insolence and idleness of the strong, the ignorance and brutishness of the weak, horrible poverty everywhere, overcrowding, degeneration, drunkenness, hypocrisy, lying — Yet in all the houses and on all the streets there is peace and quiet; of the fifty thousand people who live in our town there is not one who would cry out, who would vent his indignation aloud. We see the people who go to market, eat by day, sleep by night, who babble nonsense, marry, grow old, good-naturedly drag their dead to the cemetery, but we do not see or hear those who suffer, and what is terrible in life goes on somewhere behind the scenes. Everything is peaceful and quiet and only mute statistics protest: so many people gone out of their minds, so many gallons of vodka drunk, so many children dead from malnutrition — And such a state of things is evidently necessary; obviously the happy man is at ease only because the unhappy ones bear their burdens in silence, and if there were not this silence, happiness would be impossible. It is a general hypnosis. Behind the door of every contented, happy man there ought to be someone standing with a little hammer and continually reminding him with a knock that there are unhappy people, that however happy he may be, life will sooner or later show him its claws, and trouble will come to him — illness, poverty, losses, and then no one will see or hear him, just as now he neither sees nor hears others. But there is no man with a hammer. The happy man lives at his ease, faintly fluttered by small daily cares, like an aspen in the wind — and all is well."

"That night I came to understand that I too had been contented and happy," Ivan Ivanych continued, getting up. "I too over the dinner table or out hunting would hold forth on how to live, what to believe, the right way to govern the people. I too would say that learning was the enemy of darkness, that education was necessary but that for the common people the three R's were sufficient for the time being. Freedom is a boon, I used to say, it is as essential as air, but we must wait awhile. Yes, that's what I used to say, and now I ask: Why must we wait?" said Ivan Ivanych, looking wrathfully at Burkin. "Why must we wait, I ask you? For what reason? I am told that nothing can be done all at once, that every idea is realized gradually, in its own time. But who is it that says so? Where is the proof that it is just? You cite the natural order of things, the law governing all phenomena, but is there law, is there order in the fact that I, a living, thinking man, stand beside a ditch and wait for it to close up of itself or fill up with silt, when I could jump over it or throw a bridge across it? And again, why must we wait? Wait, until we have no strength to live, and yet we have to live and are eager to live!

"I left my brother's place early in the morning, and ever since then it has become intolerable for me to stay in town. I am oppressed by the peace and the quiet, I am afraid to look at the windows, for there is nothing that pains me more than the spectacle of a happy family sitting at table having tea. I am an old man now and unfit for combat, I am not even capable of hating. I can only grieve inwardly, get irritated, worked up, and at night my head is ablaze with the rush of ideas and I cannot sleep. Oh, if I were young!"

Ivan Ivanych paced up and down the room excitedly and repeated, "If I were young!"

He suddenly walked up to Alyohin and began to press now one of his hands, now the other.

"Pavel Konstantinych," he said imploringly, "don't quiet down, don't let yourself be lulled to sleep! As long as you are young, strong, alert, do not cease to do good! There is no happiness and there should be none, and if life has a meaning and a purpose, that meaning and purpose is not our happiness but something greater and more rational. Do good!"

All this Ivan Ivanych said with a pitiful, imploring smile, as though he were asking a personal favour.

Afterwards all three of them sat in armchairs in different corners of the drawing room and were silent. Ivan Ivanych's story satisfied neither Burkin nor Alyohin. With the ladies and generals looking down from the golden frames, seeming alive in the dim light, it was tedious to listen to the story of the poor devil of a clerk who ate gooseberries. One felt like talking about elegant people, about women. And the fact that they were sitting in a drawing room where everything — the chandelier under its cover, the armchairs, the carpets underfoot — testified that the very people who were now looking down from the frames had once moved about here, sat and had tea, and the fact that lovely Pelageya was noiselessly moving about — that was better than any story.

Alyohin was very sleepy; he had gotten up early, before three o'clock in the morning, to get some work done, and now he could hardly keep his eyes open, but he was afraid his visitors might tell an interesting story in his absence, and he would not leave. He did not trouble to ask himself if what Ivan Ivanych had just said was intelligent or right. The guests were not talking about groats, or hay, or tar, but about something that had no direct bearing on his life, and he was glad of it and wanted them to go on.

"However, it's bedtime," said Burkin, rising. "Allow me to wish you good night."

Alyohin took leave of his guests and went downstairs to his own quarters, while they remained upstairs. They were installed for the night in a big room in which stood two old wooden beds decorated with carvings and in the corner was an ivory crucifix. The wide cool beds which had been made by the lovely Pelageya gave off a pleasant smell of clean linen.

Ivan Ivanych undressed silently and got into bed.

"Lord forgive us sinners!" he murmured, and drew the bedclothes over his head.

His pipe, which lay on the table, smelled strongly of burnt tobacco, and Burkin, who could not sleep for a long time, kept wondering where the unpleasant odour came from.

The rain beat against the window panes all night.

ℰℭ

The modern short story begins with Chekhov. Famous for both drama and short fiction, the Russian writer concentrated on ordinary people and events, his stories expressing a deep frustration with, yet celebration of, life. His letters show an emerging modernist, someone intent on creating stories that are aesthetic objects unto themselves as much as they are psychological portraitures. "Gooseberries" is more openly discursive than much of his other fiction, with the veterinarian Ivan Ivanych denouncing his brother's middle-class pretensions to two slightly bored friends. But his invective is much more than a tirade against social hypocrisy; his anger springs from an unfocused protest against human misery and our ability to insulate ourselves from it with habit and complacency. Opposed to these expostulations are the almost mute details that establish the story's emotional tone, perhaps its true content — the water adjoining the bath-hut, the odour of stale tobacco at the story's end. Helping to establish the adage that "showing" is better than "telling," Chekhov influenced numerous twentieth-century authors. When Cynthia Ozick praises Alice Munro by saying "she is our Chekhov," she pays tribute to Chekhov's enduring place in the history of short fiction.

M.T.

KATE CHOPIN   *(1851-1904)*

The Story of an Hour

K nowing that Mrs. Mallard was afflicted with a heart trouble, great care was
taken to break to her as gently as possible the news of her husband's death.
        It was her sister Josephine who told her, in broken sentences; veiled
hints that revealed in half concealing. Her husband's friend Richards was there,
too, near her. It was he who had been in the newspaper office when intelligence of
the railroad disaster was received, with Brently Mallard's name leading the list of
"killed." He had only taken the time to assure himself of its truth by a second
telegram, and had hastened to forestall any less careful, less tender friend in bearing
the sad message.

She did not hear the story as many women have heard the same, with a
paralyzed inability to accept its significance. She wept at once, with sudden, wild
abandonment, in her sister's arms. When the storm of grief had spent itself she
went away to her room alone. She would have no one follow her.

There stood, facing the open window, a comfortable, roomy armchair. Into
this she sank, pressed down by a physical exhaustion that haunted her body and
seemed to reach into her soul.

She could see in the open square before her house the tops of trees that were
all aquiver with the new spring life. The delicious breath of rain was in the air. In
the street below a peddler was crying his wares. The notes of a distant song which
someone was singing reached her faintly, and countless sparrows were twittering
in the eaves.

There were patches of blue sky showing here and there through the clouds
that had met and piled one above the other in the west facing her window.

She sat with her head thrown back upon the cushion of the chair, quite
motionless, except when a sob came up into her throat and shook her, as a child
who has cried itself to sleep continues to sob in its dreams.

She was young, with a fair, calm face, whose lines bespoke repression and
even a certain strength. But now there was a dull stare in her eyes, whose gaze was
fixed away off yonder on one of those patches of blue sky. It was not a glance of
reflection, but rather indicated a suspension of intelligent thought.

There was something coming to her and she was waiting for it, fearfully.
What was it? She did not know; it was too subtle and elusive to name. But she felt
it, creeping out of the sky, reaching toward her through the sounds, the scents, the
colour that filled the air.

Now her bosom rose and fell tumultuously. She was beginning to recognize
this thing that was approaching to possess her, and she was striving to beat it back
with her will — as powerless as her two white slender hands would have been.

When she abandoned herself a little whispered word escaped her slightly parted lips. She said it over and over under her breath: "free, free, free!" The vacant stare and the look of terror that had followed it went from her eyes. They stayed keen and bright. Her pulses beat fast, and the coursing blood warmed and relaxed every inch of her body.

She did not stop to ask if it were or were not a monstrous joy that held her. A clear and exalted perception enabled her to dismiss the suggestion as trivial.

She knew that she would weep again when she saw the kind, tender hands folded in death; the face that had never looked save with love upon her, fixed and grey and dead. But she saw beyond that bitter moment a long procession of years to come that would belong to her absolutely. And she opened and spread her arms out to them in welcome.

There would be no one to live for her during those coming years; she would live for herself. There would be no powerful will bending hers in that blind persistence with which men and women believe they have a right to impose a private will upon a fellow-creature. A kind intention or a cruel intention made the act seem no less a crime as she looked upon it in that brief moment of illumination.

And yet she had loved him — sometimes. Often she had not. What did it matter! What could love, the unsolved mystery, count for in face of this possession of self-assertion which she suddenly recognized as the strongest impulse of her being!

"Free! Body and soul free!" she kept whispering.

Josephine was kneeling before the closed door with her lips to the keyhole, imploring for admission. "Louise, open the door! I beg; open the door — you will make yourself ill. What are you doing, Louise? For heaven's sake open the door."

"Go away. I am not making myself ill." No; she was drinking in a very elixir of life through that open window.

Her fancy was running riot along those days ahead of her. Spring days, and summer days, and all sorts of days that would be her own. She breathed a quick prayer that life might be long. It was only yesterday she had thought with a shudder that life might be long.

She arose at length and opened the door to her sister's importunities. There was a feverish triumph in her eyes, and she carried herself unwittingly like a goddess of Victory. She clasped her sister's waist, and together they descended the stairs. Richards stood waiting for them at the bottom.

Some one was opening the front door with a latchkey. It was Brently Mallard who entered, a little travel-stained, composedly carrying his grip-sack and umbrella. He had been far from the scene of accident, and did not even know there had been one. He stood amazed at Josephine's piercing cry; at Richards' quick motion to screen him from the view of his wife.

But Richards was too late.

When the doctors came they said she had died of heart disease — of joy that kills.

೩೦೦೪

Kate Chopin's work was virtually unappreciated until the early 1970s, when the modern women's movement sparked a revival of interest in her. During her lifetime, Chopin had a reputation as a local colourist who wrote primarily about New Orleans culture. In 1899, she published The Awakening, *a realistic novel about the sexual and artistic awakening of a young mother who abandons her family and eventually commits suicide. The novel shocked many early twentieth-century readers unprepared to encounter such ideas in a novel — especially one by a woman. The revival of interest in her and the high esteem in which she is now held demonstrate the extent to which the popularity of a writer is closely tied to the values and assumptions (political, social, sexual) of the society in which her work is read.*

"The Story of an Hour" is typical of Chopin in both its subject matter and its artistic method. Like many modern short stories, it focuses on one incident that is presented and viewed through the distancing lens of irony. Chopin's irony still has the power to surprise — and even shock. As we read we discover that an event conventionally accompanied by grief is here welcomed with its opposite: joy. But that subversive irony is then subjected to yet another reversal in the unexpected — and ironic — final sentence.

N.C.

ELIZABETH COOK-LYNN

(b. 1930)

Loss of the Sky

In those years before the United States entered World War I, there lived near Fort Pierre, South Dakota, one Joseph Shields, a fifty-year-old Sioux Indian who in his own way knew something of the rise of brutal doctrines, something of the destruction of ancient civilizations, something of a change of worlds.

The proud owner of two hundred head of horses, he was a man who strongly reflected his Dakotah heritage, despite a rather arduous education at Carlisle, that school for Indians in the East. Through the years, as he aged, he continued to smoke in the traditional way, to take the sweat, to carry on long conversations with friends, and, when he thought no one was watching, he took his drum out into the prairie hills as the sun rose and sang the ancient songs of his people, who were called the "sun worshippers of the Plains."

Though he was somewhat Christianized by the Dominican priests who roamed the prairies, as much nomads as any Indians had ever been, Joseph never quite accepted the totality of that faith, never quite believed in the recent god of the strange blackrobes. So it was that whenever the spirit moved him in the old way, he profoundly and reverently sang to the god he knew more intimately.

Though the tyranny of those years would be evident to the world by the crushing of innocent people all over Europe, the perilousness of them seemed remote to old Shields, not at all like the years he remembered from the shadows of his past, when his family hid out in caves along the Missouri River, surreptitiously kept watch on the movements of the U.S. Army troops, wondered aloud about the business of the Seventh Cavalry, Sibley, Thompson, Sheridan, about the new troops they could not identify, who they were, and what they wanted here in Sioux Country.

These were not painful years for the old man, not like those of the past nor those to come later. In fact, Joseph had come to the time in his life when he thought of white men and their endless cruelties less and less. Instead, he placed a modicum of good faith in his own immediate world and, more specifically, in the five sons and one daughter his good wife, Ruth, had borne him.

He would go out to the corrals where his sons were working the horses, and with great pride he would watch his middle son, Teo, the finest rider anywhere around, teach his mount to neckrein or bulldog or, as in the case of some of the fresh two-year-olds, to take the saddle.

These were good years, and Joseph thought little about the marauding German armies and the war clouds hanging over the capitals of Europe. The problems of such governments did not concern him. Joseph had never exercised a vote in them, and when the Indian Commissioner came to the reservation from Washington, D.C., to talk of the grandeur of conferring citizenship upon members of the tribe, Joseph listened politely, his eyes directed at the floor. He stared for a long time and never raised his eyes, and then he turned away, walked quietly outside to his team of horses, spoke to them with sureness and authority, and drove them the fifty miles to his place. He never mentioned the matter to his wife, nor to his sons, and if he thought about it at all, it did not take on any grand significance as a noble idea.

So it was that the good weather days passed for Joseph and his family, the days when the breeds and the fullbloods gathered at the fairs to race their horses and socialize at the powwows which followed the competitions, travelling and camping at Fort Pierre, at Rapid City, on through Montana, and sometimes as far as Canada, until it was September and time for the sons and daughters to return to the Indian boarding school two hundred miles away.

Every fall, as if the Bureau of Indian Affairs was an inexorable part of the natural cycle of life, it sent big, open army trucks down to the reservation and swept up every luckless Indian kid along the Crow Creek whose parents hadn't hidden him in the timber.

And then Joseph would be left with the memories of the summer, the echoes of young voices, "*Até. . . ahitonwan*, look here." The horses would get fat and shaggy and wild from little handling through the winter. And Joseph would walk through the silent corrals.

Life went on even then, though, and Ruth would cook the fine soup made of dried corn and *ti(n)psina*, until that awful night when Teo, the middle son, the finest rider anywhere around, walked away from the darkened dormitory for the last time and slipped onto the C & NW, whose lonesome whistle had often beckoned him over the years when he would lie in bed on the second floor, unable to sleep, wishing for home.

Teo didn't go home. The school authorities would only come after him as they had done before. Instead, he rode the rails to Chicago, enlisted in the Army, and after a decent training period, was among the 14,000 troops which landed on the shores of France. It was the summer of 1917, seven years before his people were to become U.S. citizens.

Joseph weakened as the years passed. His middle son, the finest rider anywhere around, Teo, had not made it back from France. Joseph kept the paper which told of his son's bravery and his death and that his body would not be coming back. It was the last part of the message which made Joseph an old man.

Inevitably, the proper songs were sung in honour of the young warrior, and for years the anguish of Ruth's wailing songs never left Joseph's memory. Ruth cut her hair and slashed her legs, and after that she never wore the pretty beaded shawls and bright moccasins and hair pieces she loved to make.

Joseph's two hundred head of horses were neglected, became scattered and lost; some of them were stolen, but it did not matter. The old man seemed somehow compelled to sit and gaze into the distance, as if he might see Teo, tall and straight in the saddle, the middle son, the finest rider anywhere around, come over the rise, his arm lifted gently in greeting.

Joseph seldom went into the hills to pray and sing anymore, but when he did, he never failed to weep that the bones of his son, the middle son, the finest rider anywhere around, could not mingle with the bones of his grandfathers.

ഇറ

"Loss of the Sky" first appeared in a 1982 collection of stories and poems by Elizabeth Cook-Lynn titled Then Badger Said This. *The book is a poetic narrative of Sioux history from prewhite times to Reservation life in the twentieth century. Her vignettes of contemporary Sioux life are juxtaposed against tales, myths, and poems of the past, many of them clearly adapted from the Dakota language. This section was first published (with minor revisions) as "Loss of the Sky" in Cook-Lynn's collection* The Power of Horses and Other Stories *(1990). Written in an epic Homerian style that befits the construction of "new" history, the story of Joseph Shields, and his son Teo and their horses, is ultimately a story of all times and all nations. It has the breathtaking simplicity of a fable, or of an oral legend that might pass through many generations of speakers.*

Elizabeth Cook-Lynn is a member of the Crow Creek tribe of Dakota Sioux, and was born at Fort Thompson, South Dakota. Her works have been widely published in the U.S. and Canada, and she has taught at several American universities, most recently Eastern Washington State College at Cheney, Washington. She now lives and writes in Rapid City, South Dakota. She is also a grandmother, a poet, and a critic.

K.M.

LOUISE ERDRICH   *(b. 1954)*

The Bingo Van

W hen I walked into bingo that night in early spring, I didn't have a
girlfriend, a home or an apartment, a piece of land or a car, and I wasn't
tattooed yet, either. Now look at me. I'm walking the reservation road
in borrowed pants, toward a place that isn't mine, downhearted because I'm left
by a woman. All I have of my temporary riches is this black pony running across
the back of my hand — a tattoo I had Lewey's Tattoo Den put there on account of
a waking dream. I'm still not paid up. I still owe for the little horse. But if Lewey
wants to repossess it, then he'll have to catch me first.

Here's how it is on coming to the bingo hall. It's a long, low quonset barn.
Inside, there used to be a pall of smoke, but now the smoke-eater fans in the ceiling
take care of that. So upon first entering you can pick out your friends. On that
night in early spring, I saw Eber, Clay, and Robert Morrissey sitting about halfway
up toward the curtained stage with their grandmother Lulu. By another marriage,
she was my grandma, too. She had five tickets spread in front of her. The boys
each had only one. When the numbers rolled, she picked up a dabber in each hand.
It was the Earlybird game, a one-hundred-dollar prize, and nobody had got too
wound up yet or serious.

"Lipsha, go get us a Coke," said Lulu when someone else bingoed. "Yourself,
too."

I went to the concession with Eber, who had finished high school with me.
Clay and Robert were younger. We got our soft drinks and came back, set them
down, pulled up to the table, and laid out a new set of tickets before us. Like I say,
my grandmother, she played five at once, which is how you get the big money. In
the long run, much more than breaking even, she was one of those rare Chippewas
who actually profited by bingo. But, then again, it was her only way of gambling.
No pull-tabs, no blackjack, no slot machines for her. She never went into the back
room. She banked all the cash she won. I thought I should learn from Lulu
Lamartine, whose other grandsons had stiff new boots while mine were worn down
into the soft shape of moccasins. I watched her.

Concentration. Before the numbers even started, she set her mouth, snapped
her purse shut. She shook her dabbers so that the foam-rubber tips were thoroughly
inked. She looked at the time on her watch. The Coke, she took a drink of that, but
no more than a sip. She was a narrow-eyed woman with a round jaw, curled hair.
Her eyeglasses, blue plastic, hung from her neck by a gleaming chain. She raised
the ovals to her eyes as the caller took the stand. She held her dabbers poised while
he plucked the ball from the chute. He read it out: B-7. Then she was absorbed,
scanning, dabbing, into the game. She didn't mutter. She had no lucky piece to
touch in front of her. And afterward, even if she lost a blackout game by one

square, she never sighed or complained.

All business, that was Lulu. And all business paid.

I think I would have been all business too, like her, if it hadn't been for what lay behind the stage curtain to be revealed. I didn't know it, but that was what would change the order of my life. Because of the van, I'd have to get stupid first, then wise. You see, I had been floundering since high school, trying to catch my bearings in the world. It all lay ahead of me, spread out in the sun like a giveaway at a naming ceremony. Only thing was, I could not choose a prize. Something always stopped my hand before it reached.

"Lipsha Morrissey, you got to go for a vocation." That's what I told myself, in a state of nervous worry. I was getting by on almost no money, relying on my job as night watchman in a bar. That earned me a place to sleep, twenty dollars per week, and as much beef jerky, Beer Nuts, and spicy sausage sticks as I could eat.

I was now composed of these three false substances. No food in a bar has a shelf life of less than forty months. If you are what you eat, I would live forever, I thought.

And then they pulled aside the curtain, and I saw that I wouldn't live as long as I had coming unless I owned that van. It had every option you could believe — blue plush on the steering wheel, diamond side windows, and complete carpeted interior. The seats were easy chairs, with little headphones, and it was wired all through the walls. You could walk up close during intermission and touch the sides. The paint was cream, except for the design picked out in blue, which was a Sioux Drum border. In the back there was a small refrigerator and a carpeted platform for sleeping. It was a home, a portable den with front-wheel drive. I could see myself in it right off. I could see I *was* it.

On TV, they say you are what you drive. Let's put it this way: I wanted to be that van.

Now, I know that what I felt was a symptom of the national decline. You'll scoff at me, scorn me, say, What right does that waste Lipsha Morrissey, who makes his living guarding beer, have to comment outside of his own tribal boundary? But I was able to investigate the larger picture, thanks to Grandma Lulu, from whom I learned to be one-minded in my pursuit of a material object.

I went night after night to the bingo. Every hour I spent there, I grew more certain I was close. There was only one game per night at which the van was offered, a blackout game, where you had to fill every slot. The more tickets you bought, the more your chances increased. I tried to play five tickets, like Grandma Lulu did, but they cost five bucks each. To get my van, I had to shake hands with greed. I got unprincipled.

You see, my one talent in this life is a healing power I get passed down through the Pillager branch of my background. It's in my hands. I snap my fingers together so hard they almost spark. Then I blank out my mind, and I put on the touch. I had a reputation up to then for curing sore joints and veins. I could relieve ailments caused in an old person by a half century of grinding stoop-over work. I had a power in myself that flowed out, resistless. I had a richness in my dreams and waking thoughts. But I never realized I would have to give up my healing source once I started charging for my service.

You know how it is about charging. People suddenly think you are worth something. Used to be, I'd go anyplace I was called, take any price or take nothing. Once I let it get around that I charged a twenty for my basic work, however, the phone at the bar rang off the hook.

"Where's that medicine boy?" they asked. "Where's Lipsha?"

I took their money. And it's not like beneath the pressure of a twenty I didn't try, for I did try, even harder than before. I skipped my palms together, snapped my fingers, positioned them where the touch inhabiting them should flow. But when it came to blanking out my mind I consistently failed. For each time, in the center of the cloud that came down into my brain, the van was now parked, in perfect focus.

I suppose I longed for it like for a woman, except I wasn't that bad yet, and, anyway, then I did meet a woman, which set me back in my quest.

Instead of going for the van with everything, saving up to buy as many cards as I could play when they got to the special game, for a few nights I went short term, for variety, with U-Pickem cards, the kind where you have to choose the numbers for yourself.

First off, I wrote in the shoe and pants sizes of those Morrissey boys. No luck. So much for them. Next I took my birth date and a double of it — still no go. I wrote down the numbers of my grandma's address and her anniversary dates. Nothing. Then one night I realized if my U-Pickem was going to win it would be more like *revealed*, rather than a forced kind of thing. So I shut my eyes, right there in the middle of the long bingo table, and I let my mind blank out, white and fizzing like the screen of a television, until something formed. The van, as always. But on its tail this time a license plate was officially fixed and numbered. I used that number, wrote it down in the boxes, and then I bingoed.

C––>

I got two hundred dollars from that imaginary license. The money was in my pocket when I left. The next morning, I had fifty cents. But it's not like you think with Serena, and I'll explain that. She didn't want something from me; she didn't care if I had money, and she didn't ask for it. She was seventeen and had a two-year-old boy. That tells you about her life. Her last name was American Horse, an old Sioux name she was proud of even though it was strange to Chippewa country. At her older sister's house Serena's little boy blended in with the younger children, and Serena herself was just one of the teenagers. She was still in high school, a year behind the year she should have been in, and she had ambitions. Her idea was to go into business and sell her clothing designs, of which she had six books.

I don't know how I got a girl so decided in her future to go with me, even that night. Except I told myself, "Lipsha, you're a nice-looking guy. You're a winner." And for the moment I was. I went right up to her at the Coin-Op and said, "Care to dance?", which was a joke — there wasn't anyplace to dance. Yet she liked me. We had a sandwich and then she wanted to take a drive, so we tagged along with some others in the back of their car. They went straight south, toward Hoopdance, off the reservation, where action was taking place.

"Lipsha," she whispered on the way, "I always liked you from a distance."

"Serena," I said, "I liked you from a distance, too."

So then we moved close together on the car seat. My hand was on my knee, and I thought of a couple of different ways I could gesture, casually pretend to let it fall on hers, how maybe if I talked fast she wouldn't notice, in the heat of the moment, her hand in my hand, us holding hands, our lips drawn to one another. But then I decided to boldly take courage, to take her hand as, at the same time, I looked into her eyes. I did this. In the front, the others talked among themselves. Yet we just sat there. After a while she said, "You want to kiss me?"

But I answered, not planning how the words would come out, "Our first kiss has to be a magic moment only we can share."

Her eyes went wide as a deer's, and her big smile bloomed. Her skin was dark, her long hair a burnt-brown colour. She wore no jewelry, no rings, just the clothing she had sewed from her designs — a suit jacket and pair of pants that were the tan of eggshells, with symbols picked out in blue thread on the borders, the cuffs, and the hem. I took her in, admiring, for some time on that drive before I realized that the reason Serena's cute outfit nagged me so was on account of she was dressed up to match my bingo van. I could hardly tell her this surprising coincidence, but it did convince me that the time was perfect, the time was right.

They let us off at a certain place just over the reservation line, and we got out, hardly breaking our gaze from each other. You want to know what this place was? I'll tell you. O.K. So it was a motel — a long, low double row of rooms, painted white on the outside, with brown wooden doors. There was a beautiful sign set up, featuring a lake with some fish jumping out of it. We stood beside the painted water.

"I haven't done this since Jason," she said. That was the name of her two-year-old son. "I have to call up my sister first."

There was a phone near the office, inside a plastic shell. She went over there.

"He's sleeping," she said which she returned.

I went into the office, stood before the metal counter. There was a number floating in my mind.

"Is Room 22 available?" I asked.

I suppose, looking at me, I look too much like an Indian. The owner, a big sandy-haired woman in a shiny black blouse, noticed that. You get so you see it cross their face the way wind blows a disturbance on water. There was a period of contemplation, a struggle in this woman's thinking. Behind her the television whispered. Her mouth opened, but I spoke first.

"This here is Andrew Jackson," I said, tenderizing the bill. "Known for setting up our Southern relatives for the Trail of Tears. And to keep him company we got two Mr. Hamiltons."

The woman turned shrewd, and took the bills.

"No parties." She held out a key attached to a square of orange plastic.

"Just sex." I could not help but reassure her. But that was talk, big talk from a person with hardly any experience and nothing that resembled a birth-control device. I wasn't one of those so-called studs who couldn't open up their wallets without dropping a foil-wrapped square. No, Lipsha Morrissey was deep at heart a romantic, a wild-minded kind of guy, I told myself, a fool with no letup. I went out to Serena, and took her hand in mine. I was shaking inside but my voice was steady and my hands were cool.

"Let's go in." I showed the key. "Let's not think about tomorrow."

"That's how I got Jason," said Serena.

So we stood there.

"I'll go in," she said at last. "Down two blocks, there's an all-night gas station. They sell 'em."

I went. O.K. Life in this day and age might be less romantic in some ways. It seemed so in the hard twenty-four-hour fluorescent light, as I tried to choose what I needed from the rack by the counter. It was quite a display; there were dazzling choices — textures, shapes. I saw I was being watched, and I suddenly grabbed what was near my hand — two boxes, economy size.

"Heavy date?"

I suppose the guy on the late shift was bored, could not resist. His T-shirt said "Big Sky Country." He was grinning in an ugly way. So I answered.

"Not really. Fixing up a bunch of my white buddies from Montana. Trying to keep down the sheep population."

His grin stayed fixed. Maybe he had heard a lot of jokes about Montana blondes, or maybe he was from somewhere else. I looked at the boxes in my hand, put one back.

"Let me help you out," the guy said. "What you need is a bag of these."

He took down a plastic sack of little oblong party balloons, Day-Glo pinks and oranges and blues.

"Too bright," I said. "My girlfriend's a designer. She hates clashing colours." I was breathing hard suddenly, and so was he. Our eyes met and narrowed.

"What does she design?" he said. "Bedsheets?"

"What does yours design?" I said. "Wool sweaters?"

I put money between us. "For your information, my girlfriend's not only beautiful but she and I are the same species."

"Which is?"

"Take the money," I said. "Hand over my change and I'll be out of here. Don't make me do something I'd regret."

"I'd be real threatened." The guy turned from me, ringing up my sale. "I'd be shaking, except I know you Indian guys are chickenshit."

I took my package, took my change.

"Baaaaa," I said, and beat it out of there. It's strange how a bashful kind of person like me gets talkative in some of our less pleasant border-town situations.

I took a roundabout way back to Room 22 and tapped on the door. There was a little window right beside it. Serena peeked through, and let me in.

"Well," I said then, in that awkward interval, "guess we're set."

She took the bag from my hand and didn't say a word, just put it on the little table beside the bed. There were two chairs. Each of us took one. Then we sat down and turned on the television. The romance wasn't in us now for some reason, but there was something invisible that made me hopeful about the room.

It was just a small place, a modest kind of place, clean. You could smell the faint chemical of bug spray the moment you stepped inside. You could look at the television hung on the wall, or examine the picture of golden trees and a waterfall. You could take a shower for a long time in the cement shower stall, standing on your personal shower mat for safety. There was a little tin desk. You could sit down there and write a letter on a sheet of plain paper from the drawer. The lampshade was made of reeds, pressed and laced tight together. The spread on the double mattress was reddish, a rusty cotton material. There was an air-conditioner, with a fan we turned on.

"I don't know why we're here," I said at last. "I'm sorry."

Serena took a small brush from her purse.

"Comb my hair?"

I took the brush and sat on the bed, just behind her. I began at the ends, very careful, but there were hardly any tangles to begin with. Her hair was a quiet brown without variation. My hand followed the brush, smoothing after each stroke, until the fall of her hair was a hypnotizing silk. I could lift my hand away from her head and the hair would follow, electric to my touch, in soft strands that hung suspended until I returned to the brushing. She never moved, except to switch off the light and then the television. She sat down again in the total dark and said, "Please, keep on," so I did. The air got thick. Her hair got lighter, full of blue static, charged so that I was held place by the attraction. A golden spark jumped on the carpet. Serena turned toward me. Her hair floated down around her at that moment like a tent of energy.

∝

Well, the money part is not related to that. I gave it all to Serena, that's true. Her intention was to buy material and put together the creations that she drew in her notebooks. It was fashion with a Chippewa flair, as she explained it, and sure to win prizes at the state home-ec. contest. She promised to pay me interest when she opened her own shop. The next day, after we had parted, after I had checked out the bar I was supposed to night-watch, I went off to the woods to sit and think. Not about the money, which was Serena's — and good luck to her — but about her and me.

She was two years younger than me, yet she had direction and a child, while I was aimless, lost in hyperspace, using up my talent, which was already fading from my hands. I wondered what our future could hold. One thing was sure: I never knew a man to support his family by playing bingo, and the medicine calls for Lipsha were getting fewer by the week, and fewer, as my touch failed to heal people, fled from me, and lay concealed.

I sat on ground where, years ago, my greats and my great-greats, the Pillagers, had walked. The trees around me were the dense birch and oak of old woods. The lake drifted in, grey waves, white foam in a bobbing lace. Thin gulls lined themselves up on a sandbar. The sky went dark. I closed my eyes, and that is when the little black pony galloped into my mind. It sped across the choppy waves like a skipping stone, its mane a banner, its tail a flag, and vanished on the other side of the shore.

It was luck. Serena's animal. American Horse.

"This is the last night I'm going to try for the van," I told myself. I always kept three twenties stuffed inside the edging of my blanket in back of the bar. Once that stash was gone I'd make a real decision. I'd open the yellow pages at random, and where my finger pointed I would take that kind of job.

Of course, I never counted on winning the van.

I was playing for it on the shaded side of a blackout ticket, which is always hard to get. As usual, I sat with Lulu and her boys. Her vigilance helped me. She let me use her extra dabber and she sat and smoked a filter cigarette, observing the quiet frenzy that was taking place around her. Even though that van had sat on the stage for five months, even though nobody had yet won it and everyone said it was a scam, when it came to playing for it most people bought a couple of tickets. That night, I went all out and purchased eight.

A girl read out the numbers from the hopper. Her voice was clear and light on the microphone. I didn't even notice what was happening — Lulu pointed out one place I had missed on the winning ticket. Then I had just two squares left to make a bingo and I suddenly sweated, I broke out into a chill, I went cold and hot at once. After all my pursuit, after all my plans, I was N-6 and G-60. I had narrowed myself, shrunk into the spaces on the ticket. Each time the girl read a number and it wasn't that 6 or 60 I sickened, recovered, forgot to breathe.

She must have read twenty numbers out before N-6. Then right after that, G-60 rolled off her lips.

I screamed. I am ashamed to say how loud I yelled. That girl came over, got the manager, and then he checked out my numbers slow and careful while everyone hushed.

He didn't say a word. He checked them over twice. Then he pursed his lips together and wished he didn't have to say it.

"It's a bingo," he finally told the crowd.

Noise buzzed to the ceiling — talk of how close some others had come, green talk — and every eye was turned and cast on me, which was uncomfortable. I never was the center of looks before, not Lipsha, who everybody took for granted around here. Not all those looks were for the good, either. Some were plain envious and ready to believe the first bad thing a sour tongue could pin on me. It made sense in a way. Of all those who'd stalked that bingo van over the long months, I was now the only one who had not lost money on the hope.

◌◌

O.K., so what kind of man does it make Lipsha Morrissey that the keys did not tarnish his hands one slight degree, and that he beat it out that very night in the van, completing only the basic paperwork? I didn't go after Serena, and I can't tell you why. Yet I was hardly ever happier. In that van, I rode high, but that's the thing. Looking down on others, even if it's only from the seat of a van that a person never really earned, does something to the human mentality. It's hard to say. I changed. After just one evening riding the reservation roads, passing with a swish of my tires, I started smiling at the homemade hot rods, at the clunkers below me, at the old-lady cars nosing carefully up and down the gravel hills.

I started saying to myself that I should visit Serena, and a few nights later I finally did go over there. I pulled into her sister's driveway with a flourish I could not help, as the van slipped into a pothole and I roared the engine. For a moment, I sat in the dark, letting my headlamps blaze alongside the door until Serena's brother-in-law leaned out.

"Cut the lights!" he yelled. "We got a sick child."

I rolled down my window, and asked for Serena.

"It's her boy. She's in here with him." He waited. I did, too, in the dark. A dim light was on behind him and I saw some shadows, a small girl in those pajamas with the feet tacked on, someone pacing back and forth.

"You want to come in?" he called.

But here's the gist of it. I just said to tell Serena hi for me, and then I backed out of there, down the drive, and left her to fend for herself. I could have stayed there. I could have drawn my touch back from wherever it had gone to. I could have offered my van to take Jason to the I.H.S. I could have sat there in silence as a dog guards its mate, its own blood. I could have done something different from what I did, which was to hit the road for Hoopdance and look for a better time.

I cruised until I saw where the party house was located that night. I drove the van over the low curb, into the yard, and I parked there. I watched until I recognized a couple of cars and saw the outlines of Indians and mixed, so I knew that walking in would not involve me in what the newspapers term an episode. The door was white, stained and raked by a dog, with a tiny fan-shaped window. I went through and stood inside. There was movement, a kind of low-key swirl of bright hair and dark hair tossing alongside each other. There were about as many Indians as there weren't. This party was what we call around here a Hairy Buffalo, and most people were grouped around a big brown plastic garbage can that served as the punch bowl for the all-purpose stuff, which was anything that anyone brought, dumped in along with pink Hawaiian Punch. I grew up around a lot of the people, and others I knew by sight. Among those last, there was a young familiar-looking guy.

It bothered me. I recognized him, but I didn't know him. I hadn't been to school with him, or played him in any sport, because I did not play sports. I couldn't think where I'd seen him until later, when the heat went up and he took off his bomber jacket. Then "Big Sky Country" showed, plain letters on a bright-blue background.

I edged around the corner of the room, into the hall, and stood there to argue with myself. Would he recognize me, or was I just another face, a customer? He probably wasn't really from Montana, so he might not even have been insulted by our little conversation, or remember it anymore. I reasoned that he had probably picked up the shirt vacationing, though who would want to go across that border, over to where the world got meaner? I told myself that I should calm my nerves, go back into the room, have fun. What kept me from doing that was the sudden thought of Serena, of our night together and what I had bought and used.

Once I remembered, I was lost to the present moment. One part of me caught up with the other. I realized that I had left Serena to face her crisis, alone, while I took off in my brand-new van.

I have a hard time getting drunk. It's just the way I am. I start thinking and forget to fill the cup, or recall something I have got to do, and just end up walking from a party. I have put down a full can of beer before and walked out to weed my grandma's rhubarb patch, or work on a cousin's car. Now I was putting myself in Serena's place, feeling her feelings.

What would he want to do that to me for?

I heard her voice say this out loud, just behind me, where there was nothing but wall. I edged along until I came to a door, and there I went through, into a tiny bedroom full of coats, and so far nobody either making out or unconscious upon the floor. I sat on a pile of parkas and jean jackets in this little room, an alcove in the rising buzz of the party outside. I saw a phone, and I dialled Serena's number. Her sister answered.

"Thanks a lot," she said when I said it was me. "You woke up Jason."

"What's wrong with him?" I asked.

There was a silence, then Serena's voice got on the line. "I'm going to hang up."

"Don't."

"He's crying. His ears hurt so bad he can't stand it."

"I'm coming over there."

"Forget it. Forget you."

She said the money I had loaned her would be in the mail. She reminded me it was a long time since the last time I had called. And then the phone went dead. I held the droning receiver in my hand, and tried to clear my mind. The only thing I saw in it, clear as usual, was the van. I decided this was a sign for me to get in behind the wheel. I should drive straight to Serena's house, put on the touch, help her son out. So I set my drink on the windowsill. Then I slipped out the door and I walked down the porch steps, only to find them waiting.

I guess he had recognized me after all, and I guess he was from Montana. He had friends, too. They stood around the van, and their heads were level with the roof, for they were tall.

"Let's go for a ride," said the one from the all-night gas pump.

He knocked on the window of my van with his knuckles. When I told him no thanks, he started karate-kicking the door. He wore black cowboy boots, pointy-toed, with hard-edged new heels. They left ugly dents every time he landed a blow.

"Thanks anyhow," I repeated. "But the party's not over." I tried to get back into the house, but, like in a bad dream, the door was stuck, or locked. I hollered, pounded, kicked at the very marks that desperate dog had left, but the music rose and nobody heard. So I ended up in the van. They acted very gracious. They urged me to drive. They were so polite that I tried to tell myself they weren't all that bad. And sure enough, after we had drove for a while, these Montana guys said they had chipped in together to buy me a present.

"What is it?" I asked. "Don't keep me in suspense."

"Keep driving," said the pump jockey.

"I don't really go for surprises," I said. "What's your name, anyhow?"

"Marty."

"I got a cousin named Marty," I said.

"Forget it."

The guys in the back exchanged a grumbling kind of laughter, a knowing set of groans. Marty grinned, turned toward me from the passenger seat.

"If you really want to know what we're going to give you, I'll tell. It's a map. A map of Montana."

Their laughter got wild and went on for too long.

"I always liked the state," I said in a serious voice.

"No shit," said Marty. "Then I hope you like sitting on it." He signalled where I should turn, and all of a sudden I realized that Lewey's lay ahead. Lewey ran his Tattoo Den from the basement of his house, kept his equipment set up and ready for the weekend.

"Whoa," I said. I stopped the van. "You can't tattoo a person against his will. It's illegal."

"Get your lawyer on it tomorrow." Marty leaned in close for me to see his eyes. I put the van back in gear but just chugged along, desperately thinking. Lewey was a strange kind of guy, an old Dutch sailor who got beached here, about as far as you can get from salt water. I decided that I'd ask Marty, in a polite kind of way, to beat me up instead. If that failed, I would tell him that there were many states I would not mind so much — smaller, rounder ones.

"Are any of you guys from any other state?" I asked, anxious to trade.

"Kansas."

"South Dakota."

It wasn't that I really had a thing against those places, understand; it's just that the straight-edged shape is not a Chippewa preference. You look around you, and everything you see is round, everything in nature. There are no perfect boundaries, no borders. Only human-made things tend toward cubes and squares — the van, for instance. That was an example. Suddenly I realized that I was driving a wheeled version of the state of North Dakota.

"Just beat me up, you guys. Let's get this over with. I'll stop."

But they laughed, and then we were at Lewey's.

◌

The sign on his basement door said COME IN. I was shoved from behind and strapped together by five pairs of heavy, football-toughened hands. I was the first to see Lewey, I think, the first to notice that he was not just a piece of all the trash and accumulated junk that washed through the concrete-floored cellar but a person, sitting still as any statue, in a corner, on a chair that creaked and sang when he rose and walked over.

He even looked like a statue — not the type you see in history books, I don't mean those, but the kind you see for sale as you drive along the highway. He was a Paul Bunyan, carved with a chain saw. He was rough-looking, finished in big strokes.

"Please," I said, "I don't want . . ."

Marty squeezed me around the throat and tousled up my hair, like friendly.

"He's just got cold feet. Now remember, Lewey, map of Montana. You know where. And put in a lot of detail."

I tried to scream.

"Like I was thinking," Marty went on, "of those maps we did in grade school showing products from each region. Cows' heads, oil wells, those little sheaves of wheat, and so on."

"Tie him up," said Lewey. His voice was thick, with a commanding formal accent. "Then leave."

They did. They took my pants and the keys to the van. I heard the engine roar and die away, and I rolled from side to side in my strict bindings. I felt Lewey's hand on my shoulder.

"Be still." His voice had changed, now that the others were gone, to a low sound that went with his appearance and did not seem at all unkind. I looked up at him. A broke-down God is who he looked like from my worm's-eye view. His beard was pure white, long and patchy, and his big eyes frozen blue. His head was half bald, shining underneath the brilliant fluorescent tubes in the ceiling. You never know where you're going to find your twin in the world, your double. I don't mean in terms of looks — I'm talking about mind-set. You never know where you're going to find the same thoughts in another brain, but when it happens you know it right off, just like the two of you were connected by a small electrical wire that suddenly glows red-hot and sparks. That's what happened when I met Lewey Koep.

"I don't have a pattern for Montana," he told me. He untied my ropes with a few quick jerks, sneering at the clumsiness of the knots. Then he sat in his desk chair again, and watched me get my bearings.

"I don't want anything tattooed on me, Mr. Koep," I said. "It's a kind of revenge plot."

He sat in silence, in a waiting quiet, hands folded and face composed. By now I knew I was safe, but I had nowhere to go, and so I sat down on a pile of magazines. He asked, "What revenge?" and I told him the story, the whole thing right from the beginning, when I walked into the bingo hall. I left out the personal details about Serena and me, but he got the picture. I told him about the van.

"That's an unusual piece of good fortune."

"Have you ever had any? Good fortune?"

"All the time. Those guys paid plenty, for instance, though I suppose they'll want it back. You pick out a design. You can owe me."

He opened a book he had on the table, a notebook with plastic pages that clipped in and out, and handed it over to me. I didn't want a tattoo, but I didn't want to disappoint this man, either. I leafed through the dragons and the hearts, thinking how to refuse, and then suddenly I saw the horse. It was the same picture that had come into my head as I sat in the woods. Now here it was. The pony skimmed, legs outstretched, reaching for the edge of the page. I got a thought in my head, clear and vital, that this little horse would convince Serena I was serious about her.

"This one."

Lewey nodded, and heated his tools.

CR

That's how I got it put on, that little horse, and suffered pain. Now my hand won't let me rest. It throbs and aches as if it was coming alive again after a hard frost had made it numb. I know I'm going somewhere, taking this hand to Serena. Even walking down the road in a pair of big-waisted green pants belonging to Lewey Koep, toward the So Long Bar, where I keep everything I own in life, I'm going forward. My hand is a ball of pins, but when I look down I see the little black horse running hard, fast, and serious.

I'm ready for what will come next. That's why I don't fall on the ground, and I don't yell, when I come across the van in a field. At first, I think it is the dream van, the way I always see it in my vision. Then I look, and it's the real vehicle. Totalled.

My bingo van is smashed on the sides, kicked and scratched, and the insides are scattered. Stereo wires, glass, and ripped pieces of carpet are spread here and there among the new sprouts of wheat. I force open a door that is bent inward. I wedge myself behind the wheel, which is tipped over at a crazy angle, and I look out. The windshield is shattered in a sunlight burst, through which the world is cut to bits.

I've been up all night, and the day stretches long before me, so I decide to sleep where I am. Part of the seat is still wonderfully upholstered, thick and plush, and it reclines now — permanently, but so what? I relax into the small comfort, my body as warm as an animal, my thoughts drifting. I know I'll wake to nothing, but at this moment I feel rich. Sinking away, I feel like everything worth having is within my grasp. All I have to do is put my hand into the emptiness.

SOCR

Louise Erdrich is perhaps the most prolific and critically acclaimed Native American writer. She grew up in Wahpeton, North Dakota, and is a member of the Turtle Mountain Band of the Anishinabe (Chippewa), which provides the setting for virtually all of her works, including "The Bingo Van." Her desire to transmit a sense of place and the history of the people who have inhabited it likens her to one of her strongest influences, William Faulkner, and his Yoknapatawpha County. Erdrich's greatest literary debt, though, lies with her mother Rita and great-uncle Ben Gourneau, both master storytellers. "The Bingo Van" focuses on one of Erdrich's many reappearing characters, the isolated and self-deprecating Lipsha, who receives an epiphany by the end of the story, an insight that he does not share with his readers. One way of deciphering what Lipsha knows is through the supporting cast of characters, each of whom, on one level at least, exists to teach Lipsha a lesson of some kind. The two major symbols of the story, the van and the little horse, which represent, among other things, differing value systems, also act as indexes of Lipsha's final realization. One of the few generalizations about Native American writers that one might make is that they tend to use symbolism more frequently than their non-Native counterparts. This is partly due to the fact that most tribal ceremonies revolve around central symbols (and colours), and also because symbols can be such rich devices: a single object may embody and represent many different, often vibrantly contradictory, ideas.

B.S.

WILLIAM FAULKNER *(1897-1962)*

A Rose for Emily

When Miss Emily Grierson died, our whole town went to her funeral: the men through a sort of respectful affection for a fallen monument, the women mostly out of curiosity to see the inside of her house, which no one save an old manservant — a combined gardener and cook — had seen in at least ten years.

It was a big, squarish frame house that had once been white, decorated with cupolas and spires and scrolled balconies in the heavily lightsome style of the seventies, set on what had once been our most select street. But garages and cotton gins had encroached and obliterated even the august names of that neighbourhood; only Miss Emily's house was left, lifting its stubborn and coquettish decay above the cotton wagons and the gasoline pumps — an eyesore among eyesores. And now Miss Emily had gone to join the representatives of those august names where they lay in the cedar-bemused cemetery among the ranked and anonymous graves of Union and Confederate soldiers who fell at the battle of Jefferson.

Alive, Miss Emily had been a tradition, a duty, and a care; a sort of hereditary obligation upon the town, dating from that day in 1894 when Colonel Sartoris, the mayor — he who fathered the edict that no Negro woman should appear on the streets without an apron — remitted her taxes, the dispensation dating from the death of her father on into perpetuity. Not that Miss Emily would have accepted charity. Colonel Sartoris invented an involved tale to the effect that Miss Emily's father had loaned money to the town, which the town, as a matter of business, preferred this way of repaying. Only a man of Colonel Sartoris' generation and thought could have invented it, and only a woman could have believed it.

When the next generation, with its more modern ideas, became mayors and aldermen, this arrangement created some little dissatisfaction. On the first of the year they mailed her a tax notice. February came, and there was no reply. They wrote her a formal letter, asking her to call at the sheriff's office at her convenience. A week later the mayor wrote her himself, offering to call or to send his car for her, and received in reply a note on paper of an archaic shape, in a thin, flowing calligraphy in faded ink, to the effect that she no longer went out at all. The tax notice was also enclosed, without comment.

They called a special meeting of the Board of Aldermen. A deputation waited upon her, knocked at the door through which no visitor had passed since she ceased giving china-painting lessons eight or ten years earlier. They were admitted by the old Negro into a dim hall from which a stairway mounted into still more shadow. It smelled of dust and disuse — a close, dank smell. The Negro led them into the parlour. It was furnished in heavy, leather-covered furniture. When the Negro opened the blinds of one window, they could see that the leather was cracked; and when they sat down, a faint dust rose sluggishly about their thighs, spinning with slow motes in the single sun-ray. On a tarnished gilt easel before the fireplace stood a crayon portrait of Miss Emily's father.

They rose when she entered — a small, fat woman in black, with a thin gold chain descending to her waist and vanishing into her belt, leaning on an ebony cane with a tarnished gold head. Her skeleton was small and spare; perhaps that was why what would have been merely plumpness in another was obesity in her. She looked bloated, like a body long submerged in motionless water, and of that pallid hue. Her eyes, lost in the fatty ridges of her face, looked like two small pieces of coal pressed into a lump of dough as they moved from one face to another while the visitors stated their errand.

She did not ask them to sit. She just stood in the door and listened quietly until the spokesman came to a stumbling halt. Then they could hear the invisible watch ticking at the end of the gold chain.

Her voice was dry and cold. "I have no taxes in Jefferson. Colonel Sartoris explained it to me. Perhaps one of you can gain access to the city records and satisfy yourselves."

"But we have. We are the city authorities, Miss Emily. Didn't you get a notice from the sheriff, signed by him?"

"I received a paper, yes," Miss Emily said. "Perhaps he considers himself the sheriff. . . I have no taxes in Jefferson."

"But there is nothing on the books to show that, you see. We must go by the —"

"See Colonel Sartoris. I have no taxes in Jefferson."

"But, Miss Emily —"

"See Colonel Sartoris." (Colonel Sartoris had been dead almost ten years.) "I have no taxes in Jefferson. Tobe!" The Negro appeared. "Show these gentlemen out."

જી

So she vanquished them, horse and foot, just as she had vanquished their fathers thirty years before about the smell. That was two years after her father's death and a short time after her sweetheart — the one we believed would marry her — had deserted her. After her father's death she went out very little; after her sweetheart went away, people hardly saw her at all. A few of the ladies had the temerity to call, but were not received, and the only sign of life about the place was the Negro man — a young man then — going in and out with a market basket.

"Just as if a man — any man — could keep a kitchen properly," the ladies said; so they were not surprised when the smell developed. It was another link between the gross, teeming world and the high and mighty Griersons.

A neighbour, a woman, complained to the mayor, Judge Stevens, eighty years old.

"But what will you have me do about it, madam?" he said.

"Why, send her word to stop it," the woman said. "Isn't there a law?"

"I'm sure that won't be necessary," Judge Stevens said, "It's probably just a snake or a rat that nigger of hers killed in the yard. I'll speak to him about it."

The next day he received two more complaints, one from a man who came in diffident deprecation. "We really must do something about it, Judge. I'd be the last one in the world to bother Miss Emily, but we've got to do something." That night the Board of Aldermen met — three grey-beards and one younger man, a member of the rising generation.

"It's simple enough," he said. "Send her word to have her place cleaned up. Give her a certain time to do it in, and if she don't. . ."

"Dammit, sir," Judge Stevens said, "Will you accuse a lady to her face of smelling bad?"

So the next night, after midnight, four men crossed Miss Emily's lawn and slunk about the house like burglars, sniffing along the base of the brickwork and at the cellar openings while one of them performed a regular sowing motion with his hand out of a sack slung from his shoulder. They broke open the cellar door and sprinkled lime there, and in all the outbuildings. As they recrossed the lawn, a window that had been dark was lighted and Miss Emily sat in it, the light behind her, and her upright torso motionless as that of an idol. They crept quietly across the lawn and into the shadow of the locusts that lined the street. After a week or two the smell went away.

That was when people had begun to feel really sorry for her. People in our town, remembering how old lady Wyatt, her great-aunt, had gone completely crazy at last, believed that the Griersons held themselves a little too high for what they really were. None of the young men were quite good enough for Miss Emily and such. We had long thought of them as a tableau, Miss Emily a slender figure in white in the background, her father a spraddled silhouette in the foreground, his back to her and clutching a horsewhip, the two of them framed by the back-flung front door. So when she got to be thirty and was still single, we were not pleased exactly, but vindicated; even with insanity in the family she wouldn't have turned down all of her chances if they had really materialized.

When her father died, it got about that the house was all that was left to her; and in a way, people were glad. At last they could pity Miss Emily. Being left alone, and a pauper, she had become humanized. Now she too would know the old thrill and the old despair of a penny more or less.

The day after his death all the ladies prepared to call at the house and offer condolence and aid, as is our custom. Miss Emily met them at the door, dressed as usual and with no trace of grief on her face. She told them that her father was not dead. She did that for three days, with the ministers calling on her, and the doctors, trying to persuade her to let them dispose of the body. Just as they were about to resort to law and force, she broke down, and they buried her father quickly.

We did not say she was crazy then. We believed she had to do that. We remembered all the young men her father had driven away, and we knew that with nothing left, she would have to cling to that which had robbed her, as people will.

℧

She was sick for a long time. When we saw her again, her hair was cut short, making her look like a girl, with a vague resemblance to those angels in coloured church windows — sort of tragic and serene.

The town had just let the contracts for paving the sidewalks, and in the summer after her father's death they began to work. The construction company came with niggers and mules and machinery, and a foreman named Homer Barron, a Yankee — a big, dark, ready man, with a big voice and eyes lighter than his face. The little boys would follow in groups to hear him cuss the niggers, and the niggers singing in time to the rise and fall of picks. Pretty soon he knew everybody in town. Whenever you heard a lot of laughing anywhere about the square, Homer Barron would be in the center of the group. Presently we began to see him and Miss Emily on Sunday afternoons driving in the yellow-wheeled buggy and the matched team of bays from the livery stable.

At first we were glad that Miss Emily would have an interest, because the ladies all said, "Of course a Grierson would not think seriously of a Northerner, a day labourer." But there were still others, older people, who said that even grief could not cause a real lady to forget *noblesse oblige* — without calling it *noblesse oblige*. They just said, "Poor Emily. Her kinsfolk should come to her." She had some kin in Alabama; but years ago her father had fallen out with them over the estate of old lady Wyatt, the crazy woman, and there was no communication between the two families. They had not even been represented at the funeral.

And as soon as the old people said, "Poor Emily," the whispering began. "Do you suppose it's really so?" they said to one another. "Of course it is. What else could . . ." This behind their hands; rustling of craned silk and satin behind jalousies closed upon the sun of Sunday afternoon as the thin, swift clop-clop-clop of the matched team passed: "Poor Emily."

She carried her head high enough — even when we believed that she was fallen. It was as if she demanded more than ever the recognition of her dignity as the last Grierson; as if it had wanted that touch of earthiness to reaffirm her imperviousness. Like when she bought the rat poison, the arsenic. That was over a year after they had begun to say "Poor Emily," and while the two female cousins were visiting her.

"I want some poison," she said to the druggist. She was over thirty then, still a slight woman, though thinner than usual, with cold, haughty black eyes in a face the flesh of which was strained across the temples and about the eyesockets as you imagine a lighthouse-keeper's face ought to look. "I want some poison," she said.

"Yes, Miss Emily. What kind? For rats and such? I'd recom —"

"I want the best you have. I don't care what kind."

The druggist named several. "They'll kill anything up to an elephant. But what you want is —"

"Arsenic," Miss Emily said. "Is that a good one?"

"Is . . . arsenic? Yes, ma'am. But what you want —"

"I want arsenic."

The druggist looked down at her. She looked back at him, erect, her face like a strained flag. "Why, of course," the druggist said. "If that's what you want. But the law requires you to tell what you are going to use it for."

Miss Emily just stared at him, her head tilted back in order to look him eye for eye, until he looked away and went and got the arsenic and wrapped it up. The Negro delivery boy brought her the package; the druggist didn't come back. When she opened the package at home there was written on the box, under the skull and bones: "For rats."

CR

So the next day we all said, "She will kill herself"; and we said it would be the best thing. When she had first begun to be seen with Homer Barron, we had said, "She will marry him." Then we said, "She will persuade him yet," because Homer himself had remarked — he liked men, and it was known that he drank with the younger men in the Elks' Club — that he was not a marrying man. Later we said, "Poor Emily" behind the jalousies as they passed on Sunday afternoon in the glittering buggy, Miss Emily with her head high and Homer Barron with his hat cocked and a cigar in his teeth, reins and whip in a yellow glove.

Then some of the ladies began to say that it was a disgrace to the town and a bad example to the young people. The men did not want to interfere, but at last the ladies forced the Baptist minister — Miss Emily's people were Episcopal — to call upon her. He would never divulge what happened during that interview, but he refused to go back again. The next Sunday they again drove about the streets, and the following day the minister's wife wrote to Miss Emily's relations in Alabama.

So she had blood-kin under her roof again and we sat back to watch developments. At first nothing happened. Then we were sure that they were to be married. We learned that Miss Emily had been to the jeweler's and ordered a man's toilet set in silver, with the letters H.B. on each piece. Two days later we learned that she had bought a complete outfit of men's clothing, including a nightshirt, and we said, "They are married." We were really glad. We were glad because the two female cousins were even more Grierson than Miss Emily had ever been.

So we were not surprised when Homer Barron — the streets had been finished some time since — was gone. We were a little disappointed that there was not a public blowing-off, but we believed that he had gone on to prepare for Miss Emily's coming, or to give her a chance to get rid of the cousins. (By that time it was a cabal, and we were all Miss Emily's allies to help circumvent the cousins.) Sure enough, after another week they departed. And, as we had expected all along, within three days Homer Barron was back in town. A neighbour saw the Negro man admit him at the kitchen door at dusk one evening.

And that was the last we saw of Homer Barron. And of Miss Emily for some time. The Negro man went in and out with the market basket, but the front door remained closed. Now and then we would see her at a window for a moment, as the men did that night when they sprinkled the lime, but for almost six months she did not appear on the streets. Then we knew that this was to be expected too; as if that quality of her father which had thwarted her woman's life so many times had been too virulent and too furious to die.

When we next saw Miss Emily, she had grown fat and her hair was turning grey. During the next few years it grew greyer and greyer until it attained an even pepper-and-salt iron-grey, when it ceased turning. Up to the day of her death at seventy-four it was still that vigorous iron-grey, like the hair of an active man.

From that time on her front door remained closed, save for a period of six or seven years, when she was about forty, during which she gave lessons in china-painting. She fitted up a studio in one of the downstairs rooms, where the daughters and granddaughters of Colonel Sartoris' contemporaries were sent to her with the same regularity and in the same spirit that they were sent to church on Sundays with a twenty-five-cent piece for the collection plate. Meanwhile her taxes had been remitted.

Then the newer generation became the backbone and the spirit of the town, and the painting pupils grew up and fell away and did not send their children to her with boxes of colour and tedious brushes and pictures cut from the ladies' magazines. The front door closed upon the last one and remained closed for good. When the town got free postal delivery, Miss Emily alone refused to let them fasten the metal numbers above her door and attach a mailbox to it. She would not listen to them.

Daily, monthly, yearly we watched the Negro grow greyer and more stooped, going in and out with the market basket. Each December we sent her a tax notice, which would be returned by the post office a week later, unclaimed. Now and then we would see her in one of the downstairs windows — she had evidently shut up the top floor of the house — like the carven torso of an idol in a niche, looking or not looking at us, we could never tell which. Thus she passed from generation to generation — dear, inescapable, impervious, tranquil, and perverse.

And so she died. Fell ill in the house filled with dust and shadows, with only a doddering Negro man to wait on her. We did not even know she was sick; we had long since given up trying to get any information from the Negro. He talked to no one, probably not even to her, for his voice had grown harsh and rusty, as if from disuse.

She died in one of the downstairs rooms, in a heavy walnut bed with a curtain, her grey head propped on a pillow, yellow and mouldy with age and lack of sunlight.

CR

The Negro met the first of the ladies at the front door and let them in, with their hushed, sibilant voices and their quick, curious glances, and then he disappeared. He walked right through the house and out the back and was not seen again.

The two female cousins came at once. They held the funeral on the second day, with the town coming to look at Miss Emily beneath a mass of bought flowers, with the crayon face of her father musing profoundly above the bier and the ladies sibilant and macabre; and the very old men — some in their brushed Confederate uniforms — on the porch and the lawn, talking of Miss Emily as if she had been a contemporary of theirs, believing that they had danced with her and courted her perhaps, confusing time with its mathematical progression, as the old do, to whom all the past is not a diminishing road, but, instead, a huge meadow which no winter ever quite touches, divided from them now by the narrow bottleneck of the most recent decade of years.

Already we knew that there was one room in that region above stairs which no one had seen in forty years, and which would have to be forced. They waited until Miss Emily was decently in the ground before they opened it.

The violence of breaking down the door seemed to fill this room with pervading dust. A thin, acrid pall as of the tomb seemed to lie everywhere upon this room decked and furnished as for a bridal: upon the valance curtains of faded rose colour, upon the rose-shaded lights, upon the dressing table, upon the delicate array of crystal and the man's toilet things backed with tarnished silver, silver so tarnished that the monogram was obscured. Among them lay a collar and tie, as if they had just been removed, which, lifted, left upon the surface a pale crescent in the dust. Upon a chair hung the suit, carefully folded; beneath it the two mute shoes and the discarded socks.

The man himself lay in the bed.

For a long while we just stood there, looking down at the profound and fleshless grin. The body had apparently once lain in the attitude of an embrace, but now the long sleep that outlasts love, that conquers even the grimace of love, had cuckolded him. What was left of him, rotted beneath what was left of the nightshirt, had become inextricable from the bed in which he lay; and upon him and upon the pillow beside him lay that even coating of the patient and biding dust.

Then we noticed that in the second pillow was the indentation of a head. One of us lifted something from it, and leaning forward, that faint and invisible dust dry and acrid in the nostrils, we saw a long strand of iron-grey hair.

ℰↃℭℛ

Like many good stories, "A Rose for Emily" has mystery at its heart. This results partly from the chronology: the narrator, who seems to be a spokesperson for the town, begins with Emily's death and the questions it raises for us. Rather than answering them directly, he flashes back many years and works forward to her funeral and the gruesome discovery. We learn part of the truth about what happened to Homer Barron, the Yankee who had called on Miss Emily but was not a marrying man; the image of a strand of Emily's hair on the pillow beside his dead body is, of course, seriously creepy. Why did Faulkner write such a bizarre tale? This Southern Gothic horror story suggests something important about what it means to be human — how we hold on, whether to traditions or people or ways of thinking, in order to shore up our identities or find security in a changing world. Miss Emily, whose character is the biggest mystery of all, can be seen to represent the Old South, her class, her gender or, perhaps, all of those who cling to the past. Finally, there is a puzzle in the title: what is the "rose" for Emily? Who is providing the gift? And why?

A.M.

Richard Ford *(b. 1944)*

Sweethearts

I was standing in the kitchen while Arlene was in the living room saying good-bye to her ex-husband, Bobby. I had already been out to the store for groceries and come back and made coffee, and was drinking it and staring out the window while the two of them said whatever they had to say. It was a quarter to six in the morning.

This was not going to be a good day in Bobby's life, that was clear, because he was headed to jail. He had written several bad checks, and before he could be sentenced for that he had robbed a convenience store with a pistol — completely gone off his mind. And everything had gone to hell, as you might expect. Arlene had put up the money for his bail, and there was some expensive talk about an appeal. But there wasn't any use to that. He was guilty. It would cost money and then he would go to jail anyway.

Arlene had said she would drive him to the sheriff's department this morning, if I would fix him breakfast, so he could surrender on a full stomach, and that had seemed all right. Early in the morning Bobby had brought his motorcycle around to the backyard and tied up his dog to the handlebars. I had watched him from the window. He hugged the dog, kissed it on the head and whispered something in its ear, then came inside. The dog was a black Lab, and it sat beside the motorcycle now and stared with blank interest across the river at the buildings of town, where the sky was beginning to turn pinkish and the day was opening up. It was going to be our dog for a while now, I guessed.

Arlene and I had been together almost a year. She had divorced Bobby long before and had gone back to school and gotten real estate training and bought the house we lived in, then quit that and taught high school a year, and finally quit that and just went to work in a bar in town, which is where I came upon her. She and Bobby had been childhood sweethearts and run crazy for fifteen years. But when I came into the picture, things with Bobby were settled, more or less. No one had hard feelings left, and when he came around I didn't have any trouble with him. We had things we talked about — our pasts, our past troubles. It was not the worst you could hope for.

From the living room I heard Bobby say, "So how am I going to keep up my self-respect. Answer me that. That's my big problem."

"You have to get centered," Arlene said in an upbeat voice. "Be within yourself if you can."

"I feel like I'm catching a cold right now," Bobby said. "On the day I enter prison I catch cold."

"Take Contac," Arlene said. "I've got some somewhere." I heard a chair scrape the floor. She was going to get it for him.

"I already took that," Bobby said. "I had some at home."

"You'll feel better then," Arlene said. "They'll have Contac in prison."

"I put all my faith in women," Bobby said softly. "I see now that was wrong."

"I couldn't say," Arlene said. And then no one spoke.

I looked out the window at Bobby's dog. It was still staring across the river at town as if it knew about something there.

The door to the back bedroom opened then, and my daughter Cherry came out wearing her little white nightgown with red valentines on it. BE MINE was on all the valentines. She was still asleep, though she was up. Bobby's voice had waked her up.

"Did you feed my fish?" she said and stared at me. She was barefoot and holding a doll, and looked pretty as a doll herself.

"You were asleep already," I said.

She shook her head and looked at the open living-room door. "Who's that?" she said.

"Bobby's here," I said. "He's talking to Arlene."

Cherry came over to the window where I was and looked out at Bobby's dog. She liked Bobby, but she liked his dog better. "There's Buck," she said. Buck was the dog's name. A tube of sausage was lying on the sink top and I wanted to cook it, for Bobby to eat, and then have him get out. I wanted Cherry to go to school, and for the day to flatten out and hold fewer people in it. Just Arlene and me would be enough.

"You know, Bobby, sweetheart," Arlene said now in the other room, "in our own lifetime we'll see the last of the people who were born in the nineteenth century. They'll all be gone soon. Every one of them."

"We should've stayed together, I think," Bobby whispered. I was not supposed to hear that, I knew. "I wouldn't be going to prison if we'd loved each other."

"I wanted to get divorced, though," Arlene said.

"That was a stupid idea."

"Not for me it wasn't," Arlene said. I heard her stand up.

"It's water over the bridge now, I guess, isn't it?" I heard Bobby's hands hit his knees three times in a row.

"Let's watch TV," Cherry said to me, and went and turned on the little set on the kitchen table. There was a man talking on a news show.

"Not loud," I said. "Keep it soft."

"Let's let Buck in," she said. "Buck's lonely."

"Leave Buck outside," I said.

Cherry looked at me without any interest. She left her doll on top of the TV. "Poor Buck," she said. "Buck's crying. Do you hear him?"

"No," I said. "I can't hear him."

⌘

Bobby ate his eggs and stared out the window as if he was having a hard time concentrating on what he was doing. Bobby is a handsome small man with thick black hair and pale eyes. He is likable, and it is easy to see why women would like him. This morning he was dressed in jeans and a red T-shirt and boots. He looked like somebody on his way to jail.

He stared out the back window for a long time and then he sniffed and nodded. "You have to face that empty moment, Russ." He cut his eyes at me. "How often have you done that?"

"Russ's done that, Bob," Arlene said. "We've all done that now. We're adults."

"Well, that's where I am right now," Bobby said. "I'm at the empty moment here. I've lost everything."

"You're among friends, though, sweetheart." Arlene smiled. She was smoking a cigarette.

"I'm calling you up. Guess who I am," Cherry said to Bobby. She had her eyes squeezed tight and her nose and mouth pinched up together. She was moving her head back and forth.

"Who are you?" Bobby said and smiled.

"I'm the bumblebee."

"Can't you fly?" Arlene said.

"No. My wings are much too short and I'm too fat." Cherry opened her eyes at us suddenly.

"Well, you're in big trouble then," Arlene said.

"A turkey can go forty-five miles an hour," Cherry said and looked shocked.

"Go change your clothes," I said.

"Go ahead now, sweetheart." Arlene smiled at her. "I'll come help you."

Cherry squinted at Bobby, then went back to her room. When she opened her door I could see her aquarium in the dark against the wall, a pale green light with pink rocks and tiny dots of fish.

Bobby ran his hands back through his hair and stared up at the ceiling. "Okay," he said, "here's the awful criminal now, ready for jail." He looked at us then, and he looked wild, as wild and desperate as I have ever seen a man look. And it was not for no reason.

"That's off the wall," Arlene said. "That's just completely boring. I'd never be married to a man who was a fucking criminal." She looked at me, but Bobby looked at me too.

"Somebody ought to come take her away," Bobby said. "You know that, Russell? Just put her in a truck and take her away. She always has such a wonderful fucking outlook. You wonder how she got in this fix here." He looked around the little kitchen, which was shabby and white. At one time Arlene's house had been a jewelry store, and there was a black security camera above the kitchen door, though it wasn't connected now.

"Just try to be nice, Bobby," Arlene said.

"I just oughta slap you," Bobby said, and I could see his jaw muscles tighten, and I thought he might slap her then. In the bedroom I saw Cherry standing naked in the dark, sprinkling food in her aquarium. The light made her skin look the colour of water.

"Try to calm down, Bob," I said and stayed put in my chair. "We're all your friends."

"I don't know why people came out here," Bobby said. "The West is fucked up. It's ruined. I wish somebody would take me away from here."

"Somebody's going to, I guess," Arlene said, and I knew she was mad at him and I didn't blame her, though I wished she hadn't said that.

Bobby's blue eyes got small, and he smiled at her in a hateful way. I could see Cherry looking in at us. She had not heard this kind of talk yet. Jail talk. Mean talk. The kind you don't forget. "Do you think I'm jealous of you two?" Bobby said. "Is that it?"

"I don't know what you are," Arlene said.

"Well, I'm not. I'm not jealous of you two. I don't want a kid. I don't want a house. I don't want anything you got. I'd rather go to Deer Lodge." His eyes flashed out at us.

"That's lucky, then," Arlene said. She stubbed out her cigarette on her plate, blew smoke, then stood up to go help Cherry. "Here I am now, hon," she said and closed the bedroom door.

Bobby sat at the kitchen table for a while and did not say anything. I knew he was mad but that he was not mad at me. Probably, in fact, he couldn't even think why I was the one here with him now — some man he hardly knew, who slept with a woman he had loved all his life and, at that moment, thought he still loved, but who — among his other troubles — didn't love him anymore. I knew he wanted to say that and a hundred things more then. But words can seem weak. And I felt sorry for him, and wanted to be as sympathetic as I could be.

"I don't like to tell people I'm divorced, Russell," Bobby said very clearly and blinked his eyes. "Does that make any sense to you?" He looked at me as if he thought I was going to lie to him, which I wasn't.

"That makes plenty of sense," I said.

"You've been married, haven't you? You have your daughter."

"That's right," I said.

"You're divorced, aren't you?"

"Yes."

Bobby looked up at the security camera above the kitchen door, and with his finger and thumb made a gun that he pointed at the camera, and made a soft popping with his lips, then he looked at me and smiled. It seemed to make him calmer. It was a strange thing.

"Before my mother died, okay?" Bobby said, "I used to call her on the phone. And it took her a long time to get out of bed. And I used to wait and wait and wait while it rang. And sometimes I knew she just wouldn't answer it, because she couldn't get up. Right? And it would ring forever because it was me, and I was willing to wait. Sometimes I'd just let it ring, and so would she, and I wouldn't know what the fuck was going on. Maybe she was dead, right?" He shook his head.

"I'll bet she knew it was you," I said. "I bet it made her feel better."

"You think?" Bobby said.

"It's possible. It seems possible."

"What would you do, though?" Bobby said. He bit his lower lip and thought about the subject. "When would you let it stop ringing? Would you let it go twenty-five or fifty? I wanted her to have time to decide. But I didn't want to drive her crazy. Okay?"

"Twenty-five seems right," I said.

Bobby nodded. "That's interesting. I guess we all do things different. I always did fifty."

"That's fine."

"Fifty's way too many, I think."

"It's what you think *now*," I said. "But then was different."

"There's a familiar story," Bobby said.

"It's everybody's story," I said. "The then-and-now story."

"We're just short of paradise, aren't we, Russell?"

"Yes we are," I said.

Bobby smiled at me then in a sweet way, a way to let anyone know he wasn't a bad man, no matter what he'd robbed.

"What would you do if you were me," Bobby said, "if you were on your way to Deer Lodge for a year?"

I said, "I'd think about when I was going to get out, and what kind of day that was going to be, and that it wasn't very far in the future."

"I'm just afraid it'll be too noisy to sleep in there," he said and looked concerned about that.

"It'll be all right," I said. "A year can go by quick."

"Not if you never sleep," he said. "That worries me."

"You'll sleep," I said. "You'll sleep fine."

And Bobby looked at me then, across the kitchen table, like a man who knows half of something and who is supposed to know everything, who sees exactly what trouble he's in and is scared to death by it.

"I feel like a dead man, you know?" And tears suddenly came into his pale eyes. "I'm really sorry," he said. "I know you're mad at me. I'm sorry." He put his head in his hands then and cried. And I thought: What else could he do? He couldn't avoid this now. It was all right.

"It's okay, bud," I said.

"I'm happy for you and Arlene, Russ," Bobby said, his face still in tears. "You have my word on that. I just wish she and I had stayed together, and I wasn't such an asshole. You know what I mean?"

"I know exactly," I said. I did not move to touch him, though maybe I should have. But Bobby was not my brother, and for a moment I wished I wasn't tied to all this. I was sorry I had to see any of it, sorry that each of us would have to remember it.

CR

On the drive to town Bobby was in better spirits. He and Cherry sat in the back, and Arlene in the front. I drove. Cherry held Bobby's hand and giggled, and

Bobby let her put on his black silk Cam Ranh Bay jacket he had won playing cards, and Cherry said that she had been a soldier in some war.

The morning had started out sunny, but now it had begun to be foggy, though there was sun high up, and you could see the Bitterroots to the south. The river was cool and in a mist, and from the bridge you could not see the pulp yard or the motels a half mile away.

"Let's just drive, Russ," Bobby said from the backseat. "Head to Idaho. We'll all become Mormons and act right."

"That'd be good, wouldn't it?" Arlene turned and smiled at him. She wasn't mad now. It was her nicest trait, not to stay mad at anybody for long.

"Good day," Cherry said.

"Who's that talking," Bobby asked.

"I'm Paul Harvey," Cherry said.

"He always says that, doesn't he?" Arlene said.

"Good day," Cherry said again.

"That's all Cherry's going to say all day now, Daddy," Arlene said to me.

"You've got a honeybunch back here," Bobby said and tickled Cherry's ribs. "She's her daddy's girl all the way."

"Good day," Cherry said again and giggled.

"Children pick up your life, don't they, Russ?" Bobby said. "I can tell that."

"Yes, they do," I said. "They can."

"I'm not so sure about that one back there, though," Arlene said. She was dressed in a red cowboy shirt and jeans, and she looked tired to me. But I knew she didn't want Bobby to go to jail by himself.

"I am. I'm sure of it," Bobby said, and then didn't say anything else.

We were on a wide avenue where it was foggy, and there were shopping centres and drive-ins and car lots. A few cars had their headlights on, and Arlene stared out the window at the fog. "You know what I used to want to be?" she said.

"What?" I said when no one else said anything.

Arlene stared a moment out the window and touched the corner of her mouth with her fingernail and smoothed something away. "A Tri-Delt," she said and smiled. "I didn't really know what they were, but I wanted to be one. I was already married to him, then, of course. And they wouldn't take married girls in."

"That's a joke," Bobby said, and Cherry laughed.

"No. It's not a joke," Arlene said. "It's just something you don't understand and that I missed out on in life." She took my hand on the seat and kept looking out the window. And it was as if Bobby wasn't there then, as if he had already gone to jail.

"What I miss is seafood," Bobby said in an ironic way. "Maybe they'll have it in prison. You think they will?"

"I hope so, if you miss it," Arlene said.

"I bet they will," I said. "I bet they have fish of some kind in there."

"Fish and seafood aren't the same," Bobby said.

CR

We turned onto the street where the jail was. It was an older part of town and there were some old white two-storey residences that had been turned into lawyers' offices and bail bondsmen's rooms. Some bars were farther on, and the bus station. At the end of the street was the courthouse. I slowed so we wouldn't get there too fast.

"You're going to jail right now," Cherry said to Bobby.

"Isn't that something?" Bobby said. I watched him up in the rearview; he looked down at Cherry and shook his head as if it amazed him.

"I'm going to school soon as that's over," Cherry said.

"Why don't I just go to school with you?" Bobby said. "I think I'd rather do that."

"No sir," Cherry said.

"Oh Cherry, please don't make me go to jail. I'm innocent," Bobby said. "I don't want to go."

"Too bad," Cherry said and crossed her arms.

"Be nice," Arlene said. Though I know Cherry thought she was being nice. She liked Bobby.

"She's teasing, Mama. Aren't we, Cherry baby? We understand each other."

"I'm not her mama," Arlene said.

"That's right, I forgot," Bobby said. And he widened his eyes at her. "What's your hurry, Russ?" Bobby said, and I saw I had almost come to a stop in the street. The jail was a half block ahead of us. It was a tall modern building built on the back of the old stone courthouse. Two people were standing in the little front yard looking up at a window. A station wagon was parked on the street in front. The fog had begun to burn away now.

"I didn't want to rush you," I said.

"Cherry's already dying for me to go in there, aren't you, baby?"

"No, she's not. She doesn't know anything about that," Arlene said.

"You go to hell," Bobby said. And he grabbed Arlene's shoulder with his hand and squeezed it back hard against the seat. "This is not your business, it's not your business at all. Look, Russ," Bobby said, and he reached in the black plastic bag he was taking with him and pulled a pistol out of it and threw it over onto the front seat between Arlene and me. "I thought I might kill Arlene, but I changed my mind." He grinned at me, and I could tell he was crazy and afraid and at the end of all he could do to help himself anymore.

"Jesus Christ," Arlene said. "Jesus, Jesus Christ."

"Take it, goddamn it. It's for you," Bobby said with a crazy look. "It's what you wanted. Boom," Bobby said. "Boom-boom-boom."

"I'll take it," I said and pulled the gun under my leg. I wanted to get it out of sight.

"What is it?" Cherry said. "Lemme see." She pushed up to see.

"It's nothing, honey," I said. "Just something of Bobby's."

"Is it a gun?" Cherry said.

"No, sweetheart," I said, "it's not." I pushed the gun down on the floor under my foot. I did not know if it was loaded, and I hoped it wasn't. I wanted

Bobby out of the car then. I have had my troubles, but I am not a person who likes violence or guns. I pulled over to the curb in front of the jail, behind the brown station wagon. "You better make a move now," I said to Bobby. I looked at Arlene, but she was staring straight ahead. I know she wanted Bobby gone, too.

"I didn't plan this. This just happened," Bobby said. "Okay? You understand that? Nothing's planned."

"Get out," Arlene said and did not turn to look at him.

"Give Bobby back his jacket," I said to Cherry.

"Forget it, it's yours," Bobby said. And he grabbed his plastic string bag.

"She doesn't want it," Arlene said.

"Yes I do," Cherry said. "I want it."

"Okay," I said. "That's nice, sweetheart."

Bobby sat in the seat and did not move then. None of us moved in the car. I could see out the window into the little jailyard. Two Indians were sitting in plastic chairs outside the double doors. A man in a grey uniform stepped out the door and said something to them, and one got up and went inside. There was a large, red-faced woman standing on the grass, staring at our car.

I got out and walked around the car to Bobby's door and opened it. It was cool out, and I could smell the sour pulp-mill smell being held in the fog, and I could hear a car laying rubber on another street.

"Bye-bye, Bobby," Cherry said in the car. She reached over and kissed him.

"Bye-bye," Bobby said. "Bye-bye."

The man in the grey uniform had come down off the steps and stopped halfway to the car, watching us. He was waiting for Bobby, I was sure of that.

Bobby got out and stood up on the curb. He looked around and shivered. He looked cold and I felt bad for him. But I would be glad when he was gone and I could live a normal life again.

"What do we do now?" Bobby said. He saw the man in the grey uniform, but would not look at him. Cherry was saying something to Arlene in the car, but Arlene didn't say anything. "Maybe I oughta run for it," Bobby said, and I could see his pale eyes were jumping as if he was eager for something now, eager for things to happen to him. Suddenly he grabbed both my arms and pushed me back against the door and pushed his face right up to my face. "Fight me," he whispered and smiled a wild smile. "Knock the shit out of me. See what they do." I pushed against him, and for a moment he held me there, and I held him, and it was as if we were dancing without moving. And I smelled his breath and felt his cold, thin arms and his body struggling against me, and I knew what he wanted was for me not to let him go, and for all this to be a dream he could forget about.

"What're you doing?" Arlene said, and she turned around and glared at us. She was mad, and she wanted Bobby to be in jail now. "Are you kissing each other?" she said. "Is that what you're doing? Kissing good-bye?"

"We're kissing each other, that's right," Bobby said. "That's what we're doing. I always wanted to kiss Russell. We're queers." He looked at her then, and I know he wanted to say something more to her, to tell her that he hated her or that he loved her or wanted to kill her or that he was sorry. But he couldn't come to the words for that. And I felt him go rigid and shiver, and I didn't know what he would do. Though I knew that in the end he would give in to things and go along without a struggle. He was not a man to struggle against odds. That was his character, and it is the character of many people.

"Isn't this the height of something, Russell?" Bobby said, and I knew he was going to be calm now. He let go my arms and shook his head. "You and me out here like trash, fighting over a woman."

And there was nothing I could say then that would save him or make life better for him at that moment or change the way he saw things. And I went and got back in the car while Bobby turned himself in to the uniformed man who was waiting.

CR

I drove Cherry to school then, and when I came back outside Arlene had risen to a better mood and suggested that we take a drive. She didn't start work until noon, and I had the whole day to wait until Cherry came home. "We should open up some emotional distance," she said. And that seemed right to me.

We drove up onto the interstate and went toward Spokane, where I had lived once and Arlene had, too, though we didn't know each other then — the old days, before marriage and children and divorce, before we met the lives we would eventually lead, and that we would be happy with or not.

We drove along the Clark Fork for a while, above the fog that stayed with the river, until the river turned north and there seemed less reason to be driving anywhere. For a time I thought we should just drive to Spokane and put up in a motel. But that, even I knew, was not a good idea. And when we had driven on far enough for each of us to think about things besides Bobby, Arlene said, "Let's throw that gun away, Russ." I had forgotten all about it, and I moved it on the floor with my foot to where I could see it — the gun Bobby had used, I guessed, to commit crimes and steal people's money for some crazy reason. "Let's throw it in the river," Arlene said. And I turned the car around.

We drove back to where the river turned down even with the highway again, and went off on a dirt-and-gravel road for a mile. I stopped under some pine trees and picked up the gun and looked at it to see if it was loaded and found it wasn't. Then Arlene took it by the barrel and flung it out the window without even leaving the car, spun it not very far from the bank, but into deep water where it hit with no splash and was gone in an instant. "Maybe that'll change his luck," I said. And I felt better about Bobby for having the gun out of the car, as if he was safer now, in less danger of ruining his life and other people's, too.

When we had sat there for a minute or two, Arlene said, "Did he ever cry? When you two were sitting in the kitchen? I wondered about that."

"No," I said. "He was scared. But I don't blame him for that."

"What did he say?" And she looked as if the subject interested her now, whereas before it hadn't.

"He didn't say too much. He said he loved you, which I knew anyway."

Arlene looked out the side window at the river. There were still traces of fog that had not burned off in the sun. Maybe it was nine o'clock in the morning. You could hear the interstate back behind us, trucks going east at high speed.

"I'm not real unhappy that Bobby's out of the picture now. I have to say that," Arlene said. "I should be more — I guess — sympathetic. It's hard to love pain if you're me, though."

"It's not really my business," I said. And I truly did not think it was or ever would be. It was not where my life was leading me, I hoped.

"Maybe if I'm drunk enough someday I'll tell you about how we got apart," Arlene said. She opened the glove box and got out a package of cigarettes and closed the latch with her foot. "Nothing should surprise anyone, though, when the sun goes down. I'll just say that. It's all just melodrama." She thumped the pack against the heel of her hand and put her feet up on the dash. And I thought about poor Bobby, being frisked and handcuffed out in the yard of the jail and being led away to become a prisoner, like a piece of useless machinery. I didn't think anyone could blame him for anything he ever thought or said or became after that. He could die in jail and we would still be outside and free. "Would you tell me something if I asked you?" Arlene said, opening her package of cigarettes. "Your word's worth something, isn't it?"

"To me it is," I said.

She looked over at me and smiled because that was a question she had asked me before, and an answer I had said. She reached across the car seat and squeezed my hand, then looked down the gravel road to where the Clark Fork went north and the receding fog had changed the colours of the trees and made them greener and the moving water a darker shade of blue-black.

"What do you think when you get in bed with me every night? I don't know why I want to know that. I just do," Arlene said. "It seems important to me."

And in truth I did not have to think about that at all, because I knew the answer, and had thought about it already, had wondered, in fact, if it was in my mind because of the time in my life it was, or because a former husband was involved, or because I had a daughter to raise alone, and no one else I could be absolutely sure of.

"I just think," I said, "here's another day that's gone. A day I've had with you. And now it's over."

"There's some loss in that, isn't there?" Arlene nodded at me and smiled.

"I guess so," I said.

"It's not so all-bad though, is it? There can be a next day."

"That's true," I said.

"We don't know where any of this is going, do we?" she said, and she squeezed my hand tight.

"No," I said. And I knew that was not a bad thing at all, not for anyone, in any life.

"You're not going to leave me for some other woman, now, are you? You're still my sweetheart. I'm not crazy, am I?"

"I never thought that," I said.

"It's your hole card, you know," Arlene said. "You can't leave twice. Bobby proved that." She smiled at me again.

And I knew she was right about that, though I did not want to hear about Bobby anymore for a while. He and I were not alike. Arlene and I had nothing to do with him. Though I knew, then, how you became a criminal in the world and lost it all. Somehow, and for no apparent reason, your decisions got tipped over and you lost your hold. And one day you woke up and you found yourself in the very situation you said you would never ever be in, and you did not know what was most important to you anymore. And after *that*, it was all over. And I did not want that to happen to me — did not, in fact, think it ever would. I knew what love was about. It was about not giving trouble or inviting it. It was about not leaving a woman for the thought of another one. It was about never being in that place you said you'd never be in. And it was not about being alone. Never that. Never that.

ℰᴏᴄℛ

Although Richard Ford has mostly published novels, including the Pulitzer Prize winning Independence Day, *his short stories are masterful. Often set in the West, they show people suddenly finding themselves at the edge of their lives, or much later, wondering about the repercussions of such moments, perplexed at the invisible process that has somehow made them who they are, live in the manner they do. Ford's characters sense that the most bewildering thing that has happened to them is the passage of time; consequently, discovering a way to tell their stories becomes crucial as they try to navigate among events shared with others and the vicissitudes of memory. The unsettling, potentially violent dramatic situation of "Sweethearts" underscores the story's many layers of sensibility. The characters converse amongst themselves, but they're also speaking past both each other and the present to their unresolved pasts. They're voicing old angers, trying to understand feelings we don't know we have until unforeseen circumstances bring them out. It takes so long, Ford suggests, to learn our own contours. Introducing an anthology of American short fiction, Ford once wrote: "Here's a form which invites more detailed notice — displaying life not as it is, admittedly, but in flashbacks, in hyper-reality, with epiphanies and without." "Sweethearts" exemplifies Ford's aesthetic. The story offers truly startling images taken from the commonplace — the unplugged surveillance camera, the little girl with her valentine nightgown — that, hooking us deeper into the day joining this small group of people, also serve as mnemonic devices, giving us glimpses into what happens in our own lives.*

M.T.

Mavis Gallant (b. 1922)

The Moslem Wife

In the south of France, in the business room of a hotel quite near to the house
where Katherine Mansfield (whom no one in this hotel had ever heard of) was
writing "The Daughters of the Late Colonel," Netta Asher's father announced
that there would never be a man-made catastrophe in Europe again. The dead of
that recent war, the doomed nonsense of the Russian Bolsheviks had finally knocked
sense into European heads. What people wanted now was to get on with life. When
he said "life," he meant its commercial business.

Who would have contradicted Mr. Asher? Certainly not Netta. She did not
understand what he meant quite so well as his French solicitor seemed to, but she
did listen with interest and respect, and then watched him signing papers that, she
knew, concerned her for life. He was renewing the long lease her family held on
the Hotel Prince Albert and Albion. Netta was then eleven. One hundred years
should at least see her through the prime of her life, said Mr. Asher, only half
jokingly, for of course he thought his seed was immortal.

Netta supposed she might easily live to be more than a hundred — at any
rate, for years and years. She knew that her father did not want her to marry until
she was twenty-six and that she was then supposed to have a pair of children, the
elder a boy. Netta and her father and the French lawyer shook hands on the lease,
and she was given her first glass of champagne. The date on the bottle was 1909,
for the year of her birth. Netta bravely pronounced the wine delicious, but her
father said she would know much better vintages before she was through.

Netta remembered the handshake but perhaps not the terms. When the lease
had eighty-eight years to run, she married her first cousin, Jack Ross, which was
not at all what her father had had in mind. Nor would there be the useful pair of
children — Jack couldn't abide them. Like Netta he came from a hotelkeeping
family where the young were like blight. Netta had up to now never shown a scrap
of maternal feeling over anything, but Mr. Asher thought Jack might have made
an amiable parent — a kind one, at least. She consoled Mr. Asher on one count, by
taking the hotel over in his lifetime. The hotel was, to Netta, a natural life; and so
when Mr. Asher, dying, said, "She behaves as I wanted her to," he was right as far
as the drift of Netta's behaviour was concerned but wrong about its course.

The Ashers' hotel was not down on the seafront, though boats and sea could
be had from the south-facing rooms.

Across a road nearly empty of traffic were handsome villas, and behind and to
either side stood healthy olive trees and a large lemon grove. The hotel was painted a
deep ochre with white trim. It had white awnings and green shutters and black iron
balconies as lacquered and shiny as Chinese boxes. It possessed two tennis courts, a
lily pond, a sheltered winter garden, a formal rose garden, and trees full of nightingales.

In the summer dark, *belles-de-nuit* glowed pink, lemon, white, and after their evening watering they gave off a perfume that varied from plant to plant and seemed to match the petals' coloration. In May the nights were dense with stars and fireflies. From the rose garden one might have seen the twin pulse of cigarettes on a balcony, where Jack and Netta sat drinking a last brandy-and-soda before turning in. Most of the rooms were shuttered by then, for no traveller would have dreamed of being south except in winter. Jack and Netta and a few servants had the whole place to themselves. Netta would hire workmen and have the rooms that needed it repainted — the blue cardroom, and the red-walled bar, and the white dining room, where Victorian mirrors gave back glossy walls and blown curtains and nineteenth-century views of the Ligurian coast, the work of an Asher great-uncle. Everything upstairs and down was soaked and wiped and polished, and even the pictures were relentlessly washed with soft cloths and ordinary laundry soap. Netta also had the boiler overhauled and the linen mended and new monograms embroidered and the looking glasses resilvered and the shutters taken off their hinges and scraped and made spruce green again for next year's sun to fade, while Jack talked about decorators and expert gardeners and even wrote to some, and banged tennis balls against the large new garage. He also read books and translated poetry for its own sake and practised playing the clarinet. He had studied music once, and still thought that an important life, a musical life, was there in the middle distance. One summer, just to see if he could, he translated pages of St. John Perse, which were as blank as the garage wall to Netta, in any tongue.

Netta adored every minute of her life, and she thought Jack had a good life too, with nearly half the year for the pleasures that suited him. As soon as the grounds and rooms and cellar and roof had been put to rights, she and Jack packed and went travelling somewhere. Jack made plans. He was never so cheerful as when buying Baedekers and dragging out their stickered trunks. But Netta was nothing of a traveller. She would have been glad to see the same sun rising out of the same sea from the window every day until she died. She loved Jack, and what she liked best after him was the hotel. It was a place where, once, people had come to die of tuberculosis, yet it held no trace or feeling of danger. When Netta walked with her workmen through sheeted summer rooms, hearing the cicadas and hearing Jack start, stop, start some deeply alien music (alien even when her memory automatically gave her a composer's name), she was reminded that here the dead had never been allowed to corrupt the living; the dead had been dressed for an outing and removed as soon as their first muscular stiffness relaxed. Some were wheeled out in chairs, sitting, and some reclined on portable cots, as if merely resting.

That is why there is no bad atmosphere here, she would say to herself. Death has been swept away, discarded. When the shutters are closed on a room, it is for sleep or for love. Netta could think this easily because neither she nor Jack was ever sick. They knew nothing about insomnia, and they made love every day of their lives — they had married in order to be able to.

Spring had been the season for dying in the old days. Invalids who had struggled through the dark comfort of winter took fright as the night receded. They felt without protection. Netta knew about this, and about the difference between darkness and brightness, but neither affected her. She was not afraid of death or of the dead — they were nothing but cold, heavy furniture. She could have tied jaws shut and weighted eyelids with native instinctiveness, as other women were born knowing the temperature of an infant's milk.

"There are no ghosts," she could say, entering the room where her mother, then her father had died. "If there were, I would know."

Netta took it for granted, now she was married, that Jack felt as she did about light, dark, death, and love. They were as alike in some ways (none of them physical) as a couple of twins, spoke much the same language in the same accents, had the same jokes — mostly about other people — and had been together as much as their families would let them for most of their lives. Other men seemed dull to Netta — slower, perhaps, lacking the spoken shorthand she had with Jack. She never mentioned this. For one thing, both of them had the idea that, being English, one must not say too much. Born abroad, they worked hard at an Englishness that was innocently inaccurate, rooted mostly in attitudes. Their families had been innkeepers along this coast for a century, even before Dr. James Henry Bennet had discovered "the Genoese Rivieras." In one of his guides to the region, a "Mr. Ross" is mentioned as a hotel owner who will accept English bank checks, and there is a "Mr. Asher," reliable purveyor of English groceries. The most trustworthy shipping agents in 1860 are the Montale brothers, converts to the Anglican Church, possessors of a British *laissez-passer* to Malta and Egypt. These families, by now plaited like hair, were connections of Netta's and Jack's and still in business from beyond Marseilles to Genoa. No wonder that other men bored her, and that each thought the other both familiar and unique. But of course they were unalike too. When once someone asked them, "Are you related to Montale, the poet?" Netta answered, "What poet?" and Jack said, "I wish we were."

There were no poets in the family. Apart from the great-uncle who had painted landscapes, the only person to try anything peculiar had been Jack, with his music. He had been allowed to study, up to a point; his father had been no good with hotels — had been a failure, in fact, bailed out four times by his cousins, and it had been thought, for a time, that Jack Ross might be a dunderhead too. Music might do him; he might not be fit for anything else.

Information of this kind about the meaning of failure had been gleaned by Netta years before, when she first became aware of her little cousin. Jack's father and mother — the commercial blunderers — had come to the Prince Albert and Albion to ride out a crisis. They were somewhere between undischarged bankruptcy and annihilation, but one was polite: Netta curtsied to her aunt and uncle. Her eyes were on Jack. She could not read yet, though she could sift and classify attitudes. She drew near him, sucking her lower lip, her hands behind her back. For the first time she was conscious of the beauty of another child. He was younger than Netta, imprisoned in a portable-fence arrangement in which he moved tirelessly, crabwise, hanging on a barrier he could easily have climbed. He was as fair as his Irish mother and sunburned a deep brown. His blue gaze was not a baby's — it was too challenging. He was naked except for shorts that were large and seemed about to fall down. The sunburn, the undress were because his mother was reckless and rather odd. Netta — whose mother was perfect — wore boots, stockings, a longsleeved frock, and a white sun hat. She heard the adults laugh and say that Jack looked like a prizefighter. She walked around his prison, staring, and the blue-eyed fighter stared back.

The Rosses stayed a long time, while the family sent telegrams and tried to raise money for them. No one looked after Jack much. He would lie on a marble step of the staircase watching the hotel guests going into the cardroom or the dining room. One night, for a reason that remorse was to wipe out in a minute, Netta gave him such a savage kick (though he was not really in her way) that one of his legs remained paralyzed for a long time.

"*Why* did you do it?" her father asked her — this in the room where she was shut up on bread and water. Netta didn't know. She loved Jack, but who would believe it now? Jack learned to walk, then to run, and in time to ski and play tennis; but her lifelong gift to him was a loss of balance, a sudden lopsided bend of a knee. Jack's parents had meantime been given a small hotel to run at Bandol. Mr. Asher, responsible for a bank loan, kept an eye on the place. He went often, in a hotel car with a chauffeur, Netta perched beside him. When, years later, the families found out that the devoted young cousins had become lovers, they separated them without saying much. Netta was too independent to be dealt with. Besides, her father did not want a rift; his wife had died, and he needed Netta. Jack, whose claim on music had been the subject of teasing until now, was suddenly sent to study in England. Netta saw that he was secretly dismayed. He wanted to be almost anything as long as it was impossible, and then only as an act of grace. Netta's father did think it was his duty to tell her that marriage was, at its best, a parched arrangement, intolerable without a flow of golden guineas and fresh blood. As cousins, Jack and Netta could not bring each other anything except stale money. Nothing stopped them: they were married four months after Jack became twenty-one. Netta heard someone remark at her wedding, "She doesn't need a husband," meaning perhaps the practical, matter-of-fact person she now seemed to be. She did have the dry, burned-out look of someone turned inward. Her dark eyes glowed out of a thin face. She had the shape of a girl of fourteen. Jack, who was large, and fair, and who might be stout at forty if he wasn't careful, looked exactly his age, and seemed quite ready to be married.

Netta could not understand why, loving Jack as she did, she did not look more like him. It had troubled her in the past when they did not think exactly the same thing at almost the same time. During the secret meetings of their long engagement she had noticed how even before a parting they were nearly apart — they had begun to "unmesh," as she called it. Drinking a last drink, usually in the buffet of a railway station, she would see that Jack was somewhere else, thinking about the next-best thing to Netta. The next-best thing might only be a book he wanted to finish reading, but it was enough to make her feel exiled. He often told Netta, "I'm not holding on to you. You're free," because he thought it needed saying, and of course he wanted freedom for himself. But to Netta "freedom" had a cold sound. Is that what I do want, she would wonder. Is that what I think he should offer? Their partings were often on the edge of parting forever, not just because Jack had said or done or thought the wrong thing but because between them they generated the high sexual tension that leads to quarrels. Barely ten minutes after agreeing that no one in the world could possibly know what they knew, one of them, either one, could curse the other out over something trivial. Yet they were, and remained, much in love, and when they were apart Netta sent him letters that were almost despairing with enchantment.

Jack answered, of course, but his letters were cautious. Her exploration of feeling was part of an unlimited capacity she seemed to have for passionate behaviour, so at odds with her appearance, which had been dry and sardonic even in childhood. Save for an erotic sentence or two near the end (which Netta read first) Jack's messages might have been meant for any girl cousin he particularly liked. Love was memory, and he was no good at the memory game; he needed Netta there. The instant he saw her he knew all he had missed. But Netta, by then, felt forgotten, and she came to each new meeting aggressive and hurt, afflicted with the physical signs of her doubts and injuries — cold sores, rashes, erratic periods, mysterious temperatures. If she tried to discuss it he would say, "We aren't going over all that again, are we?" Where Netta was concerned he had settled for the established faith, but Netta, who had a wilder, more secret God, wanted a prayer a minute, not to speak of unending miracles and revelations.

When they finally married, both were relieved that the strain of partings and of tense disputes in railway stations would come to a stop. Each privately blamed the other for past violence, and both believed that once they could live openly, without interference, they would never have a disagreement again. Netta did not want Jack to regret the cold freedom he had vainly tried to offer her. He must have his liberty, and his music, and other people, and, oh, anything he wanted — whatever would stop him from saying he was ready to let her go free. The first thing Netta did was to make certain they had the best room in the hotel. She had never actually owned a room until now. The private apartments of her family had always been surrendered in a crisis: everyone had packed up and moved as beds were required. She and Jack were hopelessly untidy, because both had spent their early years moving down hotel corridors, trailing belts and raincoats, with tennis shoes hanging from knotted strings over their shoulders, their arms around books and sweaters and grey flannel bundles. Both had done lessons in the corners of lounges, with cups and glasses rattling, and other children running, and English voices louder than anything. Jack, who had been vaguely educated, remembered his boarding schools as places where one had a permanent bed. Netta chose for her marriage a south-facing room with a large balcony and an awning of dazzling white. It was furnished with lemonwood that had been brought to the Riviera by Russians for their own villas long before. To the lemonwood Netta's mother had added English chintzes; the result, in Netta's eyes, was not bizarre but charming. The room was deeply mirrored; when the shutters were closed on hot afternoons a play of light became as green as a forest on the walls, and as blue as seawater in the glass. A quality of suspension, of disbelief in gravity, now belonged to Netta. She became tidy, silent, less introspective, as watchful and as reflective as her bedroom mirrors. Jack stayed as he was, luckily; any alteration would have worried her, just as a change in an often-read story will trouble a small child. She was intensely, almost unnaturally happy.

One day she overheard an English doctor, whose wife played bridge every afternoon at the hotel, refer to her, to Netta, as "the little Moslem wife." It was said affectionately, for the doctor liked her. She wondered if he had seen through walls and had watched her picking up the clothing and the wet towels Jack left strewn like clues to his presence. The phrase was collected and passed from mouth to mouth in the idle English colony. Netta, the last person in the world deliberately to eavesdrop (she lacked that sort of interest in other people), was sharp of hearing where her marriage was concerned. She had a special antenna for Jack, for his shades of meaning, secret intentions, for his innocent contradictions. Perhaps "Moslem wife" meant several things, and possibly it was plain to anyone with eyes that Jack, without meaning a bit of harm by it, had a way with women. Those he attracted were a puzzling lot, to Netta. She had already catalogued them — elegant elderly parties with tongues like carving knives; gentle, clever girls who flourished on the unattainable; untouchable-daughter types, canny about their virginity, wondering if Jack would be father enough to justify the sacrifice. There was still another kind — tough, sunburned, clad in dark colours — who made Netta think in the vocabulary of horoscopes: Her gem — diamonds. Her colour — black. Her language — worse than Netta's. She noticed that even when Jack had no real use for a woman he never made it apparent; he adopted anyone who took a liking to him. He assumed — Netta thought — a tribal, paternal air that was curious in so young a man. The plot of attraction interested him, no matter how it turned out. He was like someone reading several novels at once, or like someone playing simultaneous chess.

Netta did not want her marriage to become a world of stone. She said nothing except, "Listen, Jack, I've been at this hotel business longer than you have. It's wiser not to be too pally with the guests." At Christmas the older women gave him boxes of expensive soap. "They must think someone around here wants a good wash," Netta remarked. Outside their fenced area of private jokes and private love was a landscape too open, too light-drenched, for serious talk. And then, when? Jack woke up quickly and early in the morning and smiled as naturally as children do. He knew where he was and the day of the week and the hour. The best moment of the day was the first cigarette. When something bloody happened, it was never before six in the evening. At night he had a dark look that went with a dark mood, sometimes. Netta would tell him that she could see a cruise ship floating on the black horizon like a piece of the Milky Way, and she would get that look for an answer. But it never lasted. His memory was too short to let him sulk, no matter what fragment of night had crossed his mind. She knew, having heard other couples all her life, that at least she and Jack never made the conjugal sounds that passed for conversation and that might as well have been bow-wow and quack quack.

If, by chance, Jack found himself drawn to another woman, if the tide of attraction suddenly ran the other way, then he would discover in himself a great need to talk to his wife. They sat out on their balcony for much of one long night and he told her about his Irish mother. His mother's eccentricity — "Vera's dottiness," where the family was concerned — had kept Jack from taking anything seriously. He had been afraid of pulling her mad attention in his direction. Countless times she had faked tuberculosis and cancer and announced her own imminent death. A telephone call from a hospital had once declared her lost in a car crash.

"It's a new life, a new life," her husband had babbled, coming away from the phone. Jack saw his father then as beautiful. Women are beautiful when they fall in love, said Jack; sometimes the glow will last a few hours, sometimes even a day or two.

"You know," said Jack, as if Netta knew, "the look of amazement on a girl's face . . ."

Well, that same incandescence had suffused Jack's father when he thought his wife had died, and it continued to shine until a taxi deposited dotty Vera with her cheerful announcement that she had certainly brought off a successful April Fool. After Jack's father died she became violent. "Getting away from her was a form of violence in me," Jack said. "But I did it." That was why he was secretive; that was why he was independent. He had never wanted any woman to get her hands on his life.

Netta heard this out calmly. Where his own feelings were concerned she thought he was making them up as he went along. The garden smelled coolly of jasmine and mimosa. She wondered who his new girl was, and if he was likely to blurt out a name. But all he had been working up to was that his mother — mad, spoiled, devilish, whatever she was — would need to live with Jack and Netta, unless Netta agreed to giving her an income. An income would let her remain where she was — at the moment, in a Rudolf Steiner community in Switzerland, devoted to medieval gardening and to getting the best out of Goethe. Netta's father's training prevented even the thought of spending the money in such a manner.

"You won't regret all you've told me, will you?" she asked. She saw that the new situation would be her burden, her chain, her mean little joke sometimes. Jack scarcely hesitated before saying that where Netta mattered he could never regret anything. But what really interested him now was his mother.

"Lifts give her claustrophobia," he said. "She mustn't be higher than the second floor." He sounded like a man bringing a legal concubine into his household, scrupulously anxious to give all his women equal rights. "And I hope she will make friends," he said. "It won't be easy, at her age. One can't live without them." He probably meant that he had none. Netta had been raised not to expect to have friends: you could not run a hotel and have scores of personal ties. She expected people to be polite and punctual and to mean what they said, and that was the end of it. Jack gave his friendship easily, but he expected considerable diversion in return.

Netta said dryly, "If she plays bridge, she can play with Mrs. Blackley." This was the wife of the doctor who had first said "Moslem wife." He had come down here to the Riviera for his wife's health; the two belonged to a subcolony of flat-dwelling expatriates. His medical practice was limited to hypochondriacs and rheumatic patients. He had time on his hands: Netta often saw him in the hotel reading room, standing, leafing — he took pleasure in handling books. Netta, no reader, did not like touching a book unless it was new. The doctor had a trick of speech Jack loved to imitate: he would break up his words with an extra syllable, some words only, and at that not every time. "It is all a matter of stu-hyle," he said, for "style," or, Jack's favourite, "Oh, well, in the end it all comes down to su-hex." "Uh-hebb and flo-ho of hormones" was the way he once described the behaviour of saints — Netta had looked twice at him over that. He was a firm agnostic and the first person from whom Netta heard there existed a magical Dr. Freud. When Netta's father had died of pneumonia, the doctor's "I'm su-horry, Netta" had been so heartfelt she could not have wished it said another way.

His wife, Georgina, could lower her blood pressure or stop her heartbeat nearly at will. Netta sometimes wondered why Dr. Blackley had brought her to a soft climate rather than to the man at Vienna he so admired. Georgina was well enough to play fierce bridge, with Jack and anyone good enough. Her husband usually came to fetch her at the end of the afternoon when the players stopped for tea. Once, because he was obliged to return at once to a patient who needed him, she said, "Can't you be competent about anything?" Netta thought she understood, then, his resigned repetition of "It's all su-hex." "Oh, don't explain. You bore me," said his wife, turning her back.

Netta followed him out to his car. She wore an India shawl that had been her mother's. The wind blew her hair; she had to hold it back. She said, "Why don't you kill her?"

"I am not a desperate person," he said. He looked at Netta, she looking up at him because she had to look up to nearly everyone except children, and he said. "I've wondered why we haven't been to bed."

"Who?" said Netta. "You and your wife? Oh. You mean me." She was not offended, she just gave the shawl a brusque tug and said, "Not a hope. Never with a guest," though of course that was not the reason.

"You might have to, if the guest were a maharaja," he said, to make it all harmless. "I am told it is pu-hart of the courtesy they expect."

"We don't get their trade," said Netta. This had not stopped her liking the doctor. She pitied him, rather, because of his wife, and because he wasn't Jack and could not have Netta.

"I do love you," said the doctor, deciding finally to sit down in his car. "Ee-nee-ormously." She watched him drive away as if she loved him too, and might never see him again. It never crossed her mind to mention any of this conversation to Jack.

✧

That very spring, perhaps because of the doctor's words, the hotel did get some maharaja trade — three little sisters with ebony curls, men's eyebrows, large heads, and delicate hands and feet. They had four rooms, one for their governess. A chauffeur on permanent call lodged elsewhere. The governess, who was Dutch, had a perfect triangle of a nose and said "whom" for "who," pronouncing it "whum." The girls were to learn French, tennis, and swimming. The chauffeur arrived with a hairdresser, who cut their long hair; it lay on the governess's carpet, enough to fill a large pillow. Their toe- and fingernails were filed to points and looked like a kitten's teeth. They came smiling down the marble staircase, carrying new tennis racquets, wearing blue linen skirts and navy blazers. Mrs. Blackley glanced up from the bridge game as they went by the cardroom. She had been one of those opposed to their having lessons at the English Lawn Tennis Club, for reasons that were, to her, perfectly evident.

She said, loudly, "They'll have to be in white."

"End whay, pray?" cried the governess, pointing her triangle nose.

"They can't go on the courts except in white. It is a private club. Entirely white."

"Whum do they all think they are?" the governess asked, prepared to stalk on. But the girls, with their newly cropped heads, and their vulnerable necks showing, caught the drift and refused to go.

"Whom indeed," said Georgina Blackley, fiddling with her bridge hand and looking happy.

"My wife's seamstress could run up white frocks for them in a minute," said Jack. Perhaps he did not dislike children all that much.

"Whom could," muttered Georgina.

But it turned out that the governess was not allowed to choose their clothes, and so Jack gave the children lessons at the hotel. For six weeks they trotted around the courts looking angelic in blue, or hopelessly foreign, depending upon who saw them. Of course they fell in love with Jack, offering him a passionate loyalty they had nowhere else to place. Netta watched the transfer of this gentle, anxious gift. After they departed, Jack was bad-tempered for several evenings and then never spoke of them again; they, needless to say, had been dragged from him weeping.

When this happened the Rosses had been married nearly five years. Being childless but still very loving, they had trouble deciding which of the two would be the child. Netta overheard "He's a darling, but she's a sergeant major and no mistake. And so *mean*." She also heard "He's a lazy bastard. He bullies her. She's a fool." She searched her heart again about children. Was it Jack or had it been Netta who had first said no? The only child she had ever admired was Jack, and not as a child but as a fighter, defying her. She and Jack were not the sort to have animal children, and Jack's dotty mother would probably soon be child enough for any couple to handle. Jack still seemed to adopt, in a tribal sense of his, half the women who fell in love with him. The only woman who resisted adoption was Netta — still burned-out, still ardent, in a manner of speaking still fourteen. His mother had turned up meanwhile, getting down from a train wearing a sly air of enjoying her own jokes, just as she must have looked on the day of the April Fool. At first she was no great trouble, though she did complain about an ulcerated leg. After years of pretending, she at last had something real. Netta's policy of silence made Jack's mother confident. She began to make a mockery of his music: "All that money gone for nothing!" Or else, "The amount we wasted on schools! The hours he's thrown away with his nose in a book. All that reading — if at least it had got him somewhere." Netta noticed that he spent more time playing bridge and chatting to cronies in the bar now. She thought hard, and decided not to make it her business. His mother had once been pretty; perhaps he still saw her that way. She came of a ramshackle family with a usable past; she spoke of the Ashers and the Rosses as if she had known them when they were tinkers. English residents who had a low but solid barrier with Jack and Netta were fences-down with his mad mother: they seemed to take her at her own word when it was about herself. She began then to behave like a superior sort of guest, inviting large parties to her table for meals, ordering special wines and dishes at inconvenient hours, standing endless rounds of drinks in the bar.

Netta told herself, Jack wants it this way. It is his home too. She began to live a life apart, leaving Jack to his mother. She sat wearing her own mother's shawl, hunched over a new, modern adding machine, punching out accounts. "Funny couple," she heard now. She frowned, smiling in her mind; none of these people knew what bound them, or how tied they were. She had the habit of dodging out of her mother-in-law's parties by saying, "I've got such an awful lot to do." It made them laugh, because they thought this was Netta's term for slave-driving the servants. They thought the staff did the work, and that Netta counted the profits and was too busy with bookkeeping to keep an eye on Jack — who now, at twenty-six, was as attractive as he ever would be.

A woman named Iris Cordier was one of Jack's mother's new friends. Tall, loud, in winter dully pale, she reminded Netta of a blond penguin. Her voice moved between a squeak and a moo, and was a mark of the distinguished literary family to which her father belonged. Her mother, a Frenchwoman, had been in and out of nursing homes for years. The Cordiers haunted the Riviera, with Iris looking after her parents and watching their diets. Now she lived in a flat somewhere in Roquebrune with the survivor of the pair — the mother, Netta believed. Iris paused and glanced in the business room where Mr. Asher had signed the hundred-year lease. She was on her way to lunch — Jack's mother's guest, of course.

"I say, aren't you Miss Asher?"

"I was." Iris, like Dr. Blackley, was probably younger than she looked. Out of her own childhood Netta recalled a desperate adolescent Iris with middle-aged parents clamped like handcuffs on her life. "How is your mother?" Netta had been about to say "How is Mrs. Cordier?" but it sounded servile.

"I didn't know you knew her."

"I remember her well. Your father too. He was a nice person."

"And still is," said Iris, sharply. "He lives with me, and he always will. French daughters don't abandon their parents." No one had ever sounded more English to Netta. "And your father and mother?"

"Both dead now. I'm married to Jack Ross."

"Nobody told me," said Iris, in a way that made Netta think, Good Lord, Iris too? Jack could not possibly seem like a patriarchal figure where she was concerned; perhaps this time the game was reversed and Iris played at being tribal and maternal. The idea of Jack, or of any man, flinging himself on that iron bosom made Netta smile. As if startled, Iris covered her mouth. She seemed to be frightened of smiling back.

Oh, well, and what of it, Iris too, said Netta to herself, suddenly turning back to her accounts. As it happened, Netta was mistaken (as she never would have been with a bill). That day Jack was meeting Iris for the first time.

The upshot of these errors and encounters was an invitation to Roquebrune to visit Iris's father. Jack's mother was ruthlessly excluded, even though Iris probably owed her a return engagement because of the lunch. Netta supposed that Iris had decided one had to get past Netta to reach Jack — an inexactness if ever there was one. Or perhaps it was Netta Iris wanted. In that case the error became a farce. Netta had almost no knowledge of private houses. She looked around at something that did not much interest her, for she hated to leave her own home, and saw Iris's father, apparently too old and shaky to get out of his armchair. He smiled and he nodded, meanwhile stroking an aged cat. He said to Netta, "You resemble your mother. A sweet woman. Obliging and quiet. I used to tell her that I longed to live in her hotel and be looked after."

Not by me, thought Netta.

Iris's amber bracelets rattled as she pushed and pulled everyone through introductions. Jack and Netta had been asked to meet a young American Netta had often seen in her own bar, and a couple named Sandy and Sandra Braunsweg, who turned out to be Anglo-Swiss and twins. Iris's long arms were around them as she cried to Netta, "Don't you know these babies?" They were, like the Rosses, somewhere in their twenties. Jack looked on, blue-eyed, interested, smiling at everything new. Netta supposed that she was now seeing some of the rather hard-up snobbish — snobbish what? "Intelligumhen-sia," she imagined Dr. Blackley supplying. Having arrived at a word, Netta was ready to go home; but they had only just arrived. The American turned to Netta. He looked bored, and astonished by it. He needs the word for "bored," she decided. Then he can go home, too. The Riviera was no place for Americans. They could not sit all day waiting for mail and the daily papers and for the clock to show a respectable drinking time. They made the best of things when they were caught with a house they'd been rash enough to rent unseen. Netta often had them then *en pension* for meals: a hotel dining room was one way of meeting people. They paid a fee to use the tennis courts, and they liked the bar. Netta would notice then how Jack picked up any accent within hearing.

Jack was now being attentive to the old man, Iris's father. Though this was none of Mr. Cordier's business, Jack said, "My wife and I are first cousins, as well as second cousins twice over."

"You don't look it."

Everyone began to speak at once, and it was a minute or two before Netta heard Jack again. This time he said, "We are from a family of great..." It was lost. What now? Great innkeepers? Worriers? Skinflints? Whatever it was, old Mr. Cordier kept nodding to show he approved.

"We don't see nearly enough of young men like you," he said.

"True!" said Iris loudly. "We live in a dreary world of ill women down here." Netta thought this hard on the American, on Mr. Cordier, and on the male Braunsweg twin, but none of them looked offended. "I've got no time for women," said Iris. She slapped down a glass of whiskey so that it splashed, and rapped on a table with her knuckles. "Shall I tell you why? Because women don't tick over. They just simply don't tick over." No one disputed this. Iris went on: Women were underinformed. One could have virile conversations only with men. Women were attached to the past through fear, whereas men had a fearless sense of history. "Men tick," she said, glaring at Jack.

"I am not attached to a past," said Netta, slowly. "The past holds no attractions." She was not used to general conversation. She thought that every word called for consideration and for an answer. "Nothing could be worse than the way we children were dressed. And our mothers — the hard waves of their hair, the white lips. I think of those pale profiles and I wonder if those women were ever young."

Poor Netta, who saw herself as profoundly English, spread consternation by being suddenly foreign and gassy. She talked the English of expatriate children, as if reading aloud. The twins looked shocked. But she had appealed to the American. He sat beside her on a scuffed velvet sofa. He was so large that she slid an inch or so in his direction when he sat down. He was Sandra Braunsweg's special friend: they had been in London together. He was trying to write.

"What do you mean?" said Netta. "Write what?"

"Well — a novel, to start," he said. His father had staked him to one year, then another. He mentioned all that Sandra had borne with, how she had actually kicked and punched him to keep him from being too American. He had embarrassed her to death in London by asking a waitress, "Miss, where's the toilet?"

Netta said, "Didn't you mind being corrected?"

"Oh, no. It was just friendly."

Jack meanwhile was listening to Sandra telling about her English forebears and her English education. "I had many years of undeniably excellent schooling," she said. "Mitten Todd."

"What's that?" said Jack.

"It's near Bristol. I met excellent girls from Italy, Spain. I took *him* there to visit," she said, generously including the American. "I said, 'Get a yellow necktie.' He went straight out and bought one. I wore a little Schiaparelli. Bought in Geneva but still a real. . . A yellow jacket over a grey. . . Well, we arrived at my excellent old school, and even though the day was drizzly I said, 'Put the top of the car back.' He did so at once, and then he understood. The interior of the car harmonized perfectly with the yellow and grey." The twins were orphaned. Iris was like a mother.

"When Mummy died we didn't know where to put all the Chippendale," said Sandra, "Iris took a lot of it."

Netta thought, She is so silly. How can he respond? The girl's dimples and freckles and soft little hands were nothing Netta could have ever described: she had never in her life thought a word like "pretty." People were beautiful or they were not. Her happiness had always been great enough to allow for despair. She knew that some people thought Jack was happy and she was not.

"And what made you marry your young cousin?" the old man boomed at Netta. Perhaps his background allowed him to ask impertinent questions; he must have been doing so nearly forever. He stroked his cat; he was confident. He was spokesman for a roomful of wondering people.

"Jack was a moody child and I promised his mother I would look after him," said Netta. In her hopelessly un-English way she believed she had said something funny.

CR

At eleven o'clock the hotel car expected to fetch the Rosses was nowhere. They trudged home by moonlight. For the last hour of the evening Jack had been skewered on virile conversations, first with Iris, then with Sandra, to whom Netta had already given "Chippendale" as a private name. It proved that Iris was right about concentrating on men and their ticking — Jack even thought Sandra rather pretty.

"Prettier than me?" said Netta, without the faintest idea what she meant, but aware she had said something stupid.

"Not so attractive," said Jack. His slight limp returned straight out of childhood. *She* had caused his accident.

"But she's not always clear," said Netta. "Mitten Todd, for example."

"Who're you talking about?"

"Who are *you*?"

"Iris, of course."

As if they had suddenly quarrelled they fell silent. In silence they entered their room and prepared for bed. Jack poured a whiskey, walked on the clothes he had dropped, carried his drink to the bathroom. Through the half-shut door he called suddenly, "Why did you say that asinine thing about promising to look after me?"

"It seemed so unlikely, I thought they'd laugh." She had a glimpse of herself in the mirrors picking up his shed clothes.

He said, "Well, is it true?"

She was quiet for such a long time that he came to see if she was still in the room. She said, "No, your mother never said that or anything like it."

"We shouldn't have gone to Roquebrune," said Jack. "I think those bloody people are going to be a nuisance. Iris wants her father to stay here, with the cat, while she goes to England for a month. How do we get out of that?"

"By saying no."

"I'm rotten at no."

"I told you not to be too pally with women," she said, as a joke again, but jokes were her way of having floods of tears.

Before this had a chance to heal, Iris's father moved in, bringing his cat in a basket. He looked at his room and said, "Medium large." He looked at his bed and said, "Reasonably long." He was, in short, daft about measurements. When he took books out of the reading room, he was apt to return them with "This volume contains about 70,000 words" written inside the back cover.

Netta had not wanted Iris's father, but Jack had said yes to it. She had not wanted the sick cat, but Jack had said yes to that too. The old man, who was lost without Iris, lived for his meals. He would appear at the shut doors of the dining room an hour too early, waiting for the menu to be typed and posted. In a voice that matched Iris's for carrying power, he read aloud, alone: "Consommé. Good Lord, again? Is there a choice between the fish and the cutlet? I can't possibly eat all of that. A bit of salad and a boiled egg. That's all I could possibly want." That was rubbish, because Mr. Cordier ate the menu and more, and if there were two puddings, or a pudding and ice cream, he ate both and asked for pastry, fruit, and cheese to follow. One day, after Dr. Blackley had attended him for faintness, Netta passed a message on to Iris, who had been back from England for a fortnight now but seemed in no hurry to take her father away.

"Keith Blackley thinks your father should go on a diet."

"He can't," said Iris. "Our other doctor says dieting causes cancer."

"You can't have heard that properly," Netta said.

"It is like those silly people who smoke to keep their figures," said Iris. "Dieting."

"Blackley hasn't said he should smoke, just that he should eat less of everything."

"My father has never smoked in his life," Iris cried. "As for his diet, I weighed his food out for years. He's not here forever. I'll take him back as soon as he's had enough of hotels."

He stayed for a long time, and the cat did too, and a nuisance they both were to the servants. When the cat was too ailing to walk, the old man carried it to a path behind the tennis courts and put it down on the gravel to die. Netta came out with the old man's tea on a tray (not done for everyone, but having him out of the way was a relief) and she saw the cat lying on its side, eyes wide, as if profoundly thinking. She saw unlicked dirt on its coat and ants exploring its paws. The old man sat in a garden chair, wearing a panama hat, his hands clasped on a stick. He called, "Oh, Netta, take her away. I am too old to watch anything die. I know what she'll do," he said, indifferently, his voice falling as she came near. "Oh, I know that. Turn on her back and give a shriek. I've heard it often."

Netta disburdened her tray onto a garden table and pulled the tray cloth under the cat. She was angered at the haste and indecency of the ants. "It would be polite to leave her," she said. "She doesn't want to be watched."

"I always sit here," said the old man.

Jack, making for the courts with Chippendale, looked as if the sight of the two conversing amused him. Then he understood and scooped up the cat and tray cloth and went away with the cat over his shoulder. He laid it in the shade of a Judas tree, and within an hour it was dead. Iris's father said, "I've got no one to talk to here. That's my trouble. That shroud was too small for my poor Polly. Ask my daughter to fetch me."

Jack's mother said that night, "I'm sure you wish that I had a devoted daughter to take me away too." Because of the attention given the cat she seemed to feel she had not been nuisance enough. She had taken to saying, "My leg is dying before I am," and imploring Jack to preserve her leg, should it be amputated, and make certain it was buried with her. She wanted Jack to be close by at nearly any hour now, so that she could lean on him. After sitting for hours at bridge she had trouble climbing two flights of stairs; nothing would induce her to use the lift.

"Nothing ever came of your music," she would say, leaning on him. "Of course, you have a wife to distract you now. I needed a daughter. Every woman does." Netta managed to trap her alone, and forced her to sit while she stood over her. Netta said, "Look, Aunt Vera, I forbid you, I absolutely forbid you, do you hear, to make a nurse of Jack, and I shall strangle you with my own hands if you go on saying nothing came of his music. You are not to say it in my hearing or out of it. Is that plain?"

Jack's mother got up to her room without assistance. About an hour later the gardener found her on a soft bed of wallflowers. "An inch to the left and she'd have landed on a rake," he said to Netta. She was still alive when Netta knelt down. In her fall she had crushed the plants, the yellow minted *giroflées de Nice*. Netta thought that she was now, at last, for the first time, inhaling one of the smells of death. Her aunt's arms and legs were turned and twisted; her skirt was pulled so that her swollen leg showed. It seemed that she had jumped carrying her walking stick — it lay across the path. She often slept in an armchair, afternoons, with one eye slightly open. She opened that eye now and, seeing she had Netta, said, "My son." Netta was thinking, I have never known her. And if I knew her, then it was Jack or myself I could not understand. Netta was afraid of giving orders, and of telling people not to touch her aunt before Dr. Blackley could be summoned, because she knew that she had always been mistaken. Now Jack was there, propping his mother up, brushing leaves and earth out of her hair. Her head dropped on his shoulder. Netta thought from the sudden heaviness that her aunt had died, but she sighed and opened that one eye again, saying this time, "Doctor?" Netta left everyone doing the wrong things to her dying — no, her murdered — aunt. She said quite calmly into a telephone, "I am afraid that my aunt must have jumped or fallen from the second floor."

Jack found a letter on his mother's night table that began, "Why blame Netta? I forgive." At dawn he and Netta sat at a card table with yesterday's cigarettes still not cleaned out of the ashtray, and he did not ask what Netta had said or done that called for forgiveness. They kept pushing the letter back and forth. He would read it and then Netta would. It seemed natural for them to be silent. Jack had sat beside his mother for much of the night. Each of them then went to sleep for an hour, apart, in one of the empty rooms, just as they had done in the old days when their parents were juggling beds and guests and double and single quarters. By the time the doctor returned for his second visit Jack was neatly dressed and seemed wide awake. He sat in the bar drinking black coffee and reading a travel book of Evelyn Waugh's called *Labels*. Netta, who looked far more untidy and underslept, wondered if Jack wished he might leave now, and sail from Monte Carlo on the Stella Polaris.

Dr. Blackley said, "Well, you are a dim pair. She is not in pu-hain, you know." Netta supposed this was the roundabout way doctors have of announcing death, very like "Her sufferings have ended." But Jack, looking hard at the doctor, had heard another meaning. "Jumped or fell," said Dr. Blackley. "She neither fell nor jumped. She is up there enjoying a damned good thu-hing."

Netta went out and through the lounge and up the marble steps. She sat down in the shaded room on the chair where Jack had spent most of the night. Her aunt did not look like anyone Netta knew, not even like Jack. She stared at the alien face and said, "Aunt Vera, Keith Blackley says there is nothing really the matter. You must have made a mistake. Perhaps you fainted on the path, overcome by the scent of wallflowers. What would you like me to tell Jack?"

Jack's mother turned on her side and slowly, tenderly, raised herself on an elbow. "Well, Netta," she said, "I daresay the fool is right. But as I've been given a lot of sleeping stuff, I'd as soon stay here for now."

Netta said, "Are you hungry?"

"I should very much like a ham sandwich on English bread, and about that much gin with a lump of ice."

∝

She began coming down for meals a few days later. They knew she had crept down the stairs and flung her walking stick over the path and let herself fall hard on a bed of wallflowers — had even plucked her skirt up for a bit of accuracy; but she was also someone returned from beyond the limits, from the other side of the wall. Once she said, "It was like diving and suddenly realizing there was no water in the sea." Again, "It is not true that your life rushes before your eyes. You can see the flowers floating up to you. Even a short fall takes a long time."

Everyone was deeply changed by this incident. The effect on the victim herself was that she got religion hard.

"We are all hopeless nonbelievers!" shouted Iris, drinking in the bar one afternoon. "At least, I hope we are. But when I see you, Vera, I feel there might be something in religion. You look positively temperate."

"I am allowed to love God, I hope," said Jack's mother.

Jack never saw or heard his mother anymore. He leaned against the bar, reading. It was his favourite place. Even on the sunniest of afternoons he read by the red-shaded light. Netta was present only because she had supplies to check. Knowing she ought to keep out of this, she still said, "Religion is more than love. It is supposed to tell you why you exist and what you are expected to do about it."

"You have no religious feelings at all?" This was the only serious and almost the only friendly question Iris was ever to ask Netta.

"None," said Netta. "I'm running a business."

"I love God as Jack used to love music," said his mother. "At least he said he did when we were paying for lessons."

"Adam and Eve had God," said Netta. "They had nobody *but* God. A fat lot of good that did them." This was as far as their dialectic went. Jack had not moved once except to turn pages. He read steadily but cautiously now, as if every author had a design on him. That was one effect of his mother's incident. The other was that he gave up bridge and went back to playing the clarinet. Iris hammered out an accompaniment on the upright piano in the old music room, mostly used for listening to radio broadcasts. She was the only person Netta had ever heard who could make Mozart sound like an Irish jig. Presently Iris began to say that it was time Jack gave a concert. Before this could run into a crisis Iris changed her mind and said what he wanted was a holiday. Netta thought he needed something: he seemed to be exhausted by love, friendship, by being a husband, someone's son, by trying to make a world out of reading and sense out of life. A visit to England to meet some stimulating people, said Iris. To help Iris with her tiresome father during the journey. To visit art galleries and bookshops and go to concerts. To meet people. To talk.

This was a hot, troubled season, and many persons were planning journeys

— not to meet other people but for fear of a war. The hotel had emptied out by the end of March. Netta, whose father had known there would never be another catastrophe, had her workmen come in, as usual. She could hear the radiators being drained and got ready for painting as she packed Jack's clothes. They had never been separated before. They kept telling each other that it was only for a short holiday — for three or four weeks. She was surprised at how neat marriage was, at how many years and feelings could be folded and put under a lid. Once, she went to the window so that he would not see her tears and think she was trying to blackmail him. Looking out, she noticed the American, Chippendale's lover, idly knocking a tennis ball against the garage, as Jack had done in the early summers of their life; he had come round to the hotel looking for a partner, but that season there were none. She suddenly knew to a certainty that if Jack were to die she would search the crowd of mourners for a man she could live with. She would not return from the funeral alone.

Grief and memory, yes, she had said to herself, but what about three o'clock in the morning?

CR

By June nearly everyone Netta knew had vanished, or, like the Blackleys, had started to pack. Netta had new tablecloths made, and ordered new white awnings, and two dozen rosebushes from the nursery at Cap Ferrat. The American came over every day and followed her from room to room, talking. He had nothing better to do. The Swiss twins were in England. His father, who had been backing his writing career until now, had suddenly changed his mind about it — now, when he needed money to get out of Europe. He had projects for living on his own, but they required a dose of funds. He wanted to open a restaurant on the Riviera where nothing but chicken pie would be served. Or else a vast and expensive café where people would pay to make their own sandwiches. He said that he was seeing the food of the future, but all that Netta could see was customers asking for their money back. He trapped her behind the bar and said he loved her; Netta made other women look like stuffed dolls. He could still remember the shock of meeting her, the attraction, the brilliant answer she had made to Iris about attachments to the past.

Netta let him rave until he asked for a loan. She laughed and wondered if it was for the chicken-pie restaurant. No — he wanted to get on a boat sailing from Cannes. She said, quite cheerfully, "I can't be Venus and Barclays Bank. You have to choose."

He said, "Can't Venus ever turn up with a letter of credit?"

She shook her head. "Not a hope."

But when it was July and Jack hadn't come back, he cornered her again. Money wasn't in it now: his father had not only relented but had virtually ordered him home. He was about twenty-two, she guessed. He could still plead successfully for parental help and for indulgence from women. She said, no more than affectionately, "I'm going to show you a very pretty room."

A few days later Dr. Blackley came alone to say goodbye.

"Are you really staying?" he asked.

"I am responsible for the last eighty-one years of this lease," said Netta. "I'm going to be thirty. It's a long tenure. Besides, I've got Jack's mother and she won't leave. Jack has a chance now to visit America. It doesn't sound sensible to me, but she writes encouraging him. She imagines him suddenly very rich and sending for her. I've discovered the limit of what you can feel about people. I've discovered something else," she said abruptly. "It is that sex and love have nothing in common. Only a coincidence, sometimes. You think the coincidence will go on and so you get married. I suppose that is what men are born knowing and women learn by accident."

"I'm su-horry."

"For God's sake, don't be. It's a relief."

She had no feeling of guilt, only of amazement. Jack, as a memory, was in a restricted area — the tennis courts, the cardroom, the bar. She saw him at bridge with Mrs. Blackley and pouring drinks for temporary friends. He crossed the lounge jauntily with a cluster of little dark-haired girls wearing blue. In the mirrored bedroom there was only Netta. Her dreams were cleansed of him. The looking glasses still held their blue-and-silver-water shadows, but they lost the habit of giving back the moods and gestures of a Moslem wife.

◌

About five years after this, Netta wrote to Jack. The war had caught him in America, during the voyage his mother had so wanted him to have. His limp had kept him out of the Army. As his mother (now dead) might have put it, all that reading had finally got him somewhere: he had spent the last years putting out a two-pager on aspects of European culture — part of a scrupulous effort Britain was making for the West. That was nearly all Netta knew. A Belgian Red Cross official had arrived, apparently in Jack's name, to see if she was still alive. She sat in her father's business room, wearing a coat and a shawl because there was no way of heating any part of the hotel now, and she tried to get on with the letter she had been writing in her head, on and off, for many years.

"In June, 1940, we were evacuated," she started, for the tenth or eleventh time. "I was back by October. Italians had taken over the hotel. They used the mirror behind the bar for target practice. Oddly enough it was not smashed. It is covered with spiderwebs, and the bullet hole is the spider. I had great trouble over Aunt Vera, who disappeared and was found finally in one of the attic rooms.

"The Italians made a pet of her. Took her picture. She enjoyed that. Everyone who became thin had a desire to be photographed, as if knowing they would use this intimidating evidence against those loved ones who had missed being starved. Guilt for life. After an initial period of hardship, during which she often had her picture taken at her request, the Italians brought food and looked after her, more than anyone. She was their mama. We were annexed territory and in time we had the same food as the Italians. The thin pictures of your mother are here on my desk.

"She buried her British passport and would never say where. Perhaps under the Judas tree with Mr. Cordier's cat, Polly. She remained just as mad and just as spoiled, and that became dangerous when life stopped being ordinary. She complained about me to the Italians. At that time a complaint was a matter of prison and of death if it was made to the wrong person. Luckily for me, there was also the right person to take the message.

"A couple of years after that, the Germans and certain French took over and the Italians were shut up in another hotel without food or water, and some people risked their well-being to take water to them (for not everyone preferred the new situation, you can believe me). When she was dying I asked her if she had a message for one Italian officer who had made such a pet of her and she said, 'No, why?' She died without a word for anybody. She was buried as 'Rossini,' because the Italians had changed people's names. She had said she was French, a Frenchwoman named Ross, and so some peculiar civil status was created for us — the two Mrs. Rossinis.

"The records were topsy-turvy; it would have meant going to the Germans and explaining my dead aunt was British, and of course I thought I would not. The death certificate and permission to bury are for a Vera Rossini. I have them here on my desk for you with her pictures.

"You are probably wondering where I have found all this writing paper. The Germans left it behind. When we were being shelled I took what few books were left in the reading room down to what used to be the wine cellar and read by candlelight. You are probably wondering where the candles came from. A long story. I even have paint for the radiators, large buckets that have never been opened.

"I live in one room, my mother's old sitting room. The business room can be used but the files are gone. When the Italians were here your mother was their mother, but I was not their Moslem wife, although I still had respect for men. One yelled '*Luce, luce,*' because your mother was showing a light. She said, 'Bugger you, you little toad.' He said, 'Granny, I said "*luce,*" not "*Duce.*" '

"Not long ago we crept out of our shelled homes, looking like cave dwellers. When you see the hotel again, it will be functioning. I shall have painted the radiators. Long shoots of bramble come in through the cardroom windows. There are drifts of leaves in the old music room and I saw scorpions and heard their rustling like the rustle of death. Everything that could have been looted has gone. Sheets, bedding, mattresses. The neighbours did quite a lot of that. At the risk of their lives. When the Italians were here we had rice and oil. Your mother, who was crazy, used to put out grains to feed the mice.

"When the Germans came we had to live under Vichy law, which meant each region lived on what it could produce. As ours produces nothing, we got quite thin again. Aunt Vera died plump. Do you know what it means when I say she used to complain about me?

"Send me some books. As long as they are in English. I am quite sick of the three other languages in which I've heard so many threats, such boasting, such a lot of lying.

"For a time I thought people would like to know how the Italians left and the Germans came in. It was like this: They came in with the first car moving slowly, flying the French flag. The highest-ranking French official in the region. Not a German. No, just a chap getting his job back. The Belgian Red Cross people were completely uninterested and warned me that no one would ever want to hear.

"I suppose that you already have the fiction of all this. The fiction must be different, oh very different, from Italians sobbing with homesickness in the night. The Germans were not real, they were especially got up for the events of the time. Sat in the white dining room, eating with whatever plates and spoons were not broken or looted, ate soups that were mostly water, were forbidden to complain. Only in retreat did they develop faces and I noticed then that some were terrified and many were old. A radio broadcast from some untouched area advised the local population not to attack them as they retreated, it would make wild animals of them. But they were attacked by some young boys shooting out of a window and eight hostages were taken, including the son of the man who cut the maharaja's daughters' black hair, and they were shot and left along the wall of a café on the more or less Italian side of the border. And the man who owned the café was killed too, but later, by civilians — he had given names to the Gestapo once, or perhaps it was something else. He got on the wrong side of the right side at the wrong time, and he was thrown down the deep gorge between the two frontiers.

"Up in one of the hill villages Germans stayed till no one was alive. I was at that time in the former wine cellar, reading books by candlelight.

"The Belgian Red Cross team found the skeleton of a German deserter in a cave and took back the helmet and skull to Knokke-le-Zoute as souvenirs.

"My war has ended. Our family held together almost from the Napoleonic adventures. It is shattered now. Sentiment does not keep families whole — only mutual pride and mutual money."

¨

This true story sounded so implausible that she decided never to send it. She wrote a sensible letter asking for sugar and rice and for new books; nothing must be older than 1940.

Jack answered at once: there were no new authors (he had been asking people). Sugar was unobtainable, and there were queues for rice. Shoes had been rationed. There were no women's stockings but lisle, and the famous American legs looked terrible. You could not find butter or meat or tinned pineapple. In restaurants, instead of butter you were given miniature golf balls of cream cheese. He supposed that all this must sound like small beer to Netta.

A notice arrived that a CARE package awaited her at the post office. It meant that Jack had added his name and his money to a mailing list. She refused to sign for it; then she changed her mind and discovered it was not from Jack but from the American she had once taken to such a pretty room. Jack did send rice and sugar and delicious coffee but he forgot about books. His letters followed; sometimes three arrived in a morning. She left them sealed for days. When she sat down to answer, all she could remember were implausible things.

Iris came back. She was the first. She had grown puffy in England — the result of drinking whatever alcohol she could get her hands on and grimly eating her sweets allowance: there would be that much less gin and chocolate for the Germans if ever they landed. She put her now wide bottom on a comfortable armchair — one of the few chairs the first wave of Italians had not burned with cigarettes or idly hacked at with daggers — and said Jack had been living with a woman in America and to spare the gossip had let her be known as his wife. Another Mrs. Ross? When Netta discovered it was dimpled Chippendale, she laughed aloud.

"I've seen them," said Iris. "I mean I saw them together. King Charles and a spaniel. Jack wiped his feet on her."

Netta's feelings were of lightness, relief. She would not have to tell Jack about the partisans hanging by the neck in the arches of the Place Masséna at Nice. When Iris had finished talking, Netta said, "What about his music?"

"I don't know."

"How can you not know something so important."

"Jack had a good chance at things, but he made a mess of everything," said Iris. "My father is still living. Life really is too incredible for some of us."

A dark girl of about twenty turned up soon after. Her costume, a grey dress buttoned to the neck, gave her the appearance of being in uniform. She unzipped a military-looking bag and cried, in an unplaceable accent, "*Ha*llo, *ha*llo, Mrs. Ross? A few small gifts for you," and unpacked a bottle of Haig, four tins of corned beef, a jar of honey, and six pairs of American nylon stockings, which Netta had never seen before, and were as good to have under a mattress as gold. Netta looked up at the tall girl.

"Remember? I was the middle sister. With," she said gravely, "the typical middle-sister problems." She scarcely recalled Jack, her beloved. The memory of Netta had grown up with her. "I remember you laughing," she said, without loving that memory. She was a severe, tragic girl. "You were the first adult I ever heard laughing. At night in bed I could hear it from your balcony. You sat smoking with, I suppose, your handsome husband. I used to laugh just to hear you."

She had married an Iranian journalist. He had discovered that political prisoners in the United States were working under lamentable conditions in tin mines. President Truman had sent them there. People from all over the world planned to unite to get them out. The girl said she had been to Germany and to Austria, she had visited camps, they were all alike, and that was already the past, and the future was the prisoners in the tin mines.

Netta said, "In what part of the country are these mines?"

The middle sister looked at her sadly and said, "Is there more than one part?"

For the first time in years, Netta could see Jack clearly. They were silently sharing a joke; he had caught it too. She and the girl lunched in a corner of the battered dining room. The tables were scarred with initials. There were no tablecloths. One of the great-uncle's paintings still hung on a wall. It showed the Quai Laurenti, a country road alongside the sea. Netta, who had no use for the past, was discovering a past she could regret. Out of a dark, gentle silence — silence imposed by the impossibility of telling anything real — she counted the cracks in the walls. When silence failed she heard power saws ripping into olive trees and a lemon grove. With a sense of deliverance she understood that soon there would be nothing left to spoil. Her great-uncle's picture, which ought to have changed out of sympathetic magic, remained faithful. She regretted everything now, even the three anxious little girls in blue linen. Every calamitous season between then and now seemed to descend directly from Georgina Blackley's having said "white" just to keep three children in their place. Clad in buttoned-up grey, the middle sister now picked at corned beef and said she had hated her father, her mother, her sisters, and most of all the Dutch governess.

"Where is she now?" said Netta.

"Dead, I hope." This was from someone who had visited camps. Netta sat listening, her cheek on her hand. Death made death casual: she had always known. Neither the vanquished in their flight nor the victors returning to pick over rubble seemed half so vindictive as a tragic girl who had disliked her governess.

CR

Dr. Blackley came back looking positively cheerful. In those days men still liked soldiering. It made them feel young, if they needed to feel it, and it got them away from home. War made the break few men could make on their own. The doctor looked years younger, too, and very fit. His wife was not with him. She had survived everything, and the hardships she had undergone had completely restored her to health — which had made it easy for her husband to leave her. Actually, he had never gone back, except to wind up the matter.

"There are things about Georgina I respect and admire," he said, as husbands will say from a distance. His war had been in Malta. He had come here, as soon as he could, to the shelled, gnawed, tarnished coast (as if he had not seen enough at Malta) to ask Netta to divorce Jack and to marry him, or live with him — anything she wanted, on any terms.

But she wanted nothing — at least, not from him.

"Well, one can't defeat a memory," he said. "I always thought it was mostly su-hex between the two of you."

"So it was," said Netta. "So far as I remember."

"Everyone noticed. You would vanish at odd hours. Dis-huppear."

"Yes, we did."

"You can't live on memories," he objected. "Though I respect you for being faithful, of course."

"What you are talking about is something of which one has no specific memory," said Netta. "Only of seasons. Places. Rooms. It is as abstract to remember as to read about. That is why it is boring in talk except as a joke, and boring in books except for poetry."

"You never read poetry."

"I do now."

"I guessed that," he said.

"That lack of memory is why people are unfaithful, as it is so curiously called. When I see closed shutters I know there are lovers behind them. That is how the memory works. The rest is just convention and small talk."

"Why lovers? Why not someone sleeping off the wine he had for lunch?"

"No. Lovers."

"A middle-aged man cutting his toenails in the bathtub," he said with unexpected feeling. "Wearing bifocal lenses so that he can see his own feet."

"No, lovers. Always."

He said, "Have you missed him?"

"Missed who?"

"Who the bloody hell are we talking about?"

"The Italian commander billeted here. He was not a guest. He was here by force. I was not breaking a rule. Without him I'd have perished in every way. He may be home with his wife now. Or in that fortress near Turin where he sent other men. Or dead." She looked at the doctor and said, "Well, what would you like me to do? Sit here and cry?"

"I can't imagine you with a brute."

"I never said that."

"Do you miss him still?"

"The absence of Jack was like a cancer which I am sure has taken root, and of which I am bound to die," said Netta.

"You'll bu-hury us all," he said, as doctors tell the condemned.

"I haven't said I won't." She rose suddenly and straightened her skirt, as she used to do when hotel guests became pally. "Conversation over," it meant.

"Don't be too hard on Jack," he said.

"I am hard on myself," she replied.

After he had gone he sent her a parcel of books, printed on greyish paper, in warped wartime covers. All of the titles were, to Netta, unknown. There was *Fireman Flower* and *The Horse's Mouth* and *Four Quartets* and *The Stuff to Give the Troops* and *Better Than a Kick in the Pants* and *Put Out More Flags*. A note added that the next package would contain Henry Green and Dylan Thomas. She guessed he would not want to be thanked, but she did so anyway. At the end of her letter was "Please remember, if you mind too much, that I said no to you once before." Leaning on the bar, exactly as Jack used to, with a glass of the middle sister's drink at hand, she opened *Better Than a Kick in the Pants* and read, ". . . two Fascists came in, one of them tall and thin and tough looking; the other smaller, with only one arm and an empty sleeve pinned up to his shoulder. Both of them were quite young and wore black shirts."

Oh, thought Netta, I am the only one who knows all this. No one will ever realize how much I know of the truth, the truth, the truth, and she put her head on her hands, her elbows on the scarred bar, and let the first tears of her after-war run down her wrists.

☙

The last to return was the one who should have been first. Jack wrote that he was coming down from the north as far as Nice by bus. It was a common way of travelling and much cheaper than by train. Netta guessed that he was mildly hard up and that he had saved nothing from his war job. The bus came in at six, at the foot of the Place Masséna. There was a deep-blue late-afternoon sky and pale sunlight. She could hear birds from the public gardens nearby. The Place was as she had always seen it, like an elegant drawing room with a blue ceiling. It was nearly empty. Jack looked out on this sunlighted, handsome space and said, "Well,

I'll just leave my stuff at the bus office, for the moment" — perhaps noticing that Netta had not invited him anywhere. He placed his ticket on the counter, and she saw that he had not come from far away: he must have been moving south by stages. He carried an aura of London pub life; he had been in London for weeks.

A frowning man hurrying to wind things up so he could have his first drink of the evening said, "The office is closing and we don't keep baggage here."

"People used to be nice," Jack said.

"Bus people?"

"Just people."

She was hit by the sharp change in his accent. As for the way of speaking, which is something else again, he was like the heir to great estates back home after a Grand Tour. Perhaps the estates had run down in his absence. She slipped the frowning man a thousand francs, a new pastel-tinted bill, on which the face of a calm girl glowed like an opal. She said, "We shan't be long."

She set off over the Place, walking diagonally — Jack beside her, of course. He did not ask where they were headed, though he did make her smile by saying, "Did you bring a car?," expecting one of the hotel cars to be parked nearby, perhaps with a driver to open the door; perhaps with cold chicken and wine in a hamper, too. He said, "I'd forgotten about having to tip for every little thing." He did not question his destination, which was no farther than a café at the far end of the square. What she felt at that instant was intense revulsion. She thought, I don't want him, and pushed away some invisible flying thing — a bat or a blown paper. He looked at her with surprise. He must have been wondering if hardship had taught Netta to talk in her mind.

This is it, the freedom he was always offering me, she said to herself, smiling up at the beautiful sky.

They moved slowly along the nearly empty square, pausing only when some worn-out Peugeot or an old bicycle, finding no other target, made a swing in their direction. Safely on the pavement, they walked under the arches where partisans had been hanged. It seemed to Netta the bodies had been taken down only a day or so before. Jack, who knew about this way of dying from hearsay, chose a café table nearly under a poor lad's bound, dangling feet.

"I had a woman next to me on the bus who kept a hedgehog all winter in a basketful of shavings," he said. "He can drink milk out of a wineglass." He hesitated. "I'm sorry about the books you asked for. I was sick of books by then. I was sick of rhetoric and culture and patriotic crap."

"I suppose it is all very different over there," said Netta.

"God, yes."

He seemed to expect her to ask questions, so she said, "What kind of clothes do they wear?"

"They wear quite a lot of plaids and tartans. They eat at peculiar hours. You'll see them eating strawberries and cream just when you're thinking of having a drink."

She said, "Did you visit the tin mines, where Truman sends his political prisoners?"

"*Tin* mines?" said Jack. "No."

"Remember the three little girls from the maharaja trade?"

Neither could quite hear what the other had to say. They were partially deaf to each other.

Netta continued softly, "Now, as I understand it, she first brought an American to London, and then she took an Englishman to America."

He had too much the habit of women, he was playing too close a game, to waste points saying, "Who? What?"

"It was over as fast as it started," he said. "But then the war came and we were stuck. She became a friend," he said. "I'm quite fond of her" — which Netta translated as, "It is a subterranean river that may yet come to light." "You wouldn't know her," he said. "She's very different now. I talked so much about the south, down here, she finally found some land going dirt cheap at Bandol. The mayor arranged for her to have an orchard next to her property, so she won't have neighbours. It hardly cost her anything. He said to her, 'You're very pretty.' "

"No one ever had a bargain in property because of a pretty face," said Netta.

"Wasn't it lucky," said Jack. He could no longer hear himself, let alone Netta. "The war was unsettling, being in America. She minded not being active. Actually she was using the Swiss passport, which made it worse. Her brother was killed over Bremen. She needs security now. In a way it was sorcerer and apprentice between us, and she suddenly grew up. She'll be better off with a roof over her head. She writes a little now. Her poetry isn't bad," he said, as if Netta had challenged its quality.

"Is she at Bandol now, writing poetry?"

"Well, no." He laughed suddenly. "There isn't a roof yet. And, you know, people don't sit writing that way. They just think they're going to."

"Who has replaced you?" said Netta. "Another sorcerer?"

"Oh, *he* . . . he looks like George II in a strong light. Or like Queen Anne. Queen Anne and Lady Mary, somebody called them." Iris, that must have been. Queen Anne and Lady Mary wasn't bad — better than King Charles and his spaniel. She was beginning to enjoy his story. He saw it, and said lightly, "I was too preoccupied with you to manage another life. I couldn't see myself going on and on away from you. I didn't want to grow middle-aged at odds with myself."

But he had lost her; she was enjoying a reverie about Jack now, wearing one of those purple sunburns people acquire at golf. She saw him driving an open car, with large soft freckles on his purple skull. She saw his mistress's dog on the front seat and the dog's ears flying like pennants. The revulsion she felt did not lend distance but brought a dreamy reality closer still. He must be thirty-four now, she said to herself. A terrible age for a man who has never imagined thirty-four.

"Well, perhaps you have made a mess of it," she said, quoting Iris.

"What mess? I'm here. *He* —"

"Queen Anne?"

"Yes, well, actually Gerald is his name; he wears nothing but brown. Brown suit, brown tie, brown shoes. I said, '*He* can't go to Mitten Todd. He won't match.' "

"Harmonize," she said.

"That's it. Harmonize with the —"

"What about Gerald's wife? I'm sure he has one."

"Lucretia."

"No, really?"

"On my honour. When I last saw them they were all together, talking."

Netta was remembering what the middle sister had said about laughter on the balcony. She couldn't look at him. The merest crossing of glances made her start laughing rather wildly into her hands. The hysterical quality of her own laughter caught her in midair. What were they talking about? He hitched his chair nearer and dared to take her wrist.

"Tell me, now," he said as if they were to be two old confidence men getting their stories straight. "What about you? Was there ever . . . " The glaze of laughter had not left his face and voice. She saw that he would make her his business, if she let him. Pulling back, she felt another clasp, through a wall of fog. She groped for this other, invisible hand, but it dissolved. It was a lost, indifferent hand; it no longer recognized her warmth. She understood: He is dead . . . Jack, closed to ghosts, deaf to their voices, was spared this. He would be spared everything, she saw. She envied him his imperviousness, his true unhysterical laughter.

Perhaps that's why I kicked him, she said. I was always jealous. Not of women. Of his short memory, his comfortable imagination. And I am going to be thirty-seven and I have a dark, an accurate, a deadly memory.

He still held her wrist and turned it another way, saying, "Look, there's paint on it."

"Oh, God, where is the waiter?" she cried, as if that were the one important thing. Jack looked his age, exactly. She looked like a burned-out child who had been told a ghost story. Desperately seeking the waiter, she turned to the café behind them and saw the last light of the long afternoon strike the mirror above the bar — a flash in a tunnel; hands juggling with fire. That unexpected play, at a remove, borne indoors, displayed to anyone who could stare without blinking, was a complete story. It was the brightness on the looking glass, the only part of a life, or a love, or a promise, that could never be concealed, changed, or corrupted.

Not a hope, she was trying to tell him. He could read her face now. She reminded herself, If I say it, I am free. I can finish painting the radiators in peace. I can read every book in the world. If I had relied on my memory for guidance, I would never have crept out of the wine cellar. Memory is what ought to prevent you from buying a dog after the first dog dies, but it never does. It should at least keep you from saying yes twice to the same person.

"I've always loved you," he chose to announce — it really was an announcement, in a new voice that stated nothing except facts.

The dark, the ghosts, the candlelight, her tears on the scarred bar — *they* were real. And still, whether she wanted to see it or not, the light of imagination danced all over the square. She did not dare to turn again to the mirror, lest she confuse the two and forget which light was real. A pure white awning on a cross street seemed to her to be of indestructible beauty. The window it sheltered was hollowed with sadness and shadow. She said with the same deep sadness, "I believe you." The wave of revulsion receded, sucked back under another wave — a powerful adolescent craving for something simple, such as true love.

Her face did not show this. It was set in adolescent stubbornness, and this was one of their old, secret meetings when, sullen and hurt, she had to be coaxed into life as Jack wanted it lived. It was the same voyage, at the same rate of speed. The Place seemed to her to be full of invisible traffic — first a whisper of tires, then a faint, high screeching, then a steady roar. If Jack heard anything, it could be only the blood in the veins and his loud, happy thought. To a practical romantic like Jack, dying to get Netta to bed right away, what she was hearing was only the uh-hebb and flo-ho of hormones, as Dr. Blackley said. She caught a look of amazement on his face: *Now* he knew what he had been deprived of. *Now* he remembered. It had been Netta, all along.

Their evening shadows accompanied them over the long square. "I still have a car," she remarked. "But no petrol. There's a train." She did keep on hearing a noise, as of heavy traffic rushing near and tearing away. Her own quiet voice carried across it, saying, "Not a hope." He must have heard that. Why, it was as loud as a shout. He held her arm lightly. He was as buoyant as morning. This was his morning — the first light on the mirror, the first cigarette. He pulled her into an archway where no one could see. What could I do, she asked her ghosts, but let my arm be held, my steps be guided?

Later, Jack said that the walk with Netta back across the Place Masséna was the happiest event of his life. Having no reliable counter-event to put in its place, she let the memory stand.

෫෫෬

Though born in Montréal, Mavis Gallant has lived and worked in Paris for most of her life. Her stories often concern — recalling Henry James — "the international theme," and their historical and political sophistication has won them wide acclaim. "The Moslem Wife," published in 1976, is the story of Netta and her husband Jack, who is also her first cousin. The story covers the years around the Second World War, so we become intently aware of the passage of time, of change. Ironically, though Netta has acute powers of insight, she is unable to change her life, while Jack, the passive victim of chance and opportunity, suffers less — in fact is happy. Mirrors, and light, become metaphors for the way Netta sees things indirectly, as reflections. "The Moslem Wife" is a title given by others to characterize her apparent subservience to her husband. She is constructed by others, by what they say and do — starting of course with her father. In the end, even after she has broken with Jack, and admitted her contempt for him, she takes him back. She does so because "the light of imagination" falls momentarily on her world, and "a pure white awning on a cross street seemed to her to be of indestructible beauty." Now, her old life is restored. But whose life is it? She is "coaxed into life as Jack wanted it." Her defeat verges on a generous openness to Jack's temperament, to his words. This all happens in the presence of light, as if her loss is a gift.

A.S.

Charlotte Perkins Gilman *(1860-1935)*

The Yellow Wall-paper

I t is very seldom that mere ordinary people like John and myself secure ancestral halls for the summer.

A colonial mansion, a hereditary estate, I would say a haunted house, and reach the height of romantic felicity — but that would be asking too much of fate!

Still I will proudly declare that there is something queer about it.

Else, why should it be let so cheaply? And why have stood so long untenanted?

John laughs at me, of course, but one expects that in marriage.

John is practical in the extreme. He has no patience with faith, an intense horror of superstition, and he scoffs openly at any talk of things not to be felt and seen and put down in figures.

John is a physician, and *perhaps* — (I would not say it to a living soul, of course, but this is dead paper and a great relief to my mind) — *perhaps* that is one reason I do not get well faster.

You see, he does not believe I am sick!

And what can one do?

If a physician of high standing, and one's own husband, assures friends and relatives that there is really nothing the matter with one but temporary nervous depression — a slight hysterical tendency — what is one to do?

My brother is also a physician, and also of high standing, and he says the same thing.

So I take phosphates or phosphites — whichever it is — and tonics, and journeys, and air, and exercise, and am absolutely forbidden to "work" until I am well again.

Personally, I disagree with their ideas.

Personally, I believe that congenial work, with excitement and change, would do me good.

But what is one to do?

I did write for a while in spite of them; but it *does* exhaust me a good deal — having to be so sly about it, or else meet with heavy opposition.

I sometimes fancy that in my condition if I had less opposition and more society and stimulus — but John says the very worst thing I can do is to think about my condition, and I confess it always makes me feel bad.

So I will let it alone and talk about the house.

The most beautiful place! It is quite alone, standing well back from the road, quite three miles from the village. It makes me think of English places that you read about, for there are hedges and walls and gates that lock, and lots of separate little houses for the gardeners and people.

There is a *delicious* garden! I never saw such a garden — large and shady, full of box-bordered paths, and lined with long grape-covered arbours with seats under them.

There were greenhouses, but they are all broken now.

There was some legal trouble, I believe, something about the heirs and co-heirs; anyhow, the place has been empty for years.

That spoils my ghostliness, I am afraid, but I don't care — there is something strange about the house — I can feel it.

I even said so to John one moonlight evening, but he said what I felt was a *draught*, and shut the window.

I get unreasonably angry with John sometimes. I'm sure I never used to be so sensitive. I think it is due to this nervous condition.

But John says if I feel so, I shall neglect proper self-control; so I take pains to control myself — before him, at least, and that makes me very tired.

I don't like our room a bit. I wanted one downstairs that opened on the piazza and had roses all over the window, and such pretty old-fashioned chintz hangings! But John would not hear of it.

He said there was only one window and not room for two beds, and no near room for him if he took another.

He is very careful and loving, and hardly lets me stir without special direction.

I have a schedule prescription for each hour in the day; he takes all care from me, and so I feel basely ungrateful not to value it more.

He said we came here solely on my account, that I was to have perfect rest and all the air I could get. "Your exercise depends on your strength, my dear," said he, "and your food somewhat on your appetite; but air you can absorb all the time." So we took the nursery at the top of the house.

It is a big, airy room, the whole floor nearly, with windows that look all ways, and air and sunshine galore. It was nursery first and then playroom and gymnasium, I should judge; for the windows are barred for little children, and there are rings and things in the walls.

The paint and paper look as if a boys' school had used it. It is stripped off — the paper — in great patches all around the head of my bed, about as far as I can reach, and in a great place on the other side of the room low down. I never saw a worse paper in my life.

One of those sprawling flamboyant patterns committing every artistic sin.

It is dull enough to confuse the eye in following, pronounced enough to constantly irritate and provoke study, and when you follow the lame uncertain curves for a little distance they suddenly commit suicide — plunge off at outrageous angles, destroy themselves in unheard of contradictions.

The colour is repellent, almost revolting; a smouldering unclean yellow, strangely faded by the slow-turning sunlight.

It is a dull yet lurid orange in some places, a sickly sulphur tint in others.

No wonder the children hated it! I should hate it myself if I had to live in this room long.

There comes John, and I must put this away — he hates to have me write a word.

C3

We have been here two weeks, and I haven't felt like writing before, since that first day.

I am sitting by the window now, up in this atrocious nursery, and there is nothing to hinder my writing as much as I please, save lack of strength.

John is away all day, and even some nights when his cases are serious.

I am glad my case is not serious!

But these nervous troubles are dreadfully depressing.

John does not know how much I really suffer. He knows there is no *reason* to suffer, and that satisfies him.

Of course it is only nervousness. It does weigh on me so not to do my duty in any way!

I meant to be such a help to John, such a real rest and comfort, and here I am a comparative burden already!

Nobody would believe what an effort it is to do what little I am able — to dress and entertain, and order things.

It is fortunate Mary is so good with the baby. Such a dear baby!

And yet I *cannot* be with him, it makes me so nervous.

I suppose John never was nervous in his life. He laughs at me so about this wall-paper!

At first he meant to repaper the room, but afterwards he said that I was letting it get the better of me, and that nothing was worse for a nervous patient than to give way to such fancies.

He said that after the wall-paper was changed it would be the heavy bedstead, and then the barred windows, and then that gate at the head of the stairs, and so on.

"You know the place is doing you good," he said, "and really, dear, I don't care to renovate the house just for a three months' rental."

"Then do let us go downstairs," I said. "There are such pretty rooms there."

Then he took me in his arms and called me a blessed little goose, and said he would go down cellar, if I wished, and have it whitewashed into the bargain.

But he is right enough about the beds and windows and things.

It is as airy and comfortable a room as anyone need wish, and, of course, I would not be so silly as to make him uncomfortable just for a whim.

I'm really getting quite fond of the big room, all but that horrid paper.

Out of one window I can see the garden, those mysterious deep-shaded arbours, the riotous old-fashioned flowers, and bushes and gnarly trees.

Out of another I get a lovely view of the bay and a little private wharf belonging to the estate. There is a beautiful shaded lane that runs down there from the house. I always fancy I see people walking in these numerous paths and arbours, but John has cautioned me not to give way to fancy in the least. He says that with my imaginative power and habit of story-making, a nervous weakness like mine is sure to lead to all manner of excited fancies, and that I ought to use my will and good sense to check the tendency. So I try.

I think sometimes that if I were only well enough to write a little it would relieve the press of ideas and rest me.

But I find I get pretty tired when I try.

It is so discouraging not to have any advice and companionship about my work. When I get really well, John says we will ask Cousin Henry and Julia down for a long visit; but he says he would as soon put fireworks in my pillow-case as to let me have those stimulating people about now.

I wish I could get well faster.

But I must not think about that. This paper looks to me as if it *knew* what a vicious influence it had!

There is a recurrent spot where the pattern lolls like a broken neck and two bulbous eyes stare at you upside down.

I get positively angry with the impertinence of it and the everlastingness. Up and down and sideways they crawl, and those absurd, unblinking eyes are everywhere. There is one place where two breadths didn't match, and the eyes go all up and down the line, one a little higher than the other.

I never saw so much expression in an inanimate thing before, and we all know how much expression they have! I used to lie awake as a child and get more entertainment and terror out of blank walls and plain furniture than most children could find in a toy-store.

I remember what a kindly wink the knobs of our big, old bureau used to have, and there was one chair that always seemed like a strong friend.

I used to feel that if any of the other things looked too fierce I could always hop into that chair and be safe.

The furniture in this room is no worse than inharmonious, however, for we had to bring it all from downstairs. I suppose when this was used as a playroom they had to take the nursery things out, and no wonder! I never saw such ravages as the children have made here.

The wall-paper, as I said before, is torn off in spots, and it sticketh closer than a brother — they must have had perseverance as well as hatred.

Then the floor is scratched and gouged and splintered, the plaster itself is dug out here and there, and this great heavy bed, which is all we found in the room, looks as if it had been through the wars.

But I don't mind it a bit — only the paper.

There comes John's sister. Such a dear girl as she is, and so careful of me! I must not let her find me writing.

She is a perfect and enthusiastic housekeeper, and hopes for no better profession. I verily believe she thinks it is the writing which made me sick!

But I can write when she is out, and see her a long way off from these windows.

There is one that commands the road, a lovely shaded winding road, and one that just looks off over the country. A lovely country, too, full of great elms and velvet meadows.

This wall-paper has a kind of sub-pattern in a different shade, a particularly irritating one, for you can only see it in certain lights, and not clearly then.

But in the places where it isn't faded and where the sun is just so — I can see a strange, provoking, formless sort of figure, that seems to skulk about behind that silly and conspicuous front design.

There's sister on the stairs!

CR

Well, the Fourth of July is over! The people are all gone, and I am tired out. John thought it might do me good to see a little company, so we just had mother and Nellie and the children down for a week.

Of course I didn't do a thing. Jennie sees to everything now.

But it tired me all the same.

John says if I don't pick up faster he shall send me to Weir Mitchell in the fall.

But I don't want to go there at all. I had a friend who was in his hands once, and she says he is just like John and my brother, only more so!

Besides, it is such an undertaking to go so far.

I don't feel as if it was worth while to turn my hand over for anything, and I'm getting dreadfully fretful and querulous.

I cry at nothing, and cry most of the time.

Of course I don't when John is here, or anybody else, but when I am alone.

And I am alone a good deal just now. John is kept in town very often by serious cases, and Jennie is good and lets me alone when I want her to.

So I walk a little in the garden or down that lovely lane, sit on the porch under the roses, and lie down up here a good deal.

I'm getting really fond of the room in spite of the wall-paper. Perhaps *because* of the wall-paper.

It dwells in my mind so!

I lie here on this great immovable bed — it is nailed down, I believe — and follow that pattern about by the hour. It is as good as gymnastics, I assure you. I start, we'll say, at the bottom, down in the corner over there where it has not been touched, and I determine for the thousandth time that I *will* follow that pointless pattern to some sort of conclusion.

I know a little of the principle of design, and I know this thing was not arranged on any laws of radiation, or alternation, or repetition, or symmetry, or anything else that I ever heard of.

It is repeated, of course, by the breadths, but not otherwise.

Looked at in one way, each breadth stands alone, the bloated curves and flourishes — a kind of "debased Romanesque" with *delirium tremens* — go waddling up and down in isolated columns of fatuity.

But, on the other hand, they connect diagonally, and the sprawling outlines run off in great slanting waves of optic horror, like a lot of wallowing sea-weeds in full chase.

The whole thing goes horizontally, too, at least it seems so, and I exhaust myself trying to distinguish the order of its going in that direction.

They have used a horizontal breadth for a frieze, and that adds wonderfully to the confusion.

There is one end of the room where it is almost intact, and there, when the crosslights fade and the low sun shines directly upon it, I can almost fancy radiation after all — the interminable grotesques seem to form around a common centre and rush off in headlong plunges of equal distraction.

It makes me tired to follow it. I will take a nap I guess.

છ

I don't know why I should write this.

I don't want to.

I don't feel able.

And I know John would think it absurd. But I *must* say what I feel and think in some way — it is such a relief!

But the effort is getting to be greater than the relief.

Half the time now I am awfully lazy, and lie down ever so much.

John says I mustn't lose my strength, and has me take cod liver oil and lots of tonics and things, to say nothing of ale and wine and rare meat.

Dear John! He loves me very dearly, and hates to have me sick. I tried to have a real earnest reasonable talk with him the other day, and tell him how I wish he would let me go and make a visit to Cousin Henry and Julia.

But he said I wasn't able to go, nor able to stand it after I got there; and I did not make out a very good case for myself, for I was crying before I had finished.

It is getting to be a great effort for me to think straight. Just this nervous weakness I suppose.

And dear John gathered me up in his arms, and just carried me upstairs and laid me on the bed, and sat by me and read to me till it tired my head.

He said I was his darling and his comfort and all he had, and that I must take care of myself for his sake, and keep well.

He says no one but myself can help me out of it, that I must use my will and self-control and not let any silly fancies run away with me.

There's one comfort, the baby is well and happy, and does not have to occupy this nursery with the horrid wall-paper.

If we had not used it, that blessed child would have! What a fortunate escape! Why, I wouldn't have a child of mine, an impressionable little thing, live in such a room for worlds.

I never thought of it before, but it is lucky that John kept me here after all, I can stand it so much easier than a baby, you see.

Of course I never mention it to them any more — I am too wise — but I keep watch of it all the same.

There are things in that paper that nobody knows about but me, or ever will.

Behind that outside pattern the dim shapes get clearer every day.

It is always the same shape, only very numerous.

And it is like a woman stooping down and creeping about behind that pattern. I don't like it a bit. I wonder — I begin to think — I wish John would take me away from here!

CR

It is so hard to talk with John about my case, because he is so wise, and because he loves me so.

But I tried it last night.

It was moonlight. The moon shines in all around just as the sun does.

I hate to see it sometimes, it creeps so slowly, and always comes in by one window or another.

John was asleep and I hated to waken him, so I kept still and watched the moonlight on that undulating wall-paper till I felt creepy.

The faint figure behind seemed to shake the pattern, just as if she wanted to get out.

I got up softly and went to feel and see if the paper *did* move, and when I came back John was awake.

"What is it, little girl?" he said. "Don't go walking about like that — you'll get cold."

I thought it was a good time to talk, so I told him that I really was not gaining here, and that I wished he would take me away.

"Why, darling!" said he. "Our lease will be up in three weeks, and I can't see how to leave before.

"The repairs are not done at home, and I cannot possibly leave town just now. Of course if you were in any danger, I could and would, but you really are better, dear, whether you can see it or not. I am a doctor, dear, and I know. You are gaining flesh and colour, your appetite is better, I feel really much easier about you."

"I don't weigh a bit more," said I, "nor as much; and my appetite may be better in the evening when you are here, but it is worse in the morning when you are away!"

"Bless her little heart!" said he with a big hug, "she shall be as sick as she pleases! But now let's improve the shining hours by going to sleep, and talk about it in the morning!"

"And you won't go away?" I asked gloomily.

"Why, how can I, dear? It is only three weeks more and then we will take a nice little trip of a few days while Jennie is getting the house ready. Really, dear, you are better!"

"Better in body perhaps —" I began, and stopped short, for he sat up straight and looked at me with such a stern, reproachful look that I could not say another word.

"My darling," said he, "I beg of you, for my sake and for our child's sake, as well as for your own, that you will never for one instant let that idea enter your mind! There is nothing so dangerous, so fascinating, to a temperament like yours. It is a false and foolish fancy. Can you not trust me as a physician when I tell you so?"

So of course I said no more on that score, and we went to sleep before long. He thought I was asleep first, but I wasn't, and lay there for hours trying to decide whether that front pattern and the back pattern really did move together or separately.

CR

On a pattern like this, by daylight, there is a lack of sequence, a defiance of law, that is a constant irritant to a normal mind.

The colour is hideous enough, and unreliable enough, and infuriating enough, but the pattern is torturing.

You think you have mastered it, but just as you get well underway in following, it turns a back-somersault and there you are. It slaps you in the face, knocks you down, and tramples upon you. It is like a bad dream.

The outside pattern is a florid arabesque, reminding one of a fungus. If you can imagine a toadstool in joints, an interminable string of toadstools, budding and sprouting in endless convolutions — why, that is something like it.

That is, sometimes!

There is one marked peculiarity about this paper, a thing nobody seems to notice but myself, and that is that it changes as the light changes.

When the sun shoots in through the east window — I always watch for that first long, straight ray — it changes so quickly that I never can quite believe it.

That is why I watch it always.

By moonlight — the moon shines in all night when there is a moon — I wouldn't know it was the same paper.

At night in any kind of light, in twilight, candlelight, lamplight, and worst of all by moonlight, it becomes bars! The outside pattern, I mean, and the woman behind it is as plain as can be.

I didn't realize for a long time what the thing was that showed behind, that dim sub-pattern, but now I am quite sure it is a woman.

By daylight she is subdued, quiet. I fancy it is the pattern that keeps her so still. It is so puzzling. It keeps me quiet by the hour.

I lie down ever so much now. John says it is good for me, and to sleep all I can.

Indeed he started the habit by making me lie down for an hour after each meal.

It is a very bad habit I am convinced, for you see I don't sleep.

And that cultivates deceit, for I don't tell them I'm awake — O no!

The fact is I am getting a little afraid of John.

He seems very queer sometimes, and even Jennie has an inexplicable look.

It strikes me occasionally, just as a scientific hypothesis, that perhaps it is the paper!

I have watched John when he did not know I was looking, and come into the room suddenly on the most innocent excuses, and I've caught him several times *looking at the paper!* And Jennie too. I caught Jennie with her hand on it once.

She didn't know I was in the room, and when I asked her in a quiet, a very quiet voice, with the most restrained manner possible, what she was doing with the paper — she turned around as if she had been caught stealing, and looked quite angry — asked me why I should frighten her so!

Then she said that the paper stained everything it touched, that she had found yellow smooches on all my clothes and John's, and she wished we would be more careful!

Did not that sound innocent? But I know she was studying that pattern, and I am determined that nobody shall find it out but myself!

CR

Life is very much more exciting now than it used to be. You see I have something more to expect, to look forward to, to watch. I really do eat better, and am more quiet than I was.

John is so pleased to see me improve! He laughed a little the other day, and said I seemed to be flourishing in spite of my wall-paper.

I turned it off with a laugh. I had no intention of telling him it was *because* of the wall-paper — he would make fun of me. He might even want to take me away.

I don't want to leave now until I have found it out. There is a week more, and I think that will be enough.

CR

I'm feeling ever so much better! I don't sleep much at night, for it is so interesting to watch developments; but I sleep a good deal during the daytime.

In the daytime it is tiresome and perplexing.

There are always new shoots on the fungus, and new shades of yellow all over it. I cannot keep count of them, though I have tried conscientiously.

It is the strangest yellow, that wall-paper! It makes me think of all the yellow things I ever saw — not beautiful ones like buttercups, but old foul, bad yellow things.

But there is something else about that paper — the smell! I noticed it the moment we came into the room, but with so much air and sun it was not bad. Now we have had a week of fog and rain, and whether the windows are open or not, the smell is here.

It creeps all over the house.

I find it hovering in the dining-room, skulking in the parlour, hiding in the hall, lying in wait for me on the stairs.

It gets into my hair.

Even when I go to ride, if I turn my head suddenly and surprise it — there is that smell!

Such a peculiar odour, too! I have spent hours in trying to analyze it, to find what it smelled like.

It is not bad — at first — and very gentle, but quite the subtlest, most enduring odour I ever met.

In this damp weather it is awful, I wake up in the night and find it hanging over me.

It used to disturb me at first. I thought seriously of burning the house — to reach the smell.

But now I am used to it. The only thing I can think of that it is like is the *colour* of the paper! A yellow smell.

There is a very funny mark on this wall, low down, near the mopboard. A streak that runs round the room. It goes behind every piece of furniture, except the bed, a long, straight, even *smooch*, as if it had been rubbed over and over.

I wonder how it was done and who did it, and what they did it for. Round and round and round — round and round and round — it makes me dizzy!

CR

I really have discovered something at last.

Through watching so much at night, when it changes so, I have finally found out.

The front pattern *does* move — and no wonder! The woman behind shakes it!

Sometimes I think there are a great many women behind, and sometimes only one, and she crawls around fast, and her crawling shakes it all over.

Then in the very bright spots she keeps still, and in the very shady spots she just takes hold of the bars and shakes them hard.

And she is all the time trying to climb through. But nobody could climb through that pattern — it strangles so; I think that is why it has so many heads.

They get through, and then the pattern strangles them off and turns them upside down, and makes their eyes white!

If those heads were covered or taken off it would not be half so bad.

CR

I think that woman gets out in the daytime!

And I'll tell you why — privately — I've seen her!

I can see her out of every one of my windows!

It is the same woman, I know, for she is always creeping, and most women do not creep by daylight.

I see her in that long shaded lane, creeping up and down. I see her in those dark grape arbours, creeping all around the garden.

I see her on that long road under the trees, creeping along, and when a carriage comes she hides under the blackberry vines.

I don't blame her a bit. It must be very humiliating to be caught creeping by daylight!

I always lock the door when I creep by daylight. I can't do it at night, for I know John would suspect something at once.

And John is so queer now, that I don't want to irritate him. I wish he would take another room! Besides, I don't want anybody to get that woman out at night but myself.

I often wonder if I could see her out of all the windows at once.

But, turn as fast as I can, I can only see out of one at one time.

And though I always see her, she *may* be able to creep faster than I can turn!

I have watched her sometimes away off in the open country, creeping as fast as a cloud shadow in a high wind.

CR

If only that top pattern could be gotten off from the under one! I mean to try it, little by little.

I have found out another funny thing, but I shan't tell it this time! It does not do to trust people too much.

There are only two more days to get this paper off, and I believe John is beginning to notice. I don't like the look in his eyes.

And I heard him ask Jennie a lot of professional questions about me. She had a very good report to give.

She said I slept a good deal in the daytime.

John knows I don't sleep very well at night, for all I'm so quiet!

He asked me all sorts of questions, too, and pretended to be very loving and kind.

As if I couldn't see through him!

Still, I don't wonder he acts so, sleeping under this paper for three months.

It only interests me, but I feel sure John and Jennie are affected by it.

CR

Hurrah! This is the last day, but it is enough. John is to stay in town over night, and won't be out until this evening.

Jennie wanted to sleep with me — the sly thing! — but I told her I should undoubtedly rest better for a night all alone.

That was clever, for really I wasn't alone a bit! As soon as it was moonlight and that poor thing began to crawl and shake the pattern, I got up and ran to help her.

I pulled and she shook, I shook and she pulled, and before morning we had peeled off yards of that paper.

A strip about as high as my head and half around the room.

And then when the sun came and that awful pattern began to laugh at me, I declared I would finish it to-day!

We go away to-morrow, and they are moving all my furniture down again to leave things as they were before.

Jennie looked at the wall in amazement, but I told her merrily that I did it out of pure spite at the vicious thing.

She laughed and said she wouldn't mind doing it herself, but I must not get tired.

How she betrayed herself that time!

But I am here, and no person touches this paper but me — not *alive!*

She tried to get me out of the room — it was too patent! But I said it was so quiet and empty and clean now that I believed I would lie down again and sleep all I could; and not to wake me even for dinner — I would call when I woke.

So now she is gone, and the servants are gone, and the things are gone, and there is nothing left but that great bedstead nailed down, with the canvas mattress we found on it.

We shall sleep downstairs to-night, and take the boat home to-morrow.

I quite enjoy the room, now it is bare again.

How those children did tear about here!

This bedstead is fairly gnawed!

But I must get to work.

I have locked the door and thrown the key down into the front path.

I don't want to go out, and I don't want to have anybody come in, till John comes.

I want to astonish him.

I've got a rope up here that even Jennie did not find. If that woman does get out, and tries to get away, I can tie her!

But I forgot I could not reach far without anything to stand on!

This bed will *not* move!

I tried to lift and push it until I was lame, and then I got so angry I bit off a little piece at one corner — but it hurt my teeth.

Then I peeled off all the paper I could reach standing on the floor. It sticks horribly and the pattern just enjoys it! All those strangled heads and bulbous eyes and waddling fungus growths just shriek with derision!

I am getting angry enough to do something desperate. To jump out of the window would be admirable exercise, but the bars are too strong even to try.

Besides, I wouldn't do it. Of course not. I know well enough that a step like that is improper and might be misconstrued.

I don't like to *look* out of the windows even — there are so many of those creeping women, and they creep so fast.

I wonder if they all come out of that wall-paper as I did?

But I am securely fastened now by my well-hidden rope — you don't get *me* out in the road there!

I suppose I shall have to get back behind the pattern when it comes night, and that is hard!

It is so pleasant to be out in this great room and creep around as I please!

I don't want to go outside. I won't, even if Jennie asks me to.

For outside you have to creep on the ground, and everything is green instead of yellow.

But here I can creep smoothly on the floor, and my shoulder just fits in that long smooch around the wall, so I cannot lose my way.

Why, there's John at the door!

It is no use, young man, you can't open it!

How he does call and pound!

Now he's crying for an axe.

It would be a shame to break down that beautiful door!

"John dear!" said I in the gentlest voice, "the key is down by the front steps, under a plantain leaf!"

That silenced him for a few moments.

Then he said — very quietly indeed — "Open the door, my darling!"

"I can't," said I. "The key is down by the front door under a plantain leaf!"

And then I said it again, several times, very gently and slowly, and said it so often that he had to go and see, and he got it of course, and came in. He stopped short by the door.

"What is the matter?" he cried. "For God's sake, what are you doing!"

I kept on creeping just the same, but I looked at him over my shoulder.

"I've got out at last," said I, "in spite of you and Jane! And I've pulled off most of the paper, so you can't put me back!"

Now why should that man have fainted? But he did, and right across my path by the wall, so that I had to creep over him every time!

ଚୈଠ୫

In addition to being a creative writer, Charlotte Perkins Gilman was well known during her lifetime as a social reformer and cultural critic. Despite being regarded as a feminist writer (the word feminist *was coined in 1891), Gilman preferred to be called a humanist. Her reformist principles are reflected in "The Yellow Wall-paper," a short story that has as one of its avowed purposes the criticism of Dr. S. Weir Mitchell's celebrated "rest cures," which nearly drove Gilman herself to madness and suicide. But this auto-biography is fictionalized to reveal the healing power that the nameless protagonist receives from the "work" of the imagination. The main character comes to realize that she has the ability to imagine new possibilities for herself beyond her husband and his patriarchal medical profession. Her escape from a male-dominated world remains ambivalent, however, since she must "creep" like a beast. Yet, through her rebellious acts of writing, and reading her fragmented self into the wallpaper, she wins our sympathy and admiration because she endures "unheard-of contradictions." She must endure not only the unheard-of freedom her fancy uncovers outside the severely restricted roles imposed upon women, but also the "formless figure" of her own identity.*

G.S.

NICOLAI GOGOL   *(1809-1852)*

The Overcoat

In the department . . . but perhaps it is just as well not to say in which department. There is nothing more touchy and ill-tempered in the world than departments, regiments, government offices, and indeed any kind of official body. Nowadays every private individual takes a personal insult to be an insult against society at large. I am told that not so very long ago a police commissioner (I don't remember of what town) sent in a petition to the authorities in which he stated in so many words that all Government decrees had been defied and his own sacred name most decidedly taken in vain. And in proof he attached to his petition an enormous volume of some highly romantic work in which a police commissioner figured on almost every tenth page, sometimes in a very drunken state. So to avoid all sorts of unpleasant misunderstandings, we shall refer to the department in question as *a certain department*.

And so in *a certain department* there served *a certain Civil Servant*, a Civil Servant who cannot by any stretch of the imagination be described as in any way remarkable. He was in fact a somewhat short, somewhat pockmarked, somewhat red-haired man, who looked rather short-sighted and was slightly bald on the top of his head, with wrinkles on both cheeks, and a rather sallow complexion. There is nothing we can do about it: it is all the fault of the St. Petersburg climate. As for his rank (for with us rank is something that must be stated before anything else), he was what is known as a perpetual titular councillor, the ninth rank among the fourteen ranks into which our Civil Service is divided, a rank which, as every one knows, has been sneered at and held up to scorn by all sorts of writers who have the praiseworthy habit of setting upon those who cannot hit back. The Civil Servant's surname was Bashmachkin. From this it can be clearly inferred that it had once upon a time originated from the Russian word *bashmak*, to wit, shoe. But when, at what precise date, and under what circumstances the metamorphosis took place, must for ever remain a mystery. His father, grandfather, and, why, even his brother-in-law as well as all the rest of the Bashmachkins always walked about in boots, having their soles repaired no more than three times a year. His name and patronymic were Akaky Akakyevich. The reader may think it a little odd, not to say somewhat *recherché,* but we can assure him that we wasted no time in searching for this name and that it happened in the most natural way that no other name could be given to him, and the way it came about is as follows:

Akaky Akakyevich was born, if my memory serves me right, on the night of 23rd March. His mother of blessed memory, the wife of a Civil Servant and a most excellent woman in every respect, took all the necessary steps for the child to be christened. She was still lying in bed, facing the door, and on her right stood the godfather, Ivan Ivanovich Yeroshkin, a most admirable man, who was a head clerk at the Supreme Court, and the godmother, Arina Semyonovna Byelobrúshkina, the wife of the district police inspector, a most worthy woman. The mother was presented with the choice of three names, namely, Mokkia, Sossia, or, it was suggested, the child might be called after the martyr Khozdazat. "Oh dear," thought his late mother, "they're all such queer names!" To please her, the calendar was opened at another place, but again the three names that were found were rather uncommon, namely, Trifily, Dula and Varakhassy. "Bother," said the poor woman, "what queer names! I've really never heard such names! Now if it had only been Varadat or Varukh, but it would be Trifily and Varakhassy!" Another page was turned and the names in the calendar were Pavsikakhy and Vakhtissy. "Well," said the mother, "I can see that such is the poor innocent infant's fate. If that is so, let him rather be called after his father. His father was Akaky, so let the son be Akaky, too." It was in this way that he came to be called Akaky. The child was christened, and during the ceremony he began to cry and pulled such a face that it really seemed as though he had a premonition that he would be a titular councillor one day. Anyway, that is how it all came to pass.

We have told how it had come about at such length because we are anxious that the reader should realize himself that it could not have happened otherwise, and that to give him any other name was quite out of the question.

When and at what precise date Akaky had entered the department, and who had appointed him to it, is something that no one can remember. During all the years he had served in that department many directors and other higher officials had come and gone, but he still remained in exactly the same place, in exactly the same position, in exactly the same job, doing exactly the same kind of work, to wit, copying official documents. Indeed, with time the belief came to be generally held that he must have been born into the world entirely fitted out for his job, in his Civil Servant's uniform and a bald patch on his head. No particular respect was shown him in the department. Not only did the caretakers not get up from their seats when he passed by, but they did not even vouchsafe a glance at him, just as if a common fly had flown through the waiting-room. His superiors treated him in a manner that could be best described as frigidly despotic. Some assistant head clerk would just shove a paper under his nose without even saying, "Please copy it," or "Here's an interesting, amusing little case!" or something in a similarly pleasant vein as is the custom in all well-regulated official establishments. And he would accept it without raising his eyes from the paper, without looking up to see who had put it on his desk, or whether indeed he had any right to put it there. He just took it and immediately settled down to copy it. The young clerks laughed and cracked jokes about him, the sort of jokes young clerks could be expected to crack. They told stories about him in his presence, stories that were specially invented about him. They joked about his landlady, an old woman of seventy, who they claimed beat him, or they asked him when he was going to marry her. They also showered bits of torn paper on his head and called them snow. But never a word did Akaky say to it all, as though unaware of the presence of his tormentors in the office. It did not even interfere with his work; for while these rather annoying practical jokes were played on him he never made a single mistake in the document he was copying. It was only when the joke got too unbearable, when somebody jogged his arm and so interfered with his work, that he would say, "Leave me alone, gentlemen. Why do you pester me?" There was a strange note in the words and in the voice in which they were uttered: there was something in it that touched one's heart with pity. Indeed, one young man who had only recently been appointed to the department and who, following the example of the others, tried to have some fun at his expense, stopped abruptly at Akaky's mild expostulation, as though stabbed through the heart; and since then everything seemed to have changed in him and he saw everything in quite a different light. A kind of unseen power made him keep away from his colleagues whom at first he had taken for decent, well-bred men. And for a long time afterwards, in his happiest moments, he would see the shortish Civil Servant with the bald patch on his head, uttering those pathetic words, "Leave me alone! Why do you pester me?" And in those pathetic words he seemed to hear others: "I am your brother." And the poor young man used to bury his face in his hands, and many a time in his life he would shudder when he perceived how much inhumanity there was in man, how much savage brutality there lurked beneath the most refined, cultured manners, and, dear Lord, even in the man the world regarded as upright and honourable. . . .

It would be hard to find a man who lived so much for his job. It was not sufficient to say that he worked zealously. No, his work was a labour of love to him. There, in that copying of his, he seemed to see a multifarious and pleasant world of his own. Enjoyment was written on his face; some letters he was particularly fond of, and whenever he had the chance of writing them, he was beside himself with joy, chuckling to himself, winking and helping them on with his lips, so that you could, it seemed, read on his face every letter his pen was forming with such care. If he had been rewarded in accordance with his zeal, he would to his own surprise have got as far as a state councillorship; but, as the office wits expressed it, all he got for his pains was a metal disc in his button-hole and a stitch in his side. Still it would be untrue to say that no one took any notice of him. One director, indeed, being a thoroughly good man and anxious to reward him for his long service, ordered that he should be given some more responsible work than his usual copying, that is to say, he was told to prepare a report for another department of an already concluded case; all he had to do was to alter the title at the top of the document and change some of the verbs from the first to the third person singular. This, however, gave him so much trouble that he was bathed in perspiration and kept mopping his forehead until at last he said, "No, I can't do it. You'd better give me something to copy." Since then they let him carry on with his copying for ever. Outside this copying nothing seemed to exist for him. He never gave a thought to his clothes: his uniform was no longer green, but of some nondescript rusty white. His collar was very short and narrow so that his neck, though it was not at all long, looked as if it stuck a mile out of the collar, like the necks of the plaster kittens with wagging heads, scores of which are carried about on their heads by street-vendors of non-Russian nationality. And something always seemed to cling to his uniform: either a straw or some thread. He possessed, besides, the peculiar knack when walking in the street of passing under a window just at the time when some rubbish was tipped out of it, and for this reason he always carried about on his hat bits of watermelon or melon rind and similar trash. He had never in his life paid the slightest attention to what was going on daily in the street, and in this he was quite unlike his young colleagues in the Civil Service, who are famous as observers of street life, their eagle-eyed curiosity going even so far as to notice that the strap under the trousers of some man on the pavement on the other side of the street has come undone, a thing which never fails to bring a malicious grin to their faces. But even if Akaky did look at anything, he saw nothing but his own neat lines, written out in an even hand, and only if a horse's muzzle, appearing from goodness knows where, came to rest on his shoulder and blew a gale on his cheek from its nostrils, did he become aware of the fact that he was not in the middle of a line, but rather in the middle of the street.

On his arrival home, he would at once sit down at the table, quickly gulp down his cabbage soup, eat a piece of beef with onions without noticing what it tasted like, eating whatever Providence happened to send at the time, flies and all. Noticing that his stomach was beginning to feel full, he would get up from the table, fetch his inkwell and start copying the papers he had brought home with him. If, however, there were no more papers to copy, he would deliberately make another copy for his own pleasure, intending to keep it for himself, especially if the paper was remarkable not so much for the beauty of its style as for the fact of being addressed to some new or important person.

Even at those hours when all the light has faded from the grey St. Petersburg sky, and the Civil Service folk have taken their fill of food and dined each as best he could, according to his salary and his personal taste; when all have had their rest after the departmental scraping of pens, after all the rush and bustle, after their own and other people's indispensable business had been brought to a conclusion, and anything else restless man imposes upon himself of his own free will had been done, and even much more than is necessary; when every Civil Servant is hastening to enjoy as best he can the remaining hours of his leisure — one more enterprising rushing off to the theatre, another going for a stroll to stare at some silly women's hats, a third going to a party to waste his time paying compliments to some pretty girl, the star of some small Civil Service circle, while a fourth — as happens in nine cases out of ten — paying a call on a fellow Civil Servant living on the third or fourth floor in a flat of two small rooms with a tiny hall or kitchen, with some pretensions to fashion — a lamp or some other article that has cost many self-denying sacrifices, such as doing without dinners or country outings; in short, even when all the Civil Servants have dispersed among the tiny flats of their friends to play a stormy game of whist, sipping tea from glasses and nibbling a penny biscuit, or inhaling the smoke of their long pipes and, while dealing the cards, retailing the latest high society scandal (for every Russian is so devotedly attached to high society that he cannot dispense with it for a moment), or, when there is nothing else to talk about, telling the old chestnut about the fortress commandant who was told that the tail of the horse of Falconnetti's statue of Peter I had been docked — in short, even while every government official in the capital was doing his best to enjoy himself, Akaky Akakyevich made no attempt to woo the fair goddess of mirth and jollity. No one could possibly ever claim to have seen him at a party. Having copied out documents to his heart's content, he went to bed, smiling in anticipation of the pleasures the next day had in store for him and wondering what the good Lord would send him to copy. So passed the peaceful life of a man who knew how to be content with his lot on a salary of four hundred roubles a year; and it might have flowed on as happily to a ripe old age, were it not for the various calamities which beset the lives not only of titular, but of privy, actual, court, and any other councillors, even those who give no counsel to any man, nor take any from anyone, either.

There is in St. Petersburg a great enemy of all those who receive a salary of four hundred roubles a year, or thereabouts. This enemy is none other than our northern frost, though you will hear people say that it is very good for the health. At nine o'clock in the morning, just at the hour when the streets are full of Civil Servants on their way to their departments, he starts giving such mighty and stinging filips to all noses without exception, that the poor fellows simply do not know where to put them. At a time when the foreheads of even those who occupy the highest positions in the State ache with the frost, and tears start to their eyes, the poor titular councillors are sometimes left utterly defenceless. Their only salvation lies in running as fast as they can in their thin, threadbare overcoats through five or six streets and then stamping their feet vigorously in the vestibule, until they succeed in unfreezing their faculties and abilities, frozen on the way, and are once more able to tackle the affairs of State.

Akaky had for some time been feeling that the fierce cold seemed to have no difficulty at all in penetrating to his back and shoulders, however fast he tried to sprint across the legal distance from his home to the department. It occurred to him at length that his overcoat might not be entirely blameless for this state of affairs. On examining it thoroughly at home, he discovered that in two or three places, to wit, on the back and round the shoulders, it looked like some coarse homespun cotton; the cloth had worn out so much that it let through the wind, and the lining had all gone to pieces. It must be mentioned here that Akaky's overcoat, too, had been the butt of the departmental wits; it had been even deprived of the honourable name of overcoat and had been called a *capote*. And indeed it was of a most peculiar cut: its collar had shrunk in size more and more every year, for it was used to patch the other parts. The patching did no credit to the tailor's art and the result was that the final effect was somewhat baggy and far from beautiful. Having discovered what was wrong with his overcoat, Akaky decided that he would have to take it to Petrovich, a tailor who lived somewhere on the fourth floor up some back stairs and who, in spite of the disadvantage of having only one eye and pock marks all over his face, carried on a rather successful trade in mending the trousers and frock-coats of government clerks and other gentlemen whenever, that is to say, he was sober and was not hatching some other scheme in his head.

We really ought not to waste much time over this tailor; since, however, it is now the fashion that the character of every person in a story must be delineated fully, then by all means let us have Petrovich, too. To begin with, he was known simply by his Christian name of Grigory, and had been a serf belonging to some gentleman or other; he began calling himself Petrovich only after he had obtained his freedom, when he started drinking rather heavily every holiday, at first only on the great holidays, and thereafter on any church holiday, on any day, in fact, marked with a cross in the calendar. So far as that went, he was true to the traditions of his forebears and in his altercations with his wife on this subject he would call her a worldly woman and a German. Having mentioned his wife, we had better say a word or two about her also; to our great regret, however, we know very little about her, except that Petrovich had a wife, who wore a bonnet, and not a kerchief; there appears to be some doubt as to whether she was goodlooking or not, but on the whole it does not seem likely that she had very much to boast of in that respect; at any rate, only guardsmen were ever known to peer under her bonnet when meeting her in the street, twitching their moustaches and emitting a curious kind of grunt at the same time.

While ascending the stairs leading to Petrovich's flat — the stairs which, to do them justice, were soaked with water and slops and saturated with a strong spirituous smell which irritates the eyes and which, as the whole world knows, is a permanent feature of all the back stairs of St. Petersburg houses — while ascending the stairs, Akaky was already wondering how much Petrovich would ask for mending his overcoat, and made up his mind not to give him more than two roubles. The door of Petrovich's flat was open because his wife had been frying some fish and had filled the whole kitchen with smoke, so that even the cockroaches could no longer be seen. Akaky walked through the kitchen, unnoticed even by Mrs. Petrovich, and, at last, entered the tailor's room where he beheld Petrovich sitting on a large table of unstained wood with his legs crossed under him like a Turkish pasha. His feet, as is the custom of tailors when engaged in their work, were bare. The first thing that caught his eye was Petrovich's big toe, which Akaky knew very well indeed, with its deformed nail as thick and hard as the shell of a tortoise. A skein of silk and cotton thread hung about Petrovich's neck, and on his knees lay some tattered piece of clothing. He had for the last minute or two been trying to thread his needle and, failing every time, he was terribly angry with the dark room and even with the thread itself, muttering under his breath, "Won't you go through, you beast? You'll be the death of me yet, you slut!" Akaky could not help feeling sorry that he had come just at the moment when Petrovich was angry: he liked to place an order with Petrovich only when the tailor was a bit merry, or when he had, as his wife put it, "been swilling his corn-brandy, the one-eyed devil!" When in such a state, Petrovich was as a rule extremely amenable and always gave in and agreed to any price, and even bowed and thanked him. It was true that afterwards his wife would come to see Akaky and tell him with tears in her eyes that her husband had been drunk and had therefore charged him too little; but all Akaky had to do was to add another ten-copeck piece and the thing was settled. But now Petrovich was to all appearances sober as a judge and, consequently, rather bad-tempered, intractable and liable to charge any old price. Akaky realized that and was about, as the saying is, to beat a hasty retreat, but it was too late: Petrovich had already screwed up his only eye and was looking at him steadily. Akaky had willy-nilly to say, "Good morning, Petrovich!" "Good morning, sir. How are you?" said Petrovich, fixing his eye on Akaky's hands in an effort to make out what kind of offering he had brought.

"Well, you see, Petrovich, I — er — have come — er — about that, you know . . ." said Akaky.

It might be as well to explain at once that Akaky mostly talked in prepositions, adverbs, and, lastly, such parts of speech as have no meaning whatsoever. If the matter was rather difficult, he was in the habit of not finishing the sentences, so that often having begun his speech with, "This is — er — you know . . . a bit of that, you know . . ." he left it at that, forgetting to finish the sentence in the belief that he had said all that was necessary.

"What's that you've got there, sir?" said Petrovich, scrutinizing at the same time the whole of Akaky's uniform with his one eye, from the collar to the sleeves, back, tails and button-holes, which was all extremely familiar to him, since it was his own handiwork. Such is the immemorial custom among tailors; it is the first thing a tailor does when he meets one of his customers.

"Well, you see, Petrovich, I've come about this here, you know . . . this overcoat of mine. The cloth, you know. . . . You see, it's really all right everywhere, in fact, excellent. . . . I mean, it's in fine condition here and — er — all over. Looks a bit dusty, I know, and you might get the impression that it was old, but as a matter of fact it's as good as new, except in one place where it's a bit — er — a bit, you know. . . . On the back, I mean, and here on the shoulder. . . . Looks as though it was worn through a bit, and on the other shoulder too, just a trifle, you see. . . . Well, that's really all. Not much work in it. . . ."

Petrovich took the *capote*, first spread it on the table, examined it for a long time, shook his head, and stretched out his hand to the window for his round snuff-box with a portrait of some general, though which particular general it was impossible to say, for the place where the face should have been had been poked in by a finger and then pasted over with a square bit of paper. Having treated himself to a pinch of snuff, Petrovich held the overcoat out in his hands against the light and gave it another thorough examination, and again shook his head; he then turned it with the lining upwards and again shook his head, again took off the lid with the general pasted over with paper, and, filling his nose with snuff, replaced the lid, put away the snuff-box and, at last, said, "No, sir. Impossible to mend it. There's nothing left of it."

Akaky's heart sank at those words. "Why is it impossible, Petrovich?" he said, almost in the imploring voice of a child. "It's only on the shoulders that it's a bit worn, and I suppose you must have bits of cloth somewhere. . . ."

"Oh, I've got plenty of bits of cloth, sir, lots of 'em," said Petrovich. "But you see, sir, you can't sew 'em on. The whole coat's rotten. Touch it with a needle and it will fall to pieces."

"Well, if it falls to pieces, all you have to do is to patch it up again."

"Why, bless my soul, sir, and what do you suppose the patches will hold on to? What am I to sew them on to? Can't you see, sir, how badly worn it is? You can't call it cloth any more: one puff of wind and it will be blown away."

"But please strengthen it a bit. I mean, it can't be just — er — really, you know . . ."

"No, sir," said Petrovich firmly, "it can't be done. Too far gone. Nothing to hold it together. All I can advise you to do with it, sir, is to cut it up when winter comes and make some rags to wrap round your feet, for socks, sir, are no damned good at all: there's no real warmth in 'em. It's them Germans, sir, what invented socks to make a lot of money (Petrovich liked to get in a word against the Germans on every occasion). As for your overcoat, sir, I'm afraid you'll have to get a new one."

At the word "new" a mist suddenly spread before Akaky's eyes and everything in the room began swaying giddily. The only thing he could still see clearly was the general's face pasted over with paper on the lid of Petrovich's snuffbox.

"How do you mean, a new one?" he said, still as though speaking in a dream. "Why, I haven't got the money for it."

"Well, sir, all I can say is that you just must get yourself a new one," said Petrovich with callous indifference.

"Well, and if . . . I mean, if I had to get a new one . . . how much, I mean . . ."

"How much will it come to, sir?"

"Yes."

"Well, sir, I suppose you'll have to lay out three fifty-rouble notes or more," said Petrovich pursing his lips significantly.

He had a great fondness for strong effects, Petrovich had. He liked to hit a fellow on the head suddenly and then steal a glance at him to see what kind of a face the stunned person would pull after his words.

"One hundred and fifty roubles for an overcoat!" cried poor Akaky in a loud voice, probably raising his voice to such a pitch for the first time in his life, for he was always distinguished by the softness of his voice.

"Yes, sir," said Petrovich. "And that, too, depends on the kind of coat you have. If you have marten for your collar and a silk lining for your hood, it might cost you two hundred."

"Now look here, Petrovich . . ." said Akaky in a beseeching voice, not hearing, or at any rate doing his best not to hear, what Petrovich was saying, and paying no attention whatever to the effect the tailor was trying to create. "Please, my dear fellow, just mend it somehow, so that I could still use it a bit longer, you know. . . ."

"No, sir, it will merely mean a waste of my work and your money," said Petrovich.

After such a verdict Akaky left Petrovich's room feeling completely crushed, while the tailor remained in the same position a long time after he had gone, without going back to his work, his lips pursed significantly. He was greatly pleased that he had neither demeaned himself nor let down the sartorial art.

In the street Akaky felt as though he were in a dream. "So that's how it stands, is it?" he murmured to himself. "I really didn't think that it would turn out like that, you know. . . ." Then after a pause he added, "Well, that's that. There's a real surprise for you. . . . I never thought that it would end like that. . . ." There followed another long pause, after which he said, "So that's how it is! What a sudden . . . I mean, what a terrible blow! Who could have . . . What an awful business!"

Having delivered himself thus, he walked on, without noticing it, in quite the opposite direction from his home. On the way a chimney-sweep brushed the whole of his sooty side against him and blackened his shoulder; from the top of a house that was being built a whole handful of lime fell upon him. But he was aware of nothing, and only when some time later he knocked against a policeman who, placing his halberd near him, was scattering some snuff from a horn on a calloused fist, did he recover a little, and that, too, only because the policeman said, "Now then, what are you pushing against me for? Can't you see where you're going? Ain't the pavement big enough for you?" This made him look up and retrace his steps.

But it was not until he had returned home that he began to collect his thoughts and saw his position as it really was. He began discussing the matter with himself, not in broken sentences, but frankly and soberly, as though talking to a wise friend with whom it was possible to discuss one's most intimate affairs.

"No, no," said Akaky, "it's pretty clear that it is impossible to talk to Petrovich now. He's a bit, you know . . . Been thrashed by his wife, I shouldn't wonder. I'd better go and see him next Sunday morning, for after all the drink he'll have had on Saturday night he'll still be screwing up his one eye, and he'll be very sleepy and dying for another drink to help him on his feet again, and his wife won't give him any money, so that if I come along and give him ten copecks or a little more he'll be more reasonable and change his mind about the overcoat, and then, you know . . ."

So Akaky reasoned with himself, and he felt greatly reassured.

Sunday came at last and, noticing from a distance that Petrovich's wife had left the house to go somewhere, he went straight in. To be sure, Petrovich did glower after his Saturday night's libations, and he could barely hold up his head, which seemed to be gravitating towards the floor, and he certainly looked very sleepy; and yet, in spite of this condition, no sooner did he hear what Akaky had come for than it seemed as if the devil himself had nudged him.

"Quite impossible, sir," he said. "You'll have to order a new one." Akaky immediately slipped a ten-copeck piece into his hand. "Thank you very much, sir," said Petrovich. "Very kind of you, I'm sure. I'll get a bit a' strength in me body and drink to your health, sir. But if I were you, sir, I'd stop worrying about that overcoat of yours. No good at all. Can't do nothing with it. Mind, I can promise you one thing, though: I'll make you a lovely new overcoat. That I will, sir."

Akaky tried to say something about mending the old one, but Petrovich would not even listen to him and said, "Depend upon it, sir, I'll make you a new one. Do my best for you, I will, sir. Might even while we're about it, sir, and seeing as how it's now the fashion, get a silver-plated clasp for the collar."

It was then that Akaky at last realized that he would have to get a new overcoat, and his heart failed him. And how indeed was he to do it? What with? Where was he to get the money? There was of course the additional holiday pay he could count on; at least there was a good chance of his getting that holiday bonus. But supposing he did get it, all that money had already been divided up and disposed of long ago. There was that new pair of trousers he must get; then there was that long-standing debt he owed the shoemaker for putting new tops to some old boots; he had, moreover, to order three shirts from the seamstress as well as two pairs of that particular article of underwear which cannot be decently mentioned in print — in short, all the money would have to be spent to the last penny, and even if the director of the department were to be so kind as to give him a holiday bonus of forty-five or even fifty roubles instead of forty, all that would remain of it would be the veriest trifle, which in terms of overcoat finance would be just a drop in the ocean. Though he knew perfectly well, of course, that Petrovich was sometimes mad enough to ask so utterly preposterous a price that even his wife could not refrain from exclaiming, "Gone off his head completely, the silly old fool! One day he accepts work for next to nothing, and now the devil must have made him ask more than he is worth himself !" — though he knew perfectly well, of course, that Petrovich would undertake to make him the overcoat for eighty roubles, the question still remained: where was he to get the eighty roubles? At a pinch he could raise half of it. Yes, he could find half of it all right and perhaps even a little more, but where was he to get the other half? . . .

But first of all the reader had better be told where Akaky hoped to be able to raise the first half.

Akaky was in the habit of putting away a little from every rouble he spent in a box which he kept locked up and which had a little hole in the lid through which money could be dropped. At the end of every six months he counted up the accumulated coppers and changed them into silver. As he had been saving up for a long time, there had accumulated in the course of several years a sum of over forty roubles. So he had half of the required sum in hand; but where was he to get the other half? Where was he to get another forty roubles?

Akaky thought and thought and then he decided that he would have to cut down his ordinary expenses for a year at least: do without a cup of tea in the evenings; stop burning candles in the evening and, if he had some work to do, go to his landlady's room and work by the light of her candle; when walking in the street, try to walk as lightly as possible on the cobbles and flagstones, almost on tiptoe, so as not to wear out the soles of his boots too soon; give his washing to the laundress as seldom as possible, and to make sure that it did not wear out, to take it off as soon as he returned home and wear only his dressing-gown of twilled cotton cloth, a very old garment that time itself had spared. To tell the truth, Akaky at first found it very hard to get used to such economy, but after some time he got used to it all right and everything went with a swing; he did not even mind going hungry in the evenings, for spiritually he was nourished well enough, since his thoughts were full of the great idea of his future overcoat. His whole existence indeed seemed now somehow to have become fuller, as though he had got married, as though there was someone at his side, as though he was never alone, but some agreeable helpmate had consented to share the joys and sorrows of his life, and this sweet helpmate, this dear wife of his, was no other than the selfsame overcoat with its thick padding of cotton-wool and its strong lining that would last a lifetime. He became more cheerful and his character even got a little firmer, like that of a man who knew what he was aiming at and how to achieve that aim. Doubt vanished, as though of its own accord, from his face and from his actions, and so did indecision and, in fact, all the indeterminate and shilly-shallying traits of his character. Sometimes a gleam would appear in his eyes and through his head there would flash the most bold and audacious thought, to wit, whether he should not after all get himself a fur collar of marten. All these thoughts about his new overcoat nearly took his mind off his work at the office, so much so that once, as he was copying out a document, he was just about to make a mistake, and he almost cried out, "Oh dear!" in a loud voice, and crossed himself. He went to see Petrovich at least once a month to discuss his overcoat, where it was best to buy the cloth, and what colour and at what price, and though looking a little worried, he always came back home well satisfied, reflecting that the time was not far off when he would pay for it all and when his overcoat would be ready.

As a matter of fact the whole thing came to pass much quicker than he dreamed. Contrary to all expectations, the director gave Akaky Akakyevich not forty or forty-five, but sixty roubles! Yes, a holiday bonus of sixty roubles. Whether he, too, had been aware that Akaky wanted a new overcoat, or whether it happened by sheer accident, the fact remained that Akaky had an additional twenty roubles. This speeded up the whole course of events. Another two or three months of a life on short commons and Akaky had actually saved up about eighty roubles. His pulse, generally sluggish, began beating fast. The very next day he went with Petrovich to the shops. They bought an excellent piece of cloth, and no wonder! For the matter had been carefully discussed and thought over for almost six months, and scarcely a month had passed without enquiries being made at the shops about prices, so as to make quite sure that the cloth they needed was not too expensive; and the result of all that foresight was that, as Petrovich himself admitted, they could not have got a better cloth. For the lining they chose calico, but of such fine and strong quality that, according to Petrovich, it was much better than silk and was actually much more handsome and glossy. They did not buy marten for a fur collar, for as a matter of fact it was rather expensive, but they chose cat fur instead, the best cat they could find in the shop, cat which from a distance could always be mistaken for marten. Petrovich took only two weeks over the overcoat, and that, too, because there was so much quilting to be done; otherwise it would have been ready earlier. For his work Petrovich took twelve roubles — less than that was quite out of the question: he had used nothing but silk thread in the sewing of it, and it was sewn with fine, double seams, and Petrovich had gone over each seam with his own teeth afterwards, leaving all sorts of marks on them.

It was . . . It is hard to say on what day precisely it was, but there could be no doubt at all that the day on which Petrovich at last delivered the overcoat was one of the greatest days in Akaky's life. He brought it rather early in the morning, just a short time before Akaky had to leave for the department. At no other time would the overcoat have been so welcome, for the time of rather sharp frosts had just begun, and from all appearances it looked as if the severity of the weather would increase. Petrovich walked in with the overcoat as a good tailor should. His face wore an expression of solemn gravity such as Akaky had never seen on it before. He seemed to be fully conscious of the fact that he had accomplished no mean thing and that he had shown by his own example the gulf that separated the tailors who merely relined a coat or did repairs from those who made new coats. He took the overcoat out of the large handkerchief in which he had brought it. (The handkerchief had just come from the laundress: it was only now that he folded it and put it in his pocket for use.) Having taken out the overcoat, he looked very proudly about him and, holding it in both hands, threw it very smartly over Akaky's shoulders, then he gave it a vigorous pull and, bending down, smoothed it out behind with his hand; then he draped it round Akaky, throwing it open in front a little. Akaky, who was no longer a young man, wanted to try it on with his arms in the sleeves, and Petrovich helped him to put his hands through the sleeves, and — it was all right even when he wore it with his arms in the sleeves. In fact, there could be no doubt at all that the overcoat was a perfect fit. Petrovich did not let this opportunity pass without observing that it was only because he lived in a back street and had no signboard and because he had known Akaky Akakyevich so long that he had charged him so little for making the overcoat. If he had ordered it on Nevsky Avenue, they would have charged him seventy-five roubles for the work alone. Akaky had no desire to discuss the matter with Petrovich and, to tell the truth, he was a little frightened of the big sums which Petrovich was so fond of tossing about with the idea of impressing people. He paid him, thanked him, and left immediately for the department in his new overcoat. Petrovich followed him into the street where he remained standing a long time on one spot, admiring his handiwork from a distance; then he purposely went out of his way so that he could by taking a short-cut by a side street rush out into the street again and have another look at the overcoat, this time from the other side, that is to say, from the front.

Meanwhile Akaky went along as if walking on air. Not for a fraction of a second did he forget that he had a new overcoat on his back, and he could not help smiling to himself from time to time with sheer pleasure at the thought of it. And really it had two advantages: one that it was warm, and the other that it was good. He did not notice the distance and found himself suddenly in the department. He took off the overcoat in the hall, examined it carefully and entrusted it to the special care of the door-keeper. It is not known how the news of Akaky's new overcoat had spread all over the department, but all at once every one knew that Akaky had discarded his *capote* and had a fine new overcoat. They all immediately rushed out into the hall to have a look at Akaky's new overcoat. Congratulations and good wishes were showered upon him. At first Akaky just smiled, then he felt rather embarrassed. But when all surrounded him and began telling him that he ought to celebrate his acquisition of a new overcoat and that the least he could do was to invite them all to a party, Akaky Akakyevich was thrown into utter confusion and did not know what to do, what to say to them all, or how to extricate himself from that very awkward situation. He even tried a few minutes later with the utmost good humour to assure them, blushing to the roots of his hair, that it was not a new overcoat at all, that it was just . . . well, you know . . . just his old overcoat. At last one of the clerks, and, mind, not just any clerk, but no less a person than the assistant head clerk of the office, wishing to show no doubt that he, for one, was not a proud man and did not shun men more humble than himself, said, "So be it!

I will give a party instead of Akaky Akakyevich. I invite you all, gentlemen, this evening to tea at my place. As a matter of fact, it happens to be my birthday." The Civil Servants naturally wished him many happy returns of the day and accepted his invitation with alacrity. Akaky tried at first to excuse himself, but everybody told him that it was not done and that he ought to be ashamed of himself, and he just could not wriggle out of it. However, he felt rather pleased afterwards, for it occurred to him that this would give him a chance of taking a walk in the evening in his new overcoat.

That day was to Akaky like a great festival. He came home in a most happy frame of mind, took off his overcoat, hung it with great care on the wall, stood for some time admiring the cloth and lining, and then produced his old overcoat, which had by then gone to pieces completely, just to compare the two. He looked at it and could not help chuckling out loud: what a difference! And he kept smiling to himself all during dinner when he thought of the disgraceful state of his old overcoat. He enjoyed his dinner immensely and did no copying at all afterwards, not one document did he copy, but just indulged himself a little by lying down on his bed until dusk. Then, without dawdling unnecessarily, he dressed, threw the overcoat over his shoulders, and went out into the street.

Unfortunately we cannot say where precisely the Civil Servant who was giving the party lived. Our memory is beginning to fail us rather badly and everything in St. Petersburg, all the streets and houses, has become so blurred and mixed up in our head that we find it very difficult indeed to sort it out properly. Be that as it may, there can be no doubt that the Civil Servant in question lived in one of the best parts of the town, which means of course that he did not live anywhere near Akaky Akakyevich. At first Akaky had to pass through some deserted streets, very poorly lighted, but as he got nearer to the Civil Servant's home the streets became more crowded and more brilliantly illuminated. There certainly were more people in the streets, the women were well dressed and the men even wore beaver collars. There were fewer poor peasant cabmen with their grate-like wooden sledges studded with brass nails; on the contrary, the cabmen were mostly fine fellows in crimson velvet caps with lacquered sledges and bearskin covers, and carriages with sumptuously decorated boxes drove at a great speed through the streets, their wheels crunching on the snow.

Akaky looked at it all as though he had never seen anything like it in his life, and indeed he had not left his room in the evening for several years. He stopped before a lighted shop window and for some minutes looked entranced at a painting of a beautiful woman who was taking off a shoe and showing a bare leg, a very shapely leg, too; and behind her back a gentleman had stuck his head through the door of another room, a gentleman with fine side-whiskers and a handsome imperial on his chin. Akaky shook his head and grinned, and then went on his way. Why did he grin? It might have been because he had seen something he had never seen before, but a liking for which is buried deep down inside every one of us, or because (like many another Civil Servant) he thought to himself, "Oh, those damned Frenchmen! What a people they are, to be sure! If they set their heart on something, something . . . well, something of that kind, you know, then it is something . . .

well, something of that kind. . . ." But perhaps he never even said anything at all to himself. How indeed is one to delve into a man's mind and find out what he is thinking about? At last he reached the house where the young assistant head clerk of his office lived.

The assistant head clerk lived in great style: there was a lamp burning on the stairs, and his flat was on the second floor. As he entered the hall, Akaky saw on the floor rows upon rows of galoshes. Among them in the middle of the room stood a *samovar*, hissing and letting off clouds of steam. The walls were covered with overcoats and cloaks, some even with beaver collars and velvet revers. A confused buzz of conversation came from the other side of the wall, and it grew very clear and loud when the door opened and a footman came out with a trayful of empty tea-glasses, a jug of cream and a basket of biscuits. It was evident that the Civil Servants had been there for some time and had already finished their first glass of tea.

After hanging up his overcoat himself, Akaky entered the room, and there flashed upon his sight simultaneously candles, Civil Servants, pipes, card-tables, while his ears were filled with the confused sound of continuous conversation, which came from every corner of the room, and the noise of moving chairs. He stood in the middle of the room, looking rather forlorn and trying desperately to think what he ought to do. But his presence had already been noticed and he was welcomed with loud shouts, and everybody immediately went into the hall to inspect his overcoat anew. Though feeling rather embarrassed at first, Akaky, being of a singularly ingenuous nature, could not help being pleased to hear how everybody praised his overcoat. Then, of course, they forgot all about him and his overcoat and crowded, as was to be expected, round the card-tables set out for whist.

All this — the noise, the talk, and the crowd of people — was very strange and bewildering to Akaky. He simply did not know what to do, where to put his hands and feet, or his whole body; at length he sat down by the card players, looked at the cards, studied the face of one player, then of another, and after a little time began to feel bored and started yawning, particularly as it was getting late and it was long past his bedtime. He tried to take leave of his host, but they would not let him go, saying that they had to drink a glass of champagne in honour of his new overcoat. In about an hour supper was served. It consisted of a mixed salad, cold veal, meat pie, cream pastries, and champagne. They made Akaky drink two glasses of champagne, after which he felt that everything got much jollier in the room. However, he could not forget that it was already midnight and that it was high time he went home. To make sure that his host would not detain him on one pretext or another, he stole out of the room and found his overcoat in the hall. The overcoat, he noticed not without a pang of regret, was lying on the floor. He picked it up, shook it, removed every speck of dust from it and, putting it over his shoulders, went down the stairs into the street.

It was still light in the street. A few small grocers' shops, those round-the-clock clubs of all sorts of servants, were still open; from those which were already closed a streak of light still streamed through the crack under the door, showing that there was still some company there, consisting most probably of maids and men-servants who were finishing their talk and gossip, leaving their masters completely at a loss to know where they were. Akaky walked along feeling very happy and even set off running after some lady (goodness knows why) who passed him like a streak of lightning, every part of her body in violent motion. However, he stopped almost at once and went on at a slow pace as before, marvelling himself where that unusual spurt of speed had come from. Soon he came to those never-ending, deserted streets, which even in daytime are not particularly cheerful, let alone at night. Now they looked even more deserted and lonely; there were fewer street lamps and even those he came across were extinguished: the municipal authorities seemed to be sparing of oil. He now came into the district of wooden houses and fences; there was not a soul to be seen anywhere, only the snow gleamed on the streets, and hundreds of dismal, low hovels with closed shutters which seemed to have sunk into a deep sleep stretched in a long, dark line before him. Soon he approached the spot where the street was intersected by an immense square with houses dimly visible on the other side, a square that looked to him like a dreadful desert.

A long way away — goodness knows where — he could see the glimmer of a light coming from some sentry-box, which seemed to be standing at the edge of the world. Akaky's cheerfulness faded perceptibly as he entered the square. He entered it not without a kind of involuntary sensation of dread, as though feeling in his bones that something untoward was going to happen. He looked back, and then cast a glance at either side of him: it was just as though the sea were all round him. "Much better not to look," he thought to himself, and, shutting his eyes, he walked on, opening them only to have a look how far the end of the square was. But what he saw was a couple of men standing right in front of him, men with moustaches, but what they were he could not make out in the darkness. He felt dazed and his heart began beating violently against his ribs. "Look, here is my overcoat!" one of the men said in a voice of thunder, grabbing him by the collar. Akaky was about to scream, "Help!" but the other man shook his fist in his face, a fist as big as a Civil Servant's head, and said, "You just give a squeak!" All poor Akaky knew was that they took off his overcoat and gave him a kick which sent him sprawling on the snow. He felt nothing at all any more. A few minutes later he recovered sufficiently to get up, but there was not a soul to be seen anywhere. He felt that it was terribly cold in the square and that his overcoat had gone. He began to shout for help, but his voice seemed to be too weak to carry to the end of the square. Feeling desperate and without ceasing to shout, he ran across the square straight to the sentry-box beside which stood a policeman who, leaning on his halberd, seemed to watch the running figure with mild interest, wondering no doubt why the devil a man was running towards him, screaming his head off while still a mile away. Having run up to the police constable, Akaky started shouting at him in a gasping voice that he was asleep and did not even notice that a man had been robbed under his very nose. The policeman said that he saw nothing, or rather that all he did see was that two men had stopped him (Akaky) in the middle of the square, but he supposed that they were his friends; and he advised Akaky, instead of standing there and abusing him for nothing, to go and see the police inspector next morning, for the inspector was quite sure to find the men who had taken his overcoat.

Akaky Akakyevich came running home in a state of utter confusion. His hair, which still grew, though sparsely, over his temples and at the back of his head, was terribly tousled; his chest, arms and trousers were covered with snow. His old landlady, awakened by the loud knocking at the door, jumped hurriedly out of bed and with only one slipper on ran to open the door, modestly clasping her chemise to her bosom with one hand. When she opened the door and saw the terrible state Akaky was in, she fell back with a gasp. He told her what had happened to him, and she threw up her arms in dismay and said that he ought to go straight to the district police commissioner, for the police inspector was quite sure to swindle him, promise him all sorts of things and then leave him in the lurch; it would be much better if he went to the district police commissioner who, it seemed, was known to her, for Anna, the Finnish girl who was once her cook, was now employed by the district commissioner of police as a nurse, and, besides, she had seen him often as he drove past the house, and he even went to church every Sunday and always, while saying his prayers, looked round at everybody very cheerfully, so that, judging from all appearances, he must be a kind-hearted man.

Having listened to that piece of advice, Akaky wandered off sadly to his room, and how he spent that night we leave it to those to judge who can enter into the position of another man. Early next morning he went to see the district police commissioner, but they told him that he was still asleep. He came back at ten o'clock and again they said he was asleep. He came back at eleven o'clock and was told that the police commissioner was not at home. He came back at lunch-time, but the clerks in the waiting-room would not admit him on any account unless he told them first what he had come for and what it was all about and what had happened. So that in the end Akaky felt for the first time in his life that he had to assert himself and he told them bluntly that he had come to see the district commissioner of police personally, that they had no right to refuse to admit him, that he had come from the department on official business, and that if he lodged a complaint against them, they would see what would happen. The clerks dared say nothing to this and one of them went to summon the commissioner.

The police commissioner took rather a curious view of Akaky's story of the loss of his overcoat. Instead of concentrating on the main point of the affair, he began putting all sorts of questions to Akaky which had nothing to do with it, such as why he was coming home so late, and was he sure he had not been to any disorderly house the night before, so that Akaky felt terribly embarrassed and went away wondering whether the police were ever likely to take the necessary steps to retrieve his overcoat.

That day (for the first time in his life) he did not go to the department. Next day he appeared looking very pale and wearing his old *capote*, which was in a worse state than ever. Many of his colleagues seemed moved by the news of the robbery of his overcoat, though there were a few among them who could not help pulling poor Akaky's leg even on so sad an occasion. It was decided to make a special collection for Akaky, but they only succeeded in collecting a trifling sum, for the clerks in his office had already spent a great deal on subscribing to a fund for a portrait of the director and also on some kind of a book, at the suggestion of one of the departmental chiefs, who was a friend of the author. Anyway, the sum collected was a trifling one. One Civil Servant, however, moved by compassion, decided to help Akaky with some good advice at any rate, and he told him that he should not go to the district police inspector, for though it might well happen that the district police inspector, anxious to win the approbation of his superiors, would somehow or other find his overcoat, Akaky would never be able to get it out of the police station unless he could present all the necessary legal proofs that the overcoat belonged to him. It would therefore be much better if Akaky went straight to a certain Very Important Person, for the Very Important Person could, by writing and getting into touch with the right people, give a much quicker turn to the whole matter.

Akaky Akakyevich (what else could he do?) decided to go and see the Very Important Person. What position the Very Important Person occupied and what his job actually was has never been properly ascertained and still remains unknown. Suffice it to say that the Very Important Person had become a Very Important Person only quite recently, and that until then he was quite an unimportant person. Moreover, his office was not even now considered of much importance as compared with others of greater importance. But there will always be people who regard as important what in the eyes of other people is rather unimportant. However, the Very Important Person did his best to increase his importance in all sorts of ways, to wit, he introduced a rule that his subordinates should meet him on the stairs when he arrived at his office; that no one should be admitted to his office unless he first petitioned for an interview, and that everything should be done according to the strictest order: the collegiate registrar was first to report to the provincial secretary, the provincial secretary to the titular councillor or whomsoever it was he had to report to, and that only by such a procedure should any particular business reach him. In Holy Russia, we are sorry to say, every one seems to be anxious to ape every one else and each man copies and imitates his superior. The story is even told of some titular councillor who, on being made chief of some small office, immediately partitioned off a special room for himself, calling it "the presence chamber," and placed two commissionaires in coats with red collars and galloons at the door with instructions to take hold of the door handle and open the door to any person who came to see him, though there was hardly room in "the presence chamber" for an ordinary writing-desk.

The manners and habits of the Very Important Person were very grand and impressive, but not very subtle. His whole system was based chiefly on strictness. "Strictness, strictness, and *again* strictness!" he usually declared, and at the penultimate word he usually peered very significantly into the face of the man he was addressing. There seemed to be no particular reason for this strictness, though, for the dozen or so Civil Servants who composed the whole administrative machinery of his office were held in a proper state of fear and trembling, anyhow. Seeing him coming from a distance they all stopped their work immediately and, standing at attention, waited until the chief had walked through the room. His usual conversation with any of his subordinates was saturated with strictness and consisted almost entirely of three phrases: "How dare you, sir? Do you know who you're talking to, sir? Do you realize who is standing before you, sir?" Still, he was really a good fellow at heart, was particularly pleasant with his colleagues, and quite obliging, too; but his new position went to his head. Having received the rank of general, he got all confused, was completely nonplussed and did not know what to do. In the presence of a man equal to him in rank, he was just an ordinary fellow, quite a decent fellow, and in many ways even a far from stupid fellow; but whenever he happened to be in company with men even one rank lower than he, he seemed to be lost; he sat silent and his position was really pitiable, more particularly as he himself felt that he could have spent the time so much more enjoyably. A strong desire could sometimes be read in his eyes to take part in some interesting conversation or join some interesting people, but he was always stopped by the thought: would it not mean going a little too far on his part? Would it not be mistaken for familiarity and would he not thereby lower himself in the estimation of everybody? As a consequence of this reasoning he always found himself in a position where he had to remain silent, delivering himself only from time to time of a few monosyllables, and in this way he won for himself the unenviable reputation of being an awful bore.

It was before this sort of Very Important Person that our Akaky presented himself, and he presented himself at the most inopportune moment he could possibly have chosen, very unfortunate for himself, though not so unfortunate for the Very Important Person.

At the time of Akaky's arrival the Very Important Person was in his private office, having a very pleasant talk with an old friend of his, a friend of his childhood, who had only recently arrived in St. Petersburg and whom he had not seen for several years. It was just then that he was informed that a certain Bashmachkin wanted to see him. "Who's that?" he asked abruptly, and he was told, "Some Civil Servant." "Oh," said the Very Important Person, "let him wait. I'm busy now."

Now we believe it is only fair to state here that the Very Important Person had told a thumping lie. He was not busy at all. He had long ago said all he had to say to his old friend, and their present conversation had for some time now been punctuated by long pauses, interrupted by the one or the other slapping his friend on the knee and saying, "Ah, Ivan Abramovich!" or "Yes, yes, quite right, Stepan Varlamovich!" However, he asked the Civil Servant to wait, for he wanted to show his friend, who had left the Civil Service long ago and had been spending all his time at his country house, how long he kept Civil Servants cooling their heels in his anteroom. At last, having talked, or rather kept silent as long as they liked, having enjoyed a cigar in comfortable arm-chairs with sloping backs, he seemed to remember something suddenly and said to his secretary, who was standing at the door with a sheaf of documents in his hand, "Isn't there some Civil Servant waiting to see me? Tell him to come in, please."

Seeing Akaky's humble appearance and old uniform, he turned to him and said shortly, "What do you want?" in an abrupt and firm voice, which he had specially rehearsed in the solitude of his room in front of a looking-glass a week before he received his present post and the rank of general.

Akaky, who had long since been filled with the proper amount of fear and trembling, felt rather abashed and explained as well as he could and as much as his stammering would let him, with the addition of the more than usual number of "wells" and "you knows," that his overcoat was quite a new overcoat, and that he had been robbed in a most shameless fashion, and that he was now applying to his excellency in the hope that his excellency might by putting in a word here and there or doing this or that, or writing to the Commissioner of Police of the Metropolis, or to some other person, get his overcoat back. For some unknown reason the general considered such an approach as too familiar. "What do you mean, sir?" he said in his abrupt voice. "Don't you know the proper procedure? What have you come to me for? Don't you know how things are done? In the first place you should have sent in a petition about it to my office. Your petition, sir, would have been placed before the chief clerk, who would have transferred it to my secretary, and my secretary would have submitted it to me. . . ."

"But, your excellency," said Akaky, trying to summon the handful of courage he had (it was not a very big handful, anyway), and feeling at the same time that he was perspiring all over, "I took the liberty, your excellency, of troubling you personally because — er — because, sir, secretaries are, well, you know, rather unreliable people. . . ."

"What? What did you say, sir?" said the Very Important Person. "How dare you speak like this, sir? Where did you get the impudence to speak like this, sir? Where did you get these extraordinary ideas from, sir? What's the meaning of this mutinous spirit that is now spreading among young men against their chiefs and superiors?" The Very Important Person did not seem to have noticed that Akaky Akakyevich was well over fifty, and it can only be supposed, therefore, that if he called him a young man he meant it only in a relative sense, that is to say, that compared with a man of seventy Akaky was a young man. "Do you realize, sir, who you are talking to? Do you understand, sir, who is standing before you? Do you understand it, sir? Do you understand it, I ask you?"

Here he stamped his foot and raised his voice to so high a pitch that it was not Akaky Akakyevich alone who became terrified. Akaky was on the point of fainting. He staggered, trembled all over, and could not stand on his feet. Had it not been for the door-keepers, who ran up to support him, he would have collapsed on the ground. He was carried out almost unconscious. The Very Important Person, satisfied that the effect he had produced exceeded all expectations and absolutely in raptures over the idea that a word of his could actually throw a man into a faint, glanced at his friend out of the corner of his eye, wondering what impression he had made on him; and he was pleased to see that his friend was rather in an uneasy frame of mind himself and seemed to show quite unmistakable signs of fear.

Akaky could not remember how he had descended the stairs, or how he had got out into the street. He remembered nothing. His hands and feet had gone dead. Never in his life had he been so hauled over the coals by a general, and not his own general at that. He walked along in a blizzard, in the teeth of a howling wind, which was sweeping through the streets, with his mouth agape and constantly stumbling off the pavement; the wind, as is its invariable custom in St. Petersburg, blew from every direction and every side street all at once. His throat became inflamed in no time at all, and when at last he staggered home he was unable to utter a word. He was all swollen, and he took to his bed. So powerful can a real official reprimand be sometimes!

Next day Akaky was in a high fever. Thanks to the most generous assistance of the St. Petersburg climate, his illness made much more rapid progress than could have been expected, and when the doctor arrived he merely felt his pulse and found nothing to do except prescribe a poultice, and that only because he did not want to leave the patient without the beneficent aid of medicine; he did, though, express his opinion then and there that all would be over in a day and a half. After which he turned to the landlady and said, "No need to waste time, my dear lady. You'd better order a deal coffin for him at once, for I don't suppose he can afford an oak coffin, can he?"

Did Akaky Akakyevich hear those fateful words and, if he did hear them, did they produce a shattering effect upon him? Did he at that moment repine at his wretched lot in life? It is quite impossible to say, for the poor man was in a delirium and a high fever. Visions, one stranger than another, haunted him incessantly: one moment he saw Petrovich and ordered him to make an overcoat with special traps for thieves, whom he apparently believed to be hiding under his bed, so that he called to his landlady every minute to get them out of there, and once he even asked her to get a thief from under his blanket; another time he demanded to be told why his old *capote* was hanging on the wall in front of him when he had a new overcoat; then it seemed to him that he was standing before the general and listening to his reprimand, which he so well deserved, saying, "Sorry, your excellency!" and, finally, he let out a stream of obscenities, shouting such frightful words that his dear old landlady kept crossing herself, having never heard him use such words, particularly as they seemed always to follow immediately upon the words "your excellency." He raved on and no sense could be made of his words, except that it was quite evident that his incoherent words and thoughts all revolved about one and the same overcoat. At length poor Akaky Akakyevich gave up the ghost.

Neither his room nor his belongings were put under seal because, in the first place, he had no heirs, and in the second there was precious little inheritance he left behind, comprising as it did all in all a bundle of quills, a quire of white Government paper, three pairs of socks, a few buttons that had come off his trousers, and the *capote* with which the reader has already made his acquaintance. Who finally came into all this property, goodness only knows, and I must confess that the author of this story was not sufficiently interested to find out. Akaky Akakyevich was taken to the cemetery and buried. And St. Petersburg carried on without Akaky, as though he had never lived there. A human being just disappeared and left no trace, a human being whom no one ever dreamed of protecting, who was not dear to anyone, whom no one thought of taking any interest in, who did not attract the attention even of a naturalist who never fails to stick a pin through an ordinary fly to examine it under the microscope; a man who bore meekly the sneers and insults of his fellow Civil Servants in the department and who went to his grave because of some silly accident, but who before the very end of his life did nevertheless catch a glimpse of a Bright Visitant in the shape of an overcoat, which for a brief moment brought a ray of sunshine into his drab, poverty-stricken life, and upon whose head afterwards disaster had most pitilessly fallen, as it falls upon the heads of the great ones of this earth! . . .

A few days after his death a caretaker was sent to his room from the department to order him to present himself at the office at once: the chief himself wanted to see him! But the caretaker had to return without him, merely reporting that Akaky Akakyevich could not come, and to the question, "Why not?" he merely said, "He can't come, sir, 'cause he's dead. That's why, sir. Been buried these four days, he has, sir." It was in this way that the news of his death reached the department, and on the following day a new clerk was sitting in his place, a much taller man, who did not write letters in Akaky's upright hand, but rather sloping and aslant.

But who could have foreseen that this was not the last of Akaky Akakyevich and that he was destined to be the talk of the town for a few days after his death, as though in recompense for having remained unnoticed all through his life. But so it fell out, and our rather poor story quite unexpectedly acquired a most fantastic ending.

Rumours suddenly spread all over St. Petersburg that a ghost in the shape of a Government clerk had begun appearing near Kalinkin Bridge and much farther afield, too, and that this ghost was looking for some stolen overcoat and, under the pretext of recovering this lost overcoat, was stripping overcoats off the backs of all sorts of people, irrespective of their rank or calling: overcoats with cat fur, overcoats with beaver fur, raccoon, fox and bear fur-coats, in fact, overcoats with every kind of fur or skin that men have ever made use of to cover their own. One of the departmental clerks had seen the ghost with his own eyes and at once recognized Akaky Akakyevich; but that frightened him so much that he took to his heels and was unable to get a better view of the ghost, but merely saw how he shook a finger at him threateningly from a distance. From all sides complaints were incessantly heard to the effect that the backs and shoulders, not only of titular councillors, but also of court councillors, were in imminent danger of catching cold as a result of this frequent pulling off of overcoats. The police received orders to catch the ghost at all costs, dead or alive, and to punish him in the most unmerciful manner as an example to all other ghosts, and they nearly did catch it. A police constable whose beat included Kiryushkin Lane had actually caught the ghost by his collar on the very scene of his latest crime, in the very act of attempting to pull a frieze overcoat off the back of some retired musician who had once upon a time tootled on a flute. Having caught him by the collar, the policeman shouted to two of his comrades to come to his help, and when those arrived he told them to hold the miscreant while he reached for his snuff-box which he kept in one of his boots, to revive his nose which had been frostbitten six times in his life; but the snuff must have been of a kind that even a ghost could not stand. For no sooner had the policeman, closing his right nostril with a finger, inhaled with his left nostril half a handful of snuff than the ghost sneezed so violently that he splashed the eyes of all three. While they were raising their fists to wipe their eyes, the ghost had vanished completely, so that they were not even sure whether he had actually been in their hands. Since that time policemen were in such terror of the dead that they were even afraid to arrest the living, merely shouting from a distance, "Hi, you there, move along, will you?" and the ghost of the Civil Servant began to show himself beyond Kalinkin Bridge, causing alarm and dismay among all law-abiding citizens of timid dispositions.

We seem, however, to have completely forgotten a certain Very Important Person who, as a matter of fact, was the real cause of the fantastic turn this otherwise perfectly true story has taken. To begin with, we think it is only fair to make it absolutely clear that the Very Important Person felt something like a twinge of compunction soon after the departure of poor Akaky Akakyevich, whom he had taken to task so severely. Sympathy for a fellow human being was not alien to him; his heart was open to all kinds of kindly impulses in spite of the fact that his rank often prevented them from coming to the surface. As soon as the friend he had not seen for so long had left, he felt even a little worried about poor Akaky, and since that day he could not get the pale face of the meek little Government clerk out of his head, the poor Civil Servant who could not take an official reprimand like a man. In fact, he worried so much about him that a week later he sent one of his own clerks to Akaky to find out how he was getting on, whether his overcoat had turned up, and whether it was not really possible to help him in any way. When he learnt that Akaky had died suddenly of a fever he was rather upset and all day long his conscience troubled him, and he was in a bad mood. Wishing to distract himself a little and forget the unpleasant incident, he went to spend an evening with one of his friends, where he found quite a large company and, what was even better, they all seemed to be almost of the same rank as he, so that there was nothing at all to disconcert him. This had a most wonderful effect on his state of mind. He let himself go, became a very pleasant fellow to talk to, affable and genial, and spent a very agreeable evening. At dinner he drank a few glasses of champagne, which, as is generally acknowledged, is quite an excellent way of getting rid of gloomy thoughts. The champagne led him to introduce a certain change into his programme for that night, to wit, he decided not to go home at once, but first visit a lady friend of his, a certain Karolina Ivanovna, presumably of German descent, with whom he was on exceedingly friendly terms. It should be explained here that the Very Important Person was not a young man, that he was a good husband and a worthy father of a family. Two sons, one of whom was already in Government service, and a very sweet sixteen-year-old daughter, whose little nose was perhaps a thought too arched, but who was very pretty none the less, came every morning to kiss his hand, saying, "*Bonjour, papa.*" His wife, who was still in the prime of life and not at all bad-looking, first gave him her hand to kiss and then, turning it round, kissed his hand. But the Very Important Person, who was very satisfied indeed with these domestic pleasantries, thought it only right to have a lady friend in another part of the town for purely friendly relations. This lady friend was not a bit younger or better-looking than his wife, but there it is: such is the way of the world, and it is not our business to pass judgment upon it. And so the Very Important Person descended the stairs, sat down in his sledge,

said to his coachman, "To Karolina Ivanovna," and, wrapping himself up very
snugly in his warm overcoat, gave himself up completely to the enjoyment of his
pleasant mood, than which nothing better could happen to a Russian, that is to say,
the sort of mood when you do not yourself have to think of anything, while thoughts,
one more delightful than another, come racing through your head without even
putting you to the trouble of chasing after them or looking for them. Feeling very
pleased, he recalled without much effort all the pleasant happenings of the evening,
all the witty sayings, which had aroused peals of laughter among the small circle
of friends, many of which he even now repeated softly to himself, finding them
every bit as funny as they were the first time he heard them, and it is therefore little
wonder that he chuckled happily most of the time. The boisterous wind, however,
occasionally interfered with his enjoyment, for, rushing out suddenly from heaven
knew where and for a reason that was utterly incomprehensible, it cut his face like
a knife, covering it with lumps of snow, swelling out his collar like a sail, or
suddenly throwing it with supernatural force over his head and so causing him
incessant trouble to extricate himself from it. All of a sudden the Very Important
Person felt that somebody had seized him very firmly by the collar. Turning round,
he saw a small-sized man in an old, threadbare Civil Service uniform, and it was
not without horror that he recognized Akaky Akakyevich. The Civil Servant's
face was white as snow and looked like that of a dead man. But the horror of the
Very Important Person increased considerably when he saw that the mouth of the
dead man became twisted and, exhaling the terrible breath of the grave, Akaky's
ghost uttered the following words, "Aha! So here you are! I've — er — collared
you at last! . . . It's your overcoat I want, sir! You didn't care a rap for mine, did
you? Did nothing to get it back for me, and abused me into the bargain! All right,
then, give me yours now!" The poor Very Important Person nearly died of fright.
Unbending as he was at the office and generally in the presence of his inferiors,
and though one look at his manly appearance and figure was enough to make
people say, "Ugh, what a Tartar!" nevertheless in this emergency he, like many
another man of athletic appearance, was seized with such terror that he began, not
without reason, to apprehend a heart attack. He threw off his overcoat himself and
shouted to his driver in a panic-stricken voice, "Home, quick!" The driver,
recognizing the tone which was usually employed in moments of crisis and was
quite often accompanied by something more forceful, drew in his head between
his shoulders just to be on the safe side, flourished his whip and raced off as swift
as an arrow. In a little over six minutes the Very Important Person was already at
the entrance of his house.

Pale, frightened out of his wits, and without his overcoat, he arrived home
instead of going to Karolina Ivanovna's, and somehow or other managed to stagger
to his room. He spent a very restless night, so that next morning at breakfast his
daughter told him outright, "You look very pale today, Papa!" But Papa made no
reply. Not a word did he say to any one about what had happened to him, where he
had been and where he had intended to go.

This incident made a deep impression upon the Very Important Person. It
was not so frequently now that his subordinates heard him say, "How dare you,

sir? Do you realize who you're talking to, sir?" And if he did say it, it was only after he had heard what it was all about.

But even more remarkable was the fact that since then the appearance of the Civil Servant's ghost had completely ceased. It can only be surmised that he was very pleased with the general's overcoat which must have fitted him perfectly; at least nothing was heard any more of people who had their overcoats pulled off their backs. Not that there were not all sorts of busybodies who would not let well alone and who went on asserting that the ghost of the Civil Servant was still appearing in the more outlying parts of the town. Indeed, a Kolomna policeman saw with his own eyes the ghost appear from behind a house; but having rather a frail constitution — once an ordinary young pig, rushing out of a house, had sent him sprawling, to the great delight of some cabbies who were standing round and whom, for such an insult, he promptly fined two copecks each for snuff — he dared not stop the ghost, but merely followed it in the dark until, at last, it suddenly looked round and, stopping dead in its tracks, asked, "What do *you* want?" at the same time displaying a fist of a size that was never seen among the living. The police constable said, "Nothing," and turned back at once. This ghost however, was much taller; it had a pair of huge moustachios, and walking apparently in the direction of Obukhov Bridge, it disappeared into the darkness of the night.

ℰʘℭ

Nicolai Gogol seems to have lived in two centuries at once. His fiction and drama are ensconced in nineteenth-century Czarist Russia, yet his technique and ironic sensibility belong to our own time, when "downsizing" and information technology threaten to eradicate individual autonomy and make personal history irrelevant. A classic blending of realism and the fantastic, "The Overcoat" is both a critique of a bureaucratized state and a ghost story. Akaky Akakyevich is a human photocopier, a man whose inner life is so utterly barren that his greatest joy is to bring his meaningless work home with him at night and make it his entertainment. The physical necessity to purchase a new overcoat quickly becomes an obsession that grants the poor clerk temporary spiritual nourishment; the coat acquires the status of a fetish, a physical object onto which Akaky projects his most intense desires, needs, and fears. This story, however, is much more than a pre-Marxist analysis of commodification and the alienation of the worker. If the loss of the overcoat directly leads to Akaky's death, it also allows Gogol's prolix and gently brutal narrator to change the direction of his satire, as he then creates a miniature psychological portrait of the Very Important Person, a new and surprisingly ludicrous story in itself. "The Overcoat" offers much more than incisive social commentary; as an experiment in narrative voice, it is concerned with the art of story-telling as much as anything else.

M.T.

Nathaniel Hawthorne

(1804-1864)

Young Goodman Brown

Young Goodman Brown came forth, at sunset, into the street of Salem village, but put his head back, after crossing the threshold, to exchange a parting kiss with his young wife. And Faith, as the wife was aptly named, thrust her own pretty head into the street, letting the wind play with the pink ribbons of her cap, while she called to Goodman Brown.

"Dearest heart," whispered she, softly and rather sadly, when her lips were close to his ear, "pr'y thee, put off your journey until sunrise, and sleep in your own bed tonight. A lone woman is troubled with such dreams and such thoughts, that she's afeard of herself, sometimes. Pray, tarry with me this night, dear husband, of all nights in the year!"

"My love and my Faith," replied young Goodman Brown, "of all nights in the year, this one night must I tarry away from thee. My journey, as thou callest it, forth and back again, must needs be done 'twixt now and sunrise. What, my sweet, pretty wife, dost thou doubt me already, and we but three months married!"

"Then, God bless you!" said Faith, with the pink ribbons, "and may you find all well, when you come back."

"Amen!" cried Goodman Brown. "Say thy prayers, dear Faith, and go to bed at dusk, and no harm will come to thee."

So they parted; and the young man pursued his way, until, being about to turn the corner by the meeting-house, he looked back, and saw the head of Faith still peeping after him, with a melancholy air, in spite of her pink ribbons.

"Poor little Faith!" thought he, for his heart smote him. "What a wretch am I, to leave her on such an errand! She talks of dreams, too. Methought, as she spoke, there was trouble in her face, as if a dream had warned her what work is to be done tonight. But, no, no! 'twould kill her to think it. Well; she's a blessed angel on earth; and after this one night, I'll cling to her skirts and follow her to Heaven."

With this excellent resolve for the future, Goodman Brown felt himself justified in making more haste on his present evil purpose. He had taken a dreary road, darkened by all the gloomiest trees of the forest, which barely stood aside to let the narrow path creep through, and closed immediately behind. It was all as lonely as could be; and there is this peculiarity in such a solitude, that the traveller knows not who may be concealed by the innumerable trunks and the thick boughs overhead; so that, with lonely footsteps, he may yet be passing through an unseen multitude.

"There may be a devilish Indian behind every tree," said Goodman Brown, to himself; and he glanced fearfully behind him, as he added, "What if the devil himself should be at my very elbow!"

His head being turned back, he passed a crook of the road, and looking forward again, beheld the figure of a man, in grave and decent attire, seated at the foot of an old tree. He arose, at Goodman Brown's approach, and walked onward, side by side with him.

"You are late, Goodman Brown," said he. "The clock of the Old South was striking as I came through Boston; and that is full fifteen minutes agone."

"Faith kept me back awhile," replied the young man, with a tremor in his voice, caused by the sudden appearance of his companion, though not wholly unexpected.

It was now deep dusk in the forest, and deepest in that part of it where these two were journeying. As nearly as could be discerned, the second traveller was about fifty years old, apparently in the same rank of life as Goodman Brown, and bearing a considerable resemblance to him, though perhaps more in expression than features. Still, they might have been taken for father and son. And yet, though the elder person was as simply clad as the younger, and as simple in manner too, he had an indescribable air of one who knew the world, and would not have felt abashed at the governor's dinner-table, or in King William's court, were it possible that his affairs should call him thither. But the only thing about him, that could be fixed upon as remarkable, was his staff, which bore the likeness of a great black snake, so curiously wrought, that it might almost be seen to twist and wriggle itself, like a living serpent. This, of course, must have been an ocular deception, assisted by the uncertain light.

"Come, Goodman Brown!" cried his fellow-traveller, "this is a dull pace for the beginning of a journey. Take my staff, if you are so soon weary."

"Friend," said the other, exchanging his slow pace for a full stop, "having kept covenant by meeting thee here, it is my purpose now to return whence I came. I have scruples, touching the matter thou wot'st of."

"Sayest thou so?" replied he of the serpent, smiling apart. "Let us walk on, nevertheless, reasoning as we go, and if I convince thee not, thou shalt turn back. We are but a little way in the forest, yet."

"Too far, too far!" exclaimed the goodman, unconsciously resuming his walk. "My father never went into the woods on such an errand, nor his father before him. We have been a race of honest men and good Christians, since the days of the martyrs. And shall I be the first of the name of Brown, that ever took this path, and kept —"

"Such company, thou wouldst say," observed the elder person, interpreting his pause. "Well said, Goodman Brown! I have been as well acquainted with your family as with ever a one among the Puritans; and that's no trifle to say. I helped your grandfather, the constable, when he lashed the Quaker woman so smartly through the streets of Salem. And it was I that brought your father a pitch-pine knot, kindled at my own hearth, to set fire to an Indian village, in King Philip's war. They were my good friends, both; and many a pleasant walk have we had along this path, and returned merrily after midnight. I would fain be friends with you, for their sake."

"If it be as thou sayest," replied Goodman Brown, "I marvel they never spoke of these matters. Or, verily, I marvel not, seeing that the least rumour of the sort would have driven them from New-England. We are a people of prayer, and good works, to boot, and abide no such wickedness."

"Wickedness or not," said the traveller with the twisted staff, "I have a very general acquaintance here in New-England. The deacons of many a church have drunk the communion wine with me; the selectmen, of divers towns, make me their chairman; and a majority of the Great and General Court are firm supporters of my interest. The governor and I, too — but these are state-secrets."

"Can this be so!" cried Goodman Brown, with a stare of amazement at his undisturbed companion. "Howbeit, I have nothing to do with the governor and council; they have their own ways, and are no rule for a simple husbandman, like me. But, were I to go on with thee, how should I meet the eye of that good old man, our minister, at Salem village? Oh, his voice would make me tremble, both Sabbath-day and lecture-day!"

Thus far, the elder traveller had listened with due gravity, but now burst into a fit of irrepressible mirth, shaking himself so violently, that his snake-like staff actually seemed to wriggle in sympathy.

"Ha! ha! ha!" shouted he, again and again; then composing himself, "Well, go on, Goodman Brown, go on; but pr'y thee, don't kill me with laughing!"

"Well, then, to end the matter at once," said Goodman Brown, considerably nettled, "there is my wife, Faith. It would break her dear little heart; and I'd rather break my own!"

"Nay, if that be the case," answered the other, "e'en go thy ways, Goodman Brown. I would not, for twenty old women like the one hobbling before us, that Faith should come to any harm."

As he spoke, he pointed his staff at a female figure on the path, in whom Goodman Brown recognized a very pious and exemplary dame, who had taught him his catechism, in youth, and was still his moral and spiritual adviser, jointly with the minister and Deacon Gookin.

"A marvel, truly, that Goody Cloyse should be so far in the wilderness, at nightfall!" said he. "But, with your leave, friend, I shall take a cut through the woods, until we have left this Christian woman behind. Being a stranger to you, she might ask whom I was consorting with, and whither I was going."

"Be it so," said his fellow-traveller. "Betake you to the woods, and let me keep the path."

Accordingly, the young man turned aside, but took care to watch his companion, who advanced softly along the road, until he had come within a staff's length of the old dame. She, meanwhile, was making the best of her way, with singular speed for so aged a woman, and mumbling some indistinct words, a prayer, doubtless, as she went. The traveller put forth his staff, and touched her withered neck with what seemed the serpent's tail.

"The devil!" screamed the pious old lady.

"Then Goody Cloyse knows her old friend?" observed the traveller, confronting her, and leaning on his writhing stick.

"Ah, forsooth, and is it your worship, indeed?" cried the good dame. "Yea, truly is it, and in the very image of my old gossip, Goodman Brown, the grandfather of the silly fellow that now is. But — would your worship believe it? — my broomstick hath strangely disappeared, stolen, as I suspect, by that unhanged witch, Goody Cory, and that, too, when I was all anointed with the juice of smallage and cinque-foil and wolf's-bane —"

"Mingled with fine wheat and the fat of a new-born babe," said the shape of old Goodman Brown.

"Ah, your worship knows the receipt," cried the old lady, cackling aloud. "So, as I was saying, being all ready for the meeting, and no horse to ride on, I made up my mind to foot it; for they tell me, there is a nice young man to be taken into communion tonight. But now your good worship will lend me your arm, and we shall be there in a twinkling."

"That can hardly be," answered her friend. "I may not spare you my arm, Goody Cloyse, but here is my staff, if you will."

So saying, he threw it down at her feet, where, perhaps, it assumed life, being one of the rods which its owner had formerly lent to the Egyptian Magi. Of this fact, however, Goodman Brown could not take cognizance. He had cast up his eyes in astonishment, and looking down again, beheld neither Goody Cloyse nor the serpentine staff, but his fellow-traveller alone, who waited for him as calmly as if nothing had happened.

"That old woman taught me my catechism!" said the young man; and there was a world of meaning in this simple comment.

They continued to walk onward, while the elder traveller exhorted his companion to make good speed and persevere in the path, discoursing so aptly, that his arguments seemed rather to spring up in the bosom of his auditor, than to be suggested by himself. As they went, he plucked a branch of maple, to serve for a walking-stick, and began to strip it of the twigs and little boughs, which were wet with evening dew. The moment his fingers touched them, they became strangely withered and dried up, as with a week's sunshine. Thus the pair proceeded, at a good free pace, until suddenly, in a gloomy hollow of the road, Goodman Brown sat himself down on the stump of a tree, and refused to go any farther.

"Friend," said he, stubbornly, "my mind is made up. Not another step will I budge on this errand. What if a wretched old woman do choose to go to the devil, when I thought she was going to Heaven! Is that any reason why I should quit my dear Faith, and go after her?"

"You will think better of this, by-and-by," said his acquaintance, composedly. "Sit here and rest yourself awhile; and when you feel like moving again, there is my staff to help you along."

Without more words, he threw his companion the maple stick, and was as speedily out of sight, as if he had vanished into the deepening gloom. The young man sat a few moments, by the road-side, applauding himself greatly, and thinking with how clear a conscience he should meet the minister, in his morning-walk, nor shrink from the eye of good old Deacon Gookin. And what calm sleep would be his, that very night, which was to have been spent so wickedly, but purely and sweetly now, in the arms of Faith! Amidst these pleasant and praiseworthy meditations, Goodman Brown heard the tramp of horses along the road, and deemed it advisable to conceal himself within the verge of the forest, conscious of the guilty purpose that had brought him thither, though now so happily turned from it.

On came the hoof-tramps and the voices of the riders, two grave old voices, conversing soberly as they drew near. These mingled sounds appeared to pass along the road, within a few yards of the young man's hiding-place; but owing, doubtless, to the depth of the gloom, at that particular spot, neither the travellers nor their steeds were visible. Though their figures brushed the small boughs by the wayside, it could not be seen that they intercepted, even for a moment, the faint gleam from the strip of bright sky, athwart which they must have passed. Goodman Brown alternately crouched and stood on tiptoe, pulling aside the branches, and thrusting forth his head as far as he durst, without discerning so much as a shadow. It vexed him the more, because he could have sworn, were such a thing possible, that he recognized the voices of the minister and Deacon Gookin, jogging along quietly, as they were wont to do, when bound to some ordination or ecclesiastical council. While yet within hearing, one of the riders stopped to pluck a switch.

"Of the two, reverend Sir," said the voice like the deacon's, "I had rather miss an ordination-dinner than tonight's meeting. They tell me that some of our community are to be here from Falmouth and beyond, and others from Connecticut and Rhode-Island; besides several of the Indian powows, who, after their fashion, know almost as much deviltry as the best of us. Moreover, there is a goodly young woman to be taken into communion."

"Mighty well, Deacon Gookin!" replied the solemn old tones of the minister. "Spur up, or we shall be late. Nothing can be done, you know, until I get on the ground."

The hoofs clattered again, and the voices, talking so strangely in the empty air, passed on through the forest, where no church had ever been gathered, nor solitary Christian prayed. Whither, then, could these holy men be journeying, so deep into the heathen wilderness? Young Goodman Brown caught hold of a tree, for support, being ready to sink down on the ground, faint and overburthened with the heavy sickness of his heart. He looked up to the sky, doubting whether there really was a Heaven above him. Yet, there was the blue arch, and the stars brightening in it.

"With Heaven above, and Faith below, I will yet stand firm against the devil!" cried Goodman Brown.

While he still gazed upward, into the deep arch of the firmament, and had lifted his hands to pray, a cloud, though no wind was stirring, hurried across the zenith, and hid the brightening stars. The blue sky was still visible, except directly overhead, where this black mass of cloud was sweeping swiftly northward. Aloft in the air, as if from the depths of the cloud, came a confused and doubtful sound of voices. Once, the listener fancied that he could distinguish the accents of towns-people of his own, men and women, both pious and ungodly, many of whom he had met at the communion-table, and had seen others rioting at the tavern. The next moment, so indistinct were the sounds, he doubted whether he had heard aught but the murmur of the old forest, whispering without a wind. Then came a stronger swell of those familiar tones, heard daily in the sunshine, at Salem village, but never, until now, from a cloud of night. There was one voice, of a young woman, uttering lamentations, yet with an uncertain sorrow, and entreating for some favour, which, perhaps, it would grieve her to obtain. And all the unseen multitude, both saints and sinners, seemed to encourage her onward.

"Faith!" shouted Goodman Brown, in a voice of agony and desperation; and the echoes of the forest mocked him, crying — "Faith! Faith!" as if bewildered wretches were seeking her, all through the wilderness.

The cry of grief, rage, and terror, was yet piercing the night, when the unhappy husband held his breath for a response. There was a scream, drowned immediately in a louder murmur of voices, fading into far-off laughter, as the dark cloud swept away, leaving the clear and silent sky above Goodman Brown. But something fluttered lightly down through the air, and caught on the branch of a tree. The young man seized it, and beheld a pink ribbon.

"My Faith is gone!" cried he, after one stupefied moment. "There is no good on earth; and sin is but a name. Come, devil! for to thee is this world given."

And maddened with despair, so that he laughed loud and long, did Goodman Brown grasp his staff and set forth again, at such a rate, that he seemed to fly along the forest-path, rather than to walk or run. The road grew wilder and drearier, and more faintly traced, and vanished at length, leaving him in the heart of the dark wilderness, still rushing onward, with the instinct that guides mortal man to evil. The whole forest was peopled with frightful sounds; the creaking of the trees, the howling of wild beasts, and the yell of Indians; while, sometimes, the wind tolled like a distant church-bell, and sometimes gave a broad roar around the traveller, as if all Nature were laughing him to scorn. But he was himself the chief horror of the scene, and shrank not from its other horrors.

"Ha! ha! ha!" roared Goodman Brown, when the wind laughed at him. "Let us hear which will laugh loudest! Think not to frighten me with your deviltry! Come witch, come wizard, come Indian powow, come devil himself! and here comes Goodman Brown. You may as well fear him as he fear you!"

In truth, all through the haunted forest, there could be nothing more frightful than the figure of Goodman Brown. On he flew, among the black pines, brandishing his staff with frenzied gestures, now giving vent to an inspiration of horrid blasphemy, and now shouting forth such laughter, as set all the echoes of the forest laughing like demons around him. The fiend in his own shape is less hideous, than when he rages in the breast of man. Thus sped the demoniac on his course, until, quivering among the trees, he saw a red light before him, as when the felled trunks and branches of a clearing have been set on fire, and throw up their lurid blaze against the sky, at the hour of midnight. He paused, in a lull of the tempest that had driven him onward, and heard the swell of what seemed a hymn, rolling solemnly from a distance, with the weight of many voices. He knew the tune; it was a familiar one in the choir of the village meeting-house. The verse died heavily away, and was lengthened by a chorus, not of human voices, but of all the sounds of the benighted wilderness, pealing in awful harmony together. Goodman Brown cried out; and his cry was lost to his own ear, by its unison with the cry of the desert.

In the interval of silence, he stole forward, until the light glared full upon his eyes. At one extremity of an open space, hemmed in by the dark wall of the forest, arose a rock, bearing some rude, natural resemblance either to an altar or a pulpit, and surrounded by four blazing pines, their tops aflame, their stems untouched, like candles at an evening meeting. The mass of foliage, that had overgrown the summit of the rock, was all on fire, blazing high into the night, and fitfully illuminating the whole field. Each pendent twig and leafy festoon was in a blaze. As the red light arose and fell, a numerous congregation alternately shone forth, then disappeared in shadow, and again grew, as it were, out of the darkness, peopling the heart of the solitary woods at once.

"A grave and dark-clad company!" quoth Goodman Brown.

In truth, they were such. Among them, quivering to-and-fro, between gloom and splendour, appeared faces that would be seen, next day, at the council-board of the province, and others which, Sabbath after Sabbath, looked devoutly heavenward, and benignantly over the crowded pews, from the holiest pulpits in the land. Some affirm, that the lady of the governor was there. At least, there were high dames well known to her, and wives of honoured husbands, and widows, a great multitude, and ancient maidens, all of excellent repute, and fair young girls, who trembled, lest their mothers should espy them. Either the sudden gleams of light, flashing over the obscure field, bedazzled Goodman Brown, or he recognized a score of the church-members of Salem village, famous for their especial sanctity. Good old Deacon Gookin had arrived, and waited at the skirts of that venerable saint, his revered pastor. But, irreverently consorting with these grave, reputable, and pious people, these elders of the church, these chaste dames and dewy virgins, there were men of dissolute lives and women of spotted fame, wretches given over to all mean and filthy vice, and suspected even of horrid crimes. It was strange to see, that the good shrank not from the wicked, nor were the sinners abashed by the saints. Scattered, also, among their pale-faced enemies, were the Indian priests, or powows, who had often scared their native forest with more hideous incantations than any known to English witchcraft.

"But, where is Faith?" thought Goodman Brown; and, as hope came into his heart, he trembled.

Another verse of the hymn arose, a slow and mournful strain, such as the pious love, but joined to words which expressed all that our nature can conceive of sin, and darkly hinted at far more. Unfathomable to mere mortals is the lore of fiends. Verse after verse was sung, and still the chorus of the desert swelled between, like the deepest tone of a mighty organ. And, with the final peal of that dreadful anthem, there came a sound, as if the roaring wind, the rushing streams, the howling beasts, and every other voice of the unconverted wilderness, were mingling and according with the voice of guilty man, in homage to the prince of all. The four blazing pines threw up a loftier flame, and obscurely discovered shapes and visages of horror on the smoke-wreaths, above the impious assembly. At the same moment, the fire on the rock shot redly forth, and formed a glowing arch above its base, where now appeared a figure. With reverence be it spoken, the figure bore no slight similitude, both in garb and manner, to some grave divine of the New-England churches.

"Bring forth the converts!" cried a voice, that echoed through the field and rolled into the forest.

At the word, Goodman Brown stepped forth from the shadow of the trees, and approached the congregation, with whom he felt a loathful brotherhood, by the sympathy of all that was wicked in his heart. He could have well nigh sworn, that the shape of his own dead father beckoned him to advance, looking downward from a smoke-wreath, while a woman, with dim features of despair, threw out her hand to warn him back. Was it his mother? But he had no power to retreat one step, nor to resist, even in thought, when the minister and good old Deacon Gookin seized his arms, and led him to the blazing rock. Thither came also the slender form of a veiled female, led between Goody Cloyse, that pious teacher of the catechism, and Martha Carrier, who had received the devil's promise to be queen of hell. A rampant hag was she! And there stood the proselytes, beneath the canopy of fire.

"Welcome, my children," said the dark figure, "to the communion of your race! Ye have found, thus young, your nature and your destiny. My children, look behind you!"

They turned; and flashing forth, as it were, in a sheet of flame, the fiend-worshippers were seen; the smile of welcome gleamed darkly on every visage.

"There," resumed the sable form, "are all whom ye have reverenced from youth. Ye deemed them holier than yourselves, and shrank from your own sin, contrasting it with their lives of righteousness, and prayerful aspirations heavenward. Yet, here are they all, in my worshipping assembly! This night it shall be granted you to know their secret deeds; how hoary-bearded elders of the church have whispered wanton words to the young maids of their households; how many a woman, eager for widow's weeds, has given her husband a drink at bed-time, and let him sleep his last sleep in her bosom; how beardless youths have made haste to inherit their fathers' wealth; and how fair damsels — blush not, sweet ones! — have dug little graves in the garden, and bidden me, the sole guest, to an infant's funeral. By the sympathy of your human hearts for sin, ye shall scent out all the places — whether in church, bed-chamber, street, field, or forest — where crime has been committed, and shall exult to behold the whole earth one stain of guilt, one mighty bloodspot. Far more than this! It shall be yours to penetrate, in every bosom, the deep mystery of sin, the fountain of all wicked arts, and which inexhaustibly supplies more evil impulses than human power — than my power, at its utmost! — can make manifest in deeds. And now, my children, look upon each other."

They did so; and, by the blaze of the hell-kindled torches, the wretched man beheld his Faith, and the wife her husband, trembling before that unhallowed altar.

"Lo! there ye stand, my children," said the figure, in a deep and solemn tone, almost sad, with its despairing awfulness, as if his once angelic nature could yet mourn for our miserable race. "Depending upon one another's hearts, ye had still hoped, that virtue were not all a dream. Now are ye undeceived! Evil is the nature of mankind. Evil must be your only happiness. Welcome, again, my children, to the communion of your race!"

"Welcome!" repeated the fiend-worshippers, in one cry of despair and triumph.

And there they stood, the only pair, as it seemed, who were yet hesitating on the verge of wickedness, in this dark world. A basin was hollowed, naturally, in the rock. Did it contain water, reddened by the lurid light? or was it blood? or, perchance, a liquid flame? Herein did the Shape of Evil dip his hand, and prepare to lay the mark of baptism upon their foreheads, that they might be partakers of the mystery of sin, more conscious of the secret guilt of others, both in deed and thought, than they could now be of their own. The husband cast one look at his pale wife, and Faith at him. What polluted wretches would the next glance shew them to each other, shuddering alike at what they disclosed and what they saw!

"Faith! Faith!" cried the husband. "Look up to Heaven, and resist the Wicked One!"

Whether Faith obeyed, he knew not. Hardly had he spoken, when he found himself amid calm night and solitude, listening to a roar of the wind, which died heavily away through the forest. He staggered against the rock and felt it chill and damp, while a hanging twig, that had been all on fire, besprinkled his cheek with the coldest dew.

The next morning, young Goodman Brown came slowly into the street of Salem village, staring around him like a bewildered man. The good old minister was taking a walk along the graveyard, to get an appetite for breakfast and meditate his sermon, and bestowed a blessing, as he passed, on Goodman Brown. He shrank from the venerable saint, as if to avoid an anathema. Old Deacon Gookin was at domestic worship, and the holy words of his prayer were heard through the open window. "What God doth the wizard pray to?" quoth Goodman Brown. Goody Cloyse, that excellent old Christian, stood in the early sunshine, at her own lattice, catechising a little girl, who had brought her a pint of morning's milk. Goodman Brown snatched away the child, as from the grasp of the fiend himself. Turning the corner by the meeting-house, he spied the head of Faith, with the pink ribbons, gazing anxiously forth, and bursting into such joy at sight of him, that she skipped along the street, and almost kissed her husband before the whole village. But, Goodman Brown looked sternly and sadly into her face, and passed on without a greeting.

Had Goodman Brown fallen asleep in the forest, and only dreamed a wild dream of a witch-meeting?

Be it so, if you will. But, alas! it was a dream of evil omen for young Goodman Brown. A stern, a sad, a darkly meditative, a distrustful, if not a desperate man, did he become, from the night of that fearful dream. On the Sabbath-day, when the congregation were singing a holy psalm, he could not listen, because an anthem of sin rushed loudly upon his ear, and drowned all the blessed strain. When the minister spoke from the pulpit, with power and fervid eloquence, and, with his hand on the open Bible, of the sacred truths of our religion, and of saint-like lives and triumphant deaths, and of future bliss or misery unutterable, then did Goodman Brown turn pale, dreading, lest the roof should thunder down upon the grey blasphemer and his hearers. Often, awakening suddenly at midnight, he shrank from the bosom of

Faith, and at morning or eventide, when the family knelt down at prayer, he scowled, and muttered to himself, and gazed sternly at his wife, and turned away. And when he had lived long, and was borne to his grave, a hoary corpse, followed by Faith, an aged woman, and children and grandchildren, a goodly procession, besides neighbours, not a few, they carved no hopeful verse upon his tombstone; for his dying hour was gloom.

ℰ⟩⟨ℛ

Nathaniel Hawthorne was born in Salem, Massachusetts, the descendant of a prominent Puritan family that included a judge at the Salem witchcraft trials. Hawthorne's own ambivalent attitudes toward Puritan beliefs are implicit in his work, including the celebrated The Scarlet Letter *(1850) as well as in many short stories such as "Young Goodman Brown." His ambivalence arises from a deep preoccupation with the tumultuous drama of the human soul in its struggles between faith and doubt, guilt and sin. Imaginatively revising allegory as a form, Hawthorne depicts his characters as the embodiment not only of moral concepts but also of psychological traits associated with the dark side of our nature. Thus his stories end not with a clearly stated moral, but with an ambiguous tension. Is this story a dream, a vision reflecting the state of Young Goodman Brown's soul? If Hawthorne refuses to provide a clear "moral," what does this story teach us?*

C.M.

A Clean, Well-Lighted Place

It was late and every one had left the café except an old man who sat in the shadow the leaves of the tree made against the electric light. In the daytime the street was dusty, but at night the dew settled the dust and the old man liked to sit late because he was deaf and now at night it was quiet and he felt the difference. The two waiters inside the café knew that the old man was a little drunk, and while he was a good client they knew that if he became too drunk he would leave without paying, so they kept watch on him.

"Last week he tried to commit suicide," one waiter said.

"Why?"

"He was in despair."

"What about?"

"Nothing."

"How do you know it was nothing?"

"He has plenty of money."

They sat together at a table that was close against the wall near the door of the café and looked at the terrace where the tables were all empty except where the old man sat in the shadow of the leaves of the tree that moved slightly in the wind. A girl and a soldier went by in the street. The street light shone on the brass number on his collar. The girl wore no head covering and hurried beside him.

"The guard will pick him up," one waiter said.

"What does it matter if he gets what he's after?"

"He had better get off the street now. The guard will get him. They went by five minutes ago."

The old man sitting in the shadow rapped on his saucer with his glass. The younger waiter went over to him.

"What do you want?"

The old man looked at him. "Another brandy," he said.

"You'll be drunk," the waiter said. The old man looked at him. The waiter went away.

"He'll stay all night," he said to his colleague. "I'm sleepy now. I never get into bed before three o'clock. He should have killed himself last week."

The waiter took the brandy bottle and another saucer from the counter inside the café and marched out to the old man's table. He put down the saucer and poured the glass full of brandy.

"You should have killed yourself last week," he said to the deaf man. The old man motioned with his finger. "A little more," he said. The waiter poured on into the glass so that the brandy slopped over and ran down the stem into the top saucer of the pile. "Thank you," the old man said. The waiter took the bottle back inside the café. He sat down at the table with his colleague again.

"He's drunk now," he said.

"He's drunk every night."

"What did he want to kill himself for?"

"How should I know."

"How did he do it?"

"He hung himself with a rope."

"Who cut him down?"

"His niece."

"Why did they do it?"

"Fear for his soul."

"How much money has he got?"

"He's got plenty."

"He must be eighty years old."

"Anyway I should say he was eighty."

"I wish he would go home. I never get to bed before three o'clock. What kind of hour is that to go to bed?"

"He stays up because he likes it."

"He's lonely. I'm not lonely. I have a wife waiting in bed for me."

"He had a wife once too."

"A wife would be no good to him now."

"You can't tell. He might be better with a wife."

"His niece looks after him."

"I know. You said she cut him down."

"I wouldn't want to be that old. An old man is a nasty thing."

"Not always. This old man is clean. He drinks without spilling. Even now, drunk. Look at him."

"I don't want to look at him. I wish he would go home. He has no regard for those who must work."

The old man looked from his glass across the square, then over at the waiters.

"Another brandy," he said, pointing to his glass. The waiter who was in a hurry came over.

"Finished," he said, speaking with that omission of syntax stupid people employ when talking to drunken people or foreigners. "No more tonight. Close now."

"Another," said the old man.

"No. Finished." The waiter wiped the edge of the table with a towel and shook his head.

The old man stood up, slowly counted the saucers, took a leather coin purse from his pocket and paid for the drinks, leaving half a peseta tip.

The waiter watched him go down the street, a very old man walking unsteadily but with dignity.

"Why didn't you let him stay and drink?" the unhurried waiter asked. They were putting up the shutters. "It is not half-past two."

"I want to go home to bed."

"What is an hour?"

"More to me than to him."

"An hour is the same."

"You talk like an old man yourself. He can buy a bottle and drink at home."

"It's not the same."

"No, it is not," agreed the waiter with a wife. He did not wish to be unjust. He was only in a hurry.

"And you? You have no fear of going home before your usual hour?"

"Are you trying to insult me?"

"No, hombre, only to make a joke."

"No," the waiter who was in a hurry said, rising from pulling down the metal shutters. "I have confidence. I am all confidence."

"You have youth, confidence, and a job," the older waiter said. "You have everything."

"And what do you lack?"

"Everything but work."

"You have everything I have."

"No. I have never had confidence and I am not young."

"Come on. Stop talking nonsense and lock up."

"I am of those who like to stay late at the café," the older waiter said. "With all those who do not want to go to bed. With all those who need a light for the night."

"I want to go home and into bed."

"We are of two different kinds," the older waiter said. He was now dressed to go home. "It is not only a question of youth and confidence although those things are very beautiful. Each night I am reluctant to close up because there may be some one who needs the café."

"Hombre, there are bodegas open all night long."

"You do not understand. This is a clean and pleasant café. It is well lighted. The light is very good and also, now, there are shadows of the leaves."

"Good night," said the younger waiter.

"Good night," the other said. Turning off the electric light he continued the conversation with himself. It is the light of course but it is necessary that the place be clean and pleasant. You do not want music. Certainly you do not want music. Nor can you stand before a bar with dignity although that is all that is provided for these hours. What did he fear? It was not fear or dread. It was a nothing that he knew too well. It was all a nothing and a man was nothing too. It was only that and light was all it needed and a certain cleanness and order. Some lived in it and never felt it but he knew it all was nada y pues nada y nada y pues nada. Our nada who art in nada, nada be thy name thy kingdom nada thy will be nada in nada as it is in nada. Give us this nada our daily nada and nada us our nada as we nada our nadas and nada us not into nada but deliver us from nada; pues nada. Hail nothing full of nothing, nothing is with thee. He smiled and stood before a bar with a shining steam pressure coffee machine.

"What's yours?" asked the barman.

"Nada."

"Otro loco mas," said the barman and turned away.

"A little cup," said the waiter.

The barman poured it for him.

"The light is very bright and pleasant but the bar is unpolished," the waiter said.

The barman looked at him but did not answer. It was too late at night for conversation.

"You want another copita?" the barman asked.

"No, thank you," said the waiter and went out. He disliked bars and bodegas. A clean, well-lighted café was a very different thing. Now, without thinking further, he would go home to his room. He would lie in the bed and finally, with daylight, he would go to sleep. After all, he said to himself, it is probably only insomnia. Many must have it.

ℼ)(ℽ

Perhaps the most noticeable feature of "A Clean, Well-Lighted Place" is its style, one which leaves out almost everything that can be left out. Despite this, the story is rich and suggestive. Why?

Hemingway was a newspaper reporter before he became a short story writer, a novelist and, eventually, a Nobel laureate. This was probably good training: he had to report as much as possible in as few words as possible, leaving out whatever was not absolutely necessary. This story does just that. It leaves out a lot of things that we might ordinarily expect to find. We learn a few facts: the old man tried to hang himself but was cut down by his niece; the old man has "plenty" of money yet is "in despair"; the young waiter is married and wants to close up early to get home to his wife; the older waiter wants to keep the café open for the benefit of "all those who need a light for the night."

But these bare facts, flatly narrated, hardly explain the story's effect on most readers. The story suggests far more than it says. Human existence in this story has been reduced to its minimal need: not to be alone. At the heart of the story is "nada": nothing. And the only thing that can be counterbalanced to "nada" is a "clean, well-lighted place" where, for a brief moment, "light," "cleanness" and " order" — the irreducible minima of life — can just stave off the night that waits outside the tiny café.

By paring away everything that is unessential, Hemingway's style reveals what he considers essential.

N.C.

LINDA HOGAN   (b. 1947)

Aunt Moon's Young Man

T hat autumn when the young man came to town, there was a deep blue sky.
On their way to the fair, the wagons creaked into town. One buckboard,
driven by cloudy white horses, carried a grunting pig inside its wooden
slats. Another had cages of chickens. In the heat, the chickens did not flap their
wings. They sounded tired and old, and their shoulders drooped like old men.

There was tension in the air. Those people who still believed in omens would
turn to go home, I thought, white chicken feathers caught on the wire cages they
brought, reminding us all that the cotton was poor that year and that very little of
it would line the big trailers outside the gins.

A storm was brewing over the plains, and beneath its clouds a few people
from the city drove dusty black motorcars through town, angling around the statue
of General Pickens on Main Street. They refrained from honking at the wagons
and the white, pink-eyed horses. The cars contained no animal life, just neatly
folded stacks of quilts, jellies, and tomato relish, large yellow gourds, and pumpkins
that looked like the round faces of children through half-closed windows.

"The biting flies aren't swarming today," my mother said. She had her hair
done up in rollers. It was almost dry. She was leaning against the window frame,
looking at the ink-blue trees outside. I could see Bess Evening's house through the
glass, appearing to sit like a small, hand-built model upon my mother's shoulder.
My mother was a dreamer, standing at the window with her green dress curved
over her hip.

Her dress was hemmed slightly shorter on one side than on the other. I decided
not to mention it. The way she leaned, with her abdomen tilted out, was her natural
way of standing. She still had good legs, despite the spidery blue veins she said
came from carrying the weight of us kids inside her for nine months each. She also
blamed us for her few grey hairs.

She mumbled something about "the silence before the storm" as I joined her
at the window.

She must have been looking at the young man for a long time, pretending to
watch the sky. He was standing by the bushes and the cockscombs. There was a
flour sack on the ground beside him. I thought at first it might be filled with
something he brought for the fair, but the way his hat sat on it and a pair of black
boots stood beside it, I could tell it held his clothing, and that he was passing
through Pickens on his way to or from some city.

"It's mighty quiet for the first day of fair," my mother said. She sounded far
away. Her eyes were on the young stranger. She unrolled a curler and checked a
strand of hair.

We talked about the weather and the sky, but we both watched the young man. In the deep blue of sky his white shirt stood out like a light. The low hills were fire-gold and leaden.

One of my mother's hands was limp against her thigh. The other moved down from the rollers and touched the green cloth at her chest, playing with a flaw in the fabric.

"Maybe it was the tornado," I said about the stillness in the air. The tornado had passed through a few days ago, touching down here and there. It exploded my cousin's house trailer but it left his motorcycle, standing beside it, untouched. "Tornadoes have no sense of value," my mother had said. "They are always taking away the saints and leaving behind the devils."

The young man stood in that semi-slumped, half-straight manner of fullblood Indians. Our blood was mixed like Heinz 57, and I always thought of purebloods as better than us. While my mother eyed his plain moccasins, she patted her rolled hair as if to put it in order. I was counting the small brown flowers in the blistered wallpaper, the way I counted ceiling tiles in the new school, and counted each step when I walked.

I pictured Aunt Moon inside her house up on my mother's shoulder. I imagined her dark face above the yellow oilcloth, her braids reflecting the yellow as they separated dried plants. She would rise slowly, as I'd seen her do, take a good long time to brush out her hair, and braid it once again. She would pet her dog, Mister, with long slow strokes while she prepared herself for the fair.

My mother moved aside, leaving the house suspended in the middle of the window, where it rested on a mound of land. My mother followed my gaze. She always wanted to know what I was thinking or doing. "I wonder," she said, "why in tarnation Bess's father built that house up there. It gets all the heat and wind."

I stuck up for Aunt Moon. "She can see everything from there, the whole town and everything."

"Sure, and everything can see her. A wonder she doesn't have ghosts."

I wondered what she meant by that, everything seeing Aunt Moon. I guessed by her lazy voice that she meant nothing. There was no cutting edge to her words.

"And don't call her Aunt Moon." My mother was reading my mind again, one of her many tricks. "I know what you're thinking," she would say when I thought I looked expressionless. "You are thinking about finding Mrs. Mark's ring and holding it for a reward."

I would look horrified and tell her that she wasn't even lukewarm, but the truth was that I'd been thinking exactly those thoughts. I resented my mother for guessing my innermost secrets. She was like God, everywhere at once knowing everything. I tried to concentrate on something innocent. I thought about pickles. I was safe; she didn't say a word about dills or sweets.

Bess, Aunt Moon, wasn't really my aunt. She was a woman who lived alone and had befriended me. I liked Aunt Moon and the way she moved, slowly, taking up as much space as she wanted and doing it with ease. She had wide lips and straight eyelashes.

Aunt Moon dried medicine herbs in the manner of her parents. She knew about plants, both the helpful ones and the ones that were poisonous in all but the smallest of doses. And she knew how to cut wood and how to read the planets. She told me why I was stubborn. It had to do with my being born in May. I believed her because my father was born a few days after me, and he was stubborn as all get out, even compared to me.

Aunt Moon was special. She had life in her. The rest of the women in town were cold in the eye and fretted over their husbands. I didn't want to be like them. They condemned the men for drinking and gambling, but even after the loudest quarrels, ones we'd overhear, they never failed to cook for their men. They'd cook platters of lard-fried chicken, bowls of mashed potatoes, and pitchers of creamy flour gravy.

Bess called those meals "sure death by murder."

Our town was full of large and nervous women with red spots on their thin-skinned necks, and we had single women who lived with brothers and sisters or took care of an elderly parent. Bess had comments on all of these: "They have eaten their anger and grown large," she would say. And there were the sullen ones who took care of men broken by the war, women who were hurt by the men's stories of death and glory but never told them to get on with living, like I would have done.

Bessie's own brother, J.D., had gone to the war and returned with softened, weepy eyes. He lived at the veterans' hospital and he did office work there on his good days. I met him once and knew by the sweetness of his eyes that he had never killed anyone, but something about him reminded me of the lonely old shacks out on cotton farming land. His eyes were broken windows.

"Where do you think that young man is headed?" my mother asked.

Something in her voice was wistful and lonely. I looked at her face, looked out the window at the dark man, and looked back at my mother again. I had never thought about her from inside the skin. She was the mind reader in the family, but suddenly I knew how she did it. The inner workings of the mind were clear in her face, like words in a book. I could even feel her thoughts in the pit of my stomach. I was feeling embarrassed at what my mother was thinking when the stranger crossed the street. In front of him an open truck full of prisoners passed by. They wore large white shirts and pants, like immigrants from Mexico. I began to count the flowers in the wallpaper again, and the truckful of prisoners passed by, and when it was gone, the young man had also vanished into thin air.

Besides the young man, another thing I remember about the fair that year was the man in the bathroom. On the first day of the fair, the prisoners were bending over like great white sails, their black and brown hands stuffing trash in canvas bags. Around them the children washed and brushed their cows and raked fresh straw about their pigs. My friend Elaine and I escaped the dust-laden air and went into the women's public toilets, where we shared a stolen cigarette. We heard someone open the door, and we fanned the smoke. Elaine stood on the toilet seat so her sisters wouldn't recognize her shoes. Then it was silent, so we opened the stall and stepped out. At first the round dark man, standing by the door, looked like a woman, but then I noticed the day's growth of beard at his jawline. He wore a blue work shirt and a little straw hat. He leaned against the wall, his hand moving inside his pants. I grabbed Elaine, who was putting lipstick on her cheeks like rouge, and pulled her outside the door, the tube of red lipstick still in her hand.

Outside, we nearly collapsed by a trash can, laughing. "Did you see that? It was a man! A man! In the women's bathroom." She smacked me on the back.

We knew nothing of men's hands inside their pants, so we began to follow him like store detectives, but as we rounded a corner behind his shadow, I saw Aunt Moon walking away from the pigeon cages. She was moving slowly with her cane, through the path's sawdust, feathers, and sand.

"Aunt Moon, there was a man in the bathroom," I said, and then remembered the chickens I wanted to tell her about. Elaine ran off. I didn't know if she was still following the man or not, but I'd lost interest when I saw Aunt Moon.

"Did you see those chickens that lay the green eggs?" I asked Aunt Moon.

She wagged her head no, so I grabbed her free elbow and guided her past the pigeons with curly feathers and the turkeys with red wattles, right up to the chickens.

"They came all the way from South America. They sell for five dollars, can you imagine?" Five dollars was a lot for chickens when we were still recovering from the Great Depression, men were still talking about what they'd done with the CCC, and children still got summer complaint and had to be carried around crippled for months.

She peered into the cage. The eggs were smooth and resting in the straw. "I'll be" was all she said.

I studied her face for a clue as to why she was so quiet, thinking she was mad or something. I wanted to read her thoughts as easily as I'd read my mother's. In the strange light of the sky, her eyes slanted a bit more than usual. I watched her carefully. I looked at the downward curve of her nose and saw the young man reflected in her eyes. I turned around.

On the other side of the cage that held the chickens from Araucania was the man my mother had watched. Bess pretended to be looking at the little Jersey cattle in the distance, but I could tell she was seeing that man. He had a calm look on his face and his dark chest was smooth as oil where his shirt was opened. His eyes were large and black. They were fixed on Bess like he was a hypnotist or something magnetic that tried to pull Bess Evening toward it, even though her body stepped back. She did step back, I remember that, but even so, everything in her went forward, right up to him.

I didn't know if it was just me or if his presence charged the air, but suddenly the oxygen was gone. It was like the fire at the Fisher Hardware when all the air was drawn into the flame. Even the chickens clucked softly, as if suffocating, and the cattle were more silent in the straw. The pulse in everything changed.

I don't know what would have happened if the rooster hadn't crowed just then, but he did, and everything returned to normal. The rooster strutted and we turned to watch him.

Bessie started walking away and I went with her. We walked past the men and boys who were shooting craps in a cleared circle. One of them rubbed the dice between his hands as we were leaving, his eyes closed, his body's tight muscles willing a winning throw. He called me Lady Luck as we walked by. He said,

"There goes Lady Luck," and he tossed the dice.

At dinner that evening we could hear the dance band tuning up in the makeshift beer garden, playing a few practice songs to the empty tables with their red cloths. They played "The Tennessee Waltz." For a while, my mother sang along with it. She had brushed her hair one hundred strokes and now she was talking and regretting talking all at the same time. "He was such a handsome man," she said. My father wiped his face with a handkerchief and rested his elbows on the table. He chewed and looked at nothing in particular. "For the longest time he stood there by the juniper bushes."

My father drank some coffee and picked up the newspaper. Mother cleared the table, one dish at a time and not in stacks like usual. "His clothes were neat. He must not have come from very far away." She moved the salt shaker from the end of the table to the center, then back again.

"I'll wash," I volunteered.

Mother said, "Bless you," and touched herself absently near the waist, as if to remove an apron. "I'll go get ready for the dance," she said.

My father turned a page of the paper.

The truth was, my mother was already fixed up for the dance. Her hair looked soft and beautiful. She had slipped into her new dress early in the day, "to break it in," she said. She wore nylons and she was barefoot and likely to get a runner. I would have warned her, but it seemed out of place, my warning. Her face was softer than usual, her lips painted to look full, and her eyebrows were much darker than usual.

"Do you reckon that young man came here for the rodeo?" She hollered in from the living room, where she powdered her nose. Normally she made up in front of the bathroom mirror, but the cabinet had been slammed and broken mysteriously one night during an argument so we had all taken to grooming ourselves in the small framed mirror in the living room.

I could not put my finger on it, but all the women at the dance that night were looking at the young man. It wasn't exactly that he was handsome. There was something else. He was alive in his whole body while the other men walked with great effort and stiffness, even those who did little work and were still young. Their male bodies had no language of their own in the way that his did. The women themselves seemed confused and lonely in the presence of the young man, and they were ridiculous in their behaviour, laughing too loud, blushing like schoolgirls, or casting him a flirting eye. Even the older women were brighter than usual. Mrs. Tubby, whose face was usually as grim as the statue of General Pickens, the Cherokee hater, played with her necklace until her neck had red lines from the chain. Mrs. Tens twisted a strand of her hair over and over. Her sister tripped over a chair because she'd forgotten to watch where she was going.

The men, sneaking drinks from bottles in paper bags, did not notice any of the fuss.

Maybe it was his hands. His hands were strong and dark.

I stayed late, even after wives pulled their husbands away from their ball game talk and insisted they dance.

My mother and father were dancing. My mother smiled up into my father's face as he turned her this way and that. Her uneven skirt swirled a little around her legs. She had a run in her nylons, as I predicted. My father, who was called Peso by the townspeople, wore his old clothes. He had his usual look about him, and I noticed that faraway, unfocused gaze on the other men too. They were either distant or they were present but rowdy, embarrassing the women around them with the loud talk of male things: work and hunting, fights, this or that pretty girl. Occasionally they told a joke, like, "Did you hear the one about the travelling salesman?"

The dancers whirled around the floor, some tapping their feet, some shuffling, the women in new dresses and dark hair all curled up like in movie magazines, the men with new leather boots and crew cuts. My dad's rear stuck out in back, the way he danced. His hand clutched my mother's waist.

That night, Bessie arrived late. She was wearing a white dress with a full gathered skirt. The print was faded and I could just make out the little blue stars on the cloth. She carried a yellow shawl over her arm. Her long hair was braided as usual in the manner of the older Chickasaw women, like a wreath on her head. She was different from the others with her bright shawls. Sometimes she wore a heavy shell necklace or a collection of bracelets on her arm. They jangled when she talked with me, waving her hands to make a point. Like the time she told me that the soul is a small woman inside the eye who leaves at night to wander to new places.

No one had ever known her to dance before, but that night the young man and Aunt Moon danced together among the artificial geraniums and plastic carnations. They held each other gently like two breakable vases. They didn't look at each other or smile the way the other dancers did; that's how I knew they liked each other. His large dark hand was on the small of her back. Her hand rested tenderly on his shoulder. The other dancers moved away from them and there was empty space all around them.

My father went out into the dark to smoke and to play a hand or two of poker. My mother went to sit with some of the other women, all of them pulling their damp hair away from their necks and letting it fall back again, or furtively putting on lipstick, fanning themselves, and sipping their beers.

"He puts me in the mind of a man I once knew," said Mrs. Tubby.

"Look at them," said Mrs. Tens. "Don't you think he's young enough to be her son?"

With my elbows on my knees and my chin in my hands, I watched Aunt Moon step and square when my mother loomed up like a shadow over the bleachers where I sat.

"Young lady," she said in a scolding voice. "You were supposed to go home and put the children to bed."

I looked from her stern face to my sister Susan, who was like a chubby angel sleeping beside me. Peso Junior had run off to the gambling game, where he was pushing another little boy around. My mother followed my gaze and looked at Junior. She put her hands on her hips and said, "Boys!"

My sister Roberta, who was twelve, had stayed close to the women all night, listening to their talk about the fullblood who had come to town for a rodeo or something and who danced so far away from Bessie that they didn't look friendly at all except for the fact that the music had stopped and they were still waltzing.

CR

Margaret Tubby won the prize money that year for the biggest pumpkin. It was 220.4 centimeters in circumference and weighed 190 pounds and had to be carried on a stretcher by the volunteer firemen. Mrs. Tubby was the town's chief social justice. She sat most days on the bench outside the grocery store. Sitting there like a full-chested hawk on a fence, she held court. She had watched Bess Evening for years with her sharp gold eyes. "This is the year I saw it coming," she told my mother, as if she'd just been dying for Bess to go wrong. It showed up in the way Bess walked, she said, that the woman was coming to a no good end just like the rest of her family had done.

"When do you think she had time to grow that pumpkin?" Mother asked as we escaped Margaret Tubby's court on our way to the store. I knew what she meant, that Mrs. Tubby did more time with gossip than with her garden.

Margaret was even more pious than usual at that time of year when the green tent revival followed on the heels of the fair, when the pink-faced men in white shirts arrived and, really, every single one of them was a preacher. Still, Margaret Tubby kept her prize money to herself and didn't give a tithe to any church.

With Bess Evening carrying on with a stranger young enough to be her son, Mrs. Tubby succeeded in turning the church women against her once and for all. When Bessie walked down the busy street, one of the oldest dances of women took place, for women in those days turned against each other easily, never thinking they might have other enemies. When Bess appeared, the women stepped away. They vanished from the very face of earth that was named Comanche Street. They disappeared into the Oklahoma redstone shops like swallows swooping into their small clay nests. The women would look at the new bolts of red cloth in Terwilligers with feigned interest, although they would never have worn red, even to a dog fight. They'd purchase another box of face powder in the five and dime, or drink cherry phosphates at the pharmacy without so much as tasting the flavour.

But Bessie was unruffled. She walked on in the empty mirage of heat, the sound of her cane blending in with horse hooves and the rhythmic pumping of oil wells out east.

At the store, my mother bought corn meal, molasses, and milk. I bought penny candy for my younger sisters and for Peso Junior with the money I earned by helping Aunt Moon with her remedies. When we passed Margaret Tubby on the way out, my mother nodded at her, but said to me, "That pumpkin grew fat on gossip. I'll bet she fed it with nothing but all-night rumours." I thought about the twenty-five-dollar prize money and decided to grow pumpkins next year.

My mother said, "Now don't you get any ideas about growing pumpkins, young lady. We don't have room enough. They'd crowd out the cucumbers and tomatoes."

My mother and father won a prize that year, too. For dancing. They won a horse lamp for the living room. "We didn't even know it was a contest," my mother said, free from the sin of competition. Her face was rosy with pleasure and pride. She had the life snapping out of her like hot grease, though sometimes I saw that life turn to a slow and restless longing, like when she daydreamed out the window where the young man had stood that day.

Passing Margaret's post and giving up on growing a two-hundred-pound pumpkin, I remembered all the things good Indian women were not supposed to do. We were not supposed to look into the faces of men. Or laugh too loud. We were not supposed to learn too much from books because that kind of knowledge was a burden to the soul. Not only that, it always took us away from our loved ones. I was jealous of the white girls who laughed as loud as they wanted and never had rules. Also, my mother wanted me to go to college no matter what anyone else did or thought. She said I was too smart to stay home and live a life like hers, even if the other people thought book learning would ruin my life.

Aunt Moon with her second sight and heavy breasts managed to break all the rules. She threw back her head and laughed out loud, showing off the worn edges of her teeth. She didn't go to church. She did a man's work, cared for animals, and chopped her own wood. The gossiping women said it was a wonder Bessie Evening was healthy at all and didn't have female problems — meaning with her body, I figured.

The small woman inside her eye was full and lonely at the same time.

Bess made tonics, remedies, and cures. The church women, even those who gossiped, slipped over to buy Bessie's potions at night and in secret. They'd never admit they swallowed the "snake medicine," as they called it. They'd say to Bess, "What have you got to put the life back in a man? My sister has that trouble, you know." Or they'd say, "I have a friend who needs a cure for the sadness." They bought remedies for fever and for coughing fits, for sore muscles and for sleepless nights.

Aunt Moon had learned the cures from her parents, who were said to have visited their own sins upon their children, both of whom were born out of wedlock from the love of an old Chickasaw man and a young woman from one of those tribes up north. Maybe a Navajo or something, the people thought.

But Aunt Moon had numerous talents and I respected them. She could pull cotton, pull watermelons, and pull babies with equal grace. She even delivered those scrub cattle, bred with Holsteins too big for them, caesarean. In addition to that, she told me the ways of the world and not just about the zodiac or fortune cards. "The United States is in love with death," she would say. "They sleep with it better than with lovers. They celebrate it on holidays, the Fourth of July, even in spring when they praise the loss of a good man's body."

She would tend her garden while I'd ask questions. What do you think about heaven? I wanted to know. She'd look up and then get back to pulling the weeds. "You and I both would just grump around up there with all those righteous people. Women like us weren't meant to live on golden streets. We're Indians," she'd say as she cleared out the space around a bean plant. "We're like these beans. We grew up from mud." And then she'd tell me how the people emerged right along with the crawdads from the muddy female swamps of the land. "And what is gold anyway? Just something else that comes from mud. Look at the conquistadors." She pulled a squash by accident. "And look at the sad women of this town, old already and all because of gold." She poked a hole in the ground and replanted the roots of the squash. "Their men make money, but not love. They give the women gold rings, gold-rimmed glasses, gold teeth, but their skin dries up for lack of love. Their hearts are little withered raisins." I was embarrassed by the mention of making love, but I listened to her words.

℞

This is how I came to call Bessie Evening by the name of Aunt Moon: She'd been teaching me that animals and all life should be greeted properly as our kinfolk. "Good day, Uncle," I learned to say to the longhorn as I passed by on the road. "Good morning, cousins. Is there something you need?" I'd say to the sparrows. And one night when the moon was passing over Bessie's house, I said, "Hello, Aunt Moon. I see you are full of silver again tonight." It was so much like Bess Evening, I began to think, that I named her after the moon. She was sometimes full and happy, sometimes small and weak. I began saying it right to her ears: "Auntie Moon, do you need some help today?"

She seemed both older and younger than thirty-nine to me. For one thing, she walked with a cane. She had developed some secret ailment after her young daughter died. My mother said she needed the cane because she had no mortal human to hold her up in life, like the rest of us did.

But the other thing was that she was full of mystery and she laughed right out loud, like a Gypsy, my mother said, pointing out Bessie's blue-painted walls, bright clothes and necklaces, and all the things she kept hanging from her ceiling. She decorated outside her house, too, with bits of blue glass hanging from the trees, and little polished quartz crystals that reflected rainbows across the dry hills.

Aunt Moon had solid feet, a light step, and a face that clouded over with emotion and despair one moment and brightened up like light the next. She'd beam and say to me, "Sassafras will turn your hair red," and throw back her head to laugh, knowing full well that I would rinse my dull hair with sassafras that very night, ruining my mother's pans.

I sat in Aunt Moon's kitchen while she brewed herbals in white enamel pans on the woodstove. The insides of the pans were black from sassafras and burdock and other plants she picked. The kitchen smelled rich and earthy. Some days it was hard to breathe from the combination of woodstove heat and pollen from the plants, but she kept at it and her medicine for cramps was popular with the women in town.

Aunt Moon made me proud of my womanhood, giving me bags of herbs and an old eagle feather that had been doctored by her father back when people used to pray instead of going to church. "The body divines everything," she told me, and sometimes when I was with her, I knew the older Indian world was still here and I'd feel it in my skin and hear the night sounds speak to me, hear the voice of water tell stories about people who lived here before, and the deep songs came out from the hills.

One day I found Aunt Moon sitting at her table in front of a plate of untouched toast and wild plum jam. She was weeping. I was young and didn't know what to say, but she told me more than I could ever understand. "Ever since my daughter died," she told me, "my body aches to touch her. All the mourning has gone into my bones." Her long hair was loose that day and it fell down her back like a waterfall, almost to the floor.

After that I had excuses on the days I saw her hair loose. "I'm putting up new wallpaper today," I'd say, or "I have to help Mom can peaches," which was the truth.

"Sure," she said, and I saw the tinge of sorrow around her eyes even though she smiled and nodded at me.

Canning the peaches, I asked my mother what it was that happened to Aunt Moon's daughter.

"First of all," my mother set me straight, "her name is Bess, not Aunt Moon." Then she'd tell the story of Willow Evening. "That pretty child was the light of that woman's eye," my mother said. "It was all so fast. She was playing one minute and the next she was gone. She was hanging on to that wooden planter and pulled it right down onto her little chest."

My mother touched her chest. "I saw Bessie lift it like it weighed less than a pound — did I already tell you that part?"

All I had seen that day was Aunt Moon holding Willow's thin body. The little girl's face was already gone to ashes and Aunt Moon blew gently on her daughter's skin, even though she was dead, as if she could breathe the life back into her one more time. She blew on her skin the way I later knew that women blow sweat from lovers' faces, cooling them. But I knew nothing of any kind of passion then.

The planter remained on the dry grassy mound of Aunt Moon's yard, and even though she had lifted it, no one else, not even my father, could move it. It was still full of earth and dead geraniums, like a monument to the child.

"That girl was all she had," my mother said through the steam of boiling water. "Hand me the ladle, will you?"

The peaches were suspended in sweet juice in their clear jars. I thought of our lives — so short, the skin so soft around us that we could be gone any second from our living — thought I saw Willow's golden brown face suspended behind glass in one of the jars.

⚬

The men first noticed the stranger, Isaac, when he cleaned them out in the poker game that night at the fair. My father, who had been drinking, handed over the money he'd saved for the new bathroom mirror and took a drunken swing at the young man, missing him by a foot and falling on his bad knee. Mr. Tubby told his wife he lost all he'd saved for the barber shop business, even though everyone in town knew he drank it up long before the week of the fair. Mr. Tens lost his Mexican silver ring. It showed up later on Aunt Moon's hand.

Losing to one another was one thing. Losing to Isaac Cade meant the dark young man was a card sharp and an outlaw. Even the women who had watched the stranger all that night were sure he was full of demons.

The next time I saw Aunt Moon, it was the fallow season of autumn, but she seemed new and fresh as spring. Her skin had new light. Gathering plants, she smiled at me. Her cane moved aside the long dry grasses to reveal what grew underneath. Mullein was still growing, and holly.

I sat at the table while Aunt Moon ground yellow ochre in a mortar. Isaac came in from fixing the roof. He touched her arm so softly I wasn't sure she felt it. I had never seen a man touch a woman that way.

He said hello to me and he said, "You know those fairgrounds? That's where the three tribes used to hold sings." He drummed on the table, looking at me, and sang one of the songs. I said I recognized it, a song I sometimes dreamed I heard from the hill.

A red handprint appeared on his face, like one of those birthmarks that only show up in the heat or under the strain of work or feeling.

"How'd you know about the fairgrounds?" I asked him.

"My father was from here." He sat still, as if thinking himself into another time. He stared out the window at the distances that were in between the blue curtains.

I went back to Aunt Moon's the next day. Isaac wasn't there, so Aunt Moon and I tied sage in bundles with twine. I asked her about love.

"It comes up from the ground just like corn," she said. She pulled a knot tighter with her teeth.

Later, when I left, I was still thinking about love. Outside where Bess had been planting, black beetles were digging themselves under the turned soil, and red ants had grown wings and were starting to fly.

When I returned home, my mother was sitting outside the house on a chair. She pointed at Bess Evening's house. "With the man there," she said, "I think it best you don't go over to Bessie's house anymore."

I started to protest, but she interrupted. "There are no ands, ifs, or buts about it."

I knew it was my father who made the decision. My mother had probably argued my point and lost to him again, and lost some of her life as well. She was slowed down to a slumberous pace. Later that night as I stood by my window looking toward Aunt Moon's house, I heard my mother say, "God damn them all and this whole damned town."

"There now," my father said. "There now."

∞

"She's as dark and stained as those old black pans she uses," Margaret Tubby said about Bess Evening one day. She had come to pick up a cake from Mother for the church bake sale. I was angered by her words. I gave her one of those "looks could kill" faces, but I said nothing. We all looked out the window at Aunt Moon. She was standing near Isaac, looking at a tree. It leapt into my mind suddenly, like lightning, that Mrs. Tubby knew about the blackened pans. That would mean she had bought cures from Aunt Moon. I was smug about this discovery.

Across the way, Aunt Moon stood with her hand outstretched, palm up. It was filled with roots or leaves. She was probably teaching Isaac about the remedies. I knew Isaac would teach her things also, older things, like squirrel sickness and porcupine disease that I'd heard about from grandparents.

Listening to Mrs. Tubby, I began to understand why, right after the fair, Aunt Moon had told me I would have to fight hard to keep my life in this town. Mrs. Tubby said, "Living out of wedlock! Just like her parents." She went on, "History repeats itself."

I wanted to tell Mrs. Tubby a thing or two myself. "History, my eye," I wanted to say. "You're just jealous about the young man." But Margaret Tubby was still angry that her husband had lost his money to the stranger, and also because she probably still felt bad about playing with her necklace like a young girl that night at the fair. My mother said nothing, just covered the big caramel cake and handed it over to Mrs. Tubby. My mother looked like she was tired of fools and that included me. She looked like the woman inside her eye had just wandered off.

I began to see the women in Pickens as ghosts. I'd see them in the library looking at the stereopticons, and in the ice cream parlour. The more full Aunt Moon grew, the more drawn and pinched they became.

The church women echoed Margaret. "She's as stained as her pans," they'd say, and they began buying their medicines at the pharmacy. It didn't matter that their coughs returned and that their children developed more fevers. It didn't matter that some of them could not get pregnant when they wanted to or that Mrs. Tens grew thin and pale and bent. They wouldn't dream of lowering themselves to buy Bessie's medicines.

౷

My mother ran hot water into the tub and emptied one of her packages of bubble powder into it. "Take a bath," she told me. "It will steady your nerves."

I was still crying, standing it the window, looking out at Aunt Moon's house through the rain.

The heavy air had been broken by an electrical storm earlier that day. In a sudden crash, the leaves flew off their trees, the sky exploded with lightning, and thunder rumbled the earth. People went to their doors to watch. It scared me. The clouds turned green and it began to hail and clatter.

That was when Aunt Moon's old dog, Mister, ran off, went running like crazy through the town. Some of the older men saw him on the street. They thought he was hurt and dying because of the way he ran and twitched. He butted right into a tree and the men thought maybe he had rabies or something. They meant to put him out of his pain. One of them took aim with a gun and shot him, and when the storm died down and the streets misted over, everything returned to heavy stillness and old Mister was lying on the edge of the Smiths' lawn. I picked him up and carried his heavy body up to Aunt Moon's porch. I covered him with sage, like she would have done.

Bess and Isaac had gone over to Alexander that day to sell remedies. They missed the rain, and when they returned, they were happy about bringing home bags of beans, ground corn, and flour.

I guess it was my mother who told Aunt Moon about her dog.

That evening I heard her wailing. I could hear her from my window and I looked out and saw her with her hair all down around her shoulders like a black shawl. Isaac smoothed back her hair and held her. I guessed that all the mourning was back in her bones again, even for her little girl, Willow.

That night my mother sat by my bed. "Sometimes the world is a sad place," she said and kissed my hot forehead. I began to cry again.

"Well, she still has the burro," my mother said, neglecting to mention Isaac.

I began to worry about the burro and to look after it. I went over to Aunt Moon's against my mother's wishes, and took carrots and sugar to the grey burro. I scratched his big ears.

By this time, most of the younger and healthier men had signed up to go to Korea and fight for their country. Most of the residents of Pickens were mixed-blood Indians and they were even more patriotic than white men. I guess they wanted to prove that they were good Americans. My father left and, we saw him off at the depot. I admit I missed him saying to me, "The trouble with you is you think too much." Old Peso, always telling people what their problems were. Margaret Tubby's lazy son had enlisted because, as his mother had said, "It would make a man of him," and when he was killed in action, the townspeople resented Isaac, Bess Evening's young man, even more since he did not have his heart set on fighting the war.

CR

Aunt Moon was pregnant the next year when the fair came around again, and she was just beginning to show. Margaret Tubby had remarked that Bess was visiting all those family sins on another poor child.

This time I was older. I fixed Mrs. Tubby in my eyes and I said, "Mrs. Tubby, you are just like history, always repeating yourself."

She pulled her head back into her neck like a turtle. My mother said, "Hush, Sis. Get inside the house." She put her hands on her hips. "I'll deal with you later." She almost added, "Just wait till your father gets home."

Later, I felt bad, talking that way to Margaret Tubby so soon after she lost her son.

Shortly after the fair, we heard that the young man inside Aunt Moon's eye was gone. A week passed and he didn't return. I watched her house from the window and I knew, if anyone stood behind me, the little house was resting up on my shoulder.

Mother took a nap and I grabbed the biscuits off the table and snuck out.

"I didn't hear you come in," Aunt Moon said to me.

"I didn't knock," I told her. "My mom just fell asleep. I thought it'd wake her up."

Aunt Moon's hair was down. Her hands were on her lap. A breeze came in the window. She must not have been sleeping and her eyes looked tired. I gave her the biscuits I had taken off the table. I lied and told her my mother had sent them over. We ate one.

Shortly after Isaac was gone, Bess Evening again became the focus of the town's women. Mrs. Tubby said, "Bessie would give you the shirt off her back. She never deserved a no good man who would treat her like dirt and then run off." Mrs. Tubby went over to Bess Evening's and bought enough cramp remedy from the pregnant woman to last her and her daughters for the next two years.

Mrs. Tens lost her pallor. She went to Bessie's with a basket of jellies and fruits, hoping in secret that Bess would return Mr. Tens's Mexican silver ring now that the young man was gone.

The women were going to stick by her; you could see their squared shoulders. They no longer hid their purchases of herbs. They forgot how they'd looked at Isaac's black eyes and lively body with longing that night of the dance. If they'd had dowsing rods, the split willow branches would have flown up to the sky, so much had they twisted around the truth of things and even their own natures. Isaac was the worst of men. Their husbands, who were absent, were saints who loved them. Every morning when my mother said her prayers and forgot she'd damned the town and everybody in it, I heard her ask for peace for Bessie Evening, but she never joined in with the other women who seemed happy over Bessie's tragedy.

Isaac was doubly condemned in his absence. Mrs. Tubby said, "What kind of fool goes off to leave a woman who knows about tea leaves and cures for diseases of the body and the mind alike? I'll tell you what kind, a card shark, that's what."

Someone corrected her. "Card *sharp*, dearie, not *shark*."

Who goes off and leaves a woman whose trees are hung with charming stones, relics, and broken glass, a woman who hangs sage and herbs to dry on her walls and whose front porch is full of fresh-cut wood? Those women, how they wanted to comfort her, but Bess Evening would only go to the door, leave them standing outside on the steps, and hand their herbs to them through the screen.

My cousins from Denver came for the fair. I was going to leave with them and get a job in the city for a year or so, then go on to school. My mother insisted she could handle the little ones alone now that they were bigger, and that I ought to go. It was best I made some money and learned what I could, she said.

"Are you sure?" I asked while my mother washed her hair in the kitchen sink.

"I'm sure as the night's going to fall." She sounded light-hearted, but her hands stopped moving and rested on her head until the soap lather began to disappear. "Besides, your dad will probably be home any day now."

I said, "Okay then, I'll go. I'll write you all the time." I was all full of emotion, but I didn't cry.

"Don't make promises you can't keep," my mother said, wrapping a towel around her head.

I went to the dance that night with my cousins, and out in the trees I let Jim Tens kiss me and promised him that I would be back. "I'll wait for you," he said. "And keep away from those city boys."

I meant it when I said, "I will."

He walked me home, holding my hand. My cousins were still at the dance.

Mom would complain about their late city hours. Once she even told us that city people eat supper as late as eight o'clock P.M. We didn't believe her.

After Jim kissed me at the door, I watched him walk down the street. I was surprised that I didn't feel sad.

I decided to go to see Aunt Moon one last time. I was leaving at six in the morning and was already packed and I had taken one of each herb sample I'd learned from Aunt Moon, just in case I ever needed them.

I scratched the burro's grey face at the lot and walked up toward the house. The window was gold and filled with lamplight. I heard an owl hooting in the distance and stopped to listen.

I glanced in the window and stopped in my tracks. The young man, Isaac, was there. He was speaking close to Bessie's face. He put his finger under her chin and lifted her face up to his. He was looking at her with soft eyes and I could tell there were many men and women living inside their eyes that moment. He held her cane across the back of her hips. With it, he pulled her close to him and held her tight, his hands on the cane pressing her body against his. And he kissed her. Her hair was down around her back and shoulders and she put her arms around his neck. I turned to go. I felt dishonest and guilty for looking in at them. I began to run.

I ran into the bathroom and bent over the sink to wash my face. I wiped Jim Tens's cold kiss from my lips. I glanced up to look at myself in the mirror, but my face was nothing, just shelves of medicine bottles and aspirin. I had forgotten the mirror was broken.

From the bathroom door I heard my mother saying her prayers, fervently, and louder than usual. She said, "Bless Sis's Aunt Moon and bless Isaac, who got arrested for trading illegal medicine for corn, and forgive him for escaping from jail."

She said this so loud, I thought she was talking to me. Maybe she was. Now how did she read my mind again? It made me smile, and I guessed I was reading hers.

All the next morning, driving through the deep blue sky, I thought how all the women had gold teeth and hearts like withered raisins. I hoped Jim Tens would marry one of the Tubby girls. I didn't know if I'd ever go home or not. I had Aunt Moon's herbs in my bag, and the eagle feather wrapped safe in a scarf. And I had a small, beautiful woman in my eye.

℘℧

Poet, fiction writer, and essayist Linda Hogan was born in Denver, but grew up in Colorado Springs and in Germany. Although there were no books in her home, Hogan used the stories of her Chickasaw father and uncle as her literary resources. Like most of her work, this story is set in Oklahoma (a Choctaw word that can mean both "red earth" and "red people"). It opens on the first day of the fair in autumn — three tribes used to hold sings on the exact location of the fairground — and closes with men gradually returning, or not returning, from the war. There is much to puzzle over in this story. Why the title? Why is Aunt Moon, a social outcast, so important to the narrator? Why does the narrator finally decide not to save herself for Jim Tens? What is the purpose of the peculiar scene with the man in the woman's bathroom? What does Aunt Moon mean when she says "the United States is in love with death"? Perhaps the most baffling claim by Aunt Moon is that "the soul is a small woman inside the eye." This phrase is repeated, with variations, several times throughout the story, and it is supported by a network of sight imagery: eyes, mirrors, windows, reflections. How do we reconcile this rather mystical equation of soul, woman, and sight with the essential earthiness and sensuality of Aunt Moon and her young man, whose relationship causes most of the action of the story?

B.S.

SHIRLEY JACKSON
(1916-1965)

The Lottery

The morning of June 27th was clear and sunny, with the fresh warmth of a full-summer day; the flowers were blossoming profusely and the grass was richly green. The people of the village began to gather in the square, between the post office and the bank, around ten o'clock; in some towns there were so many people that the lottery took two days and had to be started on June 26th, but in this village, where there were only about three hundred people, the whole lottery took less than two hours, so it could begin at ten o'clock in the morning and still be through in time to allow the villagers to get home for noon dinner.

The children assembled first, of course. School was recently over for the summer, and the feeling of liberty sat uneasily on most of them; they tended to gather together quietly for a while before they broke into boisterous play, and their talk was still of the classroom and the teacher, of books and reprimands. Bobby Martin had already stuffed his pockets full of stones, and the other boys soon followed his example, selecting the smoothest and roundest stones; Bobby and Harry Jones and Dickie Delacroix — the villagers pronounced this name "Dellacroy" — eventually made a great pile of stones in one corner of the square and guarded it against the raids of the other boys. The girls stood aside, talking among themselves, looking over their shoulders at the boys, and the very small children rolled in the dust or clung to the hands of their older brothers or sisters.

Soon the men began to gather, surveying their own children, speaking of planting and rain, tractors and taxes. They stood together, away from the pile of stones in the corner, and their jokes were quiet and they smiled rather than laughed. The women, wearing faded house dresses and sweaters, came shortly after their menfolk. They greeted one another and exchanged bits of gossip as they went to join their husbands. Soon the women, standing by their husbands, began to call to their children, and the children came reluctantly, having to be called four or five times. Bobby Martin ducked under his mother's grasping hand and ran, laughing, back to the pile of stones, His father spoke up sharply, and Bobby came quickly and took his place between his father and his oldest brother.

The lottery was conducted — as were the square dances, the teen-age club, the Halloween program — by Mr. Summers, who had time and energy to devote to civic activities. He was a round-faced, jovial man and he ran the coal business, and people were sorry for him, because he had no children and his wife was a scold. When he arrived in the square, carrying the black wooden box, there was a murmur of conversation among the villagers, and he waved and called, "Little late today, folks." The postmaster, Mr. Graves, followed him, carrying a three-legged stool, and the stool was put in the center of the square and Mr. Summers set the black box down on it. The villagers kept their distance, leaving a space between themselves and the stool, and when Mr. Summers said, "Some of you fellows want to give me a hand?" there was a hesitation before two men, Mr. Martin and his oldest son, Baxter, came forward to hold the box steady on the stool while Mr. Summers stirred up the papers inside it.

The original paraphernalia for the lottery had been lost long ago, and the black box now resting on the stool had been put into use even before Old Man Warner, the oldest man in town, was born. Mr. Summers spoke frequently to the villagers about making a new box, but no one liked to upset even as much tradition as was represented by the black box. There was a story that the present box had been made with some pieces of the box that had preceded it, the one that had been constructed when the first people settled down to make a village here. Every year, after the lottery, Mr. Summers began talking again about a new box, but every year the subject was allowed to fade off without anything's being done. The black box grew shabbier each year; by now it was no longer completely black but splintered badly along one side to show the original wood colour, and in some places faded or stained.

Mr. Martin and his oldest son, Baxter, held the black box securely on the stool until Mr. Summers had stirred the papers thoroughly with his hand. Because so much of the ritual had been forgotten or discarded, Mr. Summers had been successful in having slips of paper substituted for the chips of wood that had been used for generations. Chips of wood, Mr. Summers had argued, had been all very well when the village was tiny, but now that the population was more than three hundred and likely to keep on growing, it was necessary to use something that would fit more easily into the black box. The night before the lottery, Mr. Summers and Mr. Graves made up the slips of paper and put them in the box, and it was then taken to the safe of Mr. Summers' coal company and locked up until Mr. Summers was ready to take it to the square next morning. The rest of the year, the box was put away, sometimes one place, sometimes another; it had spent one year in Mr. Graves's barn and another year underfoot in the post office, and sometimes it was set on a shelf in the Martin grocery and left there.

There was a great deal of fussing to be done before Mr. Summers declared the lottery open. There were the lists to make up — of heads of families, heads of households in each family, members of each household in each family. There was the proper swearing-in of Mr. Summers by the postmaster, as the official of the lottery; at one time, some people remembered, there had been a recital of some sort, performed by the official of the lottery, a perfunctory, tuneless chant that had been rattled off duly each year; some people believed that the official of the lottery used to stand just so when he said or sang it, others believed that he was supposed to walk among the people, but years and years ago this part of the ritual had been allowed to lapse. There had been, also, a ritual salute, which the official of the lottery had had to use in addressing each person who came up to draw from the box, but this also had changed with time, until now it was felt necessary only for the official to speak to each person approaching. Mr. Summers was very good at all this; in his clean white shirt and blue jeans, with one hand resting carelessly on the black box, he seemed very proper and important as he talked interminably to Mr. Graves and the Martins.

Just as Mr. Summers finally left off talking and turned to the assembled villagers, Mrs. Hutchinson came hurriedly along the path to the square, her sweater thrown over her shoulders, and slid into place in the back of the crowd. "Clean forgot what day it was," she said to Mrs. Delacroix, who stood next to her, and they both laughed softly. "Thought my old man was out back stacking wood," Mrs. Hutchinson went on, "and then I looked out the window and the kids was gone, and then I remembered it was the twenty-seventh and came a-running." She dried her hands on her apron, and Mrs. Delacroix said, "You're in time, though. They're still talking away up there."

Mrs. Hutchinson craned her neck to see through the crowd and found her husband and children standing near the front. She tapped Mrs. Delacroix on the arm as a farewell and began to make her way through the crowd. The people separated good-humouredly to let her through; two or three people said, in voices just loud enough to be heard across the crowd, "Here comes your Missus, Hutchinson," and "Bill, she made it after all." Mrs. Hutchinson reached her husband, and Mr. Summers, who had been waiting, said cheerfully, "Thought we were going to have to get on without you, Tessie." Mrs. Hutchinson said, grinning, "Wouldn't have me leave m'dishes in the sink, now, would you, Joe?," and soft laughter ran through the crowd as the people stirred back into position after Mrs. Hutchinson's arrival.

"Well, now," Mr. Summers said soberly, "guess we better get started, get this over with, so's we can go back to work. Anybody ain't here?"

"Dunbar," several people said. "Dunbar, Dunbar."

Mr. Summers consulted his list. "Clyde Dunbar," he said. "That's right. He's broke his leg, hasn't he? Who's drawing for him?"

"Me, I guess," a woman said, and Mr. Summers turned to look at her. "Wife draws for her husband," Mr. Summers said. "Don't you have a grown boy to do it for you, Janey?" Although Mr. Summers and everyone else in the village knew the answer perfectly well, it was the business of the official of the lottery to ask such questions formally. Mr. Summers waited with an expression of polite interest while Mrs. Dunbar answered.

"Horace's not but sixteen yet," Mrs. Dunbar said regretfully. "Guess I gotta fill in for the old man this year."

"Right," Mr. Summers said. He made a note on the list he was holding. Then he asked, "Watson boy drawing this year?"

A tall boy in the crowd raised his hand. "Here," he said. "I'm drawing for m'mother and me." He blinked his eyes nervously and ducked his head as several voices in the crowd said things like "Good fellow, Jack," and "Glad to see your mother's got a man to do it."

"Well," Mr. Summers said, "guess that's everyone. Old Man Warner make it?"

"Here," a voice said, and Mr. Summers nodded.

ɔ઼

A sudden hush fell on the crowd as Mr. Summers cleared his throat and looked at the list. "All ready?" he called. "Now, I'll read the names — heads of families first — and the men come up and take a paper out of the box. Keep the paper folded in your hand without looking at it until everyone has had a turn. Everything clear?"

The people had done it so many times that they only half listened to the directions; most of them were quiet, wetting their lips, not looking around. Then Mr. Summers raised one hand high and said, "Adams." A man disengaged himself from the crowd and came forward. "Hi, Steve," Mr. Summers said, and Mr. Adams said, "Hi, Joe." They grinned at one another humourlessly and nervously. Then Mr. Adams reached into the black box and took out a folded paper. He held it firmly by one corner as he turned and went hastily back to his place in the crowd, where he stood a little apart from his family, not looking down at his hand.

"Allen," Mr. Summers said. "Anderson. . . . Bentham."

"Seems like there's no time at all between lotteries any more," Mrs. Delacroix said to Mrs. Graves in the back row. "Seems like we got through with the last one only last week."

"Time sure goes fast," Mrs. Graves said.

"Clark. . . . Delacroix."

"There goes my old man," Mrs. Delacroix said. She held her breath while her husband went forward.

"Dunbar," Mr. Summers said, and Mrs. Dunbar went steadily to the box while one of the women said, "Go on, Janey," and another said, "There she goes."

"We're next," Mrs. Graves said. She watched while Mr. Graves came around from the side of the box, greeted Mr. Summers gravely, and selected a slip of paper from the box. By now, all through the crowd there were men holding the small folded papers in their large hands, turning them over and over nervously. Mrs. Dunbar and her two sons stood together, Mrs. Dunbar holding the slip of paper.

"Harburt. . . . Hutchinson."

"Get up there, Bill," Mrs. Hutchinson said, and the people near her laughed. "Jones."

"They do say," Mr. Adams said to Old Man Warner, who stood next to him, "that over in the north village they're talking of giving up the lottery."

Old Man Warner snorted, "Pack of crazy fools," he said. "Listening to the young folks, nothing's good enough for *them*. Next thing you know, they'll be wanting to go back to living in caves, nobody work any more, live *that* way for a while. Used to be a saying about 'Lottery in June, corn be heavy soon.' First thing you know, we'd all be eating stewed chickweed and acorns. There's *always* been a lottery," he added petulantly. "Bad enough to see young Joe Summers up there joking with everybody."

"Some places have already quit lotteries," Mrs. Adams said.

"Nothing but trouble in *that*," Old Man Warner said stoutly. "Pack of young fools."

"Martin." And Bobby Martin watched his father go forward. "Overdyke . . . . Percy."

"I wish they'd hurry," Mrs. Dunbar said to her older son. "I wish they'd hurry."

"They're almost through," her son said.

"You get ready to run tell Dad," Mrs. Dunbar said.

Mr. Summers called his own name and then stepped forward precisely and selected a slip from the box. Then he called, "Warner."

"Seventy-seventh year I been in the lottery," Old Man Warner said as he went through the crowd. "Seventy-seventh time."

"Watson." The tall boy came awkwardly through the crowd. Someone said, "Don't be nervous, Jack," and Mr. Summers said, "Take your time, son."

"Zanini."

∝

After that, there was a long pause, a breathless pause, until Mr. Summers, holding his slip of paper in the air, said, "All right, fellows." For a minute, no one moved, and then all the slips of paper were opened. Suddenly, all the women began to speak at once, saying, "Who is it?," "Who's got it?," "Is it the Dunbars?," "Is it the Watsons?" Then the voices began to say, "It's Hutchinson. It's Bill," "Bill Hutchinson's got it."

"Go tell your father," Mrs. Dunbar said to her older son.

People began to look around to see the Hutchinsons. Bill Hutchinson was standing quiet, staring down at the paper in his hand. Suddenly, Tessie Hutchinson shouted to Mr. Summers, "You didn't give him time enough to take any paper he wanted. I saw you. It wasn't fair!"

"Be a good sport, Tessie," Mrs. Delacroix called, and Mrs. Graves said, "All of us took the same chance."

"Shut up, Tessie," Bill Hutchinson said.

"Well, everyone," Mr. Summers said, "that was done pretty fast, and now we've got to be hurrying a little more to get done in time." He consulted his next list. "Bill," he said, "you draw for the Hutchinson family. You got any other households in the Hutchinsons?"

"There's Don and Eva," Mrs. Hutchinson yelled. "Make *them* take their chance!"

"Daughters draw for their husbands' families, Tessie," Mr. Summers said gently. "You know that as well as anyone else."

"It wasn't *fair*," Tessie said.

"I guess not, Joe," Bill Hutchinson said regretfully. "My daughter draws with her husband's family, that's only fair. And I've got no other family except the kids."

"Then, as far as drawing for families is concerned, it's you," Mr. Summers said in explanation, "and as far as drawing for households is concerned, that's you, too. Right?"

"Right," Bill Hutchinson said.

"How many kids, Bill?" Mr. Summers asked formally.

"Three," Bill Hutchinson said. "There's Bill, Jr., and Nancy, and little Dave. And Tessie and me."

"All right, then," Mr. Summers said. "Harry, you got their tickets back?"

Mr. Graves nodded and held up the slips of paper. "Put them in the box, then," Mr. Summers directed. "Take Bill's and put it in."

"I think we ought to start over," Mrs. Hutchinson said, as quietly as she could, "I tell you it wasn't *fair*. You didn't give him time enough to choose. *Every*body saw that."

Mr. Graves had selected the five slips and put them in the box, and he dropped all the papers but those onto the ground, where the breeze caught them and lifted them off.

"Listen, everybody," Mrs. Hutchinson was saying to the people around her.

"Ready, Bill?" Mr. Summers asked, and Bill Hutchinson, with one quick glance around at his wife and children, nodded.

"Remember," Mr. Summers said, "take the slips and keep them folded until each person has taken one. Harry, you help little Dave." Mr. Graves took the hand of the little boy, who came willingly with him up to the box. "Take a paper out of the box, Davy," Mr. Summers said. Davy put his hand into the box and laughed. "Take just *one* paper," Mr. Summers said. "Harry, you hold it for him." Mr. Graves took the child's hand and removed the folded paper from the tight fist and held it while little Dave stood next to him and looked up at him wonderingly.

"Nancy next," Mr. Summers said. Nancy was twelve, and her school friends breathed heavily as she went forward, switching her skirt, and took a slip daintily from the box. "Bill, Jr.," Mr. Summers said, and Billy, his face red and his feet over-large, nearly knocked the box over as he got a paper out. "Tessie," Mr. Summers said. She hesitated for a minute, looking around defiantly, and then set her lips and went up to the box. She snatched a paper out and held it behind her.

"Bill," Mr. Summers said, and Bill Hutchinson reached into the box and felt around, bringing his hand out at last with the slip of paper in it.

The crowd was quiet. A girl whispered, "I hope it's not Nancy," and the sound of the whisper reached the edges of the crowd.

"It's not the way it used to be," Old Man Warner said clearly. "People ain't the way they used to be."

"All right," Mr. Summers said. "Open the papers. Harry, you open little Dave's."

Mr. Graves opened the slip of paper and there was a general sigh through the crowd as he held it up and everyone could see that it was blank. Nancy and Bill, Jr., opened theirs at the same time, and both beamed and laughed, turning around to the crowd and holding their slips of paper above their heads.

"Tessie," Mr. Summers said. There was a pause, and then Mr. Summers looked at Bill Hutchinson, and Bill unfolded his paper and showed it. It was blank.

"It's Tessie," Mr. Summers said, and his voice was hushed. "Show us her paper, Bill."

Bill Hutchinson went over to his wife and forced the slip of paper out of her hand. It had a black spot on it, the black spot Mr. Summers had made the night before with the heavy pencil in the coal-company office. Bill Hutchinson held it up, and there was a stir in the crowd.

"All right, folks," Mr. Summers said. "Let's finish quickly."

Although the villagers had forgotten the ritual and lost the original black box, they still remembered to use stones. The pile of stones the boys had made earlier was ready; there were stones on the ground with the blowing scraps of paper that had come out of the box. Mrs. Delacroix selected a stone so large she had to pick it up with both hands and turned to Mrs. Dunbar. "Come on," she said. "Hurry up."

Mrs. Dunbar had small stones in both hands, and she said, gasping for breath, "I can't run at all. You'll have to go ahead and I'll catch up with you."

The children had stones already, and someone gave little Davy Hutchinson a few pebbles.

Tessie Hutchinson was in the center of a cleared space by now, and she held her hands out desperately as the villagers moved in on her. "It isn't fair," she said. A stone hit her on the side of the head.

Old Man Warner was saying, "Come on, come on, everyone." Steve Adams was in the front of the crowd of villagers, with Mrs. Graves beside him.

"It isn't fair, it isn't right," Mrs. Hutchinson screamed, and then they were upon her.

৪১০৫৪

Though she published twelve major works and numerous short stories, Shirley Jackson is best known for this "horror classic," which first appeared in The New Yorker *in June 1948. The story provoked strong reactions, which Jackson herself classified as "bewilderment, speculation, and plain old-fashioned abuse." Jackson refused to tell readers what the story meant. However, her husband, literary critic Stanley Edgar Hyman, reported that "she was always proud that the Union of South Africa banned 'The Lottery,' and she felt that they at least understood the story." Like Jackson's other short fiction, "The Lottery" focuses on a woman's defeat and victimization, but can be read as a post-war allegory about the potential dangers of tradition and conformity. Critics have emphasized the story's ritual elements, particularly its focus on the scapegoat, the supposedly random victim sacrificed to atone for society's sins. But is Tessie really a random victim, or is she, as a woman, the most logical victim of patriarchal culture? Does Summers, the leading official of the town, use his power to rig the lottery? The story's power lies in the way it lulls us with its innocent beginning, and then shocks us into asking these questions — into considering how the lottery may still be happening among us. Like the New Testament narrative of the woman taken in adultery, Jackson's story asks us to look at the stones in our own hands.*

T.G.

James Joyce (1882-1941)

Araby

North Richmond Street, being blind, was a quiet street except at the hour when the Christian Brothers' School set the boys free. An uninhabited house of two storeys stood at the blind end, detached from its neighbours in a square ground. The other houses of the street, conscious of decent lives within them, gazed at one another with brown imperturbable faces.

The former tenant of our house, a priest, had died in the back drawing-room. Air, musty from having been long enclosed, hung in all the rooms, and the waste room behind the kitchen was littered with old useless papers. Among these I found a few paper-covered books, the pages of which were curled and damp: *The Abbot*, by Walter Scott, *The Devout Communicant* and *The Memoirs of Vidocq*. I liked the last best because its leaves were yellow. The wild garden behind the house contained a central apple-tree and a few straggling bushes under one of which I found the late tenant's rusty bicycle-pump. He had been a very charitable priest; in his will he had left all his money to institutions and the furniture of his house to his sister.

When the short days of winter came, dusk fell before we had well eaten our dinners. When we met in the street the houses had grown sombre. The space of sky above us was the colour of ever-changing violet and towards it the lamps of the street lifted their feeble lanterns. The cold air stung us and we played till our bodies glowed. Our shouts echoed in the silent street. The career of our play brought us through the dark muddy lanes behind the houses, where we ran the gauntlet of the rough tribes from the cottages, to the back doors of the dark dripping gardens where odours arose from the ashpits, to the dark odorous stables where a coachman smoothed and combed the horse or shook music from the buckled harness. When we returned to the street, light from the kitchen windows had filled the areas. If my uncle was seen turning the corner, we hid in the shadow until we had seen him safely housed. Or if Mangan's sister came out on the doorstep to call her brother in to his tea, we watched her from our shadow peer up and down the street. We waited to see whether she would remain or go in and, if she remained, we left our shadow and walked up to Mangan's steps resignedly. She was waiting for us, her figure defined by the light from the half-opened door. Her brother always teased her before he obeyed, and I stood by the railings looking at her. Her dress swung as she moved her body, and the soft rope of her hair tossed from side to side.

Every morning I lay on the floor in the front parlour watching her door. The blind was pulled down to within an inch of the sash so that I could not be seen. When she came out on the doorstep my heart leaped. I ran to the hall, seized my books and followed her. I kept her brown figure always in my eye and, when we came near the point at which our ways diverged, I quickened my pace and passed her. This happened morning after morning. I had never spoken to her, except for a few casual words, and yet her name was like a summons to all my foolish blood.

Her image accompanied me even in places the most hostile to romance. On Saturday evenings when my aunt went marketing I had to go to carry some of the parcels. We walked through the flaring streets, jostled by drunken men and bargaining women, amid the curses of labourers, the shrill litanies of shop-boys who stood on guard by the barrels of pigs' cheeks, the nasal chanting of street-singers, who sang a *come-all-you* about O'Donovan Rossa, or a ballad about the troubles in our native land. These noises converged in a single sensation of life for me: I imagined that I bore my chalice safely through a throng of foes. Her name sprang to my lips at moments in strange prayers and praises which I myself did not understand. My eyes were often full of tears (I could not tell why) and at times a flood from my heart seemed to pour itself out into my bosom. I thought little of the future. I did not know whether I would ever speak to her or not or, if I spoke to her, how I could tell her of my confused adoration. But my body was like a harp and her words and gestures were like fingers running upon the wires.

One evening I went into the back drawing-room in which the priest had died. It was a dark rainy evening and there was no sound in the house. Through one of the broken panes I heard the rain impinge upon the earth, the fine incessant needles of water playing in the sodden beds. Some distant lamp or lighted window gleamed below me. I was thankful that I could see so little. All my senses seemed to desire to veil themselves and, feeling that I was about to slip from them, I pressed the palms of my hands together until they trembled, murmuring: *O love! O love!* many times.

At last she spoke to me. When she addressed the first words to me I was so confused that I did not know what to answer. She asked me was I going to *Araby*. I forget whether I answered yes or no. It would be a splendid bazaar, she said; she would love to go.

"And why can't you?" I asked.

While she spoke she turned a silver bracelet round and round her wrist. She could not go, she said, because there would be a retreat that week in her convent. Her brother and two other boys were fighting for their caps and I was alone at the railings. She held one of the spikes, bowing her head towards me. The light from the lamp opposite our door caught the white curve of her neck, lit up her hair that rested there and, falling, lit up the hand upon the railing. It fell over one side of her dress and caught the white border of a petticoat, just visible as she stood at ease.

"It's well for you," she said.

"If I go," I said, "I will bring you something."

What innumerable follies laid waste my waking and sleeping thoughts after that evening! I wished to annihilate the tedious intervening days. I chafed against the work of school. At night in my bedroom and by day in the classroom her image came between me and the page I strove to read. The syllables of the word *Araby* were called to me through the silence in which my soul luxuriated and cast an Eastern enchantment over me. I asked for leave to go to the bazaar on Saturday night. My aunt was surprised and hoped it was not some Freemason affair. I answered few questions in class. I watched my master's face pass from amiability to sternness; he hoped I was not beginning to idle. I could not call my wandering thoughts together. I had hardly any patience with the serious work of life which, now that it stood between me and my desire, seemed to me child's play, ugly monotonous child's play.

On Saturday morning I reminded my uncle that I wished to go to the bazaar in the evening. He was fussing at the hallstand, looking for the hat-brush, and answered me curtly:

"Yes, boy, I know."

As he was in the hall I could not go into the front parlour and lie at the window. I left the house in bad humour and walked slowly towards the school. The air was pitilessly raw and already my heart misgave me.

When I came home to dinner my uncle had not yet been home. Still it was early. I sat staring at the clock for some time and, when its ticking began to irritate me, I left the room. I mounted the staircase and gained the upper part of the house. The high cold empty gloomy rooms liberated me and I went from room to room singing. From the front window I saw my companions playing below in the street. Their cries reached me weakened and indistinct and, leaning my forehead against the cool glass, I looked over at the dark house where she lived. I may have stood there for an hour, seeing nothing but a brown-clad figure cast by my imagination, touched discreetly by the lamplight at the curved neck, at the hand upon the railings and at the border below the dress.

When I came downstairs again I found Mrs. Mercer sitting at the fire. She was an old garrulous woman, a pawnbroker's widow, who collected used stamps for some pious purpose. I had to endure the gossip of the tea-table. The meal was prolonged beyond an hour and still my uncle did not come. Mrs. Mercer stood up to go: she was sorry she couldn't wait any longer, but it was after eight o'clock and she did not like to be out late, as the night air was bad for her. When she had gone I began to walk up and down the room, clenching my fists. My aunt said:

"I'm afraid you may put off your bazaar for this night of Our Lord."

At nine o'clock I heard my uncle's latchkey in the hall door. I heard him talking to himself and heard the hallstand rocking when it had received the weight of his overcoat. I could interpret these signs. When he was midway through his dinner I asked him to give me the money to go to the bazaar. He had forgotten.

"The people are in bed and after their first sleep now," he said.

I did not smile. My aunt said to him energetically:

"Can't you give him the money and let him go? You've kept him late enough as it is."

My uncle said he was very sorry he had forgotten. He said he believed in the old saying: "All work and no play makes Jack a dull boy." He asked me where I was going and, when I had told him a second time, he asked me did I know *The Arab's Farewell to his Steed*. When I left the kitchen he was about to recite the opening lines of the piece to my aunt.

I held a florin tightly in my hand as I strode down Buckingham Street towards the station. The sight of the streets thronged with buyers and glaring with gas recalled to me the purpose of my journey. I took my seat in a third-class carriage of a deserted train. After an intolerable delay the train moved out of the station slowly. It crept onward among ruinous houses and over the twinkling river. At Westland Row Station a crowd of people pressed to the carriage doors; but the porters moved them back, saying that it was a special train for the bazaar. I remained alone in the bare carriage. In a few minutes the train drew up beside an improvised wooden platform. I passed out on to the road and saw by the lighted dial of a clock that it was ten minutes to ten. In front of me was a large building which displayed the magical name.

I could not find any sixpenny entrance and, fearing that the bazaar would be closed, I passed in quickly through a turnstile, handing a shilling to a weary-looking man. I found myself in a big hall girdled at half its height by a gallery. Nearly all the stalls were closed and the greater part of the hall was in darkness. I recognized a silence like that which pervades a church after a service. I walked into the centre of the bazaar timidly. A few people were gathered about the stalls which were still open. Before a curtain, over which the words *Café Chantant* were written in coloured lamps, two men were counting money on a salver. I listened to the fall of the coins.

Remembering with difficulty why I had come, I went over to one of the stalls and examined porcelain vases and flowered tea-sets. At the door of the stall a young lady was talking and laughing with two young gentlemen. I remarked their English accents and listened vaguely to their conversation.

"O, I never said such a thing!"

"O, but you did!"

"O, but I didn't!"

"Didn't she say that?"

"Yes. I heard her."

"O, there's a . . . fib!"

Observing me, the young lady came over and asked me did I wish to buy anything. The tone of her voice was not encouraging; she seemed to have spoken to me out of a sense of duty. I looked humbly at the great jars that stood like eastern guards at either side of the dark entrance to the stall and murmured:

"No, thank you."

The young lady changed the position of one of the vases and went back to the two young men. They began to talk of the same subject. Once or twice the young lady glanced at me over her shoulder.

I lingered before her stall, though I knew my stay was useless, to make my interest in her wares seem the more real. Then I turned away slowly and walked down the middle of the bazaar. I allowed the two pennies to fall against the sixpence in my pocket. I heard a voice call from one end of the gallery that the light was out. The upper part of the hall was now completely dark.

Gazing up into the darkness I saw myself as a creature driven and derided by vanity; and my eyes burned with anguish and anger.

∞α

Reading this story for the first time, we are likely to wonder where the narrator's final words come from. Joyce has seemingly given us a story about a young boy's first crush, told from the point of view of an older, wiser narrator; nothing prepares us for the anguish his younger self feels when he cannot bring his beloved a gift from Araby. Re-reading the story, however, we notice images of blindness and religious devotion that tell us something more about his feelings. The street he lives on is "blind"; his senses, as he walks through the house thinking of her, "seemed to desire to veil themselves." He never sees her entirely: she is always standing in a slanting light that reveals "the white curve of her neck," the "soft rope of her hair," "the border of her petticoat." Yet she seems the one light in a world made up of dark muddy lanes, ashpits, and "drunken men and bargaining women." When he tells us "I imagined that I bore my chalice safely through a throng of foes," we see something religious in his devotion to her, and sense that his failure to bring her a gift is the failure of a heroic quest.

Born in Dublin, Joyce left Ireland in 1902 to spend the rest of his life in exile, writing about the very land and culture he had left. "Araby" comes from his 1914 collection of short stories, Dubliners.

K.W.

THOMAS KING *(b. 1943)*

A Seat in the Garden

Joe Hovaugh settled into the garden on his knees and began pulling at the wet, slippery weeds that had sprung up between the neat rows of beets. He trowelled his way around the zucchini and up and down the lines of carrots, and he did not notice the big Indian at all until he stopped at the tomatoes, sat back, and tried to remember where he had set the ball of twine and the wooden stakes.

The big Indian was naked to the waist. His hair was braided and wrapped with white ermine and strips of red cloth. He wore a single feather held in place by a leather band stretched around his head, and, even though his arms were folded tightly across his chest, Joe could see the glitter and flash of silver and turquoise on each finger.

"If you build it, they will come," said the big Indian.

Joe rolled forward and shielded his eyes from the morning sun.

"If you build it, they will come," said the big Indian again.

"Christ sakes," Joe shouted. "Get the hell out of the corn, will ya!"

"If you build it . . ."

"Yeah, yeah. Hey! This is private property. You people ever hear of private property?"

". . . they will come."

Joe struggled to his feet and got his shovel from the shed. But when he got back to the garden, the big Indian was gone.

"Alright!" Joe shouted and drove the nose of the shovel into the ground. "Come out of that corn!"

The corn stalks were only about a foot tall. Nevertheless, Joe walked each row, the shovel held at the ready just in case the big Indian tried to take him by surprise.

CR

When Red Mathews came by in the afternoon, Joe poured him a cup of coffee and told him about the big Indian and what he had said, and Red told Joe that he had seen the movie.

"Wasn't a movie, Red, damn it. It was a real Indian. He was just standing there in the corn."

"You probably scared him away."

"You can't let them go standing in your garden whenever they feel like it."

"That's the truth."

CR

The next day, when Joe came out to the garden to finish staking the tomatoes, the big Indian was waiting for him. The man looked as though he was asleep, but, as soon as he saw Joe, he straightened up and crossed his arms on his chest.

"You again!"

"If you build it . . ."

"I'm going to call the police. You hear me. The police are going to come and haul you away."

". . . they will come."

Joe turned around and marched back into the house and phoned the RCMP, who said they would send someone over that very afternoon.

"Afternoon? What am I supposed to do with him until then. Feed him lunch?"

The RCMP officer told Joe that it might be best if he stayed in his house. There was the chance, the officer said, that the big Indian might be drunk or on drugs and, if that were the case, it was better if Joe didn't antagonize him.

"He's walking on my corn. Does that mean anything to you?"

The RCMP officer assured Joe that it meant a great deal to him, that his wife was a gardener, and he knew how she would feel if someone walked on her corn.

"Still," said the officer, "it's best if you don't do anything."

What Joe did do was to call Red, and, when Red arrived, the big Indian was still in the garden waiting.

"Wow, he's a big sucker, alright," said Red. "You know, he looks a little like Jeff Chandler."

"I called the police, and they said not to antagonize him."

"Hey, there are two of us, right?"

"That's right," said Joe.

"You bet it's right."

Joe got the shovel and a hoe from the shed, and he and Red wandered out into the garden as if nothing was wrong.

"He's watching us," said Red.

"Don't step on the tomatoes," said Joe.

Joe walked around the zucchini, casually dragging the shovel behind him. Red ambled through the beets, the hoe slung over his shoulder.

"If you build it, they will come."

"Get him!" shouted Joe. And before Red could do anything, Joe was charging through the carrots, the shovel held out in front like a lance.

"Wait a minute, Joe," yelled Red, the hoe still on his shoulder. But Joe was already into the tomatoes. He was closing on the big Indian, who hadn't moved, when he stepped on the bundle of wooden stakes and went down in a heap.

"Hey," said Red. "You okay?"

Red helped Joe to his feet, and, when the two men looked around, the big Indian was gone.

"Where'd he go?" said Joe.

"Beats me," said Red. "What'd you do to get him so angry?"

Red helped Joe to the house, wrapped an ice pack on his ankle, and told him to put his leg on the chair.

"I saw a movie a couple of years back about a housing development that was built on top of an ancient Indian burial mound."

"I would have got him, if I hadn't tripped."

"They finally had to get an authentic medicine man to come in and appease the spirits."

"Did you see the look on his face when he saw me coming?"

"And you should have seen some of those spirits."

CR

When the RCMP arrived, Joe showed the officer where the Indian had stood, how he had run at him with the shovel, and how he had stumbled over the bundle of stakes.

After Joe got up and brushed himself off, the RCMP officer asked him if he recognized the big Indian.

"Not likely," said Joe. "There aren't any Indians around here."

"Yes, there are," said Red. "Remember those three guys who come around on weekends every so often."

"The old winos?" said Joe.

"They have that grocery cart, and they pick up cans."

"They don't count."

"They sit down there by the hydrangea and crush the cans and eat their lunch. Sometimes they get to singing."

"You mean drink their lunch."

"Well, they could have anything in that bottle."

"Most likely Lysol."

The RCMP officer walked through the garden with Joe and Red and made a great many notes. He shook hands with both men and told Joe to call him if there was any more trouble.

"Did you ever wonder," said Red, after the officer left, "just what he wants you to build or who 'they' are?"

"I suppose you saw a movie."

"Maybe we should ask the Indians."

"The drunks?"

"Maybe they could translate for us."

"The guy speaks English."

"That's right, Joe. God, this gets stranger all the time. Ed Ames, that's who he reminds me of."

CR

On Saturday morning, when Joe and Red walked out on the porch, the big Indian was waiting patiently for them in the corn. They were too far away to hear him, but they could see his mouth moving.

"Okay," said Red. "All we got to do is wait for the Indians to show up."

The Indians showed up around noon. One man had a green knapsack. The other two pushed a grocery cart in front of them. It was full of cans and bottles. They were old, Joe noticed, and even from the porch, he imagined he could smell them. They walked to a corner of the garden behind the hydrangea where the sprinklers didn't reach. It was a dry, scraggly wedge that Joe had never bothered to cultivate. As soon as the men stopped the cart and sat down on the ground, Red got to his feet and stretched.

"Come on. Can't hurt to talk with them. Grab a couple of beers, so they know we're friendly."

"A good whack with the shovel would be easier."

"Hey, this is kind of exciting. Don't you think this is kind of exciting?"

"I wouldn't trip this time."

When Joe and Red got to the corner, the three men were busy crushing the cans. One man would put a can on a flat stone and the second man would step on it. The third man picked up the crushed can and put it in a brown grocery bag. They were older than Joe had thought, and they didn't smell as bad as he had expected.

"Hi," said Red. "That's a nice collection of cans."

"Good morning," said the first Indian.

"Getting pretty hot," said the second Indian.

"You fellows like a drink?" said the third Indian, and he took a large glass bottle out of the knapsack.

"No thanks," said Red. "You fellows like a beer?"

"Lemon water," said the third Indian. "My wife makes it without any sugar so it's not as sweet as most people like."

"How can you guys drink that stuff?" said Joe.

"You get used to it," said the second Indian. "And it's better for you than pop."

As the first Indian twisted the lid off the bottle and took a long drink, Joe looked around to make sure none of his neighbours were watching him.

"I'll bet you guys know just about everything there is to know about Indians," said Red.

"Well," said the first Indian, "Jimmy and Frank are Nootka and I'm Cree. You guys reporters or something?"

"Reporters? No."

"You never know," said the second Indian. "Last month, a couple of reporters did a story on us. Took pictures and everything."

"It's good that these kinds of problems are brought to the public's attention," said Red.

"You bet," said the third Indian. "Everyone's got to help. Otherwise there's going to be more garbage than people."

Joe was already bored with the conversation. He looked back to see if the big Indian was still there.

"This is all nice and friendly," said Joe. "But we've got a problem that we were hoping you might be able to help us with."

"Sure," said the first Indian. "What's the problem?"

Joe snapped the tab on one of the beers, took a long swig, and jerked his thumb in the direction of the garden. "I've got this big Indian who likes to stand in my garden."

"Where?" asked the second Indian.

"Right there," said Joe.

"Right where?" asked the third Indian.

"If you build it, they will come," shouted the big Indian.

"There, there," said Joe. "Did you hear that?"

"Hear what?" said the first Indian.

"They're embarrassed," said Red under his breath. "Let me handle this."

"This is beginning to piss me off," said Joe, and he took another pull on the beer.

"We were just wondering," Red began. "If you woke up one day and found a big Indian standing in your cornfield and all he would say was, 'If you build it, they will come,' what would you do?"

"I'd stop drinking," said the second Indian, and the other two Indians covered their faces with their hands.

"No, no," said Red. "That's not what I mean. Well . . . you see that big Indian over there in the cornfield, don't you?"

The Indians looked at each other, and then they looked at Joe and Red.

"Okay," said the first Indian. "Sure, I see him."

"Oh, yeah," said the second Indian. "He's right there, all right. In the . . . beets?"

"Corn," said Joe.

"Right," said the third Indian. "In the corn. I can see him, too. Clear as day."

"That's our problem," said Red. "We think maybe he's a spirit or something."

"No, we don't," said Joe.

"Yes, we do," said Red, who was just getting going. "We figure he wants us to build something to appease him so he'll go away."

"Sort of like . . . a spirit?" said the first Indian.

"Hey," said the second Indian, "remember that movie we saw about that community that was built . . ."

"That's the one," said Red. "What we have to figure out is what he wants us to build. You guys got any ideas?"

The three Indians looked at each other. The first Indian looked at the cornfield. Then he looked at Joe and Red.

"Tell you what," he said. "We'll go over there and talk to him and see what he wants. He looks . . . Cree. You guys stay here, okay."

Joe and Red watched as the three Indians walked into the garden. They stood together facing the beets.

"Hey," shouted Joe. "You guys blind? He's behind you."

The first Indian waved his hand and smiled, and the three men turned around. Red could see them talking and he tried to watch their lips, but he couldn't figure out what they were saying. After a while, the Indians waved at the rows of carrots and came back over to where Joe and Red were waiting.

"Well," said Red. "Did you talk to him?"

"Yes," said the first Indian. "You were right. He is a spirit."

"I knew it!" shouted Red. "What does he want?"

The first Indian looked back to the cornfield. "He's tired of standing, he says. He wants a place to sit down. But he doesn't want to mess up the garden. He says he would like it if you would build him a . . . a . . . bench right about . . . here."

"A bench?" said Joe.

"That's what he said."

"So he can sit down?"

"He gets tired standing."

"The hell you say."

"Do you still see him?" asked the second Indian.

"You blind? Of course I still see him."

"Then I'd get started on the bench right away," said the third Indian.

"Come on, Red," said Joe, and he threw the empty beer can into the hydrangea and opened the other one. "We got to talk."

◌੪

Joe put the pad of paper on the kitchen table and drew a square. "This is the garden," he said. "These are the carrots. These are the beets. These are the beans. And this is the corn. The big Indian is right about here."

"That's right," said Red. "But what does it mean?"

"Here's where those winos crush their cans and drink their Lysol," Joe continued, marking a spot on the pad and drawing a line to it.

"Lemon water."

"You listening?"

"Sure."

"If you draw lines from the house to where the big Indian stands and from there to where the winos crush their cans and back to the house . . . Now do you see it?"

"Hey, that's pretty good, Joe."

"What does it remind you of?"

"A bench?"

"No," said Joe. "A triangle."

"Okay, I can see that."

"And if you look at it like this, you can see clearly that the winos and the big Indian are there, and the house where you and I are is here."

"What if you looked at it this way, Joe," said Red and he turned the paper a half turn to the right. "Now the house is there and the old guys and the big Indian are here."

"That's not the way you look at it. That's not the way it works."

"Does that mean we're not going to build the bench?"

"It's our battle plan."

"A bench might be simpler," said Red.

"I'll attack him from the house along this line. You take him from the street along that line. We'll catch him between us."

"I don't know that this is going to work."

"Just don't step on the tomatoes."

The next morning, Red waited behind the hydrangea. He was carrying the hoe and a camera. Joe crouched by the corner of the house with the shovel.

"Charge!" yelled Joe, and he broke from his hiding place and lumbered across the yard and into the garden. Red leaped through the hydrangea and struggled up the slight incline to the cornfield.

"If you build it, they will come," shouted the Indian.

"Build it yourself," shouted Joe, and he swung the shovel at the big Indian's legs. Red, who was slower, stopped at the edge of the cornfield to watch Joe whack the Indian with his shovel and to take a picture, so he saw Joe and his shovel run right through the Indian and crash into the compost mound.

"Joe, Joe . . . you alright? God, you should have seen it. You ran right through that guy. Just like he wasn't there. I got a great picture. Wait till you see the picture. Just around the eyes, he looks a little like Sal Mineo."

Red helped Joe back to the house and cleaned the cuts on Joe's face. He wrapped another ice pack on Joe's ankle and then drove down to the one-hour photo store and turned the film in. By the time he got back to the house, Joe was standing on the porch, leaning on the railing.

"You won't believe it, Joe," said Red. "Look at this."

Red fished a photograph out of the pack. It showed Joe and the shovel in mid-swing, plunging through the corn. The colours were brilliant.

Joe looked at the photograph for a minute and then he looked at the cornfield. "Where's the big Indian?"

"That's just it. He's not there."

"Christ!"

"Does that mean we're going to build the bench?"

ଔ

The bench was a handsome affair with a concrete base and a wooden seat. The Indians came by the very next Saturday with their knapsack and grocery cart, and Red could tell that they were impressed.

"Boy," said the first Indian, "that's a good-looking bench."

"You think this will take care of the problem?" asked Red.

"That Indian still in the cornfield?" said the second Indian.

"Of course he's still there," said Joe. "Can't you hear him?"

"I don't know," said the third Indian, and he twisted the lid off the bottle and took a drink. "I don't think he's one of ours."

"What should we do?"

"Don't throw your cans in the hydrangea," said the first Indian. "It's hard to get them out. We're not as young as we used to be."

ଔ

Joe and Red spent the rest of the day sitting on the porch, drinking beer, and watching the big Indian in the garden. He looked a little like Victor Mature, Red thought, now that he had time to think about it, or maybe Anthony Quinn, only he was taller. And there was an air about the man that made Red believe — believe with all his heart — that he had met this Indian before.

ଽଠଔ

Of Cherokee and Greek-German heritage, Thomas King was born and raised in the United States. After completing a Ph.D. in literature and history, he moved to Canada where he taught for a number of years at the University of Lethbridge. He is currently at the University of Guelph. King *is the author of two novels,* Medicine River *and* Green Grass, Running Water, *a collection of short stories,* One Good Story, That One, *as well as two children's books and a number of essays. He also writes the script for the satirical CBC radio comedy* The Dead Dog Café.

In its social criticism and comic mode, "A Seat in the Garden" is representative of King's writing. A story about territorial and cultural appropriation, it challenges readers to answer questions such as: Who is the big Indian? Why is it that only Joe and Red can see him? Why, in Joe's view, do the two Nootka and their Cree friend not count as "Indians"? What is the significance of the references to European American actors (Victor Mature, Anthony Quinn, Jeff Chandler) who were cast as Indians in Hollywood movies? What is the significance of the repeated statement, taken from W.P. Kinsella's Shoeless Joe *(made into the film* Field of Dreams*), "If you build it, they will come"? What does the garden setting of the story signify? How does the story relate to the trickster tradition of First Nations narratives?*

F.S.

Margaret Laurence

(1926-1987)

To Set Our House in Order

W hen the baby was almost ready to be born, something went wrong and my mother had to go into hospital two weeks before the expected time. I was wakened by her crying in the night, and then I heard my father's footsteps as he went downstairs to phone. I stood in the doorway of my room, shivering and listening, wanting to go to my mother but afraid to go lest there be some sight there more terrifying than I could bear.

"Hello — Paul?" my father said, and I knew he was talking to Dr. Cates. "It's Beth. The waters have broken, and the fetal position doesn't seem quite — well, I'm only thinking of what happened the last time, and another like that would be — I wish she were a little huskier, damn it — she's so — no, don't worry, I'm quite all right. Yes, I think that would be the best thing. Okay, make it as soon as you can, will you?"

He came back upstairs, looking bony and dishevelled in his pyjamas, and running his fingers through his sand-coloured hair. At the top of the stairs, he came face to face with Grandmother MacLeod, who was standing there in her quilted black satin dressing gown, her slight figure held straight and poised, as though she were unaware that her hair was bound grotesquely like white-feathered wings in the snare of her coarse night-time hairnet.

"What is it, Ewen?"

"It's all right, Mother. Beth's having — a little trouble. I'm going to take her into the hospital. You go back to bed."

"I told you," Grandmother MacLeod said in her clear voice, never loud, but distinct and ringing like the tap of a sterling teaspoon on a crystal goblet, "I did tell you, Ewen, did I not, that you should have got a girl in to help her with the housework? She would have rested more."

"I couldn't afford to get anyone in," my father said. "If you thought she should've rested more, why didn't you ever — oh God, I'm out of my mind tonight — just go back to bed, Mother, please. I must get back to Beth."

When my father went down to the front door to let Dr. Cates in, my need overcame my fear and I slipped into my parents' room. My mother's black hair, so neatly pinned up during the day, was startlingly spread across the white pillowcase. I stared at her, not speaking, and then she smiled and I rushed from the doorway and buried my head upon her.

"It's all right, honey," she said. "Listen, Vanessa, the baby's just going to come a little early, that's all. You'll be all right. Grandmother MacLeod will be here."

"How can she get the meals?" I wailed, fixing on the first thing that came to mind. "She never cooks. She doesn't know how."

"Yes, she does," my mother said. "She can cook as well as anyone when she has to. She's just never had to very much, that's all. Don't worry — she'll keep everything in order, and then some."

My father and Dr. Cates came in, and I had to go, without ever saying anything I had wanted to say. I went back to my own room and lay with the shadows all around me. I listened to the night murmurings that always went on in that house, sounds which never had a source, rafters and beams contracting in the dry air, perhaps, or mice in the walls, or a sparrow that had flown into the attic through the broken skylight there. After a while, although I would not have believed it possible, I slept.

The next morning I questioned my father. I believed him to be not only the best doctor in Manawaka, but also the best doctor in the whole of Manitoba, if not in the entire world, and the fact that he was not the one who was looking after my mother seemed to have something sinister about it.

"But it's always done that way, Vanessa," he explained. "Doctors never attend members of their own family. It's because they care so much about them, you see, and —"

"And what?" I insisted, alarmed at the way he had broken off. But my father did not reply. He stood there, and then he put on that difficult smile with which adults seek to conceal pain from children. I felt terrified, and ran to him, and he held me tightly.

"She's going to be fine," he said. "Honestly she is. Nessa, don't cry — "

Grandmother MacLeod appeared beside us, steel-spined despite her apparent fragility. She was wearing a purple silk dress and her ivory pendant. She looked as though she were all ready to go out for afternoon tea.

"Ewen, you're only encouraging the child to give way," she said. "Vanessa, big girls of ten don't make such a fuss about things. Come and get your breakfast. Now, Ewen, you're not to worry. I'll see to everything."

Summer holidays were not quite over, but I did not feel like going out to play with any of the kids. I was very superstitious, and I had the feeling that if I left the house, even for a few hours, some disaster would overtake my mother. I did not, of course, mention this feeling to Grandmother MacLeod, for she did not believe in the existence of fear, or if she did, she never let on. I spent the morning morbidly, in seeking hidden places in the house. There were many of these — odd-shaped nooks under the stairs, small and loosely nailed-up doors at the back of clothes closets, leading to dusty tunnels and forgotten recesses in the heart of the house where the only things actually to be seen were drab oil paintings stacked upon the rafters, and trunks full of outmoded clothing and old photograph albums. But the unseen presences in these secret places I knew to be those of every person, young or old, who had ever belonged to the house and had died, including Uncle Roderick who got killed on the Somme, and the baby who would have been my sister if only she had managed to come to life. Grandfather MacLeod, who had died a year after I was born, was present in the house in more tangible form. At the top of the main stairs hung the mammoth picture of a darkly uniformed man riding upon a horse whose prancing stance and dilated nostrils suggested that the battle was not yet over, that it might indeed continue until Judgement Day. The stern man was actually the Duke of Wellington, but at the time I believed him to be my grandfather MacLeod, still keeping an eye on things.

We had moved in with Grandmother MacLeod when the Depression got bad and she could no longer afford a housekeeper, but the MacLeod house never seemed like home to me. Its dark red brick was grown over at the front with Virginia creeper that turned crimson in the fall, until you could hardly tell brick from leaves. It boasted a small tower in which Grandmother MacLeod kept a weedy collection of anemic ferns. The veranda was embellished with a profusion of wrought-iron scrolls, and the circular rose-window upstairs contained glass of many colours which permitted an outlooking eye to see the world as a place of absolute sapphire or emerald, or if one wished to look with a jaundiced eye, a hateful yellow. In Grandmother MacLeod's opinion, these features gave the house style.

Inside, a multitude of doors led to rooms where my presence, if not actually forbidden, was not encouraged. One was Grandmother MacLeod's bedroom, with its stale and old-smelling air, the dim reek of medicines and lavender sachets. Here resided her monogrammed dresser silver, brush and mirror, nail-buffer and button hook and scissors, none of which must even be fingered by me now, for she meant to leave them to me in her will and intended to hand them over in the same flawless and unused condition in which they had always been kept. Here, too, were the silver-framed photographs of Uncle Roderick — as a child, as a boy, as a man in his Army uniform. The massive walnut spool bed had obviously been designed for queens or giants, and my tiny grandmother used to lie within it all day when she had migraine, contriving somehow to look like a giant queen.

The living room was another alien territory where I had to tread warily, for many valuable objects sat just-so on tables and mantelpiece, and dirt must not be tracked in upon the blue Chinese carpet with its birds in eternal motionless flight and its water-lily buds caught forever just before the point of opening. My mother was always nervous when I was in this room.

"Vanessa, honey," she would say, half apologetically, "why don't you go and play in the den, or upstairs?"

"Can't you leave her, Beth?" my father would say. "She's not doing any harm."

"I'm only thinking of the rug," my mother would say, glancing at Grandmother MacLeod, "and yesterday she nearly knocked the Dresden shepherdess off the mantel. I mean, she can't help it, Ewen, she has to run around —"

"Goddamn it, I know she can't help it," my father would growl, glaring at the smirking face of the Dresden shepherdess.

"I see no need to blaspheme, Ewen," Grandmother MacLeod would say quietly, and then my father would say he was sorry, and I would leave.

The day my mother went to the hospital, Grandmother MacLeod called me at lunch-time, and when I appeared, smudged with dust from the attic, she looked at me distastefully as though I had been a cockroach that had just crawled impertinently out of the woodwork.

"For mercy's sake, Vanessa, what have you been doing with yourself? Run and get washed this minute. Here, not that way — you use the back stairs, young lady. Get along now. Oh — your father phoned."

I swung around. "What did he say? How is she? Is the baby born?"

"Curiosity killed a cat," Grandmother MacLeod said, frowning. "I cannot understand Beth and Ewen telling you all these things, at your age. What sort of vulgar person you'll grow up to be, I dare not think. No, it's not born yet. Your mother's just the same. No change."

I looked at my grandmother, not wanting to appeal to her, but unable to stop myself. "Will she — will she be all right?"

Grandmother MacLeod straightened her already-straight back. "If I said definitely yes, Vanessa, that would be a lie, and the MacLeods do not tell lies, as I have tried to impress upon you before. What happens is God's will. The Lord giveth, and the Lord taketh away."

Appalled, I turned away so she would not see my face and my eyes. Surprisingly, I heard her sigh and felt her papery white and perfectly manicured hand upon my shoulder.

"When your Uncle Roderick got killed," she said, "I thought I would die. But I didn't die, Vanessa."

At lunch, she chatted animatedly, and I realized she was trying to cheer me in the only way she knew.

"When I married your Grandfather MacLeod," she related, "he said to me, 'Eleanor, don't think because we're going to the prairies that I expect you to live roughly. You're used to a proper house, and you shall have one.' He was as good as his word. Before we'd been in Manawaka three years, he'd had this place built. He earned a good deal of money in his time, your grandfather. He soon had more patients than either of the other doctors. We ordered our dinner service and all our silver from Birks' in Toronto. We had resident help in those days, of course, and never had less than twelve guests, for dinner parties. When I had a tea, it would always be twenty or thirty. Never any less than half a dozen different kinds of cake were ever served in this house. Well, no one seems to bother much these days. Too lazy, I suppose."

"Too broke," I suggested. "That's what Dad says."

"I can't bear slang," Grandmother MacLeod said. "If you mean hard up, why don't you say so? It's mainly a question of management, anyway. My accounts were always in good order, and so was my house. No unexpected expenses that couldn't be met, no fruit cellar running out of preserves before the winter was over. Do you know what my father used to say to me when I was a girl?"

"No," I said. "What?"

"God loves Order," Grandmother MacLeod replied with emphasis. "You remember that, Vanessa. God loves Order — he wants each one of us to set our house in order. I've never forgotten those words of my father's. I was a MacInnes before I got married. The MacInnes is a very ancient clan, the lairds of Morven and the constables of the Castle of Kinlochaline. Did you finish that book I gave you?"

"Yes," I said. Then, feeling some additional comment to be called for, "It was a swell book, Grandmother."

This was somewhat short of the truth. I had been hoping for her cairngorm brooch on my tenth birthday, and had received instead the plaid-bound volume entitled *The Clans and Tartans of Scotland*. Most of it was too boring to read, but I had looked up the motto of my own family and those of some of my friends' families. *Be then a wall of brass. Learn to suffer. Consider the end. Go carefully.* I had not found any of these slogans reassuring. What with Mavis Duncan learning to suffer, and Laura Kennedy considering the end, and Patsy Drummond going carefully, and I spending my time in being a wall of brass, it did not seem to me that any of us were going to lead very interesting lives. I did not say this to Grandmother MacLeod.

"The MacInnes motto is *Pleasure Arises from Work*," I said.

"Yes," she agreed proudly. "And an excellent motto it is, too. One to bear in mind."

She rose from the table, rearranging on her bosom the looped ivory beads that held the pendant on which a fullblown ivory rose was stiffly carved.

"I hope Ewen will be pleased," she said.

"What at?"

"Didn't I tell you?" Grandmother MacLeod said. "I hired a girl this morning, for the housework. She's to start tomorrow."

When my father got home that evening, Grandmother MacLeod told him her good news. He ran one hand distractedly across his forehead.

"I'm sorry, Mother, but you'll just have to unhire her. I can't possibly pay anyone."

"It seems distinctly odd," Grandmother MacLeod snapped, "that you can afford to eat chicken four times a week."

"Those chickens," my father said in an exasperated voice, "are how people are paying their bills. The same with the eggs and the milk. That scrawny turkey that arrived yesterday was for Logan MacCardney's appendix, if you must know. We probably eat better than any family in Manawaka, except Niall Cameron's. People can't entirely dispense with doctors or undertakers. That doesn't mean to say I've got any cash. Look, Mother, I don't know what's happening with Beth. Paul thinks he may have to do a Caesarean. Can't we leave all this? Just leave the house alone. Don't touch it. What does it matter?"

"I have never lived in a messy house, Ewen," Grandmother MacLeod said, "and I don't intend to begin now."

"Oh Lord," my father said. "Well, I'll phone Edna, I guess, and see if she can give us a hand, although God knows she's got enough, with the Connor house and her parents to look after."

"I don't fancy having Edna Connor in to help," Grandmother MacLeod objected.

"Why not?" my father shouted. "She's Beth's sister, isn't she?"

"She speaks in such a slangy way," Grandmother MacLeod said. "I have never believed she was a good influence on Vanessa. And there is no need for you to raise your voice to me, Ewen, if you please."

I could barely control my rage. I thought my father would surely rise to Aunt Edna's defence. But he did not.

"It'll be all right," he soothed her. "She'd only be here for part of the day, Mother. You could stay in your room."

Aunt Edna strode in the next morning. The sight of her bobbed black hair and her grin made me feel better at once. She hauled out the carpet sweeper and the weighted polisher and got to work. I dusted while she polished and swept, and we got through the living room and front hall in next to no time.

"Where's her royal highness, kiddo?" she enquired.

"In her room," I said. "She's reading the catalogue from Robinson & Cleaver."

"Good Glory, not again?" Aunt Edna cried. "The last time she ordered three linen tea-cloths and two dozen serviettes. It came to fourteen dollars. Your mother was absolutely frantic. I guess I shouldn't be saying this."

"I knew anyway," I assured her. "She was at the lace handkerchiefs section when I took up her coffee."

"Let's hope she stays there. Heaven forbid she should get onto the banqueting cloths. Well, at least she believes the Irish are good for two things — manual labour and linen-making. She's never forgotten Father used to be a blacksmith, before he got the hardware store. Can you beat it? I wish it didn't bother Beth."

"Does it?" I asked, and immediately realized this was a wrong move, for Aunt Edna was suddenly scrutinizing me.

"We're making you grow up before your time," she said. "Don't pay any attention to me, Nessa. I must've got up on the wrong side of the bed this morning."

But I was unwilling to leave the subject.

"All the same," I said thoughtfully, "Grandmother MacLeod's family were the lairds of Morven and the constables of the Castle of Kinlochaline. I bet you didn't know that."

Aunt Edna snorted. "Castle, my foot. She was born in Ontario, just like your Grandfather Connor, and her father was a horse doctor. Come on, kiddo, we'd better shut up and get down to business here."

We worked in silence for a while.

"Aunt Edna — " I said at last, "what about Mother? Why won't they let me go and see her?"

"Kids aren't allowed to visit maternity patients. It's tough for you, I know that. Look, Nessa, don't worry. If it doesn't start tonight, they're going to do the operation. She's getting the best of care."

I stood there, holding the feather duster like a dead bird in my hands. I was not aware that I was going to speak until the words came out.

"I'm scared," I said.

Aunt Edna put her arms around me, and her face looked all at once stricken and empty of defences.

"Oh, honey, I'm scared, too," she said.

It was this way that Grandmother MacLeod found us when she came stepping lightly down into the front hall with the order in her hand for two dozen lace-bordered handkerchiefs of pure Irish linen.

CR

I could not sleep that night, and when I went downstairs, I found my father in the den. I sat down on the hassock beside his chair, and he told me about the operation my mother was to have the next morning. He kept on saying it was not serious nowadays.

"But you're worried," I put in, as though seeking to explain why I was.

"I should at least have been able to keep from burdening you with it," he said in a distant voice, as though to himself. "If only the baby hadn't got itself twisted around — "

"Will it be born dead, like the little girl?"

"I don't know," my father said. "I hope not."

"She'd be disappointed, wouldn't she, if it was?" I said bleakly, wondering why I was not enough for her.

"Yes, she would," my father replied. "She won't be able to have any more, after this. It's partly on your account that she wants this one, Nessa. She doesn't want you to grow up without a brother or sister."

"As far as I'm concerned, she didn't need to bother," I retorted angrily.

My father laughed. "Well, let's talk about something else, and then maybe you'll be able to sleep. How did you and Grandmother make out today?"

"Oh, fine, I guess. What was Grandfather MacLeod like, Dad?"

"What did she tell you about him?"

"She said he made a lot of money in his time."

"Well, he wasn't any millionaire," my father said, "but I suppose he did quite well. That's not what I associate with him, though."

He reached across to the bookshelf, took out a small leather-bound volume and opened it. On the pages were mysterious marks, like doodling, only much neater and more patterned.

"What is it?" I asked.

"Greek," my father explained. "This is a play called *Antigone*. See, here's the title in English. There's a whole stack of them on the shelves there. *Oedipus Rex. Electra. Medea.* They belonged to your Grandfather MacLeod. He used to read them often."

"Why?" I enquired, unable to understand why anyone would pore over those undecipherable signs.

"He was interested in them," my father said. "He must have been a lonely man, although it never struck me that way at the time. Sometimes a thing only hits you a long time afterwards."

"Why would he be lonely?" I wanted to know.

"He was the only person in Manawaka who could read these plays in the original Greek," my father said. "I don't suppose many people, if anyone, had even read them in English translations. Maybe he would have liked to be a classical scholar — I don't know. But his father was a doctor, so that's what he was. Maybe he would have liked to talk to somebody about these plays. They must have meant a lot to him."

It seemed to me that my father was talking oddly. There was a sadness in his voice that I had never heard before, and I longed to say something that would make him feel better, but I could not, because I did not know what was the matter.

"Can you read this kind of writing?" I asked hesitantly.

My father shook his head. "Nope. I was never very intellectual, I guess. Rod was always brighter than I, in school, but even he wasn't interested in learning Greek. Perhaps he would've been later, if he'd lived. As a kid, all I ever wanted to do was go into the merchant marine."

"Why didn't you, then?"

"Oh well," my father said offhandedly, "a kid who'd never seen the sea wouldn't have made much of a sailor. I might have turned out to be the seasick type."

I had lost interest now that he was speaking once more like himself.

"Grandmother MacLeod was pretty cross today about the girl," I remarked.

"I know," my father nodded. "Well, we must be as nice as we can to her, Nessa, and after a while she'll be all right."

Suddenly I did not care what I said.

"Why can't she be nice to us for a change?" I burst out. "We're always the ones who have to be nice to her."

My father put his hand down and slowly tilted my head until I was forced to look at him.

"Vanessa," he said, "she's had troubles in her life which you really don't know much about. That's why she gets migraine sometimes and has to go to bed. It's not easy for her these days, either — the house is still the same, so she thinks other things should be, too. It hurts her when she finds they aren't."

"I don't see —" I began.

"Listen," my father said, "you know we were talking about what people are interested in, like Grandfather MacLeod being interested in Greek plays? Well, your grandmother was interested in being a lady, Nessa, and for a long time it seemed to her that she was one."

I thought of the Castle of Kinlochaline, and of horse doctors in Ontario.

"I didn't know —" I stammered.

"That's usually the trouble with most of us," my father said. "You go on up to bed now. I'll phone tomorrow from the hospital as soon as the operation's over."

I did sleep at last, and in my dreams I could hear the caught sparrow fluttering in the attic, and the sound of my mother crying, and the voices of the dead children.

◌

My father did not phone until afternoon. Grandmother MacLeod said I was being silly, for you could hear the phone ringing all over the house, but nevertheless I refused to move out of the den. I had never before examined my father's books, but now, at a loss for something to do, I took them out one by one and read snatches here and there. After I had been doing this for several hours, it dawned on me that most of the books were of the same kind. I looked again at the titles.

Seven-League Boots. Arabia Deserta. The Seven Pillars of Wisdom. Travels in Tibet. Count Lucknor the Sea Devil. And a hundred more. On a shelf by themselves were copies of the *National Geographic* magazine, which I looked at often enough, but never before with the puzzling compulsion which I felt now, as though I were on the verge of some discovery, something which I had to find out and yet did not want to know. I riffled through the picture-filled pages. Hibiscus and wild orchids grew in a soft-petalled confusion. The Himalayas stood lofty as gods, with the morning sun on their peaks of snow. Leopards snarled from the vined depths of a thousand jungles. Schooners buffetted their white sails like the wings of giant angels against the great sea winds.

"What on earth are you doing?" Grandmother MacLeod enquired waspishly, from the doorway. "You've got everything scattered all over the place. Pick it all up this minute, Vanessa, do you hear?"

So I picked up the books and magazines, and put them all neatly away, as I had been told to do.

When the telephone finally rang, I was afraid to answer it. At last I picked it up. My father sounded faraway, and the relief in his voice made it unsteady.

"It's okay, honey. Everything's fine. The boy was born alive and kicking after all. Your mother's pretty weak, but she's going to be all right."

I could hardly believe it. I did not want to talk to anyone. I wanted to be by myself, to assimilate the presence of my brother, towards whom, without ever having seen him yet, I felt such tenderness and such resentment.

That evening, Grandmother MacLeod approached my father, who, still dazed with the unexpected gift of neither life now being threatened, at first did not take her seriously when she asked what they planned to call the child.

"Oh, I don't know. Hank, maybe, or Joe Fauntleroy, perhaps."

She ignored his levity.

"Ewen," she said, "I wish you would call him Roderick."

My father's face changed. "I'd rather not."

"I think you should," Grandmother MacLeod insisted, very quietly, but in a voice as pointed and precise as her silver nail-scissors.

"Don't you think Beth ought to decide?" my father asked.

"Beth will agree if you do."

My father did not bother to deny something that even I knew to be true. He did not say anything. Then Grandmother MacLeod's voice, astonishingly, faltered a little.

"It would mean a great deal to me," she said.

I remembered what she had told me — *When your Uncle Roderick got killed, I thought I would die. But I didn't die.* All at once, her feeling for that unknown dead man became a reality for me. And yet I held it against her, as well, for I could see that it had enabled her to win now.

"All right," my father said tiredly. "We'll call him Roderick."

Then, alarmingly, he threw back his head and laughed.

"Roderick Dhu!" he cried. "That's what you'll call him, isn't it? Black Roderick. Like before. Don't you remember? As though he were a character out of Sir Walter Scott, instead of an ordinary kid who —"

He broke off, and looked at her with a kind of desolation in his face.

"God, I'm sorry, Mother," he said. "I had no right to say that."

Grandmother MacLeod did not flinch, or tremble, or indicate that she felt anything at all.

"I accept your apology, Ewen," she said.

CҬ

My mother had to stay in bed for several weeks after she arrived home. The baby's cot was kept in my parents' room, and I could go in and look at the small creature who lay there with his tightly closed fists and his feathery black hair. Aunt Edna came in to help each morning, and when she had finished the housework, she would have coffee with my mother. They kept the door closed, but this did not prevent me from eavesdropping, for there was an air register in the floor of the spare room, which was linked somehow with the register in my parents' room. If you put your ear to the iron grille, it was almost like a radio.

"Did you mind very much, Beth?" Aunt Edna was saying.

"Oh, it's not the name I mind," my mother replied. "It's just the fact that Ewen felt he had to. You knew that Rod had only had the sight of one eye, didn't you?"

"Sure, I knew. So what?"

"There was only a year and a half between Ewen and Rod," my mother said, "so they often went around together when they were youngsters. It was Ewen's air-rifle that did it."

"Oh Lord," Aunt Edna said heavily. "I suppose she always blamed him?"

"No, I don't think it was so much that, really. It was how he felt himself. I think he even used to wonder sometimes if — but people shouldn't let themselves think like that, or they'd go crazy. Accidents do happen, after all. When the war came, Ewen joined up first. Rod should never have been in the Army at all, but he couldn't wait to get in. He must have lied about his eyesight. It wasn't so very noticeable unless you looked at him closely, and I don't suppose the medicals were very thorough in those days. He got in as a gunner, and Ewen applied to have him in the same company. He thought he might be able to watch out for him, I guess, Rod being — at a disadvantage. They were both only kids. Ewen was nineteen and Rod was eighteen when they went to France. And then the Somme. I don't know, Edna, I think Ewen felt that if Rod had had proper sight, or if he hadn't been in the same outfit and had been sent somewhere else — you know how people always think these things afterwards, not that it's ever a bit of use. Ewen wasn't there when Rod got hit. They'd lost each other somehow, and Ewen was looking for him, not bothering about anything else, you know, just frantically looking. Then he stumbled across him quite by chance. Rod was still alive, but —"

"Stop it, Beth," Aunt Edna said. "You're only upsetting yourself."

"Ewen never spoke of it to me," my mother went on, "until once his mother showed me the letter he'd written to her at the time. It was a peculiar letter, almost formal, saying how gallantly Rod had died, and all that. I guess I shouldn't have, but I told him she'd shown it to me. He was very angry that she had. And then, as though for some reason he were terribly ashamed, he said — *I had to write something to her, but men don't really die like that, Beth. It wasn't that way at all.*

It was only after the war that he decided to come back and study medicine and go into practice with his father."

"Had Rod meant to?" Aunt Edna asked.

"I don't know," my mother said slowly. "I never felt I should ask Ewen that."

Aunt Edna was gathering up the coffee things, for I could hear the clash of cups and saucers being stacked on the tray.

"You know what I heard her say to Vanessa once, Beth? *The MacLeods never tell lies.* Those were her exact words. Even then, I didn't know whether to laugh or cry."

"Please, Edna —" my mother sounded worn out now. "Don't."

"Oh Glory," Aunt Edna said remorsefully, "I've got all the delicacy of a two-ton truck. I didn't mean Ewen, for heaven's sake. That wasn't what I meant at all. Here, let me plump up your pillows for you."

Then the baby began to cry, so I could not hear anything more of interest. I took my bike and went out beyond Manawaka, riding aimlessly along the gravel highway. It was late summer, and the wheat had changed colour, but instead of being high and bronzed in the fields, it was stunted and desiccated, for there had been no rain again this year. But in the bluff where I stopped and crawled under the barbed wire fence and lay stretched out on the grass, the plentiful poplar leaves were turning to a luminous yellow and shone like church windows in the sun. I put my head down very close to the earth and looked at what was going on there. Grasshoppers with enormous eyes ticked and twitched around me, as though the dry air were perfect for their purposes. A ladybird laboured mightily to climb a blade of grass, fell off, and started all over again, seeming to be unaware that she possessed wings and could have flown up.

I thought of the accidents that might easily happen to a person — or, of course, might not happen, might happen to somebody else. I thought of the dead baby, my sister, who might as easily have been I. Would she, then, have been lying here in my place, the sharp grass making its small toothmarks on her brown arms, the sun warming her to the heart? I thought of the leather-bound volumes of Greek, and the six different kinds of iced cakes that used to be offered always in the MacLeod house, and the pictures of leopards and green seas. I thought of my brother, who had been born alive after all, and now had been given his life's name.

I could not really comprehend these things, but I sensed their strangeness, their disarray. I felt that whatever God might love in this world, it was certainly not order.

ℰↃ⊂ℛ

This is one of a series of stories by Margaret Laurence in which the adult narrator Vanessa MacLeod looks back on important aspects of her childhood. In several of the stories Vanessa's interest in writing is evident; in others, such as this one, Vanessa becomes aware of the complexity of life and is unable to share her grandmother's faith in an ordered universe.

Laurence has spoken of these stories as semi-autobiographical. The fictional town of Manawaka, birthplace of the major characters in her Canadian fiction, is loosely based on Laurence's own birthplace, the town of Neepawa in Manitoba. As she was growing up, Laurence saw nothing in her environment that could serve as material for literature. It was only after she had lived in Africa for several years and had written about African characters who recognized the importance of their ancestors that she began to recognize the importance of her own. As she turned in her writing to an examination of her own background she succeeded, as the best regional writers do, in creating out of a specific place a world which has universal application. She concentrates, not on a struggle with the land, but on the difficulty that individuals who had experienced the hardships of prairie life had in communicating freely with others and in making themselves vulnerable by expressing emotion. Grandmother MacLeod is typical of many of Laurence's characters in this inability to express her emotions.

M.W.

D.H. LAWRENCE *(1885-1930)*

Odour of Chrysanthemums

T he small locomotive engine, Number 4, came clanking, stumbling down from Selston with seven full wagons. It appeared round the corner with loud threats of speed, but the colt that it startled from among the gorse, which still flickered indistinctly in the raw afternoon, out-distanced it at a canter. A woman, walking up the railway line to Underwood, drew back into the hedge, held her basket aside, and watched the footplate of the engine advancing. The trucks thumped heavily past, one by one, with slow inevitable movement, as she stood insignificantly trapped between the jolting black wagons and the hedge; then they curved away towards the coppice where the withered oak leaves dropped noiselessly, while the birds, pulling at the scarlet hips beside the track, made off into the dusk that had already crept into the spinney. In the open, the smoke from the engine sank and cleaved to the rough grass. The fields were dreary and forsaken, and in the marshy strip that led to the whimsey, a reedy pit-pond, the fowls had already abandoned their run among the alders, to roost in the tarred fowl-house. The pit-bank loomed up beyond the pond, flames like red sores licking its ashy sides, in the afternoon's stagnant light. Just beyond rose the tapering chimneys and the clumsy black headstocks of Brinsley Colliery. The two wheels were spinning fast up against the sky, and the winding engine rapped out its little spasms. The miners were being turned up.

The engine whistled as it came into the wide bay of railway lines beside the colliery, where rows of trucks stood in harbour.

Miners, single, trailing and in groups, passed like shadows diverging home. At the edge of the ribbed level of sidings squat a low cottage, three steps down from the cinder track. A large bony vine clutched at the house, as if to claw down the tiled roof. Round the bricked yard grew a few wintry primroses. Beyond, the long garden sloped down to a bush-covered brook course. There were some twiggy apple trees, winter-crack trees, and ragged cabbages. Beside the path hung dishevelled pink chrysanthemums, like pink cloths hung on bushes. A woman came stooping out of the felt-covered fowl-house, half-way down the garden. She closed and padlocked the door, then drew herself erect, having brushed some bits from her white apron.

She was a tall woman of imperious mien, handsome, with definite black eyebrows. Her smooth black hair was parted exactly. For a few moments she stood steadily watching the miners as they passed along the railway: then she turned towards the brook course. Her face was calm and set, her mouth was closed with disillusionment. After a moment she called:

"John!" There was no answer. She waited, and then said distinctly:

"Where are you?"

"Here!" replied a child's sulky voice from among the bushes. The woman looked piercingly through the dusk.

"Are you at that brook?" she asked sternly.

For answer the child showed himself before the raspberry-canes that rose like whips. He was a small, sturdy boy of five. He stood quite still, defiantly.

"Oh!" said the mother, conciliated. "I thought you were down at that wet brook — and you remember what I told you —"

The boy did not move or answer.

"Come, come on in," she said more gently, "it's getting dark. There's your grandfather's engine coming down the line!"

The lad advanced slowly, with resentful, taciturn movement. He was dressed in trousers and waistcoat of cloth that was too thick and hard for the size of the garments. They were evidently cut down from a man's clothes.

As they went towards the house he tore at the ragged wisps of chrysanthemums and dropped the petals in handfuls along the path.

"Don't do that — it does look nasty," said his mother. He refrained, and she, suddenly pitiful, broke off a twig with three or four wan flowers and held them against her face. When mother and son reached the yard her hand hesitated, and instead of laying the flower aside, she pushed it in her apron-band. The mother and son stood at the foot of the three steps looking across the bay of lines at the passing home of the miners. The trundle of the small train was imminent. Suddenly the engine loomed past the house and came to a stop opposite the gate.

The engine-driver, a short man with round grey beard, leaned out of the cab high above the woman.

"Have you got a cup of tea?" he said in a cheery, hearty fashion.

It was her father. She went in, saying she would mash. Directly, she returned.

"I didn't come to see you on Sunday," began the little grey-bearded man.

"I didn't expect you," said his daughter.

The engine-driver winced; then, reassuming his cheery, airy manner, he said:

"Oh, have you heard then? Well, and what do you think —?"

"I think it is soon enough," she replied.

At her brief censure the little man made an impatient gesture, and said coaxingly, yet with dangerous coldness:

"Well, what's a man to do? It's no sort of life for a man of my years, to sit at my own hearth like a stranger. And if I'm going to marry again it may as well be soon as late — what does it matter to anybody?"

The woman did not reply, but turned and went into the house. The man in the engine-cab stood assertive, till she returned with a cup of tea and a piece of bread and butter on a plate. She went up the steps and stood near the footplate of the hissing engine.

"You needn't 'a' brought me bread an' butter," said her father. "But a cup of tea" — he sipped appreciatively — "it's very nice." He sipped for a moment or two, then: "I hear as Walter's got another bout on," he said.

"When hasn't he?" said the woman bitterly.

"I heerd tell of him in the 'Lord Nelson' braggin' as he was going to spend that b— afore he went: half a sovereign that was."

"When?" asked the woman.

"A' Sat'day night — I know that's true."

"Very likely," she laughed bitterly. "He gives me twenty-three shillings."

"Aye, it's a nice thing, when a man can do nothing with his money but make a beast of himself!" said the grey-whiskered man. The woman turned her head away. Her father swallowed the last of his tea and handed her the cup.

"Aye," he sighed, wiping his mouth. "It's a settler, it is —"

He put his hand on the lever. The little engine strained and groaned, and the train rumbled towards the crossing. The woman again looked across the metals. Darkness was settling over the spaces of the railway and trucks: the miners, in grey sombre groups, were still passing home. The winding-engine pulsed hurriedly, with brief pauses. Elizabeth Bates looked at the dreary flow of men, then she went indoors. Her husband did not come.

The kitchen was small and full of firelight; red coals piled glowing up the chimney mouth. All the life of the room seemed in the white, warm hearth and the steel fender reflecting the red fire. The cloth was laid for tea; cups glinted in the shadows. At the back, where the lowest stairs protruded into the room, the boy sat struggling with a knife and a piece of white wood. He was almost hidden in the shadow. It was half-past four. They had but to await the father's coming to begin tea. As the mother watched her son's sullen little struggle with the wood, she saw herself in his silence and pertinacity; she saw the father in the child's indifference to all but himself. She seemed to be occupied by her husband. He had probably gone past his home, slunk past his own door, to drink before he came in, while his dinner spoiled and wasted in waiting. She glanced at the clock, then took the potatoes to strain them in the yard. The garden and fields beyond the brook were closed in uncertain darkness. When she rose with the saucepan, leaving the drain steaming into the night behind her, she saw the yellow lamps were lit along the high road that went up the hill away beyond the space of the railway lines and the field.

Then again she watched the men trooping home, fewer now and fewer.

Indoors the fire was sinking and the room was dark red. The woman put her saucepan on the hob, and set a batter-pudding near the mouth of the oven. Then she stood unmoving. Directly, gratefully, came quick young steps to the door. Someone hung on the latch a moment, then a little girl entered and began pulling off her outdoor things, dragging a mass of curls, just ripening from gold to brown, over her eyes with her hat.

Her mother chid her for coming late from school, and said she would have to keep her at home the dark winter days.

"Why, mother, it's hardly a bit dark yet. The lamp's not lighted, and my father's not home."

"No, he isn't. But it's a quarter to five! Did you see anything of him?"

The child became serious. She looked at her mother with large, wistful blue eyes.

"No, mother, I've never seen him. Why? Has he come up an' gone past, to Old Brinsley? He hasn't, mother, 'cos I never saw him."

"He'd watch that," said the mother bitterly, "he'd take care as you didn't see him. But you may depend upon it, he's seated in the 'Prince o' Wales.' He wouldn't be this late."

The girl looked at her mother piteously.

"Let's have our teas, mother, should we?" said she.

The mother called John to table. She opened the door once more and looked out across the darkness of the lines. All was deserted: she could not hear the winding-engines.

"Perhaps," she said to herself, "he's stopped to get some ripping done."

They sat down to tea. John, at the end of the table near the door, was almost lost in the darkness. Their faces were hidden from each other. The girl crouched against the fender slowly moving a thick piece of bread before the fire. The lad, his face a dusky mark on the shadow, sat watching her who was transfigured in the red glow.

"I do think it's beautiful to look in the fire," said the child.

"Do you?" said her mother. "Why?"

"It's so red, and full of little caves — and it feels so nice, and you can fair smell it."

"It'll want mending directly," replied her mother, "and then if your father comes he'll carry on and say there never is a fire when a man comes home sweating from the pit. A public-house is always warm enough."

There was silence till the boy said complainingly: "Make haste, our Annie."

"Well, I am doing! I can't make the fire do it no faster, can I?"

"She keeps wafflin' it about so's to make'er slow," grumbled the boy.

"Don't have such an evil imagination, child," replied the mother.

Soon the room was busy in the darkness with the crisp sound of crunching. The mother ate very little. She drank her tea determinedly, and sat thinking. When she rose her anger was evident in the stern unbending of her head. She looked at the pudding in the fender, and broke out:

"It is a scandalous thing as a man can't even come home to his dinner! If it's crozzled up to a cinder I don't see why I should care. Past his very door he goes to get to a public-house, and here I sit with his dinner waiting for him —"

She went out. As she dropped piece after piece of coal on the red fire, the shadows fell on the walls, till the room was almost in total darkness.

"I canna see," grumbled the invisible John. In spite of herself, the mother laughed.

"You know the way to your mouth," she said. She set the dustpan outside the door. When she came again like a shadow on the hearth, the lad repeated, complaining sulkily:

"I canna see."

"Good gracious!" cried the mother irritably, "you're as bad as your father if it's a bit dusk!"

Nevertheless she took a paper spill from a sheaf on the mantelpiece and proceeded to light the lamp that hung from the ceiling in the middle of the room. As she reached up, her figure displayed itself just rounding with maternity.

"Oh, mother —!" exclaimed the girl.

"What?" said the woman, suspended in the act of putting the lamp-glass over the flame. The copper reflector shone handsomely on her, as she stood with uplifted arm, turning to face her daughter.

"You've got a flower in your apron!" said the child, in a little rapture at this unusual event.

"Goodness me!" exclaimed the woman, relieved. "One would think the house was afire." She replaced the glass and waited a moment before turning up the wick. A pale shadow was seen floating vaguely on the floor.

"Let me smell!" said the child, still rapturously, coming forward and putting her face to her mother's waist.

"Go along, silly!" said the mother, turning up the lamp. The light revealed their suspense so that the woman felt it almost unbearable. Annie was still bending at her waist. Irritably, the mother took the flowers out from her apron-band.

"Oh, mother — don't take them out!" Annie cried, catching her hand and trying to replace the sprig.

"Such nonsense!" said the mother, turning away. The child put the pale chrysanthemums to her lips, murmuring:

"Don't they smell beautiful!"

Her mother gave a short laugh.

"No," she said, "not to me. It was chrysanthemums when I married him, and chrysanthemums when you were born, and the first time they ever brought him home drunk, he'd got brown chrysanthemums in his button-hole."

She looked at the children. Their eyes and their parted lips were wondering. The mother sat rocking in silence for some time. Then she looked at the clock.

"Twenty minutes to six!" In a tone of fine bitter carelessness she continued: "Eh, he'll not come now till they bring him. There he'll stick! But he needn't come rolling in here in his pit-dirt, for *I* won't wash him. He can lie on the floor — Eh, what a fool I've been, what a fool! And this is what I came here for, to this dirty hole, rats and all, for him to slink past his very door. Twice last week — he's begun now —"

She silenced herself, and rose to clear the table.

While for an hour or more the children played, subduedly intent, fertile of imagination, united in fear of the mother's wrath, and in dread of their father's home-coming, Mrs. Bates sat in her rocking-chair making a 'singlet' of thick cream-coloured flannel, which gave a dull wounded sound as she tore off the grey edge. She worked at her sewing with energy, listening to the children, and her anger wearied itself, lay down to rest, opening its eyes from time to time and steadily watching, its ears raised to listen. Sometimes even her anger quailed and shrank, and the mother suspended her sewing, tracing the footsteps that thudded along the sleepers outside; she would lift her head sharply to bid the children "hush," but she recovered herself in time, and the footsteps went past the gate, and the children were not flung out of their play-world.

But at last Annie sighed, and gave in. She glanced at her wagon of slippers, and loathed the game. She turned plaintively to her mother.

"Mother!" — but she was inarticulate.

John crept out like a frog from under the sofa. His mother glanced up.

"Yes," she said, "just look at those shirt-sleeves!"

The boy held them out to survey them, saying nothing. Then somebody called in a hoarse voice away down the line, and suspense bristled in the room, till two people had gone by outside, talking.

"It is time for bed," said the mother.

"My father hasn't come," wailed Annie plaintively. But her mother was primed with courage.

"Never mind. They'll bring him when he does come — like a log." She meant there would be no scene. "And he may sleep on the floor till he wakes himself. I know he'll not go to work to-morrow after this!"

The children had their hands and faces wiped with a flannel. They were very quiet. When they had put on their night-dresses, they said their prayers, the boy mumbling. The mother looked down at them, at the brown silken bush of intertwining curls in the nape of the girl's neck, at the little black head of the lad, and her heart burst with anger at their father, who caused all three such distress. The children hid their faces in her skirts for comfort.

When Mrs. Bates came down, the room was strangely empty, with a tension of expectancy. She took up her sewing and stitched for some time without raising her head. Meantime her anger was tinged with fear.

ℭℛ

The clock struck eight and she rose suddenly, dropping her sewing on her chair. She went to the stair-foot door, opened it, listening. Then she went out, locking the door behind her.

Something scuffled in the yard, and she started, though she knew it was only the rats with which the place was over-run. The night was very dark. In the great bay of railway lines, bulked with trucks, there was no trace of light, only away back she could see a few yellow lamps at the pit-top, and the red smear of the burning pit-bank on the night. She hurried along the edge of the track, then, crossing the converging lines, came to the stile by the white gates, whence she emerged on the road. Then the fear which had led her shrank. People were walking up to New Brinsley; she saw the lights in the houses; twenty yards farther on were the broad windows of the 'Prince of Wales,' very warm and bright, and the loud voices of men could be heard distinctly. What a fool she had been to imagine that anything had happened to him! He was merely drinking over there at the 'Prince of Wales.' She faltered. She had never yet been to fetch him, and she never would go. So she continued her walk towards the long straggling line of houses, standing back on the highway. She entered a passage between the dwellings.

"Mr. Rigley? — Yes! Did you want him? No, he's not in at this minute."

The raw-boned woman leaned forward from her dark scullery and peered at the other, upon whom fell a dim light through the blind of the kitchen window.

"Is it Mrs. Bates?" she asked in a tone tinged with respect.

"Yes. I wondered if your Master was at home. Mine hasn't come yet."

" 'Asn't 'e! Oh, Jack's been 'ome an' 'ad 'is dinner an' gone out. 'E's just gone for 'alf an hour afore bedtime. Did you call at the 'Prince o' Wales'?"

"No —"

"No, you didn't like —! It's not very nice." The other woman was indulgent. There was an awkward pause. "Jack never said nothink about — about your Master," she said.

"No! — I expect he's stuck in there!"

Elizabeth Bates said this bitterly, and with recklessness. She knew that the woman across the yard was standing at her door listening, but she did not care. As she turned:

"Stop a minute! I'll go an' ask Jack if 'e knows anythink," said Mrs. Rigley.

"Oh, no — I wouldn't like to put —!"

"Yes, I will, if you'll just step inside an' see as th' childer doesn't come downstairs and set theirselves afire."

Elizabeth Bates, murmuring a remonstrance, stepped inside. The other woman apologized for the state of the room.

The kitchen needed apology. There were little frocks and trousers and childish undergarments on the squab and on the floor, and a litter of playthings everywhere. On the black American cloth of the table were pieces of bread and cake, crusts, slops, and a teapot with cold tea.

"Eh, ours is just as bad," said Elizabeth Bates, looking at the woman, not at the house. Mrs. Rigley put a shawl over her head and hurried out, saying:

"I shanna be a minute."

The other sat, noting with faint disapproval the general untidiness of the room. Then she fell to counting the shoes of various sizes scattered over the floor. There were twelve. She sighed and said to herself, "No wonder!" — glancing at the litter. There came the scratching of two pairs of feet on the yard, and the Rigleys entered. Elizabeth Bates rose. Rigley was a big man, with very large bones. His head looked particularly bony. Across his temple was a blue scar, caused by a wound got in the pit, a wound in which the coal-dust remained blue like tattooing.

" 'Asna 'e come whoam yit?" asked the man, without any form of greeting, but with deference and sympathy. "I couldna say wheer he is — 'e's non ower theer!" — he jerked his head to signify the 'Prince of Wales.'

" 'E's 'appen gone up to th' 'Yew,' " said Mrs. Rigley.

There was another pause. Rigley had evidently something to get off his mind:

"Ah left 'im finishin' a stint," he began. "Loose-all 'ad bin gone about ten minutes when we com'n away, an' I shouted 'Are ter comin', Walt?' an' 'e said, 'Go on, Ah shanna be but a'ef a minnit,' so we com'n ter th' bottom, me an' Bowers, thinkin' as 'e wor just behint, an' 'ud come up i' th' next bantle —"

He stood perplexed, as if answering a charge of deserting his mate. Elizabeth Bates, now again certain of disaster, hastened to reassure him:

"I expect 'e's gone up to th' 'Yew Tree,' as you say. It's not the first time. I've fretted myself into a fever before now. He'll come home when they carry him."

"Ay, isn't it too bad!" deplored the other woman.

"I'll just step up to Dick's an' see if 'e *is* theer," offered the man, afraid of appearing alarmed, afraid of taking liberties.

"Oh, I wouldn't think of bothering you that far," said Elizabeth Bates, with emphasis, but he knew she was glad of his offer.

As they stumbled up the entry, Elizabeth Bates heard Rigley's wife run across the yard and open her neighbour's door. At this, suddenly all the blood in her body seemed to switch away from her heart.

"Mind!" warned Rigley. "Ah've said many a time as Ah'd fill up them ruts in this entry, sumb'dy 'll be breakin' their legs yit."

She recovered herself and walked quickly along with the miner.

"I don't like leaving the children in bed, and nobody in the house," she said.

"No, you dunna!" he replied courteously. They were soon at the gate of the cottage.

"Well, I shanna be many minnits. Dunna you be frettin' now, 'e'll be all right," said the butty.

"Thank you very much, Mr. Rigley," she replied.

"You're welcome!" he stammered, moving away. "I shanna be many minnits."

The house was quiet. Elizabeth Bates took off her hat and shawl, and rolled back the rug. When she had finished, she sat down. It was a few minutes past nine. She was startled by the rapid chuff of the winding-engine at the pit, and the sharp whirr of the brakes on the rope as it descended. Again she felt the painful sweep of her blood, and she put her hand to her side, saying aloud, "Good gracious! — it's only the nine o'clock deputy going down," rebuking herself.

She sat still, listening. Half an hour of this, and she was wearied out.

"What am I working myself up like this for?" she said pitiably to herself, "I s'll only be doing myself some damage."

She took out her sewing again.

At a quarter to ten there were footsteps. One person! She watched for the door to open. It was an elderly woman, in a black bonnet and a black woollen shawl — his mother. She was about sixty years old, pale, with blue eyes, and her face all wrinkled and lamentable. She shut the door and turned to her daughter-in-law peevishly.

"Eh, Lizzie, whatever shall we do, whatever shall we do!" she cried.

Elizabeth drew back a little, sharply.

"What is it, mother?" she said.

The elder woman seated herself on the sofa.

"I don't know, child, I can't tell you!" — she shook her head slowly. Elizabeth sat watching her, anxious and vexed.

"I don't know," replied the grandmother, sighing very deeply. "There's no end to my troubles, there isn't. The things I've gone through, I'm sure it's enough —!" She wept without wiping her eyes, the tears running.

"But, mother," interrupted Elizabeth, "what do you mean? What is it?"

The grandmother slowly wiped her eyes. The fountains of her tears were stopped by Elizabeth's directness. She wiped her eyes slowly.

"Poor child! Eh, you poor thing!" she moaned. "I don't know what we're going to do, I don't — and you as you are — it's a thing, it is indeed!"

Elizabeth waited.

"Is he dead?" she asked, and at the words her heart swung violently, though she felt a slight flush of shame at the ultimate extravagance of the question. Her words sufficiently frightened the old lady, almost brought her to herself.

"Don't say so, Elizabeth! We'll hope it's not as bad as that; no, may the Lord spare us that, Elizabeth. Jack Rigley came just as I was sittin' down to a glass afore going to bed, an' 'e said, ''Appen you'll go down th' line, Mrs. Bates. Walt's had an accident. 'Appen you'll go an' sit wi' her till we can get him home.' I hadn't time to ask him a word afore he was gone. An' I put my bonnet on an' come straight down, Lizzie. I thought to myself, 'Eh, that poor blessed child, if anybody should come an' tell her of a sudden, there's no knowin' what'll 'appen to 'er.' You mustn't let it upset you, Lizzie — or you know what to expect. How long is it, six months — or is it five, Lizzie? Ay!" — the old woman shook her head — "time slips on, it slips on! Ay!"

Elizabeth's thoughts were busy elsewhere. If he was killed — would she be able to manage on the little pension and what she could earn? — she counted up rapidly. If he was hurt — they wouldn't take him to the hospital — how tiresome he would be to nurse! — but perhaps she'd be able to get him away from the drink and his hateful ways. She would — while he was ill. The tears offered to come to her eyes at the picture. But what sentimental luxury was this she was beginning? She turned to consider the children. At any rate she was absolutely necessary for them. They were her business.

"Ay!" repeated the old woman, "it seems but a week or two since he brought me his first wages. Ay — he was a good lad, Elizabeth, he was, in his way. I don't know why he got to be such a trouble, I don't. He was a happy lad at home, only full of spirits. But there's no mistake he's been a handful of trouble, he has! I hope the Lord'll spare him to mend his ways. I hope so, I hope so. You've had a sight o' trouble with him, Elizabeth, you have indeed. But he was a jolly enough lad wi' me, he was, I can assure you. I don't know how it is. . . ."

The old woman continued to muse aloud, a monotonous irritating sound, while Elizabeth thought concentratedly, startled once, when she heard the winding-engine chuff quickly, and the brakes skirr with a shriek. Then she heard the engine more slowly, and the brakes made no sound. The old woman did not notice. Elizabeth waited in suspense. The mother-in-law talked, with lapses into silence.

"But he wasn't your son, Lizzie, an' it makes a difference. Whatever he was, I remember him when he was little an' I learned to understand him and to make allowances. You've got to make allowances for them —"

It was half-past ten, and the old woman was saying: "But it's trouble from beginning to end; you're never too old for trouble, never too old for that —" when the gate banged back, and there were heavy feet on the steps.

"I'll go, Lizzie, let me go," cried the old woman, rising. But Elizabeth was at the door. It was a man in pit-clothes.

"They're bringin' 'im, Missis," he said. Elizabeth's heart halted a moment.

Then it surged on again, almost suffocating her.

"Is he — is it bad?" she asked.

The man turned away, looking at the darkness:

"The doctor says 'e'd been dead hours. 'E saw 'im i' th' lamp-cabin."

The old woman, who stood just behind Elizabeth, dropped into a chair, and folded her hands, crying: "Oh, my boy, my boy!"

"Hush!" said Elizabeth, with a sharp twitch of a frown. "Be still, mother, don't waken th' children: I wouldn't have them down for anything!"

The old woman moaned softly, rocking herself. The man was drawing away. Elizabeth took a step forward.

"How was it?" she asked.

"Well, I couldn't say for sure," the man replied, very ill at ease. " 'E wor finishin' a stint an' th' butties 'ad gone, an' a lot o' stuff come down atop 'n 'im."

"And crushed him?" cried the widow, with a shudder.

"No," said the man, "it fell at th' back of 'im. 'E wor under th' face, an' it niver touched 'im. It shut 'im in. It seems 'e wor smothered."

Elizabeth shrank back. She heard the old woman behind her cry:

"What? — what did 'e say it was?"

The man replied, more loudly: " 'E wor smothered!"

Then the old woman wailed aloud, and this relieved Elizabeth.

"Oh, mother," she said, putting her hand on the old woman, "don't waken th' children, don't waken th' children."

She wept a little, unknowing, while the old mother rocked herself and moaned. Elizabeth remembered that they were bringing him home, and she must be ready. "They'll lay him in the parlour," she said to herself, standing a moment pale and perplexed.

Then she lighted a candle and went into the tiny room. The air was cold and damp, but she could not make a fire, there was no fireplace. She set down the candle and looked round. The candlelight glittered on the lustre-glasses, on the two vases that held some of the pink chrysanthemums, and on the dark mahogany. There was a cold, deathly smell of chrysanthemums in the room. Elizabeth stood looking at the flowers. She turned away, and calculated whether there would be room to lay him on the floor, between the couch and the chiffonier. She pushed the chairs aside. There would be room to lay him down and to step round him. Then she fetched the old red tablecloth, and another old cloth, spreading them down to save her bit of carpet. She shivered on leaving the parlour; so, from the dresser-drawer she took a clean shirt and put it at the fire to air. All the time her mother-in-law was rocking herself in the chair and moaning.

"You'll have to move from there, mother," said Elizabeth. "They'll be bringing him in. Come in the rocker."

The old mother rose mechanically, and seated herself by the fire, continuing to lament. Elizabeth went into the pantry for another candle, and there, in the little pent-house under the naked tiles, she heard them coming. She stood still in the pantry doorway, listening. She heard them pass the end of the house, and come awkwardly down the three steps, a jumble of shuffling footsteps and muttering voices. The old woman was silent. The men were in the yard.

Then Elizabeth heard Matthews, the manager of the pit, say: "You go in first, Jim. Mind!"

The door came open, and the two women saw a collier backing into the room, holding one end of a stretcher, on which they could see the nailed pit-boots of the dead man. The two carriers halted, the man at the head stooping to the lintel of the door.

"Wheer will you have him?" asked the manager, a short, white-bearded man.

Elizabeth roused herself and came from the pantry carrying the unlighted candle.

"In the parlour," she said.

"In there, Jim!" pointed the manager, and the carriers backed round into the tiny room. The coat with which they had covered the body fell off as they awkwardly turned through the two doorways, and the women saw their man, naked to the waist, lying stripped for work. The old woman began to moan in a low voice of horror.

"Lay th' stretcher at th' side," snapped the manager, "an put 'im on th' cloths. Mind now, mind! Look you now —!"

One of the men had knocked off a vase of chrysanthemums. He stared awkwardly, then they set down the stretcher. Elizabeth did not look at her husband. As soon as she could get in the room, she went and picked up the broken vase and the flowers.

"Wait a minute!" she said.

The three men waited in silence while she mopped up the water with a duster.

"Eh, what a job, what a job, to be sure!" the manager was saying, rubbing his brow with trouble and perplexity. "Never knew such a thing in my life, never! He'd no business to ha' been left. I never knew such a thing in my life! Fell over him clean as a whistle, an' shut him in. Not four foot of space, there wasn't — yet it scarce bruised him."

He looked down at the dead man, lying prone, half naked, all grimed with coal-dust.

" ' 'Sphyxiated,' the doctor said. It is the most terrible job I've ever known. Seems as if it was done o' purpose. Clean over him, an' shut 'im in, like a mouse-trap" — he made a sharp, descending gesture with his hand.

The colliers standing by jerked aside their heads in hopeless comment.

The horror of the thing bristled upon them all.

Then they heard the girl's voice upstairs calling shrilly: "Mother, mother — who is it? Mother, who is it?"

Elizabeth hurried to the foot of the stairs and opened the door:

"Go to sleep!" she commanded sharply. "What are you shouting about? Go to sleep at once — there's nothing —"

Then she began to mount the stairs. They could hear her on the boards, and on the plaster floor of the little bedroom. They could hear her distinctly:

"What's the matter now? — what's the matter with you, silly thing?" — her voice was much agitated, with an unreal gentleness.

"I thought it was some men come," said the plaintive voice of the child.

"Has he come?"

"Yes, they've brought him. There's nothing to make a fuss about. Go to sleep now, like a good child."

They could hear her voice in the bedroom, they waited whilst she covered the children under the bedclothes.

"Is he drunk?" asked the girl, timidly, faintly.

"No! No — he's not! He — he's asleep."

"Is he asleep downstairs?"

"Yes — and don't make a noise."

There was silence for a moment, then the men heard the frightened child again: "What's that noise?"

"It's nothing, I tell you, what are you bothering for?"

The noise was the grandmother moaning. She was oblivious of everything, sitting on her chair rocking and moaning. The manager put his hand on her arm and bade her "Sh — sh!!"

The old woman opened her eyes and looked at him. She was shocked by this interruption, and seemed to wonder.

"What time is it?" the plaintive thin voice of the child, sinking back unhappily into sleep, asked this last question.

"Ten o'clock," answered the mother more softly. Then she must have bent down and kissed the children.

Matthews beckoned to the men to come away. They put on their caps and took up the stretcher. Stepping over the body, they tiptoed out of the house. None of them spoke till they were far from the wakeful children.

When Elizabeth came down she found her mother alone on the parlour floor, leaning over the dead man, the tears dropping on him.

"We must lay him out," the wife said. She put on the kettle, then returning knelt at the feet, and began to unfasten the knotted leather laces. The room was clammy and dim with only one candle, so that she had to bend her face almost to the floor. At last she got off the heavy boots and put them away.

"You must help me now," she whispered to the old woman. Together they stripped the man.

When they arose, saw him lying in the naïve dignity of death, the women stood arrested in fear and respect. For a few moments they remained still, looking down, the old mother whimpering. Elizabeth felt countermanded. She saw him, how utterly inviolable he lay in himself. She had nothing to do with him. She could not accept it. Stooping, she laid her hand on him, in claim. He was still warm, for the mine was hot where he had died. His mother had his face between her hands, and was murmuring incoherently. The old tears fell in succession as drops from wet leaves; the mother was not weeping, merely her tears flowed. Elizabeth embraced the body of her husband, with cheek and lips. She seemed to be listening, inquiring, trying to get some connection. But she could not. She was driven away. He was impregnable.

She rose, went into the kitchen, where she poured warm water into a bowl, brought soap and flannel and a soft towel.

"I must wash him," she said.

Then the old mother rose stiffly, and watched Elizabeth as she carefully washed his face, carefully brushing the big blond moustache from his mouth with the flannel. She was afraid with a bottomless fear, so she ministered to him. The old woman, jealous, said:

"Let me wipe him!" — and she kneeled on the other side drying slowly as Elizabeth washed, her big black bonnet sometimes brushing the dark head of her daughter-in-law. They worked thus in silence for a long time. They never forgot it was death, and the touch of the man's dead body gave them strange emotions, different in each of the women; a great dread possessed them both, the mother felt the lie was given to her womb, she was denied; the wife felt the utter isolation of the human soul, the child within her was a weight apart from her.

At last it was finished. He was a man of handsome body, and his face showed no traces of drink. He was blond, full-fleshed, with fine limbs. But he was dead.

"Bless him," whispered his mother, looking always at his face, and speaking out of sheer terror. "Dear lad — bless him!" She spoke in a faint, sibilant ecstasy of fear and mother love.

Elizabeth sank down again to the floor, and put her face against his neck, and trembled and shuddered. But she had to draw away again. He was dead, and her living flesh had no place against his. A great dread and weariness held her: she was so unavailing. Her life was gone like this.

"White as milk he is, clear as a twelve-month baby, bless him, the darling!" the old mother murmured to herself. "Not a mark on him, clear and clean and white, beautiful as ever a child was made," she murmured with pride. Elizabeth kept her face hidden.

"He went peaceful, Lizzie — peaceful as sleep. Isn't he beautiful, the lamb? Ay — he must ha' made his peace, Lizzie. 'Appen he made it all right, Lizzie, shut in there. He'd have time. He wouldn't look like this if he hadn't made his peace. The lamb, the dear lamb. Eh, but he had a hearty laugh. I loved to hear it. He had the heartiest laugh, Lizzie, as a lad —"

Elizabeth looked up. The man's mouth was fallen back, slightly open under the cover of the moustache. The eyes, half shut, did not show glazed in the obscurity. Life with its smoky burning gone from him, had left him apart and utterly alien to her. And she knew what a stranger he was to her. In her womb was ice of fear, because of this separate stranger with whom she had been living as one flesh. Was this what it all meant — utter, intact separateness, obscured by heat of living? In dread she turned her face away. The face was too deadly. There had been nothing between them, and yet they had come together, exchanging their nakedness repeatedly. Each time he had taken her, they had been two isolated beings, far apart as now. He was no more responsible than she. The child was like ice in her womb. For as she looked at the dead man, her mind, cold and detached, said clearly: "Who am I? What have I been doing? I have been fighting a husband who did not exist. *He* existed all the time. What wrong have I done? What was that I have been living with? There lies the reality, this man." And her soul died in her for fear: she knew she had never seen him, he had never seen her, they had met in the dark and had fought in the dark, not knowing whom they met nor whom they fought. And now she saw, and turned silent in seeing. For she had been wrong. She had said he was something he was not; she had felt familiar with him. Whereas he was apart all the while, living as she never lived, feeling as she never felt.

In fear and shame she looked at his naked body, that she had known falsely. And he was the father of her children. Her soul was torn from her body and stood apart. She looked at his naked body and was ashamed, as if she had denied it. After all, it was itself. It seemed awful to her. She looked at his face, and she turned her own face to the wall. For his look was other than hers, his way was not her way. She had denied him what he was — she saw it now. She had refused him as himself. And this had been her life, and his life. She was grateful to death, which restored the truth. And she knew she was not dead.

And all the while her heart was bursting with grief and pity for him. What had he suffered? What stretch of horror for this helpless man! She was rigid with agony. She had not been able to help him. He had been cruelly injured, this naked man, this other being, and she could make no reparation. There were the children — but the children belonged to life. This dead man had nothing to do with them. He and she were only channels through which life had flowed to issue in the children. She was a mother — but how awful she knew it now to have been a wife. And he, dead now, how awful he must have felt it to be a husband. She felt that in the next world he would be a stranger to her. If they met there, in the beyond, they would only be ashamed of what had been before. The children had come, for some mysterious reason, out of both of them. But the children did not unite them. Now he was dead, she knew how eternally he was apart from her, how eternally he had nothing more to do with her. She saw this episode of her life closed. They had denied each other in life. Now he had withdrawn. An anguish came over her. It was finished then: it had become hopeless between them long before he died. Yet he had been her husband. But how little!

"Have you got his shirt, 'Lizabeth?"

Elizabeth turned without answering, though she strove to weep and behave as her mother-in-law expected. But she could not, she was silenced. She went into the kitchen and returned with the garment.

"It is aired," she said, grasping the cotton shirt here and there to try. She was almost ashamed to handle him; what right had she or anyone to lay hands on him; but her touch was humble on his body. It was hard work to clothe him. He was so heavy and inert. A terrible dread gripped her all the while: that he could be so heavy and utterly inert, unresponsive, apart. The horror of the distance between them was almost too much for her — it was so infinite a gap she must look across.

At last it was finished. They covered him with a sheet and left him lying, with his face bound. And she fastened the door of the little parlour, lest the children should see what was lying there. Then, with peace sunk heavy on her heart, she went about making tidy the kitchen. She knew she submitted to life, which was her immediate master. But from death, her ultimate master, she winced with fear and shame.

ഇൽ

Simple in plot though it may be, this story has the stark power of a Greek tragedy. Its inexorable fatality and recognition of guilt unfold against a background of gathering darkness that entraps the characters in their very humanity and social circumstances. Though the story appears merely to concern the failure of one marriage of incompatible partners, it has larger implications about the isolation and alienation we all try to overcome by forming relationships — relationships that are often doomed by the difficulty of knowing, and accepting, others as free individuals who must be embraced for their very differences and faults.

Lawrence's presentation of this dilemma is moving, as is the way he relates human failure to the social conditions that control our lives. The story's opening paragraphs vividly observe but also symbolize the situation of early twentieth-century British working people, whose lives are dominated by industrialism. Ford Madox Ford, editor of The English Review *— to whom the story was sent shortly before World War I — immediately recognized the authenticity of Lawrence's precise sensory details. "You know," he wrote, "that this fellow . . . writes from the inside. . . . this man knows. . . . You can trust him for the rest." Other elements to note are the story's various ironies, its contrasts of characters and images, and the exact nature of Elizabeth Bates's "epiphany."*

R.H.

The Ones Who Walk Away from Omelas

(Variations on a theme by William James)

With a clamour of bells that set the swallows soaring, the Festival of Summer came to the city Omelas, bright-towered by the sea. The rigging of the boats in harbour sparkled with flags. In the streets between houses with red roofs and painted walls, between old moss-grown gardens and under avenues of trees, past great parks and public buildings, processions moved. Some were decorous: old people in long stiff robes of mauve and grey, grave master workmen, quiet, merry women carrying their babies and chatting as they walked. In other streets the music beat faster, a shimmering of gong and tambourine, and the people went dancing, the procession was a dance. Children dodged in and out, their high calls rising like the swallows' crossing flights over the music and the singing. All the processions wound towards the north side of the city, where on the great water-meadow called the Green Fields boys and girls, naked in the bright air, with mud-stained feet and ankles and long, lithe arms, exercised their restive horses before the race. The horses wore no gear at all but a halter without bit. Their manes were braided with streamers of silver, gold, and green. They flared their nostrils and pranced and boasted to one another; they were vastly excited, the horse being the only animal who has adopted our ceremonies as his own. Far off to the north and west the mountains stood up half encircling Omelas on her bay. The air of morning was so clear that the snow still crowning the Eighteen Peaks burned with white-gold fire across the miles of sunlit air, under the dark blue of the sky. There was just enough wind to make the banners that marked the racecourse snap and flutter now and then. In the silence of the broad green meadows one could hear the music winding through the city streets, farther and nearer and ever approaching, a cheerful faint sweetness of the air that from time to time trembled and gathered together and broke out into the great joyous clanging of the bells.

Joyous! How is one to tell about joy? How describe the citizens of Omelas?

They were not simple folk, you see, though they were happy. But we do not say the words of cheer much any more. All smiles have become archaic. Given a description such as this one tends to make certain assumptions. Given a description such as this one tends to look next for the King, mounted on a splendid stallion and surrounded by his noble knights, or perhaps in a golden litter borne by great-muscled slaves. But there was no king. They did not use swords, or keep slaves. They were not barbarians. I do not know the rules and laws of their society, but I suspect that they were singularly few. As they did without monarchy and slavery, so they also got on without the stock exchange, the advertisement, the secret police, and the bomb. Yet I repeat that these were not simple folk, not dulcet shepherds, noble savages, bland utopians. They were not less complex than us. The trouble is that we have a bad habit, encouraged by pedants and sophisticates, of considering happiness as something rather stupid. Only pain is intellectual, only evil interesting. This is the treason of the artist: a refusal to admit the banality of evil and the terrible boredom of pain. If you can't lick 'em, join 'em. If it hurts, repeat it. But to praise despair is to condemn delight, to embrace violence is to lose hold of everything else. We have almost lost hold; we can no longer describe a happy man, nor make any celebration of joy. How can I tell you about the people of Omelas? They were not naïve and happy children — though their children were, in fact, happy. They were mature, intelligent, passionate adults whose lives were not wretched. O miracle! but I wish I could describe it better. I wish I could convince you. Omelas sounds in my words like a city in a fairy tale, long ago and far away, once upon a time. Perhaps it would be best if you imagined it as your own fancy bids, assuming it will rise to the occasion, for certainly I cannot suit you all. For instance, how about technology? I think that there would be no cars or helicopters in and above the streets; this follows from the fact that the people of Omelas are happy people. Happiness is based on a just discrimination of what is necessary, what is neither necessary nor destructive, and what is destructive. In the middle category, however — that of the unnecessary but undestructive, that of comfort, luxury, exuberance, etc. — they could perfectly well have central heating, subway trains, washing machines, and all kinds of marvelous devices not yet invented here, floating light-sources, fuelless power, a cure for the common cold. Or they could have none of that: it doesn't matter. As you like it. I incline to think that people from towns up and down the coast have been coming in to Omelas during the last days before the Festival on very fast little trains and double-decked trams, and that the train station of Omelas is actually the handsomest building in town, though plainer than the magnificent Farmers' Market. But even granted trains, I fear that Omelas so far strikes some of you as goody-goody. Smiles, bells, parades, horses, bleh. If so, please add an orgy. If an orgy would help, don't hesitate. Let us not, however, have temples from which issue beautiful nude priests and priestesses already half in ecstasy and ready to copulate with any man or woman, lover or stranger, who desires union with the deep godhead of the blood, although that was my first idea. But really it would be better not to have any temples in Omelas — at least, not manned temples. Religion yes, clergy no. Surely the beautiful nudes can just wander about, offering themselves like divine soufflés to the hunger of the needy and the rapture of the flesh. Let them join the processions. Let tambourines be struck above the copulations, and the glory of desire be proclaimed upon the gongs, and (a not unimportant point) let the offspring of these delightful rituals be beloved and looked after by all. One thing I know there is none of in Omelas is guilt. But what else should there be? I thought at first there were no drugs, but that is puritanical. For those who like it, the faint insistent sweetness of *drooz* may perfume the ways of the city, *drooz* which first brings a great lightness and brilliance to the mind and limbs, and then after some hours a dreamy languor, and wonderful visions at last of the very arcana and inmost secrets of the Universe, as well as exciting the pleasure of sex beyond all belief; and it is not habit-forming. For more modest tastes I think there ought to be beer. What else, what else belongs in the joyous city? The sense of victory, surely, the celebration of courage. But as we did without clergy, let us do without soldiers. The joy built upon successful slaughter is not the right kind of joy; it will not do; it is fearful and it is trivial. A boundless and generous contentment, a magnanimous triumph felt not against some outer enemy, but in communion with the finest and fairest in the souls of all men everywhere and the splendour of the world's summer: this is what swells the hearts of the people of Omelas, and the victory they celebrate is that of life. I really don't think many of them need to take *drooz*.

Most of the processions have reached the Green Fields by now. A marvelous smell of cooking goes forth from the red and blue tents of the provisioners. The faces of small children are amiably sticky; in the benign grey beard of a man a couple of crumbs of rich pastry are entangled. The youths and girls have mounted their horses and are beginning to group around the starting line of the course. An old woman, small, fat, and laughing, is passing out flowers from a basket, and tall young men wear her flowers in their shining hair. A child of nine or ten sits at the edge of the crowd, alone, playing on a wooden flute. People pause to listen, and they smile, but they do not speak to him, for he never ceases playing and never sees them, his dark eyes wholly rapt in the sweet, thin magic of the tune.

He finishes, and slowly lowers his hands holding the wooden flute.

As if that little private silence were the signal, all at once a trumpet sounds from the pavilion near the starting line: imperious, melancholy, piercing. The horses rear on their slender legs, and some of them neigh in answer. Sober-faced, the young riders stroke the horses' necks and soothe them, whispering, "Quiet, quiet, there my beauty, my hope. . . ." They begin to form in rank along the starting line. The crowds along the racecourse are like a field of grass and flowers in the wind. The Festival of Summer has begun.

Do you believe? Do you accept the festival, the city, the joy? No? Then let me describe one more thing.

In a basement under one of the beautiful public buildings of Omelas, or perhaps in the cellar of one of its more spacious private homes, there is a room. It has one locked door, and no window. A little light seeps in dustily between cracks in the boards, secondhand from a cobwebbed window somewhere across the cellar. In one corner of the little room a couple of mops, with stiff, clotted, foul-smelling heads, stand near a rusty bucket. The floor is dirt, a little damp to the touch, as cellar dirt usually is. The room is about three paces long and two wide: a mere broom closet or disused tool room. In the room a child is sitting. It could be a boy or a girl. It looks about six, but actually is nearly ten. It is feeble-minded. Perhaps it was born defective, or perhaps it has become imbecile through fear, malnutrition, and neglect. It picks its nose and occasionally fumbles vaguely with its toes or genitals, as it sits hunched in the corner farthest from the bucket and the two mops. It is afraid of the mops. It finds them horrible. It shuts its eyes, but it knows the mops are still standing there; and the door is locked; and nobody will come. The door is always locked; and nobody ever comes, except that sometimes — the child has no understanding of time or interval — sometimes the door rattles terribly and opens, and a person, or several people, are there. One of them may come in and kick the child to make it stand up. The others never come close, but peer in at it with frightened, disgusted eyes. The food bowl and the water jug are hastily filled, the door is locked, the eyes disappear. The people at the door never say anything, but the child, who has not always lived in the tool room, and can remember sunlight and its mother's voice, sometimes speaks. "I will be good," it says. "Please let me out. I will be good!" They never answer. The child used to scream for help at night, and cry a good deal, but now it only makes a kind of whining, "eh-haa, eh-haa," and it speaks less and less often. It is so thin there are no calves to its legs; its belly protrudes; it lives on a half-bowl of corn meal and grease a day. It is naked. Its buttocks and thighs are a mass of festered sores, as it sits in its own excrement continually.

They all know it is there, all the people of Omelas. Some of them have come to see it, others are content merely to know it is there. They all know that it has to be there. Some of them understand why, and some do not, but they all understand that their happiness, the beauty of their city, the tenderness of their friendships, the health of their children, the wisdom of their scholars, the skill of their makers, even the abundance of their harvest and the kindly weathers of their skies, depend wholly on this child's abominable misery.

This is usually explained to children when they are between eight and twelve, whenever they seem capable of understanding; and most of those who come to see the child are young people, though often enough an adult comes, or comes back, to see the child. No matter how well the matter has been explained to them, these young spectators are always shocked and sickened at the sight. They feel disgust, which they had thought themselves superior to. They feel anger, outrage, impotence, despite all the explanations. They would like to do something for the child. But there is nothing they can do. If the child were brought up into the sunlight out of that vile place, if it were cleaned and fed and comforted, that would be a good thing, indeed; but if it were done, in that day and hour all the prosperity and beauty and delight of Omelas would wither and be destroyed. Those are the terms. To exchange all the goodness and grace of every life in Omelas for that single, small improvement: to throw away the happiness of thousands for the chance of the happiness of one: that would be to let guilt within the walls indeed.

The terms are strict and absolute; there may not even be a kind word spoken to the child.

Often the young people go home in tears, or in a tearless rage, when they have seen the child and faced this terrible paradox. They may brood over it for weeks or years. But as time goes on they begin to realize that even if the child could be released, it would not get much good of its freedom: a little vague pleasure of warmth and food, no doubt, but little more. It is too degraded and imbecile to know any real joy. It has been afraid too long ever to be free of fear. Its habits are too uncouth for it to respond to humane treatment. Indeed, after so long it would probably be wretched without walls about it to protect it, and darkness for its eyes, and its own excrement to sit in. Their tears at the bitter injustice dry when they begin to perceive the terrible justice of reality, and to accept it. Yet it is their tears and anger, the trying of their generosity and the acceptance of their helplessness, which are perhaps the true source of the splendour of their lives. Theirs is no vapid, irresponsible happiness. They know that they, like the child, are not free. They know compassion. It is the existence of the child, and their knowledge of its existence, that makes possible the nobility of their architecture, the poignancy of their music, the profundity of their science. It is because of the child that they are so gentle with children. They know that if the wretched one were not there snivelling in the dark, the other one, the flute-player, could make no joyful music as the young riders line up in their beauty for the race in the sunlight of the first morning of summer.

Now do you believe in them? Are they not more credible? But there is one more thing to tell, and this is quite incredible.

At times one of the adolescent girls or boys who go to see the child does not go home to weep or rage, does not, in fact, go home at all. Sometimes also a man or woman much older falls silent for a day or two, and then leaves home. These people go out into the street, and walk down the street alone. They keep walking, and walk straight out of the city of Omelas, through the beautiful gates. They keep walking across the farmlands of Omelas. Each one goes alone, youth or girl, man or woman. Night falls; the traveler must pass down village streets, between the houses with yellow-lit windows, and on out into the darkness of the fields. Each alone, they go west or north, towards the mountains. They go on. They leave Omelas, they walk ahead into the darkness, and they do not come back. The place they go towards is a place even less imaginable to most of us than the city of happiness. I cannot describe it at all. It is possible that it does not exist. But they seem to know where they are going, the ones who walk away from Omelas.

$$\wp\!\supset\!\Omega\!\wp$$

Some people think that because fantastic fiction does not attempt to represent the real world as we know it, it must be escapist. And indeed much of it is, especially when it conforms closely to the familiar formulas associated with mass-market fantasy, horror, or science fiction. But good fantastic fiction has an advantage over realistic fiction: it is not tied to the specifics of history, geography, or national culture, so it can serve as a mirror to reflect universal human concerns. "The Ones Who Walk Away from Omelas," which has as its chief source an idea expressed by the American philosopher William James, is at once a utopian story, a thought-experiment, and an exercise in ethics. Le Guin invites us to participate in the construction of a believable ideal society based on the appealing sketch she gives us of the fair city of Omelas and its joyous citizens. She then reveals the city's terrible secret, and asks us how we would react if we were citizens of Omelas. Most of us think at first that we can escape a hard decision by changing the conditions — for after all Omelas exists only in our imagination. But it is not so easy to walk away from the issues raised by the story. Can we enjoy or even recognize what is good if we are unaware of its dark opposite?

N.R.

ALISTAIR MACLEOD   *(b. 1936)*

The Boat

There are times even now when I awake at four o'clock in the morning with the terrible fear that I have overslept, when I imagine that my father is waiting for me in the room below the darkened stairs or that the shorebound men are tossing pebbles against my window while blowing their hands and stomping their feet impatiently on the frozen steadfast earth. There are times when I am half out of bed and fumbling for socks and mumbling for words before I realize that I am foolishly alone, that no one waits at the base of the stairs and no boat rides restlessly in the waters by the pier.

At such times only the grey corpses on the overflowing ashtray beside my bed bear witness to the extinction of the latest spark and silently await the crushing out of the most recent of their fellows. And then because I am afraid to be alone with death, I dress rapidly, make a great to-do about clearing my throat, turn on both faucets in the sink and proceed to make loud splashing ineffectual noises. Later I go out and walk the mile to the all-night restaurant.

In the winter it is a very cold walk and there are often tears in my eyes when I arrive. The waitress usually gives a sympathetic little shiver and says, "Boy, it must be really cold out there; you got tears in your eyes."

"Yes," I say, "it sure is; it really is."

And then the three or four of us who are always in such places at such times make uninteresting little protective chitchat until the dawn reluctantly arrives. Then I swallow the coffee which is always bitter and leave with a great busy rush because by that time I have to worry about being late and whether I have a clean shirt and whether my car will start and about all the other countless things one must worry about when he teaches at a great Midwestern university. And I know then that that day will go by as have all the days of the past ten years, for the call and the voices and the shapes and the boat were not really there in the early morning's darkness and I have all kinds of comforting reality to prove it. They are only shadows and echoes, the animals a child's hands make on the wall by lamplight, and the voices from the rain barrel: the cuttings from an old movie made in the black and white of long ago.

I first became conscious of the boat in the same way and at almost the same time that I became aware of the people it supported. My earliest recollection of my father is a view from the floor of gigantic rubber boots and then of being suddenly elevated and having my face pressed against the stubble of his cheek, and of how it tasted of salt and of how he smelled of salt from his red-soled rubber boots to the shaggy whiteness of his hair.

When I was very small, he took me for my first ride in the boat. I rode the half-mile from our house to the wharf on his shoulders and I remember the sound

278

of his rubber boots galumphing along the gravel beach, the tune of the indecent little song he used to sing, and the odour of the salt.

The floor of the boat was permeated with the same odour and in its constancy I was not aware of change. In the harbour we made our little circle and returned. He tied the boat by its painter, fastened the stern to its permanent anchor and lifted me high over his head to the solidity of the wharf. Then he climbed up the little iron ladder that led to the wharf's cap, placed me once more upon his shoulders and galumphed off again.

When we returned to the house everyone made a great fuss over my precocious excursion and asked, "How did you like the boat?" "Were you afraid in the boat?" "Did you cry in the boat?" They repeated "the boat" at the end of all their questions and I knew it must be very important to everyone.

My earliest recollection of my mother is of being alone with her in the mornings while my father was away in the boat. She seemed to be always repairing clothes that were "torn in the boat," preparing food "to be eaten in the boat" or looking for "the boat" through our kitchen window which faced upon the sea. When my father returned about noon, she would ask, "Well, how did things go in the boat today?" It was the first question I remember asking: "Well, how did things go in the boat today?" "Well, how did things go in the boat today?"

The boat in our lives was registered at Port Hawkesbury. She was what Nova Scotians called a Cape Island boat and was designed for the small inshore fishermen who sought the lobsters of the spring and the mackerel of summer and later the cod and haddock and hake. She was thirty-two feet long and nine wide, and was powered by an engine from a Chevrolet truck. She had a marine clutch and a high-speed reverse gear and was painted light green with the name *Jenny Lynn* stencilled in black letters on her bow and painted on an oblong plate across her stern. Jenny Lynn had been my mother's maiden name and the boat was called after her as another link in the chain of tradition. Most of the boats that berthed at the wharf bore the names of some female member of their owner's household.

I say this now as if I knew it all then. All at once, all about boat dimensions and engines, and as if on the day of my first childish voyage I noticed the difference between a stencilled name and a painted name. But of course it was not that way at all, for I learned it all very slowly and there was not time enough.

I learned first about our house which was one of about fifty which marched around the horseshoe of our harbour and the wharf which was its heart. Some of them were so close to the water that during a storm the sea spray splashed against their windows while others were built farther along the beach as was the case with ours. The houses and their people, like those of the neighbouring towns and villages, were the result of Ireland's discontent and Scotland's Highland Clearances and America's War of Independence. Impulsive emotional Catholic Celts who could not bear to live with England and shrewd determined Protestant Puritans who, in the years after 1776, could not bear to live without.

The most important room in our house was one of those oblong old-fashioned kitchens heated by a wood- and coal-burning stove. Behind the stove was a box of kindling and beside it a coal scuttle. A heavy wooden table with leaves that expanded or reduced its dimensions stood in the middle of the floor. There were five wooden homemade chairs which had been chipped and hacked by a variety of knives. Against the east wall, opposite the stove, there was a couch which sagged in the middle and had a cushion for a pillow, and above it a shelf which contained matches, tobacco, pencils, odd fishhooks, bits of twine, and a tin can filled with bills and receipts. The south wall was dominated by a window which faced the sea and on the north there was a five-foot board which bore a variety of clothes hooks and the burdens of each. Beneath the board there was a jumble of odd footwear, mostly of rubber. There were also, on this wall, a barometer, a map of the marine area and a shelf which held a tiny radio. The kitchen was shared by all of us and was a buffer zone between the immaculate order of ten other rooms and the disruptive chaos of the single room that was my father's.

My mother ran her house as her brothers ran their boats. Everything was clean and spotless and in order. She was tall and dark and powerfully energetic. In later years she reminded me of the women of Thomas Hardy, particularly Eustacia Vye, in a physical way. She fed and clothed a family of seven children, making all of the meals and most of the clothes. She grew miraculous gardens and magnificent flowers and raised broods of hens and ducks. She would walk miles on berry-picking expeditions and hoist her skirts to dig for clams when the tide was low. She was fourteen years younger than my father, whom she had married when she was twenty-six and had been a local beauty for a period of ten years. My mother was of the sea as were all of her people, and her horizons were the very literal ones she scanned with her dark and fearless eyes.

Between the kitchen clothes rack and barometer, a door opened into my father's bedroom. It was a room of disorder and disarray. It was as if the wind which so often clamoured about the house succeeded in entering this single room and after whipping it into turmoil stole quietly away to renew its knowing laughter from without.

My father's bed was against the south wall. It always looked rumpled and unmade because he lay on top of it more than he slept within any folds it might have had. Beside it, there was a little brown table. An archaic goose-necked reading light, a battered table radio, a mound of wooden matches, one or two packages of tobacco, a deck of cigarette papers and an overflowing ashtray cluttered its surface. The brown larvae of tobacco shreds and the grey flecks of ash covered both the table and the floor beneath it. The once-varnished surface of the table was disfigured by numerous black scars and gashes inflicted by the neglected burning cigarettes of many years. They had tumbled from the ashtray unnoticed and branded their statements permanently and quietly into the wood until the odour of their burning caused the snuffing out of their lives. At the bed's foot there was a single window which looked upon the sea.

Against the adjacent wall there was a battered bureau and beside it there was a closet which held his single ill-fitting serge suit, the two or three white shirts that strangled him and the square black shoes that pinched. When he took off his more friendly clothes, the heavy woollen sweaters, mitts and socks which my mother knitted for him and the woollen and doeskin shirts, he dumped them unceremoniously on a single chair. If a visitor entered the room while he was lying on the bed, he would be told to throw the clothes on the floor and take their place upon the chair.

Magazines and books covered the bureau and competed with the clothes for domination of the chair. They further overburdened the heroic little table and lay on top of the radio. They filled a baffling and unknowable cave beneath the bed, and in the corner by the bureau they spilled from the walls and grew up from the floor.

The magazines were the most conventional: *Time, Newsweek, Life, Maclean's, Family Herald, Reader's Digest.* They were the result of various cut-rate subscriptions or of the gift subscriptions associated with Christmas, "the two whole years for only $3.50."

The books were more varied. There were a few hard-cover magnificents and bygone Book-of-the-Month wonders and some were Christmas or birthday gifts. The majority of them, however, were used paperbacks which came from those second-hand bookstores which advertise in the backs of magazines: "Miscellaneous Used Paperbacks 10¢ Each." At first he sent for them himself, although my mother resented the expense, but in later years they came more and more often from my sisters who had moved to the cities. Especially at first they were very weird and varied. Mickey Spillane and Ernest Haycox vied with Dostoyevsky and Faulkner, and the Penguin Poets edition of Gerard Manley Hopkins arrived in the same box as a little book on sex technique called *Getting the Most Out of Love.* The former had been assiduously annotated by a very fine hand using a very blue-inked fountain pen while the latter had been studied by someone with very large thumbs, the prints of which were still visible in the margins. At the slightest provocation it would open almost automatically to particularly graphic and well-smudged pages.

When he was not in the boat, my father spent most of his time lying on the bed in his socks, the top two buttons of his trousers undone, his discarded shirt on the ever-ready chair and the sleeves of the woollen Stanfield underwear, which he wore both summer and winter, drawn halfway up to his elbows. The pillows propped up the whiteness of his head and the goose-necked lamp illuminated the pages in his hands. The cigarettes smoked and smouldered on the ashtray and on the table and the radio played constantly, sometimes low and sometimes loud. At midnight and at one, two, three and four, one could sometimes hear the radio, his occasional cough, the rustling thud of a completed book being tossed to the corner heap, or the movement necessitated by his sitting on the edge of the bed to roll the thousandth cigarette. He seemed never to sleep, only to doze, and the light shone constantly from his window to the sea.

My mother despised the room and all it stood for and she had stopped sleeping in it after I was born. She despised disorder in rooms and in houses and in hours and in lives, and she had not read a book since high school. There she had read *Ivanhoe* and considered it a colossal waste of time. Still the room remained, like a solid rock of opposition in the sparkling waters of a clear deep harbour, opening off the kitchen where we really lived our lives, with its door always open and its contents visible to all.

The daughters of the room and of the house were very beautiful. They were tall and willowy like my mother and had her fine facial features set off by the reddish copper-coloured hair that had apparently once been my father's before it turned to white. All of them were very clever in school and helped my mother a great deal about the house. When they were young they sang and were very happy and very nice to me because I was the youngest and the family's only boy.

My father never approved of their playing about the wharf like the other children, and they went there only when my mother sent them on an errand. At such times they almost always overstayed, playing screaming games of tag or hide-and-seek in and about the fishing shanties, the piled traps and tubs of trawl, shouting down to the perch that swam languidly about the wharf's algae-covered piles, or jumping in and out of the boats that tugged gently at their lines. My mother was never uneasy about them at such times, and when her husband criticized her she would say, "Nothing will happen to them there," or "They could be doing worse things in worse places."

By about the ninth or tenth grade my sisters one by one discovered my father's bedroom and then the change would begin. Each would go into the room one morning when he was out. She would go with the ideal hope of imposing order or with the more practical objective of emptying the ashtray, and later she would be found spellbound by the volume in her hand. My mother's reaction was always abrupt, bordering on the angry. "Take your nose out of that trash and come and do your work," she would say, and once I saw her slap my youngest sister so hard that the print of her hand was scarletly emblazoned upon her daughter's cheek while the broken-spined paperback fluttered uselessly to the floor.

Thereafter my mother would launch a campaign against what she had discovered but could not understand. At times although she was not overly religious she would bring in God to bolster her arguments, saying, "In the next world God will see to those who waste their lives reading useless books when they should be about their work." Or without theological aid, "I would like to know how books help anyone to live a life." If my father were in, she would repeat the remarks louder than necessary, and her voice would carry into his room where he lay upon his bed. His usual reaction was to turn up the volume of the radio, although that action in itself betrayed the success of the initial thrust.

Shortly after my sisters began to read the books, they grew restless and lost interest in darning socks and baking bread, and all of them eventually went to work as summer waitresses in the Sea Food Restaurant. The restaurant was run by a big American concern from Boston and catered to the tourists that flooded the area during July and August. My mother despised the whole operation. She said the restaurant was not run by "our people," and "our people" did not eat there, and that it was run by outsiders for outsiders.

"Who are these people anyway?" she would ask, tossing back her dark hair, "and what do they, though they go about with their cameras for a hundred years, know about the way it is here, and what do they care about me and mine, and why should I care about them?"

She was angry that my sisters should even conceive of working in such a place and more angry when my father made no move to prevent it, and she was worried about herself and about her family and about her life. Sometimes she would say softly to her sisters, "I don't know what's the matter with my girls. It seems none of them are interested in any of the right things." And sometimes there would be bitter savage arguments. One afternoon I was coming in with three mackerel I'd been given at the wharf when I heard her say, "Well I hope you'll be satisfied when they come home knocked up and you'll have had your way."

It was the most savage thing I'd ever heard my mother say. Not just the words but the way she said them, and I stood there in the porch afraid to breathe for what seemed like the years from ten to fifteen, feeling the damp moist mackerel with their silver glassy eyes growing clammy against my leg.

Through the angle in the screen door I saw my father who had been walking into his room wheel around on one of his rubber-booted heels and look at her with his blue eyes flashing like clearest ice beneath the snow that was his hair. His usually ruddy face was drawn and grey, reflecting the exhaustion of a man of sixty-five who had been working in those rubber boots for eleven hours on an August day, and for a fleeting moment I wondered what I would do if he killed my mother while I stood there in the porch with those three foolish mackerel in my hand. Then he turned and went into his room and the radio blared forth the next day's weather forecast and I retreated under the noise and returned again, stamping my feet and slamming the door too loudly to signal my approach. My mother was busy at the stove when I came in, and did not raise her head when I threw the mackerel in a pan. As I looked into my father's room, I said, "Well how did things go in the boat today?" and he replied, "Oh not too badly, all things considered." He was lying on his back and lighting his first cigarette and the radio was talking about the Virginia coast.

All of my sisters made good money on tips. They bought my father an electric razor which he tried to use for a while and they took out even more magazine subscriptions. They bought my mother a great many clothes of the type she was very fond of, the wide-brimmed hats and the brocaded dresses, but she locked them all in trunks and refused to wear any of them.

On one August day my sisters prevailed upon my father to take some of their restaurant customers for an afternoon ride in the boat. The tourists with their expensive clothes and cameras and sunglasses awkwardly backed down the iron ladder at the wharf's side to where my father waited below, holding the rocking *Jenny Lynn* in snug against the wharf with one hand on the iron ladder and steadying his descending passengers with the other. They tried to look both prim and wind-blown like the girls in the Pepsi-Cola ads and did the best they could, sitting on the thwarts where the newspapers were spread to cover the splattered blood and fish entrails, crowding to one side so that they were in danger of capsizing the boat, taking the inevitable pictures or merely trailing their fingers through the water of their dreams.

All of them liked my father very much and, after he'd brought them back from their circles in the harbour, they invited him to their rented cabins which were located high on a hill overlooking the village to which they were so alien. He proceeded to get very drunk up there with the beautiful view and the strange company and the abundant liquor, and late in the afternoon he began to sing.

I was just approaching the wharf to deliver my mother's summons when he began, and the familiar yet unfamiliar voice that rolled down from the cabins made me feel as I had never felt before in my young life or perhaps as I had always felt without really knowing it, and I was ashamed yet proud, young yet old and saved yet forever lost, and there was nothing I could do to control my legs which trembled nor my eyes which wept for what they could not tell.

The tourists were equipped with tape recorders and my father sang for more than three hours. His voice boomed down the hill and bounced off the surface of the harbour, which was an unearthly blue on that hot August day, and was then reflected to the wharf and the fishing shanties where it was absorbed amidst the men who were baiting their lines for the next day's haul.

He sang all the old sea chanties which had come across from the old world and by which men like him had pulled ropes for generations, and he sang the East Coast sea songs which celebrated the sealing vessels of Northumberland Strait and the long liners of the Grand Banks, and of Anticosti, Sable Island, Grand Manan, Boston Harbor, Nantucket and Block Island. Gradually he shifted to the seemingly unending Gaelic drinking songs with their twenty or more verses and inevitable refrains, and the men in the shanties smiled at the coarseness of some of the verses and at the thought that the singer's immediate audience did not know what they were applauding nor recording to take back to staid old Boston. Later as the sun was setting he switched to the laments and the wild and haunting Gaelic war songs of those spattered Highland ancestors he had never seen, and when his voice ceased, the savage melancholy of three hundred years seemed to hang over the peaceful harbour and the quiet boats and the men leaning in the doorways of their shanties with their cigarettes glowing in the dusk and the women looking to the sea from their open windows with their children in their arms.

When he came home he threw the money he had earned on the kitchen table as he did with all his earnings but my mother refused to touch it and the next day he went with the rest of the men to bait his trawl in the shanties. The tourists came to the door that evening and my mother met them there and told them that her husband was not in although he was lying on the bed only a few feet away with the radio playing and the cigarette upon his lips. She stood in the doorway until they reluctantly went away.

In the winter they sent him a picture which had been taken on the day of the singing. On the back it said, "To Our Ernest Hemingway" and the "Our" was underlined. There was also an accompanying letter telling how much they had enjoyed themselves, how popular the tape was proving and explaining who Ernest Hemingway was. In a way it almost did look like one of those unshaven, taken-in-Cuba pictures of Hemingway. He looked both massive and incongruous in the setting. His bulky fisherman's clothes were too big for the green and white lawn chair in which he sat, and his rubber boots seemed to take up all of the well-clipped grass square. The beach umbrella jarred with his sunburned face and because he had already been singing for some time, his lips which chapped in the winds of spring and burned in the water glare of summer had already cracked in several places, producing tiny flecks of blood at their corners and on the whiteness of his teeth. The bracelets of brass chain which he wore to protect his wrists from chafing seemed abnormally large and his broad leather belt had been slackened and his heavy shirt and underwear were open at the throat revealing an uncultivated wilderness of white chest hair bordering on the semi-controlled stubble of his neck and chin. His blue eyes had looked directly into the camera and his hair was whiter than the two tiny clouds which hung over his left shoulder. The sea was behind him and its immense blue flatness stretched out to touch the arching blueness of the sky. It seemed very far away from him or else he was so much in the foreground that he seemed too big for it.

Each year another of my sisters would read the books and work in the restaurant. Sometimes they would stay out quite late on the hot summer nights and when they came up the stairs my mother would ask them many long and involved questions which they resented and tried to avoid. Before ascending the stairs they would go into my father's room and those of us who waited above could hear them throwing his clothes off the chair before sitting on it or the squeak of the bed as they sat on its edge. Sometimes they would talk to him a long time, the murmur of their voices blending with the music of the radio into a mysterious vapour-like sound which floated softly up the stairs.

I say this again as if it all happened at once and as if all of my sisters were of identical ages and like so many lemmings going into another sea and, again, it was of course not that way at all. Yet go they did, to Boston, to Montreal, to New York with the young men they met during the summers and later married in those far-away cities. The young men were very articulate and handsome and wore fine clothes and drove expensive cars and my sisters, as I said, were very tall and beautiful with their copper-coloured hair and were tired of darning socks and baking bread.

One by one they went. My mother had each of her daughters for fifteen years, then lost them for two and finally forever. None married a fisherman. My mother never accepted any of the young men, for in her eyes they seemed always a combination of the lazy, the effeminate, the dishonest and the unknown. They never seemed to do any physical work and she could not comprehend their luxurious vacations and she did not know whence they came nor who they were. And in the end she did not really care, for they were not of her people and they were not of her sea.

I say this now with a sense of wonder at my own stupidity in thinking I was somehow free and would go on doing well in school and playing and helping in the boat and passing into my early teens while streaks of grey began to appear in my mother's dark hair and my father's rubber boots dragged sometimes on the pebbles of the beach as he trudged home from the wharf. And there were but three of us in the house that had at one time been so loud.

Then during the winter that I was fifteen he seemed to grow old and ill at once. Most of January he lay upon the bed, smoking and reading and listening to the radio while the wind howled about the house and the needle-like snow blistered off the ice-covered harbour and the doors flew out of people's hands if they did not cling to them like death.

In February when the men began overhauling their lobster traps he still did not move, and my mother and I began to knit lobster trap headings in the evenings. The twine was as always very sharp and harsh, and blisters formed upon our thumbs and little paths of blood snaked quietly down between our fingers while the seals that had drifted down from distant Labrador wept and moaned like human children on the ice floes of the Gulf.

In the daytime my mother's brother who had been my father's partner as long as I could remember also came to work upon the gear. He was a year older than my mother and was tall and dark and the father of twelve children.

By March we were very far behind and although I began to work very hard in the evenings I knew it was not hard enough and that there were but eight weeks left before the opening of the season on May first. And I knew that my mother worried and my uncle was uneasy and that all of our very lives depended on the boat being ready with her gear and two men, by the date of May the first. And I knew then that *David Copperfield* and *The Tempest* and all of those friends I had dearly come to love must really go forever. So I bade them all good-bye.

The night after my first full day at home and after my mother had gone upstairs he called me into his room where I sat upon the chair beside his bed. "You will go back tomorrow," he said simply.

I refused then, saying I had made my decision and was satisfied.

"That is no way to make a decision," he said, "and if you are satisfied I am not. It is best that you go back." I was almost angry then and told him as all children do that I wished he would leave me alone and stop telling me what to do.

He looked at me a long time then, lying there on the same bed on which he had fathered me those sixteen years before, fathered me his only son, out of who knew what emotions when he was already fifty-six and his hair had turned to snow. Then he swung his legs over the edge of the squeaking bed and sat facing me and looked into my own dark eyes with his of crystal blue and placed his hand upon my knee. "I am not telling you to do anything," he said softly, "only asking you."

The next morning I returned to school. As I left, my mother followed me to the porch and said, "I never thought a son of mine would choose useless books over the parents that gave him life."

In the weeks that followed he got up rather miraculously and the gear was ready and the *Jenny Lynn* was freshly painted by the last two weeks of April when the ice began to break up and the lonely screaming gulls returned to haunt the silver herring as they flashed within the sea.

On the first day of May the boats raced out as they had always done, laden down almost to the gunwales with their heavy cargoes of traps. They were almost like living things as they plunged through the waters of the spring and manoeuvred between the still floating icebergs of crystal-white and emerald-green on their way to the traditional grounds that they sought out every May. And those of us who sat that day in the high school on the hill, discussing the water imagery of Tennyson, watched them as they passed back and forth beneath us until by afternoon the piles of traps which had been stacked upon the wharf were no longer visible but were spread about the bottoms of the sea. And the *Jenny Lynn* went too, all day, with my uncle tall and dark, like a latter-day Tashtego standing at the tiller with his legs wide apart and guiding her deftly between the floating pans of ice and my father in the stern standing in the same way with his hands upon the ropes that lashed the cargo to the deck. And at night my mother asked, "Well, how did things go in the boat today?"

And the spring wore on and the summer came and school ended in the third week of June and the lobster season on July first and I wished that the two things I loved so dearly did not exclude each other in a manner that was so blunt and too clear.

At the conclusion of the lobster season my uncle said he had been offered a berth on a deep-sea dragger and had decided to accept. We all knew that he was leaving the *Jenny Lynn* forever and that before the next lobster season he would buy a boat of his own. He was expecting another child and would be supporting fifteen people by the next spring and could not chance my father against the family that he loved.

I joined my father then for the trawling season, and he made no protest and my mother was quite happy. Through the summer we baited the tubs of trawl in the afternoon and set them at sunset and revisited them in the darkness of the early morning. The men would come tramping by our house at 4:00 a.m. and we would join them and walk with them to the wharf and be on our way before the sun rose out of the ocean where it seemed to spend the night. If I was not up they would toss pebbles to my window and I would be very embarrassed and tumble downstairs to where my father lay fully clothed atop his bed, reading his book and listening to his radio and smoking his cigarette. When I appeared he would swing off his bed and put on his boots and be instantly ready and then we would take the lunches my mother had prepared the night before and walk off toward the sea. He would make no attempt to wake me himself.

It was in many ways a good summer. There were few storms and we were out almost every day and we lost a minimum of gear and seemed to land a maximum of fish and I tanned dark and brown after the manner of my uncles.

My father did not tan — he never tanned — because of his reddish complexion, and the salt water irritated his skin as it had for sixty years. He burned and reburned over and over again and his lips still cracked so that they bled when he smiled, and his arms, especially the left, still broke out into the oozing saltwater boils as they had ever since as a child I had first watched him soaking and bathing them in a variety of ineffectual solutions. The chafe-preventing bracelets of brass linked chain that all the men wore about their wrists in early spring were his the full season and he shaved but painfully and only once a week.

And I saw then, that summer, many things that I had seen all my life as if for the first time and I thought that perhaps my father had never been intended for a fisherman either physically or mentally. At least not in the manner of my uncles; he had never really loved it. And I remembered that, one evening in his room when we were talking about *David Copperfield*, he had said that he had always wanted to go to the university and I had dismissed it then in the way one dismisses his father's saying he would like to be a tightrope walker, and we had gone on to talk about the Peggottys and how they loved the sea.

And I thought then to myself that there were many things wrong with all of us and all our lives and I wondered why my father, who was himself an only son, had not married before he was forty and then I wondered why he had. I even thought that perhaps he had had to marry my mother and checked the dates on the flyleaf of the Bible where I learned that my oldest sister had been born a prosaic eleven months after the marriage, and I felt myself then very dirty and debased for my lack of faith and for what I had thought and done.

And then there came into my heart a very great love for my father and I thought it was very much braver to spend a life doing what you really do not want rather than selfishly following forever your own dreams and inclinations. And I knew then that I could never leave him alone to suffer the iron-tipped harpoons which my mother would forever hurl into his soul because he was a failure as a husband and a father who had retained none of his own. And I felt that I had been very small in a little secret place within me and that even the completion of high school was for me a silly shallow selfish dream.

So I told him one night very resolutely and very powerfully that I would remain with him as long as he lived and we would fish the sea together. And he made no protest but only smiled through the cigarette smoke that wreathed his bed and replied, "I hope you will remember what you've said."

The room was now so filled with books as to be almost Dickensian, but he would not allow my mother to move or change them and he continued to read them, sometimes two or three a night. They came with great regularity now, and there were more hardcovers, sent by my sisters who had gone so long ago and now seemed so distant and so prosperous, and sent also pictures of small red-haired grandchildren with baseball bats and dolls which he placed upon his bureau and which my mother gazed at wistfully when she thought no one would see. Red-haired grandchildren with baseball bats and dolls who would never know the sea in hatred or in love.

And so we fished through the heat of August and into the cooler days of September when the water was so clear we could almost see the bottom and the white mists rose like delicate ghosts in the early morning dawn. And one day my mother said to me, "You have given added years to his life."

And we fished on into October when it began to roughen and we could no longer risk night sets but took our gear out each morning and returned at the first sign of the squalls; and on into November when we lost three tubs of trawl and the clear blue water turned to a sullen grey and the trochoidal waves rolled rough and high and washed across our bows and decks as we ran within their troughs. We wore heavy sweaters now and the awkward rubber slickers and the heavy woollen mitts which soaked and froze into masses of ice that hung from our wrists like the limbs of gigantic monsters until we thawed them against the exhaust pipe's heat. And almost every day we would leave for home, before noon, driven by the blasts of the northwest wind, coating our eyebrows with ice and freezing our eyelids closed as we leaned into a visibility that was hardly there, charting our course from the compass and the sea, running with the waves and between them but never confronting their towering might.

And I stood at the tiller now, on these homeward lunges, stood in the place and in the manner of my uncle, turning to look at my father and to shout over the roar of the engine and the slop of the sea to where he stood in the stern, drenched and dripping with the snow and the salt and the spray and his bushy eyebrows caked in ice. But on November twenty-first, when it seemed we might be making the final run of the season, I turned and he was not there and I knew even in that instant that he would never be again.

On November twenty-first the waves of the grey Atlantic are very very high and the waters are very cold and there are no signposts on the surface of the sea. You cannot tell where you have been five minutes before and in the squalls of snow you cannot see. And it takes longer than you would believe to check a boat that has been running before a gale and turn her ever so carefully in a wide and stupid circle, with timbers creaking and straining, back into the face of storm. And you know that it is useless and that your voice does not carry the length of the boat and that even if you knew the original spot, the relentless waves would carry such a burden perhaps a mile or so by the time you could return. And you know also, the final irony, that your father, like your uncles and all the men that form your past, cannot swim a stroke.

The lobster beds off the Cape Breton coast are still very rich and now, from May to July, their offerings are packed in crates of ice, and thundered by the gigantic transport trucks, day and night, through New Glasgow, Amherst, Saint John and Bangor and Portland and into Boston where they are tossed still living into boiling pots of water, their final home.

And though the prices are higher and the competition tighter, the grounds to which the *Jenny Lynn* once went remain untouched and unfished as they have for the last ten years. For if there are no signposts on the sea in storm there are certain ones in calm and the lobster bottoms were distributed in calm before any of us can remember and the grounds my father fished were those his father fished before him and there were others before and before and before. Twice the big boats have come from forty and fifty miles, lured by the promise of the grounds, and strewn the bottom with their traps and twice they have returned to find their buoys cut adrift and their gear lost and destroyed. Twice the Fisheries Officer and the Mounted Police have come and asked many long and involved questions and twice they have received no answers from the men leaning in the doors of their shanties and the women standing at their windows with their children in their arms. Twice they have gone away saying: "There are no legal boundaries in the Marine area"; "No one can own the sea"; "Those grounds don't wait for anyone."

But the men and the women, with my mother dark among them, do not care for what they say, for to them the grounds are sacred and they think they wait for me.

It is not an easy thing to know that your mother lives alone on an inadequate insurance policy and that she is too proud to accept any other aid. And that she looks through her lonely window onto the ice of winter and the hot flat calm of summer and the rolling waves of fall. And that she lies awake in the early morning's darkness when the rubber boots of the men scrunch upon the gravel as they pass beside her house on their way down to the wharf. And she knows that the footsteps never stop, because no man goes from her house, and she alone of all the Lynns has neither son nor son-in-law that walks toward the boat that will take him to the sea. And it is not an easy thing to know that your mother looks upon the sea with love and on you with bitterness because the one has been so constant and the other so untrue.

But neither is it easy to know that your father was found on November twenty-eighth, ten miles to the north and wedged between two boulders at the base of the rock-strewn cliffs where he had been hurled and slammed so many many times. His hands were shredded ribbons as were his feet which had lost their boots to the suction of the sea, and his shoulders came apart in our hands when we tried to move him from the rocks. And the fish had eaten his testicles and the gulls had pecked out his eyes and the white-green stubble of his whiskers had continued to grow in death, like the grass on graves, upon the purple, bloated mass that was his face. There was not much left of my father, physically, as he lay there with the brass chains on his wrists and the seaweed in his hair.

𝕊𝕆ℂ𝕏

With a rich, declamatory prose style, this story tells of the passing of a way of life and, paradoxically, the impossibility of completely escaping from it. Alistair MacLeod depicts a people whose heritage stretches back across time and space back to the Gaels of the Scottish Highlands, yet whose children — the future — are now leaving the fishing villages of Cape Breton for the lure of city lights, fine clothes, and an entirely different culture. The narrator's parents embody this fracturing of a way of life, this clash between tradition and the new. His mother, a striking woman of formidable strength, fears and rejects the gradually encroaching new order and desires to remain firmly rooted in the local, the known, while his father, in touch with the larger world through his wide reading and his own disappointed hopes, knows that the old ways are passing. He quietly supports his children as they seek what he had been unable to achieve: an escape from the grinding labour and ever-present danger of the fisher's life. As the story's opening and closing paragraphs make clear, however, the past can never be left behind, for it endures in one's dreams, one's memories, one's very blood.

Born in North Battleford, Saskatchewan, Alistair MacLeod returned with his parents to their native Cape Breton and received his secondary education there. After further studies in Nova Scotia, New Brunswick, and Indiana, MacLeod began a career teaching in both the United States and Canada. He is currently a professor of English and creative writing at the University of Windsor.

T.C.

KATHERINE MANSFIELD   *(1888-1923)*

The Garden-Party

A nd after all the weather was ideal. They could not have had a more perfect day for a garden-party if they had ordered it. Windless, warm, the sky without a cloud. Only the blue was veiled with a haze of light gold, as it is sometimes in early summer. The gardener had been up since dawn, mowing the lawns and sweeping them, until the grass and the dark flat rosettes where the daisy plants had been seemed to shine. As for the roses, you could not help feeling they understood that roses are the only flowers that impress people at garden-parties; the only flowers that everybody is certain of knowing. Hundreds, yes, literally hundreds, had come out in a single night; the green bushes bowed down as though they had been visited by archangels.

Breakfast was not yet over before the men came to put up the marquee.

"Where do you want the marquee put, mother?"

"My dear child, it's no use asking me. I'm determined to leave everything to you children this year. Forget I am your mother. Treat me as an honoured guest."

But Meg could not possibly go and supervise the men. She had washed her hair before breakfast, and she sat drinking her coffee in a green turban, with a dark wet curl stamped on each cheek. Jose, the butterfly, always came down in a silk petticoat and a kimono jacket.

"You'll have to go, Laura; you're the artistic one."

Away Laura flew, still holding her piece of bread-and-butter. It's so delicious to have an excuse for eating out of doors, and besides, she loved having to arrange things; she always felt she could do it so much better than anybody else.

Four men in their shirt-sleeves stood grouped together on the garden path. They carried staves covered with rolls of canvas, and they had big tool-bags slung on their backs. They looked impressive. Laura wished now that she had not got the bread-and-butter, but there was nowhere to put it, and she couldn't possibly throw it away. She blushed and tried to look severe and even a little bit short-sighted as she came up to them.

"Good morning," she said, copying her mother's voice. But that sounded so fearfully affected that she was ashamed and stammered like a little girl, "Oh — er — have you come — is it about the marquee?"

"That's right, miss," said the tallest of the men, a lanky, freckled fellow, and he shifted his tool-bag, knocked back his straw hat and smiled down at her. "That's about it."

His smile was so easy, so friendly that Laura recovered. What nice eyes he had, small, but such a dark blue! And now she looked at the others, they were smiling too. "Cheer up, we won't bite," their smile seemed to say. How very nice workmen were! And what a beautiful morning! She mustn't mention the morning;

she must be businesslike. The marquee.

"Well, what about the lily-lawn? Would that do?"

And she pointed to the lily-lawn with the hand that didn't hold the bread-and-butter. They turned, they stared in the direction. A little fat chap thrust out his under-lip, and the tall fellow frowned.

"I don't fancy it," said he. "Not conspicuous enough. You see, with a thing like a marquee," and he turned to Laura in his easy way, "you want to put it somewhere where it'll give you a bang slap in the eye, if you follow me."

Laura's upbringing made her wonder for a moment whether it was quite respectful of a workman to talk to her of bangs slap in the eye. But she did quite follow him.

"A corner of the tennis-court," she suggested. "But the band's going to be in one corner."

"H'm, going to have a band, are you?" said another of the workmen. He was pale. He had a haggard look as his dark eyes scanned the tennis-court. What was he thinking?

"Only a very small band," said Laura gently. Perhaps he wouldn't mind so much if the band was quite small. But the tall fellow interrupted.

"Look here, miss, that's the place. Against those trees. Over there. That'll do fine."

Against the karakas. Then the karaka-trees would be hidden. And they were so lovely, with their broad, gleaming leaves, and their clusters of yellow fruit. They were like trees you imagined growing on a desert island, proud, solitary, lifting their leaves and fruits to the sun in a kind of silent splendour. Must they be hidden by a marquee?

They must. Already the men had shouldered their staves and were making for the place. Only the tall fellow was left. He bent down, pinched a sprig of lavender, put his thumb and forefinger to his nose and snuffed up the smell. When Laura saw that gesture she forgot all about the karakas in her wonder at him caring for things like that — caring for the smell of lavender. How many men that she knew would have done such a thing? Oh, how extraordinarily nice workmen were, she thought. Why couldn't she have workmen for friends rather than the silly boys she danced with and who came to Sunday night supper? She would get on much better with men like these.

It's all the fault, she decided, as the tall fellow drew something on the back of an envelope, something that was to be looped up or left to hang, of these absurd class distinctions. Well, for her part, she didn't feel them. Not a bit, not an atom. . . . And now there came the chock-chock of wooden hammers. Some one whistled, some one sang out, "Are you right there, matey?" "Matey!" The friendliness of it, the — the — Just to prove how happy she was, just to show the tall fellow how at home she felt, and how she despised stupid conventions, Laura took a big bite of her bread-and-butter as she stared at the little drawing. She felt just like a work-girl.

"Laura, Laura, where are you? Telephone, Laura!" a voice cried from the house.

"Coming!" Away she skimmed, over the lawn, up the path, up the steps, across the veranda, and into the porch. In the hall her father and Laurie were brushing their hats ready to go to the office.

"I say, Laura," said Laurie very fast, "you might just give a squiz at my coat before this afternoon. See if it wants pressing."

"I will," said she. Suddenly she couldn't stop herself. She ran at Laurie and gave him a small, quick squeeze. "Oh, I do love parties, don't you?" gasped Laura.

"Ra-ther," said Laurie's warm, boyish voice, and he squeezed his sister too, and gave her a gentle push. "Dash off to the telephone, old girl."

The telephone. "Yes, yes; oh yes. Kitty? Good morning, dear. Come to lunch? Do, dear. Delighted of course. It will only be a very scratch meal — just the sandwich crusts and broken meringue-shells and what's left over. Yes, isn't it a perfect morning? Your white? Oh, I certainly should. One moment — hold the line. Mother's calling." And Laura sat back. "What, mother? Can't hear."

Mrs. Sheridan's voice floated down the stairs. "Tell her to wear that sweet hat she had on last Sunday."

"Mother says you're to wear that *sweet* hat you had on last Sunday. Good. One o'clock. Bye-bye."

Laura put back the receiver, flung her arms over her head, took a deep breath, stretched and let them fall. "Huh," she sighed, and the moment after the sigh she sat up quickly. She was still, listening. All the doors in the house seemed to open. The house was alive with soft, quick steps and running voices. The green baize door that led to the kitchen regions swung open and shut with a muffled thud. And now there came a long, chuckling absurd sound. It was the heavy piano being moved on its stiff castors. But the air! If you stopped to notice, was the air always like this? Little faint winds were playing chase, in at the tops of the windows, out at the doors. And there were two tiny spots of sun, one on the inkpot, one on a silver photograph frame, playing too. Darling little spots. Especially the one on the inkpot lid. It was quite warm. A warm little silver star. She could have kissed it.

The front door bell pealed, and there sounded the rustle of Sadie's print skirt on the stairs. A man's voice murmured; Sadie answered, careless, "I'm sure I don't know. Wait. I'll ask Mrs. Sheridan."

"What is it, Sadie?" Laura came into the hall.

"It's the florist, Miss Laura."

It was, indeed. There, just inside the door, stood a wide, shallow tray full of pots of pink lilies. No other kind. Nothing but lilies — canna lilies, big pink flowers, wide open, radiant, almost frighteningly alive on bright crimson stems.

"O-oh, Sadie!" said Laura, and the sound was like a little moan. She crouched down as if to warm herself at that blaze of lilies; she felt they were in her fingers, on her lips, growing in her breast.

"It's some mistake," she said faintly. "Nobody ever ordered so many. Sadie, go and find mother."

But at that moment Mrs. Sheridan joined them.

"It's quite right," she said calmly. "Yes, I ordered them. Aren't they lovely?" She pressed Laura's arm. "I was passing the shop yesterday, and I saw them in the window. And I suddenly thought for once in my life I shall have enough canna lilies. The garden-party will be a good excuse."

"But I thought you said you didn't mean to interfere," said Laura. Sadie had gone. The florist's man was still outside at his van. She put her arm round her mother's neck and gently, very gently, she bit her mother's ear.

"My darling child, you wouldn't like a logical mother, would you? Don't do that. Here's the man."

He carried more lilies still, another whole tray.

"Bank them up, just inside the door, on both sides of the porch, please," said Mrs. Sheridan. "Don't you agree, Laura?"

"Oh, I *do*, mother."

In the drawing-room Meg, Jose and good little Hans had at last succeeded in moving the piano.

"Now, if we put this chesterfield against the wall and move everything out of the room except the chairs, don't you think?"

"Quite."

"Hans, move these tables into the smoking-room, and bring a sweeper to take these marks off the carpet and — one moment, Hans —" Jose loved giving orders to the servants, and they loved obeying her. She always made them feel they were taking part in some drama. "Tell mother and Miss Laura to come here at once."

"Very good, Miss Jose."

She turned to Meg. "I want to hear what the piano sounds like, just in case I'm asked to sing this afternoon. Let's try over 'This Life is Weary.' "

Pom! Ta-ta-ta *Tee*-ta! The piano burst out so passionately that Jose's face changed. She clasped her hands. She looked mournfully and enigmatically at her mother and Laura as they came in.

> This Life is *Wee*-ary,
> A Tear — a Sigh.
> A Love that *Chan*-ges,
>   This life is *Wee*-ary,
> A Tear — a Sigh.
> A Love that *Chan*-ges,
> And then . . . Good-bye!

But at the word "Good-bye," and although the piano sounded more desperate than ever, her face broke into a brilliant, dreadfully unsympathetic smile.

"Aren't I in good voice, mummy?" she beamed.

> This Life is *Wee*-ary,
> Hope comes to Die,
> A Dream — a *Wa*-kening.

But now Sadie interrupted them. "What is it, Sadie?"

"If you please, m'm, cook says have you got the flags for the sandwiches?"

"The flags for the sandwiches, Sadie?" echoed Mrs. Sheridan dreamily. And the children knew by her face that she hadn't got them. "Let me see." And she said to Sadie firmly. "Tell cook I'll let her have them in ten minutes."

Sadie went.

"Now, Laura," said her mother quickly. "Come with me into the smoking-room. I've got the names somewhere on the back of an envelope. You'll have to write them out for me. Meg, go upstairs this minute and take that wet thing off your head. Jose, run and finish dressing this instant. Do you hear me, children, or shall I have to tell your father when he comes home to-night? And — and, Jose, pacify cook if you do go into the kitchen, will you? I'm terrified of her this morning."

The envelope was found at last behind the dining-room clock, though how it had got there, Mrs. Sheridan could not imagine.

"One of you children must have stolen it out of my bag, because I remember vividly — cream cheese and lemon-curd. Have you done that?"

"Yes."

"Egg and —" Mrs. Sheridan held the envelope away from her. "It looks like mice. It can't be mice, can it?"

"Olive, pet," said Laura, looking over her shoulder.

"Yes, of course, olive. What a horrible combination it sounds. Egg and olive."

They were finished at last, and Laura took them off to the kitchen. She found Jose there pacifying the cook, who did not look at all terrifying.

"I have never seen such exquisite sandwiches," said Jose's rapturous voice. "How many kinds did you say there were, cook? Fifteen?"

"Fifteen, Miss Jose."

"Well, cook, I congratulate you."

Cook swept up crusts with a long sandwich knife, and smiled broadly.

"Godber's has come," announced Sadie, issuing out of the pantry. She had seen the man pass the window.

That meant the cream puffs had come. Godber's were famous for their cream puffs. Nobody ever thought of making them at home.

"Bring them in and put them on the table, my girl," ordered cook.

Sadie brought them in and went back to the door. Of course Laura and Jose were far too grown-up to really care about such things. All the same, they couldn't help agreeing that the puffs looked very attractive. Very. Cook began arranging them, shaking off the extra icing sugar.

"Don't they carry one back to all one's parties?" said Laura.

"I suppose they do," said practical Jose, who never liked to be carried back. "They look beautifully light and feathery, I must say."

"Have one each, my dears," said cook in her comfortable voice. "Yer ma won't know."

Oh, impossible. Fancy cream puffs so soon after breakfast. The very idea made one shudder. All the same, two minutes later Jose and Laura were licking their fingers with that absorbed inward look that only comes from whipped cream.

"Let's go into the garden, out by the back way," suggested Laura. "I want to see how the men are getting on with the marquee. They're such awfully nice men."

But the back door was blocked by cook, Sadie, Godber's man and Hans.

Something had happened.

"Tuk-tuk-tuk," clucked cook like an agitated hen. Sadie had her hand clapped to her cheek as though she had toothache. Hans's face was screwed up in the effort to understand. Only Godber's man seemed to be enjoying himself; it was his story.

"What's the matter? What's happened?"

"There's been a horrible accident," said Cook. "A man killed."

"A man killed! Where? How? When?"

But Godber's man wasn't going to have his story snatched from under his very nose.

"Know those little cottages just below here, miss?" Know them? Of course, she knew them. "Well, there's a young chap living there, name of Scott, a carter. His horse shied at a traction-engine, corner of Hawke Street this morning, and he was thrown out on the back of his head. Killed."

"Dead!" Laura stared at Godber's man.

"Dead when they picked him up," said Godber's man with relish. "They were taking the body home as I come up here." And he said to the cook, "He's left a wife and five little ones."

"Jose, come here." Laura caught hold of her sister's sleeve and dragged her through the kitchen to the other side of the green baize door. There she paused and leaned against it. "Jose!" she said, horrified, "however are we going to stop everything?"

"Stop everything, Laura!" cried Jose in astonishment. "What do you mean?"

"Stop the garden-party, of course." Why did Jose pretend?

But Jose was still more amazed. "Stop the garden-party? My dear Laura, don't be so absurd. Of course we can't do anything of the kind. Nobody expects us to. Don't be so extravagant."

"But we can't possibly have a garden-party with a man dead just outside the front gate."

That really was extravagant, for the little cottages were in a lane to themselves at the very bottom of a steep rise that led up to the house. A broad road ran between. True, they were far too near. They were the greatest possible eyesore, and they had no right to be in that neighbourhood at all. They were little mean dwellings painted a chocolate brown. In the garden patches there was nothing but cabbage stalks, sick hens and tomato cans. The very smoke coming out of their chimneys was poverty-stricken. Little rags and shreds of smoke, so unlike the great silver plumes that uncurled from the Sheridans' chimneys. Washerwomen lived in the lane and sweeps and a cobbler, and a man whose house-front was studded all over with minute bird-cages. Children swarmed. When the Sheridans were little they were forbidden to set foot there because of the revolting language and of what they might catch. But since they were grown up, Laura and Laurie on their prowls sometimes walked through. It was disgusting and sordid. They came out with a shudder. But still one must go everywhere; one must see everything. So through they went.

"And just think of what the band would sound like to that poor woman," said Laura.

"Oh, Laura!" Jose began to be seriously annoyed. "If you're going to stop a band playing every time some one has an accident, you'll lead a very strenuous life. I'm every bit as sorry about it as you. I feel just as sympathetic." Her eyes hardened. She looked at her sister just as she used to when they were little and fighting together. "You won't bring a drunken workman back to life by being sentimental," she said softly.

"Drunk! Who said he was drunk?" Laura turned furiously on Jose. She said, just as they had used to say on those occasions, "I'm going straight up to tell mother."

"Do, dear," cooed Jose.

"Mother, can I come into your room?" Laura turned the big glass door-knob.

"Of course, child. Why, what's the matter? What's given you such a colour?" And Mrs. Sheridan turned round from her dressing-table. She was trying on a new hat.

"Mother, a man's been killed," began Laura.

"*Not* in the garden?" interrupted her mother.

"No, no!"

"Oh, what a fright you gave me!" Mrs. Sheridan sighed with relief, and took off the big hat and held it on her knees.

"But listen, mother," said Laura. Breathless, half-choking, she told the dreadful story. "Of course, we can't have our party, can we?" she pleaded. "The band and everybody arriving. They'd hear us, Mother; they're nearly neighbours!"

To Laura's astonishment her mother behaved just like Jose; it was harder to bear because she seemed amused. She refused to take Laura seriously.

"But, my dear child, use your common sense. It's only by accident we've heard of it. If some one had died there normally — and I can't understand how they keep alive in those poky little holes — we should still be having our party, shouldn't we?"

Laura had to say "yes" to that, but she felt it was all wrong. She sat down on her mother's sofa and pinched the cushion frill.

"Mother, isn't it really terribly heartless of us?" she asked.

"Darling!" Mrs. Sheridan got up and came over to her, carrying the hat. Before Laura could stop her she had popped it on. "My child!" said her mother, "the hat is yours. It's made for you. It's much too young for me. I have never seen you look such a picture. Look at yourself!" And she held up her hand-mirror.

"But, mother," Laura began again. She couldn't look at herself; she turned aside.

This time Mrs. Sheridan lost patience just as Jose had done.

"You are being very absurd, Laura," she said coldly. "People like that don't expect sacrifices from us. And it's not very sympathetic to spoil everybody's enjoyment as you're doing now."

"I don't understand," said Laura, and she walked quickly out of the room into her own bedroom. There, quite by chance, the first thing she saw was this charming girl in the mirror, in her black hat trimmed with gold daisies, and a long black velvet ribbon. Never had she imagined she could look like that. Is mother right? she thought. And now she hoped her mother was right. Am I being extravagant? Perhaps it was extravagant. Just for a moment she had another glimpse of that poor woman and those little children, and the body being carried into the house. But it all seemed blurred, unreal, like a picture in the newspaper. I'll remember it again after the party's over, she decided. And somehow that seemed quite the best plan. . . .

Lunch was over by half-past one. By half-past two they were all ready for the fray. The green-coated band had arrived and was established in a corner of the tennis-court.

"My dear!" trilled Kitty Maitland, "aren't they too like frogs for words? You ought to have arranged them round the pond with the conductor in the middle on a leaf."

Laurie arrived and hailed them on his way to dress. At the sight of him Laura remembered the accident again. She wanted to tell him. If Laurie agreed with the others, then it was bound to be all right. And she followed him into the hall.

"Laurie!"

"Hallo!" He was half-way upstairs, but when he turned round and saw Laura he suddenly puffed out his cheeks and goggled his eyes at her. "My word, Laura! You do look stunning," said Laurie. "What an absolutely topping hat!"

Laura said faintly "Is it?" and smiled up at Laurie and didn't tell him after all.

Soon after that people began coming in streams. The band struck up; the hired waiters ran from the house to the marquee. Wherever you looked there were couples strolling, bending to the flowers, greeting, moving on over the lawn. They were like bright birds that had alighted in the Sheridans' garden for this one afternoon, on their way to — where? Ah, what happiness it is to be with people who all are happy, to press hands, press cheeks, smile into eyes.

"Darling Laura, how well you look!"

"What a becoming hat, child!"

"Laura, you look quite Spanish. I've never seen you look so striking."

And Laura, glowing, answered softly, "Have you had tea? Won't you have an ice? The passion-fruit ices really are rather special." She ran to her father and begged him. "Daddy darling, can't the band have something to drink?"

And the perfect afternoon slowly ripened, slowly faded, slowly its petals closed.

"Never a more delightful garden-party . . ." "The greatest success . . ." "Quite the most . . ."

Laura helped her mother with the good-byes. They stood side by side in the porch till it was all over.

"All over, all over, thank heaven," said Mrs. Sheridan. "Round up the others, Laura. Let's go and have some fresh coffee. I'm exhausted. Yes, it's been very successful. But oh, these parties, these parties! Why will you children insist on giving parties!" And they all of them sat down in the deserted marquee.

"Have a sandwich, daddy dear. I wrote the flag."

"Thanks." Mr. Sheridan took a bite and the sandwich was gone. He took another. "I suppose you didn't hear of a beastly accident that happened to-day?" he said.

"My dear," said Mrs. Sheridan, holding up her hand, "we did. It nearly ruined the party. Laura insisted we should put it off."

"Oh, mother!" Laura didn't want to be teased about it.

"It was a horrible affair all the same," said Mr. Sheridan. "The chap was married too. Lived just below in the lane, and leaves a wife and half a dozen kiddies, so they say."

An awkward little silence fell. Mrs. Sheridan fidgeted with her cup. Really, it was very tactless of father . . .

Suddenly she looked up. There on the table were all those sandwiches, cakes, puffs, all uneaten, all going to be wasted. She had one of her brilliant ideas.

"I know," she said. "Let's make up a basket. Let's send that poor creature some of this perfectly good food. At any rate, it will be the greatest treat for the children. Don't you agree? And she's sure to have neighbours calling in and so on. What a point to have it all ready prepared. Laura!" She jumped up. "Get me the big basket out of the stairs cupboard."

"But, mother, do you really think it's a good idea?" said Laura.

Again, how curious, she seemed to be different from them all. To take scraps from their party. Would the poor woman really like that?

"Of course! What's the matter with you to-day? An hour or two ago you were insisting on us being sympathetic, and now —"

Oh, well! Laura ran for the basket. It was filled, it was heaped by her mother.

"Take it yourself, darling," said she. "Run down just as you are. No, wait, take the arum lilies too. People of that class are so impressed by arum lilies."

"The stems will ruin her lace frock," said practical Jose.

So they would. Just in time. "Only the basket, then. And, Laura!" — her mother followed her out of the marquee — "don't on any account —"

"What, mother?"

No, better not put such ideas into the child's head! "Nothing! Run along."

It was just growing dusky as Laura shut their garden gates. A big dog ran by like a shadow. The road gleamed white, and down below in the hollow the little cottages were in deep shade. How quiet it seemed after the afternoon. Here she was going down the hill to somewhere where a man lay dead, and she couldn't realize it. Why couldn't she? She stopped a minute. And it seemed to her that kisses, voices, tinkling spoons, laughter, the smell of crushed grass were somehow inside her. She had no room for anything else. How strange! She looked up at the pale sky, and all she thought was, "Yes, it was the most successful party."

Now the broad road was crossed. The lane began, smoky and dark. Women in shawls and men's tweed caps hurried by. Men hung over the palings; the children played in the doorways. A low hum came from the mean little cottages. In some of them there was a flicker of light, and a shadow, crab-like, moved across the window. Laura bent her head and hurried on. She wished now she had put on a coat. How her frock shone! And the big hat with the velvet streamer — if only it was another hat! Were the people looking at her? They must be. It was a mistake to have come;

she knew all along it was a mistake. Should she go back even now?

No, too late. This was the house. It must be. A dark knot of people stood outside. Beside the gate an old, old woman with a crutch sat in a chair, watching. She had her feet on a newspaper. The voices stopped as Laura drew near. The group parted. It was as though she was expected, as though they had known she was coming here.

Laura was terribly nervous. Tossing the velvet ribbon over her shoulder, she said to a woman standing by, "Is this Mrs. Scott's house?" and the woman, smiling queerly, said, "It is, my lass."

Oh, to be away from this! She actually said, "Help me, God," as she walked up the tiny path and knocked. To be away from those staring eyes, or to be covered up in anything, one of those women's shawls even. I'll just leave the basket and go, she decided. I shan't even wait for it to be emptied.

Then the door opened. A little woman in black showed in the gloom.

Laura said, "Are you Mrs. Scott?" But to her horror the woman answered, "Walk in please, miss," and she was shut in the passage.

"No," said Laura, "I don't want to come in. I only want to leave this basket. Mother sent —"

The little woman in the gloomy passage seemed not to have heard her. "Step this way, please, miss," she said in an oily voice, and Laura followed her.

She found herself in a wretched little low kitchen, lighted by a smoky lamp. There was a woman sitting before the fire.

"Em," said the little creature who had let her in. "Em! It's a young lady." She turned to Laura. She said meaningly, "I'm 'er sister, Miss. You'll excuse 'er, won't you?"

"Oh, but of course!" said Laura. "Please, don't disturb her. I — I only want to leave —"

But at that moment the woman at the fire turned round. Her face, puffed up, red, swollen eyes and swollen lips, looked terrible. She seemed as though she couldn't understand why Laura was there. What did it mean? Why was this stranger standing in the kitchen with a basket? What was it all about? And the poor face puckered up again.

"All right, my dear," said the other. "I'll thenk the young lady."

And again she began, "You'll excuse her, miss, I'm sure," and her face, swollen too, tried an oily smile.

Laura only wanted to get out, to get away. She was back in the passage. The door opened. She walked straight through into the bedroom, where the dead man was lying.

"You'd like a look at 'im, wouldn't you?" said Em's sister, and she brushed past Laura over to the bed. "Don't be afraid, my lass, —" and now her voice sounded fond and sly, and fondly she drew down the sheet — " 'e looks a picture. There's nothing to show. Come along, my dear."

Laura came.

There lay a young man, fast asleep — sleeping so soundly, so deeply, that he was far, far away from them both. Oh, so remote, so peaceful. He was dreaming.

Never wake him up again. His head was sunk in the pillow, his eyes were closed; they were blind under the closed eyelids. He was given up to his dream. What did garden-parties and baskets and lace frocks matter to him? He was far from all those things. He was wonderful, beautiful. While they were laughing and while the band was playing, this marvel had come to the lane. Happy . . . Happy. . . . All is well, said that sleeping face. This is just as it should be. I am content.

But all the same you had to cry, and she couldn't go out of the room without saying something to him. Laura gave a loud childish sob.

"Forgive my hat," she said.

And this time she didn't wait for Em's sister. She found her way out of the door, down the path, past all those dark people. At the corner of the lane she met Laurie.

He stepped out of the shadow. "Is that you, Laura?"

"Yes."

"Mother was getting anxious. Was it all right?"

"Yes, quite. Oh, Laurie!" She took his arm, she pressed up against him.

"I say, you're not crying, are you?" asked her brother.

Laura shook her head. She was.

Laurie put his arm round her shoulder. "Don't cry," he said in his warm, loving voice. "Was it awful?"

"No," sobbed Laura. "It was simply marvellous. But, Laurie —" She stopped, she looked at her brother. "Isn't life," she stammered, "isn't life —" But what life was she couldn't explain. No matter. He quite understood.

"*Isn't* it, darling?" said Laurie.

ഏറ

Together with Joyce and Lawrence, Katherine Mansfield established the British modernist short story. Without being didactic, her stories often present characters who find themselves facing situations that confute their thoroughly codified moral and psychological points of view. In "The Garden-Party," Laura tries to respond freely to experience, half recognizing that her affluent upbringing has coloured her perceptions. But she is caught in childhood; judicious yet naive, she remains dependent upon the powers that shape her life, whether they are derived from her family or more intangible cultural institutions. Mansfield focalizes much of the story through Laura's eyes, showing us, on the one hand, the exacting intimacy with which Laura apprehends the details and inconsistencies of her world, and on the other, how deeply she's internalized the ideology of her class and time. Whether she succeeds in breaking out of this heritage is debatable; certainly the ethical dilemmas enacted in the story are passed on to the reader. In a way similar to the meticulous care with which Laura's family plans the garden-party, Mansfield composes this story with details that echo throughout, often with a terrible poignancy. An imagined, blurry newspaper photograph counterpoints the turn-of-the-century aestheticization of the dead workman; his wife, dazed with grief, turns blindly toward Laura standing in the threshold of the kitchen, just as the story itself pivots on the threshold dividing life from death.

M.T.

Swimming Lessons

The old man's wheelchair is audible today as he creaks by in the hallway: on some days it's just a smooth whirr. Maybe the way he slumps in it, or the way his weight rests has something to do with it. Down to the lobby he goes, and sits there most of the time, talking to people on their way out or in. That's where he first spoke to me a few days ago. I was waiting for the elevator, back from Eaton's with my new pair of swimming-trunks.

"Hullo," he said. I nodded, smiled.

"Beautiful summer day we've got."

"Yes," I said, "it's lovely outside."

He shifted the wheelchair to face me squarely. "How old do you think I am?"

I looked at him blankly, and he said, "Go on, take a guess."

I understood the game; he seemed about seventy-five although the hair was still black, so I said, "Sixty-five?" He made a sound between a chuckle and a wheeze: "I'll be seventy-seven next month." Close enough.

I've heard him ask that question several times since, and everyone plays by the rules. Their faked guesses range from sixty to seventy. They pick a lower number when he's more depressed than usual. He reminds me of Grandpa as he sits on the sofa in the lobby, staring out vacantly at the parking lot. Only difference is, he sits with the stillness of stroke victims, while Grandpa's Parkinson's disease would bounce his thighs and legs and arms all over the place. When he could no longer hold the *Bombay Samachar* steady enough to read, Grandpa took to sitting on the veranda and staring emptily at the traffic passing outside Firozsha Baag. Or waving to anyone who went by in the compound: Rustomji, Nariman Hansotia in his 1932 Mercedes-Benz, the fat ayah Jaakaylee with her shopping-bag, the *kuchrawalli* with her basket and long bamboo broom.

The Portuguese woman across the hall has told me a little about the old man. She is the communicator for the apartment building. To gather and disseminate information, she takes the liberty of unabashedly throwing open her door when newsworthy events transpire. Not for Portuguese Woman the furtive peerings from thin cracks or spyholes. She reminds me of a character in a movie, *Barefoot In The Park* I think it was, who left empty beer cans by the landing for anyone passing to stumble and give her the signal. But PW does not need beer cans. The gutang-khutang of the elevator opening and closing is enough.

The old man's daughter looks after him. He was living alone till his stroke, which coincided with his youngest daughter's divorce in Vancouver. She returned to him and they moved into this low-rise in Don Mills. PW says the daughter talks to no one in the building but takes good care of her father.

Mummy used to take good care of Grandpa, too, till things became complicated and he was moved to the Parsi General Hospital. Parkinsonism and osteoporosis laid him low. The doctor explained that Grandpa's hip did not break because he fell, but he fell because the hip, gradually growing brittle, snapped on that fatal day. That's what osteoporosis does, hollows out the bones and turns effect into cause. It has an unusually high incidence in the Parsi community, he said, but did not say why. Just one of those mysterious things. We are the chosen people where osteoporosis is concerned. And divorce. The Parsi community has the highest divorce rate in India. It also claims to be the most westernized community in India. Which is the result of the other? Confusion again, of cause and effect.

The hip was put in traction. Single-handed, Mummy struggled valiantly with bedpans and dressings for bedsores which soon appeared like grim spectres on his back. *Mamaiji*, bent double with her weak back, could give no assistance. My help would be enlisted to roll him over on his side while Mummy changed the dressing. But after three months, the doctor pronounced a patch upon Grandpa's lungs, and the male ward of Parsi General swallowed him up. There was no money for a private nursing home. I went to see him once, at Mummy's insistence. She used to say that the blessings of an old person were the most valuable and potent of all, they would last my whole life long. The ward had rows and rows of beds; the din was enormous, the smells nauseating, and it was just as well that Grandpa passed most of his time in a less than conscious state.

But I should have gone to see him more often. Whenever Grandpa went out, while he still could in the days before parkinsonism, he would bring back pink and white sugar-coated almonds for Percy and me. Every time I remember Grandpa, I remember that; and then I think: I should have gone to see him more often. That's what I also thought when our telephone-owning neighbour, esteemed by all for that reason, sent his son to tell us the hospital had phoned that Grandpa died an hour ago.

౭

The postman rang the doorbell the way he always did, long and continuous; Mother went to open it, wanting to give him a piece of her mind but thought better of it, she did not want to risk the vengeance of postmen, it was so easy for them to destroy letters; workers nowadays thought no end of themselves, strutting around like peacocks, ever since all this Shiv Sena agitation about Maharashtra or Maharashtrians, threatening strikes and Bombay bundh *all the time, with no respect for the public; bus drivers and conductors were the worst, behaving as if they owned the buses and were doing favours to commuters, pulling the bell before you were in the bus, the driver purposely braking and moving with big jerks to make the standees lose their balance, the conductor so rude if you did not have the right change.*

But when she saw the airmail envelope with a Canadian stamp her face lit up, she said wait to the postman, and went in for a fifty paisa piece, a little baksheesh *for you, she told him, then shut the door and kissed the envelope, went in running, saying my son has written, my son has sent a letter, and Father looked up from the newspaper and said, don't get too excited, first read it, you know what kind of*

letters he writes, a few lines of empty words, I'm fine, hope you are all right, your
loving son — that kind of writing I don't call letter-writing.

Then Mother opened the envelope and took out one small page and began to
read silently, and the joy brought to her face by the letter's arrival began to ebb;
Father saw it happening and knew he was right, he said read aloud, let me also
hear what our son is writing this time, so Mother read; My dear Mummy and
Daddy, Last winter was terrible, we had record-breaking low temperatures all
through February and March, and the first official day of spring was colder than
the first official day of winter had been, but it's getting warmer now. Looks like it
will be a nice warm summer. You asked about my new apartment. It's small, but
not bad at all. This is just a quick note to let you know I'm fine, so you won't worry
about me. Hope everything is okay at home.

After Mother put it back in the envelope, Father said everything about his
life is locked in silence and secrecy, I still don't understand why he bothered to
visit us last year if he had nothing to say; every letter of his has been a quick note
so we won't worry — what does he think we worry about, his health, in that country
everyone eats well whether they work or not, he should be worrying about us with
all the black market and rationing, has he forgotten already how he used to go to
the ration-shop and wait in line every week; and what kind of apartment description
is that, not bad at all; and if it is a Canadian weather report I need from him, I can
go with Nariman Hansotia from A Block to the Cawasji Framji Memorial Library
and read all about it, there they get newspapers from all over the world.

❧

The sun is hot today. Two women are sunbathing on the stretch of patchy
lawn at the periphery of the parking lot. I can see them clearly from my kitchen.
They're wearing bikinis and I'd love to take a closer look. But I have no binoculars.
Nor do I have a car to saunter out to and pretend to look under the hood. They're
both luscious and gleaming. From time to time they smear lotion over their skin,
on the bellies, on the inside of the thighs, on the shoulders. Then one of them gets
the other to undo the string of her top and spread some there. She lies on her
stomach with the straps undone. I wait. I pray that the heat and haze make her
forget, when it's time to turn over, that the straps are undone.

But the sun is not hot enough to work this magic for me. When it's time to
come in, she flips over, deftly holding up the cups, and reties the top. They arise,
pick up towels, lotions and magazines, and return to the building.

This is my chance to see them closer. I race down the stairs to the lobby. The
old man says hullo. "Down again?"

"My mailbox," I mumble.

"It's Saturday," he chortles. For some reason he finds it extremely funny.
My eye is on the door leading in from the parking lot.

Through the glass panel I see them approaching. I hurry to the elevator and
wait. In the dimly lit lobby I can see their eyes are having trouble adjusting after
the bright sun. They don't seem as attractive as they did from the kitchen window.
The elevator arrives and I hold it open, inviting them in with what I think is a

gallant flourish. Under the fluorescent glare in the elevator I see their wrinkled skin, aging hands, sagging bottoms, varicose veins. The lustrous trick of sun and lotion and distance has ended.

I step out and they continue to the third floor. I have Monday night to look forward to, my first swimming lesson. The high school behind the apartment building is offering, among its usual assortment of macramé and ceramics and pottery classes, a class for non-swimming adults.

The woman at the registration desk is quite friendly. She even gives me the opening to satisfy the compulsion I have about explaining my non-swimming status.

"Are you from India?" she asks. I nod. "I hope you don't mind my asking, but I was curious because an Indian couple, husband and wife, also registered a few minutes ago. Is swimming not encouraged in India?"

"On the contrary," I say. "Most Indians swim like fish. I'm an exception to the rule. My house was five minutes walking distance from Chaupatty beach in Bombay. It's one of the most beautiful beaches in Bombay, or was, before the filth took over. Anyway, even though we lived so close to it, I never learned to swim. It's just one of those things."

"Well," says the woman, "that happens sometimes. Take me, for instance. I never learned to ride a bicycle. It was the mounting that used to scare me, I was afraid of falling." People have lined up behind me. "It's been very nice talking to you," she says, "hope you enjoy the course."

The art of swimming had been trapped between the devil and the deep blue sea. The devil was money, always scarce, and kept the private swimming clubs out of reach; the deep blue sea of Chaupatty beach was grey and murky with garbage, too filthy to swim in. Every so often we would muster our courage and Mummy would take me there to try and teach me. But a few minutes of paddling was all we could endure. Sooner or later something would float up against our legs or thighs or waists, depending on how deep we'd gone in, and we'd be revulsed and stride out to the sand.

Water imagery in my life is recurring. Chaupatty beach, now the high-school swimming pool. The universal symbol of life and regeneration did nothing but frustrate me. Perhaps the swimming pool will overturn that failure.

When images and symbols abound in this manner, sprawling or rolling across the page without guile or artifice, one is prone to say, how obvious, how skilless; symbols, after all, should be still and gentle as dewdrops, tiny, yet shining with a world of meaning. But what happens when, on the page of life itself, one encounters the ever-moving, all-engirdling sprawl of the filthy sea? Dewdrops and oceans both have their rightful places; Nariman Hansotia certainly knew that when he told his stories to the boys of Firozsha Baag.

The sea of Chaupatty was fated to endure the finales of life's everyday functions. It seemed that the dirtier it became, the more crowds it attracted: street urchins and beggars and beachcombers, looking through the junk that washed up. (Or was it the crowds that made it dirtier? — another instance of cause and effect blurring and evading identification.)

Too many religious festivals also used the sea as repository for their finales.

Its use should have been rationed, like rice and kerosene. On Ganesh Chaturthi, clay idols of the god Ganesh, adorned with garlands and all manner of finery, were carried in processions to the accompaniment of drums and a variety of wind instruments. The music got more frenzied the closer the procession got to Chaupatty and to the moment of immersion.

Then there was Coconut Day, which was never as popular as Ganesh Chaturthi. From a bystander's viewpoint, coconuts chucked into the sea do not provide as much of a spectacle. We used the sea, too, to deposit the leftovers from Parsi religious ceremonies, things such as flowers, or the ashes of the sacred sandalwood fire, which just could not be dumped with the regular garbage but had to be entrusted to the care of Avan Yazad, the guardian of the sea. And things which were of no use but which no one had the heart to destroy were also given to Avan Yazad. Such as old photographs.

After Grandpa died, some of his things were flung out to sea. It was high tide; we always checked the newspaper when going to perform these disposals; an ebb would mean a long walk in squelchy sand before finding water. Most of the things were probably washed up on shore. But we tried to throw them as far out as possible, then waited a few minutes; if they did not float back right away we would pretend they were in the permanent safekeeping of Avan Yazad, which was a comforting thought. I can't remember everything we sent out to sea, but his brush and comb were in the parcel, his *kusti*, and some Kemadrin pills, which he used to take to keep the parkinsonism under control.

Our paddling sessions stopped for lack of enthusiasm on my part. Mummy wasn't too keen either, because of the filth. But my main concern was the little guttersnipes, like naked fish with little buoyant penises, taunting me with their skills, swimming underwater and emerging unexpectedly all around me, or pretending to masturbate — I think they were too young to achieve ejaculation. It was embarrassing. When I look back, I'm surprised that Mummy and I kept going as long we did.

I examine the swimming-trunks I bought last week. Surf King, says the label, Made in Canada-Fabriqué Au Canada. I've been learning bits and pieces of French from bilingual labels at the supermarket too. These trunks are extremely sleek and streamlined hipsters, the distance from waistband to pouch tip the barest minimum. I wonder how everything will stay in place, not that I'm boastful about my endowments. I try them on, and feel that the tip of my member lingers perilously close to the exit. Too close, in fact, to conceal the exigencies of my swimming lesson fantasy: a gorgeous woman in the class for non-swimmers, at whose sight I will be instantly aroused, and she, spying the shape of my desire, will look me straight in the eye with her intentions; she will come home with me, to taste the pleasures of my delectable Asian brown body whose strangeness has intrigued her and unleashed uncontrollable surges of passion inside her throughout the duration of the swimming lesson.

I drop the Eaton's bag and wrapper in the garbage can. The swimming-trunks cost fifteen dollars, same as the fee for the ten weekly lessons. The garbage bag is almost full. I tie it up and take it outside. There is a medicinal smell in the hallway; the old man must have just returned to his apartment.

PW opens her door and says, "Two ladies from the third floor were lying in the sun this morning. In bikinis."

"That's nice," I say, and walk to the incinerator chute. She reminds me of Najamai in Firozsha Baag, except that Najamai employed a bit more subtlety while going about her life's chosen work.

PW withdraws and shuts her door.

ↀ

Mother had to reply because Father said he did not want to write to his son till his son had something sensible to write to him, his questions had been ignored long enough, and if he wanted to keep his life a secret, fine, he would get no letters from his father.

But after Mother started the letter he went and looked over her shoulder, telling her what to ask him, because if they kept on writing the same questions, maybe he would understand how interested they were in knowing about things over there; Father said go on, ask him what his work is at the insurance company, tell him to take some courses at night school, that's how everyone moves ahead over there, tell him not to be discouraged if his job is just clerical right now, hard work will get him ahead, remind him he is a Zoroastrian: manashni, gavashni, kunashni, *better write the translation also: good thoughts, good words, good deeds — he must have forgotten what it means, and tell him to say prayers and do* kusti *at least twice a day.*

Writing it all down sadly, Mother did not believe he wore his sudra *and* kusti *anymore, she would be very surprised if he remembered any of the prayers; when she had asked him if he needed new* sudras *he said not to take any trouble because the Zoroastrian Society of Ontario imported them from Bombay for their members, and this sounded like a story he was making up, but she was leaving it in the hands of God, ten thousand miles away there was nothing she could do but write a letter and hope for the best.*

Then she sealed it, and Father wrote the address on it as usual because his writing was much neater than hers, handwriting was important in the address and she did not want the postman in Canada to make any mistake; she took it to the post office herself, it was impossible to trust anyone to mail it ever since the postage rates went up because people just tore off the stamps for their own use and threw away the letter, the only safe way was to hand it over the counter and make the clerk cancel the stamps before your own eyes.

ↀ

Berthe, the building superintendent, is yelling at her son in the parking lot. He tinkers away with his van. This happens every fine-weathered Sunday. It must be the van that Berthe dislikes because I've seen mother and son together in other quite amicable situations.

Berthe is a big Yugoslavian with high cheekbones. Her nationality was disclosed to me by PW. Berthe speaks a very rough-hewn English, I've overheard her in the lobby scolding tenants for late rents and leaving dirty lint screens in the dryers. It's exciting to listen to her, her words fall like rocks and boulders, and one can never tell where or how the next few will drop. But her Slavic yells at her son are a different matter, the words fly swift and true, well-aimed missiles that never miss. Finally, the son slams down the hood in disgust, wipes his hands on a rag, accompanies mother Berthe inside.

Berthe's husband has a job in a factory. But he loses several days of work every month when he succumbs to the booze, a word Berthe uses often in her Slavic tirades on those days, the only one I can understand, as it clunks down heavily out of the tight-flying formation of Yugoslavian sentences. He lolls around in the lobby, submitting passively to his wife's tongue-lashings. The bags under his bloodshot eyes, his stringy moustache, stubbled chin, dirty hair are so vulnerable to the poison-laden barbs (poison works the same way in any language) emanating from deep within the powerful watermelon bosom. No one's presence can embarrass or dignify her into silence.

No one except the old man who arrives now. "Good morning," he says, and Berthe turns, stops yelling, and smiles. Her husband rises, positions the wheelchair at the favourite angle. The lobby will be peaceful as long as the old man is there.

ᘓ

It was hopeless. My first swimming lesson. The water terrified me. When did that happen, I wonder, I used to love splashing at Chaupatty, carried about by the waves. And this was only a swimming pool. Where did all that terror come from? I'm trying to remember.

Armed with my Surf King I enter the high school and go to the pool area. A sheet with instructions for the new class is pinned to the bulletin board. All students must shower and then assemble at eight by the shallow end. As I enter the showers three young boys, probably from a previous class, emerge. One of them holds his nose. The second begins to hum, under his breath: Paki Paki, smell like curry. The third says to the first two: pretty soon all the water's going to taste of curry. They leave.

It's a mixed class, but the gorgeous woman of my fantasy is missing. I have to settle for another, in a pink one-piece suit, with brown hair and a bit of a stomach. She must be about thirty-five. Plain-looking.

The instructor is called Ron. He gives us a pep talk, sensing some nervousness in the group. We're finally all in the water, in the shallow end. He demonstrates floating on the back, then asks for a volunteer. The pink one-piece suit wades forward. He supports her, tells her to lean back and let her head drop in the water.

She does very well. And as we all regard her floating body, I see what was not visible outside the pool: her bush, curly bits of it, straying out at the pink Spandex V. Tongues of water lapping against her delta, as if caressing it teasingly, make the brown hair come alive in a most tantalizing manner. The crests and troughs of little waves, set off by the movement of our bodies in a circle around her, dutifully irrigate her; the curls alternately wave free inside the crest, then adhere to her wet thighs, beached by the inevitable trough. I could watch this forever, and I wish the floating demonstration would never end.

Next we are shown how to grasp the rail and paddle, face down in the water. Between practising floating and paddling, the hour is almost gone. I have been trying to observe the pink one-piece suit, getting glimpses of her straying pubic hair from various angles. Finally, Ron wants a volunteer for the last demonstration, and I go forward. To my horror he leads the class to the deep end. Fifteen feet of water. It is so blue, and I can see the bottom. He picks up a metal hoop attached to a long wooden stick. He wants me to grasp the hoop, jump in the water, and paddle, while he guides me by the stick. Perfectly safe, he tells me. A demonstration of how paddling propels the body.

It's too late to back out; besides, I'm so terrified I couldn't find the words to do so even if I wanted to. Everything he says I do as if in a trance. I don't remember the moment of jumping. The next thing I know is, I'm swallowing water and floundering, hanging on to the hoop for dear life. Ron draws me to the rails and helps me out. The class applauds.

We disperse and one thought is on my mind: what if I'd lost my grip? Fifteen feet of water under me. I shudder and take deep breaths. This is it. I'm not coming next week. This instructor is an irresponsible person. Or he does not value the lives of non-white immigrants. I remember the three teenagers. Maybe the swimming pool is the hangout of some racist group, bent on eliminating all non-white swimmers, to keep their waters pure and their white sisters unogled.

The elevator takes me upstairs. Then gutang-khutang. PW opens her door as I turn the corridor of medicinal smells. "Berthe was screaming loudly at her husband tonight," she tells me.

"Good for her," I say, and she frowns indignantly at me.

©©

The old man is in the lobby. He's wearing thick wool gloves. He wants to know how the swimming was, must have seen me leaving with my towel yesterday. Not bad, I say.

"I used to swim a lot. Very good for the circulation." He wheezes. "My feet are cold all the time. Cold as ice. Hands too."

Summer is winding down, so I say stupidly, "Yes, it's not so warm any more."

The thought of the next swimming lesson sickens me. But as I comb through the memories of that terrifying Monday, I come upon the straying curls of brown pubic hair. Inexorably drawn by them, I decide to go.

It's a mistake, of course. This time I'm scared even to venture in the shallow end. When everyone has entered the water and I'm the only one outside, I feel a little foolish and slide in.

Instructor Ron says we should start by reviewing the floating technique. I'm in no hurry. I watch the pink one-piece pull the swim-suit down around her cheeks and flip back to achieve perfect flotation. And then reap disappointment. The pink Spandex triangle is perfectly streamlined today, nothing strays, not a trace of fuzz, not one filament, not even a sign of post-depilation irritation. Like the airbrushed parts of glamour magazine models. The barrenness of her impeccably packaged apex is a betrayal. Now she is shorn like the other women in the class. Why did she have to do it?

The weight of this disappointment makes the water less manageable, more lung-penetrating. With trepidation, I float and paddle my way through the remainder of the hour, jerking my head out every two seconds and breathing deeply, to continually shore up a supply of precious, precious air without, at the same time, seeming too anxious and losing my dignity.

I don't attend the remaining classes. After I've missed three, Ron the instructor telephones. I tell him I've had the flu and am still feeling poorly, but I'll try to be there the following week.

He does not call again. My Surf King is relegated to an unused drawer. Total losses: one fantasy plus thirty dollars. And no watery rebirth. The swimming pool, like Chaupatty beach, has produced a stillbirth. But there is a difference. Water means regeneration only if it is pure and cleansing. Chaupatty was filthy, the pool was not. Failure to swim through filth must mean something other than failure of rebirth — failure of symbolic death? Does that equal success of symbolic life? death of a symbolic failure? death of a symbol? What is the equation?

೧෭

The postman did not bring a letter but a parcel, he was smiling because he knew that every time something came from Canada his baksheesh *was guaranteed, and this time because it was a parcel Mother gave him a whole rupee, she was quite excited, there were so many stickers on it besides stamps, one for Small Parcel, another Printed Papers, a red sticker saying Insured; she showed it to Father, and opened it, then put both hands on her cheeks, not able to speak because the surprise and happiness was so great, tears came to her eyes and she could not stop smiling, till Father became impatient to know and finally got up and came to the table.*

When he saw it he was surprised and happy too, he began to grin, then hugged Mother saying our son is a writer, and we didn't even know it, he never told us a thing, here we are thinking he is still clerking away at the insurance company, and he has written a book of stories, all these years in school and college he kept his talent hidden, making us think he was just like one of the boys in the Baag, shouting and playing the fool in the compound, and now what a surprise; then Father opened the book and began reading it, heading back to the easy chair, and Mother so excited, still holding his arm, walked with him, saying it was not fair him reading it first, she wanted to read it too, and they agreed that he would read the first story, then give it to her so she could also read it, and they would take turns in that manner.

Mother removed the staples from the padded envelope in which he had mailed the book, and threw them away, then straightened the folded edges of the envelope and put it away safely with the other envelopes and letters she had collected since he left.

೧෭

The leaves are beginning to fall. The only ones I can identify are maple. The days are dwindling like the leaves. I've started a habit of taking long walks every evening. The old man is in the lobby when I leave, he waves as I go by. By the time I'm back, the lobby is usually empty.

Today I was woken up by a grating sound outside that made my flesh crawl. I went to the window and saw Berthe raking the leaves in the parking lot. Not in the expanse of patchy lawn on the periphery, but in the parking lot proper. She was raking the black tarred surface. I went back to bed and dragged a pillow over my head, not releasing it till noon.

When I return from my walk in the evening, PW, summoned by the elevator's gutang-khutang, says, "Berthe filled six big black garbage bags with leaves today."

"Six bags!" I say. "Wow!"

ೞ

Since the weather turned cold, Berthe's son does not tinker with his van on Sundays under my window. I'm able to sleep late.

Around eleven, there's a commotion outside. I reach out and switch on the clock radio. It's a sunny day, the window curtains are bright. I get up, curious, and see a black Olds Ninety-Eight in the parking lot, by the entrance to the building. The old man is in his wheelchair, bundled up, with a scarf wound several times round his neck as though to immobilize it, like a surgical collar. His daughter and another man, the car-owner, are helping him from the wheelchair into the front seat, encouraging him with words like: that's it, easy does it, attaboy. From the open door of the lobby, Berthe is shouting encouragement too, but hers is confined to one word: yah, repeated at different levels of pitch and volume, with variations on vowel-length. The stranger could be the old man's son, he has the same jet black hair and piercing eyes.

Maybe the old man is not well, it's an emergency. But I quickly scrap that thought — this isn't Bombay, an ambulance would have arrived. They're probably taking him out for a ride. If he is his son, where has he been all this time, I wonder.

The old man finally settles in the front seat, the wheelchair goes in the trunk, and they're off. The one I think is the son looks up and catches me at the window before I can move away, so I wave, and he waves back.

In the afternoon I take down a load of clothes to the laundry room. Both machines have completed their cycles, the clothes inside are waiting to be transferred to dryers. Should I remove them and place them on top of a dryer, or wait? I decide to wait. After a few minutes, two women arrive, they are in bathrobes, and smoking. It takes me a while to realize that these are the two disappointments who were sunbathing in bikinis last summer.

"You didn't have to wait, you could have removed the clothes and carried on, dear," says one. She has a Scottish accent. It's one of the few I've learned to identify. Like maple leaves.

"Well," I say, "some people might not like strangers touching their clothes."

"You're not a stranger, dear," she says, "you live in this building, we've seen you before."

"Besides, your hands are clean," the other one pipes in. "You can touch my things any time you like."

Horny old cow. I wonder what they've got on under their bathrobes. Not much, I find, as they bend over to place their clothes in the dryers.

"See you soon," they say, and exit, leaving me behind in an erotic wake of smoke and perfume and deep images of cleavages. I start the washers and depart, and when I come back later, the dryers are empty.

PW tells me, "The old man's son took him out for a drive today. He has a big beautiful black car."

I see my chance, and shoot back: "Olds Ninety-Eight."

"What?"

"The car," I explain, "it's an Oldsmobile Ninety-Eight."

She does not like this at all, my giving her information. She is visibly nettled, and retreats with a sour face.

೧೩

Mother and Father read the first five stories, and she was very sad after reading some of them, she said he must be so unhappy there, all his stories are about Bombay, he remembers every little thing about his childhood, he is thinking about it all the time even though he is ten thousand miles away, my poor son, I think he misses his home and us and everything he left behind, because if he likes it over there why would he not write stories about that, there must be so many new ideas that his new life could give him.

But Father did not agree with this, he said it did not mean that he was unhappy, all writers worked in the same way, they used their memories and experiences and made stories out of them, changing some things, adding some, imagining some, all writers were very good at remembering details of their lives.

Mother said, how can you be sure that he is remembering because he is a writer, or whether he started to write because he is unhappy and thinks of his past, and wants to save it all by making stories of it; and Father said that is not a sensible question, anyway, it is now my turn to read the next story.

೧೩

The first snow has fallen, and the air is crisp. It's not very deep, about two inches, just right to go for a walk in. I've been told that immigrants from hot countries always enjoy the snow the first year, maybe for a couple of years more, then inevitably the dread sets in, and the approach of winter gets them fretting and moping. On the other hand, if it hadn't been for my conversation with the woman at the swimming registration desk, they might now be saying that India is a nation of non-swimmers.

Berthe is outside, shovelling the snow off the walkway in the parking lot. She has a heavy, wide pusher which she wields expertly.

The old radiators in the apartment alarm me incessantly. They continue to broadcast a series of variations on death throes, and go from hot to cold and cold to hot at will, there's no controlling their temperature. I speak to Berthe about it in the lobby. The old man is there too, his chin seems to have sunk deeper into his chest, and his face is a yellowish grey.

"Nothing, not to worry about anything," says Berthe, dropping rough-hewn chunks of language around me. "Radiator no work, you tell me. You feel cold, you come to me, I keep you warm," and she opens her arms wide, laughing. I step back, and she advances, her breasts preceding her like the gallant prows of two ice-breakers. She looks at the old man to see if he is appreciating the act: "You no feel scared, I keep you safe and warm."

But the old man is staring outside, at the flakes of falling snow. What thoughts is he thinking as he watches them? Of childhood days, perhaps, and snowmen with hats and pipes, and snowball fights, and white Christmases, and Christmas trees? What will I think of, old in this country, when I sit and watch the snow come down? For me, it is already too late for snowmen and snowball fights, and all I will have is thoughts about childhood thoughts and dreams, built around snowscapes and winter-wonderlands on the Christmas cards so popular in Bombay; my snowmen and snowball fights and Christmas trees are in the pages of Enid Blyton's books, dispersed amidst the adventures of the Famous Five, and the Five Find-Outers, and the Secret Seven. My snowflakes are even less forgettable than the old man's, for they never melt.

☙

It finally happened. The heat went. Not the usual intermittent coming and going, but out completely. Stone cold. The radiators are like ice. And so is everything else. There's no hot water. Naturally. It's the hot water that goes through the rads and heats them. Or is it the other way around? Is there no hot water because the rads have stopped circulating it? I don't care, I'm too cold to sort out the cause and effect relationship. Maybe there is no connection at all.

I dress quickly, put on my winter jacket and go down to the lobby. The elevator is not working because the power is out, so I take the stairs. Several people are gathered, and Berthe has announced that she has telephoned the office, they are sending a man. I go back up the stairs. It's only one floor, the elevator is just a bad habit. Back in Firozsha Baag they were broken most of the time. The stairway enters the corridor outside the old man's apartment, and I think of his cold feet and hands. Poor man, it must be horrible for him without heat.

As I walk down the long hallway, I feel there's something different but can't pin it down. I look at the carpet, the ceiling, the wallpaper: it all seems the same. Maybe it's the freezing cold that imparts a feeling of difference.

PW opens her door: "The old man had another stroke yesterday. They took him to the hospital."

The medicinal smell. That's it. It's not in the hallway any more.

☙

In the stories that he'd read so far Father said that all the Parsi families were poor or middle-class, but that was okay; nor did he mind that the seeds for the stories were picked from the sufferings of their own lives; but there should also

*have been something positive about Parsis, there was so much to be proud of: the
great Tatas and their contribution to the steel industry, or Sir Dinshaw Petit in the
textile industry who made Bombay the Manchester of the East, or Dadabhai Naoroji
in the freedom movement, where he was the first to use the word* swaraj, *and the
first to be elected to the British Parliament where he carried on his campaign; he
should have found some way to bring some of these wonderful facts into his stories,
what would people reading these stories think, those who did not know about
Parsis — that the whole community was full of cranky, bigoted people; and in
reality it was the richest, most advanced and philanthropic community in India,
and he did not need to tell his own son that Parsis had a reputation for being
generous and family-oriented. And he could have written something also about
the historic background, how Parsis came to India from Persia because of Islamic
persecution in the seventh century, and were the descendants of Cyrus the Great
and the magnificent Persian Empire. He could have made a story of all this, couldn't
he?*

*Mother said what she liked best was his remembering everything so well,
how beautifully he wrote about it all, even the sad things, and though he changed
some of it, and used his imagination, there was truth in it.*

*My hope is, Father said, that there will be some story based on his Canadian
experience, that way we will know something about our son's life there, if not
through his letters then in his stories; so far they are all about Parsis and Bombay,
and the one with a little bit about Toronto, where a man perches on top of the
toilet, is shameful and disgusting, although it is funny at times and did make me
laugh, I have to admit, but where does he get such an imagination from, what is
the point of such a fantasy; and Mother said that she would also enjoy some stories
about Toronto and the people there; it puzzles me, she said, why he writes nothing
about it, especially since you say that writers use their own experience to make
stories out of.*

*Then Father said this is true, but he is probably not using his Toronto
experience because it is too early; what do you mean, too early, asked Mother and
Father explained it takes a writer about ten years time after an experience before
he is able to use it in his writing, it takes that long to be absorbed internally and
understood, thought out and thought about, over and over again, he haunts it and
it haunts him if it is valuable enough, till the writer is comfortable with it to be able
to use it as he wants; but this is only one theory I read somewhere, it may or may
not be true.*

*That means, said Mother, that his childhood in Bombay and our home here
is the most valuable thing in his life just now, because he is able to remember it all
to write about it, and you were so bitterly saying he is forgetting where he came
from; and that may be true, said Father, but that is not what the theory means,
according to the theory he is writing of these things because they are far enough in
the past for him to deal with objectively, he is able to achieve what critics call
artistic distance, without emotions interfering; and what do you mean emotions,
said Mother, you are saying he does not feel anything for his characters, how can
he write so beautifully about so many sad things without any feelings in his heart?*

But before Father could explain more, about beauty and emotion and inspiration and imagination, Mother took the book and said it was her turn now and too much theory she did not want to listen to, it was confusing and did not make as much sense as reading the stories, she would read them her way and Father could read them his.

C౩

My books on the windowsill have been damaged. Ice has been forming on the inside ledge, which I did not notice, and melting when the sun shines in. I spread them in a corner of the living-room to dry out.

The winter drags on. Berthe wields her snow pusher as expertly as ever, but there are signs of weariness in her performance. Neither husband nor son is ever seen outside with a shovel. Or anywhere else, for that matter. It occurs to me that the son's van is missing, too.

The medicinal smell is in the hall again, I sniff happily and look forward to seeing the old man in the lobby. I go downstairs and peer into the mailbox, see the blue and magenta of an Indian aerogramme with Don Mills, Ontario, Canada in Father's flawless hand through the slot.

I pocket the letter and enter the main lobby. The old man is there, but not in his usual place. He is not looking out through the glass door. His wheelchair is facing a bare wall where the wallpaper is torn in places. As though he is not interested in the outside world any more, having finished with all that, and now it's time to see inside. What does he see inside, I wonder? I go up to him and say hullo. He says hullo without raising his sunken chin. After a few seconds his grey countenance faces me. "How old do you think I am?" His eyes are dull and glazed; he is looking even further inside than I first presumed.

"Well, let's see, you're probably close to sixty-four."

"I'll be seventy-eight next August." But he does not chuckle or wheeze. Instead, he continues softly, "I wish my feet did not feel so cold all the time. And my hands." He lets his chin fall again.

In the elevator I start opening the aerogramme, a tricky business because a crooked tear means lost words. Absorbed in this while emerging, I don't notice PW occupying the centre of the hallway, arms folded across her chest: "They had a big fight. Both of them have left."

I don't immediately understand her agitation. "What . . . who?"

"Berthe. Husband and son both left her. Now she is all alone."

Her tone and stance suggest that we should not be standing here talking but do something to bring Berthe's family back. "That's very sad," I say, and go in. I picture father and son in the van, driving away, driving across the snow-covered country, in the dead of winter, away from wife and mother; away to where? how far will they go? Not son's van nor father's booze can take them far enough. And the further they go, the more they'll remember, they can take it from me.

C౩

All the stories were read by Father and Mother, and they were sorry when

*the book was finished, they felt they had come to know their son better now, yet
there was much more to know, they wished there were many more stories; and this
is what they mean, said Father, when they say that the whole story can never be
told, the whole truth can never be known; what do you mean, they say, asked
Mother, who they, and Father said writers, poets, philosophers. I don't care what
they say, said Mother, my son will write as much or as little as he wants to, and if
I can read it I will be happy.*

*The last story they liked the best of all because it had the most in it about
Canada, and now they felt they knew at least a little bit, even if it was a very little
bit, about his day-to-day life in his apartment; and Father said if he continues to
write about such things he will become popular because I am sure they are interested
there in reading about life through the eyes of an immigrant, it provides a different
viewpoint; the only danger is if he changes and becomes so much like them that he
will write like one of them and lose the important difference.*

෨

The bathroom needs cleaning. I open a new can of Ajax and scour the tub.
Sloshing with mug from bucket was standard bathing procedure in the bathrooms
of Firozsha Baag, so my preference now is always for a shower. I've never used
the tub as yet; besides, it would be too much like Chaupatty or the swimming pool,
wallowing in my own dirt. Still, it must be cleaned.

When I've finished, I prepare for a shower. But the clean gleaming tub and
the nearness of the vernal equinox give me the urge to do something different
today. I find the drain plug in the bathroom cabinet, and run the bath.

I've spoken so often to the old man, but I don't know his name. I should
have asked him the last time I saw him, when his wheelchair was facing the bare
wall because he had seen all there was to see outside and it was time to see what
was inside. Well, tomorrow. Or better yet, I can look it up in the directory in the
lobby. Why didn't I think of that before? It will only have an initial and a last
name, but then I can surprise him with: hullo Mr Wilson, or whatever it is.

The bath is full. Water imagery is recurring in my life: Chaupatty beach,
swimming pool, bathtub. I step in and immerse myself up to the neck. It feels
good. The hot water loses its opacity when the chlorine, or whatever it is, has
cleared. My hair is still dry. I close my eyes, hold my breath, and dunk my head.
Fighting the panic, I stay under and count to thirty. I come out, clear my lungs and
breathe deeply.

I do it again. This time I open my eyes under water, and stare blindly without
seeing, it takes all my will to keep the lids from closing. Then I am slowly able to
discern the underwater objects. The drain plug looks different, slightly distorted;
there is a hair trapped between the hole and the plug, it waves and dances with the
movement of the water. I come up, refresh my lungs, examine quickly the overwater
world of the washroom, and go in again. I do it several times, over and over. The
world outside the water I have seen a lot of, it is now time to see what is inside.

The spring session for adult non-swimmers will begin in a few days at the
high school. I must not forget the registration date.

 emdash

The dwindled days of winter are now all but forgotten; they have grown and attained a respectable span. I resume my evening walks, it's spring, and a vigorous thaw is on. The snowbanks are melting, the sound of water on its gushing, gurgling journey to the drains is beautiful. I plan to buy a book of trees, so I can identify more than the maple as they begin to bloom.

When I return to the building, I wipe my feet energetically on the mat because some people are entering behind me, and I want to set a good example. Then I go to the board with its little plastic letters and numbers. The old man's apartment is the one on the corner by the stairway, that makes it number 201. I run down the list, come to 201, but there are no little white plastic letters beside it. Just the empty black rectangle with holes where the letters would be squeezed in. That's strange. Well, I can introduce myself to him, then ask his name.

However, the lobby is empty. I take the elevator, exit at the second floor, wait for the gutang-khutang. It does not come: the door closes noiselessly, smoothly. Berthe has been at work, or has made sure someone else has. PW's cue has been lubricated out of existence.

But she must have the ears of a cockroach. She is waiting for me. I whistle my way down the corridor. She fixes me with an accusing look. She waits till I stop whistling, then says: "You know the old man died last night."

I cease groping for my key. She turns to go and I take a step towards her, my hand still in my trouser pocket. "Did you know his name?" I ask, but she leaves without answering.

emdash

Then Mother said, the part I like best in the last story is about Grandpa, where he wonders if Grandpa's spirit is really watching him and blessing him, because you know I really told him that, I told him helping an old suffering person who is near death is the most blessed thing to do, because that person will ever after watch over you from heaven, I told him this when he was disgusted with Grandpa's urine-bottle and would not touch it, would not hand it to him even when I was not at home.

Are you sure, said Father, that you really told him this, or you believe you told him because you like the sound of it, you said yourself the other day that he changes and adds and alters things in the stories but he writes it all so beautifully that it seems true, so how can you be sure; this sounds like another theory, said Mother, but I don't care, he says I told him and I believe now I told him, so even if I did not tell him then it does not matter now.

Don't you see, said Father, that you are confusing fiction with facts, fiction does not create facts, fiction can come from facts, it can grow out of facts by compounding, transposing, augmenting, diminishing, or altering them in any way; but you must not confuse cause and effect, you must not confuse what really happened with what the story says happened, you must not loose your grasp on reality, that way madness lies.

*Then Mother stopped listening because, as she told Father so often, she was
not very fond of theories, and she took out her writing pad and started a letter to
her son; Father looked over her shoulder, telling her to say how proud they were
of him and were waiting for his next book, he also said, leave a little space for me
at the end, I want to write a few lines when I put the address on the envelope.*

ΣΟΩ

This is the final story in Rohinton Mistry's first collection of stories, Tales from
Firozsha Baag *(1987), which was shortlisted for the Governor-General's Award. Mistry
records the lives of residents of a decaying middle-class apartment complex in his native
city, Bombay. Unlike the other stories in the collection, "Swimming Lessons" is narrated
from a Canadian perspective, exploring the narrator's comic, yet ironic, experience of
"immersion" in a multicultural Toronto neighbourhood. At the beginning, the narrator is
a voyeuristic outsider, an observer fantasizing about desirable but impossible relationships.
As the story progresses, he recognizes the need to see the world underwater: "The world
outside the water I have seen a lot of, it is now time to see what is inside." His sense of
living between two worlds is narrated in several ways. Letters from the narrator's parents
to their son are represented in the italicized, free-flowing idiom that he can imagine
intimately, even from a distance. In the dialogue which imagines the disagreement between
his parents, he dramatizes his internal debate between writing of the present (where he is)
or writing from the past (where he has been). He must also learn the idioms of Toronto:
snow, trees, cars. Though much there is familiar to him, much is unfamiliar, including the
swimming lessons themselves — a metaphor for his fears — his fantasies, his racial
insecurities. And it is Mistry's gaze into the underwater world of Canadian culture to record
the immigrant's experience of hybridity that is the achievement of this story.*

J.S.

KEN MITCHELL

(b. 1940)

The Great Electrical Revolution

I was only a little guy in 1937 but I can still remember Grandad being out of
work. Nobody had any money to pay him and, as he said, there wasn't much
future in bricklaying as a charity. So mostly he just sat around in his suite
above the hardware store and listened to the radio. We all listened to it when there
was nothing else to do, which was most of the time, unless you happened to be
going to school like me. Grandad stuck right there through it all, soap operas,
weather reports and quiz shows. Unless he came across a bit of cash somewhere,
and then he and Uncle Fred would go down to the beer parlour at the King William
Hotel.

Grandad and Grandma came out from the Old Country long before I was
born. When they arrived in Moose Jaw all they had was three children — Uncle
Fred, Aunt Thecla and my dad — a trunk full of working clothes and a twenty-six
pound post maul for putting up fences to keep "rogues" off Grandad's land. Rogues
meant Orangemen, cattle rustlers, and capitalists. All the way on the train out from
Montreal, he glared out the Pullman window at the endless flat, saying to his family,
"I came out here for land, b'Christ, and none of them's going to sly it on me!" He
had sworn to carve a mighty estate from the raw Saskatchewan prairie, though he
had never handled so much as a garden hoe in his life before leaving Dublin.

When he stepped off the train at the CPR station in Moose Jaw, it looked like
he was thinking of tearing it down and seeding the site to oats. It was two o'clock
in the morning, but he kept striding up and down the lobby of the station, his chest
puffed out like a bantam rooster in a chicken run. My dad and Uncle Fred and
Aunt Thecla sat on the trunk while Grandma pleaded with him to go out and find
them a place to stay. It was only later they realized he was afraid to step outside the
station. But he finally quit strutting long enough to find a porter to carry their trunk
to a hotel across the street.

The next day they went to the government land office to secure their homestead. Then Grandad and his two sons rented a democrat buggy and set out to
inspect the land they'd sailed halfway round the world to claim. Grandma and
Aunt Thecla were told to stay in the hotel room and thank the Blessed Virgin for
deliverance. They were still offering their prayers some four hours later when
Grandad burst into the room, his eyes wild and his face trembling. "Sweet Jesus
Christ," he shouted. "There's too much of it! There's just too damned much of it
out there." He staggered around the room in circles, knocking against the walls
and moaning, "Miles and miles of nothing but miles and miles." He collapsed onto
one of the beds and lay staring at the ceiling. "It'd drive us all witless in a week."

The two boys came in and told the story of their expedition to the countryside.
Grandad had started out fine, perhaps just a bit nervous. But the further they went

319

from town the more agitated and distraught he became. Soon he quit urging the horse along and let it drift to a stop. They were barely five miles from Moose Jaw when they turned around and came back with Uncle Fred driving. Grandad could only crouch on the floor of the democrat, trying to hide from the enormous sky and whispering at Fred to go faster. Grandad had come five thousand miles to the wide open spaces — only to discover he suffered from agoraphobia.

That was his last excursion onto the open prairie, though he did make one special trip to the town of Bulkhead in 1928 to fix Aunt Thecla's chimney. But that was a family favour and even then Uncle Fred had to drive him in an enclosed Ford sedan in the middle of the night, with newspapers taped to the windows so he couldn't see out. So Grandad abandoned the dream of a country manor. He took up his old trade of bricklaying in the town of Moose Jaw, where there were trees and tall buildings to protect him from the vastness. Maybe it was a fortunate turn of fate. Certainly he prospered until the Depression hit, about the time I was born.

Yet Grandad always felt somehow guilty about not settling on the land. Perhaps it was his faith in the rural life that prompted him to send my dad out to work at a cattle ranch in the hills the day after he turned sixteen. He married Aunt Thecla off to a Norwegian wheat farmer at Bulkhead. Uncle Fred was the eldest and an apprentice bricklayer so he stayed in town and lived with Grandad and Grandma in the suite above the hardware store.

I don't remember much about the ranch my father eventually took over, except whirls of dust and skinny animals dragging themselves from one side of the range to the other. Finally there were no more cattle and nothing to feed them if we did have them except wild foxtail and Russian thistle. So we moved into Moose Jaw with Grandad and Grandma and went on relief. It was better than the cattle ranch where there was nothing to do but watch tumbleweeds roll through the yard. We would've had to travel into town to collect our salted fish and government pork anyway. Grandad was happy to have us, because when my Dad went down to the rail sheds to collect our rations, he got Grandad's food as well. My Dad never complained about waiting in line for the handout, but Grandad would've starved to death first.

"Damned government drives us all to the edge. Then they expect us to queue up for the damn swill they're poisoning us with."

That was when we spent so much time listening to Grandad's radio, a great slab of black walnut he had practically stolen — or so he claimed — from a second-hand dealer on River Street. A green incandescent bulb glowed in the center of it to show when the tubes were warming up. There was a row of knobs with elaborate initials and a dial with cities like Tokyo, Madrid and Chicago. Try as we might on long winter evenings to tune the needle in and hear a show in Russian or Japanese, all we ever got was CHMJ Moose Jaw, the Buckle of the Wheat Belt.

Even so, I spent many hours on the floor in front of the cloth-covered speakers, lost to another world of mystery and imagination. When the time came that Grandad could find no more bricks to lay, he set a kitchen chair in front of the radio and sat there, not moving except to go to the King William Hotel with Uncle Fred. My Dad managed to get relief work with the city, gravelling streets for fifty cents a day.

But things grew worse. One night in the fall of 1937, the Moose Jaw Electric Light and Power Company came around and cut off our electricity for non-payment. It was hard on Grandad not to have his radio. Not only did he have nothing to do, but he had to spend all day thinking about it. So he stared out the parlour window at the back alley behind our building, and at the loading dock of the Rainbow Laundry.

That's what he was doing the day of his discovery, about the time of the Feast of the Immaculate Conception. My Dad and Uncle Fred were arguing over who had caused the Depression — R.B. Bennett or the CPR. Suddenly Grandad turned from the window with a strange look on his face. "Where does that wire go?"

"What wire?" my dad said.

"This wire, running right past the window."

He pointed to a double strand of power line that run from the pole in the back alley to the side of our building. It was a lead-in for the hardware store below.

"Holy Moses Cousin Harry," Grandad said, grinning crazily. "Isn't that a sight now?"

"You're nuts," Uncle Fred told him. "You'll never get a tap off that line there. And if you did, they'd find you out in nothing flat."

"Now father," Grandma called from the kitchen. "Don't you go and do some foolishness will get us all electrinated."

"By Jaysus." He rarely paid attention to her advice. "Cut off my power, will they?"

That night when I went to bed, I listened to him and Uncle Fred banging and scraping as they bored a hole through the parlour wall. My dad wouldn't have anything to do with it, and took my mother out to a free movie at the Co-op. He said Grandad was descending to the level of the Moose Jaw Light and Power Company.

ℂЯ

Actually, Grandad had some experience as an electrician. He had known for a long time how to run a wire from one side of the meter around to the other, to cheat the power company. I had often watched him under the meter, teetering on the rungs of our broken stepladder, yelling at Grandma to lift the damned holy candle higher, so he could see what the hell he was doing.

The next day Grandad and Uncle Fred were like a couple of children, snorting and giggling and jabbing each other in the ribs. They were waiting for the King William beer parlour to open so they could go down and tell their friends about Grandad's revenge on the power company. There they spent the afternoon like heroes, telling over and over how Grandad had spied the lead-in and how they'd bored the hole through the wall, and how justice had finally crushed the capitalist leeches. They came home for supper, but headed back immediately to the King William, where everybody was treating them to free beer.

Grandma didn't think much of their efforts, though she admitted to enjoying the music on the radio. The line came through the hole in our wall and snaked across the living room floor to the kitchen. Other cords were attached which led to the two bedrooms. Grandma muttered angrily when she had to sweep around the black tangle of wires and sockets. Never one for labour-saving gadgets, she had that quaint old country belief that electricity leaked from all the connections and swirled about the floor like demons and banshees. And with six of us living in the tiny suite, somebody was always tripping on the cords and knocking things over. But we lived with all that, because Grandad was happy again. And we might all have lived happily ever after, if Grandad and Uncle Fred could have kept their mouths shut about their revenge on the power company.

One night about a week later, we were listening to Fibber McGee and Molly, when there was a knock at the door. It was Mrs. Pisak, who lived in a tiny room down the hallway.

"Goot even," she said. "I see your power has turnt beck on."

"Ha!" Grandad barked. "We turned it on *for* 'em. Damned rogues."

"Come in and listen to the show with us," Grandma said.

Mrs. Pisak kept looking at the wires running back and forth across the parlour, and at Grandad's radio.

"Dey shut off my power too. Now I can't hear de church music."

"The dirty brigands. They'd steal pennies from the eyes of the dead!"

"So you vill turn my power beck on?"

"Hmm!" Grandad said, trying to hear Fibber and the Old-Timer. Mrs. Pizak wasn't listening to the show. Grandma and my dad watched him, not listening either. Finally he couldn't stand it. "All right, Fred. Go and fetch the brace and bit."

They bored a hole through a bedroom wall into Mrs. Pizak's cubicle and then she was on Grandad's power grid too. In fact it didn't take long before all the neighbours in the block discovered the free electricity. They all wanted to hook up. There were two whole floors of apartments above the hardware store, and soon the walls and ceilings of Grandad's suite were as full of holes as a colander, with wires running in all directions like black spaghetti. For the cost of a bottle of whiskey, people could run their lights twenty-four hours a day if they wanted. By Christmas Day, even those neighbours who paid their bills had given notice to the power company. So we enjoyed a tolerable Christmas at the end of a bad year, and Grandad and Uncle Fred got credit for it. There was a lot of celebration up and down the halls, where they were feasted as honoured guests and heroes. A euphoric feeling ran through our block, like being in a state of siege or revolution, led by my Grandad.

C⃝R

One late afternoon just after New Year's I was lying on the parlour floor, reading a second-hand *Book of Knowledge* Aunt Thecla had sent for Christmas. Grandma and my mother were knitting socks, and all three of us were listening to Major Bowes' Amateur Hour. Out of the corner of my eye, I thought I saw the radio move. I blinked and stared at it, but the big console just sat there talking about Geritol. I turned a page. Again it seemed to move with a jerk.

"Grandma, the radio moved!"

She looked up from her knitting, not believing a word I might have to say. I gave up and glared at the stupid machine. As I watched, it slid at least six inches across the parlour floor.

"Grandma, it is moving! All by itself!"

She stood up and looked at the radio, the tangle of wires across the floor, and out the parlour window.

"Larry-boy. You'd better run down the hall and fetch your grandfather. He's at the McBrides'. Number eight!"

I sprinted down the hall and pounded at the door, which someone within opened the width of a crack. "Is my Grandad in there?"

He stepped out with a glass of whiskey in his hand. "What is it, Larry?"

"Grandma says for you to come right now. There's something funny with the radio."

"My radio!" He began walking down the hall, broke into a trot then a steady gallop, holding the glass of whiskey out front so it wouldn't spill. He burst into the apartment and skidded to a halt in front of the radio, which sat in its traditional majesty, but maybe a foot to the left of his chair.

"By the Holy Toenails of Moses. What is it, woman?"

Grandma jerked her chin ominously toward the window.

Her quiet firmness usually calmed him but now in two fantastic bounds, Grandad stood glaring out the window. He turned to me with a pale face. "Larry, run and fetch your Uncle Fred."

I ran down the hallway again to number eight and fetched Uncle Fred. When we got back, Grandad was pacing in a fury, and my mother's knitting needles clattered like telegraph keys. "Have a gawk at this, Fred."

Uncle Fred and I crowded past him to see out the window. There on a pole only twenty feet from our parlour window, practically facing us eye-to-eye, was a lineman from the power company. He was replacing glass insulators along the line. God knows why he was doing it in the dead of winter, but he obviously hadn't noticed our homemade lead-in, or he would have already been pounding at our door. We could only pray he wouldn't look at the line too closely.

Once, he lifted his eyes to our window, where we stood gaping at him in the growing darkness. He raised his hand in a salute. He thought we were admiring his work!

"Wave back!" Grandad ordered and the three of us waved frantically at the lineman to make him think we appreciated his efforts, though Grandad was muttering some very ugly things about the man's ancestry.

"Look at him — as dumb as two sticks. He has to be an Orangeman. May the High King of Glory give him the mange!"

Finally, to our relief, the lineman got ready to descend the pole. He reached out his hand for support, and my heart stopped beating as his weight hung on the contraband line. Behind me, I could hear the radio slide another foot across the parlour floor. The lineman stared at the wire in his hand. He tugged experimentally, his eyes following it up to the hole through our wall. He looked at Uncle Fred and

Grandad and me, standing there at the lit-up window, with our horror-struck grins and our arms frozen above our heads in grotesque waves. Understanding spread slowly across his face.

He scrambled around to the opposite side of the pole and braced himself to give a mighty pull on our line. Simultaneously Grandad leaped into action, grabbing the wire on our side of the wall. He wrapped it round his hands and braced his feet against the baseboard. "He'll never take it from us!" The lineman gave his first vicious yank and it almost jerked Grandad smack against the wall. I remember thinking what a powerful man he must be to do that to my Grandad!

"Fred, you feather-brained idiot! Get over here and *haul* before the black-hearted son of a bitch pulls me through the wall."

Uncle Fred ran to the wire just in time, as the man on the pole gave another, mightier heave. I could see him stiffen with rage. The slender wire sawed through the hole in the wall for at least ten minutes, first one side, then the other, getting advantage. The curses on our side got very loud and bitter. I couldn't hear the lineman, but I could see him, with his mouth twisted in an awful snarl, throwing terrible looks at me and heaving on the line. He was not praying to St. Jude.

Grandad's cursing would subside periodically when Grandma warned: "Now now, Father, not in front of the boy." Then she would go back to her knitting and pretend the whole affair wasn't happening and Grandad's blasphemies would soar to monumental heights. The lineman must have been in excellent condition because our side began to play out. Grandad yelled at Grandma and my mother, even at me, to throw ourselves on the line and help. But the women refused to leave their knitting and would not allow me to be corrupted.

Grandad and Uncle Fred kept losing ground until the huge radio had slid all the way across the room and stood at their backs, hampering their exertions. "Larry. Is he weakenin' any?" He wanted desperately for me to say yes, but it was useless. "It doesn't look like it." Grandad burst out in a froth of curses I'd never heard before. A fresh attack on the line pulled his knuckles to the wall, and scraped them badly. He looked tired and beaten. All the slack in the line was taken up. He was against the wall, his head twisted, looking at me. A light flared in his eyes.

"All right, Fred. If he wants the damned thing so bad — let him have it!" They both jumped back — and nothing happened.

I could see the lineman, completely unaware of his impending disaster, literally winding himself up for an all-out assault on our wire. I wanted, out of human kindness, to shout a warning at him. But it was too late. With an incredible backward lunge, he disappeared from sight behind the power pole.

A shattering explosion of noise blasted around us, like a bomb had fallen in Grandad's suite. Every electric appliance and light they owned flew into the parlour, ricocheting off the walls, and smashing against each other. A table lamp from the bedroom careened off Uncle Fred's knee. The radio collided against the wall and was ripped off its wire. Sparking and flashing, all of Grandma's things hurled themselves against the parlour wall, popping like a string of firecrackers as the cords went zipping through the hole.

A silence fell, like a breath of air to a drowning man. The late afternoon darkness settled through the room. "Sweet Jesus," Grandad said. Then came a second uproar, a bloodcurdling series of roars and shouts as all our neighbours recovered from seeing their lamps, radios, irons, and toasters leap from their tables and collect in ruined piles of junk around the "free power" holes in their walls. Uncle Fred turned white as a sheet.

I looked out the window. The lineman sat at the foot of his pole, dazed. He looked up at me with one more hateful glare, then snipped our wire with a pair of cutters, taped the end, and marched away into the night.

Grandad stood in the darkened ruins, trying to examine his beloved radio for damage. Grandma sat in her rocking chair, knitting socks and refusing to acknowledge the disaster. It was Grandad who finally broke the silence.

"Well, they're lucky," he said. "It's just damned lucky for them they didn't scratch my radio!"

&)(&

Often regarded as a "regional artist" in the tradition of Canadian prairie realism, Ken Mitchell sets this "revolution" in Moose Jaw, his home town, and tells a story which — while in some respects a tall tale — might have happened in any prairie town during the Depression. Mitchell's "Jaw" speaks in the ethnic accents and attitudes of some of the West's colourful immigrant population, who band together in times of trouble. Populist prairie socialism, in which common people struggle against the corporation, has never been more memorably portrayed.

The unpretentious voice of the narrator is crucial to the story's paradoxical tone. He has childlike compassion for both the powerless townspeople and the government powerman, and honestly portrays the flaws in both Grandad and his beloved radio which, despite its international dials, can tune in only Moose Jaw's CHMJ. Yet cared and fought for by indomitable spirits like Grandad, the radio becomes an inspiring bridge to the world. Rooted in the local, the story speaks to universal concerns and appeals to readers all over the world, as I discovered several years ago while teaching it at Beijing University in China.

G.M.

ALICE MUNRO (b. 1931)

Boys and Girls

My father was a fox farmer. That is, he raised silver foxes, in pens; and in the fall and early winter, when their fur was prime, he killed them and skinned them and sold their pelts to the Hudson's Bay Company or the Montreal Fur Traders. These companies supplied us with heroic calendars to hang, one on each side of the kitchen door. Against a background of cold blue sky and black pine forests and treacherous northern rivers, plumed adventurers planted the flags of England or of France; magnificent savages bent their backs to the portage.

For several weeks before Christmas, my father worked after supper in the cellar of our house. The cellar was white-washed, and lit by a hundred-watt bulb over the worktable. My brother Laird and I sat on the top step and watched. My father removed the pelt inside-out from the body of the fox, which looked surprisingly small, mean and rat-like, deprived of its arrogant weight of fur. The naked, slippery bodies were collected in a sack and buried at the dump. One time the hired man, Henry Bailey, had taken a swipe at me with this sack, saying, "Christmas present!" My mother thought that was not funny. In fact she disliked the whole pelting operation — that was what the killing, skinning, and preparation of the furs was called — and wished it did not have to take place in the house. There was the smell. After the pelt had been stretched inside-out on a long board my father scraped away delicately, removing the little clotted webs of blood vessels, the bubbles of fat; the smell of blood and animal fat, with the strong primitive odour of the fox itself, penetrated all parts of the house. I found it reassuringly seasonal, like the smell of oranges and pine needles.

Henry Bailey suffered from bronchial troubles. He would cough and cough until his narrow face turned scarlet, and his light blue, derisive eyes filled up with tears; then he took the lid off the stove, and, standing well back, shot out a great clot of phlegm — hsss — straight into the heart of the flames. We admired him for this performance and for his ability to make his stomach growl at will, and for his laughter, which was full of high whistlings and gurglings and involved the whole faulty machinery of his chest. It was sometimes hard to tell what he was laughing at, and always possible that it might be us.

After we had been sent to bed we could still smell fox and still hear Henry's laugh, but these things, reminders of the warm, safe, brightly lit downstairs world, seemed lost and diminished, floating on the stale cold air upstairs. We were afraid at night in the winter. We were not afraid of *outside* though this was the time of year when snowdrifts curled around our house like sleeping whales and the wind harassed us all night, coming up from the buried fields, the frozen swamp, with its old bugbear chorus of threats and misery. We were afraid of *inside*, the room where we slept. At this time the upstairs of our house was not finished. A brick chimney went up one wall. In the middle of the floor was a square hole, with a wooden railing around it; that was where the stairs came up. On the other side of the stairwell were the things that nobody had any use for any more — a soldiery roll of linoleum, standing on end, a wicker baby carriage, a fern basket, china jugs and basins with cracks in them, a picture of the Battle of Balaclava, very sad to look at. I had told Laird, as soon as he was old enough to understand such things, that bats and skeletons lived over there; whenever a man escaped from the county jail, twenty miles away, I imagined that he had somehow let himself in the window and was hiding behind the linoleum. But we had rules to keep us safe. When the light was on, we were safe as long as we did not step off the square of worn carpet which defined our bedroom-space; when the light was off no place was safe but the beds themselves. I had to turn out the light kneeling on the end of my bed, and stretching as far as I could to reach the cord.

In the dark we lay on our beds, our narrow life rafts, and fixed our eyes on the faint light coming up the stairwell, and sang songs. Laird sang "Jingle Bells," which he would sing any time, whether it was Christmas or not, and I sang "Danny Boy." I loved the sound of my own voice, frail and supplicating, rising in the dark. We could make out the tall frosted shapes of the windows now, gloomy and white. When I came to the part, *When I am dead, as dead I well may be* — a fit of shivering caused not by the cold sheets but by pleasurable emotion almost silenced me. *You'll kneel and say, an Ave there above me* — What was an Ave? Every day I forgot to find out.

Laird went straight from singing to sleep. I could hear his long, satisfied, bubbly breaths. Now for the time that remained to me, the most perfectly private and perhaps the best time of the whole day, I arranged myself tightly under the covers and went on with one of the stories I was telling myself from night to night. These stories were about myself, when I had grown a little older; they took place in a world that was recognizably mine, yet one that presented opportunities for courage, boldness and self-sacrifice, as mine never did. I rescued people from a bombed building (it discouraged me that the real war had gone on so far away from Jubilee). I shot two rabid wolves who were menacing the schoolyard (the teachers cowered terrified at my back). I rode a fine horse spiritedly down the main street of Jubilee, acknowledging the townspeople's gratitude for some yet-to-be-worked-out piece of heroism (nobody ever rode a horse there, except King Billy in the Orangemen's Day parade). There was always riding and shooting in these stories, though I had only been on a horse twice — bareback because we did not own a saddle — and the second time I had slid right around and dropped under the horse's feet; it had stepped placidly over me. I really was learning to shoot, but I could not hit anything yet, not even tin cans on fence posts.

○？

Alive, the foxes inhabited a world my father made for them. It was surrounded by a high guard fence, like a medieval town, with a gate that was padlocked at night. Along the streets of this town were ranged large, sturdy pens. Each of them had a real door that a man could go through, a wooden ramp along the wire, for the foxes to run up and down on, and a kennel — something like a clothes chest with airholes — where they slept and stayed in winter and had their young. There were feeding and watering dishes attached to the wire in such a way that they could be emptied and cleaned from the outside. The dishes were made of old tin cans, and the ramps and kennels of odds and ends of old lumber. Everything was tidy and ingenious; my father was tirelessly inventive and his favourite book in the world was *Robinson Crusoe*. He had fitted a tin drum on a wheelbarrow, for bringing water down to the pens. This was my job in summer, when the foxes had to have water twice a day. Between nine and ten o'clock in the morning, and again after supper, I filled the drum at the pump and trundled it down through the barnyard to the pens, where I parked it, and filled my watering can and went along the streets. Laird came too, with his little cream and green gardening can, filled too full and knocking against his legs and slopping water on his canvas shoes. I had the real watering can, my father's, though I could only carry it three-quarters full.

The foxes all had names, which were printed on a tin plate and hung beside their doors. They were not named when they were born, but when they survived the first year's pelting and were added to the breeding stock. Those my father had named were called names like Prince, Bob, Wally and Betty. Those I had named were called Star or Turk, or Maureen or Diana. Laird named one Maud after a hired girl we had when he was little, one Harold after a boy at school, and one Mexico, he did not say why.

Naming them did not make pets out of them, or anything like it. Nobody but my father ever went into the pens, and he had twice had blood-poisoning from bites. When I was bringing them their water they prowled up and down on the paths they had made inside their pens, barking seldom — they saved that for nighttime, when they might get up a chorus of community frenzy — but always watching me, their eyes burning, clear gold, in their pointed, malevolent faces. They were beautiful for their delicate legs and heavy, aristocratic tails and the bright fur sprinkled on dark down their backs — which gave them their name — but especially for their faces, drawn exquisitely sharp in pure hostility, and their golden eyes.

Besides carrying water I helped my father when he cut the long grass, and the lamb's quarter and flowering money-musk, that grew between the pens. He cut with the scythe and I raked into piles. Then he took a pitchfork and threw fresh-cut grass all over the top of the pens, to keep the foxes cooler and shade their coats, which were browned by too much sun. My father did not talk to me unless it was about the job we were doing. In this he was quite different from my mother, who, if she was feeling cheerful, would tell me all sorts of things — the name of a dog she had had when she was a little girl, the names of boys she had gone out with later on when she was grown up, and what certain dresses of hers had looked like — she could not imagine now what had become of them. Whatever thoughts and stories my father had were private, and I was shy of him and would never ask him questions. Nevertheless I worked willingly under his eyes, and with a feeling of pride. One time a feed salesman came down into the pens to talk to him and my father said, "Like to have you meet my new hired man." I turned away and raked furiously, red in the face with pleasure.

"Could of fooled me," said the salesman. "I thought it was only a girl."

After the grass was cut, it seemed suddenly much later in the year. I walked on stubble in the earlier evening, aware of the reddening skies, the entering silences, of fall. When I wheeled the tank out of the gate and put the padlock on, it was almost dark. One night at this time I saw my mother and father standing talking on the little rise of ground we called the gangway, in front of the barn. My father had just come from the meathouse; he had his stiff bloody apron on, and a pail of cut-up meat in his hand.

It was an odd thing to see my mother down at the barn. She did not often come out of the house unless it was to do something — hang out the wash or dig potatoes in the garden. She looked out of place, with her bare lumpy legs, not touched by the sun, her apron still on and damp across the stomach from the supper dishes. Her hair was tied up in a kerchief, wisps of it falling out. She would tie her hair up like this in the morning, saying she did not have time to do it properly, and it would stay tied up all day. It was true, too; she really did not have time. These days our back porch was piled with baskets of peaches and grapes and pears, bought in town, and onions and tomatoes and cucumbers grown at home, all waiting to be made into jelly and jam and preserves, pickles and chili sauce. In the kitchen there was a fire in the stove all day, jars clinked in boiling water, sometimes a cheesecloth bag was strung on a pole between two chairs, straining blue-black grape pulp for jelly. I was given jobs to do and I would sit at the table peeling peaches that had been soaked in the hot water, or cutting up onions, my eyes smarting and streaming. As soon as I was done I ran out of the house, trying to get out of earshot before my mother thought of what to do next. I hated the hot dark kitchen in summer, the green blinds and the flypapers, the same old oilcloth table and wavy mirror and bumpy linoleum. My mother was too tired and preoccupied to talk to me, she had no heart to tell me about the Normal School Graduation Dance; sweat trickled over her face and she was always counting under her breath, pointing at jars, dumping cups of sugar. It seemed to me that work in the house was endless, dreary and peculiarly depressing; work done out of doors, and in my father's service, was ritualistically important.

I wheeled the tank up to the barn, where it was kept, and I heard my mother saying, "Wait till Laird gets a little bigger, then you'll have a real help."

What my father said I did not hear. I was pleased by the way he stood listening, politely as he would to a salesman or a stranger, but with an air of wanting to get on with his real work. I felt my mother had no business down here and I wanted him to feel the same way. What did she mean about Laird? He was no help to anybody. Where was he now? Swinging himself sick on the swing, going around in circles, or trying to catch caterpillars. He never once stayed with me till I was finished.

"And then I can use her more in the house," I heard my mother say. She had a dead-quiet, regretful way of talking about me that always made me uneasy. "I just get my back turned and she runs off. It's not like I had a girl in the family at all."

I went and sat on a feed bag in the corner of the barn, not wanting to appear when this conversation was going on. My mother, I felt, was not to be trusted. She was kinder than my father and more easily fooled, but you could not depend on her, and the real reasons for the things she said and did were not to be known. She loved me, and she sat up late at night making a dress of the difficult style I wanted, for me to wear when school started, but she was also my enemy. She was always plotting. She was plotting now to get me to stay in the house more, although she knew I hated it (*because* she knew I hated it) and keep me from working for my father. It seemed to me she would do this simply out of perversity, and to try her power. It did not occur to me that she could be lonely, or jealous. No grown-up could be; they were too fortunate. I sat and kicked my heels monotonously against a feedbag, raising dust, and did not come out till she was gone.

At any rate, I did not expect my father to pay any attention to what she said. Who could imagine Laird doing my work — Laird remembering the padlock and cleaning out the watering-dishes with a leaf on the end of a stick, or even wheeling the tank without it tumbling over? It showed how little my mother knew about the way things really were.

CR

I have forgotten to say what the foxes were fed. My father's bloody apron reminded me. They were fed horsemeat. At this time most farmers still kept horses, and when a horse got too old to work, or broke a leg or got down and would not get up, as they sometimes did, the owner would call my father, and he and Henry went out to the farm in the truck. Usually they shot and butchered the horse there, paying the farmer from five to twelve dollars. If they had already too much meat on hand, they would bring the horse back alive, and keep it for a few days or weeks in our stable, until the meat was needed. After the war the farmers were buying tractors and gradually getting rid of horses altogether, so it sometimes happened that we got a good healthy horse, that there was just no use for any more. If this happened in the winter we might keep the horse in our stable till spring, for we had plenty of hay and if there was a lot of snow — and the plow did not always get our road cleared — it was convenient to be able to go to town with a horse and cutter.

The winter I was eleven years old we had two horses in the stable. We did not know what names they had had before, so we called them Mack and Flora. Mack was an old black workhorse, sooty and indifferent. Flora was a sorrel mare, a driver. We took them both out in the cutter. Mack was slow and easy to handle. Flora was given to fits of violent alarm, veering at cars and even at other horses, but we loved her speed and high-stepping, her general air of gallantry and abandon. On Saturdays we went down to the stable and as soon as we opened the door on its cosy, animal-smelling darkness Flora threw up her head, rolled her eyes, whinnied despairingly and pulled herself through a crisis of nerves on the spot. It was not safe to go into her stall; she would kick.

This winter also I began to hear a great deal more on the theme my mother had sounded when she had been talking in front of the barn. I no longer felt safe. It seemed that in the minds of the people around me there was a steady undercurrent of thought, not to be deflected, on this one subject. The word *girl* had formerly seemed to me innocent and unburdened, like the word *child*; now it appeared that it was no such thing. A girl was not, as I had supposed, simply what I was; it was what I had to become. It was a definition, always touched with emphasis, with reproach and disappointment. Also it was a joke on me. Once Laird and I were fighting, and for the first time ever I had to use all my strength against him; even so, he caught and pinned my arm for a moment, really hurting me. Henry saw this, and laughed, saying, "Oh, that there Laird's gonna show you, one of these days!" Laird was getting a lot bigger. But I was getting bigger too.

My grandmother came to stay with us for a few weeks and I heard other things. "Girls don't slam doors like that." "Girls keep their knees together when they sit down." And worse still, when I asked some questions, "That's none of girls' business." I continued to slam the doors and sit as awkwardly as possible, thinking that by such measures I kept myself free.

When spring came, the horses were let out in the barnyard. Mack stood against the barn wall trying to scratch his neck and haunches, but Flora trotted up and down and reared at the fences, clattering her hooves against the rails. Snow drifts dwindled quickly, revealing the hard grey and brown earth, the familiar rise and fall of the ground, plain and bare after the fantastic landscape of winter. There was a great feeling of opening-out, of release. We just wore rubbers now, over our shoes; our feet felt ridiculously light. One Saturday we went out to the stable and found all the doors open, letting in the unaccustomed sunlight and fresh air. Henry was there, just idling around looking at his collection of calendars which were tacked up behind the stalls in a part of the stable my mother had probably never seen.

"Come to say goodbye to your old friend Mack?" Henry said. "Here, you give him a taste of oats." He poured some oats into Laird's cupped hands and Laird went to feed Mack. Mack's teeth were in bad shape. He ate very slowly, patiently shifting the oats around in his mouth, trying to find a stump of a molar to grind it on. "Poor old Mack," said Henry mournfully. "When a horse's teeth's gone, he's gone. That's about the way."

"Are you going to shoot him today?" I said. Mack and Flora had been in the stable so long I had almost forgotten they were going to be shot.

Henry didn't answer me. Instead he started to sing in a high, trembly, mocking-sorrowful voice *Oh, there's no more work, for poor Uncle Ned, he's gone where the good darkies go.* Mack's thick, blackish tongue worked diligently at Laird's hand. I went out before the song was ended and sat down on the gangway.

I had never seen them shoot a horse, but I knew where it was done. Last summer Laird and I had come upon a horse's entrails before they were buried. We had thought it was a big black snake, coiled up in the sun. That was around in the field that ran up beside the barn. I thought that if we went inside the barn, and found a wide crack or knothole to look through we would be able to see them do it. It was not something I wanted to see; just the same, if a thing really happened, it was better to see it, and know.

My father came down from the house, carrying the gun.

"What are you doing here?" he said.

"Nothing."

"Go on up and play around the house."

He sent Laird out of the stable. I said to Laird, "Do you want to see them shoot Mack?" and without waiting for an answer led him around to the front door of the barn, opened it carefully, and went in. "Be quiet or they'll hear us," I said. We could hear Henry and my father talking in the stable, then the heavy shuffling steps of Mack being backed out of his stall.

In the loft it was cold and dark. Thin, crisscrossed beams of sunlight fell through the cracks. The hay was low. It was a rolling country, hills and hollows, slipping under our feet. About four feet up was a beam going around the walls. We piled hay up in one corner and I boosted Laird up and hoisted myself. The beam was not very wide; we crept along it with our hands flat on the barn walls. There were plenty of knotholes, and I found one that gave me the view I wanted — a corner of the barnyard, the gate, part of the field. Laird did not have a knothole and began to complain.

I showed him a widened crack between two boards. "Be quiet and wait. If they hear you you'll get us in trouble."

My father came in sight carrying the gun. Henry was leading Mack by the halter. He dropped it and took out his cigarette papers and tobacco; he rolled cigarettes for my father and himself. While this was going on Mack nosed around in the old, dead grass along the fence. Then my father opened the gate and they took Mack through. Henry led Mack away from the path to a patch of ground and they talked together, not loud enough for us to hear. Mack again began searching for a mouthful of fresh grass, which was not to be found. My father walked away in a straight line, and stopped short at a distance which seemed to suit him. Henry was walking away from Mack too, but sideways, still negligently holding on to the halter. My father raised the gun and Mack looked up as if he had noticed something and my father shot him.

Mack did not collapse at once but swayed, lurched sideways and fell, first on his side; then he rolled over on his back and, amazingly, kicked his legs for a few seconds in the air. At this Henry laughed, as if Mack had done a trick for him. Laird, who had drawn a long, groaning breath of surprise when the shot was fired, said out loud, "He's not dead." And it seemed to me it might be true. But his legs stopped, he rolled on his side again, his muscles quivered and sank. The two men walked over and looked at him in a businesslike way; they bent down and examined his forehead where the bullet had gone in, and now I saw his blood on the brown grass.

"Now they just skin him and cut him up," I said. "Let's go." My legs were a little shaky and I jumped gratefully down into the hay. "Now you've seen how they shoot a horse," I said in a congratulatory way, as if I had seen it many times before. "Let's see if any barn cat's had kittens in the hay." Laird jumped. He seemed young and obedient again. Suddenly I remembered how, when he was little, I had brought him into the barn and told him to climb the ladder to the top beam. That was in the spring, too, when the hay was low. I had done it out of a need for excitement, a desire for something to happen so that I could tell about it. He was wearing a little bulky brown and white checked coat, made down from one of mine. He went all the way up, just as I told him, and sat down on the top beam with the hay far below him on one side, and the barn floor and some old machinery on the other. Then I ran screaming to my father, "Laird's up on the top beam!" My father came, my mother came, my father went up the ladder talking very quietly and brought Laird down under his arm, at which my mother leaned against the ladder and began to cry. They said to me, "Why weren't you watching him?" but nobody ever knew the truth. Laird did not know enough to tell. But whenever I saw the brown and white checked hat hanging in the closet, or at the bottom of the rag bag, which was where it ended up, I felt a weight in my stomach, the sadness of unexorcized guilt.

I looked at Laird, who did not even remember this, and I did not like the look of this thin, winter-pale face. His expression was not frightened or upset, but remote, concentrating. "Listen," I said, in an unusually bright and friendly voice, "you aren't going to tell, are you?"

"No," he said absently.

"Promise."

"Promise," he said. I grabbed the hand behind his back to make sure he was not crossing his fingers. Even so, he might have a nightmare; it might come out that way. I decided I had better work hard to get all thoughts of what he had seen out of his mind — which, it seemed to me, could not hold very many things at a time. I got some money I had saved and that afternoon we went into Jubilee and saw a show with Judy Canova, at which we both laughed a great deal. After that I thought it would be all right.

Two weeks later I knew they were going to shoot Flora. I knew from the night before, when I heard my mother ask if the hay was holding out all right, and my father said, "Well, after to-morrow there'll just be the cow, and we should be able to put her out to grass in another week." So I knew it was Flora's turn in the morning.

This time I didn't think of watching it. That was something to see just one time. I had not thought about it very often since, but sometimes when I was busy, working at school, or standing in front of the mirror combing my hair and wondering if I would be pretty when I grew up, the whole scene would flash into my mind: I would see the easy, practised way my father raised the gun, and hear Henry laughing when Mack kicked his legs in the air. I did not have any great feeling of horror and opposition, such as a city child might have had; I was too used to seeing the death of animals as a necessity by which we lived. Yet I felt a little ashamed, and there was a new wariness, a sense of holding-off, in my attitude to my father and his work.

It was a fine day, and we were going around the yard picking up tree branches that had been torn off in winter storms. This was something we had been told to do, and also we wanted to use them to make a teepee. We heard Flora whinny, and then my father's voice and Henry's shouting, and we ran down to the barnyard to see what was going on.

The stable door was open. Henry had just brought Flora out, and she had broken away from him. She was running free in the barnyard, from one end to the other. We climbed up on the fence. It was exciting to see her running, whinnying, going up on her hind legs, prancing and threatening like a horse in a Western movie, an unbroken ranch horse, though she was just an old driver, an old sorrel mare. My father and Henry ran after her and tried to grab the dangling halter. They tried to work her into a corner, and they had almost succeeded when she made a run between them, wild-eyed, and disappeared around the corner of the barn. We heard the rails clatter down as she got over the fence, and Henry yelled, "She's into the field now!"

That meant she was in the long L-shaped field that ran up by the house. If she got around the center, heading towards the lane, the gate was open; the truck had been driven into the field this morning. My father shouted to me, because I was on the other side of the fence, nearest the lane, "Go shut the gate!"

I could run very fast. I ran across the garden, past the tree where our swing was hung, and jumped across a ditch into the lane. There was the open gate. She had not got out, I could not see her up on the road; she must have run to the other end of the field. The gate was heavy. I lifted it out of the gravel and carried it across the roadway. I had it half-way across when she came in sight, galloping straight towards me. There was just time to get the chain on. Laird came scrambling through the ditch to help me.

Instead of shutting the gate, I opened it as wide as I could. I did not make any decision to do this, it was just what I did. Flora never slowed down; she galloped straight past me, and Laird jumped up and down, yelling, "Shut it, shut it!" even after it was too late. My father and Henry appeared in the field a moment too late to see what I had done. They only saw Flora heading for the township road. They would think I had not got there in time.

They did not waste any time asking about it. They went back to the barn and got the gun and the knives they used, and put these in the truck; then they turned the truck around and came bouncing up the field toward us. Laird called to them, "Let me go too, let me go too!" and Henry stopped the truck and they took him in. I shut the gate after they were all gone.

I supposed Laird would tell. I wondered what would happen to me. I had never disobeyed my father before, and I could not understand why I had done it. Flora would not really get away. They would catch up with her in the truck. Or if they did not catch her this morning somebody would see her and telephone us this afternoon or tomorrow. There was no wild country here for her to run to, only farms. What was more, my father had paid for her, we needed the meat to feed the foxes, we needed the foxes to make our living. All I had done was make more work for my father who worked hard enough already. And when my father found out about it he was not going to trust me any more; he would know that I was not entirely on his side. I was on Flora's side, and that made me no use to anybody, not even to her. Just the same, I did not regret it; when she came running at me and I held the gate open, that was the only thing I could do.

I went back to the house, and my mother said, "What's all the commotion?"

I told her that Flora had kicked down the fence and got away. "Your poor father," she said, "now he'll have to go chasing over the countryside. Well, there isn't any use planning dinner before one." She put up the ironing board. I wanted to tell her, but thought better of it and went upstairs and sat on my bed.

Lately I had been trying to make my part of the room fancy, spreading the bed with old lace curtains, and fixing myself a dressing-table with some leftovers of cretonne for a skirt. I planned to put up some kind of barricade between my bed and Laird's, to keep my section separate from his. In the sunlight, the lace curtains were just dusty rags. We did not sing at night any more. One night when I was singing Laird said, "You sound silly," and I went right on but the next night I did not start. There was not so much need to anyway, we were no longer afraid. We knew it was just old furniture over there, old jumble and confusion. We did not keep to the rules. I still stayed awake after Laird was asleep and told myself stories, but even in these stories something different was happening, mysterious alterations took place. A story might start off in the old way, with a spectacular danger, a fire or wild animals, and for a while I might rescue people; then things would change around, and instead, somebody would be rescuing me. It might be a boy from our class at school, or even Mr. Campbell, our teacher, who tickled girls under the arms. And at this point the story concerned itself at great length with what I looked like — like how long my hair was, and what kind of dress I had on; by the time I had these details worked out the real excitement of the story was lost.

It was later than one o'clock when the truck came back. The tarpaulin was over the back, which meant there was meat in it. My mother had to heat dinner up all over again. Henry and my father had changed from their bloody overalls into ordinary working overalls in the barn, and they washed their arms and necks and faces at the sink, and splashed water on their hair and combed it. Laird lifted his arm to show off a streak of blood. "We shot old Flora," he said, "and cut her up in fifty pieces."

"Well I don't want to hear about it," my mother said. "And don't come to my table like that."

My father made him go and wash the blood off.

We sat down and my father said grace and Henry pasted his chewing-gum on the end of his fork, the way he always did; when he took it off he would have us admire the pattern. We began to pass the bowls of steaming, overcooked vegetables. Laird looked across the table at me and said proudly, distinctly, "Anyway it was her fault Flora got away."

"What?" my father said.

"She could of shut the gate and she didn't. She just open' it up and Flora run out."

"Is that right?" my father said.

Everybody at the table was looking at me. I nodded, swallowing food with great difficulty. To my shame, tears flooded my eyes.

My father made a curt sound of disgust. "What did you do that for?"

I did not answer. I put down my fork and waited to be sent from the table, still not looking up.

But this did not happen. For some time nobody said anything, then Laird said matter-of-factly, "She's crying."

"Never mind," my father said. He spoke with resignation, even good humour, the words which absolved and dismissed me for good. "She's only a girl," he said.

I didn't protest that, even in my heart. Maybe it was true.

ഇറ

Alice Munro, like Mavis Gallant, has brought international celebrity to the Canadian short story. "Boys and Girls" appeared in her first published collection, Dance of the Happy Shades, *which won a Governor General's Award in 1968. The unnamed female narrator experiences the interconnectedness of reality and fiction, and the importance of becoming the teller of one's own story. She starts by giving us facts: her father, we learn immediately, is a fox farmer. But another type of story, more like a romance, keeps breaking in. We see this other story in frames: the calendar pictures with their "heroic" portraits of northern explorers; the fantasies the narrator, as a child, spins about herself; and of course the illusion that she is her father's hired man. But it turns out she is "only a girl," sentenced to a life in the shadows: her father names her and cancels her out. The turning point in the story comes when she sets the horse free, a futile gesture. It is what she does not do that is significant. Munro is writing a type of* künstlerroman, *an account of the artist's growth. With subtlety, the narrator tells us about why she is writing, where the story is coming from, over and above the strict record of events. Her father does not, we find, have the last word. She can revise the past, retell her life from her own point of view.*

A.S.

Tim O'Brien (b. 1946)

The Things They Carried

First Lieutenant Jimmy Cross carried letters from a girl named Martha, a junior at Mount Sebastian College in New Jersey. They were not love letters, but Lieutenant Cross was hoping, so he kept them folded in plastic at the bottom of his rucksack. In the late afternoon, after a day's march, he would dig his foxhole, wash his hands under a canteen, unwrap the letters, hold them with the tips of his fingers, and spend the last hour of light pretending. He would imagine romantic camping trips into the White Mountains in New Hampshire. He would sometimes taste the envelope flaps, knowing her tongue had been there. More than anything, he wanted Martha to love him as he loved her, but the letters were mostly chatty, elusive on the matter of love. She was a virgin, he was almost sure. She was an English major at Mount Sebastian, and she wrote beautifully about her professors and roommates and mid-term exams, about her respect for Chaucer and her great affection for Virginia Woolf. She often quoted lines of poetry; she never mentioned the war, except to say, Jimmy, take care of yourself. The letters weighed 10 ounces. They were signed Love, Martha, but Lieutenant Cross understood that Love was only a way of signing and did not mean what he sometimes pretended it meant. At dusk, he would carefully return the letters to his rucksack. Slowly, a bit distracted, he would get up and move among his men, checking the perimeter, then at full dark he would return to his hole and watch the night and wonder if Martha was a virgin.

CR

The things they carried were largely determined by necessity. Among the necessities or near-necessities were P-38 can openers, pocket knives, heat tabs, wristwatches, dog tags, mosquito repellent, chewing gum, candy, cigarettes, salt tablets, packets of Kool-Aid, lighters, matches, sewing kits, Military Payment Certificates, C rations, and two or three canteens of water. Together, these items weighed between 15 and 20 pounds, depending upon a man's habits or rate of metabolism. Henry Dobbins, who was a big man, carried extra rations; he was especially fond of canned peaches in heavy syrup over pound cake. Dave Jensen, who practised field hygiene, carried a toothbrush, dental floss, and several hotel-sized bars of soap he'd stolen on R&R in Sydney, Australia. Ted Lavender, who was scared, carried tranquilizers until he was shot in the head outside the village of Than Khe in mid-April. By necessity, and because it was SOP, they all carried steel helmets that weighed 5 pounds including the liner and camouflage cover. They carried the standard fatigue jackets and trousers. Very few carried underwear. On their feet they carried jungle boots — 2.1 pounds — and Dave Jensen carried three pairs of socks and a can of Dr Scholl's foot powder as a precaution against trench foot. Until he was shot, Ted Lavender carried six or seven ounces of premium dope, which for him was a necessity. Mitchell Sanders, the RTO, carried condoms. Norman Bowker carried a diary. Rat Kiley carried comic books. Kiowa, a devout Baptist, carried an illustrated New Testament that had been presented to him by his father, who taught school in Oklahoma City, Oklahoma. As a hedge against bad times however, Kiowa also carried his grandmother's distrust of the white man, his grandfather's old hunting hatchet. Necessity dictated. Because the land was mined and booby-trapped, it was SOP for each man to carry a steel-centered, nylon-covered flak jacket, which weighed 6.7 pounds, but which on hot days seemed much heavier. Because you could die so quickly, each man carried at least one large compress bandage, usually in the helmet band for easy access. Because the nights were cold, and because the monsoons were wet, each carried a green plastic poncho that could be used as a raincoat or groundsheet or makeshift tent. With its quilted liner, the poncho weighed almost two pounds, but it was worth every ounce. In April, for instance, when Ted Lavender was shot, they used his poncho to wrap him up, then to carry him across the paddy, then to lift him into the chopper that took him away.

∞

They were called legs or grunts.

To carry something was to hump it, as when Lieutenant Jimmy Cross humped his love for Martha up the hills and through the swamps. In its intransitive form, to hump meant to walk, or to march, but it implied burdens far beyond the intransitive.

Almost everyone humped photographs. In his wallet, Lieutenant Cross carried two photographs of Martha. The first was a Kodacolor snapshot signed Love, though he knew better. She stood against a brick wall. Her eyes were grey and neutral, her lips slightly open as she stared straight-on at the camera. At night, sometimes, Lieutenant Cross wondered who had taken the picture, because he knew she had boyfriends, because he loved her so much, and because he could see the shadow of the picture-taker spreading out against the brick wall. The second photograph had been clipped from the 1968 Mount Sebastian yearbook. It was an action shot — women's volleyball — and Martha was bent horizontal to the floor, reaching, the palms of her hands in sharp focus, the tongue taut, the expression frank and competitive. There was no visible sweat. She wore white gym shorts. Her legs, he thought, were almost certainly the legs of a virgin, dry and without hair, the left knee cocked and carrying her entire weight, which was just over one hundred pounds. Lieutenant Cross remembered touching that left knee. A dark theater, he remembered, and the movie was *Bonnie and Clyde*, and Martha wore a tweed skirt, and during the final scene, when he touched her knee, she turned and looked at him in a sad, sober way that made him pull his hand back, but he would always remember the feel of the tweed skirt and the knee beneath it and the sound of the gunfire that killed Bonnie and Clyde, how embarrassing it was, how slow and oppressive. He remembered kissing her good night at the dorm door. Right then, he thought, he should've done something brave. He should've carried her up the stairs to her room and tied her to the bed and touched that left knee all night long. He should've risked it. Whenever he looked at the photographs, he thought of new things he should've done.

CR

What they carried was partly a function of rank, partly of field specialty.

As a first lieutenant and platoon leader, Jimmy Cross carried a compass, maps, code books, binoculars, and a .45-caliber pistol that weighed 2.9 pounds fully loaded. He carried a strobe light and the responsibility for the lives of his men.

As an RTO, Mitchell Sanders carried the PRC-25 radio, a killer, 26 pounds with its battery.

As a medic, Rat Kiley carried a canvas satchel filled with morphine and plasma and malaria tablets and surgical tape and comic books and all the things a medic must carry, including M&Ms for especially bad wounds, for a total weight of nearly 20 pounds.

As a big man, therefore a machine gunner, Henry Dobbins carried the M-60, which weighed 23 pounds unloaded, but which was almost always loaded. In addition, Dobbins carried between 10 and 15 pounds of ammunition draped in belts across his chest and shoulders.

As PFCs or Spec 4s, most of them were common grunts and carried the standard M-16 gas-operated assault rifle. The weapon weighed 7.5 pounds unloaded, 8.2 pounds with its full 20-round magazine. Depending on numerous factors, such as topography and psychology, the riflemen carried anywhere from 12 to 20 magazines, usually in cloth bandoliers, adding on another 8.4 pounds at minimum, 14 pounds at maximum. When it was available, they also carried M-16 maintenance gear — rods and steel brushes and swabs and tubes of LSA oil — all of which weighed about a pound. Among the grunts, some carried the M-79 grenade launcher, 5.9 pounds unloaded, a reasonably light weapon except for the ammunition, which was heavy. A single round weighed 10 ounces. The typical load was 25 rounds. But Ted Lavender, who was scared, carried 34 rounds when he was shot and killed outside Than Khe, and he went down under an exceptional burden, more than 20 pounds of ammunition, plus the flak jacket and helmet and rations and water and toilet paper and tranquilizers and all the rest, plus the unweighed fear. He was dead weight. There was no twitching or flopping. Kiowa, who saw it happen, said it was like watching a rock fall, or a big sandbag or something — just boom, then down — not like the movies where the dead guy rolls around and does fancy spins and goes ass over teakettle — not like that, Kiowa said, the poor bastard just flat-fuck fell. Boom. Down. Nothing else. It was a bright morning in mid-April. Lieutenant Cross felt the pain. He blamed himself. They stripped off Lavender's canteens and ammo, all the heavy things, and Rat Kiley said the obvious, the guy's dead, and Mitchell Sanders used his radio to report one US KIA and to request a chopper. Then they wrapped Lavender in his poncho. They carried him out to a dry paddy, established security, and sat smoking the dead man's dope until the chopper came. Lieutenant Cross kept to himself. He pictured Martha's smooth young face, thinking he loved her more than anything, more than his men, and now Ted Lavender was dead because he loved her so much and could not stop thinking about her. When the dustoff arrived, they carried

Lavender aboard. Afterward they burned Than Khe. They marched until dusk, then dug their holes, and that night Kiowa kept explaining how you had to be there, how fast it was, how the poor guy just dropped like so much concrete. Boom-down, he said. Like cement.

૨

In addition to the three standard weapons — the M-60, M-16, and M-79 — they carried whatever presented itself, or whatever seemed appropriate as a means of killing or staying alive. They carried catch-as-catch-can. At various times, in various situations, they carried M-14s and CAR-15s and Swedish Ks and grease guns and captured AK-47s and Chi-Coms and RPGs and Simonov carbines and black market Uzis and .38 caliber Smith & Wesson handguns and 66 mm LAWs and shotguns and silencers and blackjacks and bayonets and C-4 plastic explosives. Lee Strunk carried a slingshot; a weapon of last resort, he called it. Mitchell Sanders carried brass knuckles. Kiowa carried his grandfather's feathered hatchet. Every third or fourth man carried a Claymore antipersonnel mine — 3.5 pounds with its firing device. They all carried fragmentation grenades — 14 ounces each. They all carried at least one M-18 coloured smoke grenade — 24 ounces. Some carried CS or tear gas grenades. Some carried white phosphorus grenades. They carried all they could bear, and then some, including a silent awe for the terrible power of the things they carried.

૨

In the first week of April, before Lavender died, Lieutenant Jimmy Cross received a good-luck charm from Martha. It was a simple pebble, an ounce at most. Smooth to the touch, it was a milky white colour with flecks of orange and violet, oval-shaped, like a miniature egg. In the accompanying letter, Martha wrote that she had found the pebble on the Jersey shoreline, precisely where the land touched water at high tide, where things came together but also separated. It was this separate-but-together quality, she wrote, that had inspired her to pick up the pebble and to carry it in her breast pocket for several days, where it seemed weightless, and then to send it through the mail, by air, as a token of her truest feelings for him. Lieutenant Cross found this romantic. But he wondered what her truest feelings were, exactly, and what she meant by separate-but-together. He wondered how the tides and waves had come into play on that afternoon along the Jersey shoreline when Martha saw the pebble and bent down to rescue it from geology. He imagined bare feet. Martha was a poet, with the poet's sensibilities, and her feet would be brown and bare, the toenails unpainted, the eyes chilly and somber like the ocean in March, and though it was painful, he wondered who had been with her that afternoon. He imagined a pair of shadows moving along the strip of sand where things came together but also separated. It was phantom jealousy, he knew, but he couldn't help himself. He loved her so much. On the march, through the hot days of early April, he carried the pebble in his mouth, turning it with his tongue, tasting sea salt and moisture. His mind wandered. He had difficulty keeping his attention on the war. On occasion he would yell at his men to spread out the column, to keep their eyes open, but then he would slip away into daydreams, just pretending, walking barefoot along the Jersey shore, with Martha, carrying nothing. He would feel himself rising. Sun and waves and gentle winds, all love and lightness.

∾

What they carried varied by mission.

When a mission took them to the mountains, they carried mosquito netting, machetes, canvas tarps, and extra bug juice.

If a mission seemed especially hazardous, or if it involved a place they knew to be bad, they carried everything they could. In certain heavily mined AOs, where the land was dense with Toe Poppers and Bouncing Betties, they took turns humping a 28-pound mine detector. With its headphones and big sensing plate, the equipment was a stress on the lower back and shoulders, awkward to handle, often useless because of the shrapnel in the earth, but they carried it anyway, partly for safety, partly for the illusion of safety.

On ambush, or other night missions, they carried peculiar little odds and ends. Kiowa always took along his New Testament and a pair of moccasins for silence. Dave Jensen carried night-sight vitamins high in carotene. Lee Strunk carried his slingshot; ammo, he claimed, would never be a problem. Rat Kiley carried brandy and M&Ms candy. Until he was shot, Ted Lavender carried the starlight scope, which weighed 6.3 pounds with its aluminum carrying case. Henry Dobbins carried his girlfriend's pantyhose wrapped around his neck as a comforter. They all carried ghosts. When dark came, they would move out single file across the meadows and paddies to their ambush coordinates, where they would quietly set up the Claymores and lie down and spend the night waiting.

Other missions were more complicated and required special equipment. In mid-April, it was their mission to search out and destroy the elaborate tunnel complexes in the Than Khe area south of Chu Lai. To blow the tunnels, they carried one-pound blocks of pentrite high explosives, four blocks to a man, 68 pounds in all. They carried wiring, detonators, and battery-powered clackers. Dave Jensen carried earplugs. Most often, before blowing the tunnels, they were ordered by higher command to search them, which was considered bad news, but by and large they just shrugged and carried out orders. Because he was a big man, Henry Dobbins was excused from tunnel duty. The others would draw numbers. Before Lavender died there were 17 men in the platoon, and whoever drew the number 17 would strip off his gear and crawl in headfirst with a flashlight and Lieutenant Cross's .45-caliber pistol. The rest of them would fan out as security. They would sit down or kneel, not facing the hole, listening to the ground beneath them, imagining cobwebs and ghosts, whatever was down there — the tunnel walls squeezing in — how the flashlight seemed impossibly heavy in the hand and how it was tunnel vision in the very strictest sense, compression in all ways, even time, and how you had to wiggle in — ass and elbows — a swallowed-up feeling — and how you found yourself worrying about odd things: Will your flashlight go dead? Do rats carry rabies? If you screamed, how far would the sound carry? Would your buddies hear it? Would they have the courage to drag you out? In some respects, though not many, the waiting was worse than the tunnel itself. Imagination was a killer.

On April 16, when Lee Strunk drew the number 17, he laughed and muttered something and went down quickly. The morning was hot and very still. Not good, Kiowa said. He looked at the tunnel opening, then out across a dry paddy toward the village of Than Khe. Nothing moved. No clouds or birds or people. As they waited, the men smoked and drank Kool-Aid, not talking much, feeling sympathy for Lee Strunk but also feeling the luck of the draw. You win some, you lose some, said Mitchell Sanders, and sometimes you settle for a rain check. It was a tired line and no one laughed.

Henry Dobbins ate a tropical chocolate bar. Ted Lavender popped a tranquilizer and went off to pee.

After five minutes, Lieutenant Jimmy Cross moved to the tunnel, leaned down, and examined the darkness. Trouble, he thought — a cave-in maybe. And then suddenly, without willing it, he was thinking about Martha. The stresses and fractures, the quick collapse, the two of them buried alive under all that weight. Dense, crushing love. Kneeling, watching the hole, he tried to concentrate on Lee Strunk and the war, all the dangers, but his love was too much for him, he felt paralyzed, he wanted to sleep inside her lungs and breathe her blood and be smothered. He wanted her to be a virgin and not a virgin, all at once. He wanted to know her. Intimate secrets: Why poetry? Why so sad? Why that greyness in her eyes? Why so alone? Not lonely, just alone — riding her bike across campus or sitting off by herself in the cafeteria — even dancing, she danced alone — and it was the aloneness that filled him with love. He remembered telling her that one evening. How she nodded and looked away. And how, later, when he kissed her, she received the kiss without returning it, her eyes wide open, not afraid, not a virgin's eyes, just flat and uninvolved.

Lieutenant Cross gazed at the tunnel. But he was not there. He was buried with Martha under the white sand at the Jersey shore. They were pressed together, and the pebble in his mouth was her tongue. He was smiling. Vaguely, he was aware of how quiet the day was, the sullen paddies, yet he could not bring himself to worry about matters of security. He was beyond that. He was just a kid at war, in love. He was twenty-four years old. He couldn't help it.

A few moments later Lee Strunk crawled out of the tunnel. He came up grinning, filthy but alive. Lieutenant Cross nodded and closed his eyes while the others clapped Strunk on the back and made jokes about rising from the dead.

Worms, Rat Kiley said. Right out of the grave. Fuckin' zombie.

The men laughed. They all felt great relief.

Spook city, said Mitchell Sanders.

Lee Strunk made a funny ghost sound, a kind of moaning, yet very happy, and right then, when Strunk made that high happy moaning sound, when he went *Ahhooooo*, right then Ted Lavender was shot in the head on his way back from peeing. He lay with his mouth open. The teeth were broken. There was a swollen black bruise under his left eye. The cheekbone was gone. Oh shit, Rat Kiley said, the guy's dead. The guy's dead, he kept saying, which seemed profound — the guy's dead. I mean really.

CR

The things they carried were determined to some extent by superstition. Lieutenant Cross carried his good-luck pebble. Dave Jensen carried a rabbit's foot. Norman Bowker, otherwise a very gentle person, carried a thumb that had been presented to him as a gift by Mitchell Sanders. The thumb was dark brown, rubbery to the touch, and weighed four ounces at most. It had been cut from a VC corpse, a boy of fifteen or sixteen. They'd found him at the bottom of an irrigation ditch, badly burned, flies in his mouth and eyes. The boy wore black shorts and sandals. At the time of his death he had been carrying a pouch of rice, a rifle, and three magazines of ammunition.

You want my opinion, Mitchell Sanders said, there's a definite moral here.

He put his hand on the dead boy's wrist. He was quiet for a time, as if counting a pulse, then he patted the stomach, almost affectionately, and used Kiowa's hunting hatchet to remove the thumb.

Henry Dobbins asked what the moral was.

Moral?

You know. *Moral.*

Sanders wrapped the thumb in toilet paper and handed it across to Norman Bowker. There was no blood. Smiling, he kicked the boy's head, watched the flies scatter, and said, It's like with that old TV show — Paladin. Have gun, will travel.

Henry Dobbins thought about it.

Yeah, well, he finally said. I don't see no moral.

There it *is*, man.

Fuck off.

CR

They carried USO stationery and pencils and pens. They carried Sterno, safety pins, trip flares, signal flares, spools of wire, razor blades, chewing tobacco, liberated joss sticks and statuettes of the smiling Buddha, candles, grease pencils, *The Stars and Stripes*, fingernail clippers, Psy Ops leaflets, bush hats, bolos, and much more. Twice a week, when the resupply choppers came in, they carried hot chow in green mermite cans and large canvas bags filled with iced beer and soda pop. They carried plastic water containers, each with a two-gallon capacity. Mitchell Sanders carried a set of starched tiger fatigues for special occasions. Henry Dobbins carried Black Flag insecticide. Dave Jensen carried empty sandbags that could be filled at night for added protection. Lee Strunk carried tanning lotion. Some things they carried in common. Taking turns, they carried the big PRC-77 scrambler radio, which weighed 30 pounds with its battery. They shared the weight of memory. They took up what others could no longer bear. Often, they carried each other, the wounded or weak. They carried infections. They carried chess sets, basketballs, Vietnamese-English dictionaries, insignias of rank, Bronze Stars and Purple Hearts, plastic cards imprinted with the Code of Conduct. They carried diseases, among them malaria and dysentery. They carried lice and ringworm and leeches and paddy algae and various rots and molds. They carried the land itself — Vietnam, the place, the soil — a powdery orange-red dust that covered their boots and fatigues and faces. They carried the sky. The whole atmosphere, they carried it, the humidity, the monsoons, the stink of fungus and decay, all of it, they carried gravity. They moved like mules. By daylight they took sniper fire, at night they were mortared, but it was not battle, it was just the endless march, village to village, without purpose, nothing won or lost. They marched for the sake of the march. They plodded along slowly, dumbly, leaning forward against the heat, unthinking, all blood and bone, simple grunts, soldiering with their legs, toiling up the hills and down into the paddies and across the rivers and up again and down, just humping, one step and then the next and then another, but no volition, no will, because it was automatic, it was anatomy, and the war was entirely a matter of posture and carriage, the hump was everything, a kind of inertia, a kind of emptiness, a dullness of desire and intellect and conscience and hope and human sensibility. Their principles were in their feet. Their calculations were biological. They had no sense of strategy or mission. They searched the villages without knowing what to look for, not caring, kicking over jars of rice, frisking children and old men, blowing tunnels, sometimes setting fires and sometimes not, then forming up and moving on to the next village, then other villages, where it would always be the same. They carried their own lives. The pressures were enormous. In the heat of early afternoon, they would remove their helmets and flak jackets, walking bare, which was dangerous but which helped ease the strain. They would often discard things along the route of march. Purely for comfort, they would throw away rations, blow their Claymores and grenades, no matter, because by nightfall the resupply choppers would arrive with more of the same, then a day or two later still more, fresh watermelons and crates of ammunition and sunglasses and woolen sweaters — the resources were stunning — sparklers for the Fourth of July, coloured eggs for Easter — it was the great American war chest — the fruits of science, the smokestacks, the canneries, the arsenals at Hartford, the Minnesota forests, the machine shops, the vast fields of corn and wheat — they carried like freight trains; they carried it on their backs and shoulders — and for all the ambiguities of Vietnam, all the mysteries and unknowns, there was at least the single abiding certainty that they would never be at a loss for things to carry.

◌

After the chopper took Lavender away, Lieutenant Jimmy Cross led his men into the village of Than Khe. They burned everything. They shot chickens and dogs, they trashed the village well, they called in artillery and watched the wreckage, then they marched for several hours through the hot afternoon, and then at dusk, while Kiowa explained how Lavender died, Lieutenant Cross found himself trembling.

He tried not to cry. With his entrenching tool, which weighed five pounds, he began digging a hole in the earth.

He felt shame. He hated himself. He had loved Martha more than his men, and as a consequence Lavender was now dead, and this was something he would have to carry like a stone in his stomach for the rest of the war.

All he could do was dig. He used his entrenching tool like an ax, slashing, feeling both love and hate, and then later, when it was full dark, he sat at the bottom of his foxhole and wept. It went on for a long while. In part, he was grieving for Ted Lavender, but mostly it was for Martha, and for himself, because she belonged to another world, which was not quite real, and because she was a junior at Mount Sebastian College in New Jersey, a poet and a virgin and uninvolved, and because he realized she did not love him and never would.

Cη

Like cement, Kiowa whispered in the dark. I swear to God — boom, down. Not a word.

I've heard this, said Norman Bowker.

A pisser, you know? Still zipping himself up. Zapped while zipping.

All right, fine. That's enough.

Yeah, but you had to see it, the guy just —

I *heard*, man. Cement. So why not shut the fuck *up*?

Kiowa shook his head sadly and glanced over at the hole where Lieutenant Jimmy Cross sat watching the night. The air was thick and wet. A warm dense fog had settled over the paddies and there was the stillness that precedes rain.

After a time Kiowa sighed.

One thing for sure, he said. The lieutenant's in some deep hurt. I mean that crying jag — the way he was carrying on — it wasn't fake or anything, it was real heavy-duty hurt. The man cares.

Sure, Norman Bowker said.

Say what you want, the man does care.

We all got problems.

Not Lavender.

No, I guess not, Bowker said. Do me a favour, though.

Shut up?

That's a smart Indian. Shut up.

Shrugging, Kiowa pulled off his boots. He wanted to say more, just to lighten up his sleep, but instead he opened his New Testament and arranged it beneath his head as a pillow. The fog made things seem hollow and unattached. He tried not to think about Ted Lavender, but then he was thinking how fast it was, no drama, down and dead and how it was hard to feel anything except surprise. It seemed unchristian. He wished he could find some great sadness, or even anger, but the emotion wasn't there and he couldn't make it happen. Mostly he felt pleased to be alive. He liked the smell of the New Testament under his cheek, the leather and ink and paper and glue, whatever the chemicals were. He liked hearing the sounds of night. Even his fatigue, it felt fine, the stiff muscles and the prickly awareness of his own body, a floating feeling. He enjoyed not being dead. Lying there, Kiowa admired Lieutenant Jimmy Cross's capacity for grief. He wanted to share the man's pain, he wanted to care as Jimmy Cross cared. And yet when he closed his eyes all he could think was Boom-down, and all he could feel was the pleasure of having his boots off and the fog curling in around him and the damp soil and the Bible smells and the plush comfort of night.

After a moment Norman Bowker sat up in the dark.

What the hell, he said. You want to talk, *talk*. Tell it to me.

Forget it.

No, man, go on. One thing I hate, it's a silent Indian.

ᘓ

For the most part they carried themselves with poise, a kind of dignity. Now and then, however, there were times of panic, when they squealed or wanted to squeal but couldn't, when they twitched and made moaning sounds and covered their heads and said Dear Jesus and flopped around on the earth and fired their weapons blindly and cringed and sobbed and begged for the noise to stop and went wild and made stupid promises to themselves and to God and to their mothers and fathers, hoping not to die. In different ways, it happened to all of them. Afterward, when the firing ended, they would blink and peek up. They would touch their bodies, feeling shame, then quickly hiding it. They would force themselves to stand. As if in slow motion, frame by frame, the world would take on the old logic — absolute silence, then the wind, then sunlight, then voices. It was the burden of being alive. Awkwardly, the men would reassemble themselves, first in private, then in groups, becoming soldiers again. They would repair the leaks in their eyes. They would check for casualties, call in dustoffs, light cigarettes, try to smile, clear their throats and spit and begin cleaning their weapons. After a time someone would shake his head and say, No lie, I almost shit my pants, and someone else would laugh, which meant it was bad, yes, but the guy had obviously not shit his pants, it wasn't that bad, and in any case nobody would ever do such a thing and then go ahead and talk about it. They would squint into the dense, oppressive sunlight. For a few moments, perhaps, they would fall silent, lighting a joint and tracking its passage from man to man, inhaling, holding in the humiliation. Scary stuff, one of them might say. But then someone else would grin or flick his eyebrows and say, Roger-dodger, almost cut me a new asshole, *almost*.

There were numerous such poses. Some carried themselves with a sort of wistful resignation, others with pride or stiff soldierly discipline or good humour or macho zeal. They were afraid of dying but they were even more afraid to show it.

They found jokes to tell.

They used a hard vocabulary to contain the terrible softness. *Greased* they'd say. *Offed, lit up, zapped while zipping*. It wasn't cruelty, just stage presence. They were actors. When someone died, it wasn't quite dying, because in a curious way it seemed scripted, and because they had their lines mostly memorized, irony mixed with tragedy, and because they called it by other names, as if to encyst and destroy the reality of death itself. They kicked corpses. They cut off thumbs. They talked grunt lingo. They told stories about Ted Lavender's supply of tranquilizers, how the poor guy didn't feel a thing, how incredibly tranquil he was.

There's a moral here, said Mitchell Sanders.

They were waiting for Lavender's chopper, smoking the dead man's dope. The moral's pretty obvious, Sanders said, and winked. Stay away from drugs. No joke, they'll ruin your day every time.

Cute, said Henry Dobbins.

Mind blower, get it? Talk about wiggy. Nothing left, just blood and brains.

They made themselves laugh.

There it is, they'd say. Over and over — there it is, my friend, there it is — as if the repetition itself were an act of poise, a balance between crazy and almost crazy, knowing without going, there it is, which meant be cool, let it ride, because Oh yeah, man, you can't change what can't be changed, there it is, there it absolutely and positively and fucking well *is*.

They were tough.

They carried all the emotional baggage of men who might die. Grief, terror, love, longing — these were intangibles, but the intangibles had their own mass and specific gravity, they had tangible weight. They carried shameful memories. They carried the common secret of cowardice barely restrained, the instinct to run or freeze or hide, and in many respects this was the heaviest burden of all, for it could never be put down, it required perfect balance and perfect posture. They carried their reputations. They carried the soldier's greatest fear, which was the fear of blushing. Men killed, and died, because they were embarrassed not to. It was what had brought them to the war in the first place, nothing positive, no dreams of glory or honour, just to avoid the blush of dishonour. They died so as not to die of embarrassment. They crawled into tunnels and walked point and advanced under fire. Each morning, despite the unknowns, they made their legs move. They endured. They kept humping. They did not submit to the obvious alternative, which was simply to close the eyes and fall. So easy, really. Go limp and tumble to the ground and let the muscles unwind and not speak and not budge until your buddies picked you up and lifted you into the chopper that would roar and dip its nose and carry you off to the world. A mere matter of falling, yet no one ever fell. It was not courage, exactly; the object was not valour. Rather, they were too frightened to be cowards.

By and large they carried these things inside, maintaining the masks of composure. They sneered at sick call. They spoke bitterly about guys who had found release by shooting off their own toes or fingers. Pussies, they'd say. Candy-asses. It was fierce, mocking talk, with only a trace of envy or awe, but even so the image played itself out behind their eyes.

They imagined the muzzle against flesh. So easy: squeeze the trigger and blow away a toe. They imagined it. They imagined the quick, sweet pain, then the evacuation to Japan, then a hospital with warm beds and cute geisha nurses.

And they dreamed of freedom birds.

At night, on guard, staring into the dark, they were carried away by jumbo jets. They felt the rush of takeoff. *Gone!* they yelled. And then velocity — wings and engines — a smiling stewardess — but it was more than a plane, it was a real bird, a big sleek silver bird with feathers and talons and high screeching. They were flying. The weights fell off; there was nothing to bear. They laughed and held on tight, feeling the cold slap of wind and altitude, soaring, thinking *It's over, I'm gone!* — they were naked, they were light and free — it was all lightness, bright and fast and buoyant, light as light, a helium buzz in the brain, a giddy bubbling in the lungs as they were taken up over the clouds and the war, beyond duty, beyond gravity and mortification and global entanglements — *Sin loi!* they yelled. *I'm sorry, motherfuckers, but I'm out of it, I'm goofed, I'm on a space cruise, I'm gone!* — and it was a restful, unencumbered sensation, just riding the light waves, sailing that big silver freedom bird over the mountains and oceans, over America, over the farms and great sleeping cities and cemeteries and highways and the golden arches of McDonald's, it was flight, a kind of fleeing, a kind of falling, falling higher and higher, spinning off the edge of the earth and beyond the sun and through the vast, silent vacuum where there were no burdens and where everything weighed exactly nothing — *Gone!* they screamed, *I'm sorry but I'm gone!* — and so at night, not quite dreaming, they gave themselves over to lightness, they were carried, they were purely borne.

CR

On the morning after Ted Lavender died, First Lieutenant Jimmy Cross crouched at the bottom of his foxhole and burned Martha's letters. Then he burned the two photographs. There was a steady rain falling, which made it difficult, but he used heat tabs and Sterno to build a small fire, screening it with his body, holding the photographs over the tight blue flame with the tips of his finger.

He realized it was only a gesture. Stupid, he thought. Sentimental, too, but mostly just stupid.

Lavender was dead. You couldn't burn the blame.

Besides, the letters were in his head. And even now, without photographs, Lieutenant Cross could see Martha playing volleyball in her white gym shorts and yellow T-shirt. He could see her moving in the rain.

When the fire died out, Lieutenant Cross pulled his poncho over his shoulders and ate breakfast from a can.

There was no great mystery, he decided.

In those burned letters Martha had never mentioned the war, except to say, Jimmy, take care of yourself. She wasn't involved. She signed the letters Love, but it wasn't love, and all the fine lines and technicalities did not matter. Virginity was no longer an issue. He hated her. Yes, he did. He hated her. Love, too, but it was a hard, hating kind of love.

The morning came up wet and blurry. Everything seemed part of everything else, the fog and Martha and the deepening rain.

He was a soldier, after all.

Half smiling, Lieutenant Jimmy Cross took out his maps. He shook his head hard, as if to clear it, then bent forward and began planning the day's march. In ten minutes, or maybe twenty, he would rouse the men and they would pack up and head west, where the maps showed the country to be green and inviting. They would do what they had always done. The rain might add some weight, but otherwise it would be one more day layered upon all the other days.

He was realistic about it. There was that new hardness in his stomach. He loved her but he hated her.

No more fantasies, he told himself.

Henceforth, when he thought about Martha, it would be only to think that she belonged elsewhere. He would shut down the daydreams. This was not Mount Sebastian, it was another world, where there were no pretty poems or mid-term exams, a place where men died because of carelessness and gross stupidity. Kiowa was right. Boom-down, and you were dead, never partly dead.

Briefly, in the rain, Lieutenant Cross saw Martha's grey eyes gazing back at him.

He understood.

It was very sad, he thought. The things men carried inside. The things men did or felt they had to do.

He almost nodded at her, but didn't.

Instead he went back to his maps. He was now determined to perform his duties firmly and without negligence. It wouldn't help Lavender, he knew that, but from this point on he would comport himself as an officer. He would dispose of his good-luck pebble. Swallow it, maybe, or use Lee Strunk's slingshot, or just drop it along the trail. On the march he would impose strict field discipline. He would be careful to send out flank security, to prevent straggling or bunching up, to keep his troops moving at the proper pace and at the proper interval. He would insist on clean weapons. He would confiscate the remainder of Lavender's dope. Later in the day, perhaps, he would call the men together and speak to them plainly. He would accept the blame for what had happened to Ted Lavender. He would be a man about it. He would look them in the eyes, keeping his chin level, and he would issue the new SOPs in a calm, impersonal tone of voice, a lieutenant's voice, leaving no room for argument or discussion. Commencing immediately, he'd tell them, they would no longer abandon equipment along the route of the march. They would police up their acts. They would get their shit together, and keep it together, and maintain it neatly and in good working order.

He would not tolerate laxity. He would show strength, distancing himself.

Among the men there would be grumbling, of course, and maybe worse, because their days would seem longer and their loads heavier, but Lieutenant Jimmy Cross reminded himself that his obligation was not to be loved but to lead. He would dispense with love; it was not now a factor. And if anyone quarreled or complained, he would simply tighten his lips and arrange his shoulders in the correct command posture. He might give a curt little nod. Or he might not. He might just shrug and say, Carry on, then they would saddle up and form into a column and move out toward the villages west of Than Khe.

౪౦ౠ

One of the foremost Vietnam War writers, Tim O'Brien has published novels and short fiction that try to make sense of the Indochina conflict. "The Things They Carried" is the title story in a fictional sequence that follows an infantry platoon in the jungle and the subsequent problems encountered by the soldiers when they return home. Self-consciously placing itself within the overall genre of war fiction, in that it replies to the work of Crane,

Hemingway, and the Hollywood film, it questions whether the miseries of combat can be expressed in aesthetic form. To the soldiers who "carry" military hardware, memories, grief, and a disembodied United States on their backs, traumatic experience doesn't offer easily understood morals or epiphanies. Instead, one of the weights they carry is the absurdity of war itself. Using an omniscient narrator who often takes on the characters' perceptions, O'Brien constructs extraordinary lists in his story, a technique often associated with surrealism and postmodernism. Because part of the story's realism involves O'Brien's use of military slang, it is helpful to know the following terms: SOP (standard operating procedure), RTO (radio and telephone operator), M & Ms (medical supplies), KIA (killed in action), AO (areas of operations). The Vietnamese phrase "Sin Loi!" means "sorry about that."

M.T.

A Good Man Is Hard to Find

The grandmother didn't want to go to Florida. She wanted to visit some of her connections in east Tennessee and she was seizing at every chance to change Bailey's mind. Bailey was the son she lived with, her only boy. He was sitting on the edge of his chair at the table, bent over the orange sports section of the *Journal.* "Now look here, Bailey," she said, "see here, read this," and she stood with one hand on her thin hip and the other rattling the newspaper at his bald head. "Here this fellow that calls himself The Misfit is aloose from the Federal Pen and headed toward Florida and you read here what it says he did to these people. Just you read it. I wouldn't take my children in any direction with a criminal like that aloose in it. I couldn't answer to my conscience if I did."

Bailey didn't look up from his reading so she wheeled around then and faced the children's mother, a young woman in slacks, whose face was as broad and innocent as a cabbage and was tied around with a green head-kerchief that had two points on the top like rabbit's ears. She was sitting on the sofa, feeding the baby his apricots out of a jar. "The children have been to Florida before," the old lady said. "You ought to take them somewhere else for a change so they would see different parts of the world and be broad. They never have been to east Tennessee."

The children's mother didn't seem to hear but the eight-year-old boy, John Wesley, a stocky child with glasses, said, "If you don't want to go to Florida, why dontcha stay at home?" He and the little girl, June Star, were reading the funny papers on the floor.

"She wouldn't stay at home to be queen for a day," June Star said without raising her yellow head.

"Yes and what would you do if this fellow, The Misfit, caught you?" the grandmother asked.

"I'd smack his face," John Wesley said.

"She wouldn't stay at home for a million bucks," June Star said. "Afraid she'd miss something. She has to go everywhere we go."

"All right, Miss," the grandmother said. "Just remember that the next time you want me to curl your hair."

June Star said her hair was naturally curly.

The next morning the grandmother was the first one in the car, ready to go. She had her big black valise that looked like the head of a hippopotamus in one corner, and underneath it she was hiding a basket with Pitty Sing, the cat, in it. She didn't intend for the cat to be left alone in the house for three days because he would miss her too much and she was afraid he might brush against one of the gas burners and accidentally asphyxiate himself. Her son, Bailey, didn't like to arrive at a motel with a cat.

She sat in the middle of the back seat with John Wesley and June Star on either side of her. Bailey and the children's mother and the baby sat in front and they left Atlanta at eight forty-five with the mileage on the car at 55890. The grandmother wrote this down because she thought it would be interesting to say how many miles they had been when they got back. It took them twenty minutes to reach the outskirts of the city.

The old lady settled herself comfortably, removing her white cotton gloves and putting them up with her purse on the shelf in front of the back window. The children's mother still had on slacks and still had her head tied up in a green kerchief, but the grandmother had on a navy blue straw sailor hat with a bunch of white violets on the brim and a navy blue dress with a small white dot in the print. Her collars and cuffs were white organdy trimmed with lace and at her neckline she had pinned a purple spray of cloth violets containing a sachet. In case of an accident, anyone seeing her dead on the highway would know at once that she was a lady.

She said she thought it was going to be a good day for driving, neither too hot nor too cold, and she cautioned Bailey that the speed limit was fifty-five miles an hour and that the patrolmen hid themselves behind billboards and small clumps of trees and sped out after you before you had a chance to slow down. She pointed out interesting details of the scenery: Stone Mountain; the blue granite that in some places came up to both sides of the highway; the brilliant red clay banks slightly streaked with purple; and the various crops that made rows of green lace-work on the ground. The trees were full of silver-white sunlight and the meanest of them sparkled. The children were reading comic magazines and their mother had gone back to sleep.

"Let's go through Georgia fast so we won't have to look at it much," John Wesley said.

"If I were a little boy," said the grandmother, "I wouldn't talk about my native state that way. Tennessee has the mountains and Georgia has the hills."

"Tennessee is just a hillbilly dumping ground," John Wesley said, "and Georgia is a lousy state too."

"You said it," June Star said.

"In my time," said the grandmother, folding her thin veined fingers, "children were more respectful of their native states and their parents and everything else. People did right then. Oh look at the cute little pickaninny!" she said and pointed to a Negro child standing in the door of a shack. "Wouldn't that make a picture, now?" she asked and they all turned and looked at the little Negro out of the back window. He waved.

"He didn't have any britches on," June Star said.

"He probably didn't have any," the grandmother explained. "Little niggers in the country don't have things like we do. If I could paint, I'd paint that picture," she said.

The children exchanged comic books.

The grandmother offered to hold the baby and the children's mother passed him over the front seat to her. She set him on her knee and bounced him and told him about the things they were passing. She rolled her eyes and screwed up her mouth and stuck her leathery thin face into his smooth bland one. Occasionally he gave her a faraway smile. They passed a large cotton field with five or six graves fenced in the middle of it, like a small island. "Look at the graveyard!" the grandmother said, pointing it out. "That was the old family burying ground. That belonged to the plantation."

"Where's the plantation?" John Wesley asked.

"Gone With the Wind," said the grandmother. "Ha. Ha."

When the children finished all the comic books they had brought, they opened the lunch and ate it. The grandmother ate a peanut butter sandwich and an olive and would not let the children throw the box and the paper napkins out the window. When there was nothing else to do they played a game by choosing a cloud and making the other two guess what shape it suggested. John Wesley took one the shape of a cow and June Star guessed a cow and John Wesley said, no, an automobile, and June Star said he didn't play fair, and they began to slap each other over the grandmother.

The grandmother said she would tell them a story if they would keep quiet. When she told a story, she rolled her eyes and waved her head and was very dramatic. She said once when she was a maiden lady she had been courted by a Mr. Edgar Atkins Teagarden from Jasper, Georgia. She said he was a very good-looking man and a gentleman and that he brought her a watermelon every Saturday afternoon with his initials cut in it, E. A. T. Well, one Saturday, she said, Mr. Teagarden brought the watermelon and there was nobody at home and he left it on the front porch and returned in his buggy to Jasper, but she never got the watermelon, she said, because a nigger boy ate it when he saw the initials, E. A. T.! This story tickled John Wesley's funny bone and he giggled and giggled but June Star didn't think it was any good. She said she wouldn't marry a man that just brought her a watermelon on Saturday. The grandmother said she would have done well to marry Mr. Teagarden because he was a gentleman and had bought Coca-Cola stock when it first came out and that he had died only a few years ago, a very wealthy man.

They stopped at The Tower for barbecued sandwiches. The Tower was a part stucco and part wood filling station and dance hall set in a clearing outside of Timothy. A fat man named Red Sammy Butts ran it and there were signs stuck here and there on the building and for miles up and down the highway saying, TRY RED SAMMY'S FAMOUS BARBECUE. NONE LIKE FAMOUS RED SAMMY'S! RED SAM! THE FAT BOY WITH THE HAPPY LAUGH. A VETERAN! RED SAMMY'S YOUR MAN!

Red Sammy was lying on the bare ground outside The Tower with his head under a truck while a grey monkey about a foot high, chained to a small chinaberry tree, chattered nearby. The monkey sprang back into the tree and got on the highest limb as soon as he saw the children jump out of the car and run toward him.

Inside, The Tower was a long dark room with a counter at one end and tables at the other and dancing space in the middle. They all sat down at a board table next to the nickelodeon and Red Sam's wife, a tall burnt-brown woman with hair and eyes lighter than her skin, came and took their order. The children's mother put a dime in the machine and played "The Tennessee Waltz," and the grandmother said that tune always made her want to dance. She asked Bailey if he would like to dance but he only glared at her. He didn't have a naturally sunny disposition like she did and trips made him nervous. The grandmother's brown eyes were very bright. She swayed her head from side to side and pretended she was dancing in her chair. June Star said play something she could tap to so the children's mother put in another dime and played a fast number and June Star stepped out onto the dance floor and did her tap routine.

"Ain't she cute?" Red Sam's wife, said, leaning over the counter. "Would you like to come be my little girl?"

"No I certainly wouldn't," June Star said. "I wouldn't live in a broken-down place like this for a million bucks!" and she ran back to the table.

"Ain't she cute?" the woman repeated, stretching her mouth politely.

"Arn't you ashamed?" hissed the grandmother.

Red Sam came in and told his wife to quit lounging on the counter, and hurry up with these people's order. His khaki trousers reached just to his hip bones and his stomach hung over them like a sack of meal swaying under his shirt. He came over and sat down at a table nearby and let out a combination sigh and a yodel. "You can't win," he said. "You can't win," and he wiped his sweating red face off with a grey handkerchief. "These days you don't know who to trust," he said. "Ain't that the truth?"

"People are certainly not nice like they used to be," said the grandmother.

"Two fellers come in here last week," Red Sammy said, "driving a Chrysler. It was a old beat-up car but it was a good one and these boys looked all right to me. Said they worked at the mill and you know I let them fellers charge the gas they bought? Now why did I do that?"

"Because you're a good man!" the grandmother said at once.

"Yes'm, I suppose so," Red Sam said as if he were struck with this answer.

His wife brought the orders, carrying the five plates all at once without a tray, two in each hand and one balanced on her arm. "It isn't a soul in this green world of God's that you can trust," she said. "And I don't count nobody out of that, not nobody," she repeated, looking at Red Sammy.

"Did you read about that criminal, The Misfit, that's escaped?" asked the grandmother.

"I wouldn't be a bit surprised if he didn't attact this place right here," said the woman. "If he hears about it being here, I wouldn't be none surprised to see him. If he hears it's two cent in the cash register, I wouldn't be a tall surprised if he . . ."

"That'll do," Red Sam said. "Go bring these people their Co'-Colas," and the woman went off to get the rest of the order.

"A good man is hard to find," Red Sammy said. "Everything is getting terrible. I remember the day you could go off and leave your screen door unlatched. Not no more."

He and the grandmother discussed better times. The old lady said that in her opinion Europe was entirely to blame for the way things were now. She said the way Europe acted you would think we were made of money and Red Sam said it was no use talking about it, she was exactly right. The children ran outside into the white sunlight and looked at the monkey in the lacy chinaberry tree. He was busy catching fleas on himself and biting each one carefully between his teeth as if it were a delicacy.

They drove off again into the hot afternoon. The grandmother took cat naps and woke up every few minutes with her own snoring. Outside of Toombsboro she woke up and recalled an old plantation that she had visited in this neighbourhood once when she was a young lady. She said the house had six white columns across the front and that there was an avenue of oaks leading up to it and two little wooden trellis arbours on either side in front where you sat down with your suitor after a stroll in the garden. She recalled exactly which road to turn off to get to it. She knew that Bailey would not be willing to lose any time looking at an old house, but the more she talked about it, the more she wanted to see it once again and find out if the little twin arbours were still standing. "There was a secret panel in this house," she said craftily, not telling the truth but wishing that she were, "and the story went that all the family silver was hidden in it when Sherman came through but it was never found . . ."

"Hey!" John Wesley said. "Let's go see it! We'll find it! We'll poke all the woodwork and find it! Who lives there? Where do you turn off at? Hey Pop, can't we turn off there?"

"We never have seen a house with a secret panel!" June Star shrieked. "Let's go to the house with the secret panel! Hey Pop, can't we go see the house with the secret panel!"

"It's not far from here, I know," the grandmother said. "It wouldn't take over twenty minutes."

Bailey was looking straight ahead. His jaw was as rigid as a horseshoe. "No," he said.

The children began to yell and scream that they wanted to see the house with the secret panel. John Wesley kicked the back of the front seat and June Star hung over her mother's shoulder and whined desperately into her ear that they never had any fun even on their vacation, that they could never do what THEY wanted to do. The baby began to scream and John Wesley kicked the back of the seat so hard that his father could feel the blows in his kidney.

"All right!" he shouted and drew the car to a stop at the side of the road. "Will you all shut up? Will you all just shut up for one second? If you don't shut up, we won't go anywhere."

"It would be very educational for them," the grandmother murmured.

"All right," Bailey said, "but get this: this is the only time we're going to stop for anything like this. This is the one and only time."

"The dirt road that you have to turn down is about a mile back," the grandmother directed. "I marked it when we passed."

"A dirt road," Bailey groaned.

After they had turned around and were headed toward the dirt road, the grandmother recalled other points about the house, the beautiful glass over the front doorway and the candle-lamp in the hall. John Wesley said that the secret panel was probably in the fireplace.

"You can't go inside this house," Bailey said. "You don't know who lives there."

"While you all talk to the people in front, I'll run around behind and get in a window," John Wesley suggested.

"We'll all stay in the car," his mother said.

They turned onto the dirt road and the car raced roughly along in a swirl of pink dust. The grandmother recalled the times when there were no paved roads and thirty miles was a day's journey. The dirt road was hilly and there were sudden washes in it and sharp curves on dangerous embankments. All at once they would be on a hill, looking down over the blue tops of trees for miles around, then the next minute, they would be in a red depression with the dust-coated trees looking down on them.

"This place had better turn up in a minute," Bailey said, "or I'm going to turn around."

The road looked as if no one had traveled on it in months.

"It's not much farther," the grandmother said and just as she said it, a horrible thought came to her. The thought was so embarrassing that she turned red in the face and her eyes dilated and her feet jumped up, upsetting her valise in the corner. The instant the valise moved, the newspaper top she had over the basket under it rose with a snarl and Pitty Sing, the cat, sprang onto Bailey's shoulder.

The children were thrown to the floor and their mother, clutching the baby, was thrown out the door onto the ground; the old lady was thrown into the front seat. The car turned over once and landed right-side-up in a gulch off the side of the road. Bailey remained in the driver's seat with the cat — grey-striped with a broad white face and an orange nose — clinging to his neck like a caterpillar.

As soon as the children saw they could move their arms and legs, they scrambled out of the car, shouting, "We've had an ACCIDENT!" The grandmother was curled up under the dashboard, hoping she was injured so that Bailey's wrath would not come down on her all at once. The horrible thought she had had before the accident was that the house she had remembered so vividly was not in Georgia but in Tennessee.

Bailey removed the cat from his neck with both hands and flung it out the window against the side of a pine tree. Then he got out of the car and started looking for the children's mother. She was sitting against the side of a red gutted ditch, holding the screaming baby, but she only had a cut down her face and a broken shoulder. "We've had an ACCIDENT!" the children screamed in a frenzy of delight.

"But nobody's killed," June Star said with disappointment as the grandmother limped out of the car, her hat still pinned to her head but the broken front brim standing up at a jaunty angle and the violet spray hanging off the side. They all sat down in the ditch, except the children, to recover from the shock. They were all shaking.

"Maybe a car will come along," said the children's mother hoarsely.

"I believe I have injured an organ," said the grandmother, pressing her side, but no one answered her. Bailey's teeth were clattering. He had on a yellow sport shirt with bright blue parrots designed in it and his face was as yellow as the shirt. The grandmother decided that she would not mention that the house was in Tennessee.

The road was about ten feet above and they could see only the tops of the trees on the other side of it. Behind the ditch they were sitting in there were more woods, tall and dark and deep. In a few minutes they saw a car some distance away on top of a hill, coming slowly as if the occupants were watching them. The grandmother stood up and waved both arms dramatically to attract their attention. The car continued to come on slowly, disappeared around a bend and appeared again, moving even slower, on top of the hill they had gone over. It was a big black battered hearse-like automobile. There were three men in it.

It came to a stop just over them and for some minutes, the driver looked down with a steady expressionless gaze to where they were sitting, and didn't speak. Then he turned his head and muttered something to the other two and they got out. One was a fat boy in black trousers and a red sweat shirt with a silver stallion embossed on the front of it. He moved around on the right side of them and stood staring, his mouth partly open in a kind of loose grin. The other had on khaki pants and a blue striped coat and a grey hat pulled down very low, hiding most of his face. He came around slowly on the left side. Neither spoke.

The driver got out of the car and stood by the side of it, looking down at them. He was an older man than the other two. His hair was just beginning to grey and he wore silver-rimmed spectacles that gave him a scholarly look. He had a long creased face and didn't have on any shirt or undershirt. He had on blue jeans that were too tight for him and he was holding a black hat and a gun. The two boys also had guns.

"We've had an ACCIDENT!" the children screamed.

The grandmother had the peculiar feeling that the bespectacled man was someone she knew. His face was as familiar to her as if she had known him all her life but she could not recall who he was. He moved away from the car and began to come down the embankment, placing his feet carefully so that he wouldn't slip. He had on tan and white shoes and no socks, and his ankles were red and thin. "Good afternoon," he said. "I see you all had you a little spill."

"We turned over twice!" said the grandmother.

"Oncet," he corrected. "We seen it happen. Try their car and see will it run, Hiram," he said quietly to the boy with the grey hat.

"What you got that gun for?" John Wesley asked. "Whatcha gonna do with that gun?"

"Lady," the man said to the children's mother, "would you mind calling them children to sit down by you? Children make me nervous. I want all you all to sit down right together there where you're at."

"What are you telling US what to do for?" June Star asked.

Behind them the line of woods gaped like a dark open mouth. "Come here," said their mother.

"Look here now," Bailey began suddenly, "we're in a predicament! We're in . . ."

The grandmother shrieked. She scrambled to her feet and stood staring. "You're The Misfit!" she said. "I recognized you at once!"

"Yes'm," the man said, smiling slightly as if he were pleased in spite of himself to be known, "but it would have been better for all of you, lady, if you hadn't reckernized me."

Bailey turned his head sharply and said something to his mother that shocked even the children. The old lady began to cry and The Misfit reddened.

"Lady," he said, "don't you get upset. Sometimes a man says things he don't mean. I don't reckon he meant to talk to you thataway."

"You wouldn't shoot a lady, would you?" the grandmother said and removed a clean handkerchief from her cuff and began to slap at her eyes with it.

The Misfit pointed the toe of his shoe into the ground and made a little hole and then covered it up again. "I would hate to have to," he said.

"Listen," the grandmother almost screamed, "I know you're a good man. You don't look a bit like you have common blood. I know you must come from nice people!"

"Yes mam," he said, "finest people in the world." When he smiled he showed a row of strong white teeth. "God never made a finer woman than my mother and my daddy's heart was pure gold," he said. The boy with the red sweat shirt had come around behind them and was standing with his gun at his hip. The Misfit squatted down on the ground. "Watch them children, Bobby Lee," he said. "You know they make me nervous." He looked at the six of them huddled together in front of him and he seemed to be embarrassed as if he couldn't think of anything to say. "Ain't a cloud in the sky," he remarked, looking up at it. "Don't see no sun but don't see no cloud neither."

"Yes, it's a beautiful day," said the grandmother. "Listen," she said, "you shouldn't call yourself The Misfit because I know you're a good man at heart. I can just look at you and tell."

"Hush!" Bailey yelled. "Hush! Everybody shut up and let me handle this!" He was squatting in the position of a runner about to sprint forward but he didn't move.

"I pre-chate that, lady," The Misfit said and drew a little circle in the ground with the butt of his gun.

"It'll take a half a hour to fix this here car," Hiram called, looking over the raised hood of it.

"Well, first you and Bobby Lee get him and that little boy to step over yonder with you," The Misfit said, pointing to Bailey and John Wesley. "The boys want to ast you something," he said to Bailey. "Would you mind stepping back in them woods there with them?"

"Listen," Bailey began, "we're in a terrible predicament! Nobody realizes what this is," and his voice cracked. His eyes were as blue and intense as the parrots in his shirt and he remained perfectly still.

The grandmother reached up to adjust her hat brim as if she were going to the woods with him but it came off in her hand. She stood staring at it and after a second she let it fall on the ground. Hiram pulled Bailey up by the arm as if he were assisting an old man. John Wesley caught hold of his father's hand and Bobby Lee followed. They went off toward the woods and just as they reached the dark edge, Bailey turned and supporting himself against a grey naked pine trunk, he shouted, "I'll be back in a minute, Mamma, wait on me!"

"Come back this instant!" his mother shrilled but they all disappeared into the woods.

"Bailey Boy!" the grandmother called in a tragic voice but she found she was looking at The Misfit squatting on the ground in front of her. "I just know you're a good man," she said desperately. "You're not a bit common!"

"Nome, I ain't a good man," The Misfit said after a second as if he had considered her statement carefully, "but I ain't the worst in the world neither. My daddy said I was a different breed of dog from my brothers and sisters. 'You know,' Daddy said, 'it's some that can live their whole life without asking about it and it's others has to know why it is, and this boy is one of the latters. He's going to be into everything!'" He put on his black hat and looked up suddenly and then away deep into the woods as if he were embarrassed again. "I'm sorry I don't have on a shirt before you ladies," he said, hunching his shoulders slightly. "We buried our clothes that we had on when we escaped and we're just making do until we can get better. We borrowed these from some folks we met," he explained.

"That's perfectly all right," the grandmother said. "Maybe Bailey has an extra shirt in his suitcase."

"I'll look and see terrectly," The Misfit said.

"Where are you taking him?" the children's mother screamed.

"Daddy was a card himself," The Misfit said. "You couldn't put anything over on him. He never got in trouble with the Authorities though. Just had the knack of handling them."

"You could be honest too if you'd only try," said the grandmother. "Think how wonderful it would be to settle down and live a comfortable life and not have to think about somebody chasing you all the time."

The Misfit kept scratching in the ground with the butt of his gun as if he were thinking about it. "Yes'm, somebody is always after you," he murmured.

The grandmother noticed how thin his shoulder blades were just behind his hat because she was standing up looking down on him. "Do you ever pray?" she asked.

He shook his head. All she saw was the black hat wiggle between his shoulder blades. "Nome," he said.

There was a pistol shot from the woods, followed closely by another. Then silence. The old lady's head jerked around. She could hear the wind move through the tree tops like a long satisfied insuck of breath. "Bailey Boy!" she called.

"I was a gospel singer for a while," The Misfit said. "I been most everything. Been in the arm service, both land and sea, at home and abroad, been twict married, been an undertaker, been with the railroads, plowed Mother Earth, been in a tornado, seen a man burnt alive oncet," and he looked up at the children's mother and the little girl who were sitting close together, their faces white and their eyes glassy. "I even seen a woman flogged," he said.

"Pray, pray," the grandmother began, "pray, pray . . ."

"I never was a bad boy that I remember of," The Misfit said in an almost dreamy voice, "but somewheres along the line I done something wrong and got sent to the penitentiary. I was buried alive," and he looked up and held her attention to him by a steady stare.

"That's when you should have started to pray," she said, "What did you do to get sent to the penitentiary that first time?"

"Turn to the right, it was a wall," The Misfit said, looking up again at the cloudless sky. "Turn to the left, it was a wall. Look up it was a ceiling, look down it was a floor. I forget what I done, lady. I set there and set there, trying to remember what it was I done and I ain't recalled it to this day. Oncet in a while, I would think it was coming to me, but it never come."

"Maybe they put you in by mistake," the old lady said vaguely.

"Nome," he said. "It wasn't no mistake. They had the papers on me."

"You must have stolen something," she said.

The Misfit sneered slightly. "Nobody had nothing I wanted," he said. "It was a head-doctor at the penitentiary said what I had done was kill my daddy but I know that for a lie. My daddy died in nineteen ought nineteen of the epidemic flu and I never had a thing to do with it. He was buried in the Mount Hopewell Baptist churchyard and you can go there and see for yourself."

"If you would pray," the old lady said, "Jesus would help you."

"That's right," The Misfit said.

"Well then, why don't you pray?" she asked trembling with delight suddenly.

"I don't want no hep," he said. "I'm doing all right by myself."

Bobby Lee and Hiram came ambling back from the woods. Bobby Lee was dragging a yellow shirt with bright blue parrots in it.

"Thow me that shirt, Bobby Lee," The Misfit said. The shirt came flying at him and landed on his shoulder and he put it on. The grandmother couldn't name what the shirt reminded her of. "No, lady," The Misfit said while he was buttoning it up, "I found out the crime don't matter. You can do one thing or you can do another, kill a man or take a tire off his car, because sooner or later you're going to forget what it was you done and just be punished for it."

The children's mother had begun to make heaving noises as if she couldn't get her breath. "Lady," he asked, "would you and that little girl like to step off yonder with Bobby Lee and Hiram and join your husband?"

"Yes, thank you," the mother said faintly. Her left arm dangled helplessly, and she was holding the baby, who had gone to sleep, in the other. "Hep that lady up, Hiram," The Misfit said as she struggled to climb out of the ditch, and Bobby Lee, you hold onto that little girl's hand."

"I don't want to hold hands with him," June Star said, "He reminds me of a pig."

The fat boy blushed and laughed and caught her by the arm and pulled her off into the woods after Hiram and her mother.

Alone with The Misfit, the grandmother found that she had lost her voice. There was not a cloud in the sky nor any sun. There was nothing around her but woods. She wanted to tell him that he must pray. She opened and closed her mouth several times before anything came out. Finally she found herself saying, "Jesus. Jesus," meaning, Jesus will help you, but the way she was saying it, it sounded as if she might be cursing.

"Yes'm," The Misfit said as if he agreed. "Jesus thown everything off balance. It was the same case with Him as with me except He hadn't committed any crime and they could prove I had committed one because they had the papers on me. Of course," he said, "they never shown me my papers. That's why I sign myself now. I said long ago, you get you a signature and sign everything you do and keep a copy of it. Then you'll know what you done and you can hold up the crime to the punishment and see do they match and in the end you'll have something to prove you ain't been treated right. I call myself The Misfit," he said, "because I can't make what all I done wrong fit what all I gone through in punishment."

There was a piercing scream from the woods, followed closely by a pistol report. "Does it seem right to you, lady, that one is punished a heap and another ain't punished at all?"

"Jesus!" the old lady cried. "You've got good blood! I know you wouldn't shoot a lady! I know you come from nice people! Pray! Jesus, you ought not to shoot a lady. I'll give you all the money I've got!"

"Lady," The Misfit said, looking beyond her far into the woods, "there never was a body that give the undertaker a tip."

There were two more pistol reports and the grandmother raised her head like a parched old turkey hen crying for water and called, "Bailey Boy, Bailey Boy!" as if her heart would break.

"Jesus was the only One that ever raised the dead," The Misfit continued, "and He shouldn't have done it. He thown everything off balance. If He did what He said, then it's nothing for you to do but thow away everything and follow Him, and if He didn't, then it's nothing for you to do but enjoy the few minutes you got left the best way you can — by killing somebody or burning down his house or doing some other meanness to him. No pleasure but meanness," he said and his voice had become almost a snarl.

"Maybe He didn't raise the dead," the old lady mumbled, not knowing what she was saying and feeling so dizzy that she sank down in the ditch with her legs twisted under her.

"I wasn't there so I can't say He didn't," The Misfit said. "I wisht I had of been there," he said, hitting the ground with his fist. "It ain't right I wasn't there because if I had been there I would of known. Listen lady," he said in a high voice, "if I had of been there I would of known and I wouldn't be like I am now." His voice seemed about to crack and the grandmother's head cleared for an instant. She saw the man's face twisted close to her own as if he were going to cry and she murmured, "Why you're one of my babies. You're one of my own children!" She reached out and touched him on the shoulder. The Misfit sprang back as if a snake had bitten him and shot her three times through the chest. Then he put his gun down on the ground and took off his glasses and began to clean them.

Hiram and Bobby Lee returned from the woods and stood over the ditch, looking down at the grandmother who half sat and half lay in a puddle of blood with her legs crossed under her like a child's and her face smiling up at the cloudless sky.

Without his glasses, The Misfit's eyes were red-rimmed and pale and defenseless-looking. "Take her off and thow her where you thown the others," he said, picking up the cat that was rubbing itself against his leg.

"She was a talker, wasn't she?" Bobby Lee said, sliding down the ditch with a yodel.

"She would of been a good woman," The Misfit said, "if it had been somebody there to shoot her every minute of her life."

"Some fun!" Bobby Lee said.

"Shut up, Bobby Lee," The Misfit said. "It's no real pleasure in life."

೮ාඋ

Although Flannery O'Connor studied creative writing at the University of Iowa and worked on her first novel in New York, most of her relatively short life was spent in the South, in Georgia where she was born. At the age of twenty-five she was diagnosed with lupus, the disease which had killed her father, and which would severely restrict her own life. Living quietly at home with her widowed mother, O'Connor continued to write her darkly humorous stories.

Despite the ardent Catholicism informing her fiction, O'Connor is no propagandist, no lay preacher. Her characters, whose authentic voices live on in the reader's mind, experience life's mystery in situations which are incongruous, even bizarre. Random acts of violence are frequently used to jar self-satisfied characters out of a sense of complacency: a disturbed adolescent girl attempts to throttle a respectable middle-aged woman in a doctor's office; a Bible salesman steals the wooden leg of a self-proclaimed nihilist. What makes a story work, according to O'Connor, is "some action, some gesture of a character that is unlike any other in the story." In "A Good Man Is Hard to Find" the grandmother's encounter with a psychopathic killer culminates in just such a gesture, one which arises from the character's sudden recognition of her own helplessness and her intimate connection to the suffering man before her.

B.M.

Frank O'Connor (1903-1966)

Guests of the Nation

At dusk the big Englishman, Belcher, would shift his long legs out of the ashes and say "Well, chums, what about it?" and Noble or me would say "All right, chum" (for we had picked up some of their curious expressions), and the little Englishman, Hawkins, would light the lamp and bring out the cards. Sometimes Jeremiah Donovan would come up and supervise the game and get excited over Hawkins's cards, which he always played badly, and shout at him as if he was one of our own "Ah, you divil, you, why didn't you play the tray?"

But ordinarily Jeremiah was a sober and contented poor devil like the big Englishman, Belcher, and was looked up to only because he was a fair hand at documents, though he was slow enough even with them. He wore a small cloth hat and big gaiters over his long pants, and you seldom saw him with his hands out of his pockets. He reddened when you talked to him, tilting from toe to heel and back, and looking down all the time at his big farmer's feet. Noble and me used to make fun of his broad accent, because we were from the town.

I couldn't at the time see the point of me and Noble guarding Belcher and Hawkins at all, for it was my belief that you could have planted that pair down anywhere from this to Claregalway and they'd have taken root there like a native weed. I never in my short experience seen two men to take to the country as they did.

They were handed on to us by the Second Battalion when the search for them became too hot, and Noble and myself, being young, took over with a natural feeling of responsibility, but Hawkins made us look like fools when he showed that he knew the country better than we did.

"You're the bloke they calls Bonaparte," he says to me. "Mary Brigid O'Connell told me to ask you what you done with the pair of her brother's socks you borrowed."

For it seemed, as they explained it, that the Second used to have little evenings, and some of the girls of the neighbourhood turned in, and, seeing they were such decent chaps, our fellows couldn't leave the two Englishmen out of them. Hawkins learned to dance "The Walls of Limerick," "The Siege of Ennis," and "The Waves of Tory" as well as any of them, though, naturally, he couldn't return the compliment, because our lads at that time did not dance foreign dances on principle.

So whatever privileges Belcher and Hawkins had with the Second they just naturally took with us, and after the first day or two we gave up all pretence of keeping a close eye on them. Not that they could have got far, for they had accents you could cut with a knife and wore khaki tunics and overcoats with civilian pants and boots. But it's my belief that they never had any idea of escaping and were quite content to be where they were.

It was a treat to see how Belcher got off with the old woman of the house where we were staying. She was a great warrant to scold, and cranky even with us, but before ever she had a chance of giving our guests, as I may call them, a lick of her tongue, Belcher had made her his friend for life. She was breaking sticks, and Belcher, who hadn't been more than ten minutes in the house, jumped up from his seat and went over to her.

"Allow me, madam," he says, smiling his queer little smile, "please allow me"; and he takes the bloody hatchet. She was struck too paralytic to speak, and after that, Belcher would be at her heels, carrying a bucket, a basket, or a load of turf, as the case might be. As Noble said, he got into looking before she leapt, and hot water, or any little thing she wanted, Belcher would have it ready for her. For such a huge man (and though I am five foot ten myself I had to look up at him) he had an uncommon shortness — or should I say lack? — of speech. It took us some time to get used to him, walking in and out, like a ghost, without a word. Especially because Hawkins talked enough for a platoon, it was strange to hear big Belcher with his toes in the ashes come out with a solitary "Excuse me, chum," or "That's right, chum." His one and only passion was cards, and I will say for him that he was a good card-player. He could have fleeced myself and Noble, but whatever we lost to him Hawkins lost to us, and Hawkins played with the money Belcher gave him.

Hawkins lost to us because he had too much old gab, and we probably lost to Belcher for the same reason. Hawkins and Noble would spit at one another about religion into the early hours of the morning, and Hawkins worried the soul out of Noble, whose brother was a priest, with a string of questions that would puzzle a cardinal. To make it worse, even in treating of holy subjects, Hawkins had a deplorable tongue. I never in all my career met a man who could mix such a variety of cursing and bad language into an argument. He was a terrible man, and a fright to argue. He never did a stroke of work, and when he had no one else to talk to, he got stuck in the old woman.

He met his match in her, for one day when he tried to get her to complain profanely of the drought, she gave him a great comedown by blaming it entirely on Jupiter Pluvius (a deity neither Hawkins nor I had ever heard of, though Noble said that among the pagans it was believed that he had something to do with the rain). Another day he was swearing at the capitalists for starting the German war when the old lady laid down her iron, puckered up her little crab's mouth, and said: "Mr. Hawkins, you can say what you like about the war, and think you'll deceive me because I'm only a simple poor countrywoman, but I know what started the war. It was the Italian Count that stole the heathen divinity out of the temple in Japan. Believe me, Mr. Hawkins, nothing but sorrow and want can follow the people that disturb the hidden powers."

A queer old girl, all right.

C੪

We had our tea one evening, and Hawkins lit the lamp and we all sat into cards. Jeremiah Donovan came in too, and sat down and watched us for a while, and it suddenly struck me that he had no great love for the two Englishmen. It came as a great surprise to me, because I hadn't noticed anything about him before.

Late in the evening a really terrible argument blew up between Hawkins and Noble, about capitalists and priests and love of your country.

"The capitalists," says Hawkins with an angry gulp, "pays the priests to tell you about the next world so as you won't notice what the bastards are up to in this."

"Nonsense, man!" says Noble, losing his temper. "Before ever a capitalist was thought of, people believed in the next world."

Hawkins stood up as though he was preaching a sermon.

"Oh, they did, did they?" he says with a sneer. "They believed all the things you believe, isn't that what you mean? And you believe that God created Adam, and Adam created Shem, and Shem created Jehoshophat. You believe all that silly old fairytale about Eve and Eden and the apple. Well, listen to me, chum. If you're entitled to hold a silly belief like that, I'm entitled to hold my silly belief — which is that the first thing your God created was a bleeding capitalist, with morality and Rolls Royce complete. Am I right, chum?" he says to Belcher.

"You're right, chum," says Belcher with his amused smile, and got up from the table to stretch his long legs into the fire and stroke his moustache. So, seeing that Jeremiah Donovan was going, and that there was no knowing when the argument about religion would be over, I went out with him. We strolled down to the village together, and then he stopped and started blushing and mumbling and saying I ought to be behind, keeping guard on the prisoners. I didn't like the tone he took with me, and anyway I was bored with life in the cottage, so I replied by asking him what the hell we wanted guarding them at all for. I told him I'd talked it over with Noble, and that we'd both rather be out with a fighting column.

"What use are those fellows to us?" says I.

He looked at me in surprise and said: "I thought you knew we were keeping them as hostages."

"Hostages?" I said.

"The enemy have prisoners belonging to us," he says, "and now they're talking of shooting them. If they shoot our prisoners, we'll shoot theirs."

"Shoot them?" I said.

"What else did you think we were keeping them for?" he says.

"Wasn't it very unforeseen of you not to warn Noble and myself of that in the beginning?" I said.

"How was it?" says he. "You might have known it."

"We couldn't know it, Jeremiah Donovan," says I. "How could we when they were on our hands so long?"

"The enemy have our prisoners as long and longer," says he.

"That's not the same thing at all," says I.

"What difference is there?" says he.

I couldn't tell him, because I knew he wouldn't understand. If it was only an old dog that was going to the vet's, you'd try and not get too fond of him, but Jeremiah Donovan wasn't a man that would ever be in danger of that.

"And when is this thing going to be decided?" says I.

"We might hear tonight," he says. "Or tomorrow or the next day at latest. So if it's only hanging round here that's a trouble to you, you'll be free soon enough."

It wasn't the hanging round that was a trouble to me at all by this time. I had worse things to worry about. When I got back to the cottage the argument was still on. Hawkins was holding forth in his best style, maintaining that there was no next world, and Noble was maintaining that there was; but I could see that Hawkins had had the best of it.

"Do you know what, chum?" he was saying with a saucy smile. "I think you're just as big a bleeding unbeliever as I am. You say you believe in the next world, and you know just as much about the next world as I do, which is sweet damn-all. What's heaven? You don't know. Where's heaven? You don't know. You know sweet damn-all! I ask you again, do they wear wings?"

"Very well, then," says Noble, "they do. Is that enough for you? They do wear wings."

"Where do they get them, then? Who makes them? Have they a factory for wings? Have they a sort of store where you hands in your chit and takes your bleeding wings?"

"You're an impossible man to argue with," says Noble. "Now, listen to me —" And they were off again.

It was long after midnight when we locked up and went to bed. As I blew out the candle I told Noble what Jeremiah Donovan was after telling me. Noble took it very quietly. When we'd been in bed about an hour he asked me did I think we ought to tell the Englishmen. I didn't think we should, because it was more than likely that the English wouldn't shoot our men, and even if they did, the brigade officers, who were always up and down with the Second Battalion and knew the Englishmen well, wouldn't be likely to want them plugged. "I think so too," says Noble. "It would be great cruelty to put the wind to them now."

"It was very unforeseen of Jeremiah Donovan anyhow," says I.

It was next morning that we found it so hard to face Belcher and Hawkins. We went about the house all day scarcely saying a word. Belcher didn't seem to notice; he was stretched into the ashes as usual, with his usual look of waiting in quietness for something unforeseen to happen, but Hawkins noticed and put it down to Noble's being beaten in the argument of the night before.

"Why can't you take a discussion in the proper spirit?" he says severely. "You and your Adam and Eve! I'm a Communist, that's what I am. Communist or anarchist, it all comes to much the same thing." And for hours he went round the house, muttering when the fit took him. "Adam and Eve! Adam and Eve! Nothing better to do with their time than picking bleeding apples!"

ରଙ

I don't know how we got through that day, but I was very glad when it was over, the tea things were cleared away, and Belcher said in his peaceable way: "Well, chums, what about it?" We sat round the table and Hawkins took out the cards, and just then I heard Jeremiah Donovan's footstep on the path and a dark presentiment crossed my mind. I rose from the table and caught him before he reached the door.

"What do you want?" I asked.

"I want those two soldier friends of yours," he says, getting red.

"Is that the way, Jeremiah Donovan?" I asked.

"That's the way. There were four of our lads shot this morning, one of them a boy of sixteen."

"That's bad," I said.

At that moment Noble followed me out, and the three of us walked down the path together, talking in whispers. Feeney, the local intelligence officer, was standing by the gate.

"What are you going to do about it?" I asked Jeremiah Donovan.

"I want you and Noble to get them out; tell them they're being shifted again; that'll be the quietest way."

"Leave me out of that," says Noble under his breath.

Jeremiah Donovan looks at him hard.

"All right," he says. "You and Feeney get a few tools from the shed and dig a hole by the far end of the bog. Bonaparte and myself will be after you. Don't let anyone see you with the tools. I wouldn't like it to go beyond ourselves."

We saw Feeney and Noble go round to the shed and went in ourselves. I left Jeremiah Donovan to do the explanations. He told them that he had orders to send them back to the Second Battalion. Hawkins let out a mouthful of curses; and you could see that though Belcher didn't say anything, he was a bit upset too. The old woman was for having them stay in spite of us, and she didn't stop advising them until Jeremiah Donovan lost his temper and turned on her. He had a nasty temper, I noticed. It was pitch-dark in the cottage by this time, but no one thought of lighting the lamp, and in the darkness the two Englishmen fetched their topcoats and said good-bye to the old woman.

"Just as a man makes a home of a bleeding place, some bastard at headquarters thinks you're too cushy and shunts you off," says Hawkins, shaking her hand.

"A thousand thanks, madam," says Belcher. "A thousand thanks for everything" — as though he'd made it up.

We went round to the back of the house and down towards the bog. It was only then that Jeremiah Donovan told them. He was shaking with excitement.

"There were four of our fellows shot in Cork this morning and now you're to be shot as a reprisal."

"What are you talking about?" snaps Hawkins. "It's bad enough being mucked about as we are without having to put up with your funny jokes."

"It isn't a joke," says Donovan. "I'm sorry, Hawkins, but it's true," and begins on the usual rigmarole about duty and how unpleasant it is.

I never noticed that people who talk a lot about duty find it much of a trouble to them.

"Oh, cut it out!" says Hawkins.

"Ask Bonaparte," says Donovan, seeing that Hawkins isn't taking him seriously. "Isn't it true, Bonaparte?"

"It is," I say, and Hawkins stops.

"Ah, for Christ's sake, chum!"

"I mean it, chum," I say.

"You don't sound as if you meant it."

"If he doesn't mean it, I do," says Donovan, working himself up.

"What have you against me, Jeremiah Donovan?"

"I never said I had anything against you. But why did your people take out four of our prisoners and shoot them in cold blood?"

He took Hawkins by the arm and dragged him on, but it was impossible to make him understand that we were in earnest. I had the Smith and Wesson in my pocket and I kept fingering it and wondering what I'd do if they put up a fight for it or ran, and wishing to God they'd do one or the other. I knew if they did run for it, that I'd never fire on them. Hawkins wanted to know was Noble in it, and when we said yes, he asked us why Noble wanted to plug him. Why did any of us want to plug him? What had he done to us? Weren't we all chums? Didn't we understand him and didn't he understand us? Did we imagine for an instant that he'd shoot us for all the so-and-so officers in the so-and-so British Army?

By this time we'd reached the bog, and I was so sick I couldn't even answer him. We walked along the edge of it in the darkness, and every now and then Hawkins would call a halt and begin all over again, as if he was wound up, about our being chums, and I knew that nothing but the sight of the grave would convince him that we had to do it. And all the time I was hoping that something would happen; that they'd run for it or that Noble would take over the responsibility from me. I had the feeling that it was worse on Noble than on me.

◌

At last we saw the lantern in the distance and made towards it. Noble was carrying it, and Feeney was standing somewhere in the darkness behind him, and the picture of them so still and silent in the bogland brought it home to me that we were in earnest, and banished the last bit of hope I had.

Belcher, on recognizing Noble, said: "Hallo, chum," in his quiet way, but Hawkins flew at him at once, and the argument began all over again, only this time Noble had nothing to say for himself and stood with his head down, holding the lantern between his legs.

It was Jeremiah Donovan who did the answering. For the twentieth time, as though it was haunting his mind, Hawkins asked if anybody thought he'd shoot Noble.

"Yes, you would," says Jeremiah Donovan.

"No, I wouldn't, damn you!"

"You would, because you'd know you'd be shot for not doing it."

"I wouldn't, not if I was to be shot twenty times over. I wouldn't shoot a pal. And Belcher wouldn't — isn't that right, Belcher?"

"That's right, chum," Belcher said, but more by way of answering the question than of joining in the argument. Belcher sounded as though whatever unforeseen thing he'd always been waiting for had come at last.

"Anyway, who says Noble would be shot if I wasn't? What do you think I'd do if I was in his place, out in the middle of a blasted bog?"

"What would you do?" asks Donovan.

"I'd go with him wherever he was going, of course. Share my last bob with him and stick by him through thick and thin. No one can ever say of me that I let down a pal."

"We had enough of this," says Jeremiah Donovan, cocking his revolver. "Is there any message you want to send?"

"No, there isn't."

"Do you want to say your prayers?"

Hawkins came out with a cold-blooded remark that even shocked me and turned on Noble again.

"Listen to me, Noble," he says. "You and me are chums. You can't come over to my side, so I'll come over to your side. That show you I mean what I say? Give me a rifle and I'll go along with you and the other lads."

Nobody answered him. We knew that was no way out.

"Hear what I'm saying?" he says. "I'm through with it. I'm a deserter or anything else you like. I don't believe in your stuff, but it's no worse than mine. That satisfy you?"

Noble raised his head, but Donovan began to speak and he lowered it again without replying.

"For the last time, have you any messages to send?" says Donovan in a cold excited sort of voice.

"Shut up, Donovan! You don't understand me, but these lads do. They're not the sort to make a pal and kill a pal. They're not the tools of any capitalist."

I alone of the crowd saw Donovan raise his Webley to the back of Hawkins's neck, and as he did so I shut my eyes and tried to pray. Hawkins had begun to say something else when Donovan fired, and as I opened my eyes at the bang, I saw Hawkins stagger at the knees and lie out flat at Noble's feet, slowly and as quiet as a kid falling asleep, with the lantern-light on his lean legs and bright farmer's boots. We all stood very still, watching him settle out in the last agony.

Then Belcher took out a handkerchief and began to tie it about his own eyes (in our excitement we'd forgotten to do the same for Hawkins), and, seeing it wasn't big enough, turned and asked for the loan of mine. I gave it to him and he knotted the two together and pointed with his foot at Hawkins.

"He's not quite dead," he says. "Better give him another."

Sure enough, Hawkins's left knee is beginning to rise. I bend down and put my gun to his head; then, recollecting myself, I get up again. Belcher understands what's in my mind.

"Give him his first," he says. "I don't mind. Poor bastard, we don't know what's happening to him now."

I knelt and fired. By this time I didn't seem to know what I was doing. Belcher, who was fumbling a bit awkwardly with the handkerchiefs, came out with a laugh as he heard the shot. It was the first time I heard him laugh and it sent a shudder down my back; it sounded so unnatural.

"Poor bugger!" he said quietly. "And last night he was so curious about it all. It's very queer, chums, I always think. Now he knows as much about it as they'll ever let him know, and last night he was all in the dark."

Donovan helped him to tie the handkerchiefs about his eyes. "Thanks, chum," he said. Donovan asked if there were any messages he wanted sent.

"No, chum," he says. "Not for me. If any of you would like to write to Hawkins's mother, you'll find a letter from her in his pocket. He and his mother were great chums. But my missus left me eight years ago. Went away with another fellow and took the kid with her. I like the feeling of a home, as you may have noticed, but I couldn't start again after that."

It was an extraordinary thing, but in those few minutes Belcher said more than in all the weeks before. It was just as if the sound of the shot had started a flood of talk in him and he could go on the whole night like that, quite happily, talking about himself. We stood round like fools now that he couldn't see us any longer. Donovan looked at Noble, and Noble shook his head. Then Donovan raised his Webley, and at that moment Belcher gives his queer laugh again. He may have thought we were talking about him, or perhaps he noticed the same thing I'd noticed and couldn't understand it.

"Excuse me, chums," he says. "I feel I'm talking the hell of a lot, and so silly, about my being so handy about a house and things like that. But this thing came on me suddenly. You'll forgive me, I'm sure."

"You don't want to say a prayer?" asks Donovan.

"No, chum," he says. "I don't think it would help. I'm ready, and you boys want to get it over."

"You understand that we're only doing our duty?" says Donovan.

Belcher's head was raised like a blind man's so that you could only see his chin and the tip of his nose in the lantern-light.

"I never could make out what duty was myself," he said. "I think you're all good lads, if that's what you mean. I'm not complaining."

Noble, just as if he couldn't bear any more of it, raised his fist at Donovan, and in a flash Donovan raised his gun and fired. The big man went over like a sack of meal, and this time there was no need for a second shot.

I don't remember much about the burying, but that it was worse than all the rest because we had to carry them to the grave. It was all mad lonely with nothing but a patch of lantern-light between ourselves and the dark, and birds hooting and screeching all round, disturbed by the guns. Noble went through Hawkins's belongings to find the letter from his mother, and then joined his hands together. He did the same with Belcher. Then, when we'd filled in the grave, we separated from Jeremiah Donovan and Feeney and took our tools back to the shed. All the way we didn't speak a word. The kitchen was dark and cold as we'd left it, and the old woman was sitting over the hearth, saying her beads. We walked past her into the room, and Noble struck a match to light the lamp. She rose quietly and came to the doorway with all her cantankerousness gone.

"What did ye do with them?" she asked in a whisper, and Noble started so that the match went out in his hand.

"What's that?" he asked without turning round.

"I heard ye," she said.

"What did you hear?" asked Noble.

"I heard ye. Do ye think I didn't hear ye, putting the spade back in the houseen?"

Noble struck another match and this time the lamp lit for him.

"Was that what ye did to them?" she asked.

Then, by God, in the very doorway, she fell on her knees and began praying, and after looking at her for a minute or two Noble did the same by the fireplace. I pushed my way out past her and left them at it. I stood at the door, watching the stars and listening to the shrieking of the birds dying out over the bogs. It is so strange what you feel at times like that that you can't describe it. Noble says he saw everything ten times the size, as though there were nothing in the whole world but that little patch of bog with the two Englishmen stiffening into it, but with me it was as if the patch of bog where the Englishmen were was a million miles away, and even Noble and the old woman, mumbling behind me, and the birds and the bloody stars were all far away, and I was somehow very small and very lost and lonely like a child astray in the snow. And anything that happened to me afterwards, I never felt the same about again.

℘)℃

In the words of the poet Yeats, Frank O'Connor (the pen name of Michael O'Donovan) did for Ireland "what Chekhov did for Russia." His more than two hundred short stories have won for him an undisputed place among the masters of the form. Born in Cork, the only child of impoverished parents, O'Connor left school at the age of fourteen, but did not cease to educate himself. He steeped himself in the Irish language, attempting translations of Gaelic poetry. Later his nationalism took the form of rebellion: he fought with the Republicans in the Civil War and was imprisoned in 1923. In his first book of short stories, Guests of the Nation, *published in 1931, O'Connor drew on this experience which had shattered most of his romantic illusions about warfare. The title story of this collection demonstrates his characteristic sympathy toward his characters. He attempts to give a voice to the "little man," to express the drama of ordinary lives. O'Connor was always concerned with getting the voices right. Rarely satisfied with his work, he revised many of his published stories, including "Guests of the Nation," whose almost phonetically transcribed Cockney dialect he modified, believing that it would distract the reader from the story's serious intent. This work, perhaps O'Connor's masterpiece, has been dramatized on several occasions, most recently providing the basis for Neil Jordan's film* The Crying Game.

B.M.

EDGAR ALLAN POE *(1809-1849)*

The Cask of Amontillado

T he thousand injuries of Fortunato I had borne as I best could; but when he ventured upon insult, I vowed revenge. You, who so well know the nature of my soul, will not suppose, however, that I gave utterance to a threat. *At length* I would be avenged; this was a point definitively settled — but the very definitiveness with which it was resolved, precluded the idea of risk. I must not only punish, but punish with impunity. A wrong is unredressed when retribution overtakes its redresser. It is equally unredressed when the avenger fails to make himself felt as such to him who has done the wrong.

It must be understood, that neither by word nor deed had I given Fortunato cause to doubt my good will. I continued, as was my wont, to smile in his face, and he did not perceive that my smile *now* was at the thought of his immolation.

He had a weak point — this Fortunato — although in other regards he was a man to be respected and even feared. He prided himself upon his connoisseurship in wine. Few Italians have the true virtuoso spirit. For the most part their enthusiasm is adopted to suit the time and opportunity — to practise imposture upon the British and Austrian *millionaires*. In painting and gemmary Fortunato, like his countrymen, was a quack — but in the matter of old wines he was sincere. In this respect I did not differ from him materially: I was skillful in the Italian vintages myself, and bought largely whenever I could.

It was about dusk, one evening during the supreme madness of the carnival season, that I encountered my friend. He accosted me with excessive warmth, for he had been drinking much. The man wore motley. He had on a tight-fitting parti-striped dress, and his head was surmounted by the conical cap and bells. I was so pleased to see him, that I thought I should never have done wringing his hand.

I said to him — "My dear Fortunato, you are luckily met. How remarkably well you are looking to-day! But I have received a pipe of what passes for Amontillado, and I have my doubts."

"How?" said he. "Amontillado? A pipe? Impossible! And in the middle of the carnival!"

"I have my doubts," I replied; "and I was silly enough to pay the full Amontillado price without consulting you in the matter. You were not to be found, and I was fearful of losing a bargain."

"Amontillado!"

"I have my doubts."

"Amontillado!"

"And I must satisfy them."

"Amontillado!"

"As you are engaged, I am on my way to Luchesi. If any one has a critical turn it is he. He will tell me — "

"Luchesi cannot tell Amontillado from Sherry."

"And yet some fools will have it that his taste is a match for your own."

"Come, let us go."

"Whither?"

"To your vaults."

"My friend, no; I will not impose upon your good nature. I perceive you have an engagement. Luchesi —"

"I have no engagement; — come."

"My friend, no. It is not the engagement, but the severe cold with which I perceive you are afflicted. The vaults are insufferably damp. They are encrusted with nitre."

"Let us go, nevertheless. The cold is merely nothing. Amontillado! You have been imposed upon. And as for Luchesi, he cannot distinguish Sherry from Amontillado."

Thus speaking, Fortunato possessed himself of my arm. Putting on a mask of black silk and drawing a *roquelaire* closely about my person, I suffered him to hurry me to my palazzo.

There were no attendants at home; they had absconded to make merry in honour of the time. I had told them that I should not return until the morning, and had given them explicit orders not to stir from the house. These orders were sufficient, I well knew, to ensure their immediate disappearance, one and all, as soon as my back was turned.

I took from their sconces two flambeaux, and giving one to Fortunato, bowed him through several suites of rooms to the archway that led into the vaults. I passed down a long and winding staircase, requesting him to be cautious as he followed. We came at length to the foot of the descent, and stood together on the damp ground of the catacombs of the Montresors.

The gait of my friend was unsteady, and the bells upon his cap jingled as he strode.

"The pipe," said he.

"It is farther on," said I; "but observe the white web-work which gleams from these cavern walls."

He turned towards me, and looked into my eyes with two filmy orbs that distilled the rheum of intoxication.

"Nitre?" he asked, at length.

"Nitre," I replied. "How long have you had that cough?"

"Ugh! ugh! ugh! — ugh! ugh! ugh! — ugh! ugh !ugh! — ugh! ugh! ugh! — ugh! ugh! ugh!"

My poor friend found it impossible to reply for many minutes.

"It is nothing," he said, at last.

"Come," I said, with decision, "we will go back; your health is precious. You are rich, respected, admired, beloved; you are happy, as once I was. You are a man to be missed. For me it is no matter. We will go back; you will be ill, and I cannot be responsible. Besides, there is Luchesi —"

"Enough," he said; "the cough is a mere nothing; it will not kill me. I shall not die of a cough."

"True — true," I replied; "and, indeed, I had no intention of alarming you unnecessarily — but you should use all proper caution. A draught of this Medoc will defend us from the damps."

Here I knocked off the neck of a bottle which I drew from a long row of its fellows that lay upon the mould.

"Drink," I said, presenting him the wine.

He raised it to his lips with a leer. He paused and nodded to me familiarly, while his bells jingled.

"I drink," he said, "to the buried that repose around us."

"And I to your long life."

He again took my arm, and we proceeded.

"These vaults," he said, "are extensive."

"The Montresors, " I replied, "were a great and numerous family."

"I forget your arms."

"A huge human foot d'or, in a field azure; the foot crushes a serpent rampant whose fangs are imbedded in the heel."

"And the motto?"

"*Nemo me impune lacessit.*"

"Good!" he said.

The wine sparkled in his eyes and the bells jingled. My own fancy grew warm with the Medoc. We had passed through long walls of piled bones, with casks and puncheons intermingling, into the inmost recesses of the catacombs. I paused again, and this time I made bold to seize Fortunato by an arm above the elbow.

"The nitre!" I said; "see, it increases. It hangs like moss upon the vaults. We are below the river's bed. The drops of moisture trickle among the bones. Come, we will go back ere it is too late. Your cough —"

"It is nothing," he said; "let us go on. But first, another draught of the Medoc."

I broke and reached him a flaçon of De Grâve. He emptied it at a breath. His eyes flashed with a fierce light. He laughed and threw the bottle upwards with a gesticulation I did not understand.

I looked at him in surprise. He repeated the movement — a grotesque one.

"You do not comprehend?" he said.

"Not I," I replied.

"Then you are not of the brotherhood."

"How?"

"You are not of the masons."

"Yes, yes," I said; "yes, yes."

"You? Impossible! A mason?"

"A mason," I replied.

"A sign," he said.

"It is this," I answered, producing a trowel from beneath the folds of my *roquelaire.*

"You jest," he exclaimed, recoiling a few paces. "But let us proceed to the Amontillado."

"Be it so," I said, replacing the tool beneath the cloak, and again offering him my arm. He leaned upon it heavily. We continued our route in search of the Amontillado. We passed through a range of low arches, descended, passed on, and descending again, arrived at a deep crypt, in which the foulness of the air caused our flambeaux rather to glow than flame.

At the most remote end of the crypt there appeared another less spacious. Its walls had been lined with human remains, piled to the vault overhead, in the fashion of the great catacombs of Paris. Three sides of this interior crypt were still ornamented in this manner. From the fourth the bones had been thrown down, and lay promiscuously upon the earth, forming at one point a mound of some size. Within the wall thus exposed by the displacing of the bones, we perceived a still interior recess, in depth about four feet, in width three, in height six or seven. It seemed to have been constructed for no especial use within itself, but formed merely the interval between two of the colossal supports of the roof of the catacombs, and was backed by one of their circumscribing walls of solid granite.

It was in vain that Fortunato, uplifting his dull torch, endeavoured to pry into the depth of the recess. Its termination the feeble light did not enable us to see.

"Proceed," I said; "herein is the Amontillado. As for Luchesi —"

"He is an ignoramus," interrupted my friend, as he stepped unsteadily forward, while I followed immediately at his heels. In an instant he had reached the extremity of the niche, and finding his progress arrested by the rock, stood stupidly bewildered. A moment more and I had fettered him to the granite. In its surface were two iron staples, distant from each other about two feet, horizontally. From one of these depended a short chain, from the other a padlock. Throwing the links about his waist, it was but the work of a few seconds to secure it. He was too much astounded to resist. Withdrawing the key I stepped back from the recess.

"Pass your hand," I said, "over the wall; you cannot help feeling the nitre. Indeed, it is *very* damp. Once more let me *implore* you to return. No? Then I must positively leave you. But I will first render you all the little attentions in my power."

"The Amontillado!" ejaculated my friend, not yet recovered from his astonishment.

"True," I replied; "the Amontillado."

As I said these words I busied myself among the pile of bones of which I have before spoken. Throwing them aside, I soon uncovered a quantity of building stone and mortar. With these materials and with the aid of my trowel, I began vigorously to wall up the entrance of the niche.

I had scarcely laid the first tier of the masonry when I discovered that the intoxication of Fortunato had in great measure worn off. The earliest indication I had of this was a low moaning cry from the depth of the recess. It was *not* the cry of a drunken man. There was then a long and obstinate silence. I laid the second tier, and the third, and the fourth; and then I heard the furious vibrations of the chain. The noise lasted for several minutes, during which, that I might hearken to it with the more satisfaction, I ceased my labours and sat down upon the bones.

When at last the clanking subsided, I resumed the trowel, and finished without interruption the fifth, the sixth, and the seventh tier. The wall was now nearly upon a level with my breast. I again paused, and holding the flambeaux over the mason-work, threw a few feeble rays upon the figure within.

A succession of loud and shrill screams, bursting suddenly from the throat of the chained form, seemed to thrust me violently back. For a brief moment I hesitated — I trembled. Unsheathing my rapier, I began to grope with it about the recess; but the thought of an instant reassured me. I placed my hand upon the solid fabric of the catacombs, and felt satisfied. I reapproached the wall. I replied to the yells of him who clamoured. I re-echoed — I aided — I surpassed them in volume and in strength. I did this, and the clamourer grew still.

It was now midnight, and my task was drawing to a close. I had completed the eighth, the ninth, and the tenth tier. I had finished a portion of the last and the eleventh; there remained but a single stone to be fitted and plastered in. I struggled with its weight; I placed it partially in its destined position. But now there came from out the niche a low laugh that erected the hairs upon my head. It was succeeded by a sad voice, which I had difficulty in recognizing as that of the noble Fortunato. The voice said —

"Ha! ha! ha! — he! he! — a very good joke, indeed — an excellent jest. We will have many a rich laugh about it at the palazzo — he! he! he! — over our wine — he! he! he!"

"The Amontillado!" I said.

"He! he! he! — he! he! he! — yes, the Amontillado. But is it not getting late? Will not they be awaiting us at the palazzo, the Lady Fortunato and the rest? Let us be gone."

"Yes," I said, "let us be gone."

"*For the love of God, Montresor!*"

"Yes," I said, "for the love of God!"

But to these words I hearkened in vain for a reply. I grew impatient. I called aloud —

"Fortunato!"

No answer. I called again —

"Fortunato!"

No answer still. I thrust a torch through the remaining aperture and let it fall within. There came forth in return only a jingling of the bells. My heart grew sick — on account of the dampness of the catacombs. I hastened to make an end of my labour. I forced the last stone into its position; I plastered it up. Against the new masonry I re-erected the old rampart of bones. For the half of a century no mortal has disturbed them. *In pace requiescat!*

ℰᏗᏉ

Horror fiction can be divided into two broad subcategories: the supernatural and the psychological. In supernatural horror, a monster from outside the natural order of the world terrorizes us, and we struggle to defeat it. Such monsters can take many forms:

cloned dinosaurs, mutated killer bees, vampires, poltergeists, space aliens. In horror of the psychological kind, there is also a monster, but it is located within ourselves, and often much harder to recognize and deal with. Many would consider psychological horror fiction, whose acknowledged master is Edgar Allan Poe, to be more terrifying at its best than the supernatural kind, and "The Cask of Amontillado" is unquestionably one of Poe's master-pieces. It seems to be a revenge tale, in which the narrator Montresor ruthlessly exacts vengeance on Fortunato by walling him up alive. But if we read the story carefully, certain disturbing questions start to dissolve our vicarious satisfaction at seeing long-delayed justice done, and make us think twice about the meaning of plot. What exactly were the insults and injuries that provoked Montresor to lead the unwitting Fortunato to such a horrible end? Who is the "You" Montresor addresses in the story's second sentence? To answer these questions, we might begin by asking ourselves about the nature of the alluring cask of amontillado that gives the story its title.

N.R.

Traplines

D ad takes the white marten from the trap.
      "Look at that, Will," he says.
      It is limp in his hands. It hasn't been dead that long.
  We tramp through the snow to the end of our trapline. Dad whistles. The
goner marten is over his shoulder. From here, it looks like Dad is wearing it. There
is nothing else in the other traps. We head back to the truck. The snow crunches.
This is the best time for trapping, Dad told me a while ago. This is when the
animals are hungry.
  Our truck rests by the roadside at an angle. Dad rolls the white marten in a
grey canvas cover separate from the others. The marten is flawless, which is rare
in these parts. I put my animals beside his and cover them. We get in the truck.
Dad turns the radio on and country twang fills the cab. We smell like sweat and oil
and pine. Dad hums. I stare out the window. Mrs. Smythe would say the trees here
are like the ones on Christmas postcards, tall and heavy with snow. They crowd
close to the road. When the wind blows strong enough, the older trees snap and
fall on the power lines.
  "Well, there's our Christmas money," Dad says, snatching a peek at the
rearview mirror.
  I look back. The wind ruffles the canvases that cover the martens. Dad is
smiling. He sits back, steering with one hand. He doesn't even mind when we are
passed by three cars. The lines in his face are loose now. He sings along with a
woman who left her husband — even that doesn't make him mad. We have our
Christmas money. At least for now, there'll be no shouting in the house. It will
take Mom and Dad a few days to find something else to fight about.
  The drive home is a long one. Dad changes the radio station twice. I search
my brain for something to say but my headache is spreading and I don't feel like
talking. He watches the road, though he keeps stealing looks at the back of the
truck. I watch the trees and the cars passing us.
  One of the cars has two women in it. The woman that isn't driving waves her
hands around as she talks. She reminds me of Mrs. Smythe. They are beside us,
then ahead of us, then gone.
  Tucca is still as we drive into it. The snow drugs it, makes it lazy. Houses
puff cedar smoke and the sweet, sharp smell gets in everyone's clothes. At school
in town, I can close my eyes and tell who's from the village and who isn't just by
smelling them.
  When we get home, we go straight to the basement. Dad gives me the ratty
martens and keeps the good ones. He made me start on squirrels when I was in
grade five. He put the knife in my hand, saying, "For Christ's sake, it's just a

squirrel. It's dead, you stupid knucklehead. It can't feel anything."

He made the first cut for me. I swallowed, closed my eyes, and lifted the knife.

"Jesus," Dad muttered. "Are you a sissy? I got a sissy for a son. Look. It's just like cutting up a chicken. See? Pretend you're skinning a chicken."

Dad showed me, then put another squirrel in front of me, and we didn't leave the basement until I got it right.

Now Dad is skinning the flawless white marten, using his best knife. His tongue is sticking out the corner of his mouth. He straightens up and shakes his skinning hand. I quickly start on the next marten. It's perfect except for a scar across its back. It was probably in a fight. We won't get much for the skin. Dad goes back to work. I stop, clench, unclench my hands. They are stiff.

"Goddamn," Dad says quietly. I look up, tensing, but Dad starts to smile. He's finished the marten. It's ready to be dried and sold. I've finished mine too. I look at my hands. They know what to do now without my having to tell them. Dad sings as we go up the creaking stairs. When we get into the hallway I breathe in, smelling fresh baked bread.

Mom is sprawled in front of the TV. Her apron is smudged with flour and she is licking her fingers. When she sees us, she stops and puts her hands in her apron pockets.

"Well?" she says.

Dad grabs her at the waist and whirls her around the living room.

"Greg! Stop it!" she says, laughing.

Flour gets on Dad and cedar chips get on Mom. They talk and I leave, sneaking into the kitchen. I swallow three aspirins for my headache, snatch two buns, and go to my room. I stop in the doorway. Eric is there, plugged into his electric guitar. He looks at the buns and pulls out an earphone.

"Give me one," he says.

I throw him the smaller bun, and he finishes it in three bites.

"The other one," he says.

I give him the finger and sit on my bed. I see him thinking about tackling me, but he shrugs and plugs himself back in. I chew on the bun, roll bits of it around in my mouth. It's still warm, and I wish I had some honey for it or some blueberry jam.

Eric leaves and comes back with six buns. He wolfs them down, cramming them into his mouth. I stick my fingers in my ears and glare at him. He can't hear himself eat. He notices me and grins. Opens his mouth so I can see. I pull out a mag and turn the pages.

Dad comes in. Eric's jaw clenches. I go into the kitchen, grabbing another bun. Mom smacks my hand. We hear Eric and Dad starting to yell. Mom rolls her eyes and puts three more loaves in the oven.

"Back later," I say.

She nods, frowning at her hands.

I walk. Think about going to Billy's house. He is seeing Elaine, though, and is getting weird. He wrote her a poem yesterday. He couldn't find anything nice to rhyme with "Elaine" so he didn't finish it.

"Pain," Craig said. "Elaine, you pain."

"Plain Elaine," Tony said.

Billy smacked Tony and they went at it in the snow. Billy gave him a face wash. That ended it, and we let Billy sit on the steps and write in peace.

"Elaine in the rain," I say, "Elaine, a flame. Cranes. Danes. Trains. My main Elaine." I kick at the slush on the ground. Billy is on his own.

I let my feet take me down the street. It starts to snow, tiny ladybug flakes. It is only four but already getting dark. Streetlights flicker on. No one but me is out walking. Snot in my nose freezes. The air is starting to burn my throat. I turn and head home. Eric and Dad should be tired by now.

Another postcard picture. The houses lining the street look snug. I hunch into my jacket. In a few weeks, Christmas lights will go up all over the village. Dad will put ours up two weeks before Christmas. We use the same set every year. We'll get a tree a week later. Mom'll decorate it. On Christmas Eve, she'll put our presents under it. Some of the presents will be wrapped in aluminum because she never buys enough wrapping paper. We'll eat turkey. Mom and Dad will go to a lot of parties and get really drunk. Eric will go to a lot of parties and get really stoned. Maybe this year I will too. Anything would be better than sitting around with Tony and Craig, listening to them gripe.

I stamp the snow off my sneakers and jeans. I open the door quietly. The TV is on loud. I can tell that it's a hockey game by the announcer's voice. I take off my shoes and jacket. The house feels really hot to me after being outside. My face starts to tingle as the skin thaws. I go into the kitchen and take another aspirin.

The kitchen could use some plants. It gets good light in the winter. Mrs. Smythe has filled her kitchen with plants, hanging the ferns by the window where the cats can't eat them. The Smythes have pictures all over their walls of places they have been — Europe, Africa, Australia. They've been everywhere. They can afford it, she says, because they don't have kids. They had one, a while ago. On the TV there's a wallet-sized picture of a dark-haired boy with his front teeth missing. He was their kid but he disappeared. Mrs. Smythe fiddles with the picture a lot.

Eric tries to sneak up behind me. His socks make a slithering sound on the floor. I duck just in time and hit him in the stomach.

He doubles over. He has a towel stretched between his hands. His choking game. He punches at me, but I hop out of the way. His fist hits the hot stove. Yelling, he jerks his hand back. I race out of the kitchen and down to the basement. Eric follows me, screaming my name. "Come out, you chicken," he says. "Come on out and fight."

I keep still behind a stack of plywood. Eric has the towel ready. After a while, he goes back upstairs and locks the door behind him.

I stand. I can't hear Mom and Dad. They must have gone out to celebrate the big catch. They'll probably find a party and go on a bender until Monday, when Dad has to go back to work. I'm alone with Eric, but he'll leave the house around ten. I can stay out of his way until then.

The basement door bursts open. I scramble under Dad's tool table. Eric must be stoned. He's probably been toking up since Mom and Dad left. Pot always makes him mean.

He laughs. "You baby. You fucking baby." He doesn't look for me that hard. He thumps loudly up the stairs, slams the door shut, then tiptoes back down and waits. He must think I'm really stupid.

We stay like this for a long time. Eric lights up. In a few minutes, the whole basement smells like pot. Dad will be pissed off if the smoke ruins the white marten. I smile, hoping it does. Eric will really get it then.

"Fuck," he says and disappears upstairs, not locking the door. I crawl out. My legs are stiff. The pot is making me dizzy.

The woodstove is cooling. I don't open it because the hinges squeal. It'll be freezing down here soon. Breathing fast, I climb the stairs. I crack the door open. There are no lights on except in our bedroom. I pull on my jacket and sneakers. I grab some bread and stuff it in my jacket, then run for the door but Eric is blocking it, leering.

"Thought you were sneaky, hey," he says.

I back into the kitchen. He follows. I wait until he is near before I bend over and ram him. He's slow because of the pot and slips to the floor. He grabs my ankle, but I kick him in the head and am out the door before he can catch me. I take the steps two at a time. Eric stands on the porch and laughs. I can't wait until I'm bigger. I'd like to smear him against a wall. Let him see what it feels like. I'd like to smear him so bad.

I munch on some bread as I head for the exit to the highway. Now the snow is coming down in thick, large flakes that melt when they touch my skin. I stand at the exit and wait.

I hear One Eye's beat-up Ford long before I see it. It clunks down the road and stalls when One Eye stops for me.

"You again. What you doing out here?" he yells at me.

"Waiting for Princess fucking Di," I say.

"Smart mouth. You keep it up and you can stay out there."

The back door opens anyway. Snooker and Jim are there. One Eye and Don Wilson are in the front. They all have silver lunch buckets at their feet.

We get into town and I say, "Could you drop me off here?"

One Eye looks back, surprised. He has forgotten about me. He frowns. "Where you going this time of night?"

"Disneyland," I say.

"Smart mouth," he says. "Don't be like your brother. You stay out of trouble."

I laugh. One Eye slows the car and pulls over. It chokes and sputters. I get out and thank him for the ride. One Eye grunts. He pulls away and I walk to Mrs. Smythe's.

ଔ

The first time I saw her house was last spring, when she invited the English class there for a barbecue. The lawn was neat and green and I only saw one dandelion. There were rose bushes in the front and raspberry bushes in the back. I went with Tony and Craig, who got high on the way there. Mrs. Smythe noticed right away. She took them aside and talked to them. They stayed in the poolroom downstairs until the high wore off.

There weren't any other kids from the village there. Only townies. Kids that Dad says will never dirty their pink hands. They were split into little groups. They talked and ate and laughed and I wandered around alone, feeling like a dork. I was going to go downstairs to Tony and Craig when Mrs. Smythe came up to me, carrying a hot dog. I never noticed her smile until then. Her blue sundress swayed as she walked.

"You weren't in class yesterday," she said.

"Stomachache."

"I was going to tell you how much I liked your essay. You must have done a lot of work on it."

"Yeah." I tried to remember what I had written.

"Which part was the hardest?" she said.

I cleared my throat. "Starting it."

"I walked right into that one," she said, laughing. I smiled.

A tall man came up and hugged her. She kissed him. "Sam," she said. "This is the student I was telling you about."

"Well, hello," Mr. Smythe said. "Great paper."

"Thanks," I said.

"Is it William or Will?" Mr. Smythe said.

"Will," I said. He held out his hand and shook mine.

"That big, huh?" he said.

Oh no, I thought, remembering what I'd written. Dad, Eric, Grandpa, and I had gone out halibut fishing once and caught a huge one. It took forever to get it in the boat and we all took turns clubbing it. But it wouldn't die, so Dad shot it. In the essay I said it was seven hundred pounds, but Mrs. Smythe had pointed out to the whole class that halibut didn't get much bigger than five hundred. Tony and Craig bugged me about that.

"Karen tells me you've written a lot about fishing," Mr. Smythe said, sounding really cheerful.

"Excuse me," Mrs. Smythe said. "That's my cue to leave. If you're smart, you'll do the same. Once you get Sam going with his stupid fish stories you can't get a word —"

Mr. Smythe goosed her. She poked him with her hot dog and left quickly. Mr. Smythe put his arm around my shoulder, shaking his head. We sat out on the patio and he told me about the time he caught a marlin and about scuba diving on the Great Barrier Reef. He went down in a shark cage once to try to film a great white eating. I told him about Uncle Bernie's gillnetter. He wanted to know if Uncle Bernie would take him out, and what gear he was going to need. We ended up in the kitchen, me using a flounder to show him how to clean a halibut.

I finally looked at the clock around eleven. Dad had said he would pick me and Tony and Craig up around eight. I didn't even know where Tony and Craig were anymore. I couldn't believe it had gotten so late without my noticing. Mrs. Smythe had gone to bed. Mr. Smythe said he would drive me home. I said that was okay, I'd hitch.

He snorted. "Karen would kill me. No, I'll drive you. Let's phone your parents and tell them you're coming home."

No one answered the phone. I said they were probably asleep. He dialed again. Still no answer.

"Looks like you've got the spare bedroom tonight," he said.

"Let me try," I said, picking up the phone. There was no answer, but after six rings I pretended Dad was on the other end. I didn't want to spend the night at my English teacher's house. Tony and Craig would never shut up about it.

"Hi, Dad," I said. "How come? I see. Car trouble. No problem. Mr. Smythe is going to drive me home. What? Sure, I —"

"Let me talk to him," Mr. Smythe said, snatching the phone. "Hello! Mr. Tate! How are you? My, my, my. Your son is a lousy liar, isn't he?" He hung up. "It's amazing how much your father sounds like a dial tone."

I picked up the phone again. "They're sleeping, that's all." Mr. Smythe watched me as I dialed. There wasn't any answer.

"Why'd you lie?" he said quietly.

We were alone in the kitchen. I swallowed. He was a lot bigger than me. When he reached over, I put my hands up and covered my face. He stopped, then took the phone out of my hands.

"It's okay," he said. "I won't hurt you. It's okay."

I put my hands down. He looked sad. That annoyed me. I shrugged, backing away. "I'll hitch," I said.

Mr. Smythe shook his head. "No, really, Karen would kill me, then she'd go after you. Come on. We'll be safer if you sleep in the spare room."

In the morning Mr. Smythe was up before I could sneak out. He was making bacon and pancakes. He asked if I'd ever done any freshwater fishing. I said no. He started talking about fishing in the Black Sea and I listened to him. He's a good cook.

Mrs. Smythe came into the kitchen dressed in some sweats and a T-shirt. She ate without saying anything and didn't look awake until she finished her coffee. Mr. Smythe phoned my house but no one answered. He asked if I wanted to go up to Old Timer's Lake with them. He had a new Sona reel he wanted to try out. I didn't have anything better to do.

The Smythes have a twenty-foot speedboat. They let me drive it around the lake a few times while Mrs. Smythe baked in the sun and Mr. Smythe put the rod together. We lazed around the beach in the afternoon, watching the people go by. Sipping their beers, the Smythes argued about who was going to drive back. We rode around the lake some more and roasted hot dogs for dinner.

CR

Their porch light is on. I go up the walk and ring the bell. Mrs. Smythe said just come in, don't bother knocking, but I can't do that. It doesn't feel right. She opens the door, smiling when she sees me. She is wearing a fluffy pink sweater. "Hi, Will. Sam was hoping you'd drop by. He says he's looking forward to beating you."

"Dream on," I say.

She laughs. "Go right in." She heads down the hall to the washroom.

I go into the living room. Mr. Smythe isn't there. The TV is on, some documentary about whales.

He's in the kitchen, scrunched over a game of solitaire. His new glasses are sliding off his nose and he looks more like a teacher than Mrs. Smythe. He scratches the beard he's trying to grow.

"Come on in," he says, patting the chair beside him.

I take a seat and watch him finish the game. He pushes his glasses up. "What's your pleasure?" he says.

"Pool," I say.

"Feeling lucky, huh?" We go down to the poolroom. "How about a little extra this week?" he says, not looking at me.

I shrug. "Sure. Dishes?"

He shakes his head. "Bigger."

"I'm not shoveling the walk," I say.

He shakes his head again. "Bigger."

"Money?

"Bigger."

"What?"

He racks up the balls. Sets the cue ball. Wipes his hands on his jeans.

"What?" I say again.

Mr. Smythe takes out a quarter. "Heads or tails?" he says, tossing it.

"Heads," I say.

He slaps the quarter on the back of his hand. "I break."

"Where? Let me see that," I say, laughing. He holds it up. The quarter is tails.

He breaks. "How'd you like to stay with us?" he says, very quietly.

"Sure," I say. "But I got to go back on Tuesday. We got to check the traplines again."

He is quiet. The balls make thunking sounds as they bounce around the table. "Do you like it here?"

"Sure," I say.

"Enough to live here?"

I'm not sure I heard him right. Maybe he's asking a different question from the one I think he's asking. I open my mouth. I don't know what to say. I say nothing.

"Those are the stakes, then," he says. "I win, you stay. You win, you stay."

He's joking. I laugh. He doesn't laugh. "You serious? " I ask.

He stands up straight. "I don't think I've ever been more serious."

The room is suddenly very small.

"Your turn," he says. "Stripes."

I scratch, missing the ball by a mile. He takes his turn.

"We don't want to push you," he says. He leans over the table, squints at a ball. "We just think that you'd be safer here. Hell, you practically live with us already." I watch my sneakers. He keeps playing. "We aren't rich. We aren't perfect. We . . ." He looks at me. "We thought maybe you'd like to try it for a couple of weeks first."

"I can't."

"You don't have to decide right now," he says. "Think about it. Take a few days."

It's my turn again but I don't feel like playing anymore. Mr. Smythe is waiting, though. I pick a ball. Aim, shoot, miss.

The game goes on in silence. Mr. Smythe wins easily. He smiles. "Well, I win. You stay."

If I wanted to get out of the room, there is only one door and Mr. Smythe is blocking it. He watches me. "Let's go upstairs," he says.

Mrs. Smythe has shut off the TV. She stands up when we come into the living room. "Will —"

"I asked him already," Mr. Smythe says.

Her head snaps around. "You what?"

"I asked him."

Her hands clench at her sides. "We were supposed to do it together, Sam." Her voice is flat. She turns to me. "You said no."

I can't look at her. I look at the walls, at the floor, at her slippers. I shouldn't have come tonight. I should have waited for Eric to leave. She stands in front of me, trying to smile. Her hands are warm on my face. "Look at me," she says. "Will? Look at me." She is trying to smile. "Hungry?" she says.

I nod. She makes a motion with her head for Mr. Smythe to follow her into the kitchen. When they're gone I sit down. It should be easy. It should be easy. I watch TV without seeing it. I wonder what they're saying about me in the kitchen.

It's now almost seven and my ribs hurt. Mostly, I can ignore it, but Eric hit me pretty hard and they're bruised. Eric got hit pretty hard by Dad, so we're even, I guess. I'm counting the days until Eric moves out. The rate he's going, he'll be busted soon anyway. Tony says the police are starting to ask questions.

It's a strange night. We all pretend that nothing has happened and Mrs. Smythe fixes some nachos. Mr. Smythe gets out a pack of Uno cards and we play a few rounds and watch the Discovery Channel. We go to bed.

I lie awake. My room. This could be my room. I already have most of my books here. It's hard to study with Eric around. I still have a headache. I couldn't get away from them long enough to sneak into the kitchen for an aspirin. I pull my T-shirt up and take a look. There's a long bruise under my ribs and five smaller ones above it. I think Eric was trying to hit my stomach but he was so wasted he kept missing. It isn't too bad. Tony's dad broke three of his ribs once. Billy got a concussion a couple of weeks ago. My dad is pretty easy. It's only Eric who really bothers me.

The Smythes keep the aspirin by the spices. I grab six, three for now and three for the morning. I'm swallowing the last one when Mr. Smythe grabs my hand. I didn't even hear him come in. I must be sleepy.

"Where'd they hit you this time?" he says.

"I got a headache," I say. "A bad one."

He pries open the hand with the aspirins in it. "How many do you plan on taking?"

"These are for later."

He sighs. I get ready for a lecture. "Go back to bed" is all he says. "It'll be okay." He sounds very tired.

"Sure," I say.

I get up around five. I leave a note saying I have things to do at home. I catch a ride with some guys coming off the graveyard shift.

෯

No one is home. Eric had a party last night. I'm glad I wasn't around. They've wrecked the coffee table and the rug smells like stale beer and cigarettes. Our bedroom is even worse. Someone puked all over Eric's bed and there are two used condoms on mine. At least none of the windows were broken this time. I start to clean my side of the room, then stop. I sit on my bed.

Mr. Smythe will be getting up soon. It's Sunday, so there'll be waffles or french toast. He'll fix a plate of bacon and eat it before Mrs. Smythe comes downstairs. He thinks she doesn't know that he does this. She'll get up around ten or eleven and won't talk to anyone until she's had about three coffees. She starts to wake up around one or two. They'll argue about something. Whose turn to take out the garbage or do the laundry. They'll read the paper.

I crawl into bed. The aspirin isn't working. I try to sleep but it really reeks in here. I have a biology test tomorrow. I forgot to bring the book back from their place. I lie there awake until our truck pulls into the driveway. Mom and Dad are fighting. They sound plastered. Mom is bitching about something. Dad is not saying anything. Doors slam.

Mom comes in first and goes straight to bed. She doesn't seem to notice the house is a mess. Dad comes in a lot slower.

"What the — Eric!" he yells. "Eric!"

I pretend to sleep. The door bangs open.

"Eric, you little bastard," Dad says, looking around. He shakes me. "Where the fuck is Eric?"

His breath is lethal. You can tell he likes his rye straight.

"How should I know?"

He rips Eric's amplifiers off the walls. He throws them down and gives them a good kick. He tips Eric's bed over. Eric is smart. He won't come home for a while. Dad will have cooled off by then and Eric can give him some money without Dad's getting pissed off. I don't move, I wait until he's out of the room before I put on a sweater. I can hear him down in the basement chopping wood. It should be around eight by now. The RinkyDink will be open in an hour.

When I go into the kitchen, Mom is there. She sees me and makes a shushing motion with her hands. She pulls out a bottle from behind the stove and sits down at the kitchen table.

"You're a good boy," she says, giggling. "You're a good boy. Help your old mother back to bed, hey."

"Sure," I say, putting an arm around her. She stands, holding onto the bottle with one hand and me with the other. "This way, my lady."

"You making fun of me?" she says, her eyes going small. "You laughing at me?" Then she laughs and we go to their room. She flops onto the bed. She takes a long drink. "You're fucking laughing at me, aren't you?"

"Mom, you're paranoid. I was making a joke."

"Yeah, you're really funny. A laugh a minute," she says, giggling again. "Real comedian."

"Yeah, that's me."

She throws the bottle at me. I duck. She rolls over and starts to cry. I cover her with the blanket and leave. The floor is sticky. Dad's still chopping wood. They wouldn't notice if I wasn't here. Maybe people would talk for a week or two, but after a while they wouldn't notice. The only people who would miss me are Tony and Craig and Billy and maybe Eric, when he got toked up and didn't have anything for target practice.

Billy is playing Mortal Kombat at the RinkyDink. He's chain-smoking. As I walk up to him, he turns around quickly.

"Oh, it's you," he says, going back to the game.

"Hi to you too," I say.

"You seen Elaine?" he says.

"Nope."

He crushes out his cigarette in the ashtray beside him. He plays for a while, loses a life, then shakes another cigarette out one-handed. He sticks it in his mouth, loses another man, then lights up. He sucks deep. "Relax," I say. "Her majesty's limo is probably stuck in traffic. She'll come."

He glares at me. "Shut up."

I go play pool with Craig, who's decided that he's James Dean. He's wearing a white T-shirt, jeans, and a black leather jacket that looks like his brother's. His hair is blow-dried and a cigarette dangles from the corner of his mouth.

"What a loser," he says.

"Who you calling a loser?"

"Billy. What a loser." He struts to the other side of the pool table.

"He's okay."

"That babe," he says. "What's-her-face. Ellen? Irma?"

"Elaine."

"Yeah, her. She's going out with him 'cause she's got a bet."

"What?"

"She's got to go out with him a month, and her friend will give her some coke."

"Billy's already giving her coke."

"Yeah. He's a loser."

I look over at Billy. He's lighting another cigarette.

"Can you imagine a townie wanting anything to do with him?" Craig says. "She's just doing it as a joke. She's going to dump him in a week. She's going to put all his stupid poems in the paper."

I see it now. There's a space around Billy. No one is going near him. He doesn't notice. Same with me. I catch some guys I used to hang out with grinning at me. When they see me looking at them, they look away.

Craig wins the game. I'm losing a lot this week.

Elaine gets to the RinkyDink after lunch. She's got some townie girlfriends with her who are tiptoeing around like they're going to get jumped. Elaine leads them right up to Billy. Everyone's watching. Billy gives her his latest poem. I wonder what he found to rhyme with "Elaine."

The girls leave. Billy holds the door open for Elaine. Her friends start to giggle. The guys standing around start to howl. They're laughing so hard they're crying. I feel sick. I think about telling Billy but I know he won't listen.

I leave the RinkyDink and go for a walk. I walk and walk and end up back in front of the RinkyDink. There's nowhere else to go. I hang out with Craig, who hasn't left the pool table.

I spend the night on his floor. Craig's parents are Jehovah's Witnesses and preach at me before I go to bed. I sit and listen because I need a place to sleep. I'm not going home until tomorrow, when Mom and Dad are sober. Craig's mom gets us up two hours before the bus that takes the village kids to school comes. They pray before we eat. Craig looks at me and rolls his eyes. People are always making fun of Craig because his parents stand on the corner downtown every Friday and hold up the *Watchtower* mags. When his parents start to bug him, he says he'll take up devil worship or astrology if they don't lay off. I think I'll ask him if he wants to hang out with me on Christmas. His parents don't believe in it.

Between classes I pass Mrs. Smythe in the hall. Craig nudges me. "Go on," he says, making sucking noises. "Go get your A."

"Fuck off," I say, pushing him.

She's talking to some girl and doesn't see me. I think about skipping English but know that she'll call home and ask where I am.

At lunch no one talks to me. I can't find Craig or Tony or Billy. The village guys who hang out by the science wing snicker as I go past. I don't stop until I get to the gym doors, where the headbangers have taken over. I don't have any money and I didn't bring a lunch, so I bum a cigarette off this girl with really tight jeans. To get my mind off my stomach I try to get her to go out with me. She looks at me like I'm crazy. When she walks away, the fringe on her leather jacket swings.

I flunk my biology test. It's multiple choice. I stare at the paper and kick myself. I know I could have passed if I'd read the chapter. Mr. Kellerman reads out the scores from lowest to highest. My name is called out third.

"Mr. Tate," he says. "Three out of thirty."

"All riiight," Craig says, slapping my back.

"Mr. Davis," Mr. Kellerman says to Craig, "three and a half."

Craig stands up and bows. The guys in the back clap. The kids in the front laugh. Mr. Kellerman reads out the rest of the scores. Craig turns to me. "Looks like I beat the Brain," he says.

"Yeah," I say. "Pretty soon you're going to be getting the Nobel Prize."

The bell rings for English. I go to my locker and take out my jacket. If she calls home no one's going to answer anyway.

I walk downtown. The snow is starting to slack off and it's even sunning a bit. My stomach growls. I haven't eaten anything since breakfast. I wish I'd gone to English. Mrs. Smythe would have given me something to eat. She always has something left over from lunch. I hunch down into my jacket.

Downtown, I go to the Paradise Arcade. All the heads hang out there. Maybe Eric'll give me some money. More like a belt, but it's worth a try. I don't see him anywhere, though. In fact, no one much is there. Just some burnouts by the pinball machines. I see Mitch and go over to him, but he's soaring, laughing at the ball going around the machine. I walk away, head for the highway, and hitch home. Mom will have passed out by now, and Dad'll be at work.

⭕

Sure enough, Mom is on the living room floor. I get her a blanket. The stove has gone out and it's freezing in here. I go into the kitchen and look through the fridge. There's one jar of pickles, some really pathetic-looking celery, and some milk that's so old it smells like cheese. There's no bread left over from Saturday. I find some Rice-A-Roni and cook it. Mom comes to and asks for some water. I bring her a glass and give her a little Rice-A-Roni. She makes a face but slowly eats it.

At six Dad comes home with Eric. They've made up. Eric has bought Dad a six-pack and they watch the hockey game together. I stay in my room. Eric has cleaned his bed by dumping his mattress outside and stealing mine. I haul my mattress back onto my bed frame. I pull out my English book. We have a grammar test this Friday. I know Mrs. Smythe will be unhappy if she has to fail me. I read the chapter on nouns and get through most of the one on verbs before Eric comes in and kicks me off the bed.

He tries to take the mattress but I punch him in the side. Eric turns and grabs my hair. "This is my bed," he says. "Understand?"

"Fuck you," I say. "You had the party. Your fucked-up friends trashed the room. You sleep on the floor."

Dad comes in and sees Eric push me against the wall and smack my face. He yells at Eric, who turns around, his fist frozen in the air. Dad rolls his sleeves up.

"You always take his side!" Eric yells. "You never take mine!"

"Pick on someone your own size," Dad says. "Unless you want to deal with me."

Eric gives me a look that says he'll settle with me later. I pick up my English book and get out. I walk around the village, staying away from the RinkyDink. It's the first place Eric will look.

I'm at the village exit. The sky is clear and the stars are popping out. Mr. Smythe will be at his telescope trying to map the Pleiades. Mrs. Smythe will be marking papers while she watches TV.

"Need a ride?" this guy says. There's a blue pickup stopped in front of me. The driver is wearing a hunting cap.

I take my hand out of my mouth. I've been chewing my knuckle like a baby. I shake my head. "I'm waiting for someone," I say.

He shrugs and takes off. I stand there and watch his headlights disappear.

They didn't really mean it. They'd get bored of me quick when they found out what I'm like. I should have just said yes. I could have stayed until they got fed up and then come home when Eric had cooled off.

Two cars pass me as I walk back to the village. I can hide at Tony's until Eric goes out with his friends and forgets this afternoon. My feet are frozen by the time I get to the RinkyDink. Tony is there.

"So. I heard Craig beat you in biology," he says.

I laugh. "Didn't it just impress you?"

"A whole half a point. Way to go," he says. "For a while there we thought you were getting townie."

"Yeah, right," I say. "Listen, I pissed Eric off —"

"Surprise, surprise."

"— and I need a place to crash. Can I sleep over?"

"Sure," he says. Mitch wanders into the RinkyDink, and a crowd of kids slowly drifts over to him. He looks around, eyeing everybody. Then he starts giving something out. Me and Tony go over.

"Wow," Tony says, after Mitch gives him something too.

"What?"

We leave and go behind the RinkyDink, where other kids are gathered. "Fucking all right," I hear Craig say, even though I can't see him.

"What?" I say. Tony opens his hand. He's holding a little vial with white crystals in it.

"Crack," he says. "Man, is he stupid. He could have made a fortune and he's just giving it away."

We don't have a pipe, and Tony wants to do this right the first time. He decides to save it for tomorrow, after he buys the right equipment. I'm hungry again. I'm about to tell him that I'm going to Billy's when I see Eric.

"Shit," I say and hide behind him.

Tony looks up. "Someone's in trou-ble," he sings.

Eric's looking for me. I hunch down behind Tony, who tries to look innocent. Eric spots him and starts to come over. "Better run," Tony whispers.

I sneak behind some other people but Eric sees me and I have to run for it anyway. Tony starts to cheer and the kids behind the RinkyDink join in. Some of the guys follow us so they'll see what happens when Eric catches up with me. I don't want to find out so I pump as hard as I can.

Eric used to be fast. I'm glad he's a dopehead now because he can't really run anymore. I'm panting and my legs are cramping but the house is in sight. I run up the stairs. The door is locked.

I stand there, hand on the knob. Eric rounds the corner to our block. There's no one behind him. I bang on the door but now I see that our truck is gone. I run around to the back but the basement door is locked too. Even the windows are locked.

Eric pops his head around the corner of the house. He grins when he sees me, then disappears. I grit my teeth and start running across our backyard. Head for Billy's. "You shithead," Eric yells. He has a friend with him, maybe Brent. I duck behind our neighbour's house. There's snow in my sneakers and all the way up my leg, but I'm sweating. I stop. I can't hear Eric. I hope I've lost him, but Eric is really pissed off and when he's pissed off he doesn't let go. I look down. My footprints are clear in the snow. I start to run again, but I hit a thick spot and have to wade through thigh-high snow. I look back. Eric is nowhere. I keep slogging. I make it to the road again and run down to the exit.

I've lost him. I'm shaking because it's cold. I can feel the sweat cooling on my skin. My breath goes back to normal. I wait for a car to come by. I've missed the night shift and the graveyard crew won't be by until midnight. It's too cold to wait that long.

A car, a red car. A little Toyota. Brent's car. I run off the road and head for a clump of trees. The Toyota pulls over and Eric gets out, yelling. I reach the trees and rest. They're waiting by the roadside. Eric is peering into the trees, trying to see me. Brent is smoking in the car. Eric crosses his arms over his chest and blows into his hands. My legs are frozen.

After a long time, a cop car cruises to a stop beside the Toyota. I wade out and wave at the two policemen. They look startled. One of them turns to Eric and Brent and asks them something. I see Eric shrug. It takes me a while to get over to where they're standing because my legs are slow.

The cop is watching me. I swear I'll never call them pigs again. I swear it. He leans over to Brent, who digs around in the glove compartment. The cop says something to his partner. I scramble down the embankment.

Eric has no marks on his face. Dad probably hit him on the back and stomach. Dad has been careful since the social worker came to our house. Eric suddenly smiles at me and holds out his hand. I move behind the police car.

"Is there a problem here?" the policeman says.

"No," Eric says. "No probulum. Li'l misunnerstanin'."

Oh, shit. He's as high as a kite. The policeman looks hard at Eric. I look at the car. Brent is staring at me, glassy-eyed. He's high too.

Eric tries again to reach out to me. I put the police car between us. The policeman grabs Eric by the arm and his partner goes and gets Brent. The policeman says something about driving under the influence but none of us are listening. Eric's eyes are on me. I'm going to pay for this. Brent is swearing. He wants a lawyer. He stumbles out of the Toyota and slips on the road. Brent and Eric are put in the backseat of the police car. The policeman comes up to me and says, "Can you make it home?"

I nod.

"Good. Go," he says.

They drive away. When I get home, I walk around the house, trying to figure out a way to break in. I find a stick and jimmy the basement door open. Just in case Eric gets out tonight, I make a bed under the tool table and go to sleep.

No one is home when I wake up. I scramble an egg and get ready for school. I sit beside Tony on the bus.

"I was expecting to see you with black eyes," he says.

My legs are still raw from last night. I have something due today but I can't remember what. If Eric is in the drunk tank, they'll let him out later.

The village guys are talking to me again. I skip gym. I skip history. I hang out with Craig and Tony in the Paradise Arcade. I'm not sure if I want to be friends with them after they joined in the chase last night, but it's better to have them on my side than not. They get a two-for-one pizza special for lunch and I'm glad I stuck with them because I'm starved. They also got some five-finger specials from Safeway. Tony is proud because he swiped a couple of bags of chips and two Pepsis and no one even noticed.

Mitch comes over to me in the bathroom.

"That was a really cheap thing to do," he says.

"What?" I haven't done anything to him.

"What? What? Getting your brother thrown in jail. Pretty crummy."

"He got himself thrown in jail. He got caught when he was high."

"That's not what he says." Mitch frowns. "He says you set him up."

"Fuck." I try to sound calm. "When'd he tell you that?"

"This morning," he says. "He's waiting for you at school."

"I didn't set him up. How could I?"

Mitch nods. He hands me some crack and says, "Hey, I'm sorry," and leaves. I look at it. I'll give it to Tony and maybe he'll let me stay with him tonight.

Billy comes into the Paradise with Elaine and her friends. He's getting some glances but he doesn't notice. He holds the chair out for Elaine, who sits down without looking at him. I don't want to be around for this. I go over to Tony.

"I'm leaving," I say.

Tony shushes me. "Watch," he says.

Elaine orders a beer. Frankie shakes his head and points to the sign that says WE DO NOT SERVE MINORS. Elaine frowns. She says something to Billy. He shrugs. She orders a Coke. Billy pays. When their Cokes come, Elaine dumps hers over Billy's head. Billy stares at her, more puzzled than anything else. Her friends start to laugh, and I get up and walk out.

I lean against the wall of the Paradise. Billy comes out a few minutes later. His face is still and pale. Elaine and her friends follow him, reciting lines from the poems he wrote her. Tony and the rest spill out too, laughing. I go back inside and trade the crack for some quarters for the video games. I keep losing. Tony wants to go now and we hitch back to the village. We raid his fridge and have chocolate ice cream coconut sundaes. Angela comes in with Di and says that Eric is looking for me. I look at Tony and he looks at me.

"Boy, are you in for it," Tony says. "You'd better stay here tonight."

When everyone is asleep, Tony pulls out a weird-looking pipe and does the crack. His face goes very dreamy and far away. A few minutes later he says, "Christ, that's great. I wonder how much Mitch has?"

I turn over and go to sleep.

CR

The next morning Billy is alone on the bus. No one wants to sit with him so there are empty seats all around him. He looks like he hasn't slept. Tony goes up to him and punches him in the arm.

"So how's Shakespeare this morning?" Tony says.

I hope Eric isn't at the school. I don't know where else I can hide.

Mrs. Smythe is waiting at the school bus stop. I sneak out the back door of the bus, with Tony and the guys pretending to fight to cover me.

We head back to the Paradise. I'm starting to smell bad. I haven't had a shower in days. I wish I had some clean clothes. I wish I had some money to buy a toothbrush. I hate the scummy feeling on my teeth. I wish I had enough for a taco or a hamburger.

Dad is at the Paradise, looking for me.

"Let's go to the Dairy Queen," he says.

He orders a coffee, a chocolate milk shake, and a cheeseburger. We take the coffee and milk shake to a back table, and I pocket the order slip. We sit there. Dad folds and unfolds a napkin.

"One of your teachers called," he says.

"Mrs. Smythe?"

"Yeah." He looks up. "Says she'd like you to stay there."

I try to read his face. His eyes are bloodshot and red-rimmed. He must have a big hangover.

The cashier calls out our number. I go up and get the cheeseburger and we split it. Dad always eats slow to make it last longer.

"Did you tell her you wanted to?"

"No," I say. "They asked me, but I said I couldn't."

Dad nods. "Did you tell them anything?"

"Like what?"

"Don't get smart," he says, sounding beat.

"I didn't say anything."

He stops chewing. "Then why'd they ask you?"

"Don't know."

"You must have told them something."

"Nope. They just asked."

"Did Eric tell them?"

I snort. "Eric? No way. They would . . . He wouldn't go anywhere near them. They're okay, Dad. They won't tell anybody."

"So you did tell them."

"I didn't. I swear I didn't. Look, Eric got me on the face a couple of times and they just figured it out."

"You're lying."

I finished my half of the cheeseburger. "I'm not lying. I didn't say anything and they won't either."

"I never touched you."

"Yeah, Eric took care of that," I say. "You seen him?"

"I kicked him out."

"You what?"

"Party. Ruined the basement," Dad says grimly. "He's old enough. Had to leave sooner or later."

He chews his last mouthful of cheeseburger. Eric will really be out of his mind now.

We drive out to check the trapline. The first trap has been tripped with a stick. Dad curses, blaming the other trappers who have lines near ours. "I'll skunk them," he says. But the last three traps have got some more martens. We even get a little lynx. Dad is happy. We go home. The basement is totally ripped apart.

Next day at school, I spend most of the time ducking from Eric and Mrs. Smythe before I finally get sick of the whole lot and go down to the Paradise. Tony is there with Billy, who asks me if I want to go to Vancouver with him until Eric cools off.

"Now?"

"No better time," he says.

I think about it. "When you leaving?"

"Tonight."

"I don't know. I don't have any money."

"Me neither," he says.

"Shit," I say. "How we going to get there? It's a zillion miles from here."

"Hitch to town, hitch to Smithers, then down to Prince George."

"Yeah, yeah, but what are we going to eat?"

He wiggles his hand. Five-finger special. I laugh.

"You change your mind," he says, "I'll be behind the RinkyDink around seven. Get some thick boots."

We're about to hitch home when I see Mrs. Smythe peer into the Paradise. It's too late to hide because she sees me. Her face stiffens. She walks over to us and the guys start to laugh. Mrs. Smythe looks at them, then at me.

"Will?" she says. "Can I talk to you outside?"

She glances around like the guys are going to jump her. I try to see what she's nervous about. Tony is grabbing his crotch. Billy is cleaning his nails. The other guys are snickering. I suddenly see them the way she does. They all have long, greasy hair, combed straight back. We're all wearing jeans, T-shirts, and sneakers. We don't look nice.

She's got on her school uniform, as she calls it. Dark skirt, white shirt, low black heels, glasses. She's watching me like she hasn't seen me before. I hope she never sees my house.

"Later?" I say. "I'm kind of busy."

She blushes, the guys laugh hard. I wish I could take the words back. "Are you sure?" she says.

Tony nudges my arm. "Why don't you introduce us to your girlfriend," he says. "Maybe she'd like —"

"Shut up," I say. Mrs. Smythe has no expression now.

"I'll talk to you later, then," she says, and turns around and walks out without looking back. If I could, I'd follow her.

Billy claps me on the shoulder. "Stay away from them," he says. "It's not worth it."

It doesn't matter. She practically said she didn't want to see me again. I don't blame her. I wouldn't want to see me again either.

She'll get into her car now and go home. She'll honk when she pulls into the driveway so Mr. Smythe will come out and help her with the groceries. She always gets groceries today. The basics and sardines. Peanut butter. I lick my lips. Diamante frozen pizzas. Oodles of Noodles. Waffles. Blueberry Mueslix.

Mr. Smythe will come out of the house, wave, come down the driveway. They'll take the groceries into the house after they kiss. They'll kick the snow off their shoes and throw something in the microwave. Watch *Cheers* reruns on Channel 8. Mr. Smythe will tell her what happened in his day. Maybe she will say what happened in hers.

We catch a ride home. Billy yabbers about Christmas in Vancouver, and how great it's going to be, the two of us, no one to boss us around, no one to bother us, going anywhere we want. I turn away from him. Watch the trees blur past. I guess anything'll be better than sitting around, listening to Tony and Craig gripe.

ℰℛ

Eden Robinson's stories reflect the changing direction of Canadian Aboriginal writing. Where earlier First Nations writers gravitated toward the literature of protest or of personal healing, Robinson's generation finds its subject matter in the horror and wonder of everyday life. "Traplines" is a chilling portrait of a teenage boy's attempt to find safe passage in a world in which the traps of alcoholism, substance abuse, violence, and faithlessness are seemingly set for children at their birth. The details the adolescent narrator, Will, selects reveal a boy who is still alive to the beauty of a flawless white marten or of heavy snow on a northern pine. However, Will's unquestioning acceptance of a life without hope, and his unswerving conviction that he does not deserve deliverance, together underscore the tragedy at the centre of the lives of adolescents like himself: the one trap from which these children have no hope of escape is the trap which they set for themselves.

G.B.

SINCLAIR ROSS *(1908-1997)*

The Painted Door

S traight across the hills it was five miles from John's farm to his father's. But in winter, with the roads impassable, a team had to make a wide detour and skirt the hills, so that from five the distance was more than trebled to seventeen.

"I think I'll walk," John said at breakfast to his wife. "The drifts in the hills wouldn't hold a horse, but they'll carry me all right. If I leave early I can spend a few hours helping him with his chores, and still be back by suppertime."

She went to the window, and thawing a clear place in the frost with her breath, stood looking across the snowswept farmyard to the huddle of stables and sheds. "There was a double wheel around the moon last night," she countered presently. "You said yourself we could expect a storm. It isn't right to leave me here alone. Surely I'm as important as your father."

He glanced up uneasily, then drinking off his coffee tried to reassure her. "But there's nothing to be afraid of — even supposing it does start to storm. You won't need to go near the stable. Everything's fed and watered now to last till night. I'll be back at the latest by seven or eight."

She went on blowing against the frosted pane, carefully elongating the clear place until it was oval-shaped and symmetrical. He watched her a moment or two longer, then more insistently repeated, "I say you won't need to go near the stable. Everything's fed and watered, and I'll see that there's plenty of wood in. That will be all right, won't it?"

"Yes — of course — I heard you —" It was a curiously cold voice now, as if the words were chilled by their contact with the frosted pane. "Plenty to eat — plenty of wood to keep me warm — what more could a woman ask for?"

"But he's an old man — living there all alone. What is it, Ann? You're not like yourself this morning."

She shook her head without turning. "Pay no attention to me. Seven years a farmer's wife — it's time I was used to staying alone."

Slowly the clear place on the glass enlarged: oval, then round, then oval again. The sun was risen above the frost mists now, so keen and hard a glitter on the snow that instead of warmth its rays seemed shedding cold. One of the two-year-old colts that had cantered away when John turned the horses out for water stood covered with rime at the stable door again, head down and body hunched, each breath a little plume of steam against the frosty air. She shivered, but did not turn. In the clear, bitter light the long white miles of prairie landscape seemed a region alien to life. Even the distant farmsteads she could see served only to intensify a sense of isolation. Scattered across the face of so vast and bleak a wilderness it was difficult to conceive them as a testimony of human hardihood and endurance. Rather they seemed futile, lost, to cower before the implacability of snow-swept earth and clear pale sun-chilled sky.

And when at last she turned from the window there was a brooding stillness in her face as if she had recognized this mastery of snow and cold. It troubled John. "If you're really afraid," he yielded, "I won't go today. Lately it's been so cold, that's all. I just wanted to make sure he's all right in case we do have a storm."

"I know — I'm not really afraid." She was putting in a fire now, and he could no longer see her face. "Pay no attention. It's ten miles there and back, so you'd better get started."

"You ought to know by now I wouldn't stay away," he tried to brighten her. "No matter how it stormed. Before we were married — remember? Twice a week I never missed and we had some bad blizzards that winter too."

He was a slow, unambitious man, content with his farm and cattle, naïvely proud of Ann. He had been bewildered by it once, her caring for a dull-witted fellow like him; then assured at last of her affection he had relaxed against it gratefully, unsuspecting it might ever be less constant than his own. Even now, listening to the restless brooding in her voice, he felt only a quick, unformulated kind of pride that after seven years his absence for a day should still concern her. While she, his trust and earnestness controlling her again:

"I know. It's just that sometimes when you're away I get lonely. . . . There's a long cold tramp in front of you. You'll let me fix a scarf around your face."

He nodded. "And on my way I'll drop in at Steven's place. Maybe he'll come over tonight for a game of cards. You haven't seen anybody but me for the last two weeks."

She glanced up sharply, then busied herself clearing the table. "It will mean another two miles if you do. You're going to be cold and tired enough as it is. When you're gone I think I'll paint the kitchen woodwork. White this time — you remember we got the paint last fall. It's going to make the room a lot lighter. I'll be too busy to find the day long."

"I will though," he insisted, "and if a storm gets up you'll feel safer, knowing that he's coming. That's what you need, maybe — someone to talk to besides me."

She stood at the stove motionless a moment, then turned to him uneasily. "Will you shave then, John — now — before you go?"

He glanced at her questioningly, and avoiding his eyes she tried to explain, "I mean — he may be here before you're back — and you won't have a chance then."

"But it's only Steven — we're not going anywhere."

"He'll be shaved, though — that's what I mean — and I'd like you too to spend a little time on yourself."

He stood up, stroking the heavy stubble on his chin. "Maybe I should — only it softens up the skin too much. Especially when I've got to face the wind."

She nodded and began to help him dress, bringing heavy socks and a big woollen sweater from the bedroom, wrapping a scarf around his face and forehead. "I'll tell Steven to come early," he said, as he went out. "In time for supper. Likely there'll be chores for me to do, so if I'm not back by six don't wait."

From the bedroom window she watched him nearly a mile along the road.

The fire had gone down when at last she turned away, and already through the house there was an encroaching chill. A blaze sprang up again when the draughts were opened, but as she went on clearing the table her movements were furtive and constrained. It was the silence weighing upon her — the frozen silence of the bitter fields and sun-chilled sky — lurking outside as if alive, relentlessly in wait, mile-deep between her now and John. She listened to it, suddenly tense, motionless. The fire crackled and the clock ticked. Always it was there. "I'm a fool," she whispered, rattling the dishes in defiance, going back to the stove to put in another fire. "Warm and safe — I'm a fool. It's a good chance when he's away to paint. The day will go quickly. I won't have time to brood."

Since November now the paint had been waiting warmer weather. The frost in the walls on a day like this would crack and peel it as it dried, but she needed something to keep her hands occupied, something to stave off the gathering cold and loneliness. "First of all," she said aloud, opening the paint and mixing it with a little turpentine, "I must get the house warmer. Fill up the stove and open the oven door so that all the heat comes out. Wad something along the window sills, to keep out the draughts. Then I'll feel brighter. It's the cold that depresses."

She moved briskly, performing each little task with careful and exaggerated absorption, binding her thoughts to it, making it a screen between herself and the surrounding snow and silence. But when the stove was filled and the windows sealed it was more difficult again. Above the quiet, steady swishing of her brush against the bedroom door the clock began to tick. Suddenly her movements became precise, deliberate, her posture self-conscious, as if someone had entered the room and were watching her. It was the silence again, aggressive, hovering. The fire spit and crackled at it. Still it was there. "I'm a fool," she repeated. "All farmers' wives have to stay alone. I mustn't give in this way. I mustn't brood. A few hours now and they'll be here."

The sound of her voice reassured her. She went on: "I'll get them a good supper — and for coffee after cards bake some of the little cakes with raisins that he likes. . . . Just three of us, so I'll watch, and let John play. It's better with four, but at least we can talk. That's all I need — someone to talk to. John never talks. He's stronger — doesn't need to. But he likes Steven — no matter what the neighbours say. Maybe he'll have him come again, and some other young people too. It's what we need, both of us, to help keep young ourselves. . . . And then before we know it we'll be into March. It's cold still in March sometimes, but you never mind the same. At least you're beginning to think about spring."

She began to think about it now. Thoughts that outstripped her words, that left her alone again with herself and the ever-lurking silence. Eager and hopeful first, then clenched, rebellious, lonely. Windows open, sun and thawing earth again, the urge of growing, living things. Then the days that began in the morning at half-past four and lasted till ten at night; the meals at which John gulped his food and scarcely spoke a word; the brute-tired stupid eyes he turned on her if ever she mentioned town or visiting.

For spring was drudgery again. John never hired a man to help him. He wanted a mortgage-free farm; then a new house and pretty clothes for her. Sometimes, because with the best of crops it was going to take so long to pay off anyway, she wondered whether they mightn't better let the mortgage wait a little. Before they were worn out, before their best years were gone. It was something of life she wanted, not just a house and furniture; something of John, not pretty clothes when she would be too old to wear them. But John of course couldn't understand. To him it seemed only right that she should have the clothes — only right that he, fit for nothing else, should slave away fifteen hours a day to give them to her. There was in his devotion a baffling, insurmountable humility that made him feel the need of sacrifice. And when his muscles ached, when his feet dragged stolidly with weariness, then it seemed that in some measure at least he was making amends for his big hulking body and simple mind. Year after year their lives went on in the same little groove. He drove his horses in the field; she milked the cows and hoed potatoes. By dint of his drudgery he saved a few months' wages, added a few dollars more each fall to his payments on the mortgage; but the only real difference that it all made was to deprive her of his companionship, to make him a little duller, older, uglier than he might otherwise have been. He never saw their lives objectively. To him it was not what he actually accomplished by means of the sacrifice that mattered, but the sacrifice itself, the gesture — something done for her sake.

And she, understanding, kept her silence. In such a gesture, however futile, there was a graciousness not to be shattered lightly. "John," she would begin sometimes, "you're doing too much. Get a man to help you — just for a month —" but smiling down at her he would answer simply, "I don't mind. Look at the hands on me. They're made for work." While in his voice there would be a stalwart ring to tell her that by her thoughtfulness she had made him only the more resolved to serve her, to prove his devotion and fidelity.

They were useless, such thoughts. She knew. It was his very devotion that made them useless, that forbade her to rebel. Yet over and over, sometimes hunched still before their bleakness, sometimes her brush making swift sharp strokes to pace the chafe and rancour that they brought, she persisted in them.

This now, the winter, was their slack season. She could sleep sometimes till eight, and John till seven. They could linger over their meals a little, read, play cards, go visiting the neighbours. It was the time to relax, to indulge and enjoy themselves; but instead, fretful and impatient, they kept on waiting for the spring. They were compelled now, not by labour, but by the spirit of labour. A spirit that pervaded their lives and brought with idleness a sense of guilt. Sometimes they did sleep late, sometimes they did play cards, but always uneasily, always reproached by the thought of more important things that might be done. When John got up at five to attend to the fire he wanted to stay up and go out to the stable. When he sat down to a meal he hurried his food and pushed his chair away again, from habit, from sheer work-instinct, even though it was only to put more wood in the stove, or go down to the cellar to cut up beets and turnips for the cows.

And anyway, sometimes she asked herself, why sit trying to talk with a man who never talked? Why talk when there was nothing to talk about but crops and cattle, the weather and the neighbours? The neighbours, too — why go visiting them when still it was the same — crops and cattle, the weather and the other neighbours?

Why go to the dances in the schoolhouse to sit among the older women, one of them now, married seven years, or to waltz with the work-bent, tired old farmers to a squeaky fiddle tune? Once she had danced with Steven six or seven times in the evening, and they had talked about it for as many months. It was easier to stay at home. John never danced or enjoyed himself. He was always uncomfortable in his good suit and shoes. He didn't like shaving in the cold weather oftener than once or twice a week. It was easier to stay at home, to stand at the window staring out across the bitter fields, to count the days and look forward to another spring.

But now, alone with herself in the winter silence, she saw the spring for what it really was. This spring — next spring — all the springs and summers still to come. While they grew old, while their bodies warped, while their minds kept shrivelling dry and empty like their lives. "I mustn't," she said aloud again. "I married him — and he's a good man. I mustn't keep on this way. It will be noon before long, and then time to think about supper. . . . Maybe he'll come early — and as soon as John is finished at the stable we can all play cards."

It was getting cold again, and she left her painting to put in more wood. But this time the warmth spread slowly. She pushed a mat up to the outside door, and went back to the window to pat down the woollen shirt that was wadded along the sill. Then she paced a few times round the room, then poked the fire and rattled the stove lids, then paced again. The fire crackled, the clock ticked. The silence now seemed more intense than ever, seemed to have reached a pitch where it faintly moaned. She began to pace on tiptoe, listening, her shoulders drawn together, not realizing for a while that it was the wind she heard, thin-strained and whimpering through the eaves.

Then she wheeled to the window, and with quick short breaths thawed the frost to see again. The glitter was gone. Across the drifts sped swift and snakelike little tongues of snow. She could not follow them, where they sprang from, or where they disappeared. It was as if all across the yard the snow were shivering awake — roused by the warnings of the wind to hold itself in readiness for the impending storm. The sky had become a sombre, whitish grey. It, too, as if in readiness, had shifted and lay close to earth. Before her as she watched a mane of powdery snow reared up breast-high against the darker background of the stable, tossed for a moment angrily, and then subsided again as if whipped down to obe-dience, and restraint. But another followed, more reckless and impatient than the first. Another reeled and dashed itself against the window where she watched. Then ominously for a while there were only the angry little snakes of snow. The wind rose, creaking the troughs that were wired beneath the eaves. In the distance, sky and prairie now were merged into one another linelessly. All round her it was gathering; already in its press and whimpering there strummed a boding of eventual fury. Again she saw a mane of snow spring up, so dense and high this time that all the sheds and stables were obscured. Then others followed, whirling fiercely out of hand; and, when at last they cleared, the stables seemed in dimmer outline than before. It was the snow beginning, long lancet shafts of it, straight from the north, borne almost level by the straining wind. "He'll be there soon," she whispered, "and coming home it will be in his back. He'll leave again right away. He saw the double wheel — he knows the kind of storm there'll be."

She went back to her painting. For a while it was easier, all her thoughts half-anxious ones of John in the blizzard, struggling his way across the hills; but petulantly again she soon began, "I knew we were going to have a storm — I told him so — but it doesn't matter what I say. Big stubborn fool — he goes his own way anyway. It doesn't matter what becomes of me. In a storm like this he'll never get home. He won't even try. And while he sits keeping his father company I can look after his stable for him, go ploughing through snowdrifts up to my knees — nearly frozen —"

Not that she meant or believed her words. It was just an effort to convince herself that she did have a grievance, to justify her rebellious thoughts, to prove John responsible for her unhappiness. She was young still, eager for excitement and distractions; and John's steadfastness rebuked her vanity, made her complaints seem weak and trivial. She went on, fretfully, "If he'd listen to me sometimes and not be so stubborn we wouldn't still be living in a house like this. Seven years in two rooms — seven years and never a new stick of furniture. . . . There — as if another coat of paint could make it different anyway."

She cleaned her brush, filled up the stove again, and went back to the window. There was a void white moment that she thought must be frost formed on the window pane; then, like a fitful shadow through the whirling snow, she recognized the stable roof. It was incredible. The sudden, maniac raging of the storm struck from her face all its pettishness. Her eyes glazed with fear a little; her lips blanched. "If he starts for home now," she whispered silently — "But he won't — he knows I'm safe — he knows Steven's coming. Across the hills he would never dare."

She turned to the stove, holding out her hands to the warmth. Around her now there seemed a constant sway and tremor, as if the air were vibrating with the shud-derings of the walls. She stood quite still, listening. Sometimes the wind struck with sharp, savage blows. Sometimes it bore down in a sustained, minute-long blast, silent with effort and intensity; then with a foiled shriek of threat wheeled away to gather and assault again. Always the eavestroughs creaked and sawed. She stared towards the window again, then detecting the morbid trend of her thoughts, prepared fresh coffee and forced herself to drink a few mouthfuls. "He would never dare," she whispered again. "He wouldn't leave the old man anyway in such a storm. Safe in here — there's nothing for me to keep worrying about. It's after one already. I'll do my baking now, and then it will be time to get supper ready for Steven."

Soon, however, she began to doubt whether Steven would come. In such a storm even a mile was enough to make a man hesitate. Especially Steven, who was hardly the one to face a blizzard for the sake of someone else's chores. He had a stable of his own to look after anyway. It would be only natural for him to think that when the storm blew up John had turned again for home. Another man would have — would have put his wife first.

But she felt little dread or uneasiness at the prospect of spending the night alone. It was the first time she had been left like this on her own resources, and her reaction, now that she could face and appraise her situation calmly, was gradually to feel it a kind of adventure and responsibility. It stimulated her. Before nightfall she must go to the stable and feed everything. Wrap up in some of John's clothes — take a ball of string in her hand, one end tied to the door, so that no matter how blinding the storm she could at least find her way back to the house. She had heard of people having to do that. It appealed to her now because suddenly it made life dramatic. She had not felt the storm yet, only watched it for a minute through the window.

It took nearly an hour to find enough string, to choose the right socks and sweaters. Long before it was time to start out she tried on John's clothes, changing and rechanging, striding around the room to make sure there would be play enough for pitching hay and struggling over snowdrifts; then she took them off again, and for a while busied herself baking the little cakes with raisins that he liked.

Night came early. Just for a moment on the doorstep she shrank back, uncertain. The slow dimming of the light clutched her with an illogical sense of abandonment. It was like the covert withdrawal of an ally, leaving the alien miles unleashed and unrestrained. Watching the hurricane of writhing snow rage past the little house she forced herself. "They'll never stand the night unless I get them fed. It's nearly dark already, and I've work to last an hour."

Timidly, unwinding a little of the string, she crept out from the shelter of the doorway. A gust of wind spun her forward a few yards, then plunged her headlong against a drift that in the dense white whirl lay invisible across her path. For nearly a minute she huddled still, breathless and dazed. The snow was in her mouth and nostrils, inside her scarf and up her sleeves. As she tried to straighten a smothering scud flung itself against her face, cutting off her breath a second time. The wind struck from all sides, blustering and furious. It was as if the storm had discovered her, as if all its forces were concentrated upon her extinction. Seized with panic suddenly she threshed out a moment with her arms, then stumbled back and sprawled her length across the drift.

But this time she regained her feet quickly, roused by the whip and batter of the storm to retaliative anger. For a moment her impulse was to face the wind and strike back blow for blow; then, as suddenly as it had come, her frantic strength gave way to limpness and exhaustion. Suddenly, a comprehension so clear and terrifying that it struck all thoughts of the stable from her mind, she realized in such a storm her puniness. And the realization gave her new strength, stilled this time to a desperate persistence. Just for a moment the wind held her, numb and swaying in its vise; then slowly, buckled far forward, she groped her way again towards the house.

Inside, leaning against the door, she stood tense and still a while. It was almost dark now. The top of the stove glowed a deep, dull red. Heedless of the storm, self-absorbed and self-satisfied, the clock ticked on like a glib little idiot. "He shouldn't have gone," she whispered silently. "He saw the double wheel — he knew. He shouldn't have left me here alone."

For so fierce now, so insane and dominant did the blizzard seem, that she could not credit the safety of the house. The warmth and lull around her was not real yet, not to be relied upon. She was still at the mercy of the storm. Only her body pressing hard like this against the door was staving it off. She didn't dare move. She didn't dare ease the ache and strain. "He shouldn't have gone," she repeated, thinking of the stable again, reproached by her helplessness. "They'll freeze in their stalls — and I can't reach them. He'll say it's all my fault. He won't believe I tried."

Then Steven came. Quickly, startled to quietness and control, she let him in and lit the lamp. He stared at her a moment, then flinging off his cap crossed to where she stood by the table and seized her arms. "You're so white — what's wrong? Look at me —" It was like him in such little situations to be masterful. "You should have known better — for a while I thought I wasn't going to make it here myself —"

"I was afraid you wouldn't come — John left early, and there was the stable —"

But the storm had unnerved her, and suddenly at the assurance of his touch and voice the fear that had been gripping her gave way to an hysteria of relief. Scarcely aware of herself she seized his arm and sobbed against it. He remained still a moment unyielding, then slipped his other arm around her shoulder. It was comforting and she relaxed against it, hushed by a sudden sense of lull and safety. Her shoulders trembled with the easing of the strain, then fell limp and still. "You're shivering," — he drew her gently towards the stove. "It's all right — nothing to be afraid of. I'm going to see to the stable."

It was a quiet, sympathetic voice, yet with an undertone of insolence, a kind of mockery even, that made her draw away quickly and busy herself putting in a fire. With his lips drawn in a little smile he watched her till she looked at him again. The smile too was insolent, but at the same time companionable; Steven's smile, and therefore difficult to reprove. It lit up his lean, still-boyish face with a peculiar kind of arrogance: features and smile that were different from John's, from other men's — wilful and derisive, yet naïvely so — as if it were less the difference itself he was conscious of, than the long-accustomed privilege that thereby fell his due. He was erect, tall, square-shouldered. His hair was dark and trim, his lips curved soft and full. While John, she made the comparison swiftly, was thickset, heavy-jowled, and stooped. He always stood before her helpless, a kind of humility and wonderment in his attitude. And Steven now smiled on her appraisingly with the worldly-wise assurance of one for whom a woman holds neither mystery nor illusion.

"It was good of you to come, Steven," she responded, the words running into a sudden, empty laugh. "Such a storm to face — I suppose I should feel flattered."

For his presumption, his misunderstanding of what had been only a momentary weakness, instead of angering quickened her, roused from latency and long disuse all the instincts and resources of her femininity. She felt eager, challenged. Something was at hand that hitherto had always eluded her, even in the early days with John, something vital, beckoning, meaningful. She didn't understand, but she knew. The texture of the moment was satisfyingly dreamlike: an incredibility perceived as such, yet acquiesced in. She was John's wife — she knew — but also she knew that Steven standing here was different from John. There was no thought or motive, no understanding of herself as the knowledge persisted. Wary and poised round a sudden little core of blind excitement she evaded him, "But it's nearly dark — hadn't you better hurry if you're going to do the chores? Don't trouble — I can get them off myself —"

An hour later when he returned from the stable she was in another dress, hair rearranged, a little flush of colour in her face. Pouring warm water for him from the kettle into the basin she said evenly, "By the time you're washed supper will be ready. John said we weren't to wait for him."

He looked at her a moment, "You don't mean you're expecting John tonight? The way it's blowing —"

"Of course." As she spoke she could feel the colour deepening in her face. "We're going to play cards. He was the one that suggested it."

He went on washing, and then as they took their places at the table, resumed, "So John's coming. When are you expecting him?"

"He said it might be seven o'clock — or a little later." Conversation with Steven at other times had always been brisk and natural, but now all at once she found it strained. "He may have work to do for his father. That's what he said when he left. Why do you ask, Steven?"

"I was just wondering — it's a rough night."

"You don't know John. It would take more than a storm to stop him."

She glanced up again and he was smiling at her. The same insolence, the same little twist of mockery and appraisal. It made her flinch, and ask herself why she was pretending to expect John — why there should be this instinct of defence to force her. This time, instead of poise and excitement, it brought a reminder that she had changed her dress and rearranged her hair. It crushed in a sudden silence, through which she heard the whistling wind again, and the creaking saw of the eaves. Neither spoke now. There was something strange, almost frightening, about this Steven and his quiet, unrelenting smile; but strangest of all was the familiarity: the Steven she had never seen or encountered, and yet had always known, always expected, always waited for. It was less Steven himself that she felt than his inevitability. Just as she had felt the snow, the silence and the storm. She kept her eyes lowered, on the window past his shoulder, on the stove, but his smile now seemed to exist apart from him, to merge and hover with the silence. She clinked a cup — listened to the whistle of the storm — always it was there. He began to speak, but her mind missed the meaning of his words. Swiftly she was making comparisons again; his face so different to John's, so handsome and young and clean-shaven. Swiftly, helplessly, feeling the imperceptible and relentless ascendancy that thereby he was gaining over her, sensing sudden menace in this new, more vital life, even as she felt drawn towards it.

The lamp between them flickered as an onslaught of the storm sent shudderings through the room. She rose to build up the fire again and he followed her. For a long time they stood close to the stove, their arms almost touching. Once as the blizzard creaked the house she spun around sharply, fancying it was John at the door; but quietly he intercepted her. "Not tonight — you might as well make up your mind to it. Across the hills in a storm like this — it would be suicide to try."

Her lips trembled suddenly in an effort to answer, to parry the certainty in his voice, then set thin and bloodless. She was afraid now. Afraid of his face so different from John's — of his smile, of her own helplessness to rebuke it. Afraid of the storm, isolating her here alone with him. They tried to play cards but she kept starting up at every creak and shiver of the walls. "It's too rough a night," he repeated. "Even for John. Just relax a few minutes — stop worrying and pay a little attention to me."

But in his tone there was a contradiction to his words. For it implied that she was not worrying — that her only concern was lest it really might be John at the door.

And the implication persisted. He filled up the stove for her, shuffled the cards — won — shuffled — still it was there. She tried to respond to his conversation, to think of the game, but helplessly into her cards instead she began to ask, Was he right? Was that why he smiled? Why he seemed to wait, expectant and assured?

The clock ticked, the fire crackled. Always it was there. Furtively for a moment she watched him as he deliberated over his hand. John, even in the days before they were married, had never looked like that. Only this morning she had asked him to shave. Because Steven was coming — because she had been afraid to see them side by side — because deep within herself she had known even then. The same knowledge, furtive and forbidden, that was flaunted now in Steven's smile. "You look cold," he said at last, dropping his cards and rising from the table. "We're not playing, anyway. Come over to the stove to a few minutes and get warm."

"But first I think we'll hang blankets over the door. When there's a blizzard like this we always do." It seemed that in sane, commonplace activity there might be release, a moment or two in which to recover herself. "John has nails to put them on. They keep out a little of the draught."

He stood on a chair for her, and hung the blankets that she carried from the bedroom. Then for a moment they stood silent, watching the blankets sway and tremble before the blade of wind that spurted around the jamb. "I forgot," she said at last, "that I painted the bedroom door. At the top there, see — I've smeared the blankets."

He glanced at her curiously, and went back to the stove. She followed him, trying to imagine the hills in such a storm, wondering whether John would come. "A man couldn't live in it," suddenly he answered her thoughts, lowering the oven door and drawing up their chairs one on each side of it. "He knows you're safe. It isn't likely that he'd leave his father, anyway."

"The wind will be in his back," she persisted. "The winter before we were married — all the blizzards that we had that year — and he never missed —"

"Blizzards like this one? Up in the hills he wouldn't be able to keep his direction for a hundred yards. Listen to it a minute and ask yourself."

His voice seemed softer, kindlier now. She met his smile a moment, its assured little twist of appraisal, then for a long time sat silent, tense, careful again to avoid his eyes.

Everything now seemed to depend on this. It was the same as a few hours ago when she braced the door against the storm. He was watching her, smiling. She dared not move, unclench her hands, or raise her eyes. The flames crackled, the clock ticked. The storm wrenched the walls as if to make them buckle in. So rigid and desperate were all her muscles set, withstanding, that the room around her seemed to swim and reel. So rigid and strained that for relief at last, despite herself, she raised her head and met his eyes again.

Intending that it should be for only an instant, just to breathe again, to ease the tension that had grown unbearable — but in his smile now, instead of the insolent appraisal that she feared, there seemed a kind of warmth and sympathy. An understanding that quickened and encouraged her — that made her wonder why but a moment ago she had been afraid. It was as if the storm had lulled, as if she had suddenly found calm and shelter.

Or perhaps, the thought seized her, perhaps instead of his smile it was she who had changed. She who, in the long, wind-creaked silence, had emerged from the increment of codes and loyalties to her real, unfettered self. She who now felt his air of appraisal as nothing more than an understanding of the unfulfilled woman that until this moment had lain within her brooding and unadmitted, reproved out of consciousness by the insistence of an outgrown, routine fidelity.

For there had always been Steven. She understood now. Seven years — almost as long as John — ever since the night they first danced together.

The lamp was burning dry, and through the dimming light, isolated in the fastness of silence and storm, they watched each other. Her face was white and struggling still. His was handsome, clean-shaven, young. Her eyes were fanatic, believing desperately, fixed upon him as if to exclude all else, as if to find justification. His were cool, bland, drooped a little with expectancy. The light kept dimming, gathering the shadows round them, hushed, conspiratorial. He was smiling still. Her hands again were clenched up white and hard.

"But he always came," she persisted. "The wildest, coldest nights — even such a night as this. There was never a storm —"

"Never a storm like this one." There was a quietness in his smile now, a kind of simplicity almost, as if to reassure her. "You were out in it yourself a few minutes. He'd have it for five miles, across the hills. . . . I'd think twice myself, on such a night, before risking even one."

ଔ

Long after he was asleep she lay listening to the storm. As a check on the draught up the chimney they had left one of the stovelids partly off, and through the open bedroom door she could see the flickerings of flame and shadow on kitchen wall. They leaped and sank fantastically. The longer she watched, the more alive they seemed to be. There was one great shadow that struggled towards her threateningly, massive and black and engulfing all the room. Again and again it advanced, about to spring, but each time a little whip of light subdued it to its place among the others on the wall. Yet though it never reached her still she cowered, feeling that gathered there was all the frozen wilderness, its heart of terror and invincibility.

Then she dozed a while, and the shadow was John. Interminably he advanced. The whips of light still flickered and coiled, but now suddenly they were swift little snakes that this afternoon she had watched twist and shiver across the snow. And they too were advancing. They writhed and vanished and came again. She lay still, paralyzed. He was over her now, so close that she could have touched him. Already it seemed that a deadly tightening hand was on her throat. She tried to scream but her lips were locked. Steven beside her slept on heedlessly.

Until suddenly as she lay staring up at him a gleam of light revealed his face. And in it was not a trace of threat or anger — only calm, and stonelike hopelessness.

That was like John. He began to withdraw, and frantically she tried to call him back. "It isn't true — not really true — listen, John —" but the words clung frozen to her lips. Already there was only the shriek of wind again, the sawing eaves, the leap and twist of shadow on the wall.

She sat up, startled now and awake. And so real had he seemed there, standing close to her, so vivid the sudden age and sorrow in his face, that at first she could not make herself understand she had been only dreaming. Against the conviction of his presence in the room it was necessary to insist over and over that he must still be with his father on the other side of the hills. Watching the shadows she had fallen asleep. It was only her mind, her imagination, distorted to a nightmare by the illogical and unadmitted dread of his return. But he wouldn't come. Steven was right. In such a storm he would never try. They were safe, alone. No one would ever know. It was only fear, morbid and irrational; only the sense of guilt that even her new-found and challenged womanhood could not entirely quell.

She knew now. She had not let herself understand or acknowledge it as guilt before, but gradually through the wind-torn silence of the night his face compelled her. The face that had watched her from the darkness with its stonelike sorrow — the face that was really John — John more than his features of mere flesh and bone could ever be.

She wept silently. The fitful gleam of light began to sink. On the ceiling and wall at last there was only a faint dull flickering glow. The little house shuddered and quailed, and a chill crept in again. Without wakening Steven she slipped out to build up the fire. It was burned to a few spent embers now, and the wood she put on seemed a long time catching light. The wind swirled through the blankets they had hung around the door, and then, hollow and moaning, roared up the chimney again, as if against its will drawn back to serve still longer with the onrush of the storm.

For a long time she crouched over the stove, listening. Earlier in the evening, with the lamp lit and the fire crackling, the house had seemed a stand against the wilderness, a refuge of feeble walls wherein persisted the elements of human meaning and survival. Now, in the cold, creaking darkness, it was strangely extinct, looted by the storm and abandoned again. She lifted the stove lid and fanned the embers till at last a swift little tongue of flame began to lick around the wood. Then she replaced the lid, extended her hands, and as if frozen in that attitude stood waiting.

It was not long now. After a few minutes she closed the draughts, and as the flames whirled back upon each other, beating against the top of the stove and sending out flickers of light again, a warmth surged up to relax her stiffened limbs.

But shivering and numb it had been easier. The bodily wellbeing that the warmth induced gave play again to an ever more insistent mental suffering. She remembered the shadow that was John. She saw him bent towards her, then retreating, his features pale and overcast with unaccusing grief. She relived their seven years together and, in retrospect, found them to be years of worth and dignity. Until crushed by it all at last, seized by a sudden need to suffer and atone, she crossed to where the draught was bitter, and for a long time stood unflinching on the icy floor.

The storm was close here. Even through the blankets she could feel a sift of snow against her face. The eaves sawed, the walls creaked, and the wind was like a wolf in howling flight.

And yet, suddenly she asked herself, hadn't there been other storms, other blizzards? And through the worst of them hadn't he always reached her?

Clutched by the thought she stood rooted a minute. It was hard now to understand how she could have so deceived herself — how a moment of passion could have quieted within her not only conscience, but reason and discretion too. John always came. There could never be a storm to stop him. He was strong, inured to the cold. He had crossed the hills since his boyhood, knew every creekbed and gully. It was madness to go on like this — to wait. While there was still time she must waken Steven, and hurry him away.

But in the bedroom again, standing at Steven's side, she hesitated. In his detachment from it all, in his quiet, even breathing, there was such sanity, such realism. For him nothing had happened; nothing would. If she wakened him he would only laugh and tell her to listen to the storm. Already it was long past midnight; either John had lost his way or not set out at all. And she knew that in his devotion there was nothing foolhardy. He would never risk a storm beyond his endurance, never permit himself a sacrifice likely to endanger her lot or future. They were both safe. No one would ever know. She must control herself — be sane like Steven.

For comfort she let her hand rest a while on Steven's shoulder. It would be easier were he awake now, with her, sharing her guilt; but gradually as she watched his handsome face in the glimmering light she came to understand that for him no guilt existed. Just as there had been no passion, no conflict. Nothing but the sane appraisal of their situation, nothing but the expectant little smile, and the arrogance of features that were different from John's. She winced deeply, remembering how she had fixed her eyes on those features, how she had tried to believe that so handsome and young, so different from John's, they must in themselves be her justification.

In the flickering light they were still young, still handsome. No longer her justification — she knew now — John was the man — but wistfully still, wondering sharply at their power and tyranny, she touched them a moment with her fingertips again.

She could not blame him. There had been no passion, no guilt; therefore there could be no responsibility. Looking down at him as he slept, half-smiling still, his lips relaxed in the conscienceless complacency of his achievement, she understood that thus he was revealed in his entirety — all there ever was or ever could be. John was the man. With him lay all the future. For tonight, slowly and contritely through the day and years to come, she would try to make amends.

Then she stole back to the kitchen, and without thought, impelled by overwhelming need again, returned to the door where the draught was bitter still. Gradually towards morning the storm began to spend itself. Its terror blast became a feeble, worn-out moan. The leap of light and shadow sank, and a chill crept in again. Always the eaves creaked, tortured with wordless prophecy. Heedless of it all the clock ticked on in idiot content.

CR

They found him the next day, less than a mile from home. Drifting with the storm he had run against his own pasture fence and, overcome, had frozen there, erect still, both hands clasping fast the wire.

"He was south of here," they said wonderingly when she told them how he had come across the hills. "Straight south — you'd wonder how he could have missed the buildings. It was the wind last night, coming every way at once. He shouldn't have tried. There was a double wheel around the moon."

She looked past them a moment, then as if to herself said simply, "If you knew him, though — John would try."

It was later, when they had left her a while to be alone with him, that she knelt and touched his hand. Her eyes dimmed, it was still such a strong and patient hand; then, transfixed, they suddenly grew wide and clear. On the palm, white even against its frozen whiteness, was a little smear of paint.

℘CR

"The Painted Door" is a powerful example of prairie realism, and the most popular of a small handful of stories written by James Sinclair Ross. Born on a farm near Shellbrook, Ross was the first Saskatchewan-born writer to establish an international reputation, and is highly praised among contemporary writers who acknowledge his literary influence. "The Painted Door" first appeared in Queen's Quarterly *in 1939, but like the rest of his eloquent tales, came to public attention in his first collection of fiction,* The Lamp at Noon and Other Stories *(1968). It quickly became the most anthologized short story in a burgeoning Canadian literature. Remarkable for its poetic simplicity, this tale is similar in many ways to Ross's major novel,* As For Me and My House, *first published in 1941 but also "discovered" in the 1960s. Aside from the prairie setting, both fictions rely on the development of a female point of view.*

Ross's strength has always been the precision of his narrative imagery. The figures of John, Ann, and Steven are presented as simple, though deep, characters with little surface complexity. Their relation to the physical world is so intense that the plot turns around their helplessness in the hostile prairie landscape. The concluding twist of this story, with the visual starkness of the "little smear of paint," maintains a resonance in the reader's mind — as well as Ann's — for a long time. It is perhaps the submerged sexual innuendoes of the rising storm and the urgent crisis of her fidelity that give the story a particular fascination for modern readers.

K.M.

John Updike (b. 1932)

Marching Through Boston

The civil rights movement had a salubrious effect on Joan Maple. A suburban mother of four, she would return late at night from a non-violence class in Roxbury with rosy cheeks and shining eyes, eager to describe, while sipping Benedictine, her indoctrination. "This huge man in overalls —"

"A Negro?" her husband asked.

"Of course. This huge man, with a *very* refined vocabulary, told us if we march anywhere, especially in the South, to let the Negro men march on the outside, because it's important for their self-esteem to be able to protect us. He told us about a New York fashion designer who went down to Selma and said she could take care of herself. Furthermore she flirted with the State troopers. They finally asked her to come home."

"I thought you were supposed to love the troopers," Richard said.

"Only abstractly. Not on your own. You mustn't do *any*thing within the movement as an individual. By flirting, she gave the trooper an opportunity to feel contempt."

"She blocked his transference, as it were."

"Don't laugh. It's all very psychological. The man told us, those who want to go, to face our ego-gratificational motives no matter how irrelevant they are and then put them behind us. Once you're in a march, you have no identity. It's elegant. It's beautiful."

He had never known her like this. It seemed to Richard that her posture was improving, her figure filling out, her skin growing lustrous, her very hair gaining body and sheen. Though he had resigned himself, through twelve years of marriage, to a rhythm of apathy and renewal, he distrusted this raw burst of beauty.

The night she returned from Alabama, it was three o'clock in the morning. He woke and heard the front door close behind her. He had been dreaming of a parallelogram in the sky that was also somehow a meteor, and the darkened house seemed quadrisected by the four sleeping children he had, with more than paternal tenderness, put to bed. He had caught himself speaking to them of Mommy as a distant departed spirit, gone to live, invisible, in the newspapers and the television set. The little girl, Bean, had burst into tears. Now the ghost closed the door and walked up the stairs, and came into his bedroom, and fell on the bed.

He switched on the light and saw her sunburned face, her blistered feet. Her ballet slippers were caked with orange mud. She had lived for three days on Coke and dried apricots; she had not gone to the bathroom for sixteen hours. The Montgomery airport had been a madhouse — nuns, social workers, divinity students fighting for space on the northbound planes. They had been in the air when they heard about Mrs. Liuzzo.

He accused her: "It could have been you."

She said, "I was always in a group." But she added guiltily, "How were the children?"

"Fine. Bean cried because she thought you were inside the television set."

"Did you see me?"

"Your parents called long distance to say they thought they did. I didn't. All I saw was Abernathy and King and their henchmen saying, 'Thass right. Say it, man. Thass sayin' it.' "

"Aren't you mean? It was very moving, except that we were all so tired. These teen-age Negro girls kept fainting; a psychiatrist explained to me that they were having psychotic breaks."

"What psychiatrist?"

"Actually, there were three of them, and they were studying to be psychiatrists in Philadelphia. They kind of took me in tow."

"I bet they did. Please come to bed. I'm very tired from being a mother."

She visited the four corners of the upstairs to inspect each sleeping child and, returning, undressed in the dark. She removed underwear she had worn for seventy hours and stood there shining; to the sleepy man in the bed it seemed a visitation, and he felt as people of old must have felt when greeted by an angel — adoring yet resentful, at this flamboyant proof of better things.

She spoke on the radio; she addressed local groups. In garages and super-markets he heard himself being pointed out as her husband. She helped organize meetings at which dapper young Negroes ridiculed and abused the applauding suburban audience. Richard marveled at Joan's public composure. Her shyness stayed with her, but it had become a kind of weapon, as if the doctrine of non-violence had given it point. Her voice, as she phoned evasive local realtors in the campaign for fair housing, grew curiously firm and rather obstinately melodious — a note her husband had never heard in her voice before. He grew jealous and irritable. He found himself insisting, at parties, on the Constitutional case for states' rights, on the misfortunes of African independence, on the tangled history of the Reconstruction. Yet she had little trouble persuading him to march with her in Boston.

He promised, though he could not quite grasp the object of the march. Indeed, his brain, as if surgically deprived, quite lacked the faculty of believing in people considered generically. All movements, of masses or of ideas supposedly embodied in masses, he secretly felt to be phantasmal. Whereas his wife, a minister's daughter, lived by abstractions; her blood returned to her heart enriched and vivified by the passage through some capillarious figment. He was struck, and subtly wounded, by the ardour with which she rewarded his promise; under his hands her body felt baroque and her skin smooth as night.

CR

The march was in April. Richard awoke that morning with a fever. He had taken something foreign into himself and his body was making resistance. Joan offered to go alone; as if something fundamental to his dignity, to their marriage, were at stake, he refused the offer. The day, dawning cloudy, had been forecast as sunny, and he wore a summer suit that enclosed his hot skin in a slipping, weightless unreality. At a highway drugstore they bought some pills designed to detonate inside him through a twelve-hour period. They parked near her aunt's house in Louisburg Square and took a taxi toward the headwaters of the march, a playground in Roxbury. The Irish driver's impassive back radiated disapproval. The cab was turned aside by a policeman; the Maples got out and walked down a broad brown boulevard lined with barbershops, shoe repair nooks, pizzerias, and friendliness associations. On stoops and stairways male Negroes loitered, blinking and muttering toward one another as if a vast, decrepit conspiracy had assigned them their positions and then collapsed.

"Lovely architecture," Joan said, pointing toward a curving side street, a neo-Georgian arc suspended in the large urban sadness.

Though she pretended to know where she was, Richard doubted that they were going the right way. But then he saw ahead of them, scattered like the anomalous objects with which Dali punctuates his perspectives, receding black groups of white clergymen. In the distance, the hot lights of police cars wheeled within a twinkling mob. As they drew nearer, coloured girls made into giantesses by bouffant hairdos materialized beside them. One wore cerise stretch pants, and the golden sandals of a heavenly cupbearer, and held pressed against her ear a transistor radio tuned to WMEX. On this thin stream of music they all together poured into a playground surrounded by a link fence.

A loose crowd of thousands swarmed on the crushed grass. Bobbing placards advertised churches, brotherhoods, schools, towns. Popsicle vendors lent an unexpected touch of carnival. Suddenly at home, Richard bought a bag of peanuts and looked around — as if this were the playground of his childhood — for friends.

But it was Joan who found some. "My God," she said. "There's my old analyst." At the fringe of some Unitarians stood a plump, doughy man with the troubled squint of a baker who has looked into too many ovens. Joan turned to go the other way.

"Don't suppress," Richard told her. "Let's go and be friendly and normal."

"It's too embarrassing."

"But it's been years since you went. You're cured."

"You don't understand. You're never cured. You just stop going."

"O.K., come this way. I think I see my Harvard section man in Plato to Dante."

But, even while arguing against it, she had been drifting them toward her psychiatrist, and now they were caught in the pull of his gaze. He scowled and came toward them, flat-footedly. Richard had never met him and, shaking hands, felt himself as a putrid heap of anecdotes, of detailed lusts and abuses. "I think I need a doctor," he madly blurted.

The other man produced, like a stiletto from his sleeve, a nimble smile. "How so?" Each word seemed precious.

"I have a fever."

"Ah." The psychiatrist turned sympathetically to Joan, and his face issued a clear commiseration: *So he is still punishing you.*

Joan said loyally, "He really does. I saw the thermometer."

"Would you like a peanut?" Richard asked. The offer felt so symbolic, so transparent, that he was shocked when the other man took one, cracked it harshly, and substantially chewed.

Joan asked, "Are you with anybody? I feel a need for group security."

"Come meet my sister." The command sounded strange to Richard; "sister" seemed a piece of psychological slang, a euphemism for "mistress."

But again things were simpler than they seemed. His sister was plainly from the same batter. Ruddy and yeasty, she seemed to have been enlarged by the exercise of good will and wore a saucer-sized S.C.L.C. button in the lapel of a coarse green suit. Richard coveted the suit; it looked warm. The day was continuing overcast and chilly. Something odd, perhaps the successive explosions of the antihistamine pill, was happening inside him, making him feel elegantly elongated; the illusion crossed his mind that he was destined to seduce this woman. She beamed and said, "My daughter Trudy and her *best* friend, Carol."

They were girls of sixteen or so, one size smaller in their bones than women. Trudy had the family pastry texture and a darting frown. Carol was homely, fragile, and touching; her upper teeth were a grey blur of braces and her arms were protectively folded across her skimpy bosom. Over a white blouse she wore only a thin blue sweater, unbuttoned. Richard told her, "You're freezing."

"I'm freezing," she said, and a small love was established between them on the basis of this demure repetition. She added, "I came along because I'm writing a term paper."

Trudy said, "She's doing a history of the labour unions," and laughed unpleasantly.

The girl shivered. "I thought they might be the same. Didn't the unions use to march?" Her voice, moistened by the obtrusion of her braces, had a sprayey faintness in the raw grey air.

The psychiatrist's sister said, "The *way* they *make* these poor children *study* nowadays! The *books* they have them *read!* Their *English* teacher *assigned* them 'Tropic of *Can*cer'! I picked it *up* and read *one page*, and Trudy reassured me, 'It's all *right*, Mother, the teacher says he's a Transcen*dent*alist!' "

It felt to Richard less likely that he would seduce her. His sense of reality was expanding in the nest of warmth these people provided. He offered to buy them all popsicles. His consciousness ventured outward and tasted the joy of so many Negro presences, the luxury of immersion in the polished shadows of their skins. He drifted happily through the crosshatch of their oblique sardonic hooting and blurred voices, searching for the popsicle vendor. The girls and Trudy's mother had said they would take one; the psychiatrist and Joan had refused. The crowd was formed of jiggling fragments. Richard waved at the rector of a church whose nursery school his children had attended; winked at a folk singer he had seen on television and who looked lost and wan in depth; assumed a stony face in passing a long-haired youth guarded by police and draped in a signboard proclaiming MARTIN LUTHER KING A TOOL OF THE COMMUNISTS; and tapped a tall bald man on the shoulder. "Remember me? Dick Maple, Plato to Dante, B-plus."

The section man turned, bespectacled and pale. It was shocking; he had aged.

∞

The march was slow to start. Trucks and police cars appeared and disappeared at the playground gate. Officious young seminarians tried to organize the crowd into lines. Unintelligible announcements crackled within the loudspeakers. Martin Luther King was a dim religious rumour on the playground plain — now here, now there, now dead, now alive. The sun showed as a kind of sore spot burning through the clouds. Carol nibbled her popsicle and shivered. Richard and Joan argued whether to march under the Danvers banner with the psychiatrist or with the Unitarians because her father was one. In the end it did not matter; King invisibly established himself at their head, a distant truck loaded with singing women lurched forward, a far corner of the crowd began to croon, "Which side are you on, boy?," and they were marching.

On Columbus Avenue they were shuffled into lines ten abreast. The Maples were separated. Joan turned up between her psychiatrist and a massive, doleful African wearing tribal scars, sneakers, and a Harvard Athletic Association sweatshirt. Richard found himself at the end of the line ahead, with Carol beside him. The man behind him, a forward-looking liberal, stepped on his heel, giving the knit of his loafer such a wrench that he had to walk the three miles through Boston with a floppy shoe and a dragging limp. He had been born in West Virginia, near the Pennsylvania line, and did not understand Boston. In ten years he had grown familiar with some of its districts, but was still surprised by the quick curving manner in which these districts interlocked. For a few blocks they marched between cheering tenements from whose topmost windows hung banners that proclaimed END DE FACTO SEGREGATION and RETIRE MRS. HICKS. Then the march turned left, and Richard was passing Symphony Hall, within whose rectangular vault he had often dreamed his way along the deep-grassed meadows of Brahms and up the agate cliffs of Strauss. At this corner, from the Stygian subway kiosk, he had emerged with Joan, Orpheus and Eurydice, when both were students; in this restaurant, a decade later, he and she, on four drinks apiece, had decided not to get a divorce that week. The new Prudential Tower, taller and somehow fainter than any other building, haunted each twist of their march, before their faces like a mirage, at their backs like a memory. A leggy nervous coloured girl wearing the orange fireman's jacket of the Security Unit shepherded their section of the line, clapping her hands, shouting freedom-song lyrics for a few bars. These songs struggled through the miles of the march, overlapping and eclipsing one another. "Which side are you on, boy, which side are you on ... like a tree-ee planted by the wah-ha-ter, we shall not be moved . . . this little light of mine, gonna shine on Boston, Mass., this little light of mine . . ." The day continued cool and without shadows. Newspapers that he had folded inside his coat for warmth slipped and slid. Carol beside him plucked at her little sweater, gathering it at her breast but unable, as if under a spell, to button it. Behind him, Joan, serenely framed between her id and superego, stepped along masterfully, swinging her arms, throwing her ballet slippers alternately outward in a confident splaying stride. ". . . let 'er shine, let 'er shine . . ."

Incredibly, they were traversing a cloverleaf, an elevated concrete arabesque devoid of cars. Their massed footsteps whispered; the city yawned beneath them. The march had no beginning and no end that Richard could see. Within him, the fever had become a small glassy scratching on the walls of the pit hollowed by the detonating pills. A piece of newspaper spilled down his legs and blew into the air. Impalpably medicated, ideally motivated, he felt, strolling along the curve of the cloverleaf, gathered within an irresistible ascent. He asked Carol, "Where are we going?"

"The newspapers said the Common."

"Do you feel faint?"

Her grey braces shyly modified her smile. "Hungry."

"Have a peanut." A few still remained in his pocket.

"Thank you." She took one. "You don't have to be paternal."

"I want to be." He felt strangely exalted and excited, as if destined to give birth. He wanted to share this sensation with Carol, but instead he asked her, "In your study of the labour movement, have you learned much about the Molly Maguires?"

"No. Were they goons or finks?"

"I think they were either coal miners or gangsters."

"Oh. I haven't studied about anything earlier than Gompers."

"I think you're wise." Suppressing the urge to tell her he loved her, he turned to look at Joan. She was beautiful, in the style of a poster, with far-seeing blue eyes and red lips parted in song.

Now they walked beneath office buildings where like mounted butterflies secretaries and dental technicians were pressed against the glass. In Copley Square, stony shoppers waited forever to cross the street. Along Boylston, there was Irish muttering; he shielded Carol with his body. The desultory singing grew defiant. The Public Garden was beginning to bloom. Worthy statues — Channing, Kosciusko, Cass, Phillips — were trundled by beneath the blurring trees; Richard's dry heart cracked like a book being opened. The march turned left down Charles and began to press against itself, to link arms, to fumble for love. He lost sight of Joan in the crush. Then they were treading on grass, on the Common, and the first drops of rain, sharp as needles, pricked their faces and hands.

CR

"Did we have to stay to hear every damn speech?" Richard asked. They were at last heading home; he felt too sick to drive and huddled, in his soaked slippery suit, toward the heater. The windshield wiper seemed to be squeaking *free-dom, free-dom.*

"I wanted to hear King."

"You heard him in Alabama."

"I was too tired to listen then."

"Did you listen this time? Didn't it seem corny and forced?"

"Somewhat. But does it matter?" Her white profile was serene; she passed a trailer truck on the right, and her window was spattered as if with applause.

"And that Abernathy. God, if he's John the Baptist, I'm Herod the Great. 'Onteel de Frenchman go back t'France, onteel de Ahrishman go back t'Ahrland, onteel de Mexican he go back tuh —' "

"Stop it."

"Don't get me wrong. I didn't mind them sounding like demagogues; what I minded was that God-awful boring phony imitation of a revival meeting. 'Thass right, yossuh. Yoh-*suh!* ' "

"Your throat sounds sore. Shouldn't you stop using it?"

"*How* could you crucify me that way? *How* could you make this miserable sick husband stand in the icy rain for hours listening to boring stupid speeches that you'd heard before anyway?"

"I didn't think the speeches were that great. But I think it was important that they were given and that people listened. You were there as a witness, Richard."

"Ah witnessed. Ah believes. Yos-suh."

"You're a very sick man."

"I know, I *know* I am. That's why I wanted to leave. Even your pasty psychiatrist left. He looked like a dunked doughnut."

"He left because of the girls."

"I loved Carol. She respected me, despite the colour of my skin."

"You didn't have to go."

"Yes I did. You somehow turned it into a point of honour. It was a sexual vindication."

"How you go on."

"'Onteel de East German goes on back t'East Germany, onteel de Luxembourgian hies hisself back to Luxembourg —' "

"Please stop it."

But he found he could not stop, and even after they reached home and she put him to bed, the children watching in alarm, his voice continued its slurred plaint. "Ah'ze all riaight, Missy, jes' a tech o' double pneu*mon*ia, don't you fret none, we'll get the cotton in."

"You're embarrassing the children."

"Shecks, doan min' me, chilluns. Ef Ah could jes' res' hyah foh a spell in de shade o' de watuhmelon patch, res' dese ol' bones . . . Lawzy, dat do feel good!"

"Daddy has a tiny cold," Joan explained.

"Will he die?" Bean asked, and burst into tears.

"Now, effen," he said, "bah some un*foh*-choonut chayance, mah spirrut should pass owen, bureh me bah de levee, so mebbe Ah kin heeah de singin' an' de banjos an' de cotton bolls a-bustin' . . . an' mebbe even de whaat folks up in de Big House kin shed a homely tear er two . . ." He was almost crying; a weird tenderness had crept over him in bed, as if he had indeed given birth, birth to this voice, a voice crying for attention from the depths of oppression. High in the window, the late afternoon sky blanched as the storm lifted. In the warmth of the bed, Richard crooned to himself, and once started up, crying out, "Missy! Missy! Doan you worreh none, ol' Tom'll see anotheh sun-up!"

But Joan was downstairs, talking firmly on the telephone.

ℬℭ

John Updike is the author of more than thirty books, including novels, essays, drama, and collections of short stories. This story is taken from Too Far to Go, *a collection depicting the Maples, a couple living in New England. Esteemed for his acute sense of detail, and his incisive, but compassionate, rendering of daily life, Updike sets "Marching Through Boston" during the civil rights movement in the 1960s, seamlessly blending the world of politics with the domestic troubles of an ordinary, faltering marriage. Much of Updike's artistry resides in his ability to sketch in the entire history of a marriage through innocuous details. Although it is narrated in third person, the story's primary focalizer is Richard Maples, and as such, we see the story mostly through his perceptions and memories. The fact that he is a lapsed Christian, and that his wife has undergone psychoanalytic treatment, are crucial interpretative models for Richard's grasp of what is happening to him. As a portrait of white, middle-class life, this story places racial struggle in the periphery; doing so, "Marching Through Boston" probes deeply into an America fractured between white and black.*

M.T.

The Watcher

I suppose it was having a bad chest that turned me into an observer, a watcher, at an early age.

"Charlie has my chest," my mother often informed friends. "A real weakness there," she would add significantly, thumping her own wishbone soundly.

I suppose I had. Family lore had me narrowly escaping death from pneumonia at the age of four. It seems I spent an entire Sunday in delirium, soaking the sheets. Dr. Carlyle was off at the reservoir rowing in his little skiff and couldn't be reached — something for which my mother illogically refused to forgive him. She was a woman who nursed and tenaciously held dark grudges. Forever after that incident the doctor was slightingly and coldly dismissed in conversation as a "man who betrayed the public's trust."

Following that spell of pneumonia, I regularly suffered from bouts of bronchitis, which often landed me in hospital in Fortune, forty miles away. Compared with the oxygen tent and the whacking great needles that were buried in my skinny rump there, being invalided at home was a piece of cake. Coughing and hacking, I would leaf through catalogues and read comic books until my head swam with print-fatigue. My diet was largely of my own whimsical choosing — hot chocolate and graham wafers were supplemented by sticky sweet coughdrops, which I downed one after another until my stomach could take no more, revolted, and tossed up the whole mess.

With the first signs of improvement in my condition my mother moved her baby to the living-room chesterfield, where she and the radio could keep me company. The electric kettle followed me and was soon burbling in the corner, jetting steam into the air to keep my lungs moist and pliable. Because I was neither quite sick nor quite well, these were the best days of my illnesses. My stay at home hadn't yet made me bored and restless, my chest no longer hurt when I breathed, and that loose pocket of rattling phlegm meant I didn't have to worry about going back to school just yet. So I luxuriated in this steamy equatorial climate, tended by a doting mother as if I were a rare tropical orchid.

My parents didn't own a television and so my curiosity and attention were focused on my surroundings during my illnesses. I tried to squeeze every bit of juice out of them. Sooner than most children I learned that if you kept quiet and still and didn't insist on drawing attention to yourself as many kids did, adults were inclined to regard you as being one with the furniture, as significant and sentient as a hassock. By keeping mum I was treated to illuminating glances into an adult world of conventional miseries and scandals.

I wasn't sure at the age of six what a miscarriage was, but I knew that Ida Thompson had had one and that now her plumbing was buggered. And watching old lady Kuznetzky hang her washing, through a living-room window trickling with condensed kettle steam, I was able to confirm for myself the rumour that the old girl eschewed panties. As she bent over to rummage in her laundry basket I caught a brief glimpse of huge, white buttocks that shimmered in the pale spring sunshine.

I also soon knew (how I don't remember exactly) that Norma Ruggs had business with the Liquor Board Store when she shuffled by our window every day at exactly 10:50 a.m. She was always at the store door at 11:00 when they unlocked and opened up for business. At 11:15 she trudged home again, a pint of ice cream in one hand, a brown paper bag disguising a bottle of fortified wine in the other, and her blotchy complexion painted a high colour of shame.

"Poor old girl," my mother would say whenever she caught sight of Norma passing by in her shabby coat and sloppy man's overshoes. They had been in high school together, and Norma had been class brain and valedictorian. She had been an obliging, dutiful girl and still was. For the wine wasn't Norma's — the ice cream was her only vice. The booze was her husband's, a vet who had come back from the war badly crippled.

All this careful study of adults may have made me old before my time. In any case it seemed to mark me in some recognizable way as being "different" or "queer for a kid." When I went to live with my grandmother in July of 1959 she spotted it right away. Of course, she was only stating the obvious when she declared me skinny and delicate, but she also noted in her vinegary voice that my eyes had a bad habit of never letting her go, and that I was the worst case of little pitchers having big ears that she had ever come across.

I ended up at my grandmother's because in May of that year my mother's bad chest finally caught up with her, much to her and everyone else's surprise. It had been pretty generally agreed by all her acquaintances that Mabel Bradley's defects in that regard were largely imagined. Not so. A government-sponsored X-ray program discovered tuberculosis, and she was packed off, pale and drawn with worry, for a stay in the sanatorium at Fort Qu'Appelle.

For roughly a month, until the school year ended, my father took charge of me and the house. He was a desolate, lanky, drooping weed of a man who had married late in life but nevertheless had been easily domesticated. I didn't like him much.

My father was badly wrenched by my mother's sickness and absence. He scrawled her long, untidy letters with a stub of gnawed pencil, and once he got shut of me, visited her every weekend. He was a soft and sentimental man whose eyes ran to water at the drop of a hat, or more accurately, death of a cat. Unlike his mother, my Grandma Bradley, he hadn't a scrap of flint or hard-headed common sense in him.

But then neither had any of his many brothers and sisters. It was as if the old girl had unflinchingly withheld the genetic code for responsibility and practicality from her pin-headed offspring. Life for her children was a series of thundering defeats, whirlwind calamities, or, at best, hurried strategic retreats. Businesses crashed and marriages failed, for they had — my father excepted — a taste for the unstable in partners marital and fiscal.

My mother saw no redeeming qualities in any of them. By and large they drank too much, talked too loudly, and raised ill-mannered children — monsters of depravity whose rudeness provided my mother with endless illustrations of what she feared I might become. "You're eating just like a pig," she would say, "exactly like your cousin Elvin." Or to my father, "You're neglecting the belt. He's starting to get as lippy as that little snot Muriel."

And in the midst, in the very eye of this familial cyclone of mishap and discontent, stood Grandma Bradley, as firm as a rock. Troubles of all kinds were laid on her doorstep. When my cousin Criselda suddenly turned big-tummied at sixteen and it proved difficult to ascertain with any exactitude the father, or even point a finger of general blame in the direction of a putative sire, she was shipped off to Grandma Bradley until she delivered. Uncle Ernie dried out on Grandma's farm and Uncle Ed hid there from several people he had sold prefab, assemble-yourself, crop-duster airplanes to.

So it was only family tradition that I should be deposited there. When domestic duties finally overwhelmed him, and I complained too loudly about fried-egg sandwiches for dinner *again*, my father left the bacon rinds hardening and curling grotesquely on unwashed plates, the slut's wool eddying along the floor in the currents of a draft, and drove the one hundred and fifty miles to the farm, *right then and there*.

My father, a dangerous man behind the wheel, took any extended trip seriously, believing the highways to be narrow, unnavigable ribbons of carnage. This trip loomed so dangerously in his mind that, rather than tear a hand from the wheel, or an eye from the road, he had me, *chronic sufferer of lung disorders*, light his cigarettes and place them carefully in his dry lips. My mother would have killed him.

"You'll love it at Grandma's," he kept saying unconvincingly, "you'll have a real boy's summer on the farm. It'll build you up, the chores and all that. And good fun too. You don't know it now, but you are living the best days of your life right now. What I wouldn't give to be a kid again. You'll love it there. There's chickens and *everything*."

CR

It wasn't exactly a lie. There were chickens. But the *everything* — as broad and overwhelming and suggestive of possibilities as my father tried to make it sound — didn't cover much. It certainly didn't comprehend a pony or a dog as I had hoped, chickens being the only livestock on the place.

It turned out that my grandmother, although she had spent most of her life on that particular piece of ground and eventually died there, didn't care much for the farm and was entirely out of sympathy with most varieties of animal life. She did keep chickens for the eggs, although she admitted that her spirits lifted considerably in the fall when it came time to butcher the hens.

Her flock was a garrulous, scraggly crew that spent their days having dust baths in the front yard, hiding their eggs, and, fleet and ferocious as hunting cheetahs, running down scuttling lizards which they trampled and pecked to death while their shiny, expressionless eyes shifted dizzily in their stupid heads. The only one of these birds I felt any compassion for was Stanley the rooster, a bedraggled male who spent his days tethered to a stake by a piece of baler twine looped around his leg. Poor Stanley crowed heart-rendingly in his captivity; his comb drooped pathetically, and he was utterly crestfallen as he lecherously eyed his bantam beauties daintily scavenging. Grandma kept him in this unnatural bondage to prevent him fertilizing the eggs and producing blood spots in the yolks. Being a finicky eater I approved this policy, but nevertheless felt some guilt over Stanley.

No, the old Bradley homestead, all that encompassed by my father's *everything*, wasn't very impressive. The two-storey house, though big and solid, needed paint and shingles. A track had been worn in the kitchen linoleum clean through to the floorboards and a long rent in the screen door had been stitched shut with waxed thread. The yard was little more than a tangle of thigh-high ragweed and sowthistle to which the chickens repaired for shade. A windbreak of spruce on the north side of the house was dying from lack of water and the competition from Scotch thistle. The evergreens were no longer green; their sere needles fell away from the branches at the touch of a hand.

The abandoned barn out back was flanked by two mountainous rotted piles of manure which I remember sprouting button mushrooms after every warm soaker of a rain. That pile of shit was the only useful thing in a yard full of junk: wrecked cars, old wagon wheels, collapsing sheds. The barn itself was mightily decayed. The paint had been stripped from its planks by rain, hail, and dry, blistering winds, and the roof sagged like a tired nag's back. For a small boy it was an ominous place on a summer day. The air was still and dark and heavy with heat. At the sound of footsteps rats squeaked and scrabbled in the empty mangers, and the sparrows which had spattered the rafters white with their dung whirred about and fluted ghostly cries.

In 1959 Grandma Bradley would have been sixty-nine, which made her a child of the gay nineties — although the supposed gaiety of that age didn't seem to have made much impress upon the development of her character. Physically she was an imposing woman. Easily six feet tall, she carried a hundred and eighty pounds on her generous frame without prompting speculation as to what she had against girdles. She could touch the floor effortlessly with the flat of her palms and pack an eighty-pound sack of chicken feed on her shoulder. She dyed her hair auburn in defiance of local mores, and never went to town to play bridge, whist, or canasta without wearing a hat and getting dressed to the teeth. Grandma loved card games of all varieties and considered anyone who didn't a mental defective.

A cigarette always smouldered in her trap. She smoked sixty a day and rolled them as thin as knitting needles in an effort at economy. These cigarettes were so wispy and delicate they tended to get lost between her swollen fingers.

And above all she believed in plain speaking. She let me know that as my father's maroon Meteor pulled out of the yard while we stood waving goodbye on the front steps.

"Let's get things straight from the beginning," she said without taking her eyes off the car as it bumped toward the grid road. "I don't chew my words twice. If you're like any of the rest of them I've had here, you've been raised as wild as a goddamn Indian. Not one of my grandchildren have been brought up to mind.

Well, you'll mind around here. I don't jaw and blow hot air to jaw and blow hot air. I belted your father when he needed it, and make no mistake I'll belt you. Is that understood?"

"Yes," I said with a sinking feeling as I watched my father's car disappear down the road, swaying from side to side as its suspension was buffeted by potholes.

"These bloody bugs are eating me alive," she said, slapping her arm. "I'm going in."

I trailed after her as she slopped back into the house in a pair of badly mauled, laceless sneakers. The house was filled with a half-light that changed its texture with every room. The venetian blinds were drawn in the parlour and some flies carved Immelmanns in the dark air that smelled of cellar damp. Others battered their bullet bodies *tip-tap*, *tip-tap* against the window panes.

In the kitchen my grandmother put the kettle on the stove to boil for tea. After she had lit one of her matchstick smokes, she inquired through a blue haze if I was hungry.

"People aren't supposed to smoke around me," I informed her. "Because of my chest. Dad can't even smoke in our house."

"That so?" she said genially. Her cheeks collapsed as she drew on her butt. I had a hint there, if I'd only known it, of how she'd look in her coffin. "You won't like it here then," she said. "I smoke all the time."

I tried a few unconvincing coughs. I was ignored. She didn't respond to the same signals as my mother.

"My mother has a bad chest, too," I said. "She's in a T.B. sanatorium."

"So I heard," my grandmother said, getting up to fetch the whistling kettle. "Oh, I suspect she'll be right as rain in no time with a little rest. T.B. isn't what it used to be. Not with all these new drugs." She considered. "That's not to say though that your father'll ever hear the end of it. Mabel was always a silly little shit that way."

I almost fell off my chair. I had never thought I'd live to hear the day my mother was called a silly little shit.

"Drink tea?" asked Grandma Bradley, pouring boiling water into a brown teapot.

I shook my head.

"How old are you anyway?" she asked.

"Eleven."

"You're old enough then," she said, taking down a cup from the shelf. "Tea gets the kidneys moving and carries off the poisons in the blood. That's why all the Chinese live to be so old. They all live to be a hundred."

"I don't know if my mother would like it," I said. "Me drinking tea."

"You worry a lot for a kid," she said, "don't you?"

I didn't know how to answer that. It wasn't a question I had ever considered. I tried to shift the conversation.

"What's there for a kid to do around here?" I said in an unnaturally inquisitive voice.

"Well, we could play cribbage," she said.

"I don't know how to play cribbage."

She was genuinely shocked. "What!" she exclaimed. "Why, you're eleven years old! Your father could count a cribbage hand when he was five. I taught all my kids to."

"I never learned how," I said. "We don't even have a deck of cards at our house. My father hates cards. Says he had too much of them as a boy."

At this my grandmother arched her eyebrows. "Is that a fact? Well, hoity-toity."

"So, since I don't play cards," I continued in a strained manner I imagined was polite, "what could I do — I mean, for fun?"

"Make your own fun," she said. "I never considered fun such a problem. Use your imagination. Take a broomstick and make like Nimrod."

"Who's Nimrod?" I asked.

"Pig ignorant," she said under her breath, and then louder, directly to me, "Ask me no questions and I'll tell you no lies. Drink your tea."

And that, for the time being, was that.

ଙ

It's all very well to tell someone to make their own fun. It's the making of it that is the problem. In a short time I was a very bored kid. There was no one to play with, no horses to ride, no gun to shoot gophers, no dog for company. There was nothing to read except the *Country Guide* and *Western Producer*. There was nothing or nobody interesting to watch. I went through my grandmother's drawers but found nothing as surprising there as I had discovered in my parents'.

Most days it was so hot that the very idea of fun boiled out of me and evaporated. I moped and dragged myself listlessly around the house in the loose-jointed, water-boned way kids have when they can't stand anything, not even their precious selves.

On my better days I tried to take up with Stanley the rooster. Scant chance of that. Tremors of panic ran through his body at my approach. He tugged desperately on the twine until he jerked his free leg out from under himself and collapsed in the dust, his heart bumping the tiny crimson scallops of his breast feathers, the black pellets of his eyes glistening, all the while shitting copiously. Finally, in the last extremes of chicken terror, he would allow me to stroke his yellow beak and finger his comb.

I felt sorry for the captive Stanley and several times tried to take him for a walk, to give him a chance to take the air and broaden his limited horizons. But this prospect alarmed him so much that I was always forced to return him to his stake in disgust while he fluttered, squawked and flopped.

So fun was a commodity in short supply. That is, until something interesting turned up during the first week of August. Grandma Bradley was dredging little watering canals with a hoe among the corn stalks on a bright blue Monday morning, and I was shelling peas into a colander on the front stoop, when a black car nosed diffidently up the road and into the yard. Then it stopped a good twenty yards short of the house as if its occupants weren't sure of their welcome. After some time, the doors opened and a man and woman got carefully out.

The woman wore turquoise-blue pedal-pushers, a sloppy black turtleneck sweater, and a gash of scarlet lipstick swiped across her white, vivid face. This was my father's youngest sister, Aunt Evelyn.

The man took her gently and courteously by the elbow and balanced her as she edged up the front yard in her high heels, careful to avoid turning an ankle on a loose stone, or in an old tire track.

The thing which immediately struck me about the man was his beard — the first I had ever seen. Beards weren't popular in 1959 — not in our part of the world. His was a randy, jutting, little goat's-beard that would have looked wicked on any other face but his. He was very tall and his considerable height was accented by a lack of corresponding breadth to his body. He appeared to have been racked and stretched against his will into an exceptional and unnatural anatomy. As he walked and talked animatedly, his free hand fluttered in front of my aunt. It sailed, twirled and gambolled on the air. Like a butterfly enticing a child, it seemed to lead her hypnotized across a yard fraught with perils for city-shod feet.

My grandmother laid down her hoe and called sharply to her daughter.

"Evvie!" she called. "Over here, Evvie!"

At the sound of her mother's voice my aunt's head snapped around and she began to wave jerkily and stiffly, striving to maintain a tottering balance on her high-heeled shoes. It wasn't hard to see that there was something not quite right with her. By the time my grandmother and I reached the pair, Aunt Evelyn was in tears, sobbing hollowly and jamming the heel of her palm into her front teeth.

The man was speaking calmly to her. "Control. Control. Deep, steady breaths. Think sea. Control. Control. Control. Think sea, Evelyn. Deep. Deep. Deep," he muttered.

"What the hell is the matter, Evelyn?" my grandmother asked sharply. "And who is *he*?"

"Evelyn is a little upset," the man said, keeping his attention focused on my aunt. "She's having one of her anxiety attacks. If you'd just give us a moment we'll clear this up. She's got to learn to handle stressful situations." He inclined his head in a priestly manner and said, "Be with the sea, Evelyn. Deep. Deep. Sink in the sea."

"It's her damn nerves again," said my grandmother.

"Yes," the man said benignly, with a smile of blinding condescension. "Sort of."

"She's been as nervous as a cut cat all her life," said my grandmother, mostly to herself.

"Momma," said Evelyn, weeping. "Momma."

"Slide beneath the waves, Evelyn. Down, down, down to the beautiful pearls," the man chanted softly. This was really something.

My grandmother took Aunt Evelyn by her free elbow, shook it, and said sharply, "Evelyn, shut up!" Then she began to drag her briskly towards the house. For a moment the man looked as if he had it in mind to protest, but in the end he meekly acted as a flanking escort for Aunt Evelyn as she was marched into the house. When I tried to follow, my grandmother gave me one of her looks and said definitely, "You find something to do out here."

I did. I waited a few minutes and then duck-walked my way under the parlour window. There I squatted with my knobby shoulder blades pressed against the siding and the sun beating into my face.

My grandmother obviously hadn't wasted any time with the social niceties. They were fairly into it.

"Lovers?" said my grandmother. "Is that what it's called now? Shack-up, you mean."

"Oh, Momma," said Evelyn, and she was crying, "it's all right. We're going to get married."

"You believe that?" said my grandmother. "You believe that geek is going to marry you?"

"Thompson," said the geek, "my name is Thompson, Robert Thompson, and we'll marry as soon as I get my divorce. Although Lord only knows when that'll be."

"That's right," said my grandmother, "Lord only knows." Then to her daughter, "You got another one. A real prize off the midway, didn't you? Evelyn, you're a certifiable lunatic."

"I didn't expect this," said Thompson. "We came here because Evelyn has had a bad time of it recently. She hasn't been eating or sleeping properly and consequently she's got herself run down. She finds it difficult to control her emotions, don't you, darling?"

I thought I heard a mild yes.

"So," said Thompson, continuing, "we decided Evelyn needs some peace and quiet before I go back to school in September."

"School," said my grandmother. "Don't tell me you're some kind of teacher?" She seemed stunned by the very idea.

"No," said Aunt Evelyn, and there was a tremor of pride in her voice that testified to her amazement that she had been capable of landing such a rare and remarkable fish. "Not a teacher. Robert's a graduate student of American Literature at the University of British Columbia."

"Hoity-toity," said Grandmother. "A graduate student. A graduate student of American Literature."

"Doctoral program," said Robert.

"And did you ever ask yourself, Evelyn, what the hell this genius is doing with you? Or is it just the same old problem with you — elevator panties? Some guy comes along and pushes the button. Up, down. Up, down."

The image this created in my mind made me squeeze my knees together deliciously and stifle a giggle.

"Mother," said Evelyn, continuing to bawl.

"Guys like this don't marry barmaids," said my grandmother.

"Cocktail hostess," corrected Evelyn. "I'm a cocktail hostess."

"You don't have to make any excuses, dear," said Thompson pompously. "Remember what I told you. You're past the age of being judged."

"What the hell is that supposed to mean?" said my grandmother. "And by the way, don't start handing out orders in my house. You won't be around long enough to make them stick."

"That remains to be seen," said Thompson.

"Let's go, Robert," said Evelyn nervously.

"Go on upstairs, Evelyn, I want to talk to your mother."

"You don't have to go anywhere," said my grandmother. "You can stay put."

"Evelyn, go upstairs." There was a pause and then I heard the sound of a chair creaking, then footsteps.

"Well," said my grandmother at last, "round one. Now for round two — get the hell out of my house."

"Can't do that."

"Why the hell not?"

"It's very difficult to explain," he said.

"Try."

"As you can see for yourself, Evelyn isn't well. She is very highly strung at the moment. I believe she is on the verge of a profound personality adjustment, a breakthrough." He paused dramatically. "Or breakdown."

"It's times like this that I wished I had a dog on the place to run off undesirables."

"The way I read it," said Thompson, unperturbed, "is that at the moment two people bulk very large in Evelyn's life. You and me. She needs the support and love of us both. You're not doing your share."

"I ought to slap your face."

"She has come home to try and get a hold of herself. We have to bury our dislikes for the moment. She needs to be handled very carefully."

"You make her sound like a trained bear. *Handled.* What that girl needs is a good talking to, and I am perfectly capable of giving her that."

"No, Mrs. Bradley," Thompson said firmly in that maddeningly self-assured tone of his. "If you don't mind me saying so, I think that's part of her problem. It's important now for you to just let Evelyn *be.*"

"Get out of my house," said my grandmother, at the end of her tether.

"I know it's difficult for you to understand," he said smoothly, "but if you understood the psychology of this you would see it's impossible for me to go; or for that matter, for Evelyn to go. If I leave she'll feel *I've* abandoned her. It can't be done. We're faced with a real psychological balancing act here."

"Now I've heard everything," said my grandmother. "Are you telling me you'd have the gall to move into a house where you're not wanted and just . . . just *stay there?*"

"Yes," said Thompson. "And I think you'll find me quite stubborn on this particular point."

"My God," said my grandmother. I could tell by her tone of voice that she had never come across anyone like Mr. Thompson before. At a loss for a suitable reply, she simply reiterated, "My God."

"I'm going upstairs now," said Thompson. "Maybe you could get the boy to bring in our bags while I see how Evelyn is doing. The car isn't locked." The second time he spoke his voice came from further away; I imagined him paused in the doorway. "Mrs. Bradley, please let's make this stay pleasant for Evelyn's sake."

She didn't bother answering him.

When I barged into the house some time later with conspicuous noisiness, I found my grandmother standing at the bottom of the stairs staring up the steps. "Well, I'll be damned," she said under her breath. "I've never seen anything like that. Goddamn freak." She even repeated it several times under her breath. "Goddamn freak. Goddamn freak."

Who could blame me if, after a boring summer, I felt my chest tighten with anticipation. Adults could be immensely interesting and entertaining if you knew what to watch for.

CR

At first things were disappointingly quiet. Aunt Evelyn seldom set forth outside the door of the room she and her man inhabited by squatters' right. There was an argument, short and sharp, between Thompson and Grandmother over this. The professor claimed no one had any business prying into what Evelyn did up there. She was an adult and had the right to her privacy and her own thoughts. My grandmother claimed *she* had a right to know what was going on up there, even if nobody else thought she did.

I could have satisfied her curiosity on that point. Not much was going on up there. Several squints through the keyhole had revealed Aunt Evelyn lolling about the bedspread in a blue housecoat, eating soda crackers and sardines, and reading a stack of movie magazines she had had me lug out of the trunk of the car.

Food, you see, was beginning to become something of a problem for our young lovers. Grandma rather pointedly set only three places for meals, and Evelyn, out of loyalty to her boyfriend, couldn't very well sit down and break bread with us. Not that Thompson didn't take such things in his stride. He sauntered casually and conspicuously about the house as if he owned it, even going so far as to poke his head in the fridge and rummage in it like some pale, hairless bear. At times like that my grandmother was capable of looking through him as if he didn't exist.

On the second day of his stay Thompson took up with me, which was all right as far as I was concerned. I had no objection. Why he decided to do this I'm not sure exactly. Perhaps he was looking for some kind of an ally, no matter how weak. Most likely he wanted to get under the old lady's skin. Or maybe he just couldn't bear not having anyone to tell how wonderful he was. Thompson was that kind of a guy.

I was certainly let in on the secret. He was a remarkable fellow. He dwelt at great length on those things which made him such an extraordinary human being. I may have gotten the order of precedence all wrong, but if I remember correctly there were three things which made Thompson very special and different from all the other people I would ever meet, no matter how long or hard I lived.

First, he was going to write a book about a poet called Allen Ginsberg which was going to knock the socks off everybody who counted. It turned out he had actually met this Ginsberg the summer before in San Francisco and asked him if he could write a book about him and Ginsberg had said, Sure, why the hell not? The way Thompson described what it would be like when he published this book left me with the impression that he was going to spend most of the rest of his life riding around on people's shoulders and being cheered by a multitude of admirers.

Second, he confessed to knowing a tremendous amount about what made other people tick and how to adjust their mainsprings when they went kaflooey. He knew all this because at one time his own mainspring had gotten a little out of sorts. But now he was a fully integrated personality with a highly creative mind and a strong intuitive sense. That's why he was so much help to Aunt Evelyn in her time of troubles.

Third, he was a Buddhist.

The only one of these things which impressed me at the time was the bit about being a Buddhist. However, I was confused, because in the *Picture Book of the World's Great Religions* which we had at home, all the Buddhists were bald, and Thompson had a hell of a lot of hair, more than I had ever seen on a man. But even though he wasn't bald, he had an idol. A little bronze statue with the whimsical smile and slightly crossed eyes which he identified as Padma-sambhava. He told me that it was a Tibetan antique he had bought in San Francisco as an object of veneration and an aid to his meditations. I asked him what a meditation was and he offered to teach me one. So I learned to recite with great seriousness and flexible intonation one of his Tibetan meditations, while my grandmother glared across her quintessentially Western parlour with unbelieving eyes.

I could soon deliver, "A king must go when his time has come. His wealth, his friends and his relatives cannot go with him. Wherever men go, wherever they stay, the effect of their past acts follows them like a shadow. Those who are in the grip of desire, the grip of existence, the grip of ignorance, move helplessly round through the spheres of life, as men or gods or as wretches in the lower regions."

Not that an eleven-year-old could make much of any of *that*.

Which is not to say that even an eleven-year-old could be fooled by Robert Thompson. In his stubbornness, egoism and blindness he was transparently un-Buddhalike. To watch him and my grandmother snarl and snap their teeth over that poor, dry bone, Evelyn, was evidence enough of how firmly bound we all are to the wretched wheel of life and its stumbling desires.

No, even his most effective weapon, his cool benevolence, that patina of patience and forbearance which Thompson displayed to Grandmother, could crack.

One windy day when he had coaxed Aunt Evelyn out for a walk I followed them at a distance. They passed the windbreak of spruce, and, at the sagging barbed-wire fence he gallantly manipulated the wires while my aunt floundered over them in an impractical dress and crinoline. It was the kind of dippy thing she would decide to wear on a hike.

Thompson strode along through the rippling grass like a wading heron, his baggy pant-legs flapping and billowing in the wind. My aunt moved along gingerly behind him, one hand modestly pinning down her wind-teased dress in the front, the other hand plastering the back of it to her behind.

It was only when they stopped and faced each other that I realized that all the time they had been traversing the field they had been arguing. A certain vaguely communicated agitation in the attitude of her figure, the way his arm stabbed at the featureless wash of sky, implied a dispute. She turned toward the house and he caught her by the arm and jerked it. In a fifties calendar fantasy her dress lifted in the wind, exposing her panties. I sank in the grass until their seed tassels trembled against my chin. I wasn't going to miss watching this for the world.

She snapped and twisted on the end of his arm like a fish on a line. Her head was flung back in an exaggerated, antique display of despair; her head rolled grotesquely from side to side as if her neck were broken.

Suddenly Thompson began striking awkwardly at her exposed buttocks and thighs with the flat of his hand. The long, gangly arm slashed like a flail as she scampered around him, the radius of her escape limited by the distance of their linked arms.

From where I knelt in the grass I could hear nothing. I was too far off. As far as I was concerned there were no cries and no pleading. The whole scene, as I remember it, was shorn of any of the personal idiosyncrasies which manifest themselves in violence. It appeared a simple case of retribution.

That night, for the first time, my aunt came down to supper and claimed her place at the table with queenly graciousness. She wore shorts, too, for the first time, and gave a fine display of mottled, discoloured thighs which reminded me of bruised fruit. She made sure, almost as if by accident, that my grandmother had a good hard look at them.

♋

Right out of the blue my grandmother said, "I don't want you hanging around that man any more. You stay away from him."

"Why?" I asked rather sulkily. He was the only company I had. Since my aunt's arrival Grandmother had paid no attention to me whatsoever.

It was late afternoon and we were sitting on the porch watching Evelyn squeal as she swung in the tire swing Thompson had rigged up for me in the barn. He had thrown a length of stray rope over the runner for the sliding door and hung a tire from it. I hadn't the heart to tell him I was too old for tire swings.

Aunt Evelyn seemed to be enjoying it though. She was screaming and girlishly kicking up her legs. Thompson couldn't be seen. He was deep in the settled darkness of the barn, pushing her back and forth. She disappeared and reappeared according to the arc which she travelled through. Into the barn, out in the sun. Light, darkness. Light, darkness.

Grandma ignored my question. "Goddamn freak," she said, scratching a match on the porch rail and lighting one of her rollies. "Wait and see, he'll get his wagon fixed."

"Aunt Evelyn likes him," I noted pleasantly, just to stir things up a bit.

"Your Aunt Evelyn's screws are loose," she said sourly. "And he's the son of a bitch who owns the screwdriver that loosened them."

"He must be an awful smart fellow to be studying to be a professor at a university," I commented. It was the last dig I could chance.

"One thing I know for sure," snapped my grandmother. "He isn't smart enough to lift the toilet seat when he pees. There's evidence enough for that."

After hearing that, I took to leaving a few conspicuous droplets of my own as a matter of course on each visit. Every little bit might help things along.

CR

I stood in his doorway and watched Thompson meditate. And don't think that, drenched in *satori* as he was, he didn't know it. He put on quite a performance sitting on the floor in his underpants. When he came out of his trance he pretended to be surprised to see me. While he dressed we struck up a conversation.

"You know, Charlie," he said while he put on his sandals (I'd never seen a grown man wear sandals in my entire life), "you remind me of my little Padma-sambhava," he said, nodding to the idol squatting on his dresser. "For a while, you know, I thought it was the smile, but it isn't. It's the eyes."

"Its eyes are crossed," I said, none too flattered at the comparison.

"No they're not," he said good-naturedly. He tucked his shirt-tail into his pants. "The artist, the maker of that image, set them fairly close together to suggest — aesthetically speaking — the intensity of inner vision, its concentration." He picked up the idol and, looking at it, said, "These are very watchful eyes, very knowing eyes. Your eyes are something like that. From your eyes I could tell you're an intelligent boy." He paused, set Padma-sambhava back on the dresser, and asked, "Are you?"

I shrugged.

"Don't be afraid to say it if you are," he said. "False modesty can be as corrupting as vanity. It took me twenty-five years to learn that."

"I usually get all A's on my report card," I volunteered.

"Well, that's something," he said, looking around the room for his belt. He picked a sweater off a chair and peered under it. "Then you see what's going on around here, don't you?" he asked. "You see what your grandmother is mistakenly trying to do?"

I nodded.

"That's right," he said. "You're a smart boy." He sat down on the bed. "Come here."

I went over to him. He took hold of me by the arms and looked into my eyes with all the sincerity he could muster. "You know, being intelligent means responsibilities. It means doing something worthwhile with your life. For instance, have you given any thought as to what you would like to be when you grow up?"

"A spy," I said.

The silly bugger laughed.

CR

It was the persistent, rhythmic thud that first woke me, and once wakened, I picked up the undercurrent of the muted clamour, of stifled struggle. The noise seeped through the beaverboard wall of the adjoining bedroom into my own, a storm of hectic urgency and violence. The floorboards of the old house squeaked; I heard what sounded like a strangled curse and moan, then a fleshy, meaty concussion which I took to be a slap. Was he killing her at last? Choking her with the silent, poisonous care necessary to escape detection?

I remembered Thompson's arm flashing frenziedly in the sunlight. My aunt's discoloured thighs. My heart creaked in my chest with fear. And after killing her? Would the madman stop? Or would he do us all in, one by one?

I got out of bed on unsteady legs. The muffled commotion was growing louder, more distinct. I padded into the hallway. The door to their bedroom was partially open, and a light showed. Terror made me feel hollow; the pit of my stomach ached.

They were both naked, something which I hadn't expected, and which came as quite a shock. What was perhaps even more shocking was the fact that they seemed not only oblivious of me, but of each other as well. She was slung around so that her head was propped on a pillow resting on the footboard of the bed. One smooth leg was draped over the edge of the bed and her heel was beating time on the floorboards (the thud which woke me) as accompaniment to Thompson's plunging body and the soft, liquid grunts of expelled air which he made with every lunge. One of her hands gripped the footboard and her knuckles were white with strain.

I watched until the critical moment, right through the growing frenzy and ardour. They groaned and panted and heaved and shuddered and didn't know themselves. At the very last he lifted his bony, hatchet face with the jutting beard to the ceiling and closed his eyes; for a moment I thought he was praying as his lips moved soundlessly. But then he began to whimper and his mouth fell open and he looked stupider and weaker than any human being I had ever seen before in my life.

℘

"Like pigs at the trough," my grandmother said at breakfast. "With the boy up there too."

My aunt turned a deep red, and then flushed again so violently that her thin lips appeared to turn blue.

I kept my head down and went on shovelling porridge. Thompson still wasn't invited to the table. He was leaning against the kitchen counter, his bony legs crossed at the ankles, eating an apple he had helped himself to.

"He didn't hear anything," my aunt said uncertainly. She whispered conspiratorially across the table to Grandmother. "Not at that hour. He'd been asleep for hours."

I thought it wise, even though it meant drawing attention to myself, to establish my ignorance. "Hear what?" I inquired innocently.

"It wouldn't do any harm if he had," said Thompson, calmly biting and chewing the temptress's fruit.

"You wouldn't see it, would you?" said Grandma Bradley. "It wouldn't matter to you what he heard? You'd think that was manly."

"Manly has nothing to do with it. Doesn't enter into it," said Thompson in that cool way he had. "It's a fact of life, something he'll have to find out about sooner or later."

Aunt Evelyn began to cry. "Nobody is ever pleased with me," she spluttered. "I'm going crazy trying to please you both. I can't do it." She began to pull nervously at her hair. "He made me," she said finally in a confessional, humble tone to her mother.

"Evelyn," said my grandmother, "you have a place here. I would never send you away. I want you here. But he has to go. I want him to go. If he is going to rub my nose in it that way he has to go. I won't have that man under my roof."

"Evelyn isn't apologizing for anything," Thompson said. "And she isn't running away either. You can't force her to choose. It isn't healthy or fair."

"There have been other ones before you," said Grandma. "This isn't anything new for Evelyn."

"Momma!"

"I'm aware of that," he said stiffly, and his face vibrated with the effort to smile. "Provincial mores have never held much water with me. I like to think I'm above all that."

Suddenly my grandmother spotted me. "What are you gawking at!" she shouted. "Get on out of here!"

I didn't budge an inch.

"Leave him alone," said Thompson.

"You'll be out of here within a week," said Grandmother. "I swear."

"No," he said smiling. "When I'm ready."

"You'll go home and go with your tail between your legs. Last night was the last straw," she said. And by God you could tell she meant it.

Thompson gave her his beatific Buddha-grin and shook his head from side to side, very, very slowly.

◌ℜ

A thunderstorm was brewing. The sky was a stew of dark, swollen cloud and a strange apple-green light. The temperature stood in the mid-nineties, not a breath of breeze stirred, my skin crawled and my head pounded above my eyes and through the bridge of my nose. There wasn't a thing to do except sit on the bottom step of the porch, keep from picking up a sliver in your ass, and scratch the dirt with a stick. My grandmother had put her hat on and driven into town on some unexplained business. Thompson and my aunt were upstairs in their bedroom, sunk in a stuporous, sweaty afternoon's sleep.

Like my aunt and Thompson, all the chickens had gone to roost to wait for rain. The desertion of his harem had thrown the rooster into a flap. Stanley trotted neurotically around his tethering post, stopping every few circuits to beat his bedraggled pinions and crow lustily in masculine outrage. I watched him for a bit without much curiosity, and then climbed off the step and walked toward him, listlessly dragging my stick in my trail.

"Here, Stanley, Stanley," I called, not entirely sure how to summon a rooster, or instil in him confidence and friendliness.

I did neither. My approach only further unhinged Stanley. His stride lengthened, the tempo of his pace increased, and his head began to dart abruptly from side to side in furtive despair. Finally, in a last desperate attempt to escape, Stanley upset himself trying to fly. He landed in a heat of disarranged, stiff, glistening feathers. I put my foot on his string and pinned him to the ground.

"Nice pretty, pretty Stanley," I said coaxingly, adopting the tone that a neighbour used with her budgie, since I wasn't sure how one talked to a bird. I slowly extended my thumb to stroke his bright-red neck feathers. Darting angrily, he struck the ball of my thumb with a snappish peck and simultaneously hit my wrist with his heel spur. He didn't hurt me, but he did startle me badly. So badly I gave a little yelp. Which made me feel foolish and more than a little cowardly.

"You son of a bitch," I said, reaching down slowly and staring into one unblinking glassy eye in which I could see my face looming larger and larger. I caught the rooster's legs and held them firmly together. Stanley crowed defiantly and showed me his wicked little tongue.

"Now, Stanley," I said, "relax, I'm just going to stroke you. I'm just going to stroke you. I'm just going to pet Stanley."

No deal. He struck furiously again with a snake-like agility, and bounded in my hand, wings beating his poultry smell into my face. A real fighting cock at last. Maybe it was the weather. Perhaps his rooster pride and patience would suffer no more indignities.

The heat, the sultry menace of the gathering storm, made me feel prickly, edgy. I flicked my middle finger smartly against his tiny chicken skull, hard enough to rattle his pea-sized brain. "You like that, buster?" I asked, and snapped him another one for good measure. He struck back again, his comb red, crested, and rubbery with fury.

I was angry myself. I turned him upside down and left him dangling, his wings drumming against the legs of my jeans. Then I righted him abruptly; he looked dishevelled, seedy and dazed.

"Okay, Stanley," I said, feeling the intoxication of power. "I'm boss here, and you behave." There was a gleeful edge to my voice, which surprised me a little. I realized I was hoping this confrontation would escalate. Wishing that he would provoke me into something.

Strange images came into my head: the bruises on my aunt's legs; Thompson's face drained of life, lifted like an empty receptacle toward the ceiling, waiting to be filled, the tendons of his neck stark and rigid with anticipation.

I was filled with anxiety, the heat seemed to stretch me, to tug at my nerves and my skin. Two drops of sweat, as large and perfectly formed as tears, rolled out of my hairline and splashed onto the rubber toes of my runners.

"Easy, Stanley," I breathed to him, "easy," and my hand crept deliberately towards him. This time he pecked me in such a way, directly on the knuckle, that it actually hurt. I took up my stick and rapped him on the beak curtly, the prim admonishment of a schoolmarm. I didn't hit him very hard, but it was hard enough to split the length of his beak with a narrow crack. The beak fissured like the nib of a fountain pen. Stanley squawked, opened and closed his beak spasmodically, bewildered by the pain. A bright jewel of blood bubbled out of the split and gathered to a trembling bead.

"There," I said excitedly, "now you've done it. How are you going to eat with a broken beak? You can't eat anything with a broken beak. You'll starve, you stupid goddamn chicken."

A wind that smelled of rain had sprung up. It ruffled his feathers until they moved with a barely discernible crackle.

"Poor Stanley," I said, and at last, numbed by the pain, he allowed me to stroke the gloss of his lacquer feathers.

I wasn't strong enough or practised enough to do a clean and efficient job of wringing his neck, but I succeeded in finishing him off after two clumsy attempts. Then, because I wanted to leave the impression that a skunk had made off with him, I punched a couple of holes in his breast with my jack knife and tried to dribble some blood on the ground. Poor Stanley produced only a few meagre spots; this corpse refused to bleed in the presence of its murderer. I scattered a handful of his feathers on the ground and buried him in the larger of the two manure piles beside the barn.

CR

"I don't think any skunk got that rooster," my grandmother said suspiciously, nudging at a feather with the toe of her boot until, finally disturbed, it was wafted away by the breeze.

Something squeezed my heart. How did she know?

"Skunks hunt at night," she said. "Must have been somebody's barn cat."

CR

"You come along with me," my grandmother said. She was standing in front of the full-length hall mirror, settling on her hat, a deadly-looking hat pin poised above her skull. "We'll go into town and you can buy a comic book at the drugstore."

It was Friday and Friday was shopping day. But Grandma didn't wheel her battered De Soto to the curb in front of the Brite Spot Grocery, she parked it in front of Maynard & Pritchard, Barristers and Solicitors.

"What are we doing here?" I asked.

Grandma was fumbling nervously with her purse. Small-town people don't like to be seen going to the lawyer's. "Come along with me. Hurry up."

"Why do I have to come?"

"Because I don't want you making a spectacle of yourself for the half-wits and loungers to gawk at," she said. "Let's not give them too much to wonder about."

Maynard & Pritchard, Barristers and Solicitors, smelled of wax and varnish and probity. My grandmother was shown into an office with a frosted pane of glass in the door and neat gilt lettering that announced it was occupied by D.F. Maynard, Q.C. I was ordered to occupy a hard chair, which I did, battering my heels on the rungs briskly enough to annoy the secretary into telling me to stop it.

My grandmother wasn't closeted long with her Queen's Counsel before the door opened and he glided after her into the passageway. Lawyer Maynard was the neatest man I had ever seen in my life. His suit fit him like a glove.

"The best I can do," he said "is send him a registered letter telling him to remove himself from the premises, but it all comes to the same thing. If that doesn't scare him off, you'll have to have recourse to the police. That's all there is to it. I told you that yesterday and you haven't told me anything new today, Edith, that would make me change my mind. Just let him know you won't put up with him any more."

"No police," she said. "I don't want the police digging in my family's business and Evelyn giving one of her grand performances for some baby-skinned constable straight out of the depot. All I need is to get her away from him for a little while, then I could tune her in. I could get through to her in no time at all."

"Well," said Maynard, shrugging, "we could try the letter, but I don't think it would do any good. He has the status of a guest in your home; just tell him to go."

My grandmother was showing signs of exasperation. "But he *doesn't* go. That's the point. I've told him and told him. But he *won't*."

"Mrs. Bradley," said the lawyer emphatically. "Edith, as a friend, don't waste your time. The police."

"I'm through wasting my time," she said.

Pulling away from the lawyer's office, my grandmother began a spirited conversation with herself. A wisp of hair had escaped from under her hat, and the dye winked a metallic red light as it jiggled up and down in the hot sunshine.

"I've told him and told him. But he won't listen. The goddamn freak thinks we're involved in a christly debating society. He thinks I don't mean business. But I mean business. I do. There's more than one way to skin a cat or scratch a dog's ass. We'll take the wheels off his little red wagon and see how she pulls."

"What about my comic book?" I said, as we drove past the Rexall.

"Shut up."

Grandma drove the De Soto to the edge of town and stopped it at the Ogdens' place. It was a service station, or rather had been until the B.A. company had taken out their pumps and yanked the franchise, or whatever you call it, on the two brothers. Since then everything had gone steadily downhill. Cracks in the window-panes had been taped with masking tape, and the roof had been patched with flattened tin cans and old licence plates. The building itself was surrounded by an acre of wrecks, sulking hulks rotten with rust, the guts of their upholstery spilled and gnawed by rats and mice.

But the Ogden brothers still carried on a business after a fashion. They stripped their wrecks for parts and were reputed to be decent enough mechanics whenever they were sober enough to turn a wrench or thread a bolt. People brought work to them whenever they couldn't avoid it, and the rest of the year gave them a wide berth.

But the Ogdens were famous for two things: their meanness and their profligacy as breeders. The place was always aswarm with kids who never seemed to wear pants except in the most severe weather, and tottered about the premises, their legs smeared with grease, shit, or various combinations of both.

"Wait here," my grandmother said, slamming the car door loudly enough to bring the two brothers out of their shop. Through the open door I saw a motor suspended on an intricate system of chains and pulleys.

The Ogdens stood with their hands in the pockets of their bib overalls while my grandmother talked to them. They were quite a sight. They didn't have a dozen teeth in their heads between them, even though the oldest brother couldn't have been more than forty. They just stood there, one sucking on a cigarette, the other on a Coke. Neither one moved or changed his expression, except once, when a tow-headed youngster piddled too close to Grandma. He was lazily and casually slapped on the side of the head by the nearest brother and ran away screaming, his stream cavorting wildly in front of him.

At last, their business concluded, the boys walked my grandmother back to the car.

"You'll get to that soon?" she said, sliding behind the wheel.

"Tomorrow all right?" said one. His words sounded all slack and chewed, issuing from his shrunken, old man's mouth.

"The sooner the better. I want that seen to, Bert."

"What seen to?" I asked.

"Bert and his brother Elwood are going to fix that rattle that's been plaguing me."

"Sure thing," said Elwood. "Nothing but clear sailing."

"What rattle?" I said.

"What rattle? What rattle? The one in the glove compartment," she said, banging it with the heel of her hand. "That rattle. You hear it?"

◌⃟

Thompson could get very edgy some days. "I should be working on my dissertation," he said, coiled in the big chair. "I shouldn't be wasting my time in this shit-hole. I should be working!"

"So why aren't you?" said Evelyn. She was spool knitting. That and reading movie magazines were the only things she ever did.

"How the christ do I work without a library? You see a goddam library within a hundred miles of this place?"

"Why do you need a library?" she said calmly. "Can't you write?"

"Write," he said, looking at the ceiling. "Write, she says. What the hell do you know about it? What the hell do *you* know about it."

"I can't see why you can't write."

"Before you write, you research. That's what you do, you *research*."

"So bite my head off. It wasn't my idea to come here."

"It wasn't me that lost my goddamn job. How the hell were we supposed to pay the rent?"

"You could have got a job."

"I'm a student. Anyway, I told you, if I get a job my wife gets her hooks into me for support. I'll starve to death before I support that bitch."

"We could go back."

"How many times does it have to be explained to you? I don't get my scholarship cheque until the first of September. We happen to be broke. Absolutely. In fact, you're going to have to hit the old lady up for gas and eating money to get back to the coast. We're stuck here. Get that into your empty fucking head. The Lord Buddha might have been able to subsist on a single bean a day; I can't."

My grandmother came into the room. The conversation stopped.

"Do you think," she said to Thompson, "I could ask you to do me a favour?"

"Why, Mrs. Bradley," he said smiling, "whatever do you mean?"

"I was wondering whether you could take my car into town to Ogdens' to get it fixed."

"Oh," said Thompson, "I don't know where it is. I don't think I'm your man."

"Ask anyone where it is. They can tell you. It isn't hard to find."

"Why would you ask me to do you a favour, Mrs. Bradley?" inquired Thompson complacently. Hearing his voice was like listening to someone drag their nails down a blackboard.

"Well, you can be goddamn sure I wouldn't," said Grandma, trying to keep a hold on herself, "except that I'm right in the middle of doing my pickling and canning. I thought you might be willing to move your lazy carcass to do something around here. Every time I turn around I seem to be falling over those legs of yours." She looked at the limbs in question as if she would like to dock them somewhere in the vicinity of the knee.

"No, I don't think I can," said Thompson easily, stroking his goat beard.

"And why the hell can't you?"

"Oh, let's just say I don't trust you, Mrs. Bradley. I don't like to leave you alone with Evelyn. Lord knows what ideas you might put in her head."

"Or take out."

"That's right. Or take out," said Thompson with satisfaction. "You can't imagine the trouble it took me to get them in there." He turned to Evelyn. "She can't imagine the trouble, can she, dear?"

Evelyn threw her spool knitting on the floor and walked out of the room.

"Evelyn's mad and I'm glad," shouted Thompson at her back. "And I know how to tease her!"

"Charlie, come here," said Grandma. I went over to her. She took me firmly by the shoulder. "From now on," said my grandma, "my family is off limits to you. I don't want to see you talking to Charlie here, or to come within sniffing distance of Evelyn."

"What do you think of that idea, Charlie?" said Thompson. "Are you still my friend or what?"

I gave him a wink my grandma couldn't see. He thought that was great; he laughed like a madman. "Superb," he said. "Superb. There's no flies on Charlie. What a diplomat."

"What the hell is the matter with you, Mr. Beatnik?" asked Grandma, annoyed beyond bearing. "What's so goddamn funny?"

"Ha ha!" roared Thompson. "What a charming notion! Me a beatnik!"

હ

Grandma Bradley held the mouthpiece of the phone very close to her lips as she spoke into it. "No, it can't be brought in. You'll have to come out here to do the job."

She listened with an intent expression on her face. Spotting me pretending to look in the fridge, she waved me out of the kitchen with her hand. I dragged myself out and stood quietly in the hallway.

"This is a party line," she said, "remember that."

Another pause while she listened.

"Okay," she said and hung up.

હ

I spent some of my happiest hours squatting in the corn patch. I was completely hidden there; even when I stood, the maturing stalks reached a foot or more above my head. It was a good place. On the hottest days it was relatively cool in that thicket of green where the shade was dark and deep and the leaves rustled and scraped and sawed dryly overhead.

Nobody ever thought to look for me there. They could bellow their bloody lungs out for me and I could just sit and watch them getting uglier and uglier about it all. There was some satisfaction in that. I'd just reach up and pluck myself a cob. I loved raw corn. The newly formed kernels were tiny, pale pearls of sweetness that gushed juice. I'd munch and munch and smile and smile and think, why don't you drop dead?

It was my secret place, my sanctuary, where I couldn't be found or touched by them. But all the same, if I didn't let them intrude on me — that didn't mean I didn't want to keep tabs on things.

At the time I was watching Thompson stealing peas at the other end of the garden. He was like some primitive man who lived in a gathering culture. My grandma kept him so hungry he was constantly prowling for food: digging in cupboards, rifling the refrigerator, scrounging in the garden.

Clad only in Bermuda shorts he was a sorry sight. His bones threatened to rupture his skin and jut out every which way. He sported a scrub-board chest with two old pennies for nipples, and a wispy garland of hair decorated his sunken breastbone. His legs looked particularly rackety; all gristle, knobs and sinew.

We both heard the truck at the same time. It came bucking up the approach, spurting gravel behind it. Thompson turned around, shaded his eyes and peered at it. He wasn't much interested. He couldn't get very curious about the natives.

The truck stopped and a man stepped out on to the running board of the '51 IHC. He gazed around him, obviously looking for something or someone. This character had a blue handkerchief sprinkled with white polka dots tied in a triangle over his face. Exactly like an outlaw in an Audie Murphy western. A genuine goddamn Jesse James.

He soon spotted Thompson standing half-naked in the garden, staring stupidly at this strange sight, his mouth bulging with peas. The outlaw ducked his head back into the cab of the truck, said something to the driver, and pointed. The driver then stepped out on to his runningboard and, standing on tippy-toe, peered over the roof of the cab at Thompson. He too wore a handkerchief tied over his mug, but his was red.

Then they both got down from the truck and began to walk very quickly towards Thompson with long, menacing strides.

"Fellows?" said Thompson.

At the sound of his voice the two men broke into a stiff-legged trot, and the one with the red handkerchief, while still moving, stooped down smoothly and snatched up the hoe that lay at the edge of the garden.

"What the hell is going on here, boys?" said Thompson, his voice pitched high with concern.

The man with the blue mask reached Thompson first. One long arm, a dirty clutch of fingers on its end, snaked out and caught him by the hair and jerked his head down. Then he kicked him in the pit of the stomach with his work boots.

"Okay, fucker," he shouted, "too fucking smart to take a fucking hint?" and he punched him on the side of the face with several short, snapping blows that actually tore Thompson's head out of his grip. Thompson toppled over clumsily and fell in the dirt. "Get fucking lost," Blue Mask said more quietly.

"Evelyn!" yelled Thompson to the house. "Jesus Christ, Evelyn!"

I was crouched lower in the corn patch and began to tremble. I was certain they were going to kill him.

"Shut up," said the man with the hoe. He glanced at the blade for a second, considered, then rotated the handle in his hands and hit Thompson a quick chop on the head with the blunt side. "Shut your fucking yap," he repeated.

"Evelyn! Evelyn! Oh God!" hollered Thompson. "I'm being murdered! For God's sake, somebody help me!" The side of his face was slick with blood.

"I told you shut up, cocksucker," said Red Mask, and kicked him in the ribs several times. Thompson groaned and hugged himself in the dust.

"Now you get lost, fucker," said the one with the hoe, "because if you don't stop bothering nice people we'll drive a spike in your skull."

"Somebody help me!" Thompson yelled at the house.

"Nobody there is going to help you," Blue Mask said. "You're all on your own, smart arse."

"You bastards," said Thompson, and spat ineffectually in their direction.

For his defiance he got struck a couple of chopping blows with the hoe. The last one skittered off his collar-bone with a sickening crunch.

"That's enough," said Red Mask, catching the handle of the hoe. "Come on."

The two sauntered back towards the truck, laughing. They weren't in any hurry to get out of there. Thompson lay on his side staring at their retreating backs. His face was wet with tears and blood.

The man with the red mask looked back over his shoulder and wiggled his ass at Thompson in an implausible imitation of effeminacy. "Was it worth it, tiger?" he shouted. "Getting your ashes hauled don't come cheap, do it?"

This set them off again. Passing me they pulled off their masks and stuffed them in their pockets. They didn't have to worry about Thompson when they had their backs to him; he couldn't see their faces. But I could. No surprise. They were the Ogden boys.

When the truck pulled out of the yard, its gears grinding, I burst out of my hiding place and ran to Thompson, who had got to his knees and was trying to stop the flow of blood from his scalp with his fingers. He was crying. Another first for Thompson. He was the first man I'd seen cry. It made me uncomfortable.

"The sons of bitches broke my ribs," he said, panting with shallow breaths. "God, I hope they didn't puncture a lung."

"Can you walk?" I asked.

"Don't think I don't know who's behind this," he said, getting carefully to his feet. His face was white. "You saw them," he said. "You saw their faces from the corn patch. We got the bastards."

He leaned a little on me as we made our way to the house. The front door was locked. We knocked. No answer. "Let me in, you old bitch!" shouted Thompson.

"Evelyn, open the goddamn door!" Silence. I couldn't hear a thing move in the house. It was as if they were all dead in there. It frightened me.

He started to kick the door. A panel splintered. "Open this door! Let me in, you old slut, or I'll kill you!"

Nothing.

"You better go," I said nervously. I didn't like this one little bit. "Those guys might come back and kill you."

"Evelyn!" he bellowed. "Evelyn!"

He kept it up for a good five minutes, alternately hammering and kicking the door, pleading with and threatening the occupants. By the end of that time he was sweating with exertion and pain. He went slowly down the steps, sobbing, beaten. "You saw them," he said, "we have the bastards dead to rights."

He winced when he eased his bare flesh onto the hot seat-covers of the car.

"I'll be back," he said, starting the motor of the car. "This isn't the end of this."

When Grandma was sure he had gone, the front door was unlocked and I was let in. I noticed my grandmother's hands trembled a touch when she lit her cigarette.

"You can't stay away from him, can you?" she said testily.

"You didn't have to do that," I said. "He was hurt. You ought to have let him in."

"I ought to have poisoned him a week ago. And don't talk about things you don't know anything about."

"Sometimes," I said, "all of you get on my nerves."

"Kids don't have nerves. Adults have nerves. They're the only ones entitled to them. And don't think I care a plugged nickel what does, or doesn't, get on your nerves."

"Where's Aunt Evelyn?"

"Your Aunt Evelyn is taken care of," she replied.

"Why wouldn't she come to the door?"

"She had her own road to Damascus. She has seen the light. Everything has been straightened out," she said. "Everything is back to normal."

C303

He looked foolish huddled in the back of the police car later that evening. When the sun began to dip, the temperature dropped rapidly, and he was obviously cold dressed only in his Bermuda shorts. Thompson sat all hunched up to relieve the strain on his ribs, his hands pressed between his knees, shivering.

My grandmother and the constable spoke quietly by the car for some time; occasionally Thompson poked his head out the car window and said something. By the look on the constable's face when he spoke to Thompson, it was obvious he didn't care for him too much. Thompson had that kind of effect on people. Several times during the course of the discussion the constable glanced my way.

I edged a little closer so I could hear what they were saying.

"He's mad as a hatter," said my grandmother. "I don't know anything about any two men. If you ask me, all this had something to do with drugs. My daughter says that this man takes drugs. He's some kind of beatnik."

"Christ," said Thompson, drawing his knees up as if to scrunch himself into a smaller, less noticeable package, "the woman is insane."

"One thing at a time, Mrs. Bradley," said the RCMP constable.

"My daughter is finished with him," she said. "He beats her, you know. I want him kept off my property."

"I want to speak to Evelyn," Thompson said. He looked bedraggled and frightened. "Evelyn and I will leave this minute if this woman wants. But I've got to talk to Evelyn."

"My daughter doesn't want to see you, mister. She's finished with you," said Grandma Bradley, shifting her weight from side to side. She turned her attention to the constable. "He beat her," she said, "bruises all over her. Can you imagine?"

"The boy knows," said Thompson desperately. "He saw them. How many times do I have to tell you?" He piped his voice to me, "Didn't you, Charlie? You saw them, didn't you?"

"Charlie?" said my grandmother. This was news to her.

I stood very still.

"Come here, son," said the constable.

I walked slowly over to them.

"Did you see the faces of the men?" the constable asked, putting a hand on my shoulder. "Do you know the men? Are they from around here?"

"How would he know?" said my grandmother. "He's a stranger."

"He knows them. At least he saw them," said Thompson. "My little Padma-sambhava never misses a trick," he said, trying to jolly me. "You see everything, don't you, Charlie? You remember everything, don't you?"

I looked at my grandmother, who stood so calmly and commandingly, waiting.

"Hey, don't look to her for the answers," said Thompson nervously. "Don't be afraid of her. You remember everything, don't you?"

He had no business begging me. I had watched their game from the sidelines long enough to know the rules. At one time he had imagined himself a winner. And now he was asking me to save him, to take a risk, when I was more completely in her clutches than he would ever be. He forgot I was a child. I depended on her.

Thompson, I saw, was powerless. He couldn't protect me. God, I remembered more than he dreamed. I remembered how his lips had moved soundlessly, his face pleading with the ceiling, his face blotted of everything but abject urgency. Praying to a simpering, cross-eyed idol. His arm flashing as he struck my aunt's bare legs. Crawling in the dirt, covered with blood.

He had taught me that "Those who are in the grip of desire, the grip of existence, the grip of ignorance, move helplessly round through the spheres of life, as men or gods or as wretches in the lower regions." Well, he was helpless now. But he insisted on fighting back and hurting the rest of us. The weak ones like Evelyn and me.

I thought of Stanley the rooster and how it had felt when the tendons separated, the gristle parted and the bones crunched under my twisting hands.

"I don't know what he's talking about," I said to the constable softly. "I didn't see anybody."

"Clear out," said my grandmother triumphantly. "Beat it."

"You dirty little son of a bitch," he said to me. "You mean little bugger."

He didn't understand much. He had forced me into the game, and now that I was a player and no longer a watcher he didn't like it. The thing was that I was good at the game. But he, being a loser, couldn't appreciate that.

Then suddenly he said, "Evelyn." He pointed to the upstairs window of the house and tried to get out of the back seat of the police car. But of course he couldn't. They take the handles off the back doors. Nobody can get out unless they are let out.

"Goddamn it!" he shouted. "Let me out! She's waving to me! She wants me!"

I admit that the figure was hard to make out at that distance. But any damn fool could see she was only waving goodbye.

♋

Charlie, the first-person narrator of this story (first published in 1980) is an outsider. This is partly due to himself (he is a sickly child) and partly due to circumstances (his mother enters a sanatorium; his father decides he can get along better without his son). One way or the other, Charlie is "different." Metaphorically, he is an orphan — and so is sent to live with his paternal grandmother for a summer. Though he is "weak" in his mother's estimation, Charlie's "watcher" status, curiously, earns him power: by being invisible to others, he is able to see them more clearly, to capture their secrets. One person who does observe him — and who at a crucial moment depends on him as a witness — is Robert Thompson, the sadistic Ph.D. student. We spot connections between Charlie's life on the margins and the desire to inflict violence. The need to be isolated is tied to the playful, the sensuous, the erotic — as when Charlie kills the rooster. He duplicates at that moment Robert's beating of Aunt Evelyn, which Charlie witnesses, and the beating Robert receives from the Ogden brothers (which, of course, causes Robert to vanish).

Charlie resumes his outsider position by the end by refusing to reveal what he has seen: he speaks silence. Charlie's "withdrawal" from action puts things back as they were, as if "nothing" has occurred.

A.S.

A Worn Path

It was December — a bright frozen day in the early morning. Far out in the country there was an old Negro woman with her head tied in a red rag, coming along a path through the pinewoods. Her name was Phoenix Jackson. She was very old and small and she walked slowly in the dark pine shadows, moving a little from side to side in her steps, with the balanced heaviness and lightness of a pendulum in a grandfather clock. She carried a thin, small cane made from an umbrella, and with this she kept tapping the frozen earth in front of her. This made a grave and persistent noise in the still air, that seemed meditative like the chirping of a solitary little bird.

She wore a dark striped dress reaching down to her shoe tops, and an equally long apron of bleached sugar sacks, with a full pocket: all neat and tidy, but every time she took a step she might have fallen over her shoelaces, which dragged from her unlaced shoes. She looked straight ahead. Her eyes were blue with age. Her skin had a pattern all its own of numberless branching wrinkles and as though a whole little tree stood in the middle of her forehead, but a golden colour ran underneath, and the two knobs of her cheeks were illumined by a yellow burning under the dark. Under the red rag her hair came down on her neck in the frailest of ringlets, still black, and with an odour like copper.

Now and then there was a quivering in the thicket. Old Phoenix said, "Out of my way, all you foxes, owls, beetles, jack rabbits, coons and wild animals! . . . Keep out from under these feet, little bob-whites. . . . Keep the big wild hogs out of my path. Don't let none of those come running my direction. I got a long way." Under her small black-freckled hand her cane, limber as a buggy whip, would switch at the brush as if to rouse up any hiding things.

On she went. The woods were deep and still. The sun made the pine needles almost too bright to look at, up where the wind rocked. The cones dropped as light as feathers. Down in the hollow was the mourning dove — it was not too late for him.

The path ran up a hill. "Seem like there is chains about my feet, time I get this far," she said, in the voice of argument old people keep to use with themselves. "Something always take a hold of me on this hill — pleads I should stay."

After she got to the top she turned and gave a full, severe look behind her where she had come. "Up through pines," she said at length. "Now down through oaks."

Her eyes opened their widest, and she started down gently. But before she got to the bottom of the hill a bush caught her dress.

Her fingers were busy and intent, but her skirts were full and long, so that before she could pull them free in one place they were caught in another. It was not possible to allow the dress to tear. "I in the thorny bush," she said. "Thorns, you doing your appointed work. Never want to let folks pass, no sir. Old eyes thought you was a pretty little *green* bush."

Finally, trembling all over, she stood free, and after a moment dared to stoop for her cane.

"Sun so high!" she cried, leaning back and looking, while the thick tears went over her eyes. "The time getting all gone here."

At the foot of this hill was a place where a log was laid across the creek.

"Now comes the trial," said Phoenix.

Putting her right foot out, she mounted the log and shut her eyes. Lifting her skirt, leveling her cane fiercely before her, like a festival figure in some parade, she began to march across. Then she opened her eyes and she was safe on the other side.

"I wasn't as old as I thought," she said.

But she sat down to rest. She spread her skirts on the bank around her and folded her hands over her knees. Up above her was a tree in a pearly cloud of mistletoe. She did not dare to close her eyes, and when a little boy brought her a plate with a slice of marble-cake on it she spoke to him. "That would be acceptable," she said. But when she went to take it there was just her own hand in the air.

So she left that tree, and had to go through a barbed-wire fence. There she had to creep and crawl, spreading her knees and stretching her fingers like a baby trying to climb the steps. But she talked loudly to herself: she could not let her dress be torn now, so late in the day, and she could not pay for having her arm or her leg sawed off if she got caught fast where she was.

At last she was safe through the fence and risen up out in the clearing. Big dead trees, like black men with one arm, were standing in the purple stalks of the withered cotton field. There sat a buzzard.

"Who you watching?"

In the furrow she made her way along.

"Glad this not the season for bulls," she said, looking sideways, "and the good Lord made his snakes to curl up and sleep in the winter. A pleasure I don't see no two-headed snake coming around that tree, where it come once. It took a while to get by him, back in the summer."

She passed through the old cotton and went into a field of dead corn. It whispered and shook and was taller than her head. "Through the maze now," she said, for there was no path.

Then there was something tall, black, and skinny there, moving before her.

At first she took it for a man. It could have been a man dancing in the field. But she stood still and listened, and it did not make a sound. It was as silent as a ghost.

"Ghost," she said sharply, "who be you the ghost of? For I have heard of nary death close by."

But there was no answer — only the ragged dancing in the wind.

She shut her eyes, reached out her hand, and touched a sleeve. She found a coat and inside that an emptiness, cold as ice.

"You scarecrow," she said. Her face lighted. "I ought to be shut up for good," she said with laughter. "My senses is gone. I too old. I the oldest people I ever know. Dance, old scarecrow," she said, "while I dancing with you."

She kicked her foot over the furrow, and with mouth drawn down, shook her head once or twice in a little strutting way. Some husks blew down and whirled in streamers about her skirts.

Then she went on, parting her way from side to side with the cane, through the whispering field. At last she came to the end, to a wagon track where the silver grass blew between the red ruts. The quail were walking around like pullets, seeming all dainty and unseen.

"Walk pretty," she said. "This the easy place. This the easy going."

She followed the track, swaying through the quiet bare fields, through the little strings of trees silver in their dead leaves, past cabins silver from weather, with the doors and windows boarded shut, all like old women under a spell sitting there. "I walking in their sleep," she said, nodding her head vigorously.

In a ravine she went where a spring was silently flowing through a hollow log. Old Phoenix bent and drank. "Sweet-gum makes the water sweet," she said, and drank more. "Nobody know who made this well, for it was here when I was born."

The track crossed a swampy part where the moss hung as white as lace from every limb. "Sleep on, alligators, and blow your bubbles." Then the track went into the road.

Deep, deep the road went down between the high green-coloured banks. Overhead the live-oaks met, and it was as dark as a cave.

A black dog with a lolling tongue came up out of the weeds by the ditch. She was meditating, and not ready, and when he came at her she only hit him a little with her cane. Over she went in the ditch, like a little puff of milkweed.

Down there, her senses drifted away. A dream visited her, and she reached her hand up, but nothing reached down and gave her a pull. So she lay there and presently went to talking. "Old woman," she said to herself, "that black dog come up out of the weeds to stall you off, and now there he sitting on his fine tail, smiling at you."

A white man finally came along and found her — a hunter, a young man, with his dog on a chain.

"Well, Granny!" he laughed. "What are you doing there?"

"Lying on my back like a June-bug waiting to be turned over, mister," she said, reaching up her hand.

He lifted her up, gave her a swing in the air, and set her down. "Anything broken, Granny?"

"No sir, them old dead weeds is springy enough," said Phoenix, when she had got her breath. "I thank you for your trouble."

"Where do you live, Granny?" he asked, while the two dogs were growling at each other.

"Away back yonder, sir, behind the ridge. You can't even see it from here."

"On your way home?"

"No sir, I going to town."

"Why, that's too far! That's as far as I walk when I come out myself, and I get something for my trouble." He patted the stuffed bag he carried, and there hung down a little closed claw. It was one of the bob-whites, with its beak hooked bitterly to show it was dead. "Now you go on home, Granny!"

"I bound to go to town, mister," said Phoenix. "The time come around."

He gave another laugh, filling the whole landscape. "I know you old coloured people! Wouldn't miss going to town to see Santa Claus!"

But something held old Phoenix very still. The deep lines in her face went into a fierce and different radiation. Without warning, she had seen with her own eyes a flashing nickel fall out of the man's pocket onto the ground.

"How old are you, Granny?" he was saying.

"There is no telling, mister," she said, "no telling."

Then she gave a little cry and clapped her hands and said, "Git on away from here, dog! Look! Look at that dog!" She laughed as if in admiration. "He ain't scared of nobody. He a big black dog." She whispered, "Sic him!"

"Watch me get rid of that cur," said the man. "Sic him, Pete! Sic him!"

Phoenix heard the dogs fighting, and heard the man running and throwing sticks. She even heard a gunshot. But she was slowly bending forward by that time, further and further forward, the lids stretched down over her eyes, as if she were doing this in her sleep. Her chin was lowered almost to her knees. The yellow palm of her hand came out from the fold of her apron. Her fingers slid down and along the ground under the piece of money with the grace and care they would have in lifting an egg from under a setting hen. Then she slowly straightened up, she stood erect, and the nickel was in her apron pocket. A bird flew by. Her lips moved. "God watching me the whole time. I come to stealing."

The man came back, and his own dog panted about them. "Well, I scared him off that time," he said, and then he laughed and lifted his gun and pointed it at Phoenix.

She stood straight and faced him.

"Doesn't the gun scare you?" he said, still pointing it.

"No, sir, I seen plenty go off closer by, in my day, and for less than what I done," she said, holding utterly still.

He smiled, and shouldered the gun. "Well, Granny," he said, "you must be a hundred years old, and scared of nothing. I'd give you a dime if I had any money with me. But you take my advice and stay home, and nothing will happen to you."

"I bound to go on my way, mister," said Phoenix. She inclined her head in the red rag. Then they went in different directions, but she could hear the gun shooting again and again over the hill.

She walked on. The shadows hung from the oak trees to the road like curtains. Then she smelled wood-smoke, and smelled the river, and she saw a steeple and the cabins on their steep steps. Dozens of little black children whirled around her. There ahead was Natchez shining. Bells were ringing. She walked on.

In the paved city it was Christmas time. There were red and green electric lights strung and crisscrossed everywhere, and all turned on in the daytime. Old

Phoenix would have been lost if she had not distrusted her eyesight and depended on her feet to know where to take her.

She paused quietly on the sidewalk where people were passing by. A lady came along in the crowd, carrying an armful of red-, green- and silver-wrapped presents; she gave off perfume like the red roses in hot summer, and Phoenix stopped her.

"Please, missy, will you lace up my shoe?" She held up her foot.

"What do you want, Grandma?"

"See my shoe," said Phoenix. "Do all right for out in the country, but wouldn't look right to go in a big building."

"Stand still then, Grandma," said the lady. She put her packages down on the sidewalk beside her and laced and tied both shoes tightly.

"Can't lace 'em with a cane," said Phoenix. "Thank you, missy. I doesn't mind asking a nice lady to tie up my shoe, when I gets out on the street."

Moving slowly and from side to side, she went into the building, and into the tower of steps, where she walked up and around until her feet knew to stop.

She entered a door, and there she saw nailed up on the wall the document that had been stamped with the gold seal and framed in the gold frame, which matched the dream that was hung up in her head.

"Here I be," she said. There was a fixed and ceremonial stiffness over her body.

"A charity case, I suppose," said an attendant who sat at the desk before her.

But Phoenix only looked above her head. There was sweat on her face, the wrinkles in her skin shone like a bright net.

"Speak up, Grandma," the woman said. "What's your name? We must have your history, you know. Have you been here before? What seems to be the trouble with you?"

Old Phoenix only gave a twitch to her face as if a fly were bothering her.

"Are you deaf?" cried the attendant.

But then the nurse came in.

"Oh, that's just old Aunt Phoenix," she said. "She doesn't come for herself — she has a little grandson. She makes these trips just as regular as clockwork. She lives away back off the Old Natchez Trace." She bent down. "Well, Aunt Phoenix, why don't you just take a seat? We won't keep you standing after your long trip." She pointed.

The old woman sat down, bolt upright in the chair.

"Now, how is the boy?" asked the nurse.

Old Phoenix did not speak.

"I said, how is the boy?"

But Phoenix only waited and stared straight ahead, her face very solemn and withdrawn into rigidity.

"Is his throat any better?" asked the nurse. "Aunt Phoenix, don't you hear me? Is your grandson's throat any better since the last time you came for the medicine?"

With her hands on her knees, the old woman waited, silent, erect and motionless, just as if she were in armour.

"You mustn't take up our time this way, Aunt Phoenix," the nurse said. "Tell us quickly about your grandson, and get it over. He isn't dead, is he?"

At last there came a flicker and then a flame of comprehension across her face, and she spoke.

"My grandson. It was my memory had left me. There I sat and forgot why I made my long trip."

"Forgot?" The nurse frowned. "After you came so far?"

Then Phoenix was like an old woman begging a dignified forgiveness for waking up frightened in the night. "I never did go to school, I was too old at the Surrender," she said in a soft voice. "I'm an old woman without an education. It was my memory fail me. My little grandson, he is just the same, and I forgot it in the coming."

"Throat never heals, does it?" said the nurse, speaking in a loud, sure voice to old Phoenix. By now she had a card with something written on it, a little list. "Yes. Swallowed lye. When was it? — January — two-three years ago —"

Phoenix spoke unasked now. "No, missy, he not dead, he just the same. Every little while his throat begin to close up again, and he not able to swallow. He not get his breath. He not able to help himself. So the time come around, and I go on another trip for the soothing medicine."

"All right. The doctor said as long as you came to get it, you could have it," said the nurse. "But it's an obstinate case."

"My little grandson, he sit up there in the house all wrapped up, waiting by himself," Phoenix went on. "We is the only two left in the world. He suffer and it don't seem to put him back at all. He got a sweet look. He going to last. He wear a little patch quilt and peep out holding his mouth open like a little bird. I remembers so plain now. I not going to forget him again, no, the whole enduring time. I could tell him from all the others in creation."

"All right." The nurse was trying to hush her now. She brought her a bottle of medicine. "Charity," she said, making a check mark in a book.

Old Phoenix held the bottle close to her eyes, and then carefully put it into her pocket.

"I thank you," she said.

"It's Christmas time, Grandma," said the attendant. "Could I give you a few pennies out of my purse?"

"Five pennies is a nickel," said Phoenix stiffly.

"Here's a nickel," said the attendant.

Phoenix rose carefully and held out her hand. She received the nickel and then fished the other nickel out of her pocket and laid it beside the new one. She stared at her palm closely, with her head on one side.

Then she gave a tap with her cane on the floor.

"This is what come to me to do," she said. "I going to the store and buy my child a little windmill they sells, made out of paper. He going to find it hard to believe there such a thing in the world. I'll march myself back where he waiting, holding it straight up in this hand."

She lifted her free hand, gave a little nod, turned around, and walked out of the doctor's office. Then her slow step began on the stairs, going down.

ℰ⊃Cℛ

Phoenix Jackson's walk, the latest of many she has made to the old Mississippi city, is, of course, more than a long trip for the medicine intended to ease the suffering of her unnamed grandson. During her journey, Phoenix meets several obstacles, among them thorns and barbed wire, a fallen log on which she must precariously cross a creek, a scarecrow futilely standing guard over the dead stalks of an abandoned cornfield, a black dog, and (significantly, the only human being she encounters until she reaches Natchez) a well-meaning yet condescending hunter. These trials are real in themselves, but their resonance makes clear that, without necessarily allegorizing the story, we can read Phoenix's journey on several levels.

Welty subtly hints at Phoenix's motivation for her trips along the "worn" path to Natchez, a delayed revelation of forgetfulness or neglect — and thus responsibility — implicit in the single word "again": "I remembers so plain now. I not going to forget him again, no, the whole enduring time. I could tell him from all the others in creation." We remain unsure whether the grandson is still alive; but what is not in doubt is Phoenix's love, a love that transcends harsh questions of guilt and redeems her as she makes her slow way along that path, secure in her faith that "God [is] watching me the whole time."

Born in Mississippi, Eudora Welty was educated there and at the University of Wisconsin. She is noted for her acuity of observation and an unfailing ear for prose rhythm. "A Worn Path" appeared in her first collection, A Curtain of Green *(1941), and has become one of the most frequently anthologized of American short stories.*

T.C.

Where Is the Voice Coming From?

The problem is to make the story.

One difficulty of this making may have been excellently stated by Teilhard de Chardin: "We are continually inclined to isolate ourselves from the things and events which surround us . . . as though we were spectators, not elements, in what goes on." Arnold Toynbee does venture, "For all that we know, Reality is the undifferentiated unity of the mystical experience," but that need not here be considered. This story ended long ago; it is one of finite acts, of orders, or elemental feelings and reactions, of obvious legal restrictions and requirements.

Presumably all the parts of the story are themselves available. A difficulty is that they are, as always, available only in bits and pieces. Though the acts themselves seem quite clear, some written reports of the acts contradict each other. As if these acts were, at one time, too well-known; as if the original nodule of each particular fact had from somewhere received non-factual accretions; or even more, as if, since the basic facts were so clear, perhaps there were a larger number of facts than any one reporter, or several, or even any reporter had ever attempted to record. About facts that are simply told by this mouth to that ear, of course, even less can be expected.

An affair seventy-five years old should acquire some of the shiny transparency of an old man's skin. It should.

Sometimes it would seem that it would be enough — perhaps more than enough — to hear the names only. The grandfather One Arrow; the mother Spotted Calf, the father Sounding Sky; the wife (wives rather, but only one of them seems to have a name, though their fathers are Napaise, Kapahoo, Old Dust, The Rump) — the one wife named, of all things, Pale Face; the cousin Going-Up-To-Sky; the brother-in-law (again, of all things) Dublin. The names of the police sound very much alike; they all begin with Constable or Corporal or Sergeant, but here and there an Inspector, then a Superintendent and eventually all the resonance of an Assistant Commissioner echoes down. More. Herself: Victoria, by the Grace of God etc., etc., QUEEN, defender of the Faith, etc., etc.; and witness "Our Right Trusty and Right Well-Beloved Cousin and Councillor the Right Honourable Sir John Campbell Hamilton-Gordon, Earl of Aberdeen; Viscount Formartine, Baron Haddo, Methlic, Tarves and Kellie in the Peerage of Scotland; Viscount Gordon of Aberdeen, County of Aberdeen in the Peerage of the United Kingdom; Baronet of Nova Scotia, Knight Grand Cross of Our Most Distinguished Order of Saint Michael and Saint George, etc., Governor General of Canada." And of course himself: in the award proclamation named "Jean-Baptiste" but otherwise known only as Almighty Voice.

But hearing cannot be enough; not even hearing all the thunder of A

Proclamation: "Now Hear Ye that a reward of FIVE HUNDRED DOLLARS will be paid to any person or persons who will give such information as will lead . . . (etc., etc.) this Twentieth day of April, in the year of Our Lord one thousand eight hundred and ninety-six, and the Fifty-ninth year of Our Reign . . ." etc. and etc.

Such hearing cannot be enough. The first item to be seen is the piece of white bone. It is almost triangular, slightly convex — concave actually as it is positioned at this moment with its corners slightly raised — graduating from perhaps a strong eighth to a weak quarter of an inch in thickness, its scattered pore structure varying between larger and smaller on its polished, certainly shiny surface. Precision is difficult since the glass showcase is at least thirteen inches deep and therefore an eye cannot be brought as close as the minute inspection of such a small, though certainly quite adequate, sample of skull would normally require. Also, because of the position it cannot be determined whether the several hairs, well over a foot long, are still in some manner attached to it or not.

The seven-pounder cannon can be seen standing almost shyly between the showcase and the interior wall. Officially it is known as a gun, not a cannon, and clearly its bore is not large enough to admit a large man's fist. Even if it can be believed that this gun was used in the 1885 Rebellion and that on the evening of Saturday, May 29, 1897 (while the nine-pounder, now unidentified, was in the process of arriving with the police on the special train from Regina), seven shells (all that were available in Prince Albert at that time) from it were sent shrieking into the poplar bluffs as night fell, clearly such shelling could not and would not disembowel the whole earth. Its carriage is now nicely lacquered, the perhaps oak spokes of its petite wheels (little higher than a knee) have been recently scraped, puttied and varnished; the brilliant burnish of its brass breeching testifies with what meticulous care charmen and women have used nationally advertised cleaners and restorers.

Though it can also be seen, even a careless glance reveals that the same concern has not been expended on the one (of two) .44 calibre 1866 model Winchesters apparently found at the last in the pit with Almighty Voice. It is also preserved in a glass case; the number 1536735 is still, though barely, distinguishable on the brass cartridge section just below the brass saddle ring. However, perhaps because the case was imperfectly sealed at one time (though sealed enough not to warrant disturbance now), or because of simple neglect, the rifle is obviously spotted here and there with blotches of rust and the brass itself reveals discolorations almost like mildew. The rifle bore, the three long strands of hair themselves, actually bristle with clots of dust. It may be that this museum cannot afford to be as concerned as the other; conversely, the disfiguration may be something inherent in the items themselves.

The small building which was the police guardroom at Duck Lake, Saskatchewan Territory, in 1895 may also be seen. It had subsequently been moved from its original place and used to house small animals, chickens perhaps, or pigs — such as a woman might be expected to have under her responsibility. It is, of course, now perfectly empty, and clean so that the public may enter with no more discomfort than a bend under the doorway and a heavy encounter with disinfectant.

The door-jamb has obviously been replaced; the bar network at one window is, however, said to be original; smooth still, very smooth. The logs inside have been smeared again and again with whitewash, perhaps paint, to an insistent point of identity-defying characterlessness. Within the small rectangular box of these logs not a sound can be heard from the streets of the, probably dead, town.

> *Hey Injun you'll get hung for stealing that steer*
> *Hey Injun for killing that government cow you'll*
> *get three weeks on the woodpile*
> *Hey Injun*

The place named Kinistino seems to have disappeared from the map but the Minnechinass Hills have not. Whether they have ever been on a map is doubtful but they will, of course, not disappear from the landscape as long as the grass grows and the rivers run. Contrary to general report and belief, the Canadian prairies are rarely, if ever, flat and the Minnechinass (spelled five different ways and translated sometimes as "The Outside Hill," sometimes as "Beautiful Bare Hills") are dissimilar from any other of the numberless hills that everywhere block out the prairie horizon. They are bare; poplars lie tattered along their tops, almost black against the straw-pale grass and sharp green against the grey soil of the ploughing laid in half-mile rectangular blocks upon their western slopes. Poles holding various wires stick out of the fields, back down the bend of the valley; what was once a farmhouse is weathering into the cultivated earth. The poplar bluff where Almighty Voice made his stand has, of course, disappeared.

The policemen he shot and killed (not the ones he wounded, of course) are easily located. Six miles east, thirty-nine miles north in Prince Albert, the English cemetery. Sergeant Colin Campbell Colebrook, North West Mounted Police Registration Number 605, lies presumably under a gravestone there. His name is seventeenth in a very long "list of non-commissioned officers and men who have died in the service since the inception of the force." The date is October 29, 1895, and the cause of death is anonymous: "Shot by escaping Indian prisoner near Prince Albert." At the foot of this grave are two others: Constable John R. Kerr, No. 3040, and Corporal C.H.S. Hockin, No. 3106. Their cause of death on May 28, 1897, is even more anonymous, but the place is relatively precise: "Shot by Indians at Min-etch-inass Hills, Prince Albert District."

The gravestone, if he has one, of the fourth man Almighty Voice killed is more difficult to locate. Mr. Ernest Grundy, postmaster at Duck Lake in 1897, apparently shut his window the afternoon of Friday, May 28, armed himself, rode east twenty miles, participated in the second charge into the bluff at about 6:30 p.m., and on the third sweep of that charge was shot dead at the edge of the pit. It would seem that he thereby contributed substantially not only to the Indians' bullet supply, but his clothing warmed them as well.

The burial place of Dublin and Going-Up-To-Sky is unknown, as is the grave of Almighty Voice. It is said that a Métis named Henry Smith lifted the latter's body from the pit in the bluff and gave it to Spotted Calf. The place of burial is not, of course, of ultimate significance. A gravestone is always less evidence than a triangular piece of skull, provided it is large enough.

Whatever further evidence there is to be gathered may rest on pictures. There are, presumably, almost numberless pictures of the policemen in the case, but the only one with direct bearing is one of Sergeant Colebrook who apparently insisted on advancing to complete an arrest after being warned three times that if he took another step he would be shot. The picture must have been taken before he joined the force; it reveals him a large-eared young man, hair brush-cut and ascot tie, his eyelids slightly drooping, almost hooded under thick brows. Unfortunately a picture of Constable R.C. Dickson, into whose charge Almighty Voice was apparently committed in that guardroom and who after Colebrook's death was convicted of negligence, sentenced to two months hard labour and discharged, does not seem to be available.

There are no pictures to be found of either Dublin (killed early by rifle fire) or Going-Up-To-Sky (killed in the pit), the two teenage boys who gave their ultimate fealty to Almighty Voice. There is, however, one said to be of Almighty Voice, Junior. He may have been born to Pale Face during the year, two hundred and twenty-one days that his father was a fugitive. In the picture he is kneeling before what could be a tent, he wears striped denim overalls and displays twin babies whose sex cannot be determined from the double-laced dark bonnets they wear. In the supposed picture of Spotted Calf and Sounding Sky, Sounding Sky stands slightly before his wife; he wears a white shirt and a striped blanket folded over his left shoulder in such a manner that the arm in which he cradles a long rifle cannot be seen. His head is thrown back; the rim of his hat appears as a black half-moon above eyes that are pressed shut as if in profound concentration; above a mouth clenched thin in a downward curve. Spotted Calf wears a long dress, a sweater which could also be a man's dress coat, and a large fringed and embroidered shawl which would appear distinctly Doukhobor in origin if the scroll patterns on it were more irregular. Her head is small and turned slightly towards her husband so as to reveal her right ear. There is what can only be called a quizzical expression on her crumpled face; it may be she does not understand what is happening and that she would have asked a question, perhaps of her husband, perhaps of the photographers, perhaps even of anyone, anywhere in the world if such questioning were possible for a Cree woman.

There is one final picture. That is one of Almighty Voice himself. At least it is purported to be of Almighty Voice himself. In the Royal Canadian Mounted Police Museum on the Barracks Grounds just off Dewdney Avenue in Regina, Saskatchewan, it lies in the same showcase, as a matter of fact immediately beside that triangular piece of skull. Both are unequivocally labelled, and it must be assumed that a police force with a world-wide reputation would not label *such* evidence incorrectly. But here emerges an ultimate problem in making the story.

There are two official descriptions of Almighty Voice. The first reads: "Height about five feet, ten inches, slight build, rather good looking, a sharp hooked nose with a remarkably flat point. Has a bullet scar on the left side of his face about 1½ inches long running from near corner of mouth towards ear. The scar cannot be noticed when his face is painted but otherwise is plain. Skin fair for an Indian."

The second description is on the Award Proclamation: "About twenty-two years old, five feet, ten inches in height, weight about eleven stone, slightly erect, neat small feet and hands; complexion inclined to be fair, wavey dark hair to shoulders, large dark eyes, broad forehead, sharp features and parrot nose with flat tip, scar on left cheek running from mouth towards ear, feminine appearance."

So run the descriptions that were, presumably, to identify a well-known fugitive in so precise a manner that an informant could collect five hundred dollars — a considerable sum when a police constable earned between one and two dollars a day. The nexus of the problems appears when these supposed official descriptions are compared to the supposed official picture. The man in the picture is standing on a small rug. The fingers on his left hand touch a curved Victorian settee, behind him a photographer's backdrop of scrolled patterns merges to vaguely paradisiacal trees and perhaps a sky. The moccasins he wears make it impossible to deduce whether his feet are "neat small." He may be five feet, ten inches tall, may weigh eleven stone, he certainly is "rather good looking" and, though it is a frontal view, it may be that the point of his long and flaring nose could be "remarkably flat." The photograph is slightly over-illuminated and so the unpainted complexion could be "inclined to be fair"; however, nothing can be seen of a scar, the hair is not wavy and shoulder-length but hangs almost to the waist in two thick straight braids worked through with beads, fur, ribbons and cords. The right hand that holds the corner of the blanket-like coat in position is large and, even in the high illumination, heavily veined. The neck is concealed under coiled beads and the forehead seems more low than "broad."

Perhaps, somehow, these picture details could be reconciled with the official description if the face as a whole were not so devastating.

On a cloth-backed sheet two feet by two and one-half feet in size, under the Great Seal of the Lion and the Unicorn, dignified by the names of the Deputy of the Minister of Justice, the Secretary of State, the Queen herself and all the heaped detail of her "Right Trusty and Right Well-beloved Cousin," this description concludes: "feminine appearance." But the picture: any face of history, any believed face that the world acknowledges as *man* — Socrates, Jesus, Attila, Genghis Khan, Mahatma Gandhi, Joseph Stalin — no believed face is more *man* than this face. The mouth, the nose, the clenched brows, the eyes — the eyes are large, yes, and dark, but even in this watered-down reproduction of unending reproductions of that original, a steady look into those eyes cannot be endured. It is a face like an axe.

CR

It is now evident that the de Chardin statement quoted at the beginning has relevance only as it proves itself inadequate to explain what has happened. At the same time, the inadequacy of Aristotle's much more famous statement becomes evident: "The true difference [between the historian and the poet] is that one relates what *has* happened, the other what *may* happen." These statements cannot explain the storymaker's activity since, despite the most rigid application of impersonal investigation, the elements of the story have now run me aground. If ever I could,

I can no longer pretend to objective, omnipotent disinterestedness. I am no longer *spectator* of what *has* happened or what *may* happen: I am become *element* in what is happening at this very moment.

For it is, of course, I myself who cannot endure the shadows on that paper which are those eyes. It is I who stand beside this broken veranda post where two corner shingles have been torn away, where barbed wire tangles the dead weeds on the edge of this field. The bluff that sheltered Almighty Voice and his two friends has not disappeared from the slope of the Minnechinass, no more than the sound of Constable Dickson's voice in that guardhouse is silent. The sound of his speaking is there even if it has never been recorded in an official report:

> *hey injun you'll get*
> *hung*
> *for stealing that steer*
> *hey injun for killing that government*
> *cow you'll get three*
> *weeks on the woodpile hey injun*

The unknown contradictory words about an unprovable act that move a boy to defiance, an implacable Cree warrior long after the three-hundred-and-fifty-year war is ended, a war already lost the day the Cree watch Cartier hoist his guns ashore at Hochelaga and they begin the long retreat west; these words of incomprehension, of threatened incomprehensible law are there to be heard just as the unmoving tableau of the three-day siege is there to be seen on the slopes of the Minnechinass. Sounding Sky is somewhere not there, under arrest, but Spotted Calf stands on a shoulder of the Hills a little to the left, her arms upraised to the setting sun. Her mouth is open. A horse rears, riderless, above the scrub willow at the edge of the bluff, smoke puffs, screams tangle in rifle barrage, there are wounds, somewhere. The bluff is so green this spring, it will not burn and the ragged line of seven police and two civilians is staggering through, faces twisted in rage, terror, and rifles sputter. Nothing moves. There is no sound of frogs in the night; twenty-seven policemen and five civilians stand in cordon at thirty-yard intervals and a body also lies in the shelter of a gully. Only a voice rises from the bluff:

> *We have fought well*
> *You have died like braves*
> *I have worked hard and am hungry*
> *Give me food*

but nothing moves. The bluff lies, a bright green island on the grassy slope surrounded by men hunched forward rigid over their long rifles, men clumped out of rifle-range, thirty-five men dressed as for fall hunting on a sharp spring day, a small gun positioned on a ridge above. A crow is falling out of the sky into the bluff, its feathers sprayed as by an explosion. The first gun and the second gun are in position, the beginning and end of the bristling surround of thirty-five Prince Albert Volunteers, thirteen civilians and fifty-six policemen in position relative to the bluff and relative to the unnumbered whites astride their horses, standing up in their carts, staring and pointing across the valley, in position relative to the bluff and the unnumbered Cree squatting silent along the higher ridges of the Hills, motionless mounds, faceless against the Sunday morning sunlight edging between and over them down along the tree tips, down into the shadows of the bluff. Nothing moves. Beside the second gun the red-coated officer has flung a handful of grass into the motionless air, almost to the rim of the red sun.

And there is a voice. It is an incredible voice that rises from among the young poplars ripped of their spring bark, from among the dead somewhere lying there, out of the arm-deep pit shorter than a man; a voice rises over the exploding smoke and thunder of guns that reel back in their positions, worked over, serviced by the grimed motionless men in bright coats and glinting buttons, a voice so high and clear, so unbelievably high and strong in its unending wordless cry.

ᘉ

The voice of "Gitchie-Manitou Wayo" — interpreted as "voice of the Great Spirit" — that is, The Almighty Voice. His death chant no less incredible in its beauty than in its incomprehensible happiness.

I say "wordless cry" because that is the way it sounds to me. I could be more accurate if I had a reliable interpreter who would make a reliable interpretation. For I do not, of course, understand the Cree myself.

ᔖᘉ

The "problem," as we read at the beginning of this narrative (first published in 1974), is "to make the story." And for a writer such as Rudy Wiebe, "story" means "truth": how to tell the truth about a historical event.

One way, of course, is by applying a historian's methods. To find the truth about the 1897 death of a Cree Warrior named Almighty Voice, consult archives, study maps, read gravestones, examine photographs. Wiebe's story takes us through such an "impersonal investigation," but it is not enough. The truth demands an imaginative, or writerly, as well as an "impersonal," or historical, approach.

The title hints at this imaginative approach: the images of voice and speaking, the question that calls for more than history to answer. Wiebe's story offers imaginative empathy — a narrator who "stands beside" the historical Almighty Voice, hearing his death chant rising from the poplar bluff, feeling the defeat in a "three-hundred-and-fifty-year war." Only by such imaginative making of the story, it claims, can we know the truth.

In his exploration of the porous border between history and fiction, Wiebe has encountered resistance to his obsession with history, as some writers see it, or his playing fast and loose with historical data, as some historians insist. To the latter, Wiebe's narrator offers the satirical disclaimer near the end of his story — mischievously acknowledging his merely subjective accuracy, while implying that history itself is an unreliable narrative. But Wiebe does not simply challenge the reliability of history. Instead, his fiction celebrates history by revealing its truths and linking them to the mysterious reliability of the storyteller's art.

G.H.

GLOSSARY

Allegory   An ancient mode of expression whose origins are religious. The term derives from Greek *allêgoria,* "speaking otherwise." An allegory is a narrative with a double meaning. Its characters, plot, and sometimes setting have a primary or literal meaning and a secondary or underlying meaning. This underlying meaning often involves spiritual, historical, or political concepts more significant than the narrative itself. An allegory has no specified length; it may be sustained throughout an entire work, or function only as an episode. Various literary forms, such as the *fable* and *parable*, may be regarded as special types of allegory.

Allusion   A reference, implicit or explicit, to an event, a person, another literary work, or a cultural artifact. In earlier times, authors assumed that the body of common knowledge shared by all would allow readers to "pick up" allusions. Modern authors, by contrast, often employ obscure allusions. Because allusion may enrich a text by bringing with it a wealth of experience and knowledge, it is closely related to the issue of *intertextuality*.

Anecdote   A short narrative account of a single event. It usually does not stand alone, but represents an episode within a longer narrative. Anecdotes serve to "humanize" individuals or to turn abstract concepts into concrete ones.

Archetype   A literary concept originating in the field of comparative anthropology (most notably J.G. Frazer's *The Golden Bough*) and in the psychology of C.G. Jung, who assumed that the experiences of our ancestors are inherited in the "collective unconscious" of all humankind. Thus, certain works of literature could stir in the reader's mind unconscious forces that he calls archetypes or "primordial images." Later archetypal critics diverge some-what from this early definition, and distance themselves from the concept of the collective unconscious. Most would widen the term to cover any narrative designs, character types, or images paradigmatic for a whole set of experiences and emotions, and which therefore seem to contain a universal truth and appeal.

Atmosphere   A term referring to the dominant mood of a literary work as created by setting (time and place), description, and tone (the *implied author*'s attitude to the subject). Atmosphere is significant since it often foreshadows events; a work's atmosphere thus fosters certain expectations in the reader.

Character   Persons presented in a narrative work. They can be major or minor, dynamic or static, consistent or inconsistent. E.M. Forster introduced the classification of characters as flat (two-dimensional) or round (three-dimensional). A flat character is built around a single quality and is static, whereas a round character is complex in temperament and capable of change.

Closure   More than simply the end or conclusion of a literary work. Closure possesses a certain aesthetic force, and gives the reader a sense of completion. It is often found in traditional narratives. On the other hand, a lack of closure is frequently associated with experimental literature. *Modernist* works, for example, are often described as open-ended or lacking closure.

Context   The notion of context gained importance with the rise of New Criticism in the 1940s. New Critics approached the literary work as a closed context, and judged the work's efficacy as an aesthetic object without referring to its historical background or the author's biography. Although by the late 1950s this mode of interpretation lost much of its force, it continues to influence literary criticism in the primary emphasis given to the individual work as such, and in the variety and subtlety of devices made available for textual analysis.

Diction   A writer's choice of words.

Diegesis   The fictional world in which narrated events occur.

Ekphrasis   The attempt in a literary work to describe or comment upon an object taken from the visual arts, for example a painting, sculpture, or film. According to W.J.T. Mitchell, ekphrastic texts manifest both a desire to claim an image's power for themselves, as well as the fear that the image will reduce them to silence. Ekphrasis thus specifically confronts the limitations and possibilities of language.

Embedded story   A story included within another; a narrative within a larger narrative.

Epiphany   The church festival commemorating the manifestation of Christ to the Gentiles; more generally, the manifestation of God's presence in the world. James Joyce gave the word a specifically literary sense. He understands epiphany as a sudden spiritual manifestation, the revelation of the essential "whatness," the soul or nature of a thing. In the analysis of literary texts, epiphany is understood as a component of the work identifiable in an image, an incident, or episode that has the effect of revealing an important insight to the fictional characters or to the reader.

Fable   An *allegorical* narrative offering a moral. The characters are often non-human or inanimate. The genre probably originated in Greece, where Aesop assembled a collection of fables in the 6ᵗʰ century BC. Compare *parable.*

Fairy tale   A folk narrative originating in the oral tradition. Through the famous collections of Charles Perrault and Jacob and Wilhelm Grimm, fairy tales became an influential literary genre. In its written form, the fairy tale tends to be a narrative in prose about the often supernatural adventures of a hero or heroine. Magic, charms, disguises, and spells are some of the major characteristics of fairy tales, which are often subtle in their interpretation of human nature and psychology.

Focalization Refers to the perceptual, emotional, and ideological perspective through which narrated events are presented. This perspective might, but does not have to, be identical to that of the narrator. In a narrative, one can distinguish between narrator and focalizer by asking "who perceives" (who is the focalizer) and "who speaks" (who is the narrator). In traditional narrative, focalization is sometimes unlocatable; we then speak of zero focalization. When focalization, however, is locatable, we can distinguish between external and internal focalization. External focalization is close to the narrating agent; here, the focalizer appears to be extradiegetic (see *diegesis*) — that is, outside the narrated events. Internal focalization, as the term suggests, puts the locus of focalization inside the represented events.

Free indirect discourse A blending of a narrator's and a character's discourse. The result displays two different voices and styles. There are a number of grammatical indicators of free indirect discourse, such as backshifting of tenses and conversion of personal and possessive pronouns. These grammatical features do not, however, appear in every instance of free indirect discourse.

Genre A kind or class of literature. The traditional division of literature into lyric, epic, and dramatic genres survives to the present day. Critics have defined numerous more limited genres; the most notable fictional genres are the short story, novel, and novella. Whereas earlier critics viewed genres as fixed literary types, it is now accepted that genres are convenient categories rather than rigid classes. Today, a genre is conceived as a set of conventions that can change over time. For the reader, such conventions function as a set of expectations, which may not, however, be satisfied, particularly by *modernist* or *postmodernist* works.

Grotesque Subversive works of literature and visual art that undermine prevailing norms. The grotesque, as Anthony di Renzo maintains, is "the product of rebellion and lively imagination that refuses to conform to the norms of the time." Grotesque was popular in the Middle Ages, when writers attacked the rigidity of Christian scholasticism. Today, the grotesque, through its bizarre and coded way of depicting the world, may attack a variety of ideologies. One is most likely to find grotesque elements in caricature, *parody*, *satire*, invective, burlesque, and black comedy.

Implied author A term introduced by Wayne Booth to refer to "the governing consciousness of the work as a whole, the source of the norms embodied in the work." The implied author must be distinguished from the real author. Whereas the "real" author may embody different ideas in different works, the implied author appears as a consistent entity with a coherent value system. Moreover, the implied author also differs from the *narrator*. While the narrator is the "speaker" in a text, the implied author has no voice; we only sense his or her presence in the design of the whole. The implied author must therefore be seen as a construct to be inferred only after the text has been interpreted.

Intertextuality   The relation of a text to other literary works: no text is an island.

Irony   Stating one thing while implying something else. This encompasses over-statement (hyperbole), understatement (meiosis), statement of the opposite, and – on occasion – statement of the obvious.

Modernism   A movement in the creative arts originating in the 1890s and influential throughout the twentieth century. Modernism involves a radical break with the traditional basis of both Western culture and art. It reached its height after the First World War, when artists experimented with new forms and a new style that would reflect contemporary disorder and destruction. Modernist fiction, such as James Joyce's *Ulysses* (1922), subverts the basic conventions of earlier prose fiction by breaking up narrative continuity, departing from standard ways of representing characters, and violating the traditional syntax and coherence of narrative language. Modernist writing presents the individual as fragmented and alienated from society, and often as deeply disturbed by the passing of time and the meaning of memory. Another distinctive trait is concern with language and with the act of writing itself; in this sense, modernist literature is often referred to as self-conscious writing.

Motif   A recurrent element (image, action, locution) that provides coherence to a text. See *theme.*

Narratee   All narrated texts are addressed to someone, but fictional texts target an imagined listener. Although some texts specifically address a narratee who shares a fictional world with the *narrator*, often as a character, most narrators speak more generally, seemingly offering their accounts to no one in particular. Narrators, however, desire to be heard and understood; by trying to detect the kind of audience they believe will be most receptive to their stories, we gain insight into a narrator's perspective on the significance of his or her story.

Narrator   The narrator is the narrative agent in a text, and must be distinguished from both the real and the *implied author*. A rough distinction can be made between third and first person ("I") narrators. Whereas third person narrators are often omniscient, first person narrators are by definition limited. Moreover, narrators can be distinguished according to narrative levels; a narrator might belong to the same reality as the characters, or he might be extra-diegetic (see *diegesis*). Moreover, narrators can be distinguished according to their level of participation in the story, their degree of perceptiveness or obtuseness, overtness or covertness, and reliability or unreliability.

Parable   A term, religious in origin, referring to a story with an ulterior meaning. Frequently, a parable is not self-explanatory and needs a key. Once the secondary meaning can be decoded, the parable reveals a moral or ethical lesson for which the narrative is an analogy. Compare *fable.*

Parody   A branch of *satire* in which an author's words, style, attitude, tone, and ideas are ridiculed through imitation and exaggeration. Parody is most effective when it maintains a subtle balance between close resemblance to the original and a deliberate distortion of its principal characteristics.

Plot   The organization of events into a narrative. It should be distinguished from the *story*.

Point of view   Refers to the intelligence through which the action of a narrative work is filtered. Most critics distinguish three basic points of view. The first, commonly found in traditional narrative, is the omniscient observer, who knows everything about every character. The second is the central observer, whose experience is rendered in the third person. As part of the fictional world, his or her knowledge is limited. The third type of point of view is the first person narrator, whose knowledge is also limited. Many variations and combinations of these points of view are possible.

Postmodernism   A group of movements originating after the Second World War and embracing, like modernism, all the creative arts. It involves both a continuation of the counter-traditional experiments of modernism, as well as attempts to break away from modernist forms that had in their turn become conventional. Postmodern fiction shares with its modernist precursors a concern for language; indeed, it often attempts to subvert the foundations of language itself. It questions writing as a reliable mode of representation, and suggests that language cannot be relied on to convey truth. Nonetheless, postmodernists maintain that we are conditioned by cultural discourse, especially as to the ways that gender, race, and class configure us. Postmodern writing sometimes appears as a pastiche of various genres (for example, narrative interspersed with news items, stories, or poems), which often undermine and contradict each other. Postmodern writing thus ultimately involves epistemological questions such as *what* and *how* we know.

Realism   According to some theorists, this term should be used only as a period designation, describing works in literature and the visual arts created between early nineteenth-century romanticism and late nineteenth-century *modernism*. Others, such as Eric Auerbach, maintain that a modernist impulse animates all Western literature. Because realist texts believe that language can be used as a kind of mirror, they imply that literature can reflect the external, social world relatively unproblematically. Realism offers intensely psychological portraits of characters who are placed in recognizable historical situations. While they are subject to change and are deeply influenced by their cultural and geographic environment, realist characters usually exhibit free will. Realist details are those moments in a text – described objects, conversations, references to the actual world – that anchor it to the reality of everyday experience.

Romance   A chivalric verse narrative originating in medieval Europe. The tone of the romance is generally light, and its focus is narrower and not as grand as that of the epic, another common medieval genre. The term's meaning changed in the nineteenth century, when certain types of historical narratives were labelled romances. Today, the term designates a narrative in prose depicting incidents that seem remote from ordinary life. Common elements are a highly imaginative narrative which lacks *verisimilitude* and which stresses action rather than *character* and event rather than development.

Satire   An approach labelled a *genre* in a different sense from, for example, the novel or the short story. Satire can alternatively be defined as an *ironic* mode or attitude appearing in a variety of genres. Critics commonly distinguish between gentle and amusing Horatian satire (associated with the classical writer Horace), and the often bitter and serious Juvenalian satire (named after the writer Juvenal).

Story   It is important to distinguish between story and *plot*. The story is a series of real or fictional events, connected by a certain logic or chronology, and involving certain actors. The plot is the organization of this series of events in a narrative.

Subtext   A text's hidden meanings, which are implied but not directly stated.

Symbol   Generally, the use of a concrete image to suggest abstract ideas. Symbols can be distinguished as natural and arbitrary. A natural symbol uses the quality of a concrete object in a metaphoric way; the brilliant light of the sun, for example, may symbolize intellectual illumination. An arbitrary symbol, on the other hand, relies on the conventional or traditional associations between a concrete object and an abstract idea that have no easily conceivable similarities. Symbols may enrich a text by generating complex associations.

Theme   A text's framing concept. The thematic approach to literature desires to uncover a text's concrete engagement with a given phenomenon, cultural dilemma, or historical situation. While a text may have "death" as its subject matter, theme arises from the act of interpretation; that is, the experience of death leads to a loss of innocence. Theme specifically involves repetition. One can detect a text's thematic interests by noting the manner in which it repeatedly develops an idea or image. It can be distinguished from *motif*, another musical term, by its greater degree of abstraction.

Verisimilitude   The quality of a text resulting from its degree of conformity to a set of "truth" norms that are external to it: a text has verisimilitude depending on the extent to which it conforms to what its readers perceive as reality.

Acknowledgements

SHERMAN ALEXIE. "The Approximate Size of My Favourite Tumour" is reprinted from *The Lone Ranger and Tonto Fistfight in Heaven* by Sherman Alexie. Copyright © 1993 by Sherman Alexie. Used by permission of Grove/Atlantic, Inc.

JAMES BALDWIN. "Sonny's Blues" was originally published in *Partisan Review*. Collected in *Going to Meet the Man* © 1965 by James Baldwin. Copyright renewed. Published by Vintage Books. Reprinted by arrangement with the James Baldwin Estate.

SANDRA BIRDSELL. "Disappearances" is reprinted from *The Two-Headed Calf* by Sandra Birdsell. Used by permission, McClelland & Stewart, Inc. *The Canadian Publishers.*

BETH BRANT. "Swimming Upstream" by Beth Brant is reprinted from *Talking Leaves: Contemporary Native American Short Stories* (Dell Publishing, 1991) by permission of the author.

BONNIE BURNARD. "Joyride" is reprinted from *Women of Influence* by Bonnie Burnard, published by Coteau Books, Regina. Used by permission of the publisher.

RAYMOND CARVER. "Cathedral" is reprinted from *Cathedral* by Raymond Carver. Copyright © 1981 by Raymond Carver. Reprinted by permission of Alfred A. Knopf Inc.

GEOFFREY CHAUCER. "The Miller's Tale" is reprinted from *The Riverside Chaucer*, Third Edition, Larry D. Benson (General Editor). Copyright © 1987 by Houghton Mifflin Company. Reprinted with permission.

ANTON CHEKHOV. "Gooseberries" by Anton Chekhov is reprinted from *The Portable Chekhov* by Anton Chekhov, edited by Avrahm Yarmolinsky. Copyright 1947, © 1968 by Viking Penguin Inc. Renewed © 1975 by Avrahm Yarmolinsky. Used by permission of Viking Penguin, a division of Penguin Putnam Inc.

KATE CHOPIN. "The Story of an Hour" is reprinted from *The Complete Works of Kate Chopin* (Louisiana State University Press, 1969).

ELIZABETH COOK-LYNN. "Loss of the Sky" is reprinted from *The Power of Horses and Other Stories* (Little, Brown and Company, 1990) by permission of the author.

LOUISE ERDRICH. "The Bingo Van" is reprinted from *Talking Leaves: Contemporary Native American Short Stories* (Dell Publishing, 1991). First published in *The New Yorker*, 1990. © Louise Erdrich. Reprinted by permission.

WILLIAM FAULKNER. "A Rose for Emily" is reprinted from *Collected Stories of William Faulkner* by William Faulkner. Copyright © 1930 and renewed 1958 by William Faulkner. Reprinted by permission of Random House, Inc.

RICHARD FORD. "Sweethearts" is reprinted from *Rock Springs* by Richard Ford. Copyright © 1987 by Richard Ford. Used by permission of Grove/Atlantic, Inc.

MAVIS GALLANT. "The Moslem Wife" is reprinted from *The Moslem Wife and Other Stories* by Mavis Gallant. Used by permission, McClelland & Stewart, Inc. *The Canadian Publishers.*

CHARLOTTE PERKINS GILMAN. "The Yellow Wall-paper" is reprinted from *Charlotte Perkins Gilman's "The Yellow Wall-paper" and the History of Its Publication and Reception: A Critical Edition and Documentary Casebook*, edited by Julie Bates Dock. Copyright © 1998 The Pennsylvania State University Press. Reproduced by permission of the publisher.

NICOLAI GOGOL. "The Overcoat" is reprinted from *The Overcoat and Other Tales of Good and Evil* by Nicolai Gogol. Copyright © 1957 by David Magarshack. Used by permission of Doubleday, a division of Bantam Doubleday Dell Publishing Group, Inc.

NATHANIEL HAWTHORNE. "Young Goodman Brown" from *Mosses from an Old Manse*, volume X of the Centenary Edition of the Works of Nathaniel Hawthorne, is reprinted by permission. Copyright © 1974 by the Ohio State University Press. All rights reserved.

ERNEST HEMINGWAY. "A Clean, Well-Lighted Place" is reprinted with permission of Scribner, a Division of Simon & Schuster, Inc., from *Winner Take Nothing* by Ernest Hemingway. Copyright 1933 by Charles Scribner's Sons. Copyright renewed © 1961 by Mary Hemingway.

LINDA HOGAN. "Aunt Moon's Young Man" is reprinted from *Talking Leaves: Contemporary Native American Short Stories* (Dell Publishing, 1991) by permission of the author.

SHIRLEY JACKSON. "The Lottery" from *The Lottery* by Shirley Jackson. Copyright © 1948,